HEARTSTOPPER

VOLUME 5

Copyright © 2023 by Alice Oseman

All rights reserved. Published by Graphix, an imprint of Scholastic Inc.,
Publishers since 1920. SCHOLASTIC, GRAPHIX, and associated logos are
trademarks and/or registered trademarks of Scholastic Inc.

The publisher does not have any control over and does not assume any
responsibility for author or third-party websites or their content.

No part of this publication may be reproduced, stored in a retrieval system,
or transmitted in any form or by any means, electronic, mechanical, photocopying,
recording, or otherwise, without written permission of the publisher.
For information regarding permission, write to Scholastic Inc., Attention:
Permissions Department, 557 Broadway, New York, NY 10012.

Heartstopper: Volume 5 was originally published in the United Kingdom
by Hachette Children's Group in 2023.

This book is a work of fiction. Names, characters, places, and incidents
are either the product of the author's imagination or are used fictitiously,
and any resemblance to actual persons, living or dead, business
establishments, events, or locales is entirely coincidental.

Library of Congress Control Number: 2019944235

ISBN 978-1-338-80750-9 (hardcover)
ISBN 978-1-338-80748-6 (paperback)

10 9 8 7 6 5 4 3   24 25 26 27

Printed in the U.S.A.   40
This edition first printing, December 2023

ALICE OSEMAN

HEARTSTOPPER

VOLUME 5

graphix

An Imprint of

■SCHOLASTIC

Sunday, March 6

I can't believe it's already the spring!

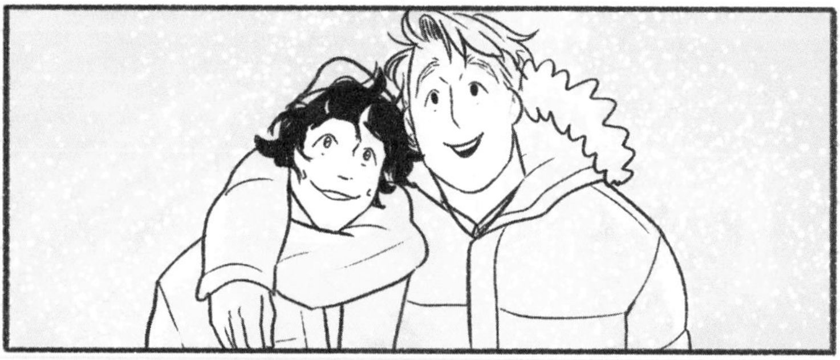

Charlie's doing a lot better now – he's back at school and back at rugby, and he's having less and less bad days.

My dad finally knows about us... actually, pretty much everyone knows we're together now.

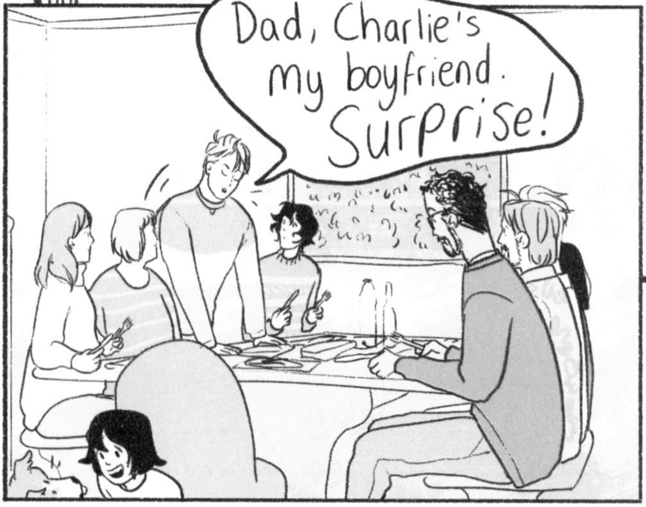
Dad, Charlie's my boyfriend. Surprise!

I guess we've come a long way. ♡

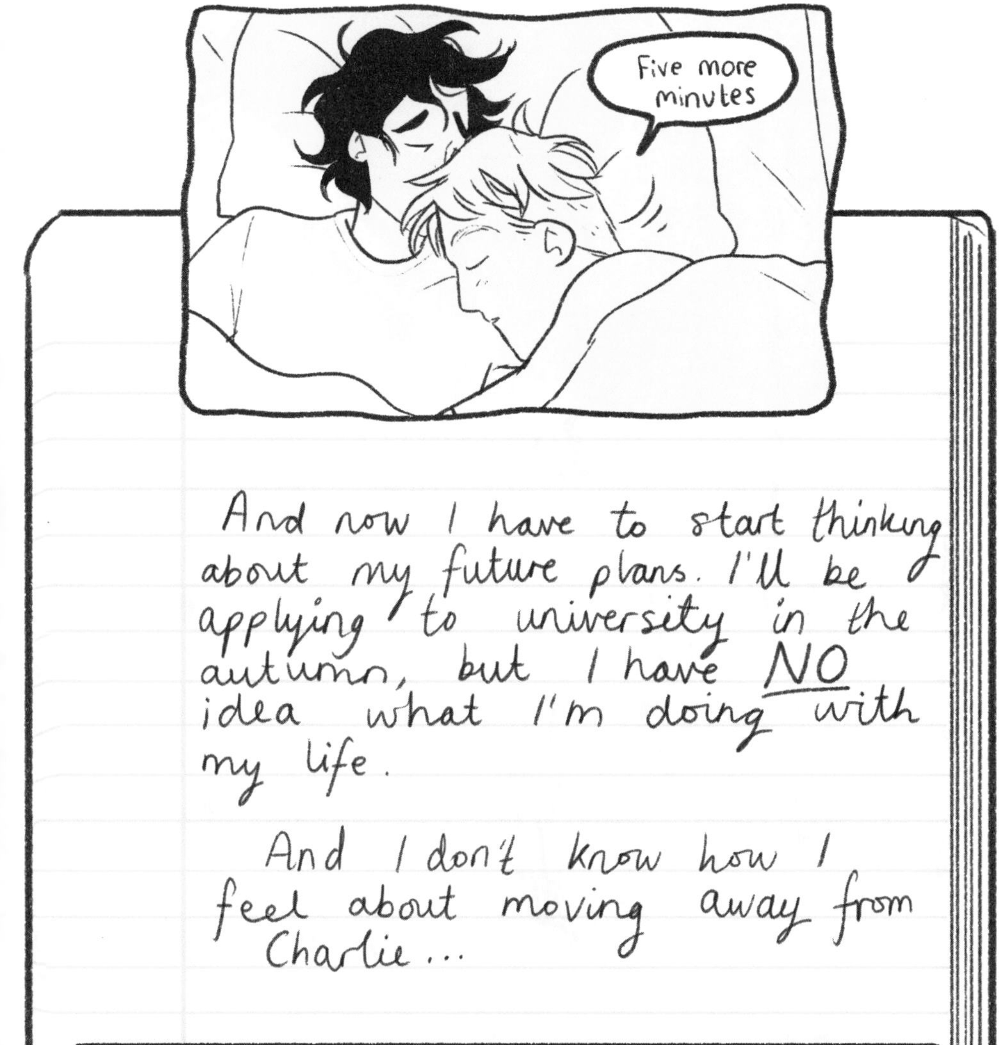
Five more minutes

And now I have to start thinking about my future plans. I'll be applying to university in the autumn, but I have NO idea what I'm doing with my life.

And I don't know how I feel about moving away from Charlie...

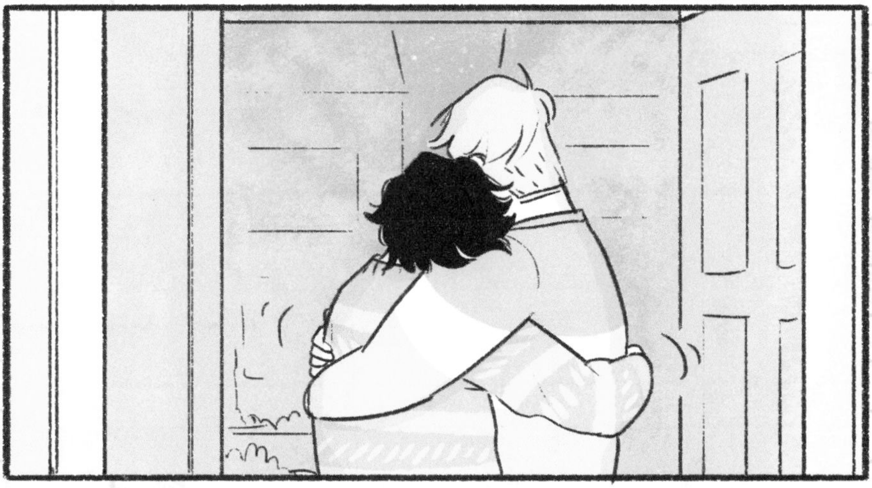

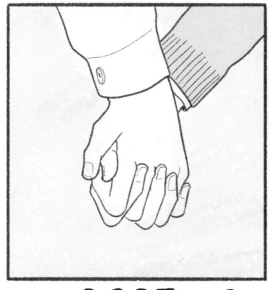

7. TOGETHER

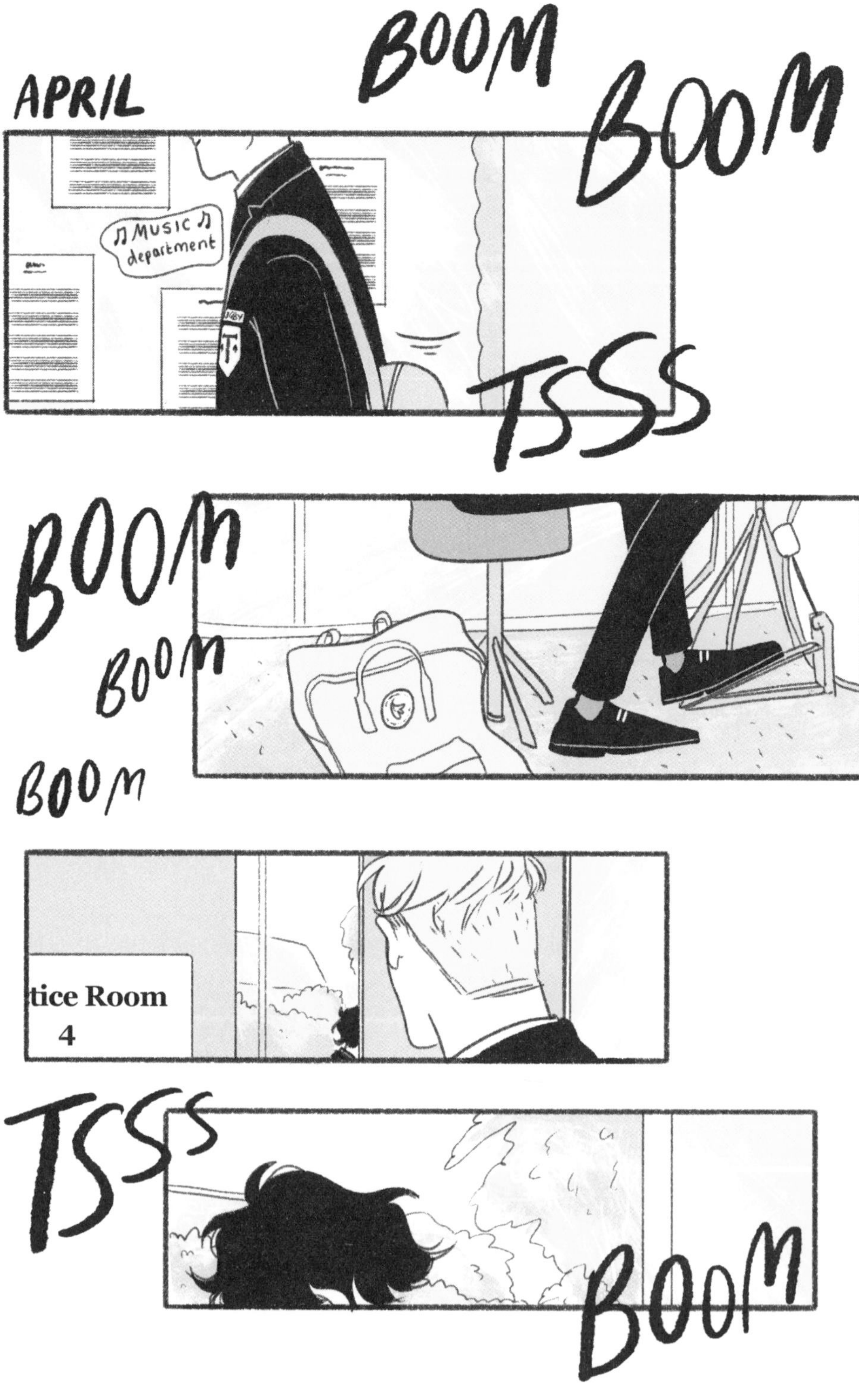
APRIL
BOOM
BOOM
MUSIC department
TSSS
BOOM
BOOM
BOOM
tice Room 4
TSSS
BOOM

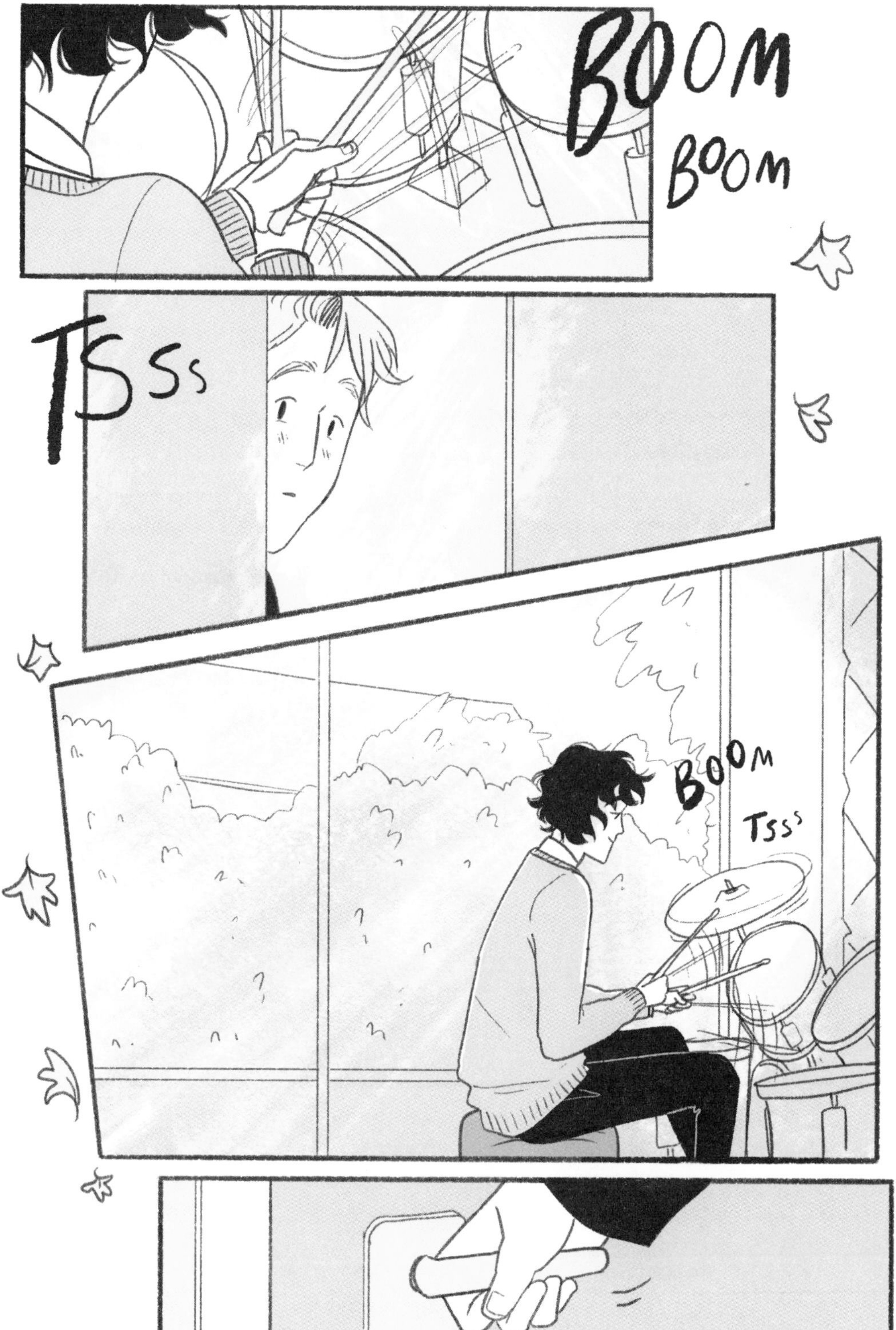
BOOM
BOOM
TSSs
BOOM
TSSs

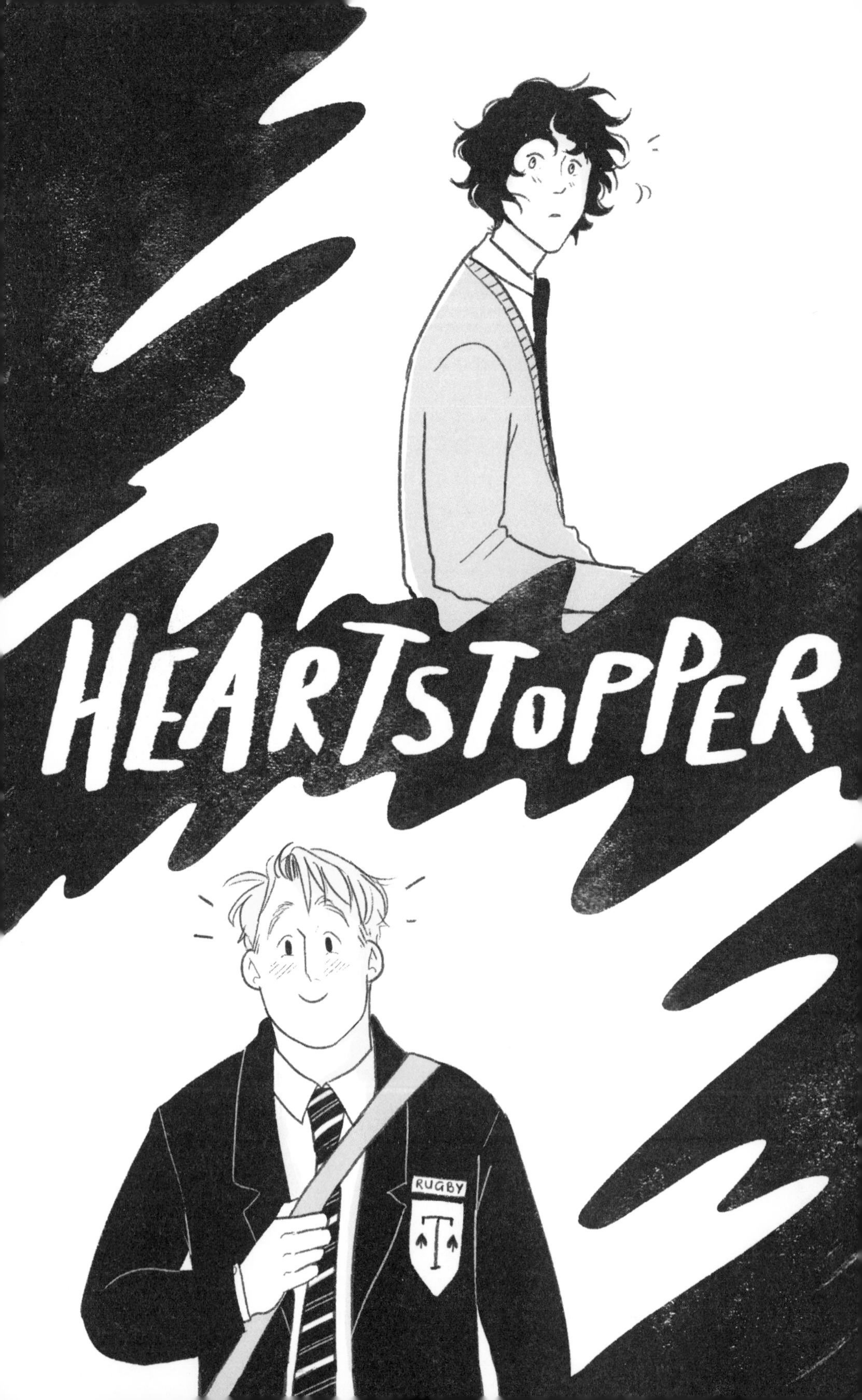
HEARTSTOPPER
RUGBY

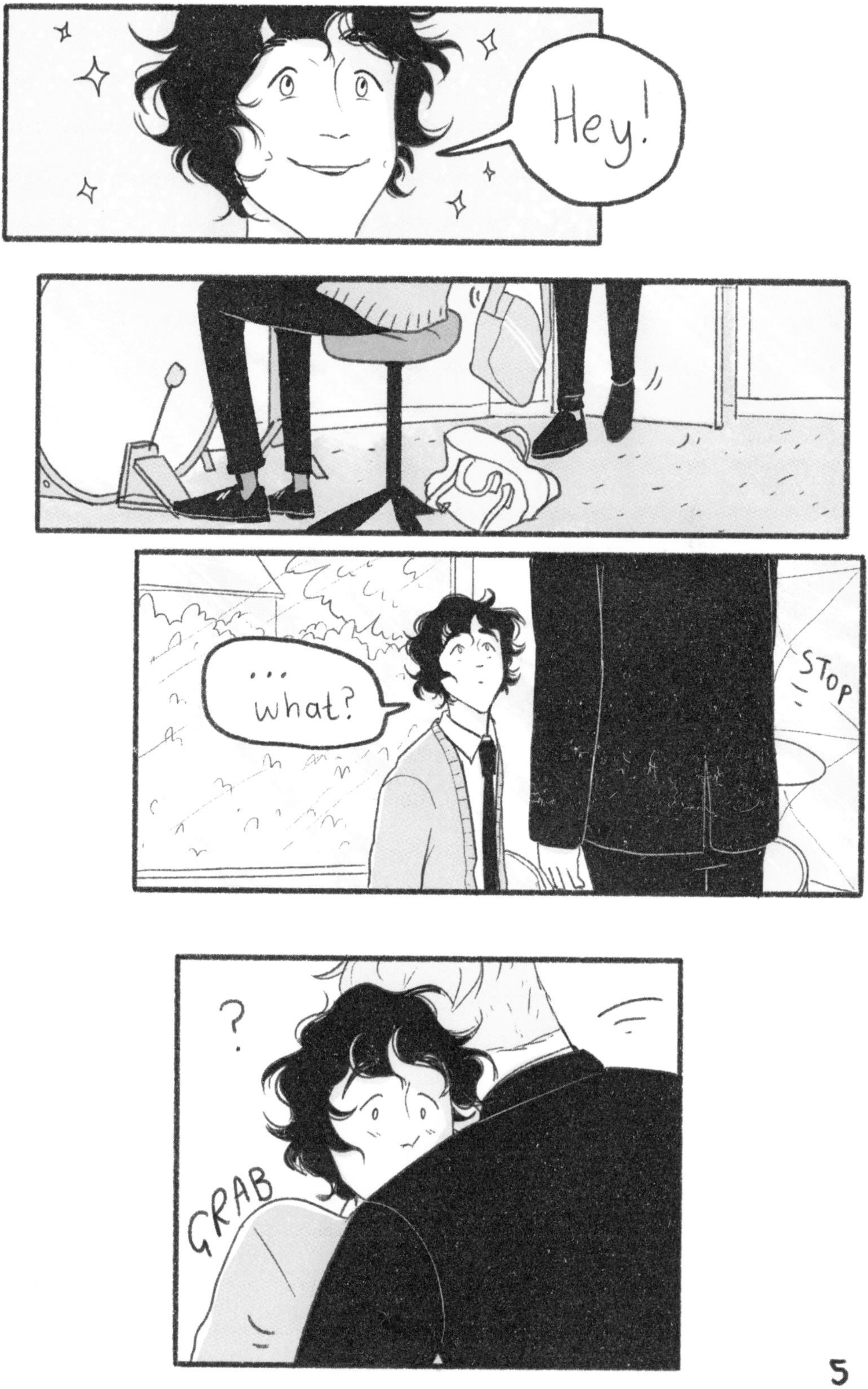
Hey!
...
what?
STOP
?
GRAB

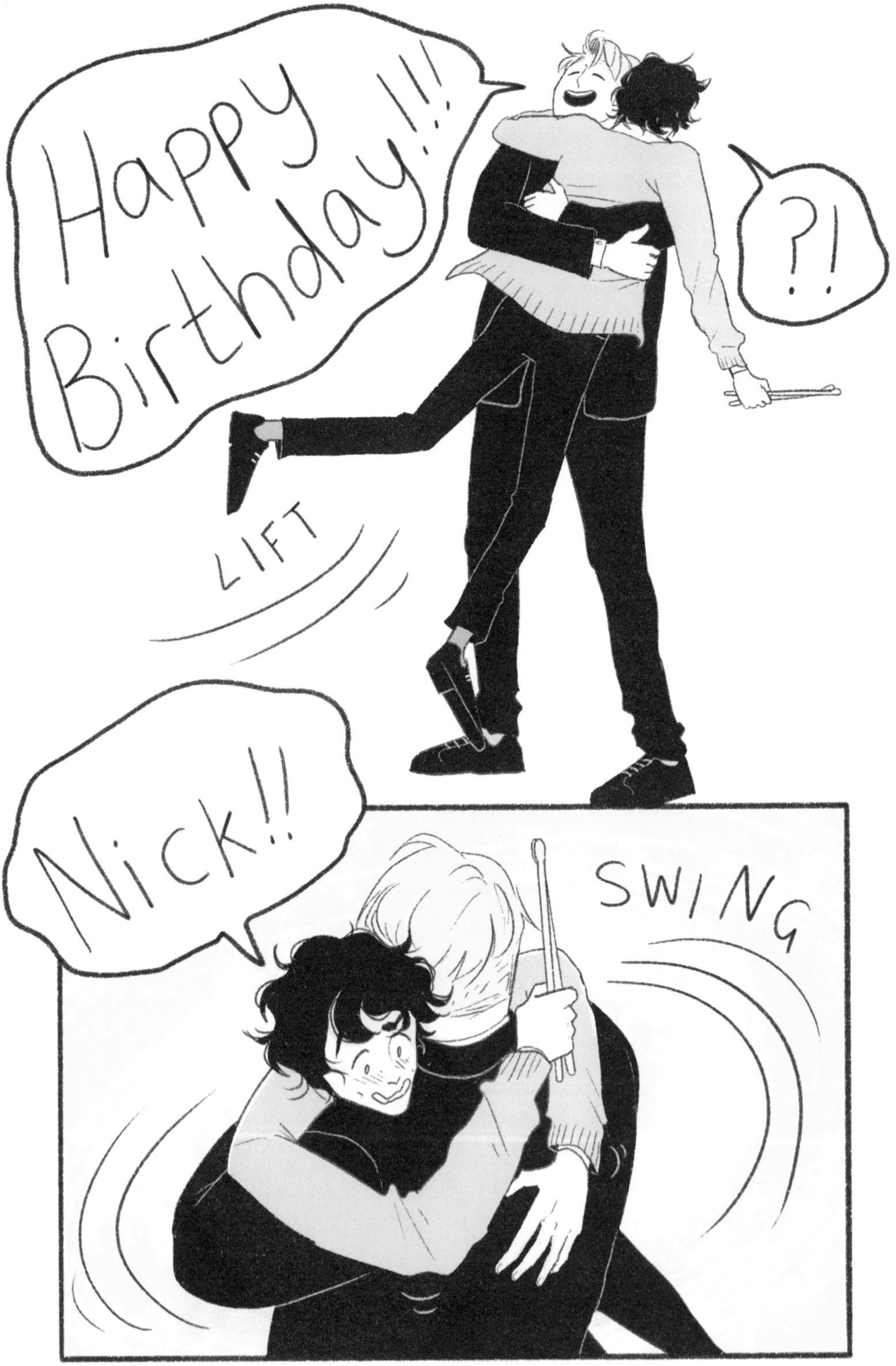
Happy Birthday!!!
?!
LIFT
Nick!!
SWING

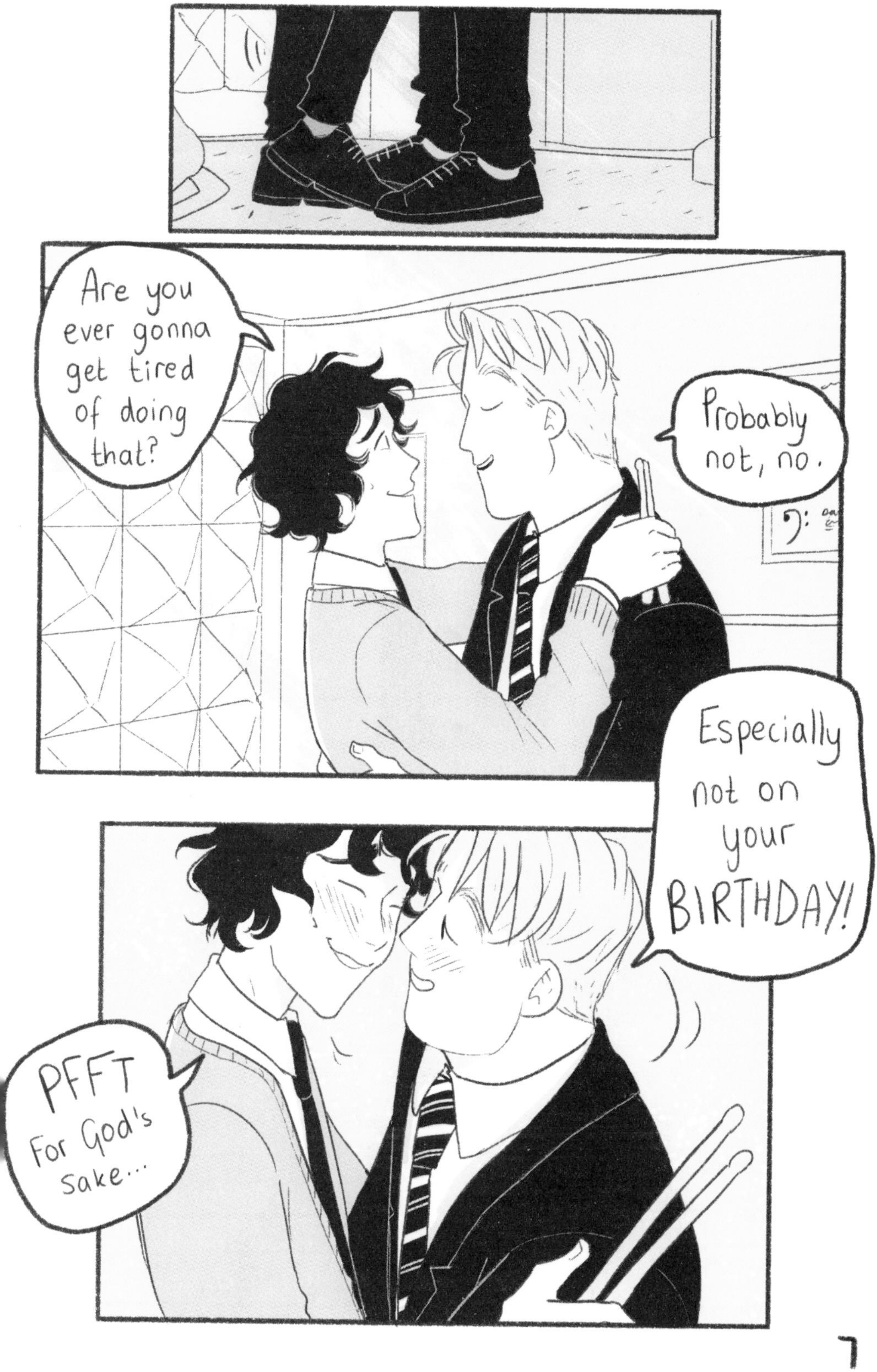
Are you ever gonna get tired of doing that?
Probably not, no.
Especially not on your BIRTHDAY!
PFFT For God's sake...

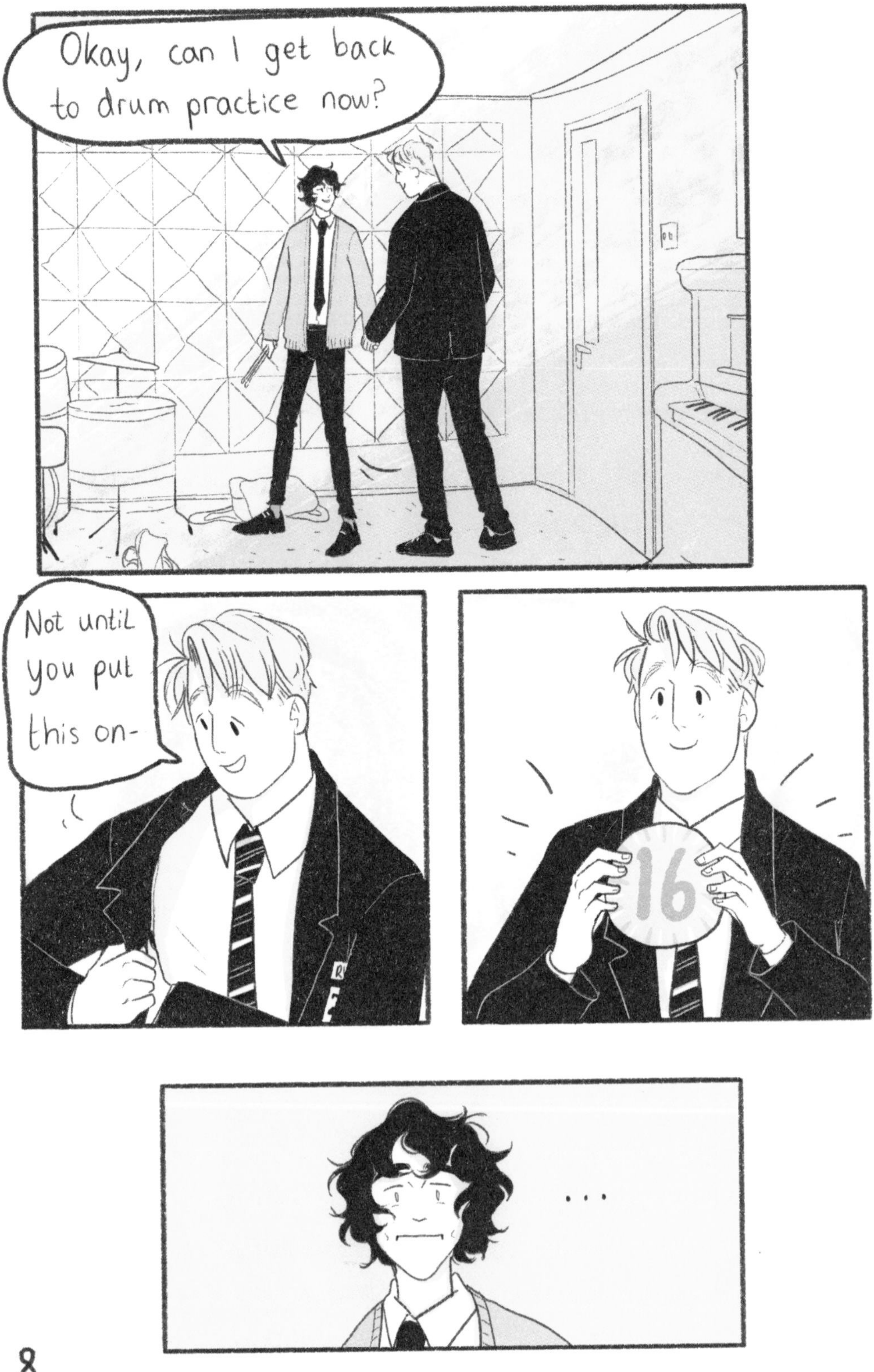
Okay, can I get back to drum practice now?
Not until you put this on-
16
...

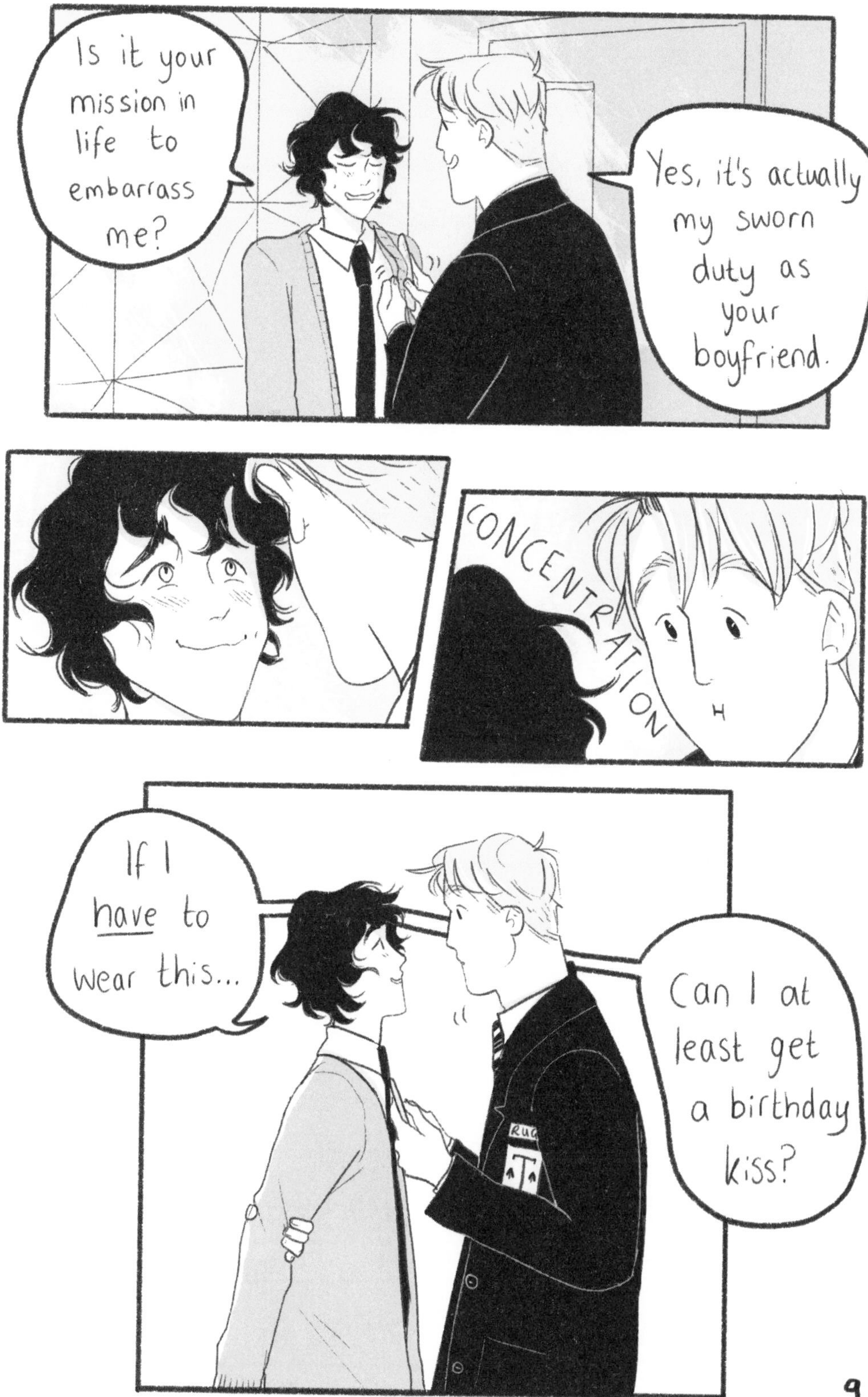
Is it your mission in life to embarrass me?
Yes, it's actually my sworn duty as your boyfriend.
CONCENTRATION
If I have to wear this...
Can I at least get a birthday kiss?

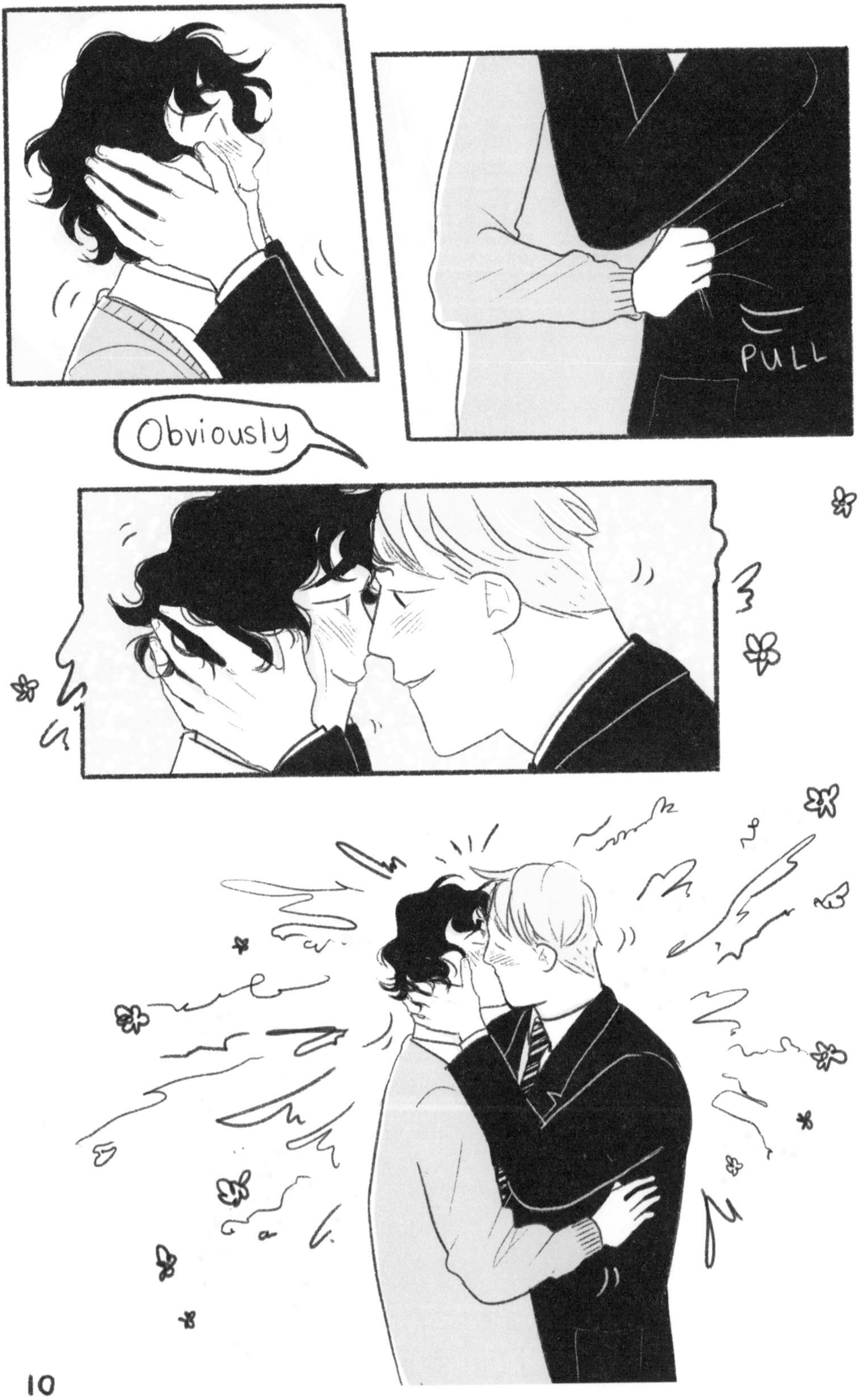
PULL
Obviously

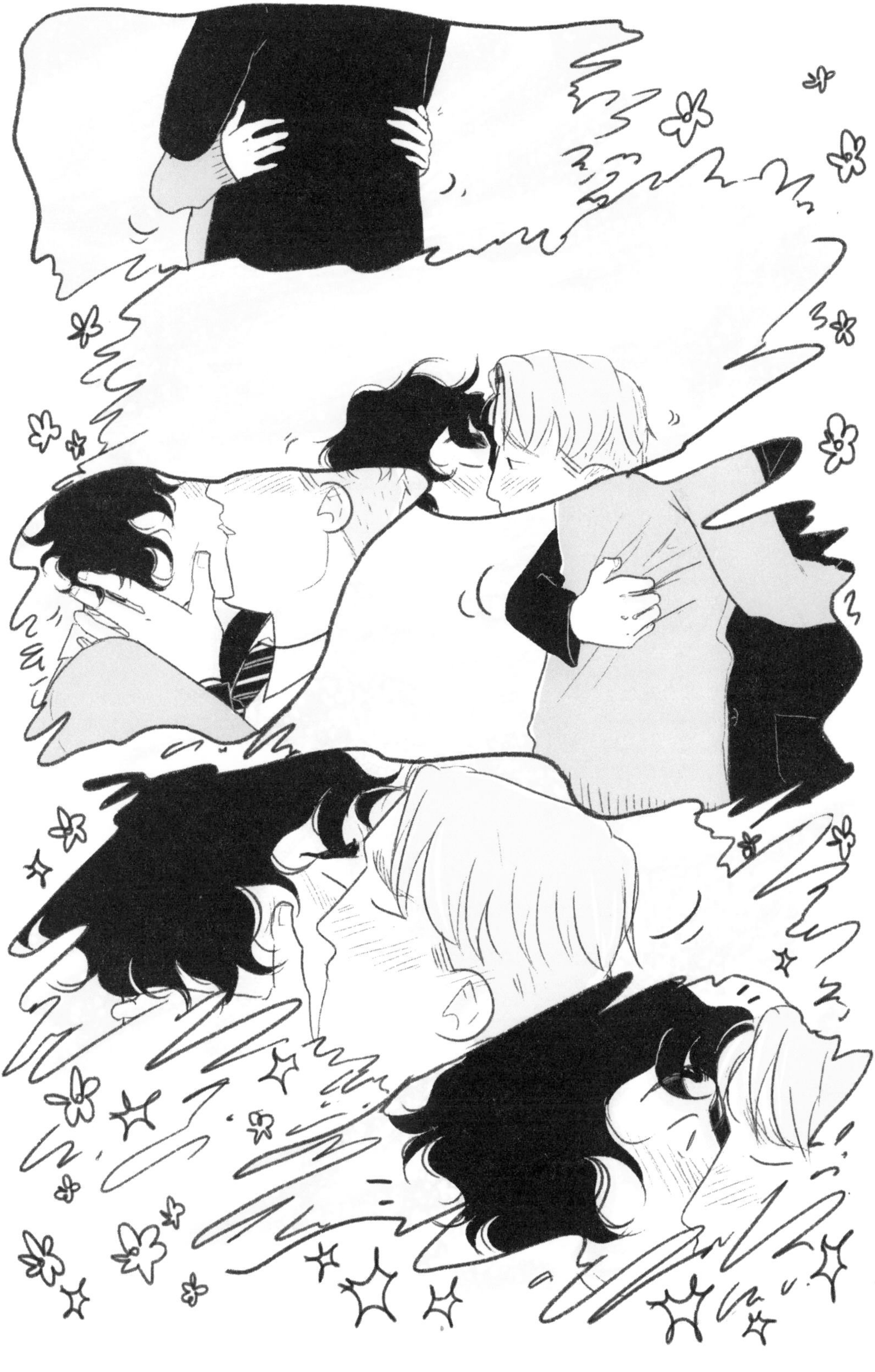

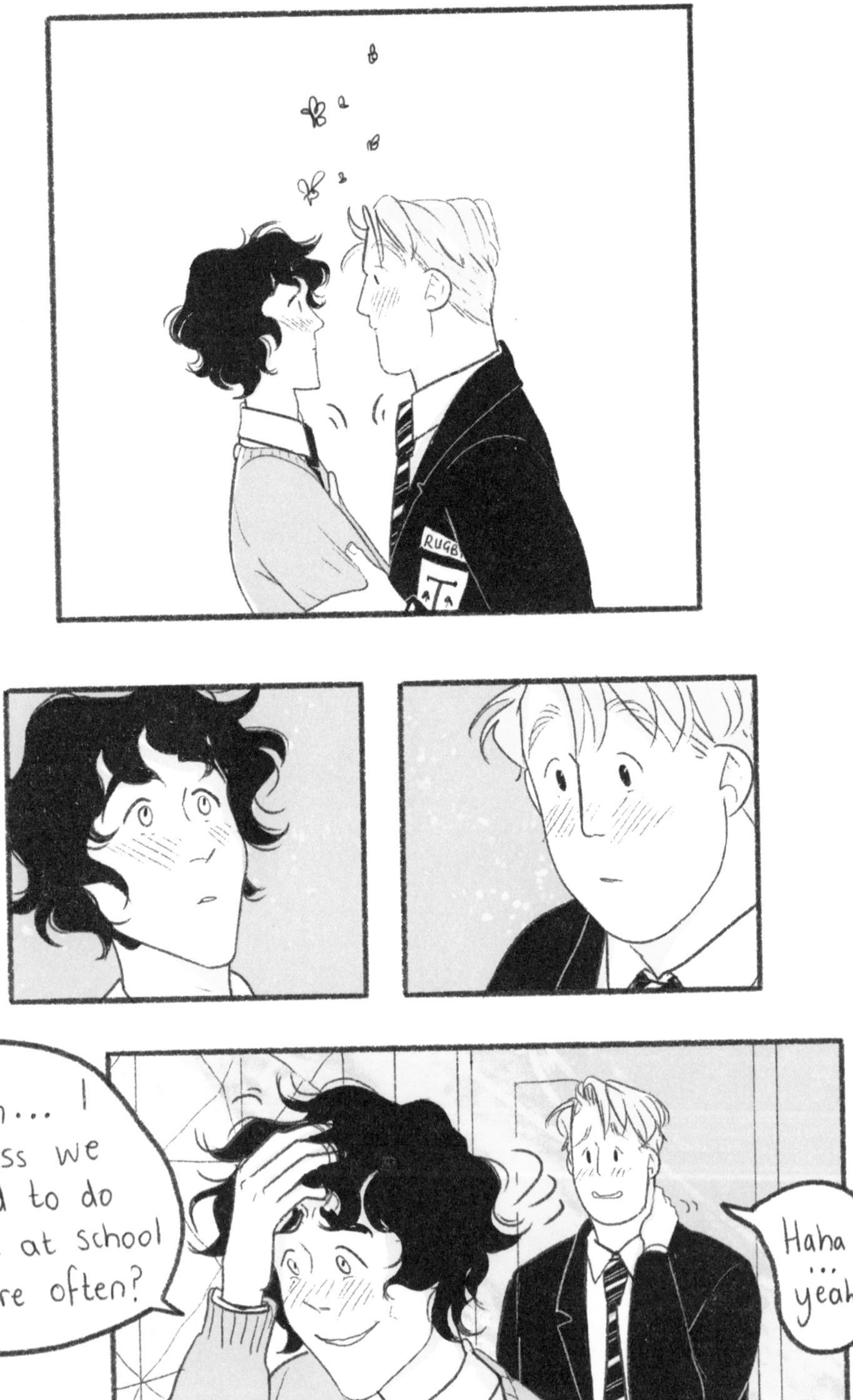
RUGBY
Um... I guess we need to do that at school more often?
Haha ... yeah

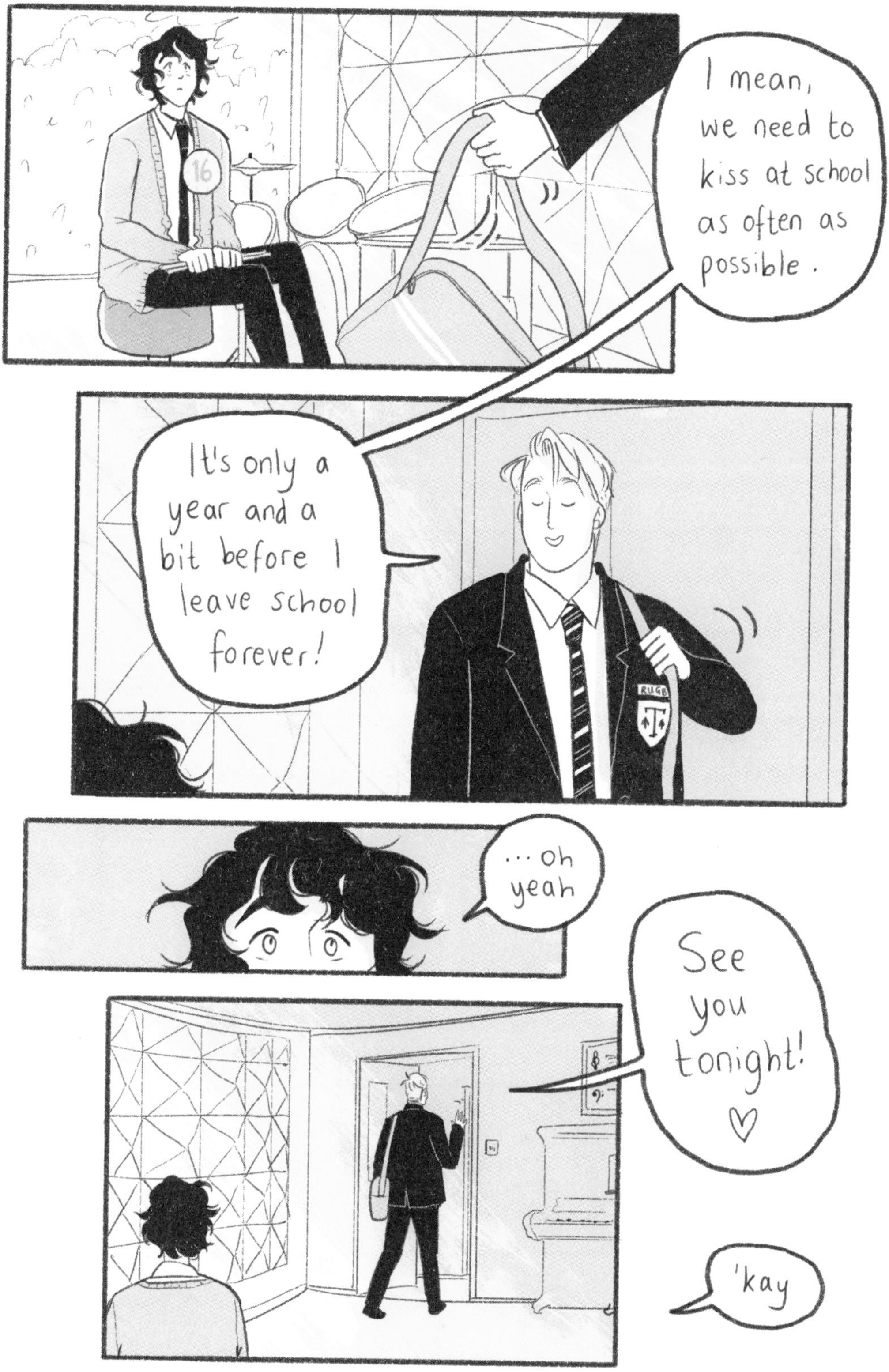
I mean, we need to kiss at school as often as possible.
It's only a year and a bit before I leave school forever!
RUGB
...oh yeah
See you tonight! ♡
'kay

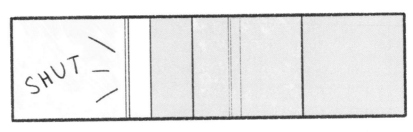

SHUT

It happened again.

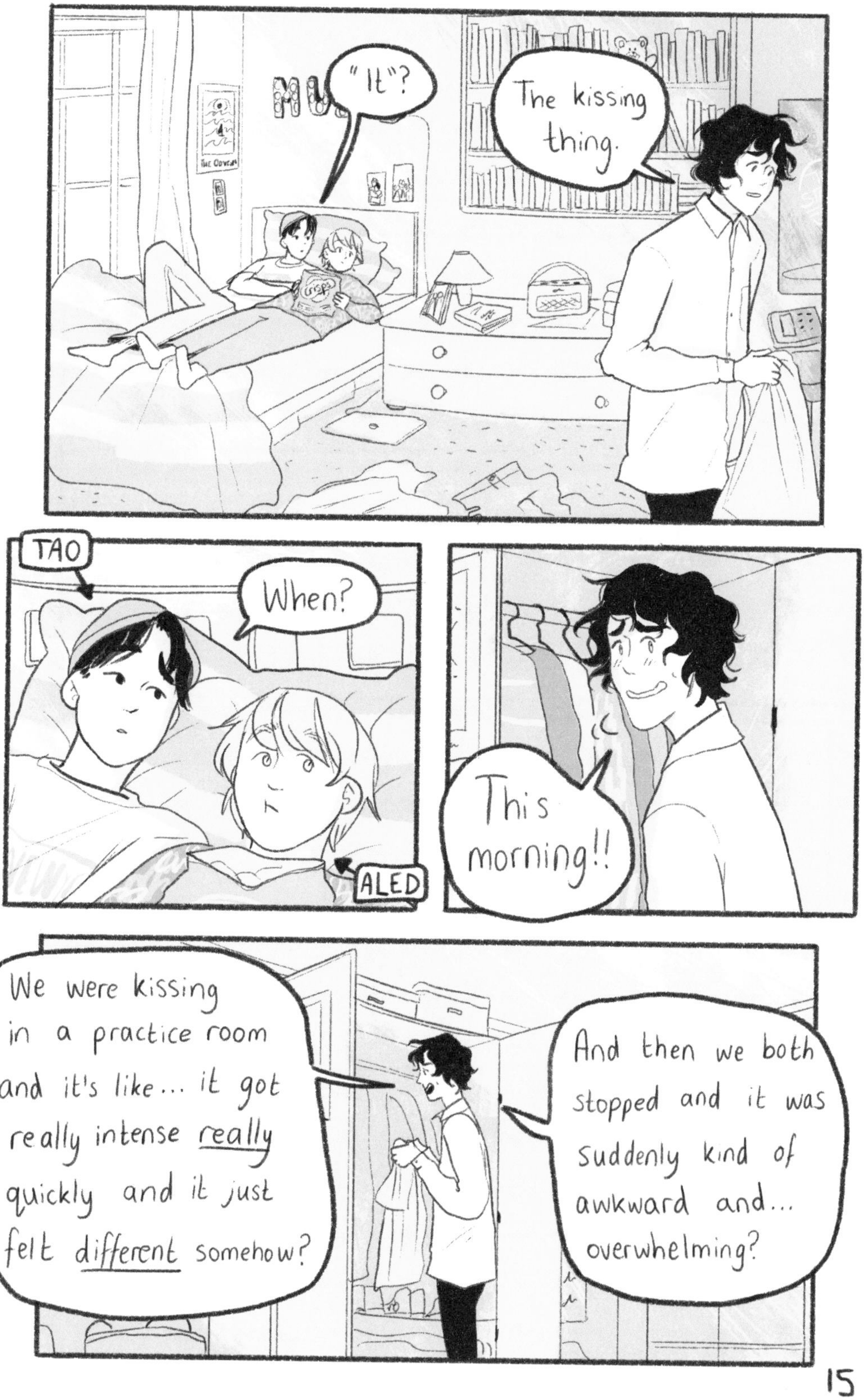
"It"?
The kissing thing.
TAO
ALED
When?
This morning!!
We were kissing in a practice room and it's like... it got really intense really quickly and it just felt different somehow?
And then we both stopped and it was suddenly kind of awkward and... overwhelming?

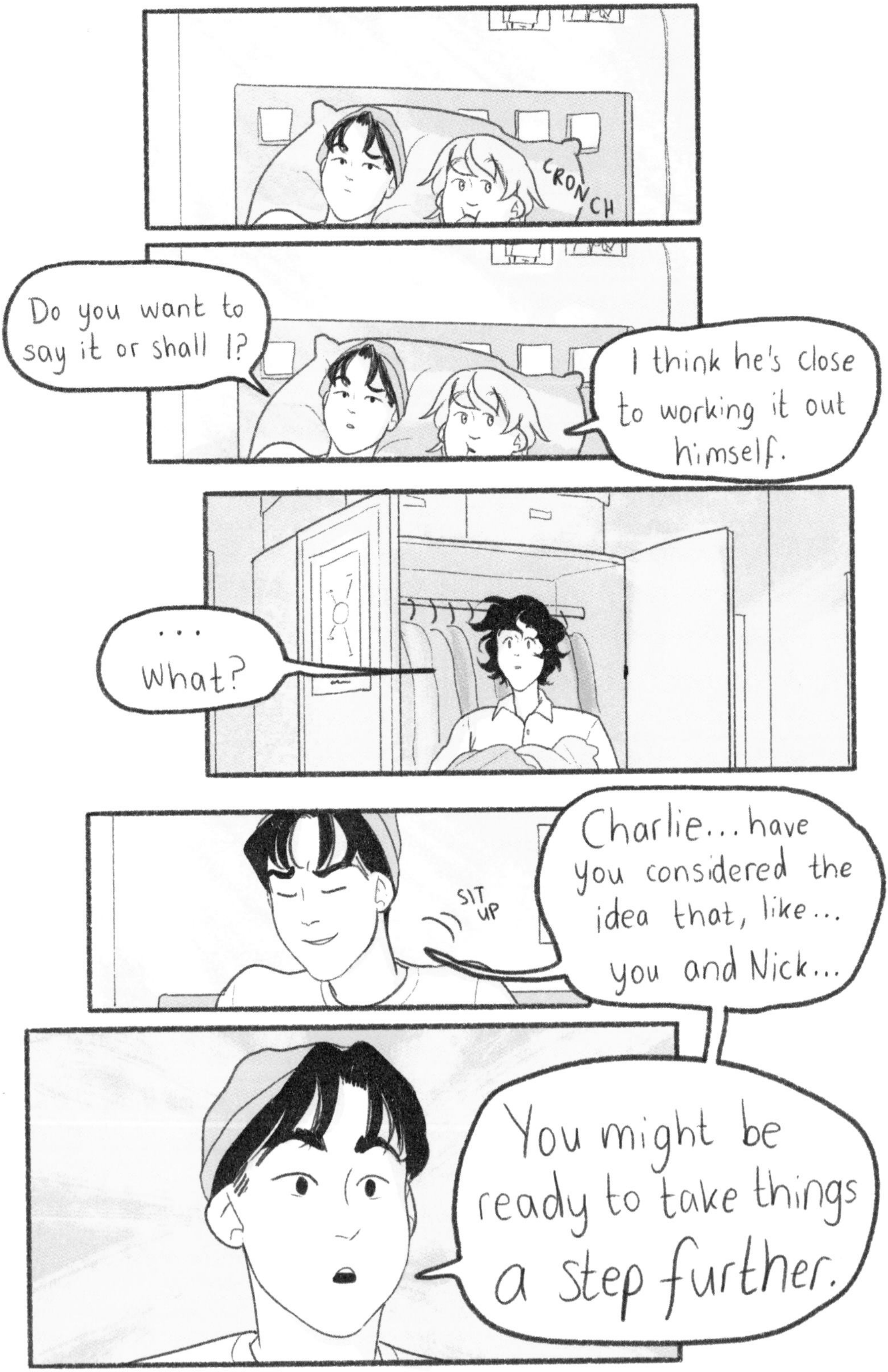
CRONCH
Do you want to say it or shall I?
I think he's close to working it out himself.
. . .
What?
SIT UP
Charlie... have you considered the idea that, like... you and Nick...
You might be ready to take things a step further.

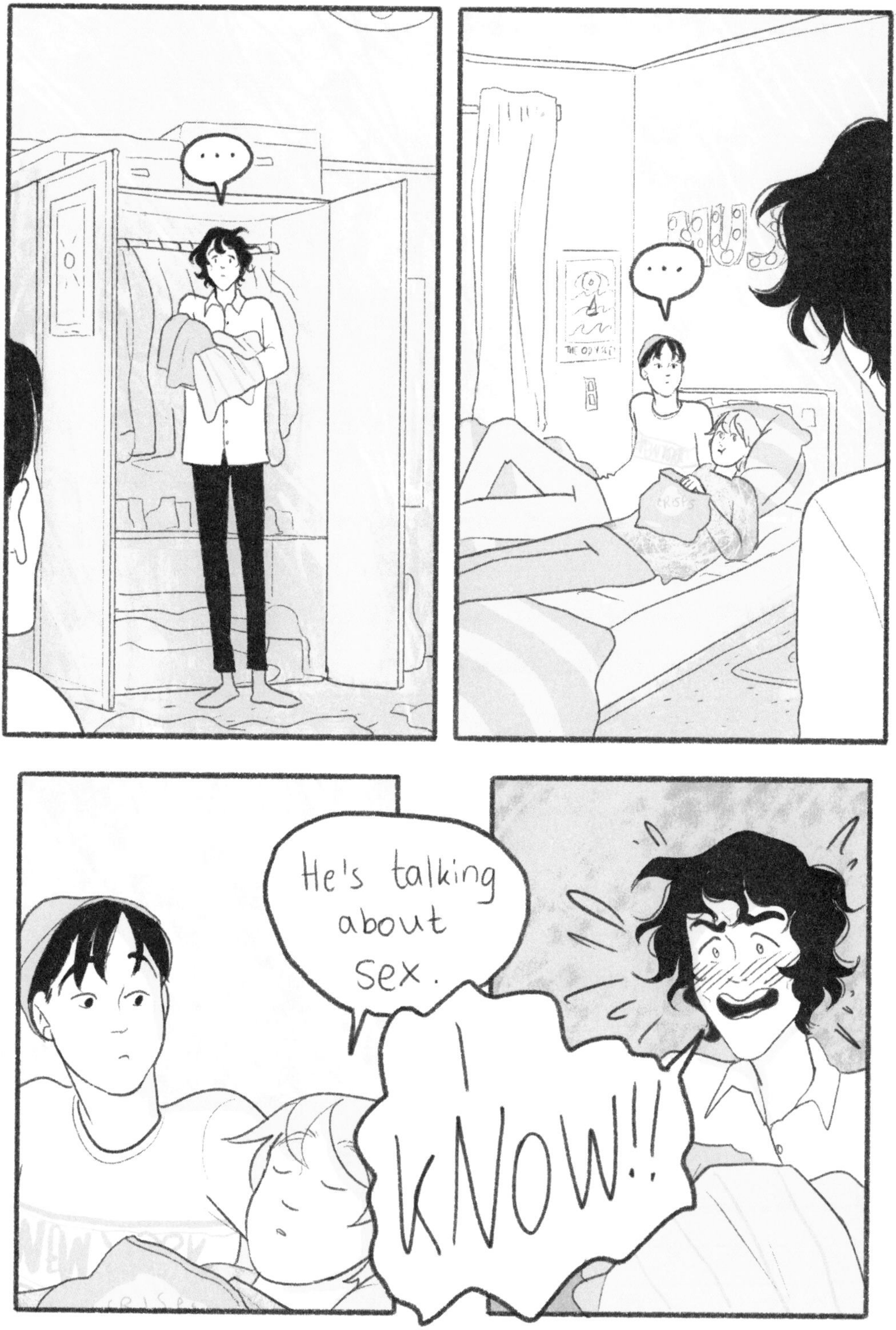
...
...
He's talking about sex.
I KNOW!!

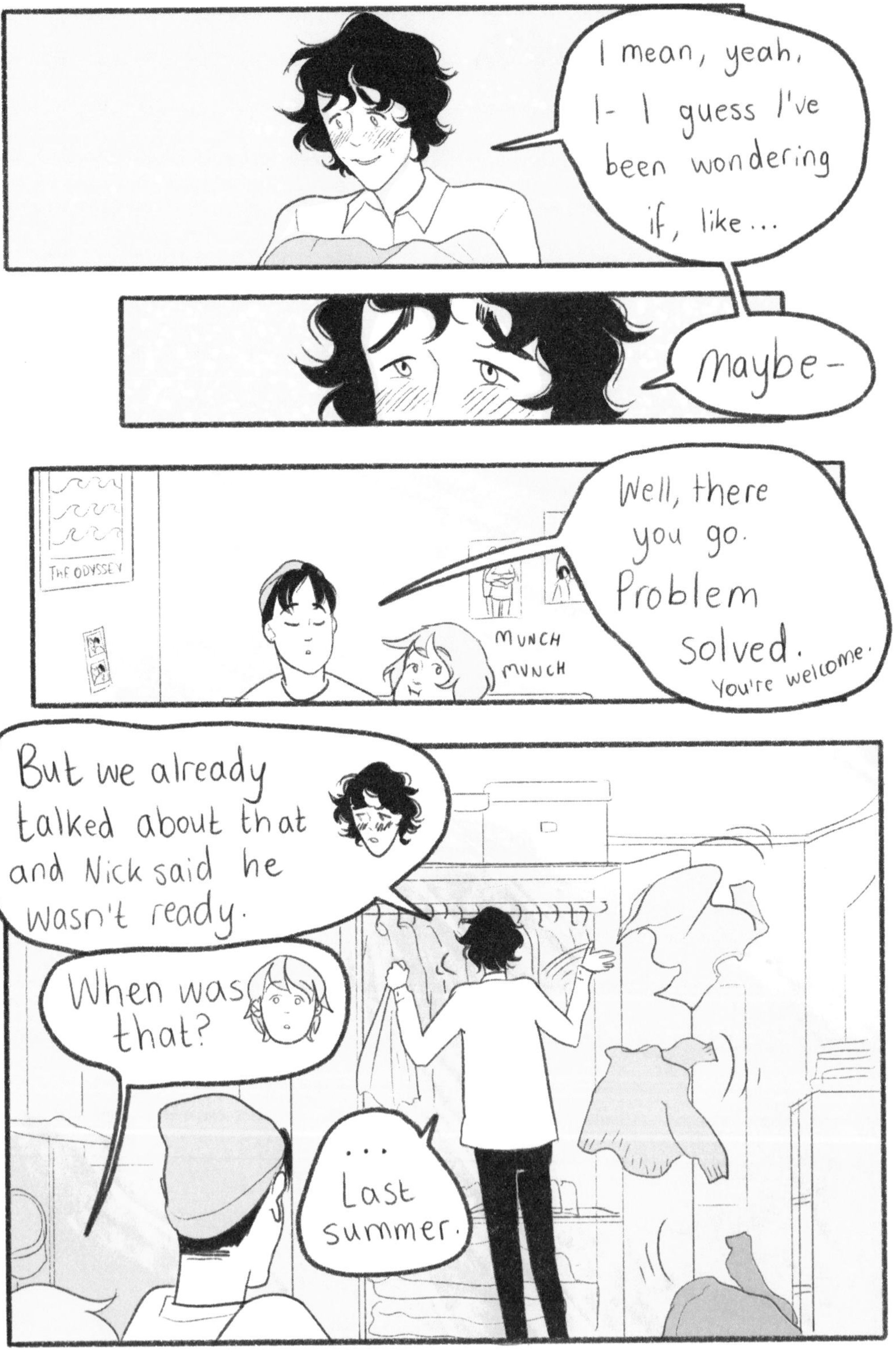
I mean, yeah, I- I guess I've been wondering if, like...
maybe-
THE ODYSSEY
MUNCH MUNCH
Well, there you go. Problem solved.
You're welcome.
But we already talked about that and Nick said he wasn't ready.
When was that?
... Last summer.

...It's literally April.

Do you think there's a possibility Nick may have changed his mind since then?

I don't know!

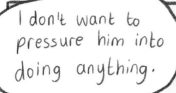

I don't want to pressure him into doing anything.

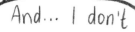

And... I don't know if I—

?

19

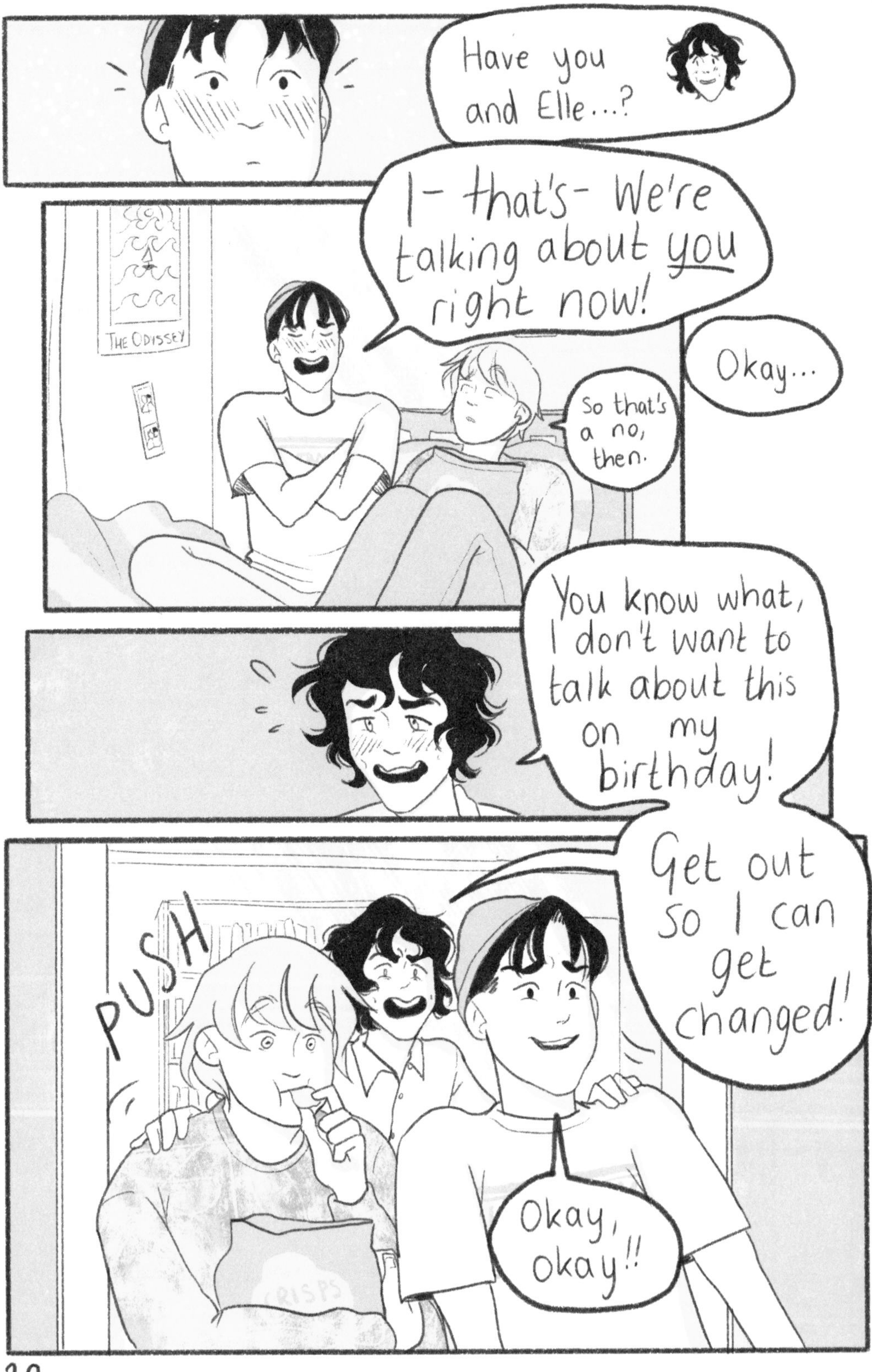
Have you and Elle...?
I- that's- We're talking about you right now!
So that's a no, then.
Okay...
THE ODISSEY
You know what, I don't want to talk about this on my birthday!
PUSH
Get out so I can get changed!
Okay, okay!!
CRISPS

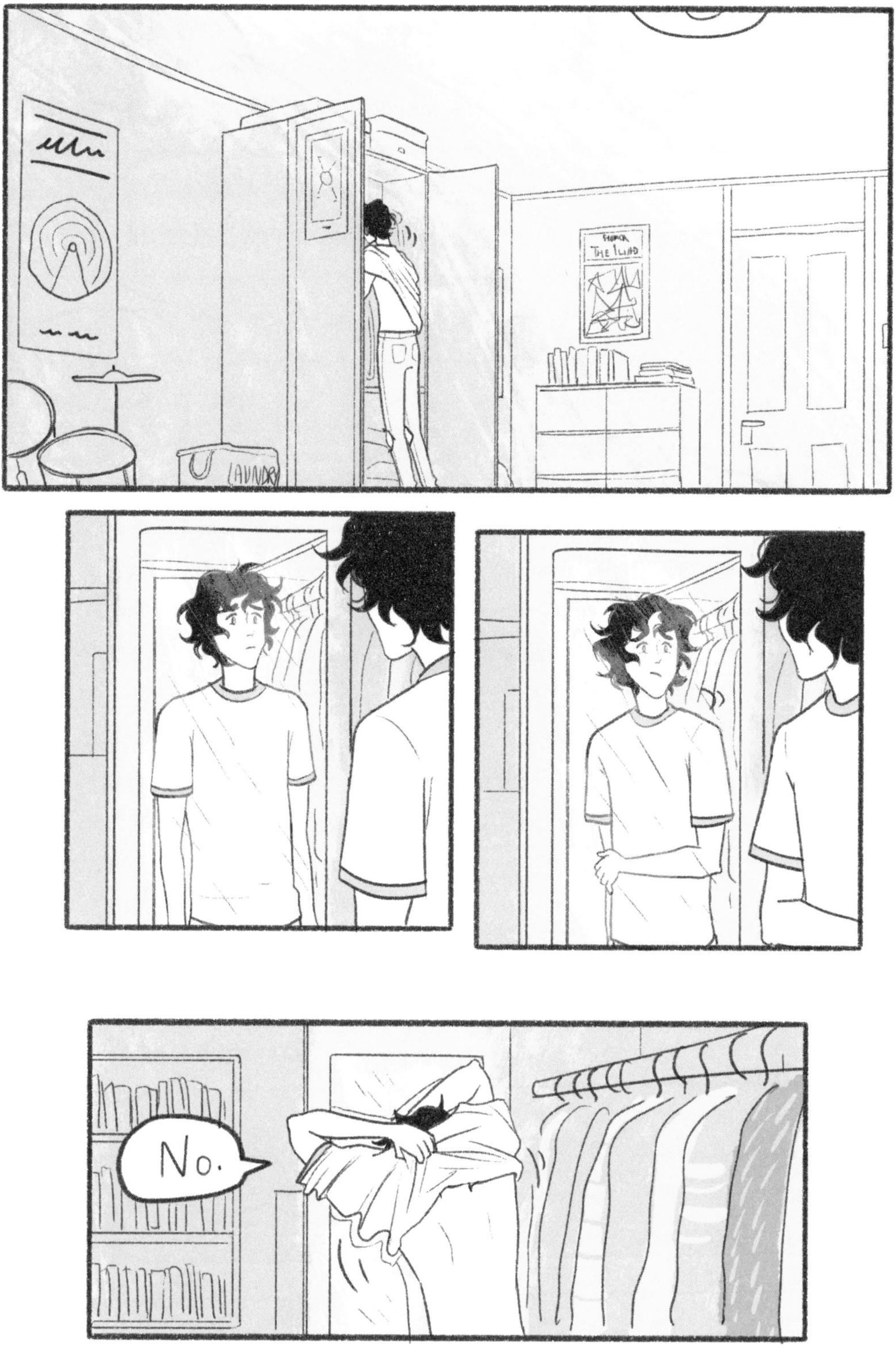
HOMER
THE ILIAD
LAUNDRY
No.

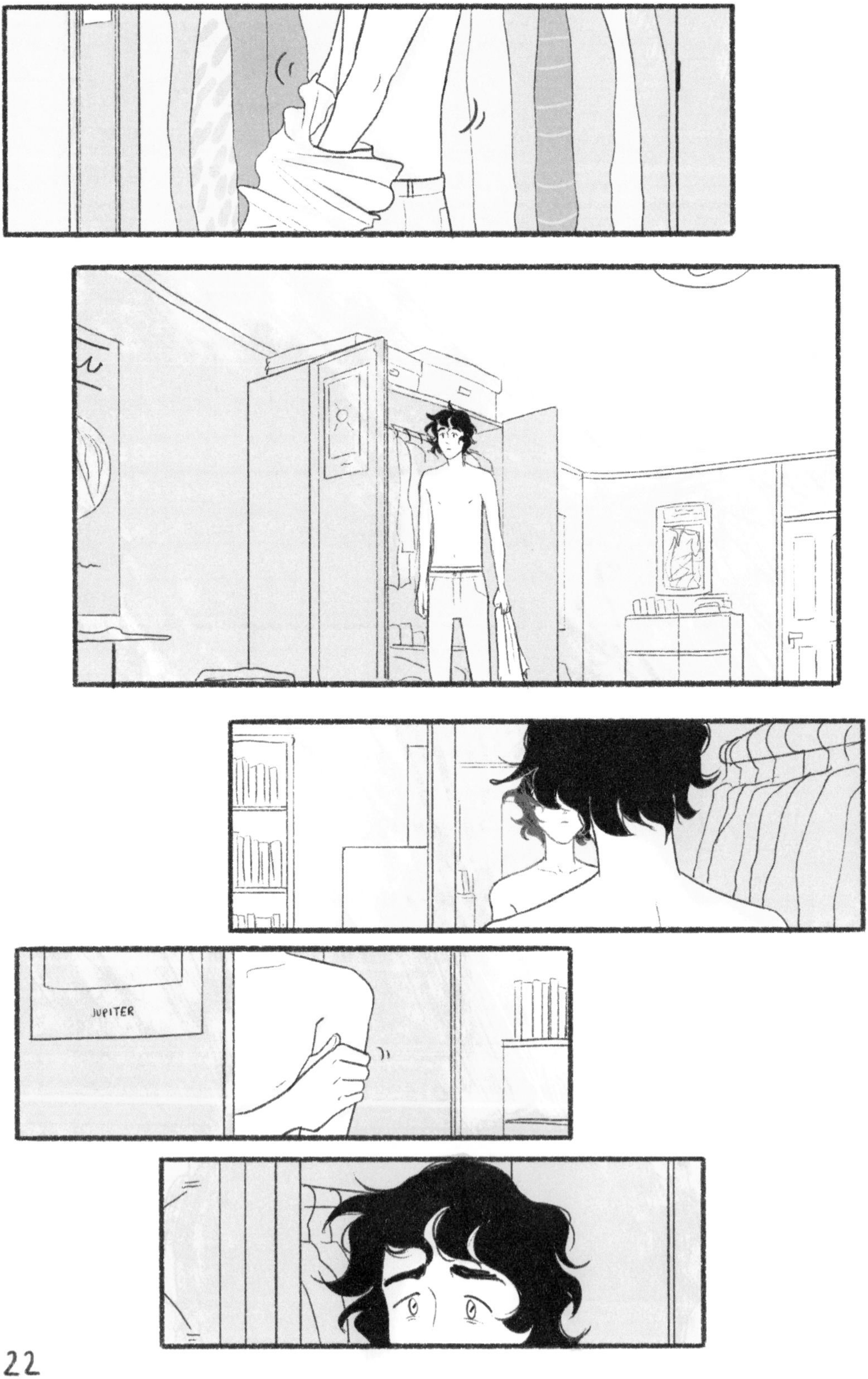
JUPITER

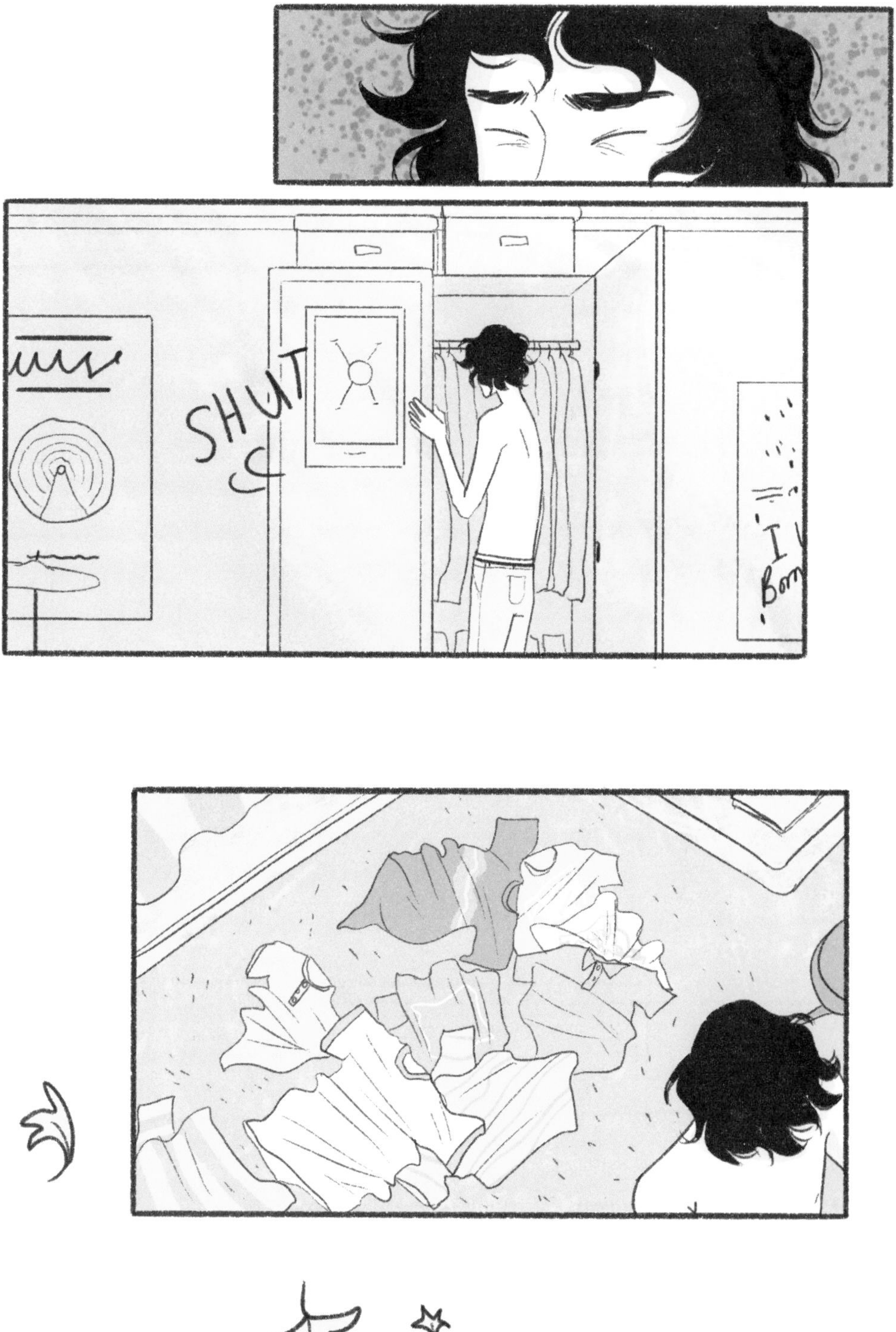
SHUT

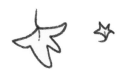

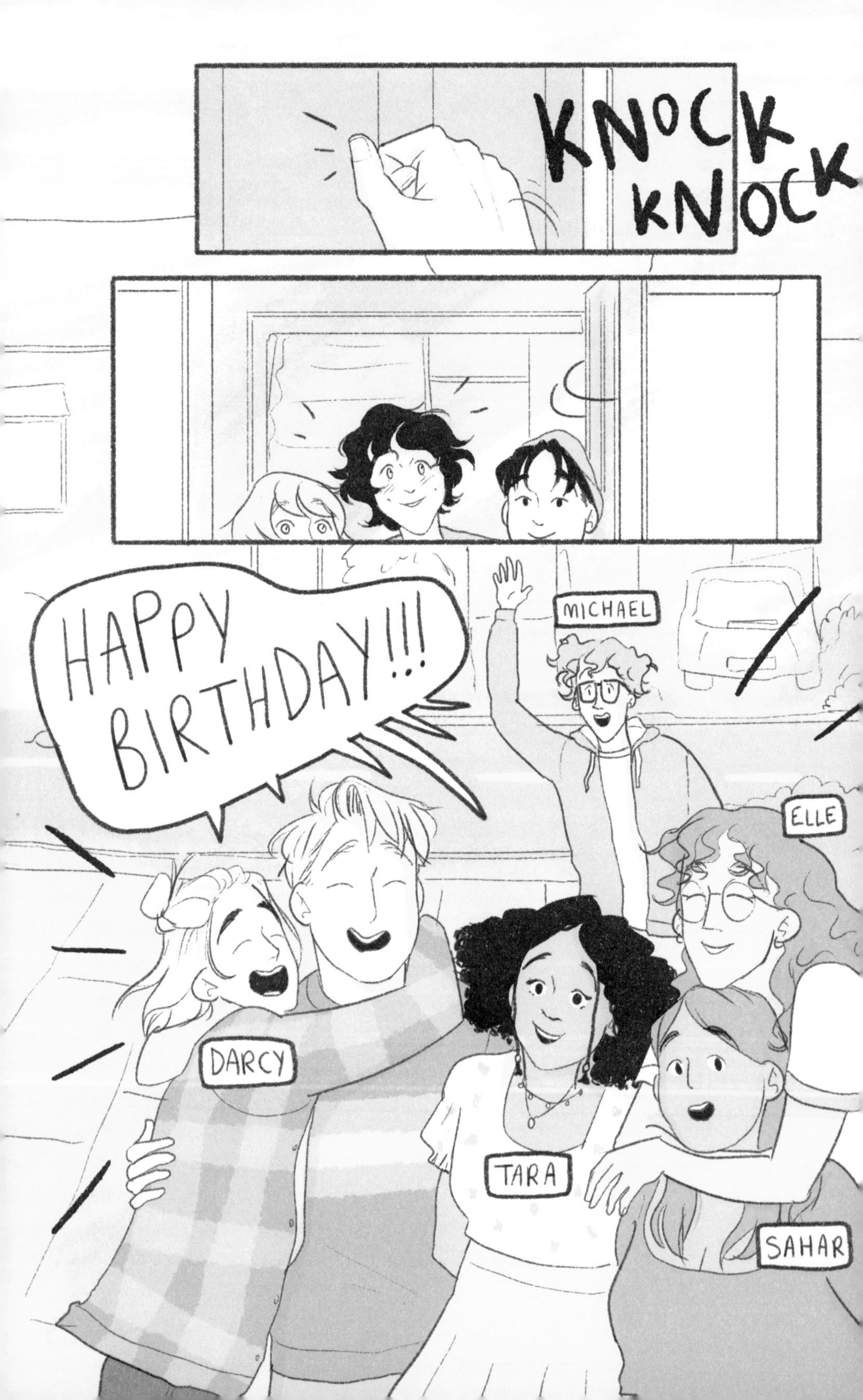

KNOCK
KNOCK
HAPPY BIRTHDAY!!!
MICHAEL
ELLE
DARCY
TARA
SAHAR

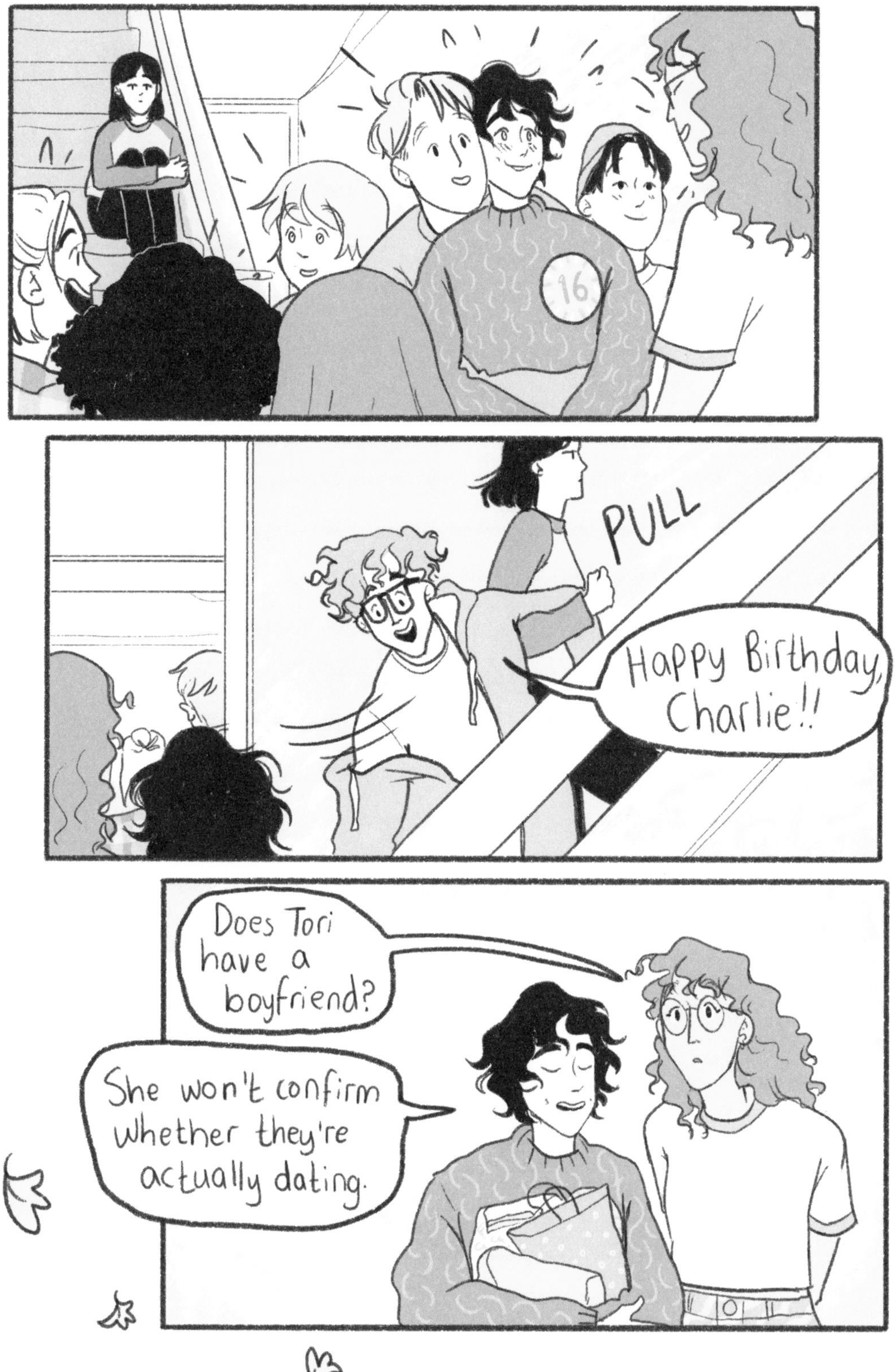
PULL
Happy Birthday, Charlie!!
Does Tori have a boyfriend?
She won't confirm whether they're actually dating.

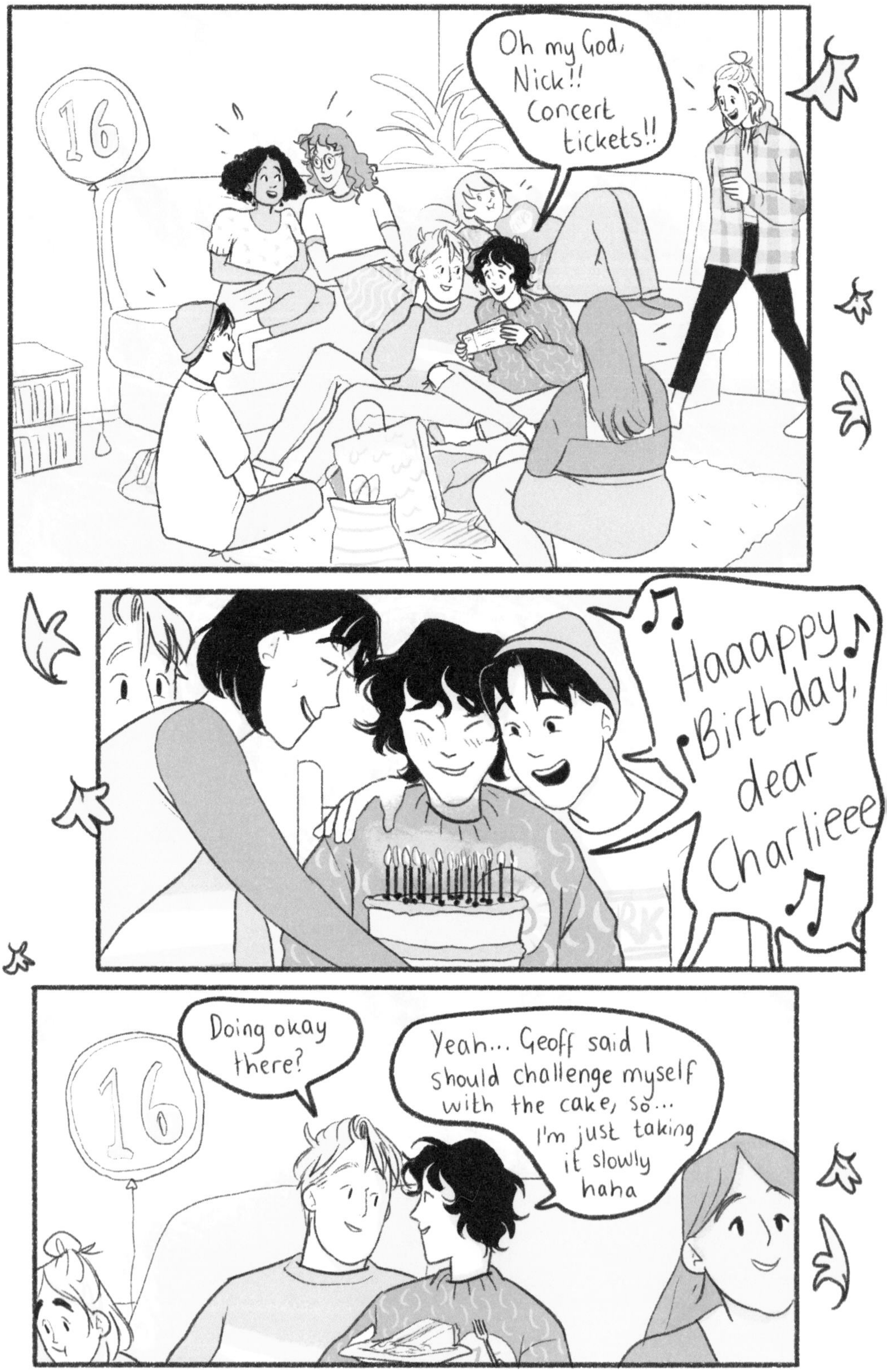
Oh my God, Nick!! Concert tickets!!
Haaappy Birthday, dear Charlieee
Doing okay there?
Yeah... Geoff said I should challenge myself with the cake, so... I'm just taking it slowly haha

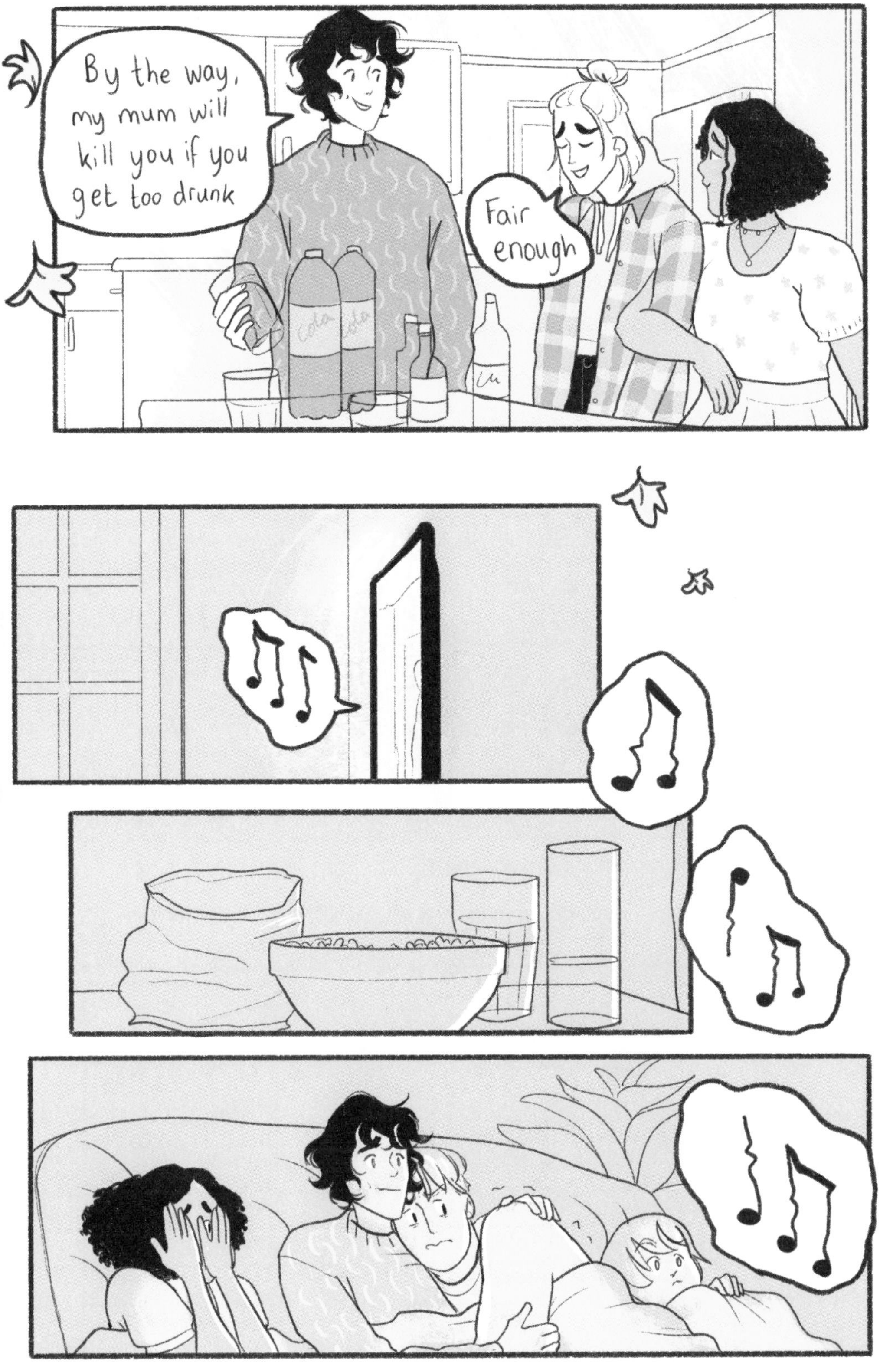
By the way, my mum will kill you if you get too drunk
Fair enough
cola
cola

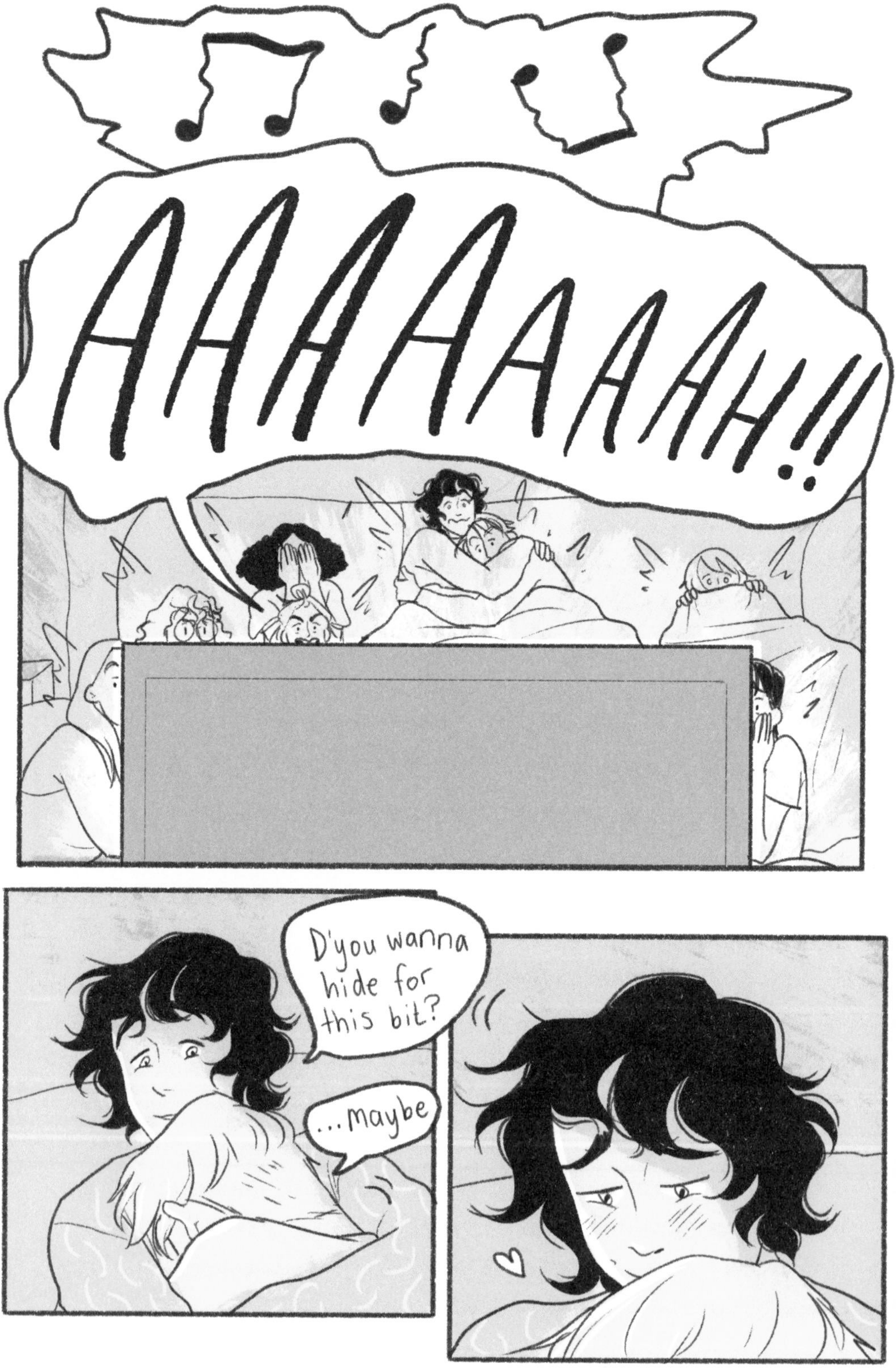
AAAAAAAAH!!
D'you wanna hide for this bit?
...maybe

Later...

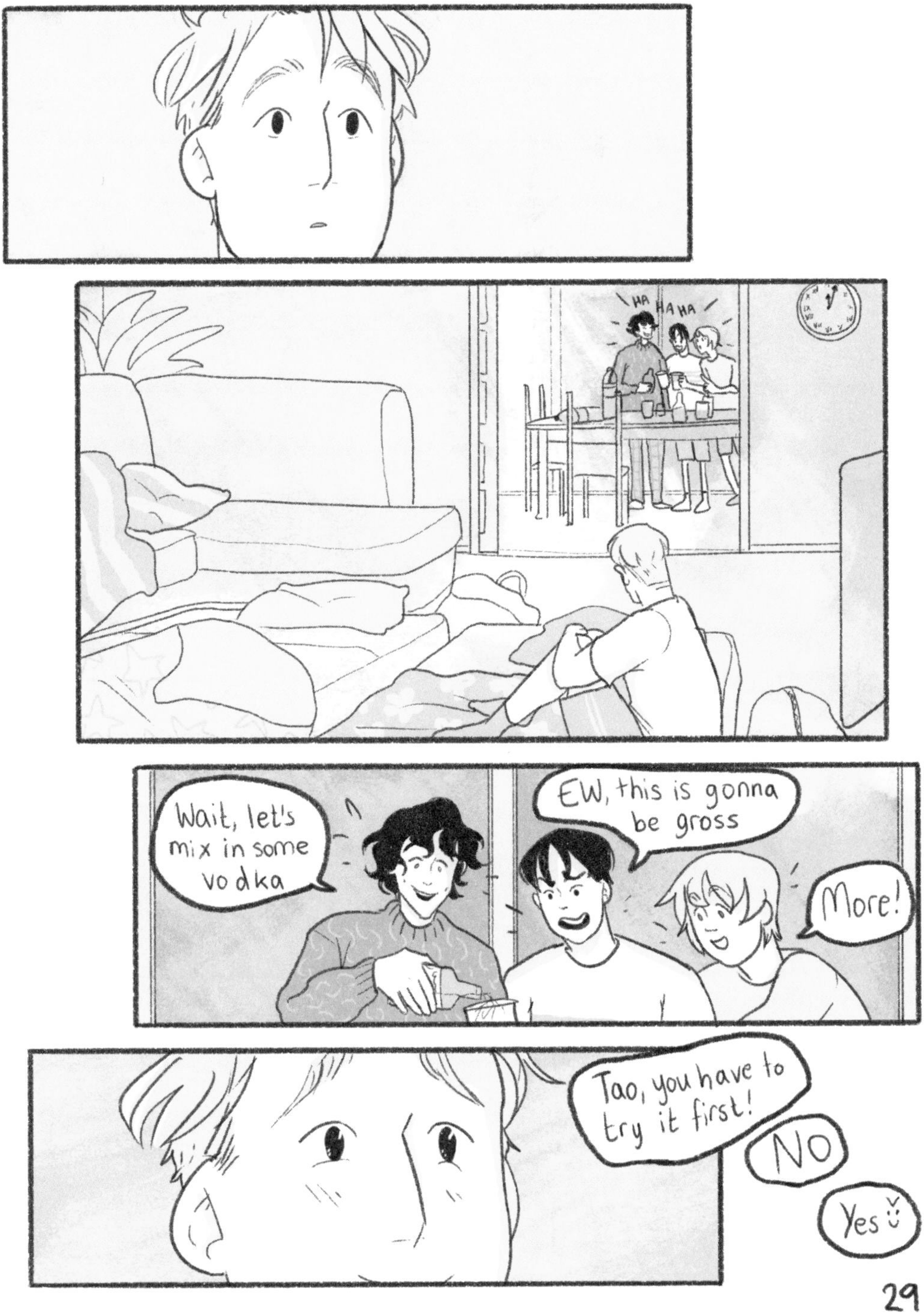
HA
HA HA
Wait, let's mix in some vodka
EW, this is gonna be gross
More!
Tao, you have to try it first!
NO
Yes

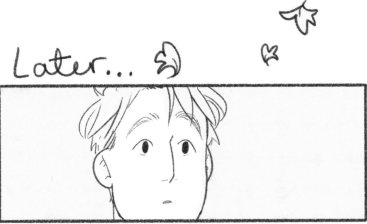

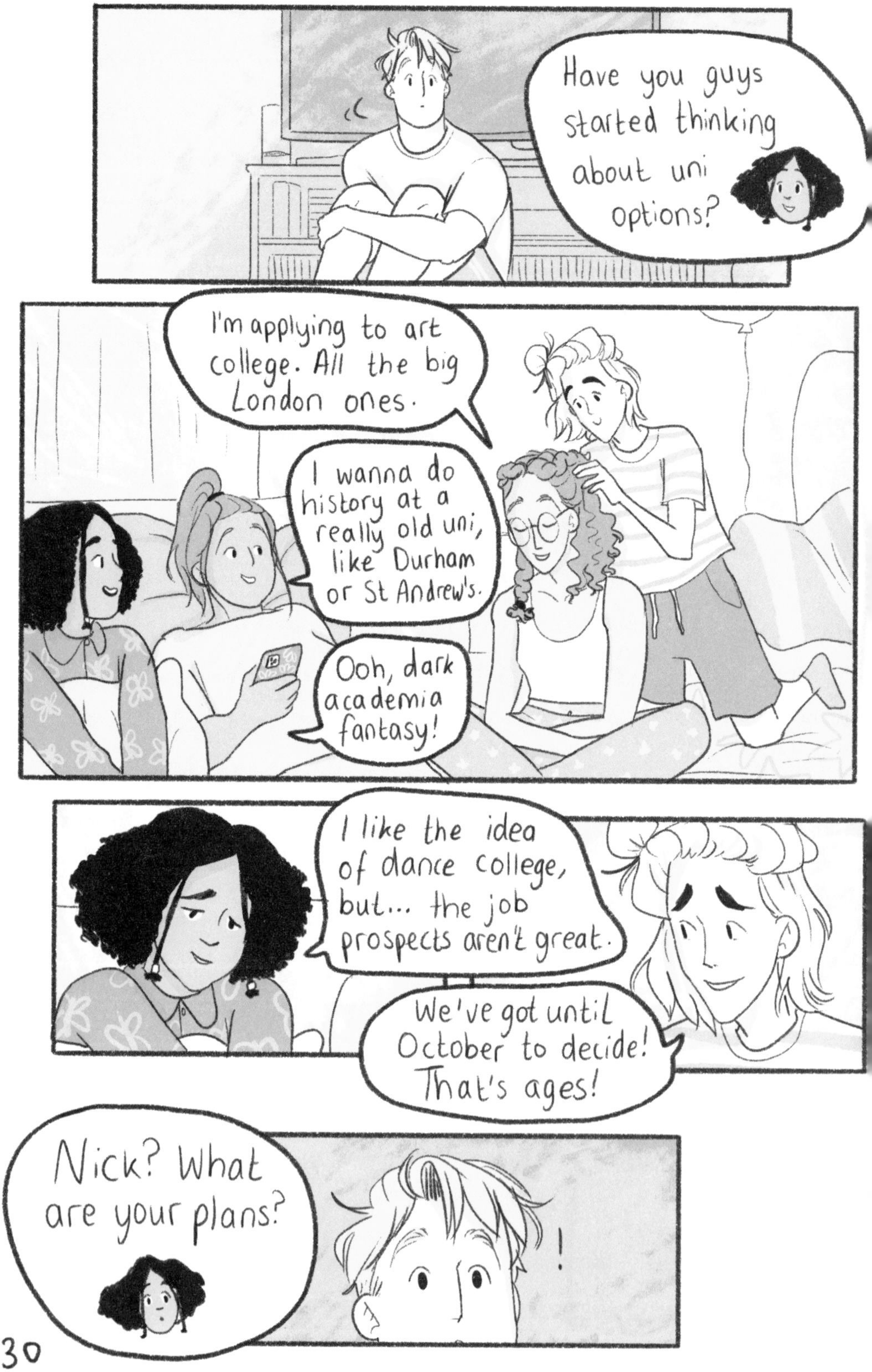
Have you guys started thinking about uni options?
I'm applying to art college. All the big London ones.
I wanna do history at a really old uni, like Durham or St Andrew's.
Ooh, dark academia fantasy!
I like the idea of dance college, but... the job prospects aren't great.
We've got until October to decide! That's ages!
Nick? What are your plans?
!

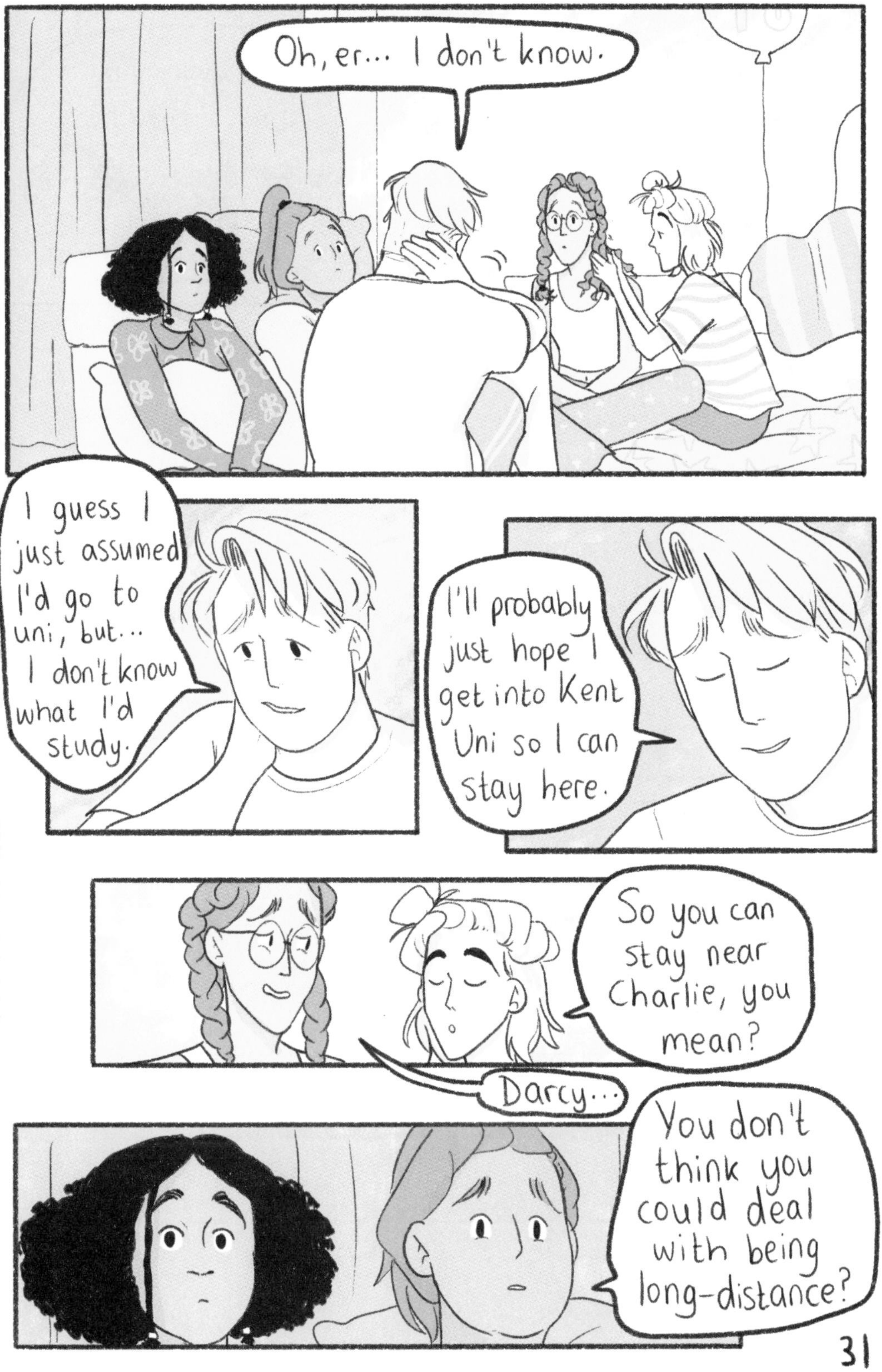
Oh, er... I don't know.
I guess I just assumed I'd go to uni, but... I don't know what I'd study.
I'll probably just hope I get into Kent Uni so I can stay here.
So you can stay near Charlie, you mean?
Darcy...
You don't think you could deal with being long-distance?

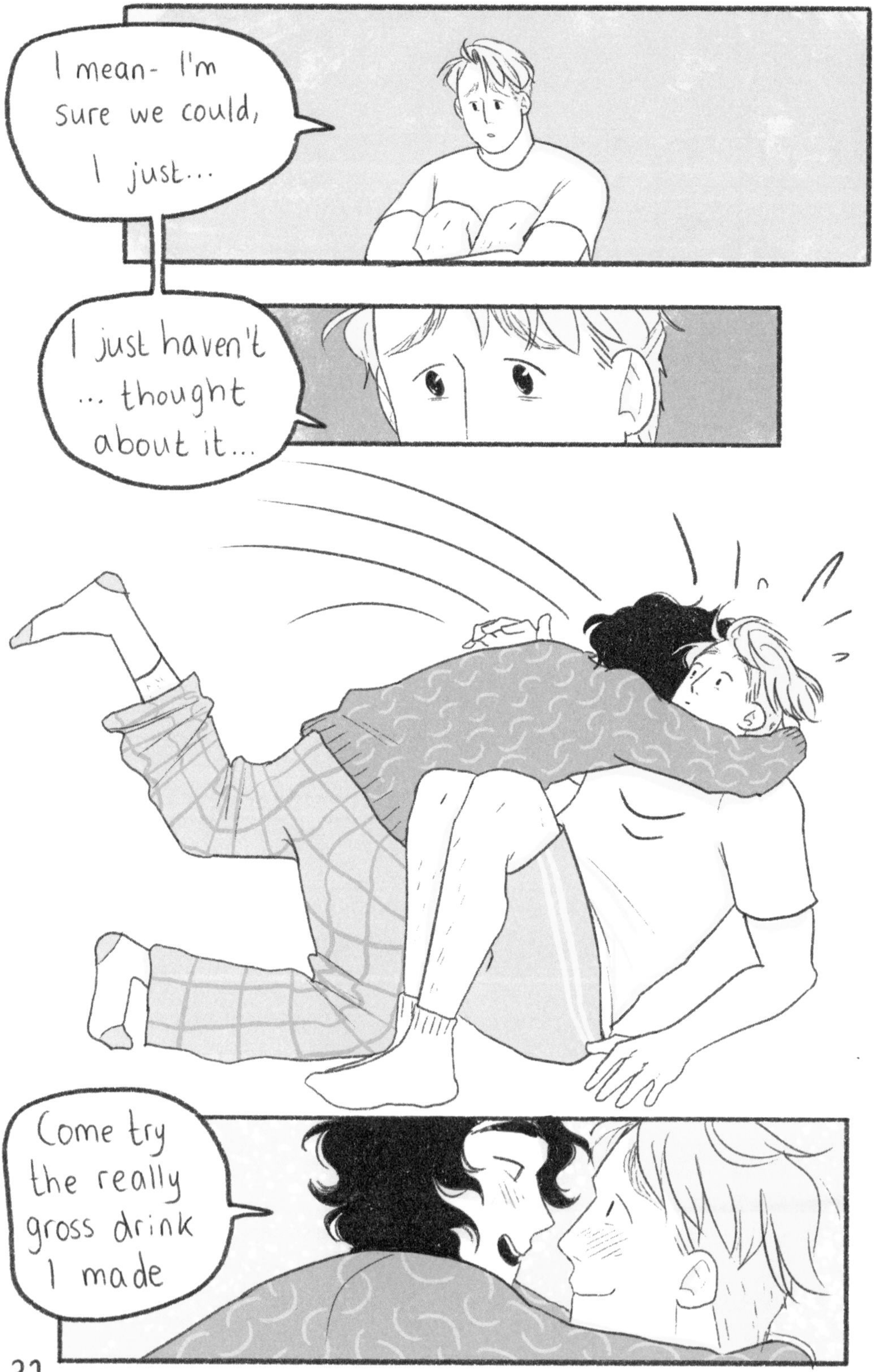
I mean- I'm sure we could, I just...
I just haven't ... thought about it...
Come try the really gross drink I made

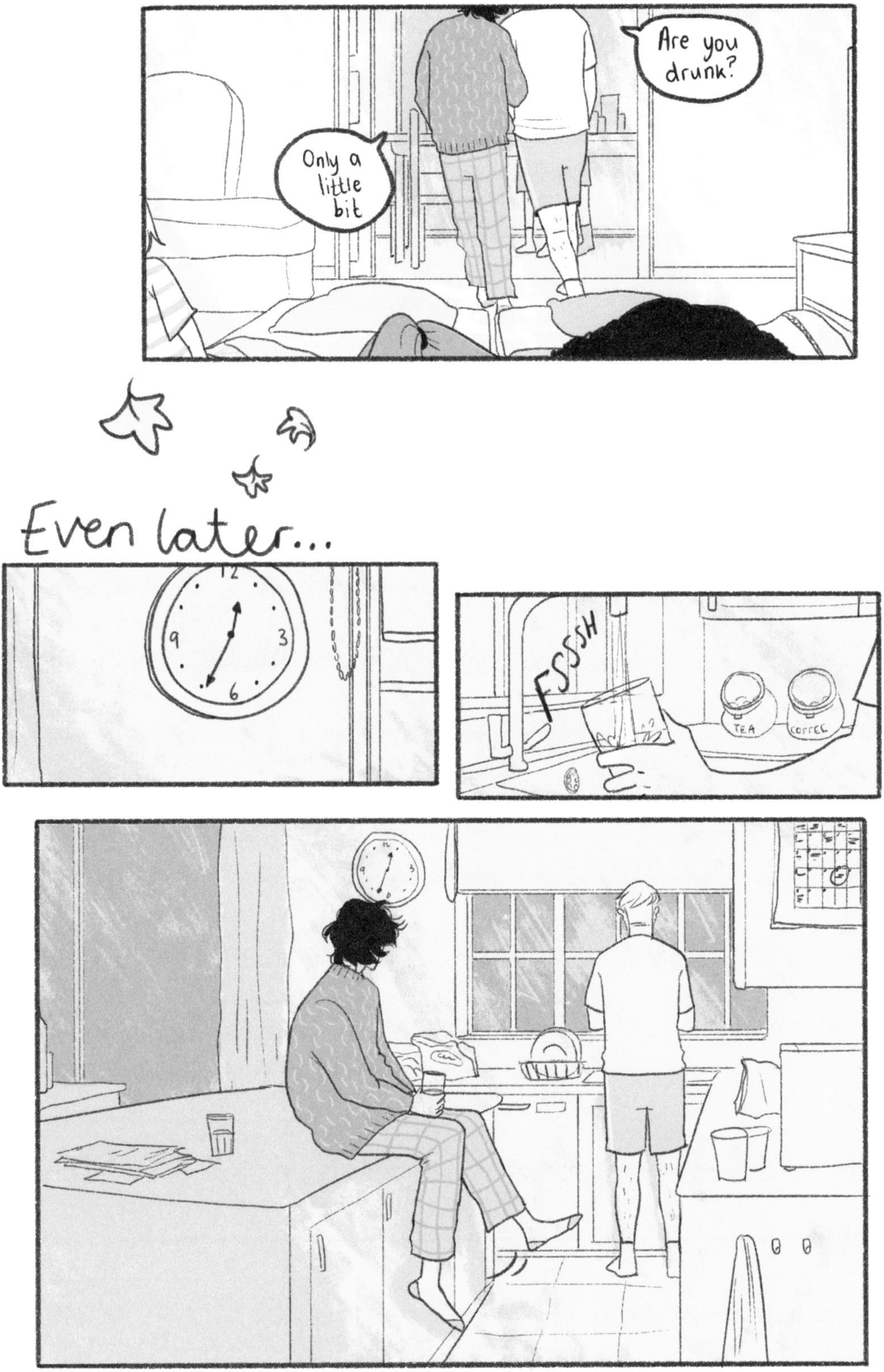
Are you drunk?
Only a little bit
Even later...
FSSSH
TEA
COFFEE

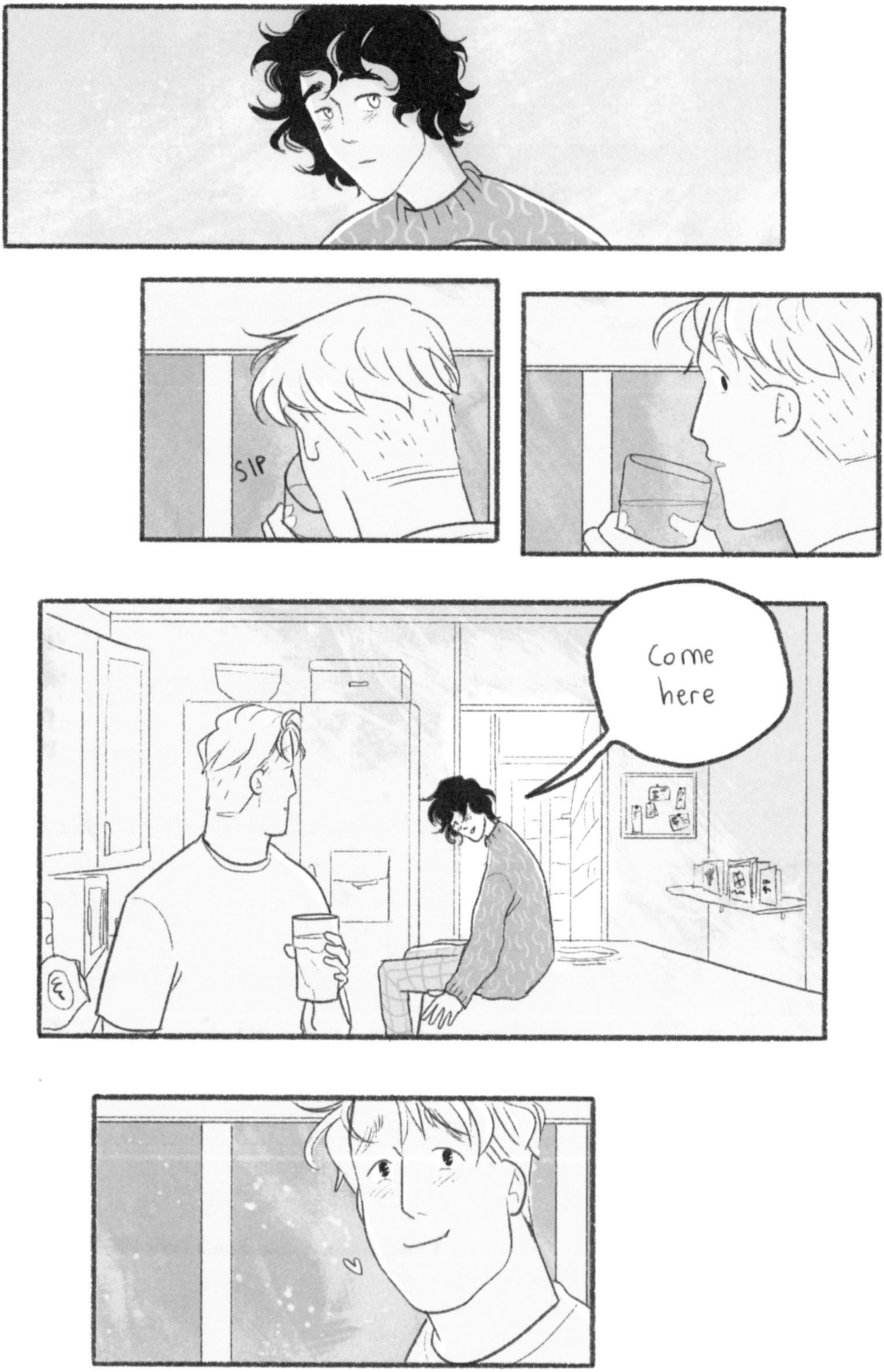
SIP
Come here

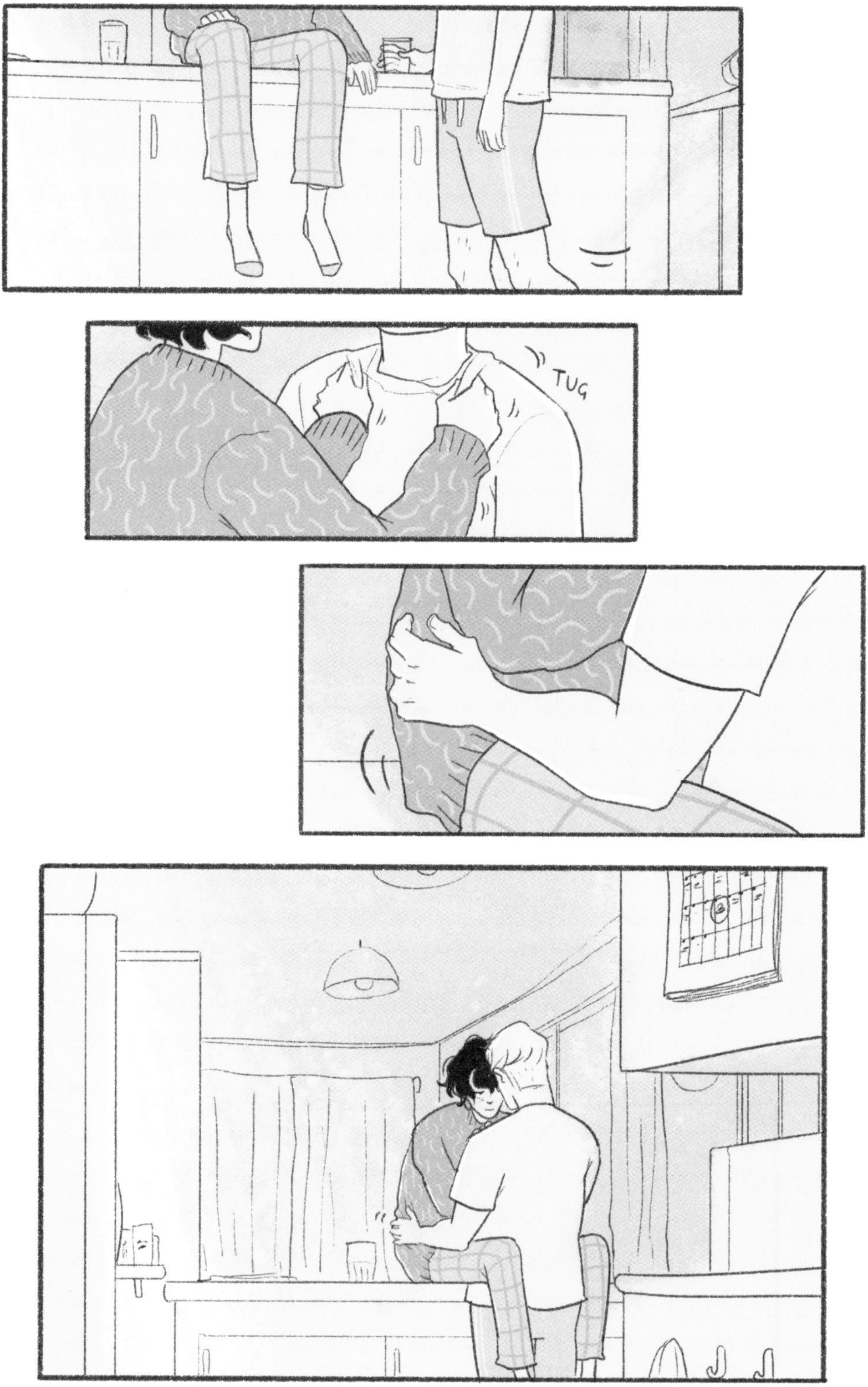
TUG

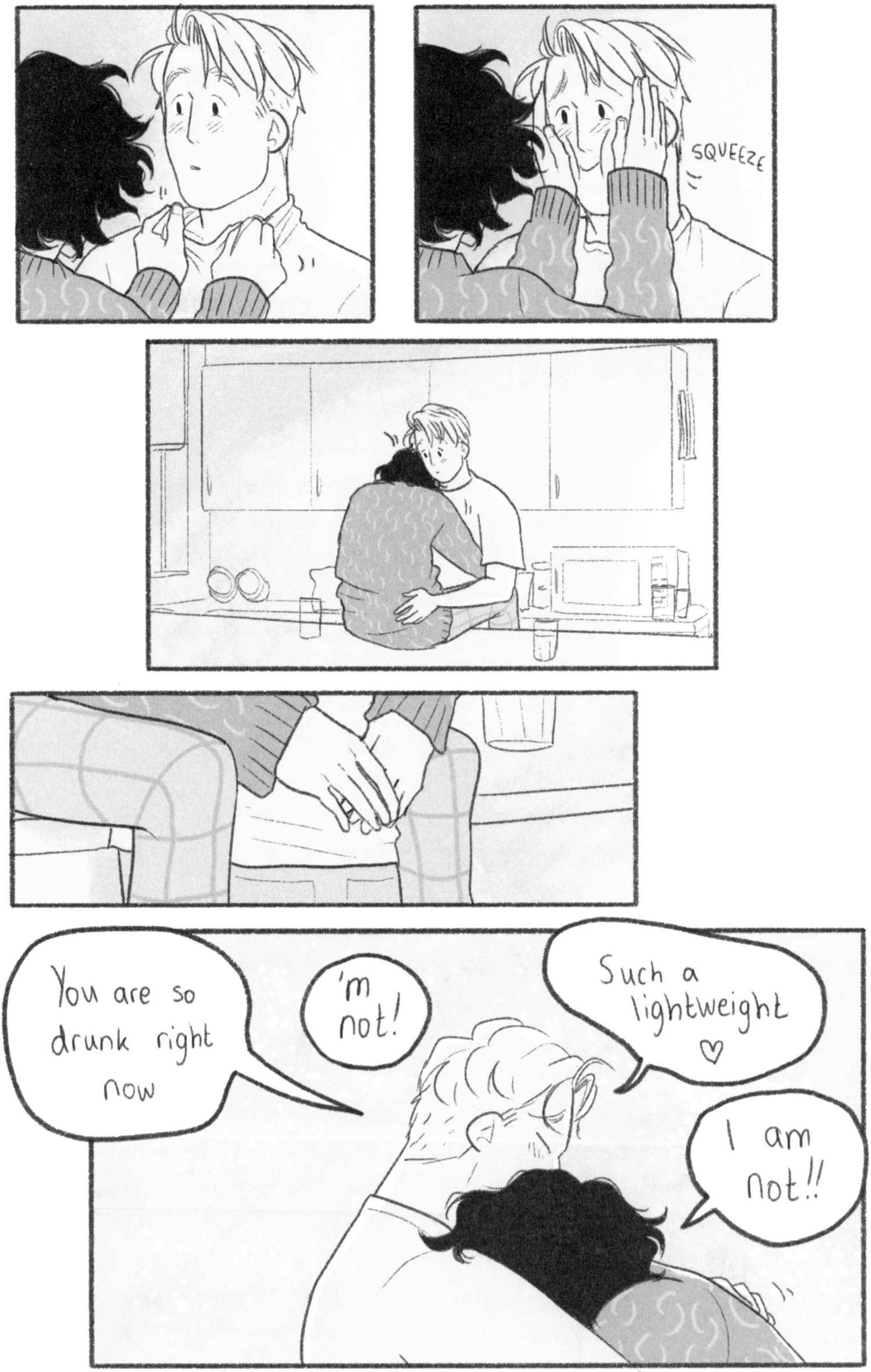
SQUEEZE
You are so drunk right now
'm not!
Such a lightweight ♡
I am not!!

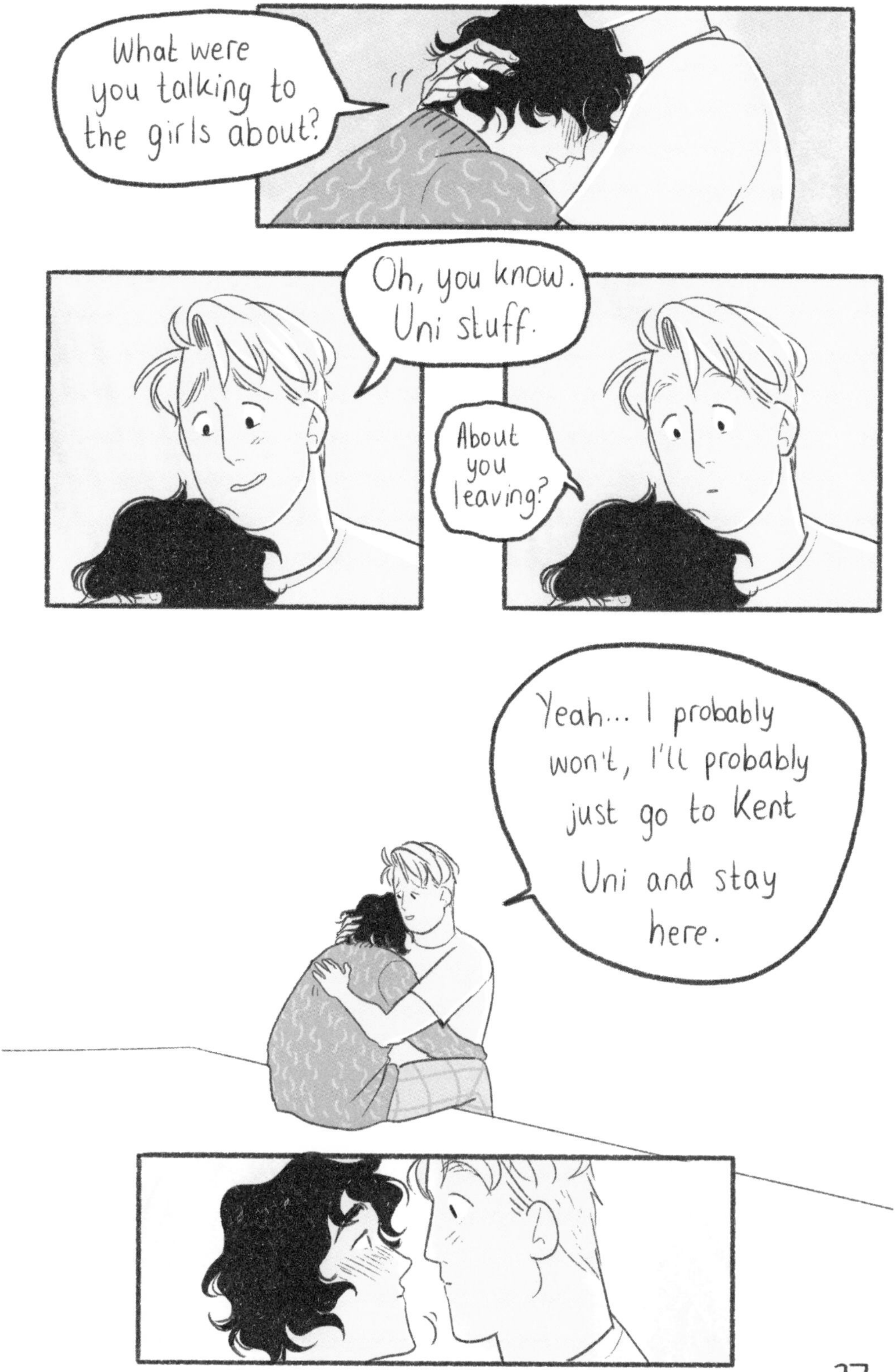
What were you talking to the girls about?
Oh, you know. Uni stuff.
About you leaving?
Yeah... I probably won't, I'll probably just go to Kent Uni and stay here.

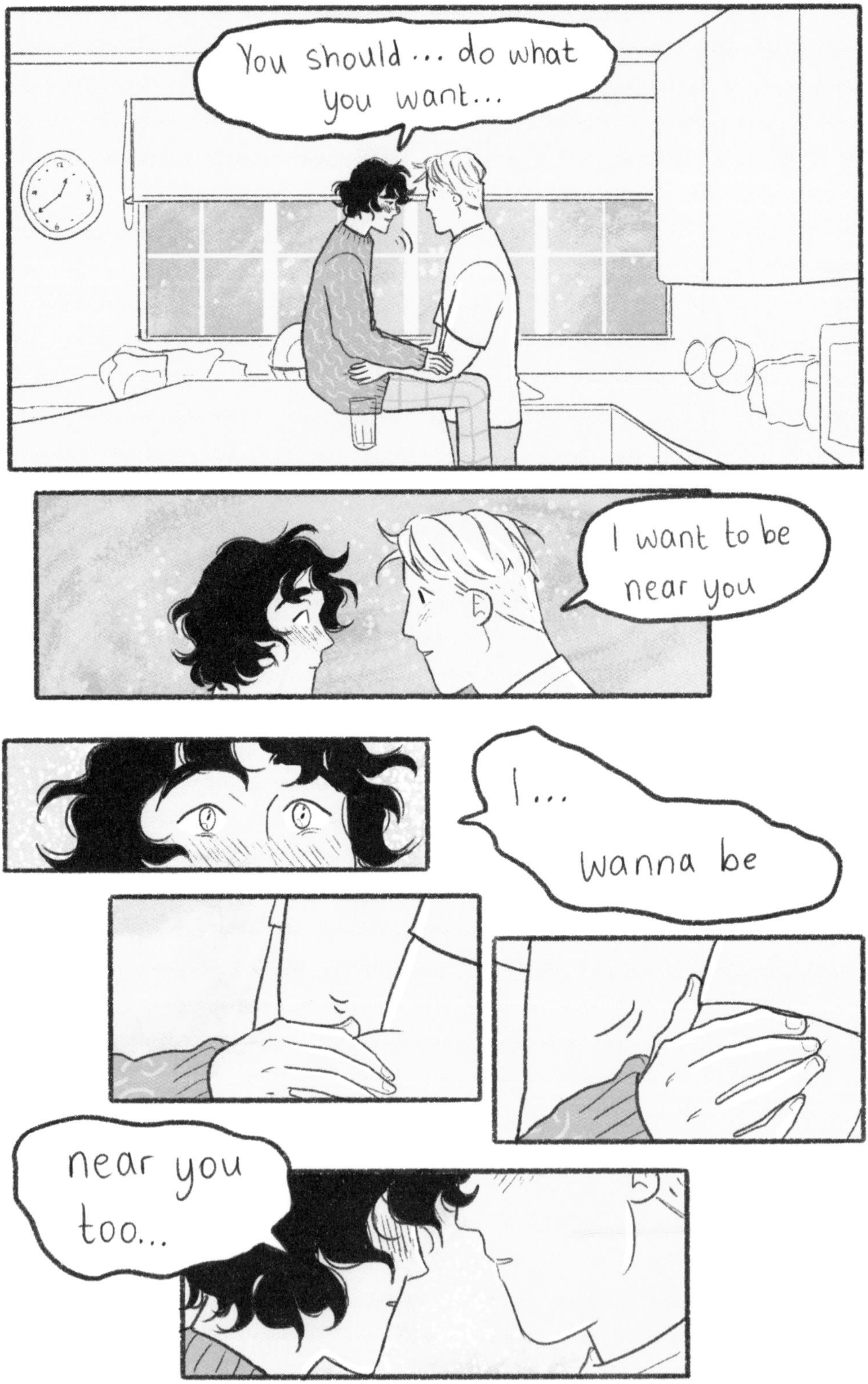
You should... do what you want...
I want to be near you
I...
wanna be
near you too...

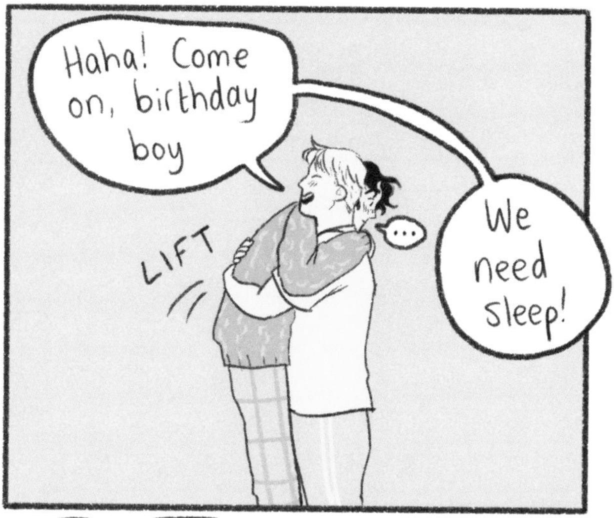
Haha! Come on, birthday boy
LIFT
...
We need sleep!

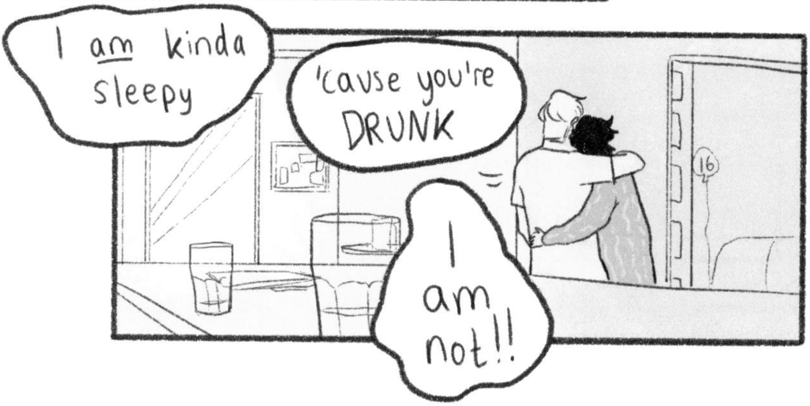
I am kinda sleepy
'Cause you're DRUNK
I am not!!
16

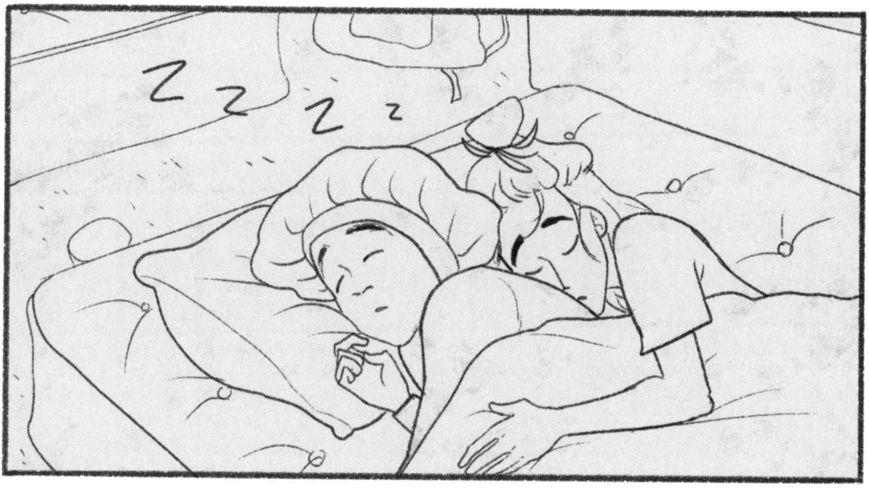
Z z Z z

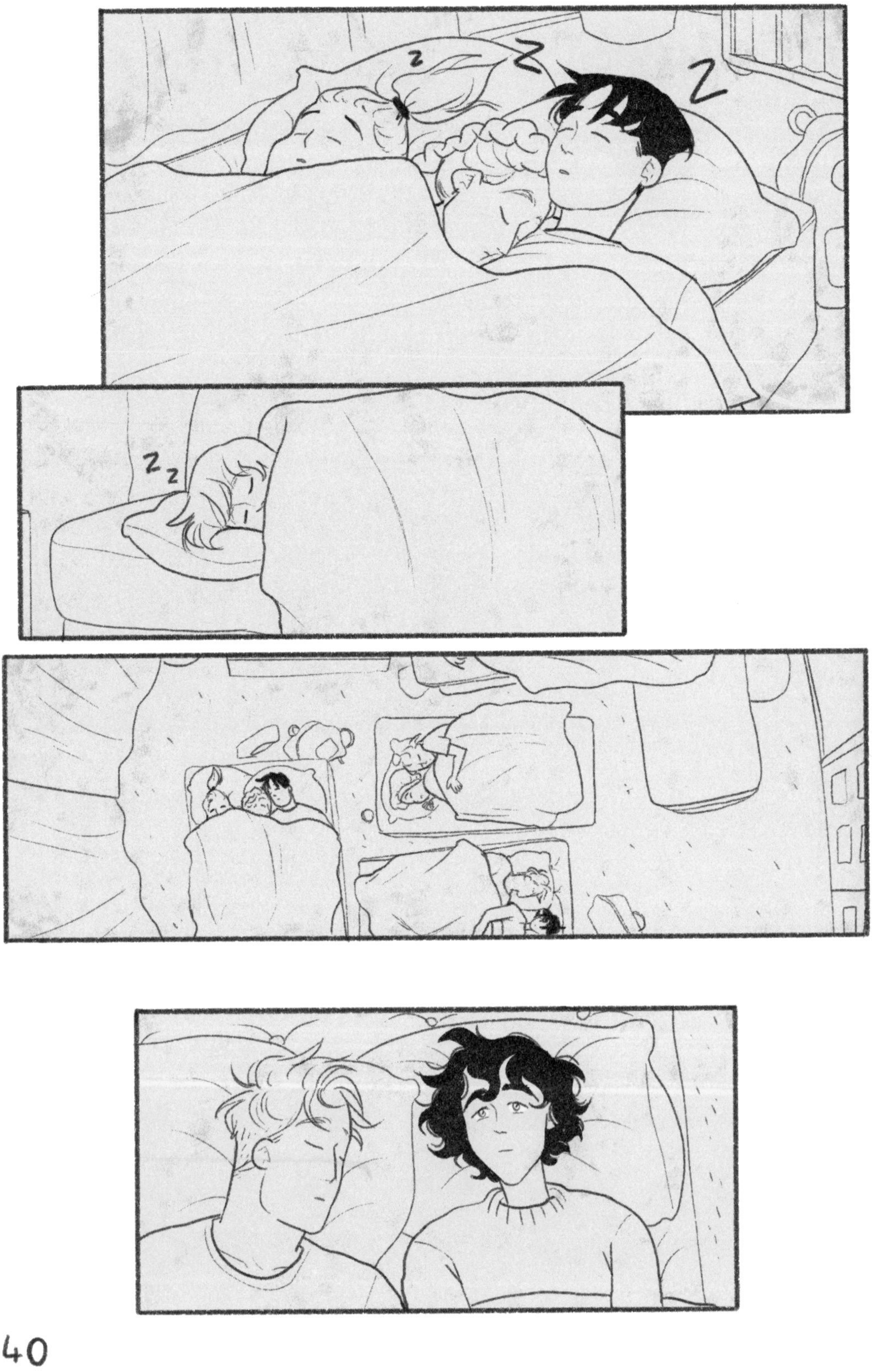
z Z Z
Z z

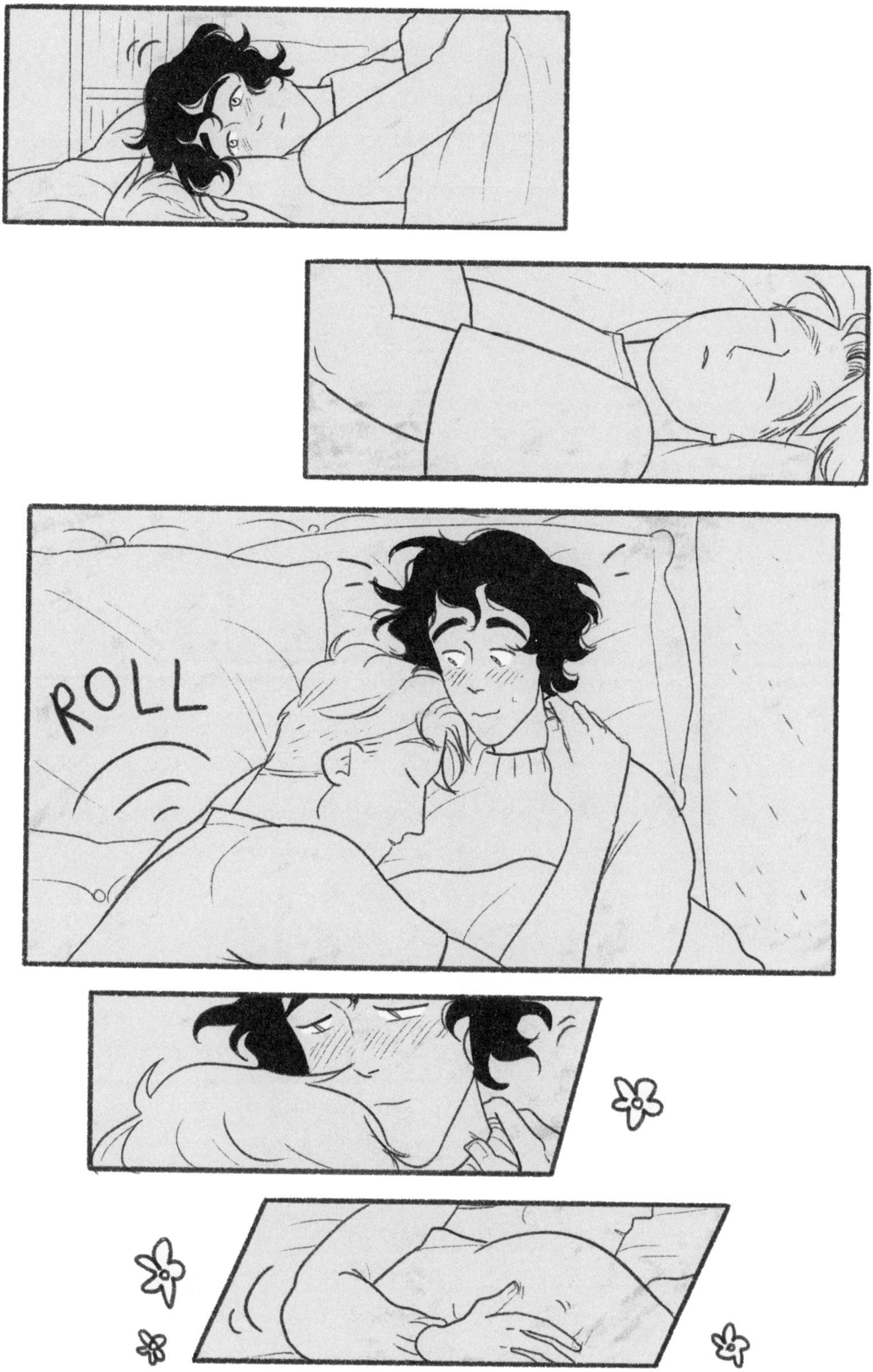
ROLL

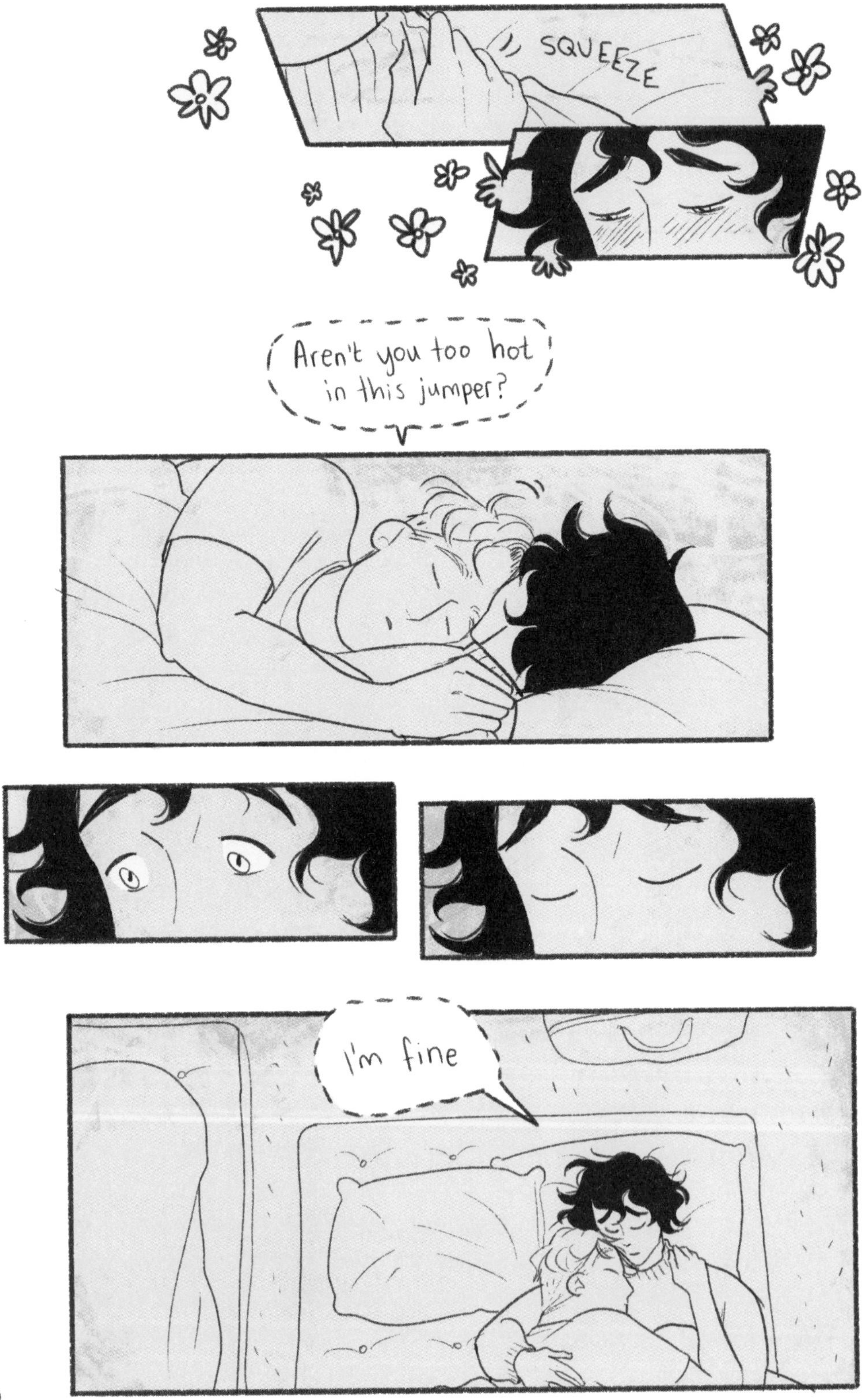
SQUEEZE
Aren't you too hot in this jumper?
I'm fine

MAY

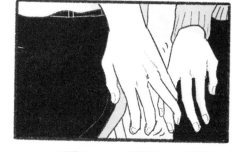

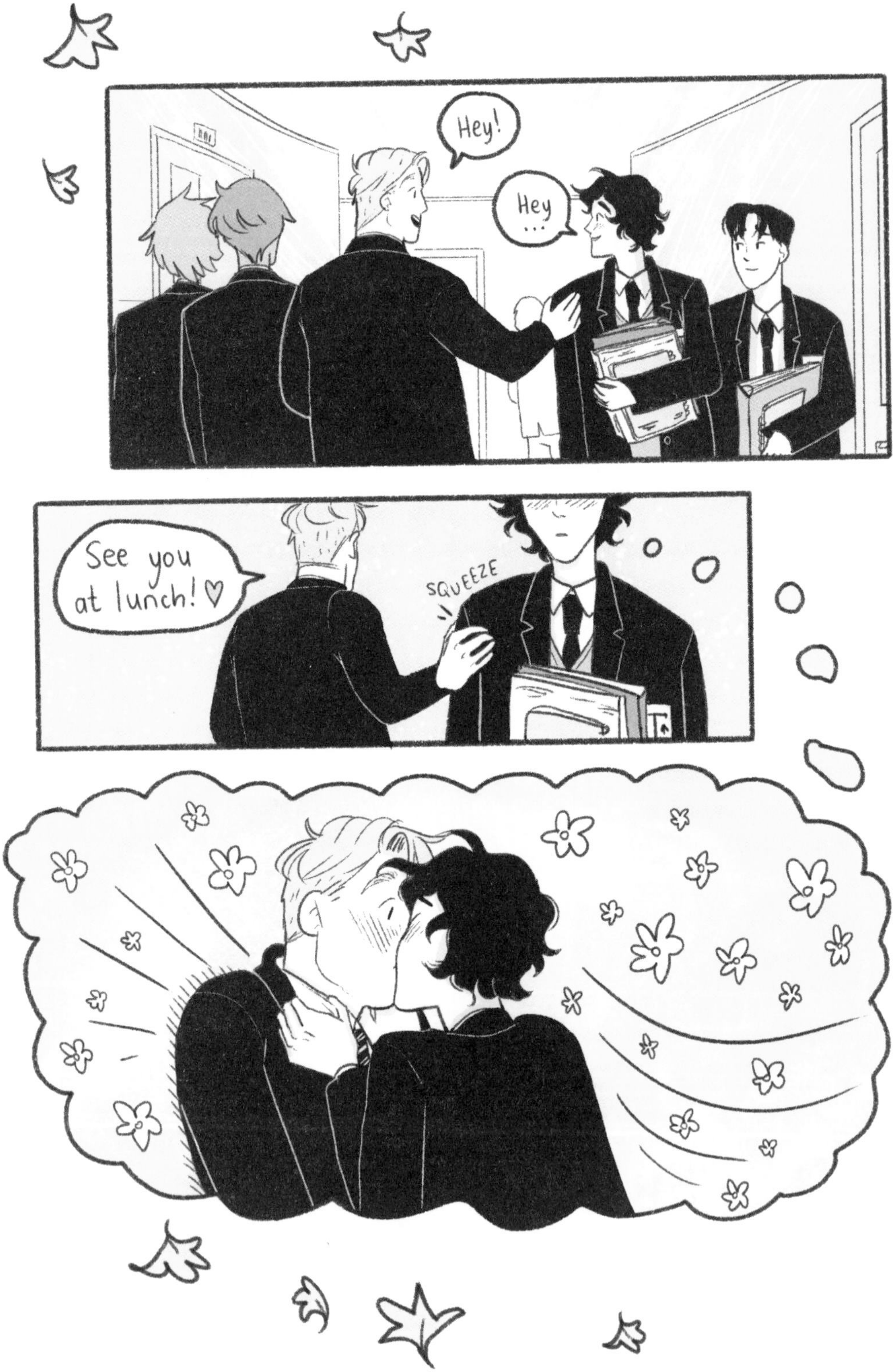
Hey!
Hey
...
See you at lunch! ♡
SQUEEZE

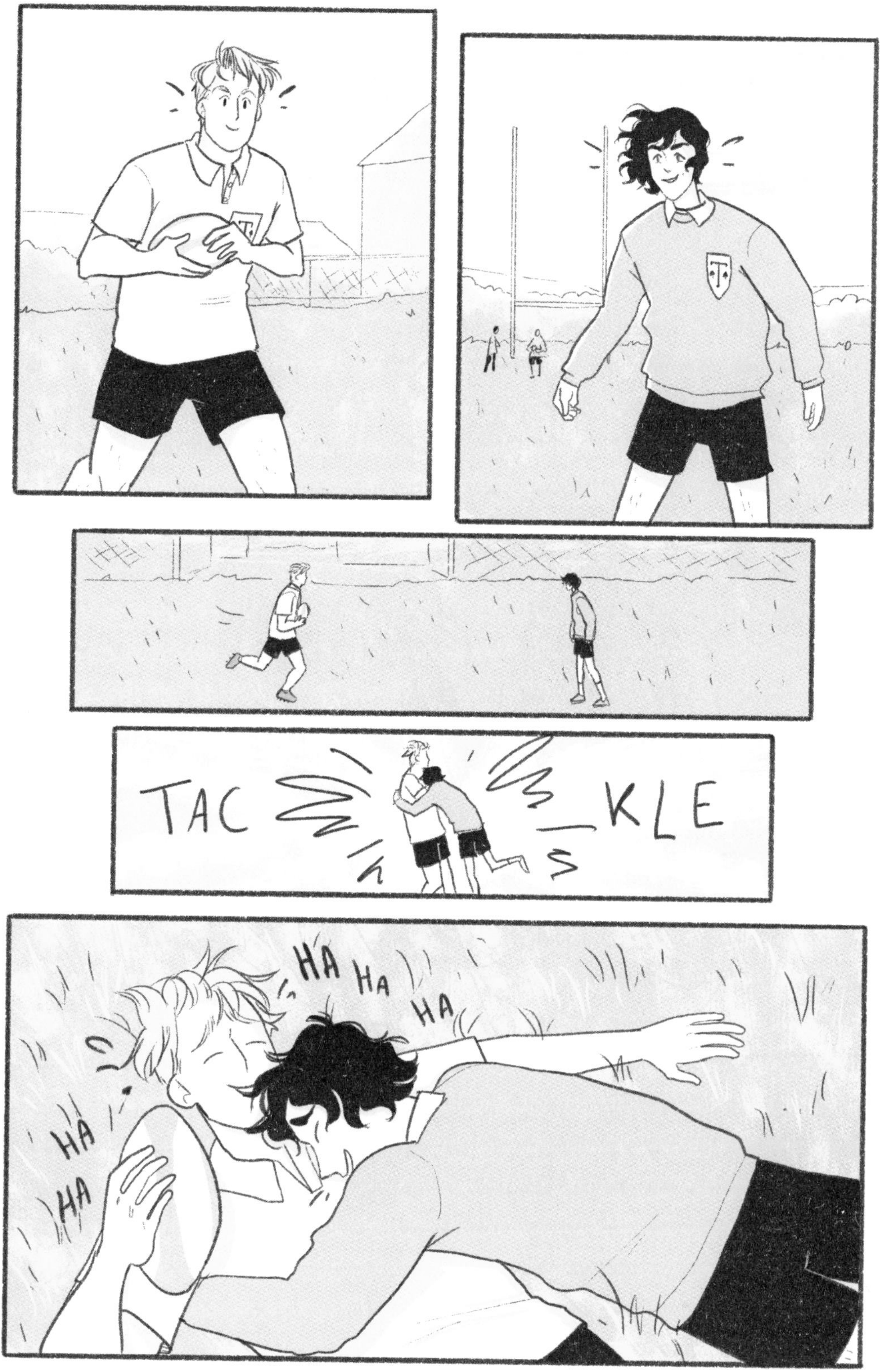
TAC KLE
HA HA HA
HA HA

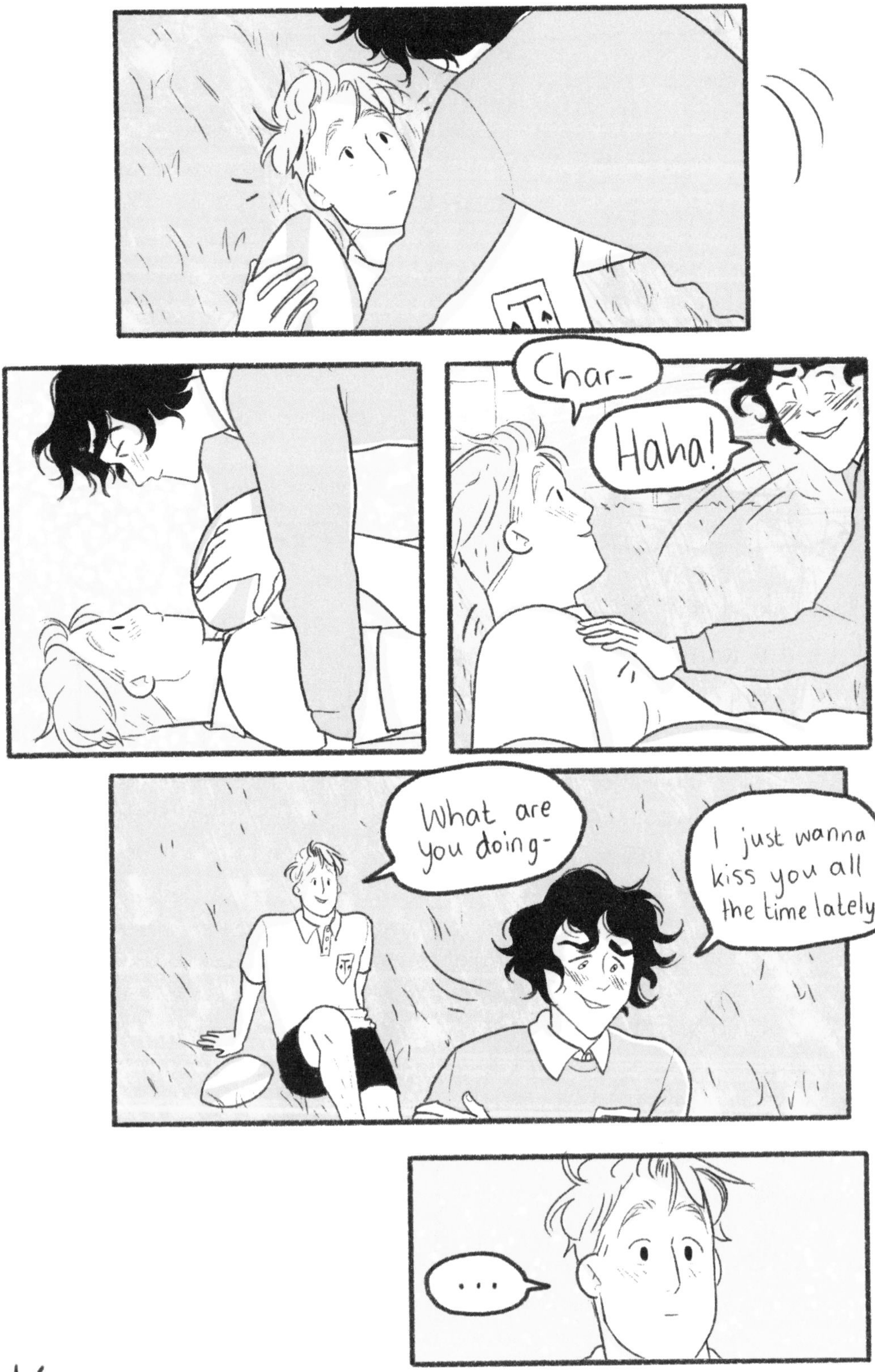
Char-
Haha!
What are you doing-
I just wanna kiss you all the time lately
...

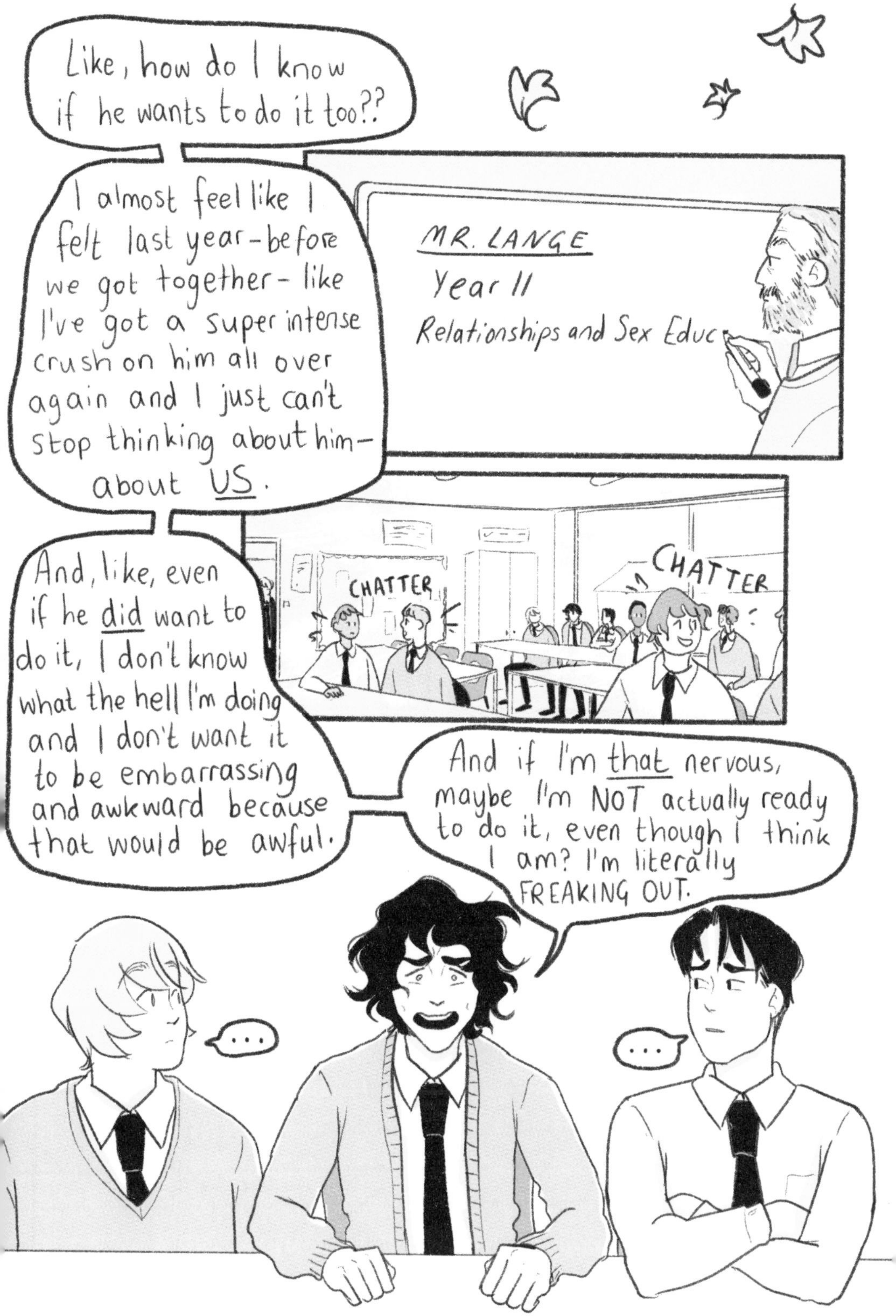
Like, how do I know if he wants to do it too??
I almost feel like I felt last year – before we got together – like I've got a super intense crush on him all over again and I just can't stop thinking about him – about US.
MR. LANGE
Year 11
Relationships and Sex Educ
CHATTER
CHATTER
And, like, even if he did want to do it, I don't know what the hell I'm doing and I don't want it to be embarrassing and awkward because that would be awful.
And if I'm that nervous, maybe I'm NOT actually ready to do it, even though I think I am? I'm literally FREAKING OUT.
...
...

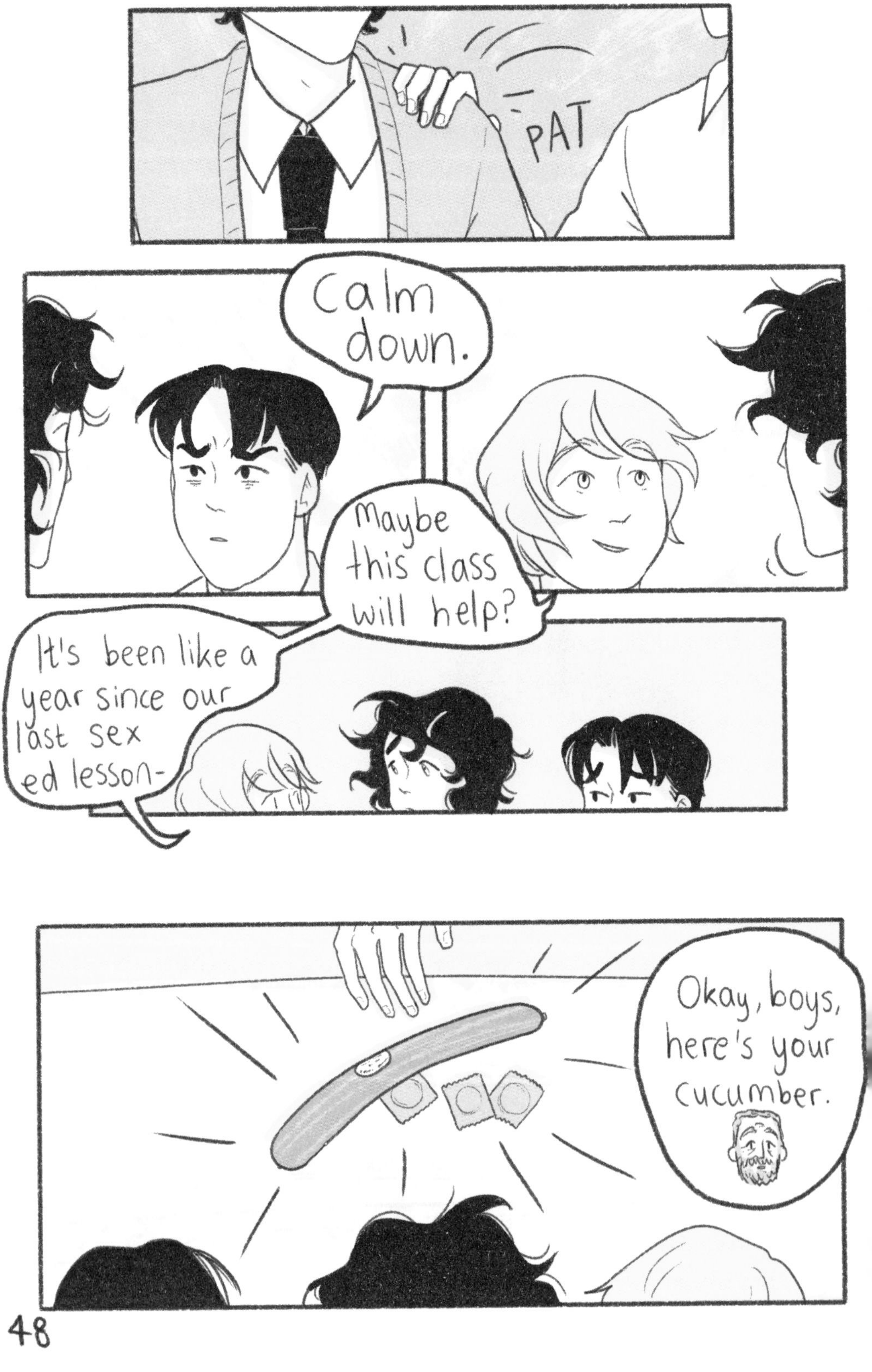
PAT
Calm down.
Maybe this class will help?
It's been like a year since our last sex ed lesson-
Okay, boys, here's your cucumber.

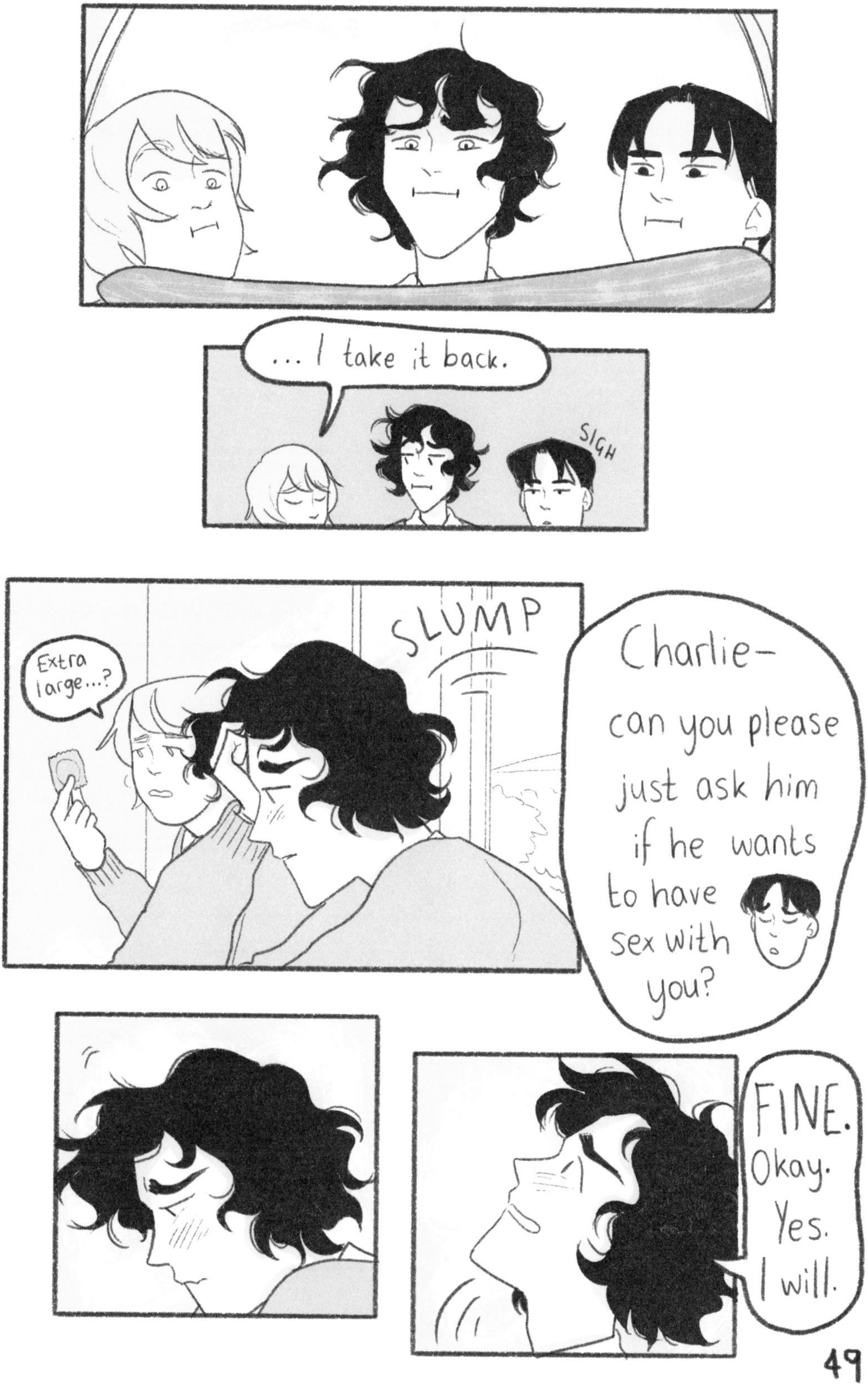
... I take it back.
SIGH
Extra large...?
SLUMP
Charlie- can you please just ask him if he wants to have sex with you?
FINE. Okay. Yes. I will.

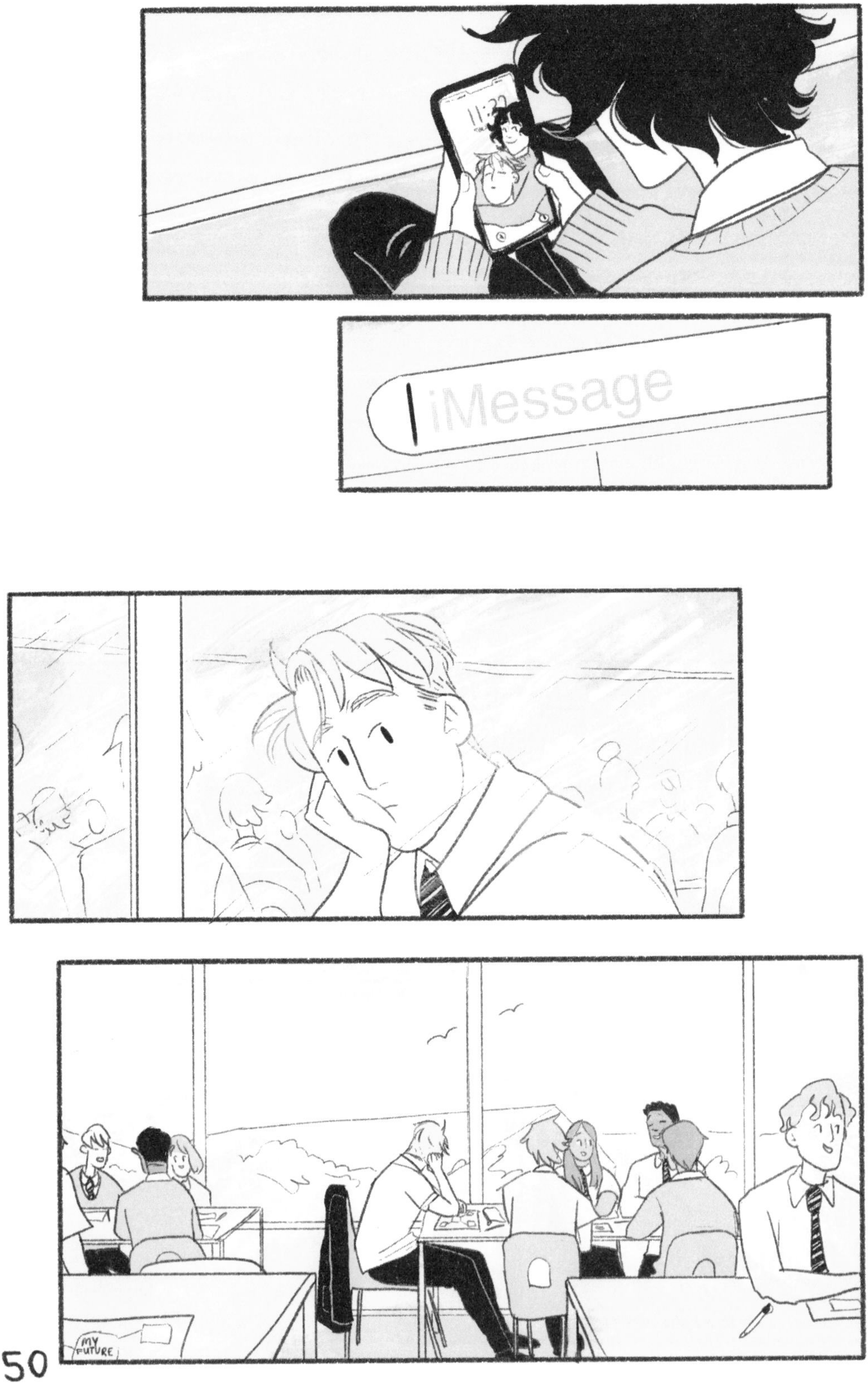
iMessage
MY FUTURE

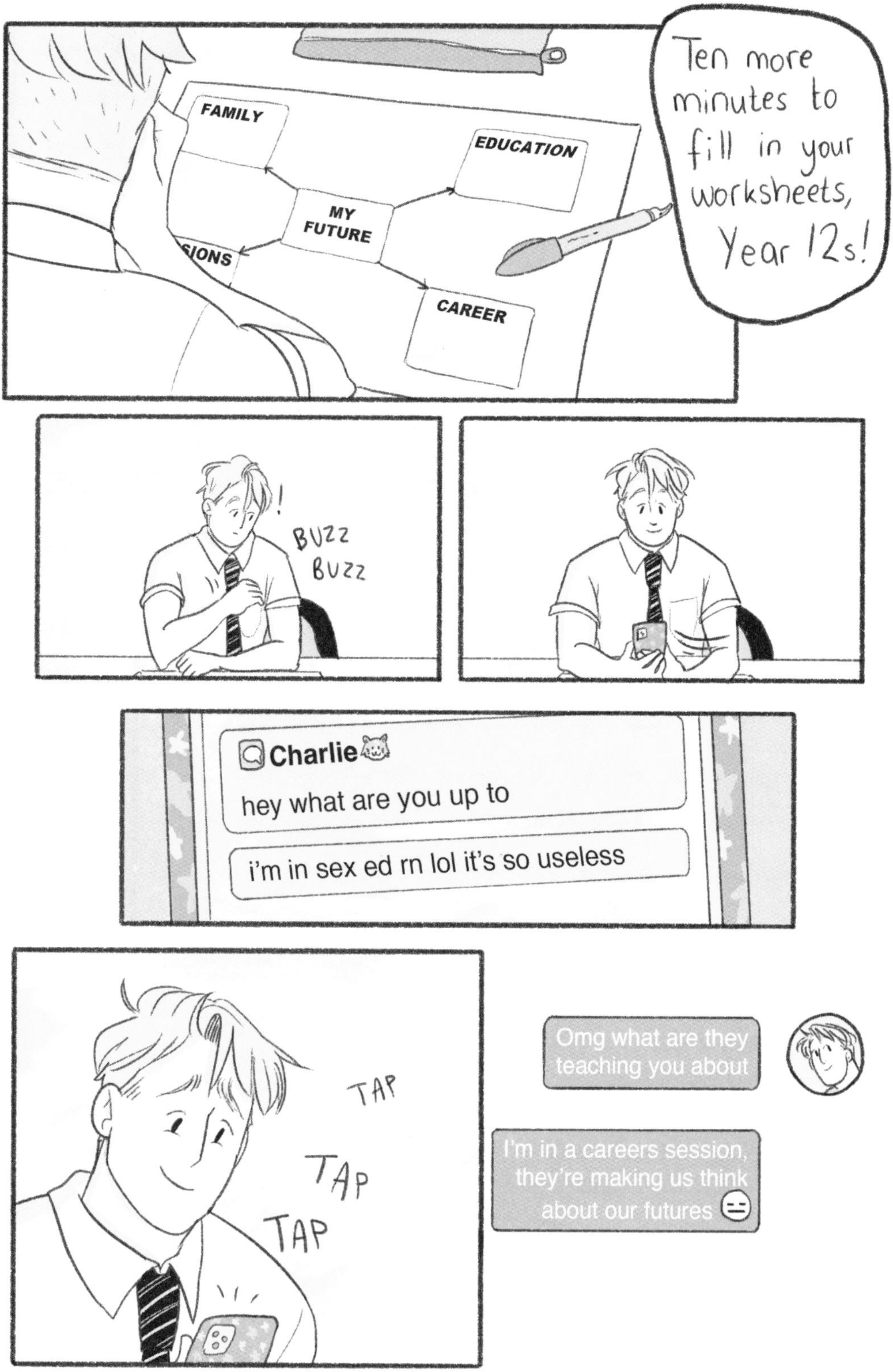
FAMILY
EDUCATION
MY FUTURE
SIONS
CAREER
Ten more minutes to fill in your worksheets, Year 12s!
!
BUZZ BUZZ
Charlie
hey what are you up to
i'm in sex ed rn lol it's so useless
TAP
TAP
TAP
Omg what are they teaching you about
I'm in a careers session, they're making us think about our futures 😑

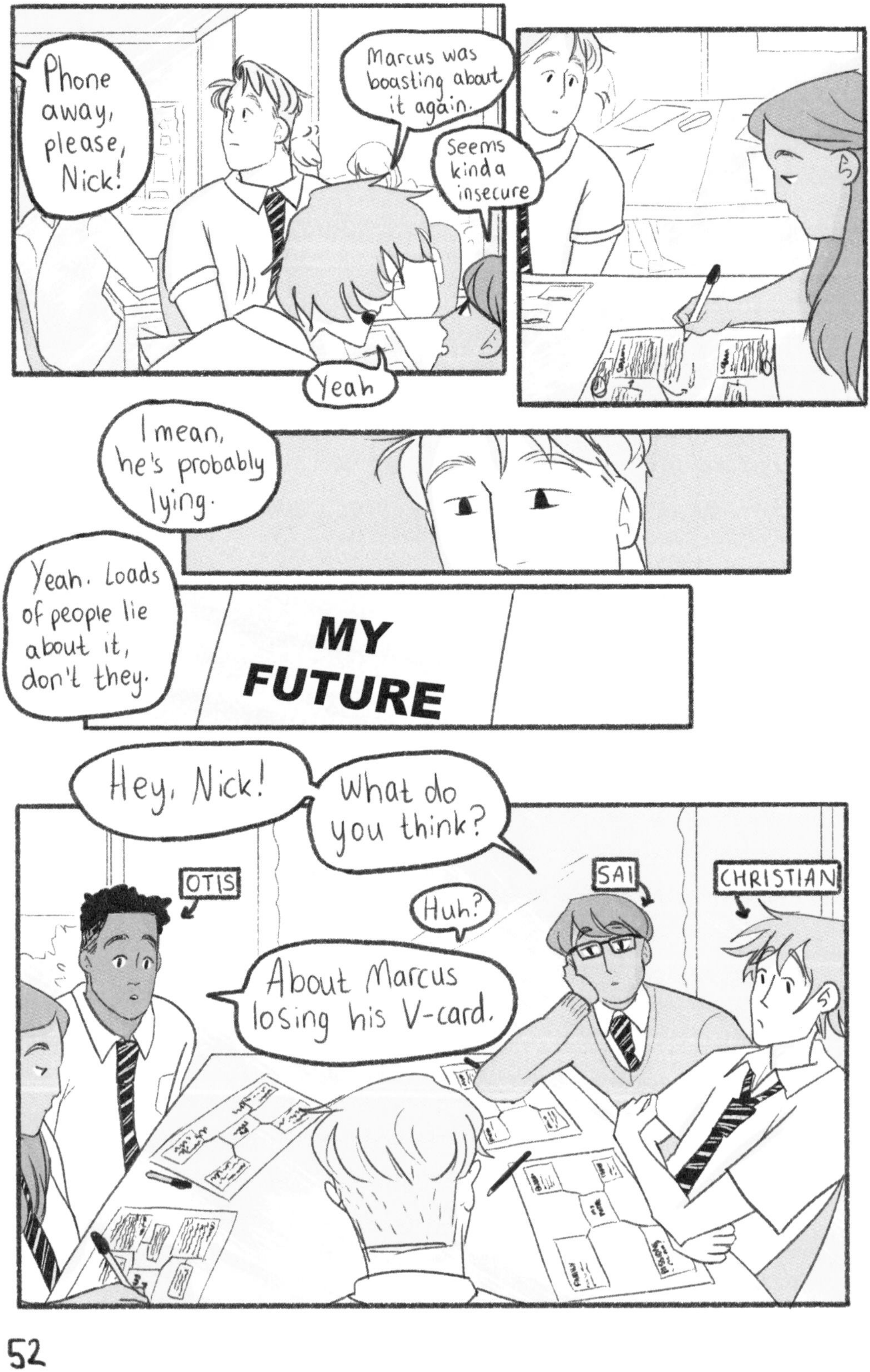
Phone away, please, Nick!
Marcus was boasting about it again.
Seems kinda insecure
Yeah
I mean, he's probably lying.
Yeah. Loads of people lie about it, don't they.
MY FUTURE
Hey, Nick!
What do you think?
OTIS
SAI
CHRISTIAN
Huh?
About Marcus losing his V-card.

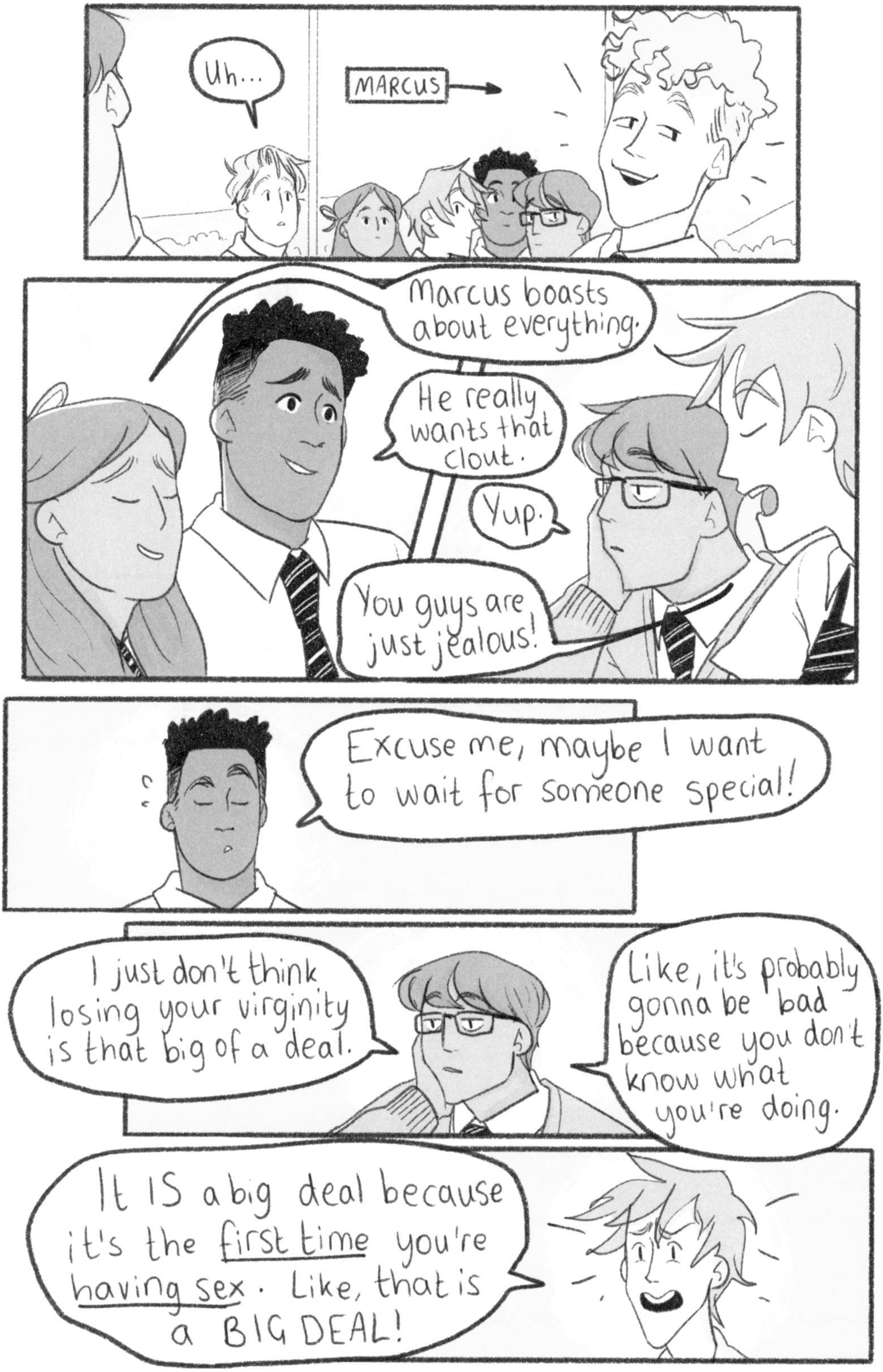
Uh...
MARCUS
Marcus boasts about everything.
He really wants that clout.
Yup.
You guys are just jealous!
Excuse me, maybe I want to wait for someone special!
I just don't think losing your virginity is that big of a deal.
Like, it's probably gonna be bad because you don't know what you're doing.
It IS a big deal because it's the first time you're having sex. Like, that is a BIG DEAL!

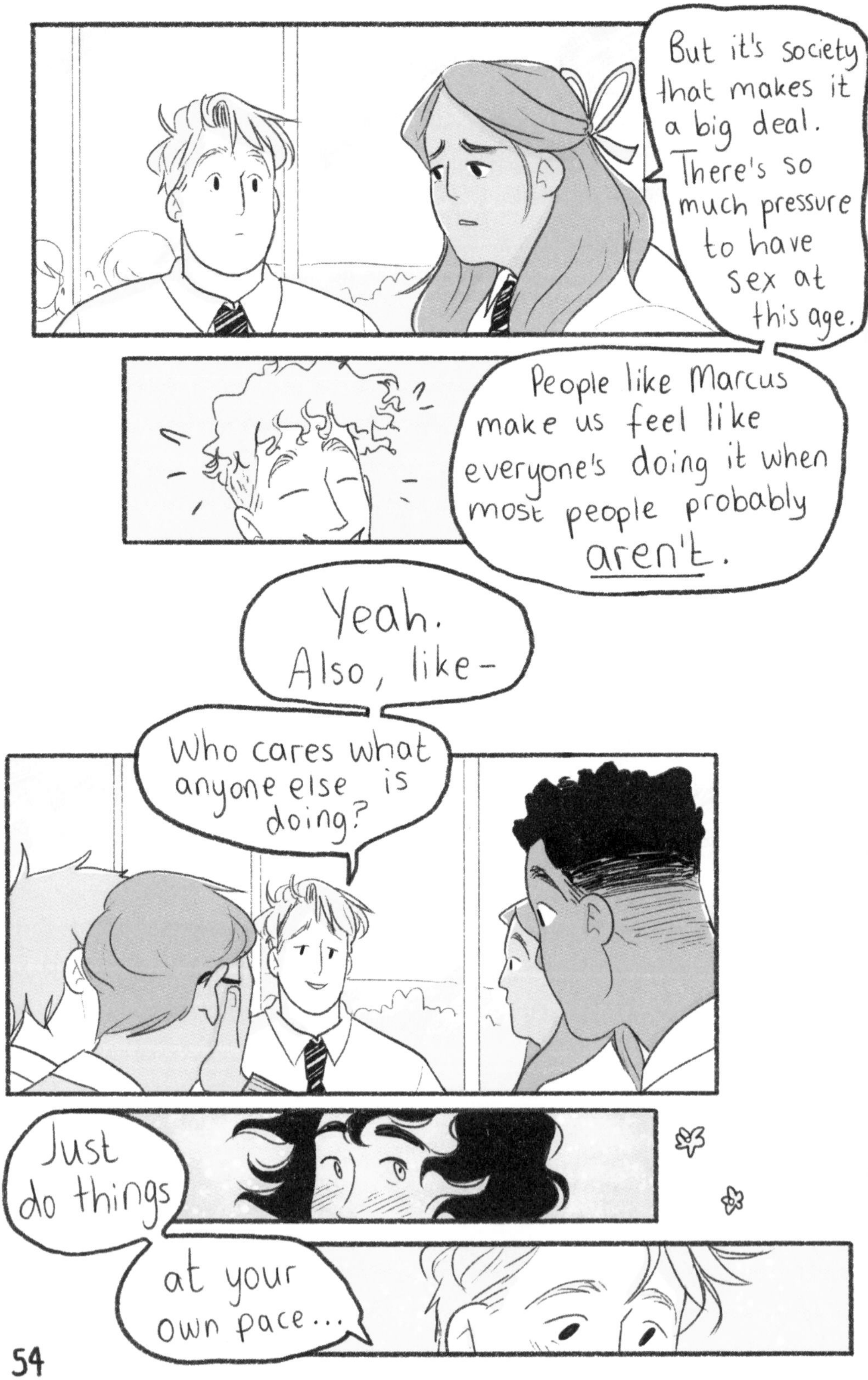
But it's society that makes it a big deal. There's so much pressure to have sex at this age.
People like Marcus make us feel like everyone's doing it when most people probably aren't.
Yeah. Also, like-
Who cares what anyone else is doing?
Just do things
at your own pace...

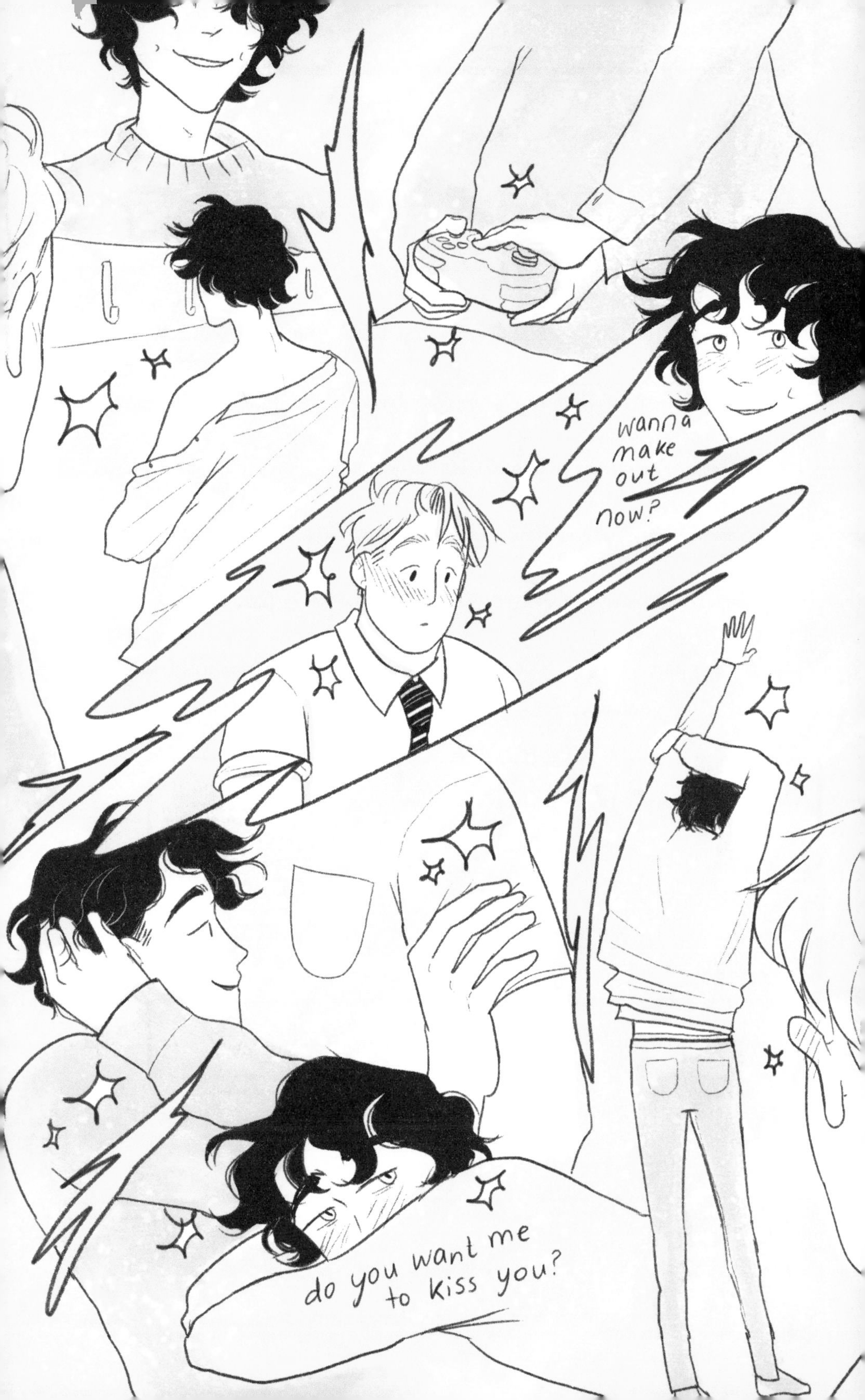
wanna make out now?
do you want me to kiss you?

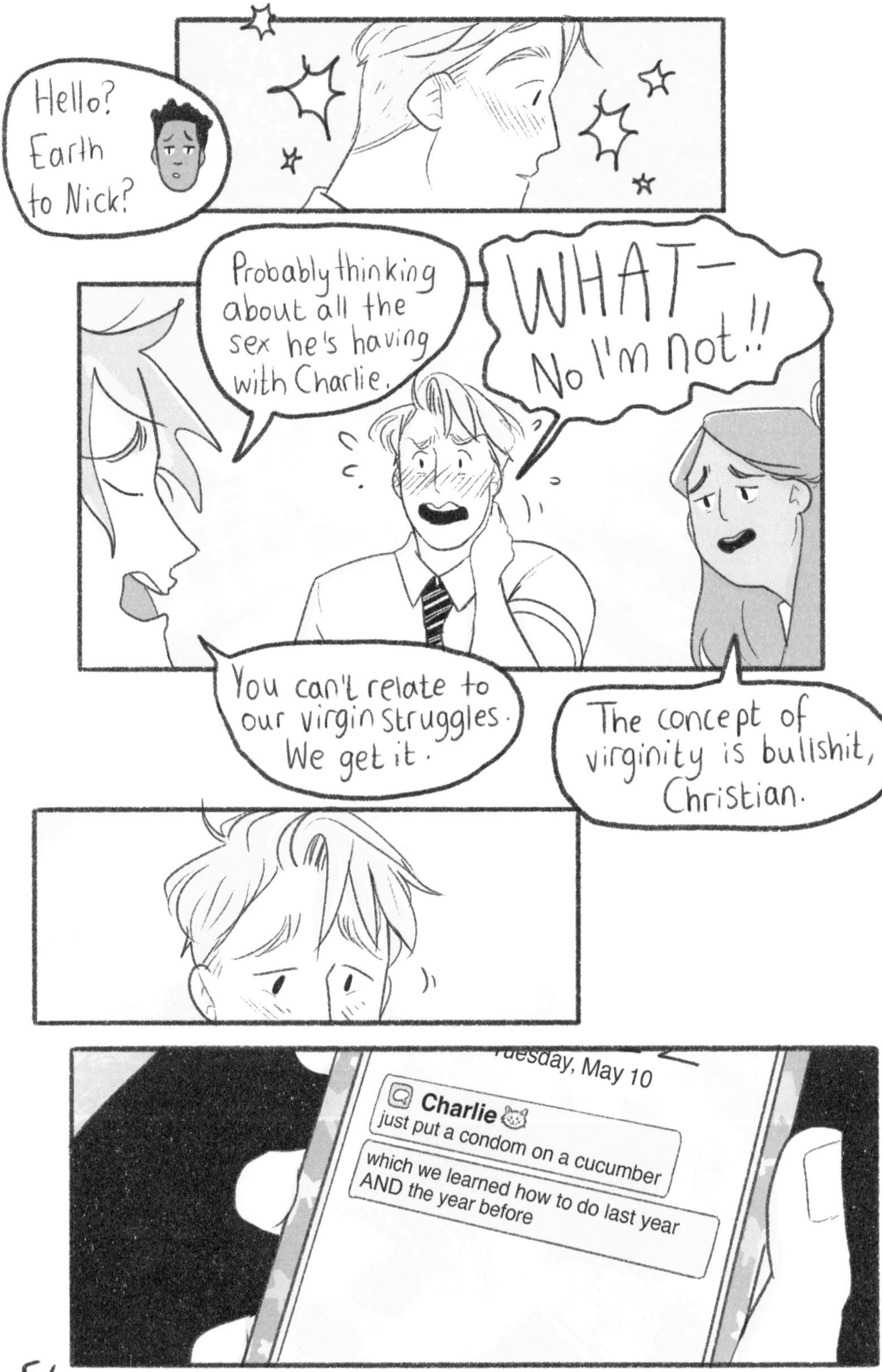
Hello? Earth to Nick?
Probably thinking about all the sex he's having with Charlie.
WHAT— No I'm not!!
You can't relate to our virgin struggles. We get it.
The concept of virginity is bullshit, Christian.
Tuesday, May 10
Charlie
just put a condom on a cucumber
which we learned how to do last year AND the year before

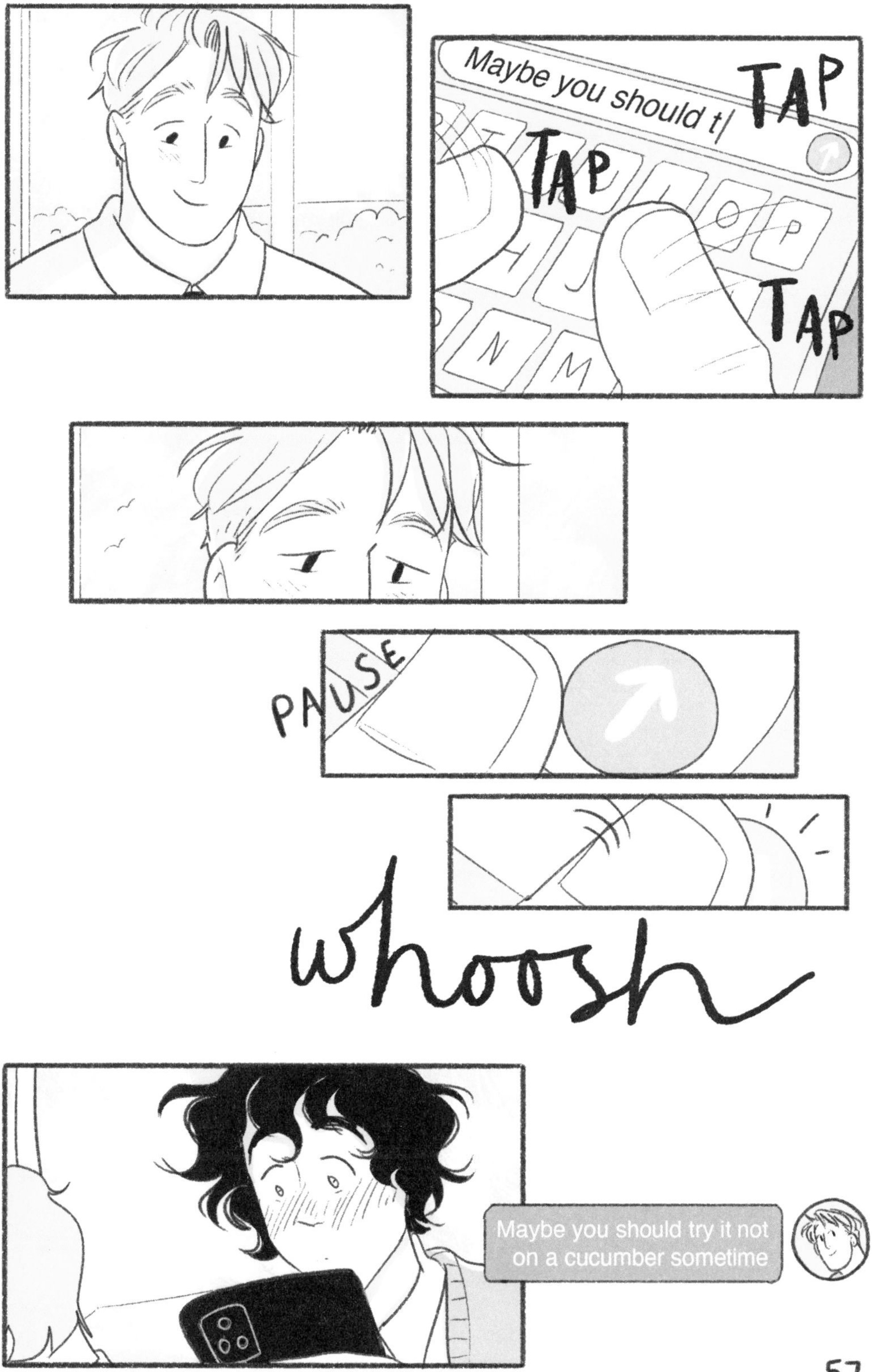
Maybe you should t|
TAP
TAP
TAP
PAUSE
whoosh
Maybe you should try it not on a cucumber sometime

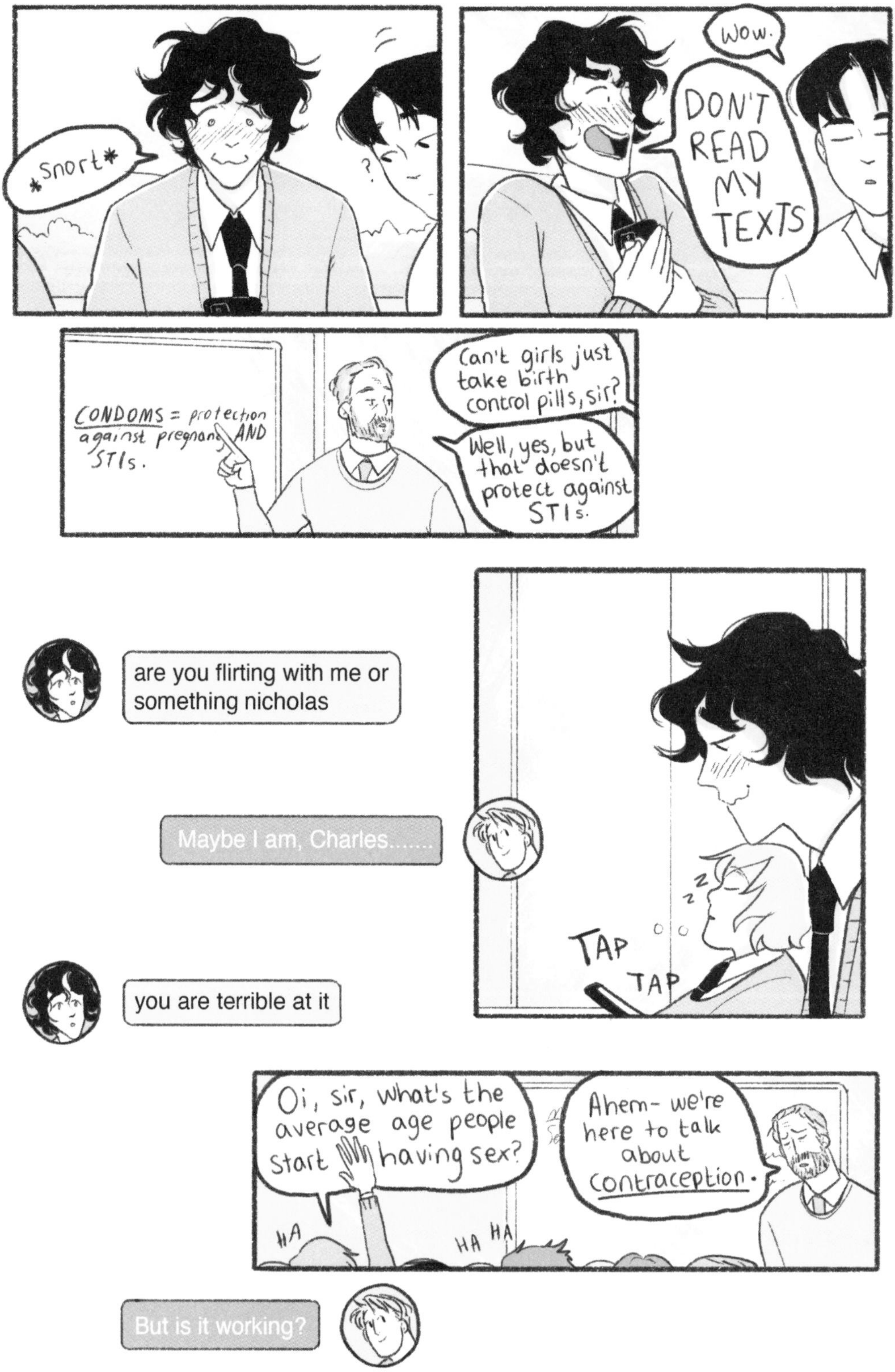
snort
?
wow.
DON'T READ MY TEXTS
CONDOMS = protection against pregnancy AND STIs.
Can't girls just take birth control pills, sir?
Well, yes, but that doesn't protect against STIs.
are you flirting with me or something nicholas
Maybe I am, Charles.......
TAP TAP
you are terrible at it
Oi, sir, what's the average age people start having sex?
Ahem- we're here to talk about contraception.
HA
HA HA
But is it working?

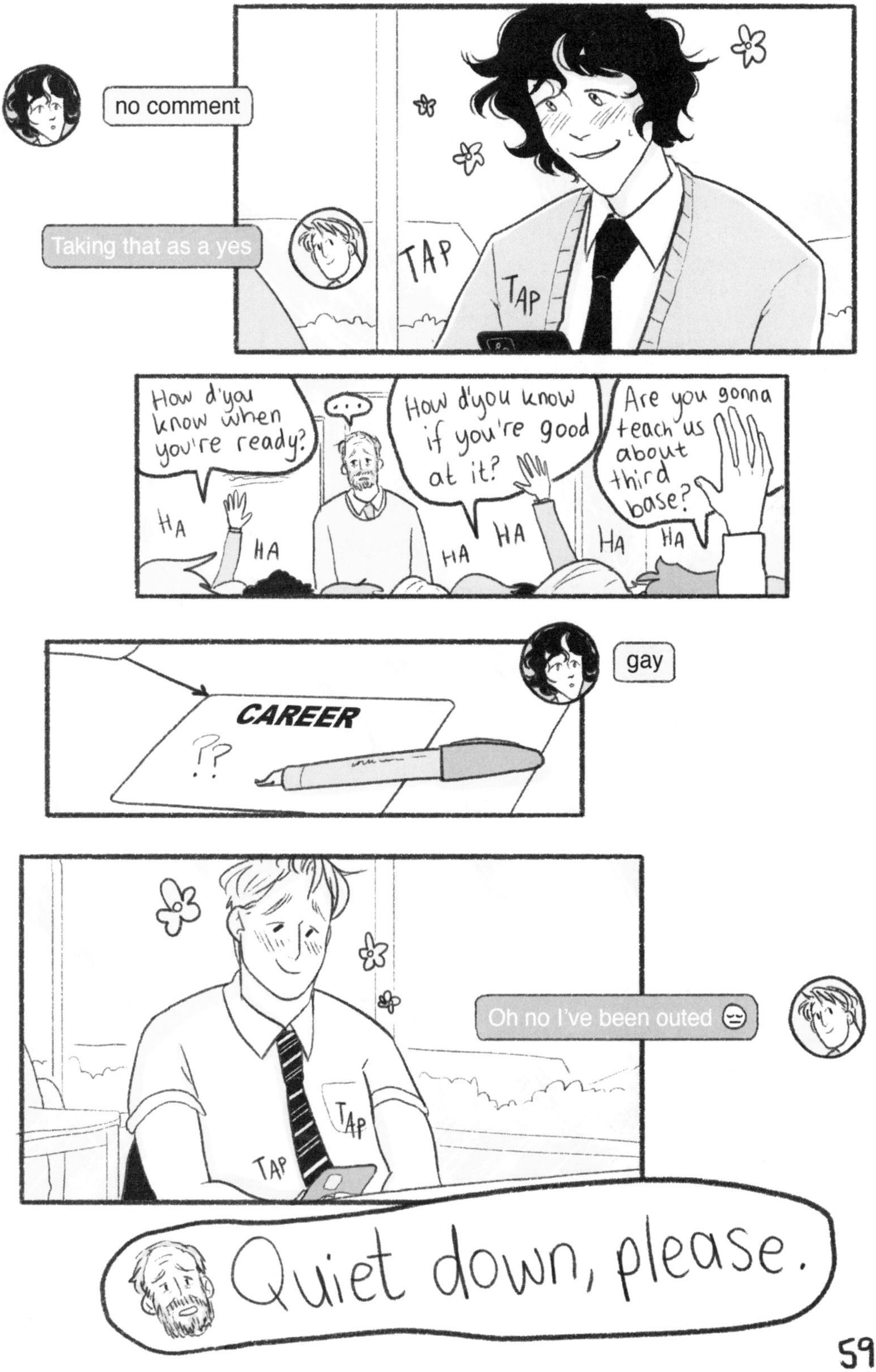
no comment
Taking that as a yes
TAP
TAP
How d'you know when you're ready?
...
How d'you know if you're good at it?
Are you gonna teach us about third base?
HA
HA
HA
HA
HA
HA
gay
CAREER
??
Oh no I've been outed
TAP
TAP
Quiet down, please.

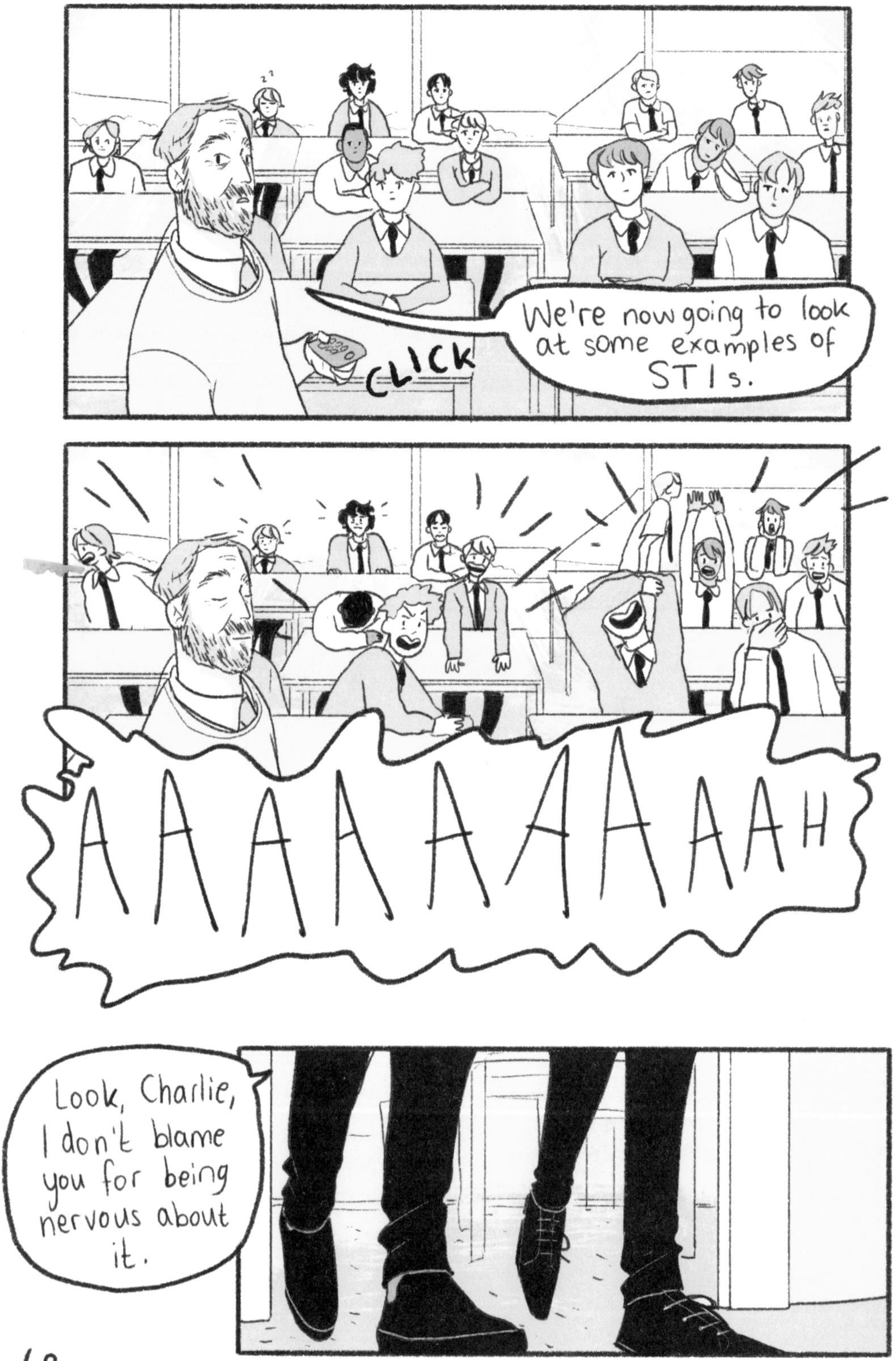
We're now going to look at some examples of STIs.
CLICK
AAAAAAAAAH
Look, Charlie, I don't blame you for being nervous about it.

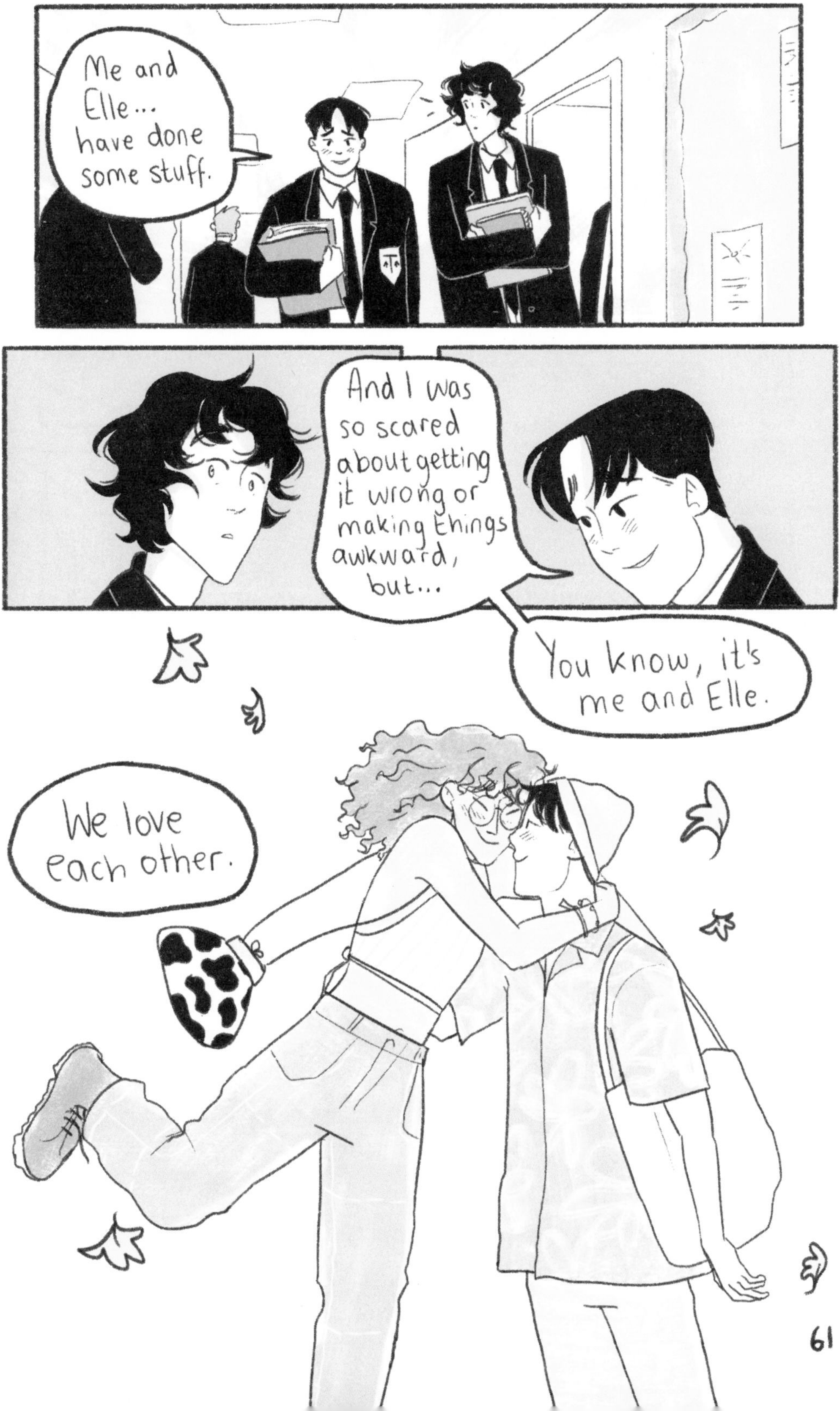
Me and Elle... have done some stuff.
And I was so scared about getting it wrong or making things awkward, but...
You know, it's me and Elle.
We love each other.

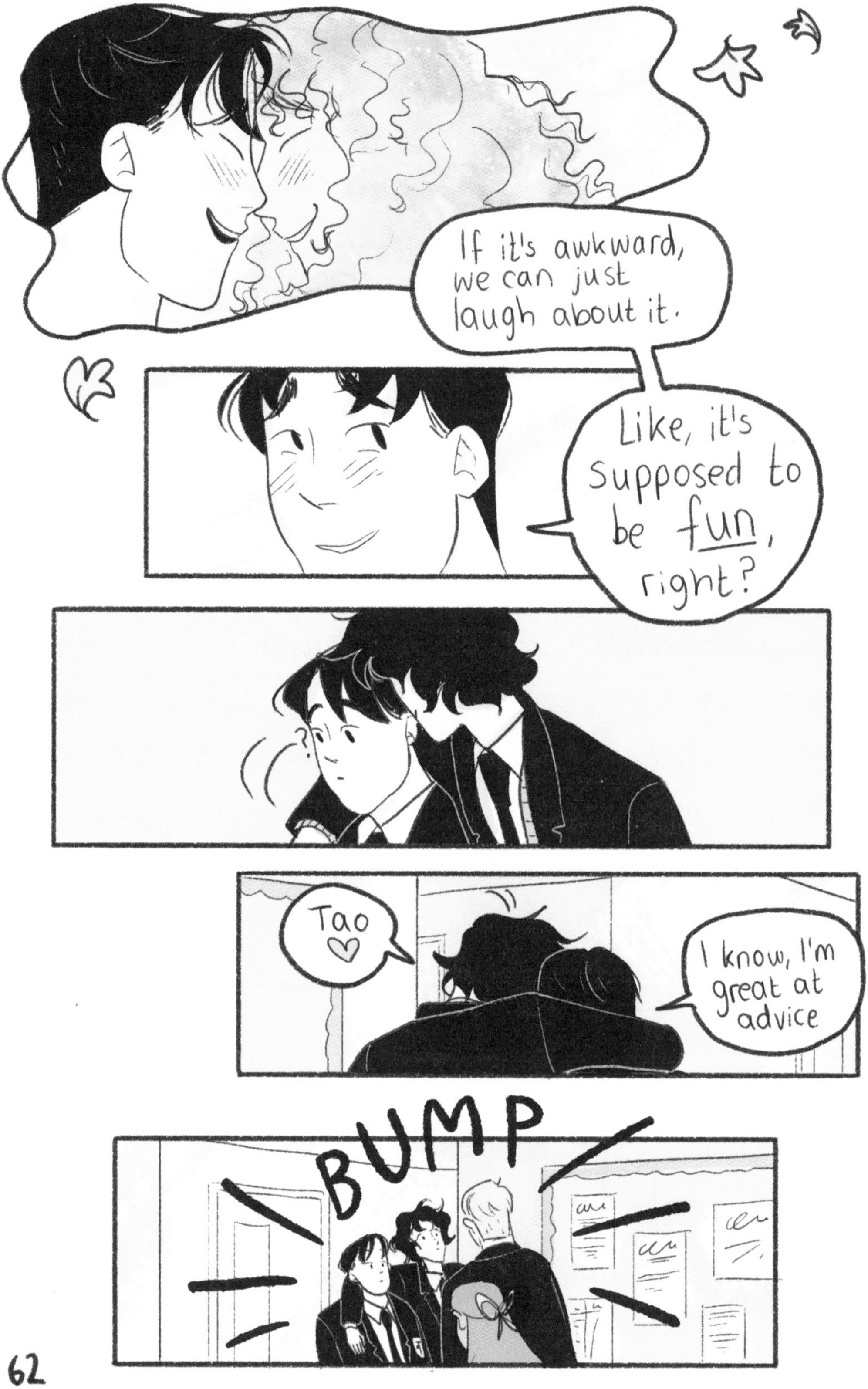
If it's awkward, we can just laugh about it.
Like, it's supposed to be fun, right?
Tao
I know, I'm great at advice
BUMP

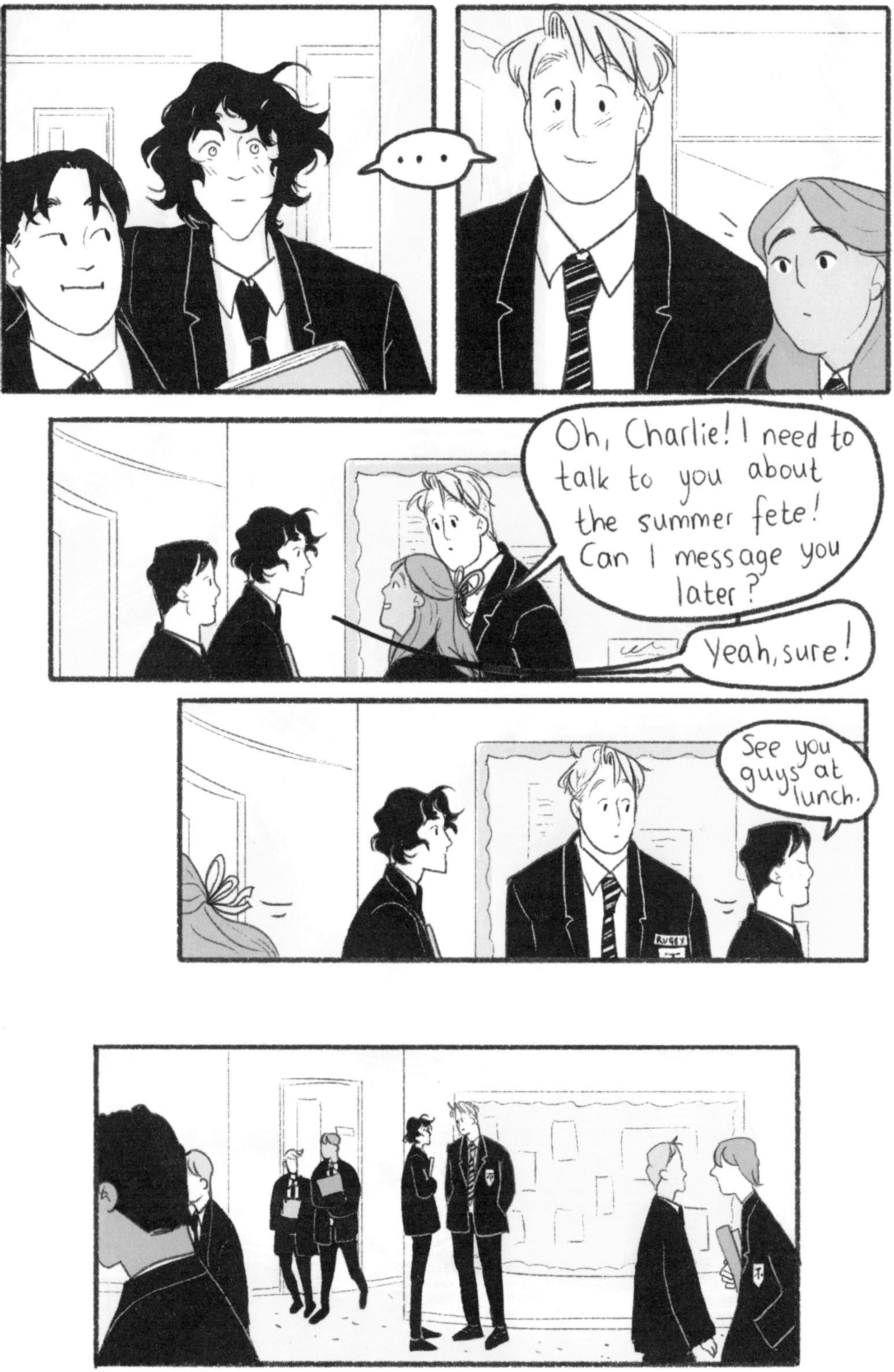
...
Oh, Charlie! I need to talk to you about the summer fete! Can I message you later?
Yeah, sure!
See you guys at lunch.
RUGBY

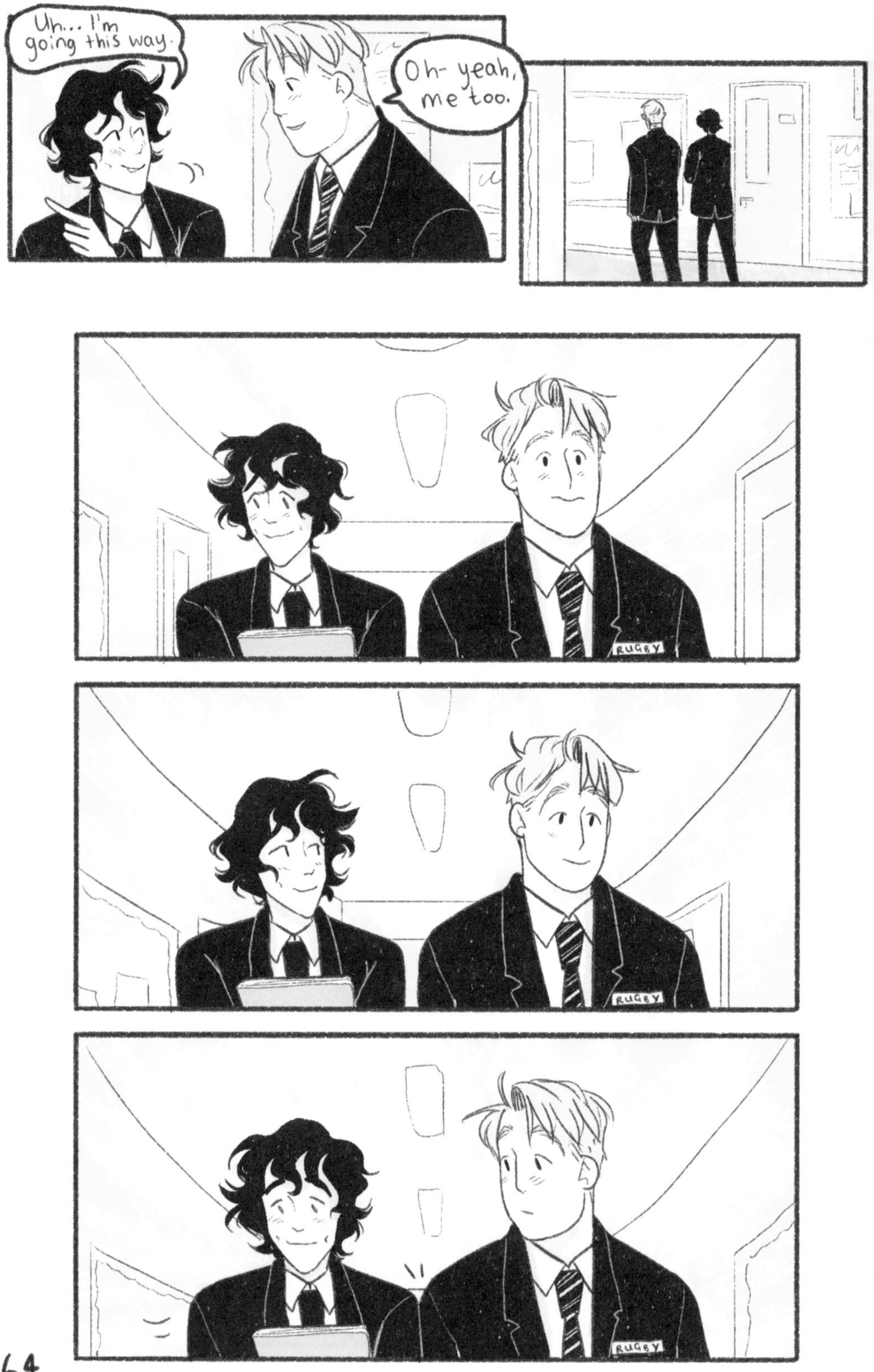
Uh... I'm going this way.
Oh- yeah, me too.
RUGBY
RUGBY
RUGBY

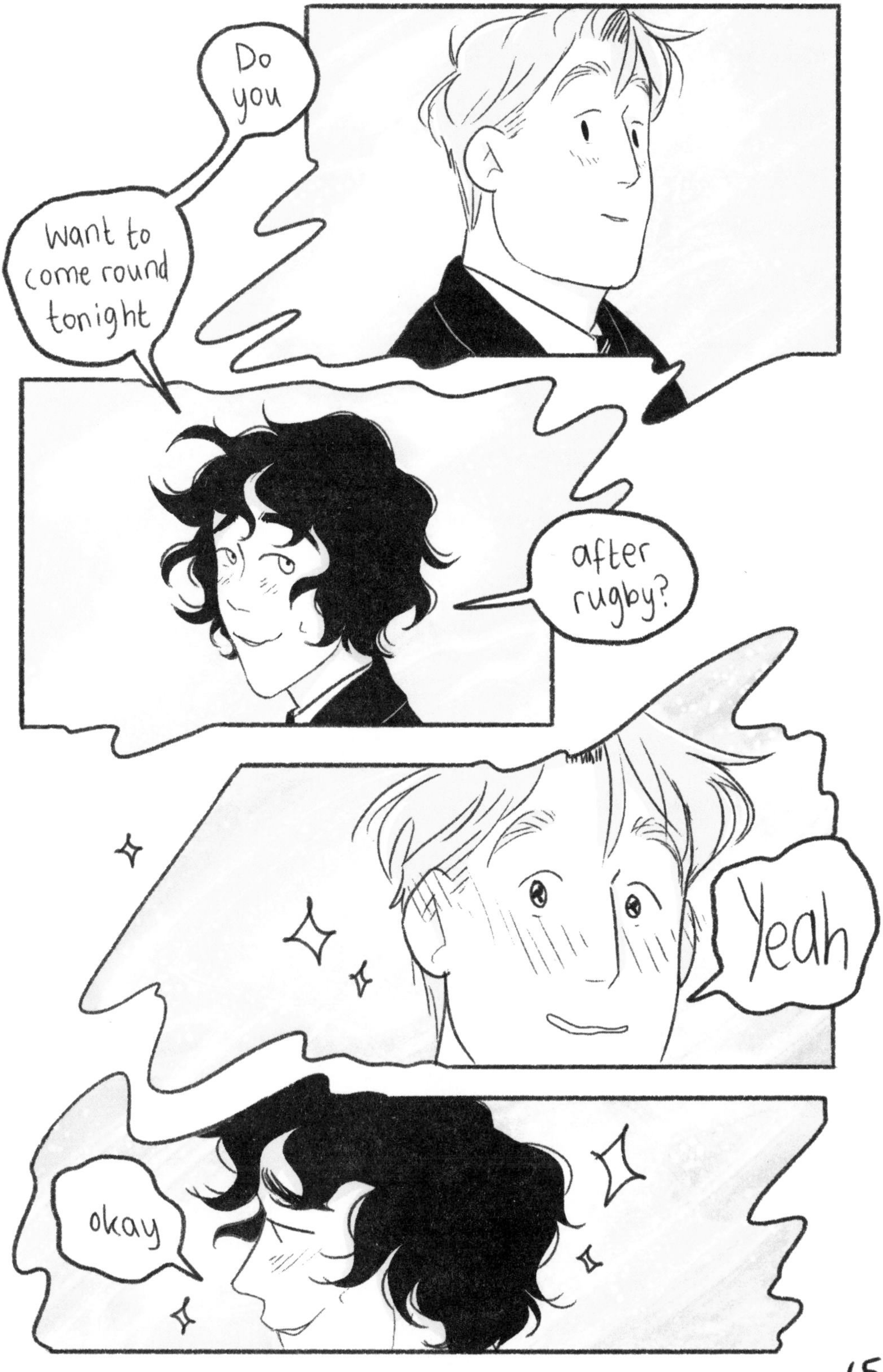
Do you
want to come round tonight
after rugby?
Yeah
okay

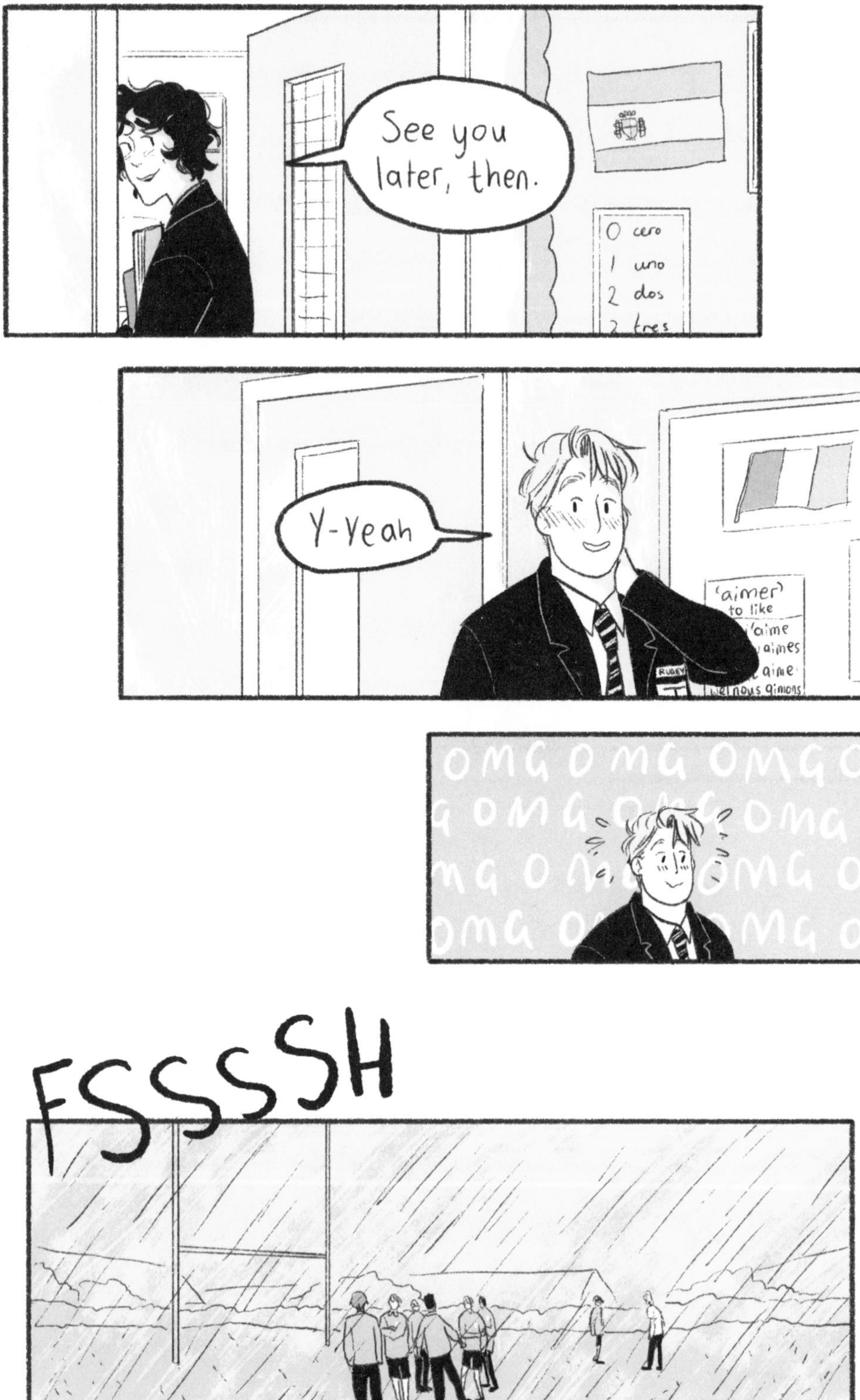
See you later, then.
0 cero
1 uno
2 dos
Y-Yeah
'aimer' to like
OMG OMG OMG
FSSSSH

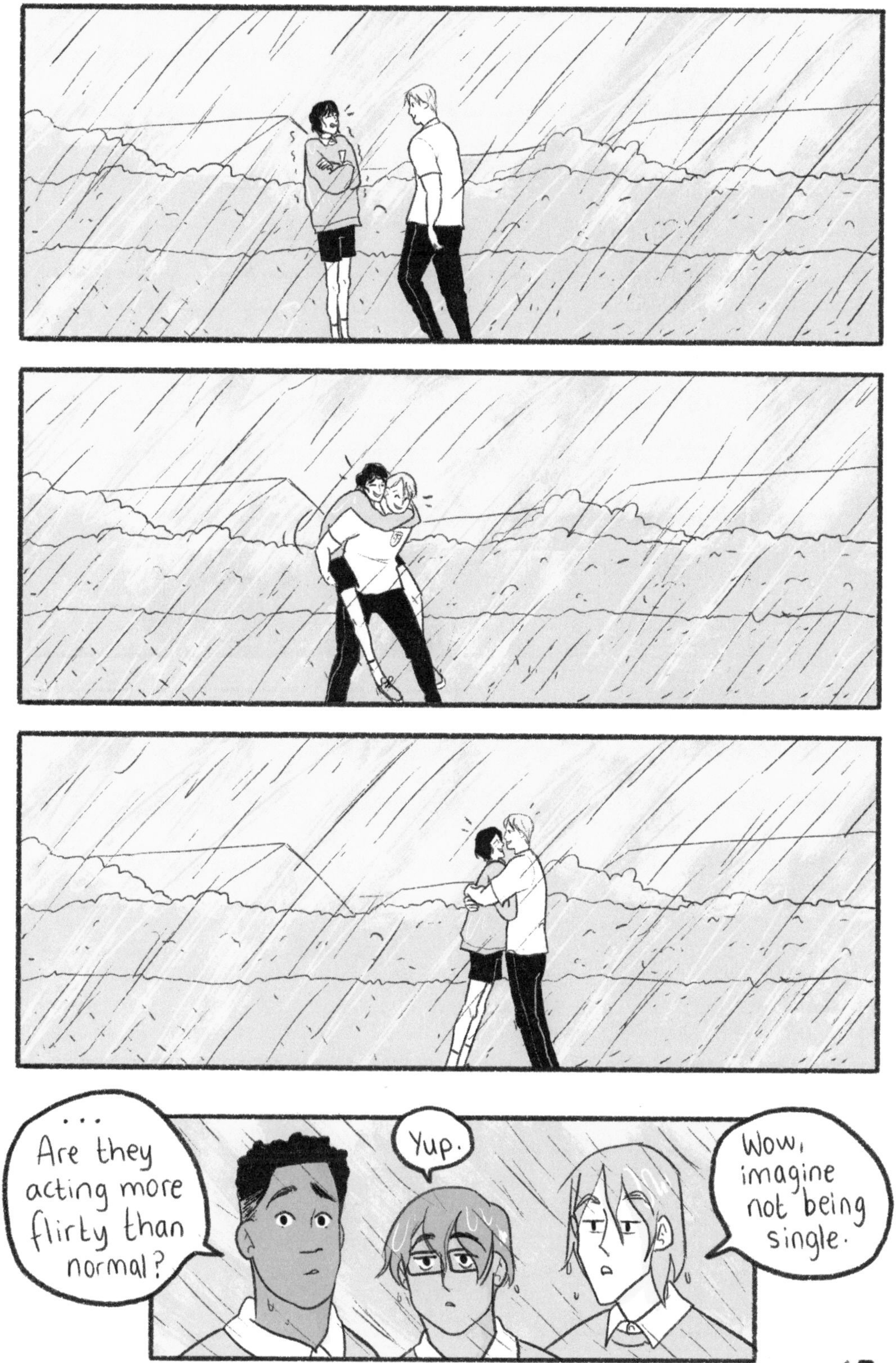
...
Are they acting more flirty than normal?
Yup.
Wow, imagine not being single.

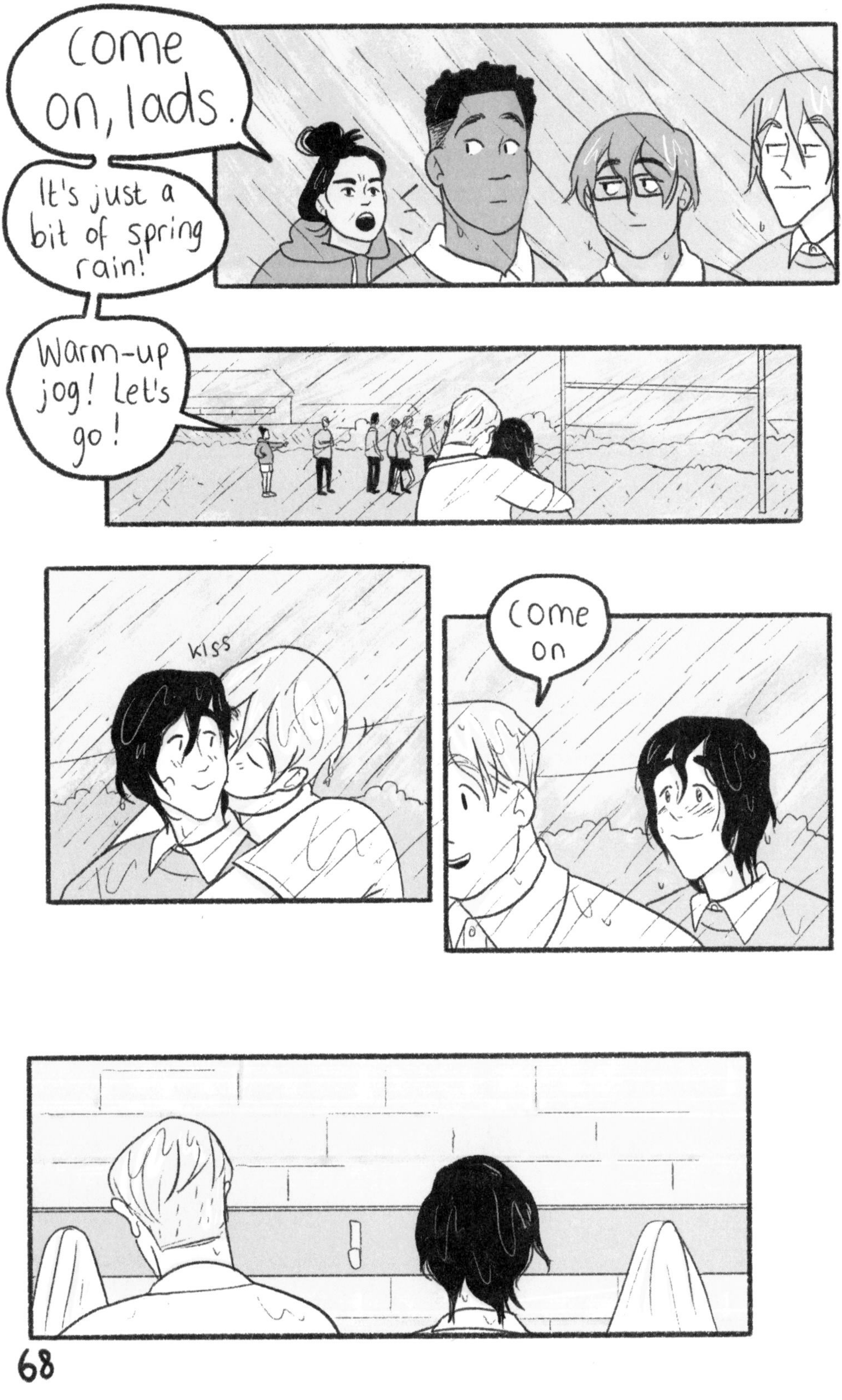
Come on, lads.
It's just a bit of spring rain!
Warm-up jog! Let's go!
KISS
Come on

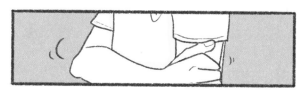

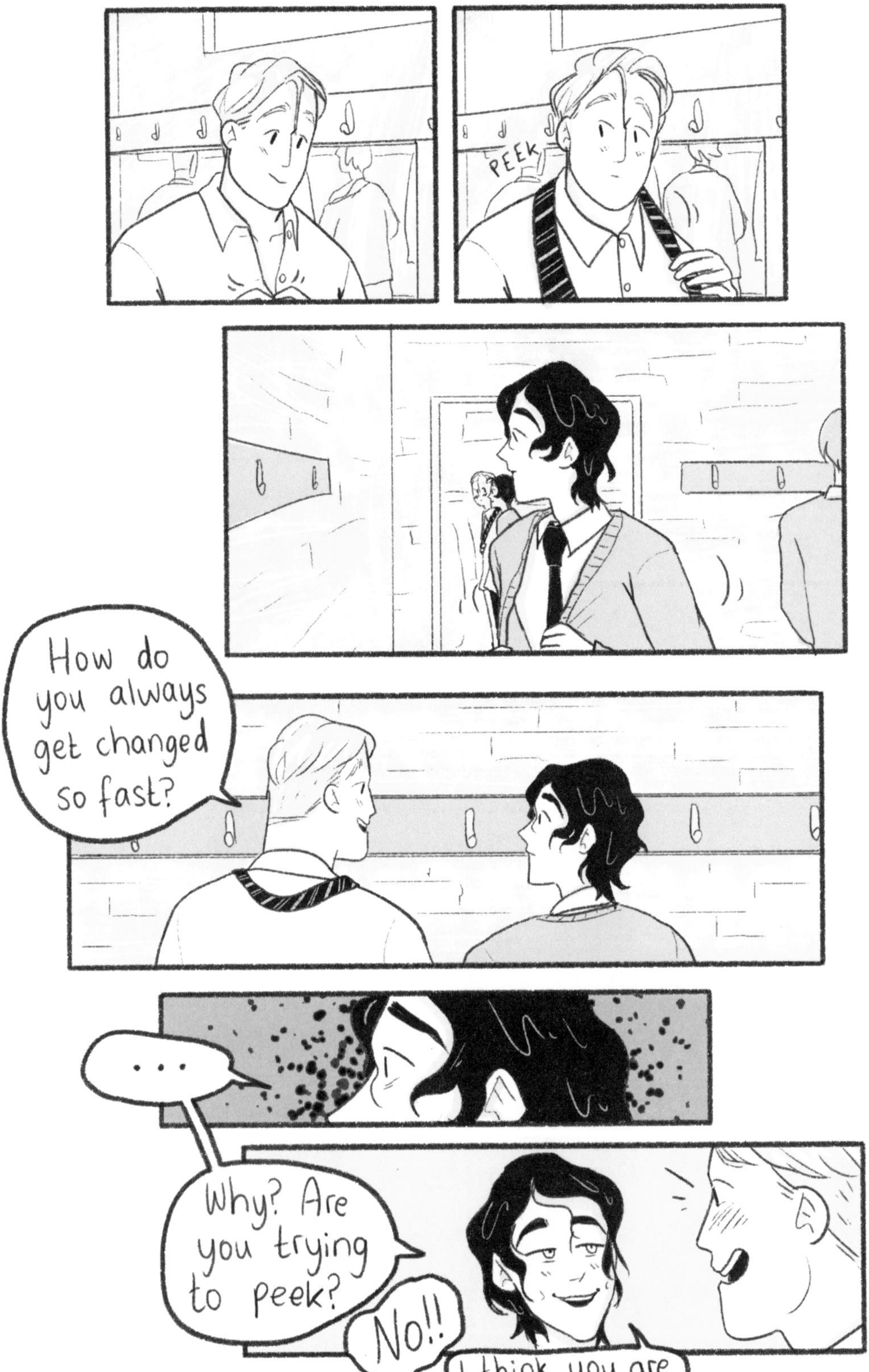
PEEK
How do you always get changed so fast?
...
Why? Are you trying to peek?
No!!
I think you are

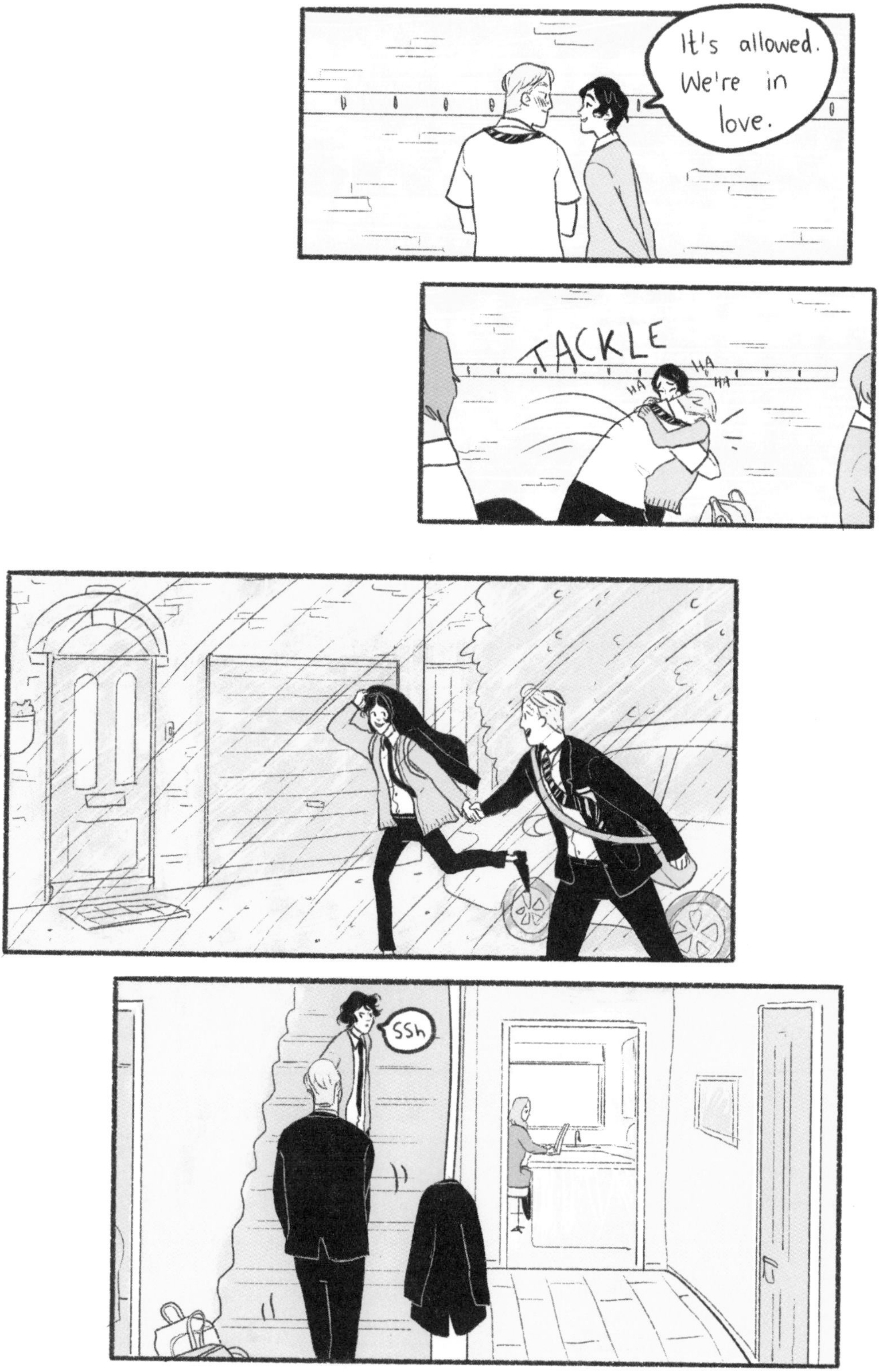
It's allowed. We're in love.
TACKLE
HA
HA
HA
SSh

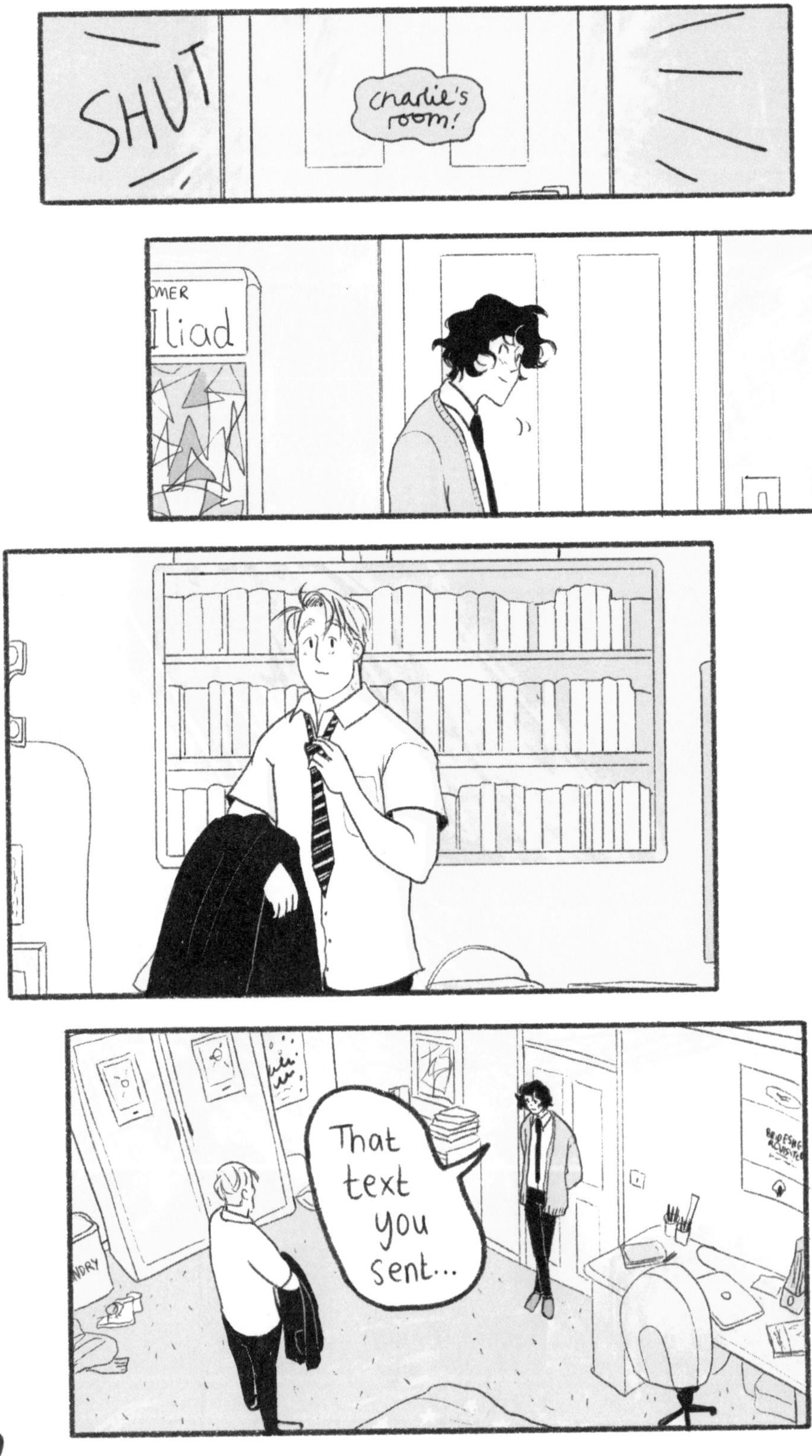
SHUT
charlie's room!
Iliad
That text you sent...

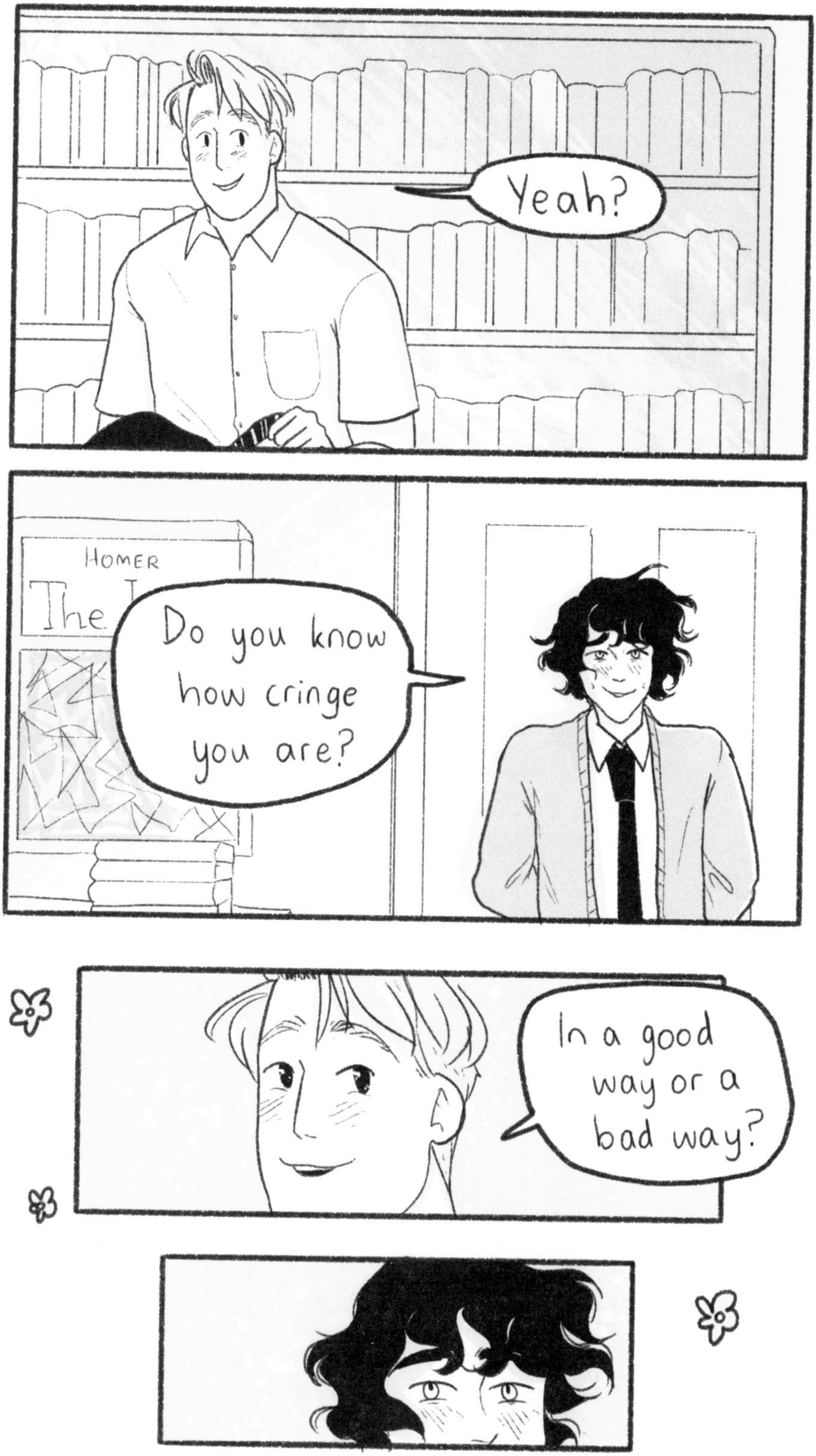
Yeah?
HOMER
The
Do you know how cringe you are?
In a good way or a bad way?

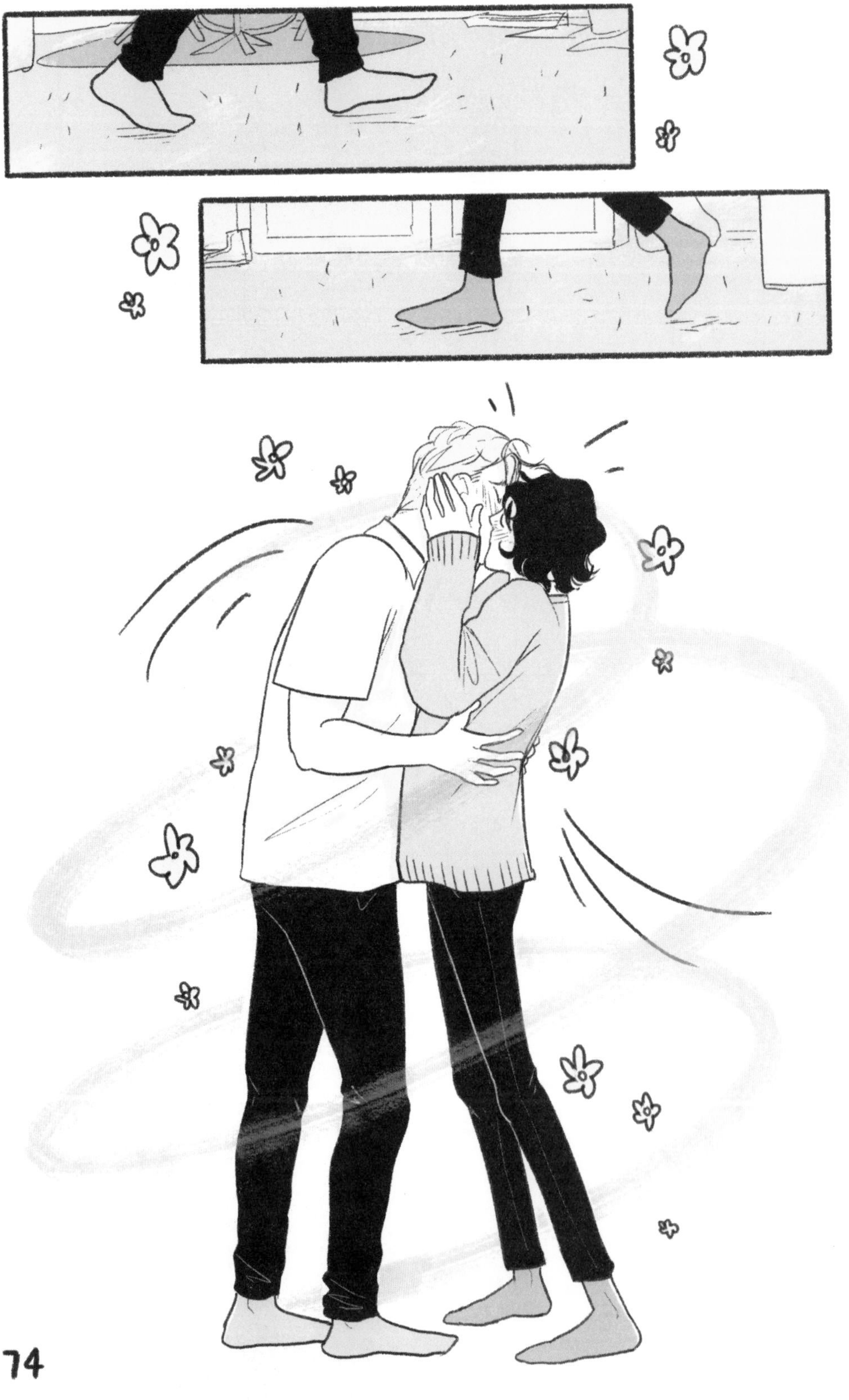

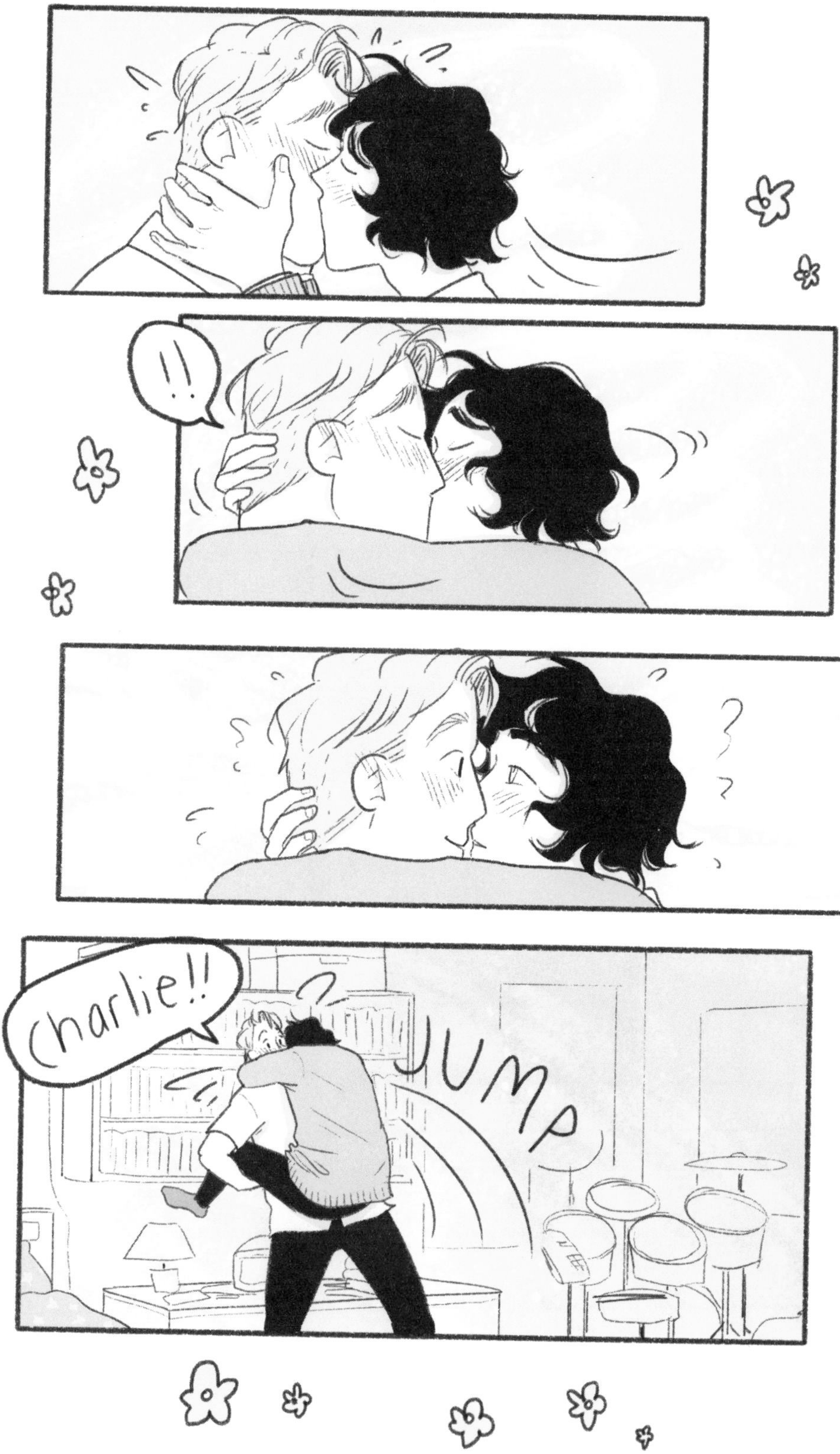
!!
Charlie!!
JUMP

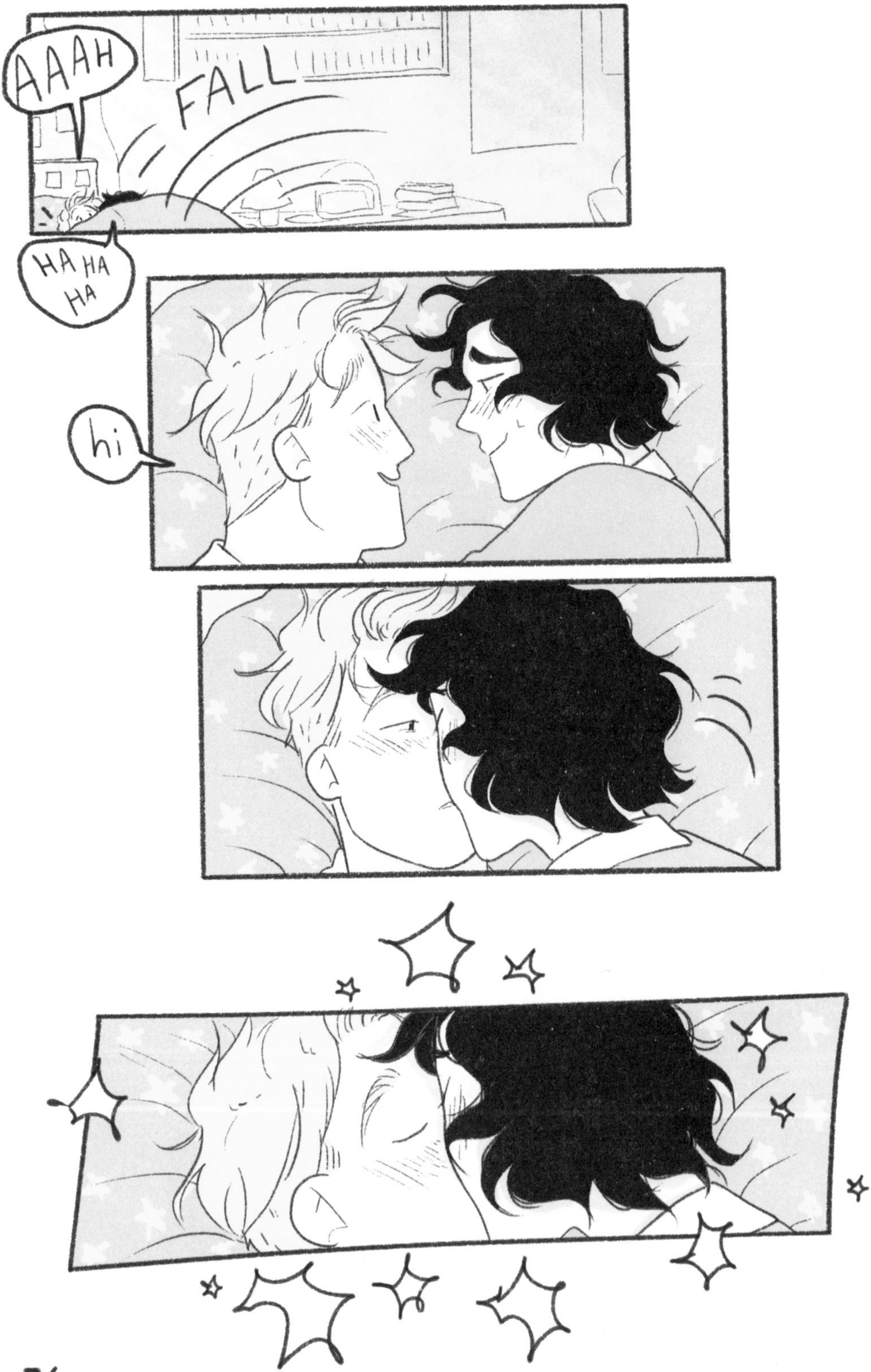
AAAH
FALL
HA HA HA HA
hi

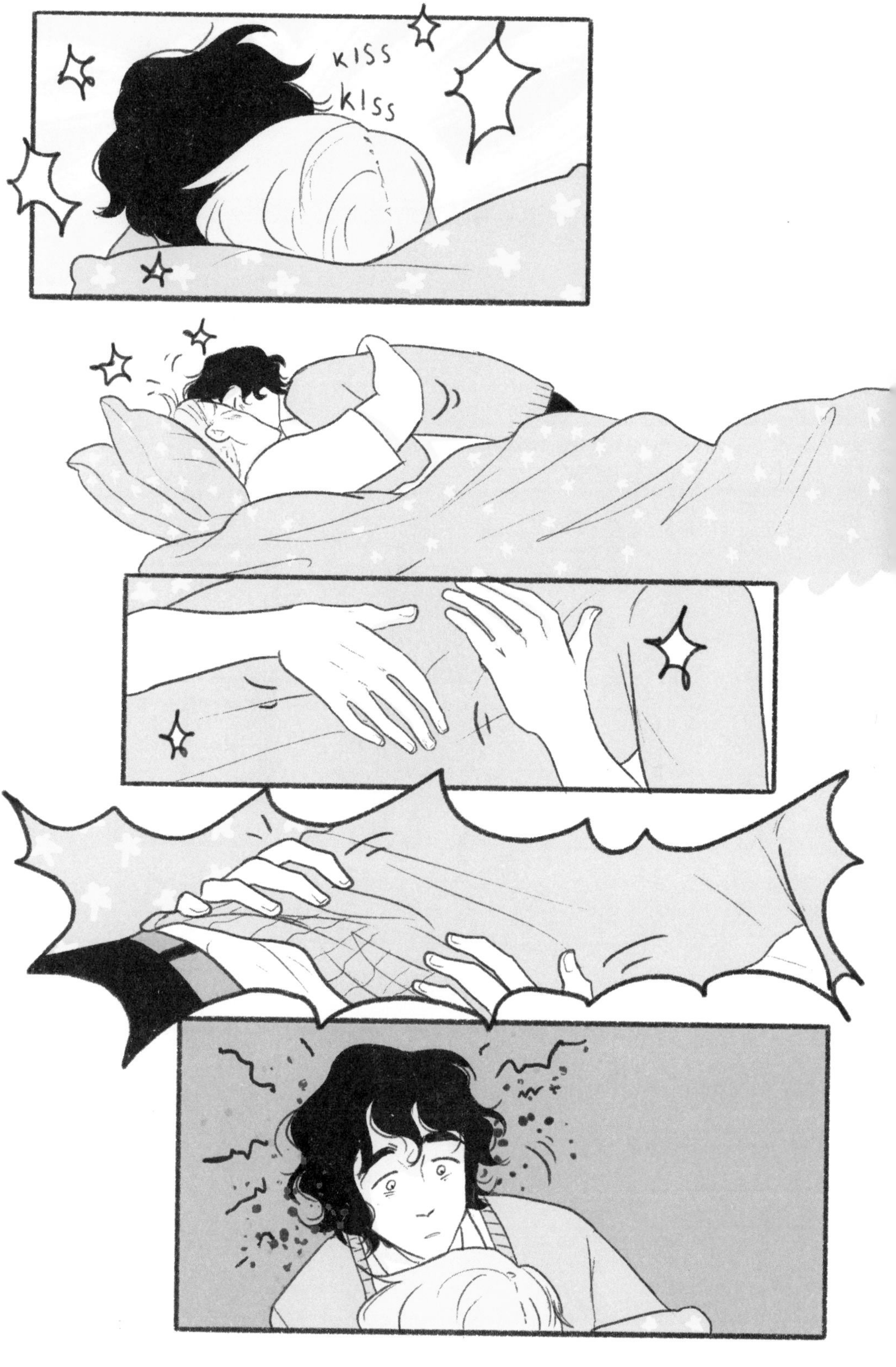
KISS
KISS

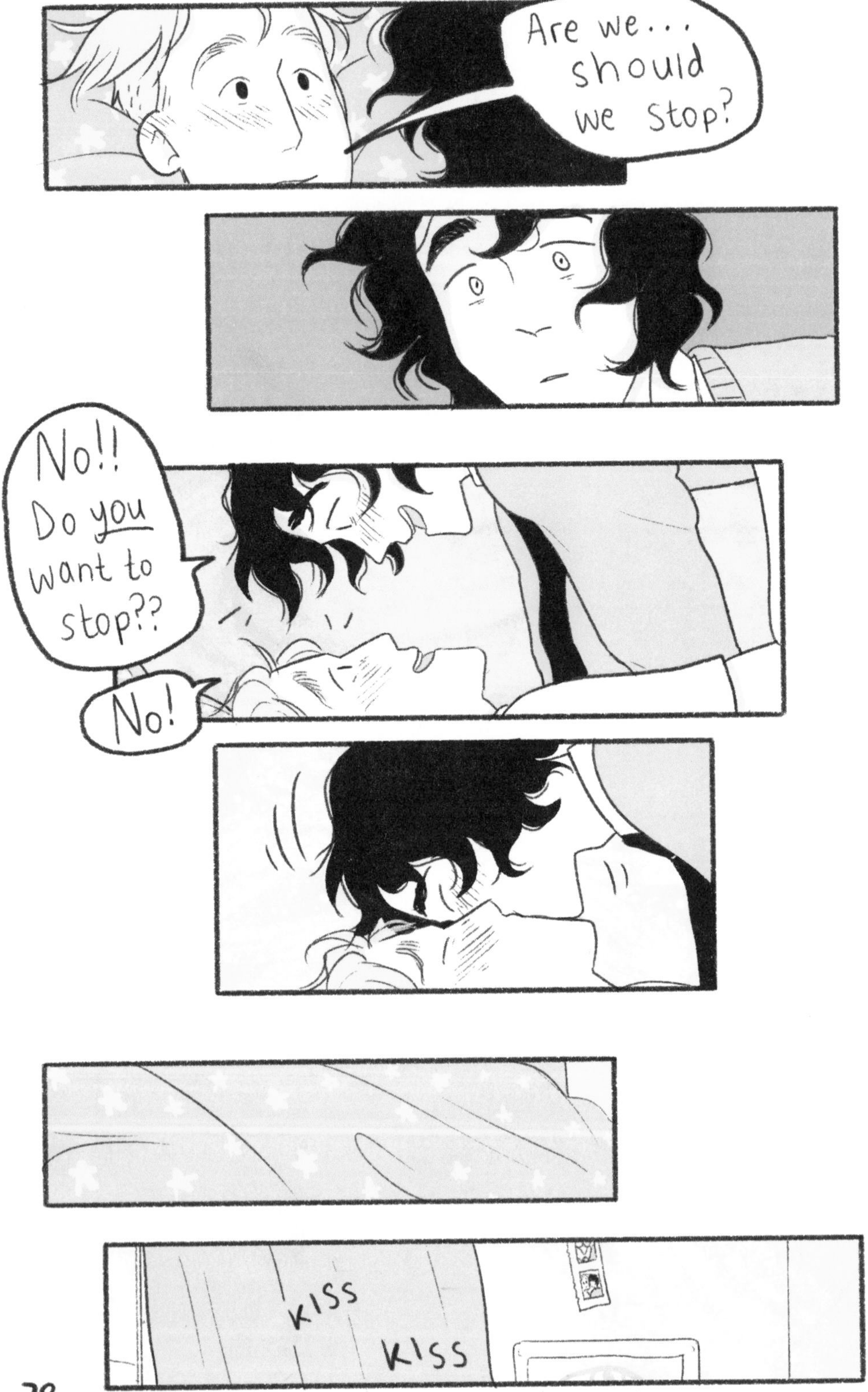
Are we... should we stop?
No!! Do you want to stop??
No!
KISS
KISS

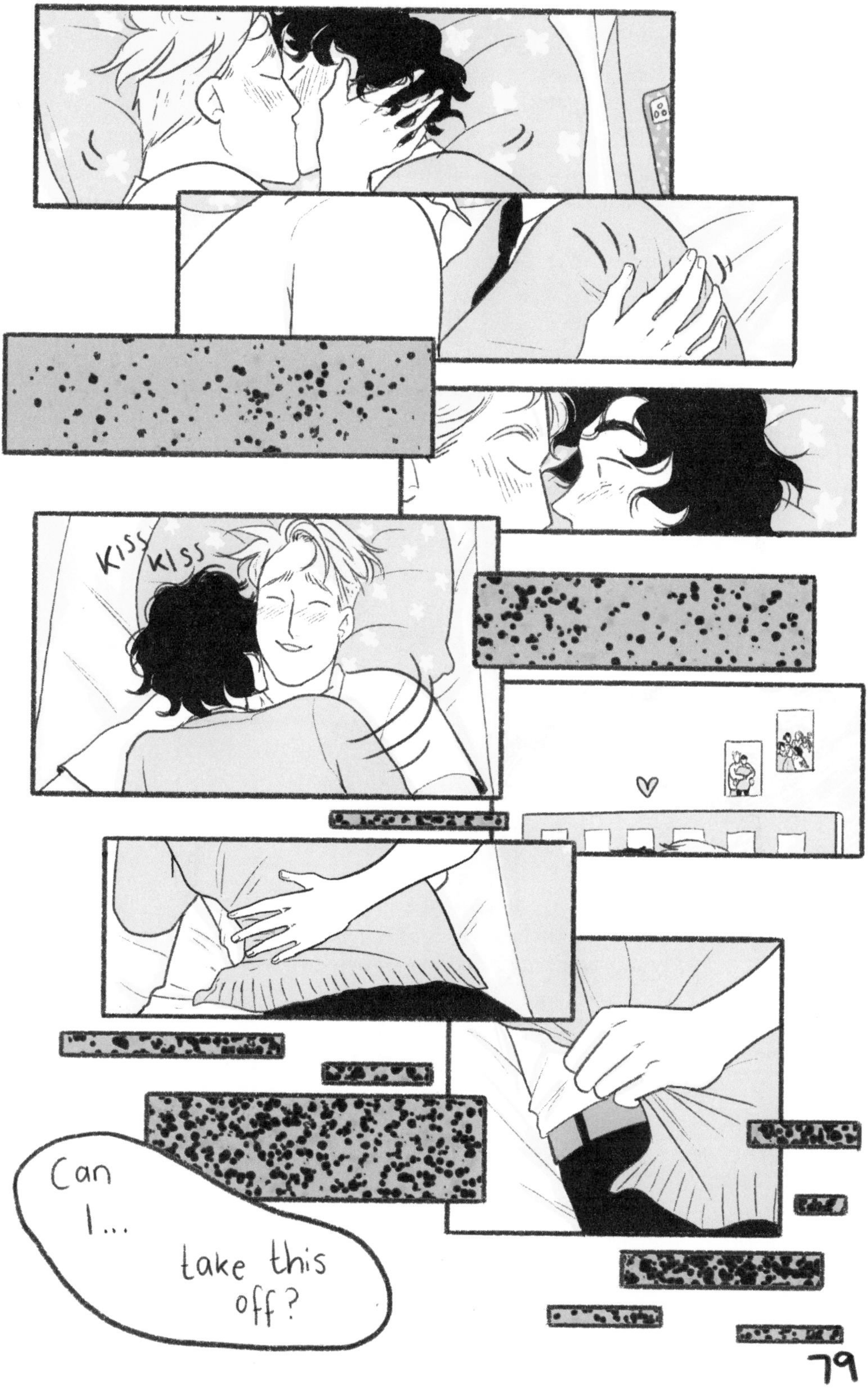
KISS KISS
Can I... take this off?

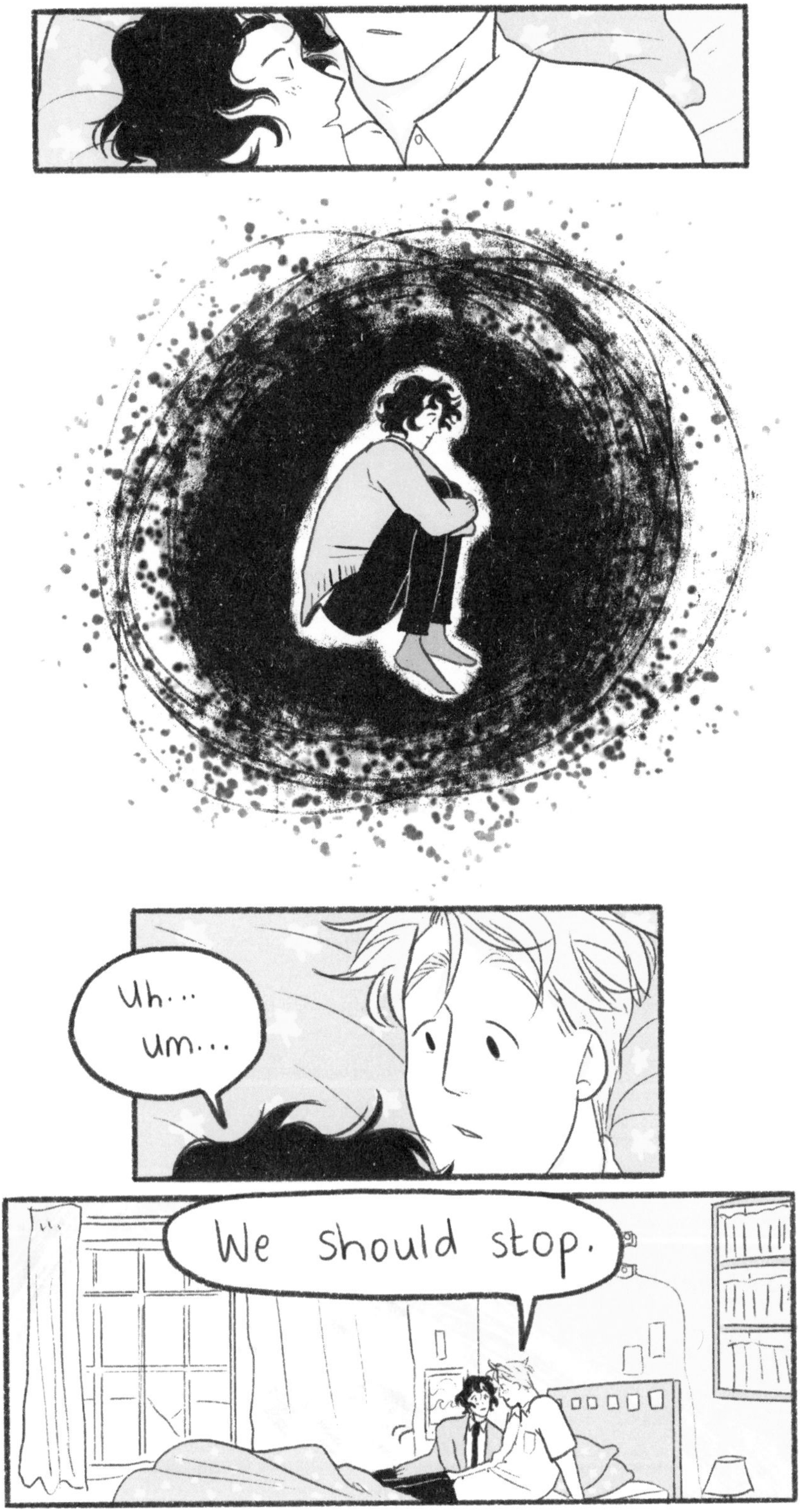
Uh...
um...
We should stop.

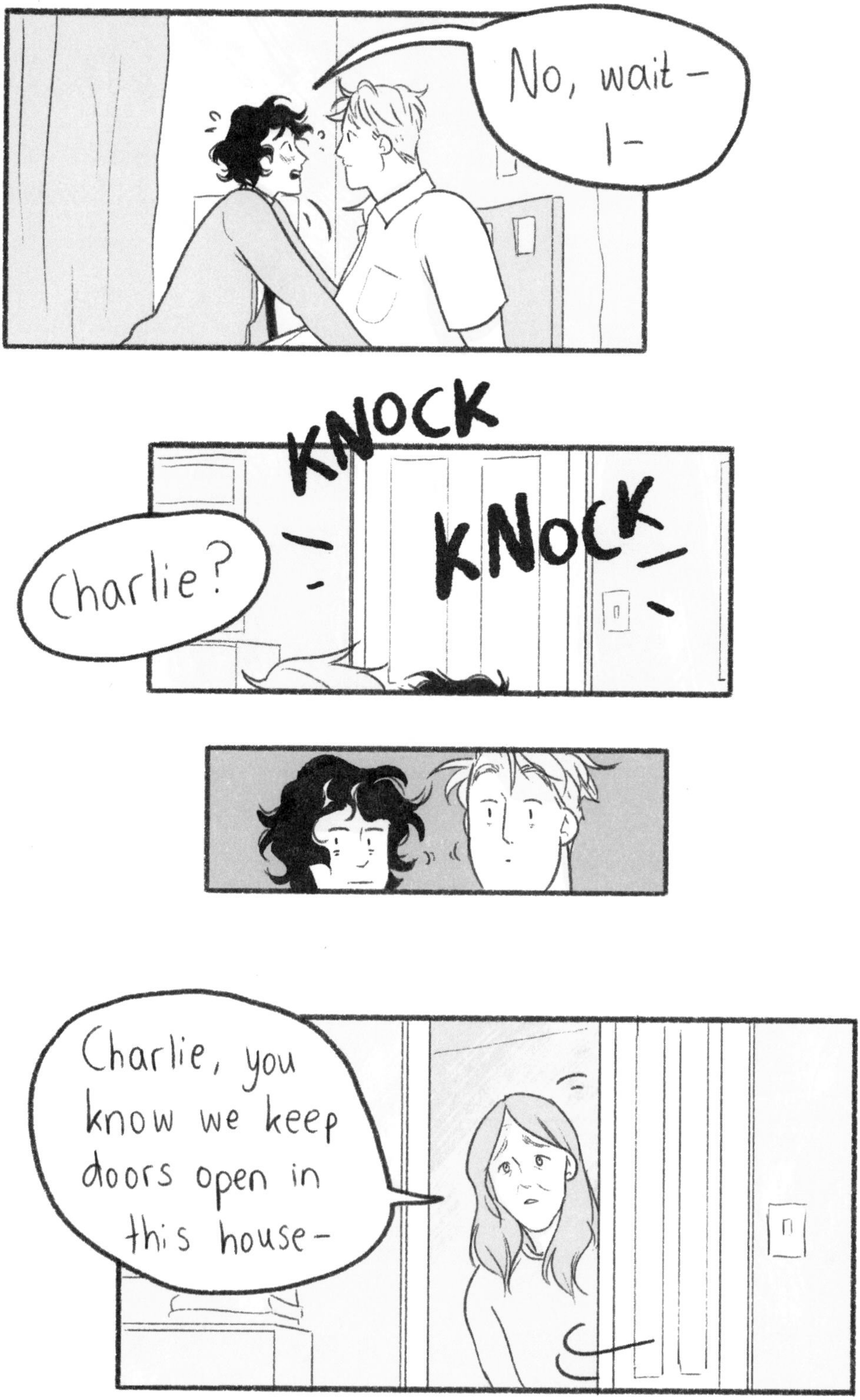
No, wait - I-
KNOCK
KNOCK
Charlie?
Charlie, you know we keep doors open in this house-

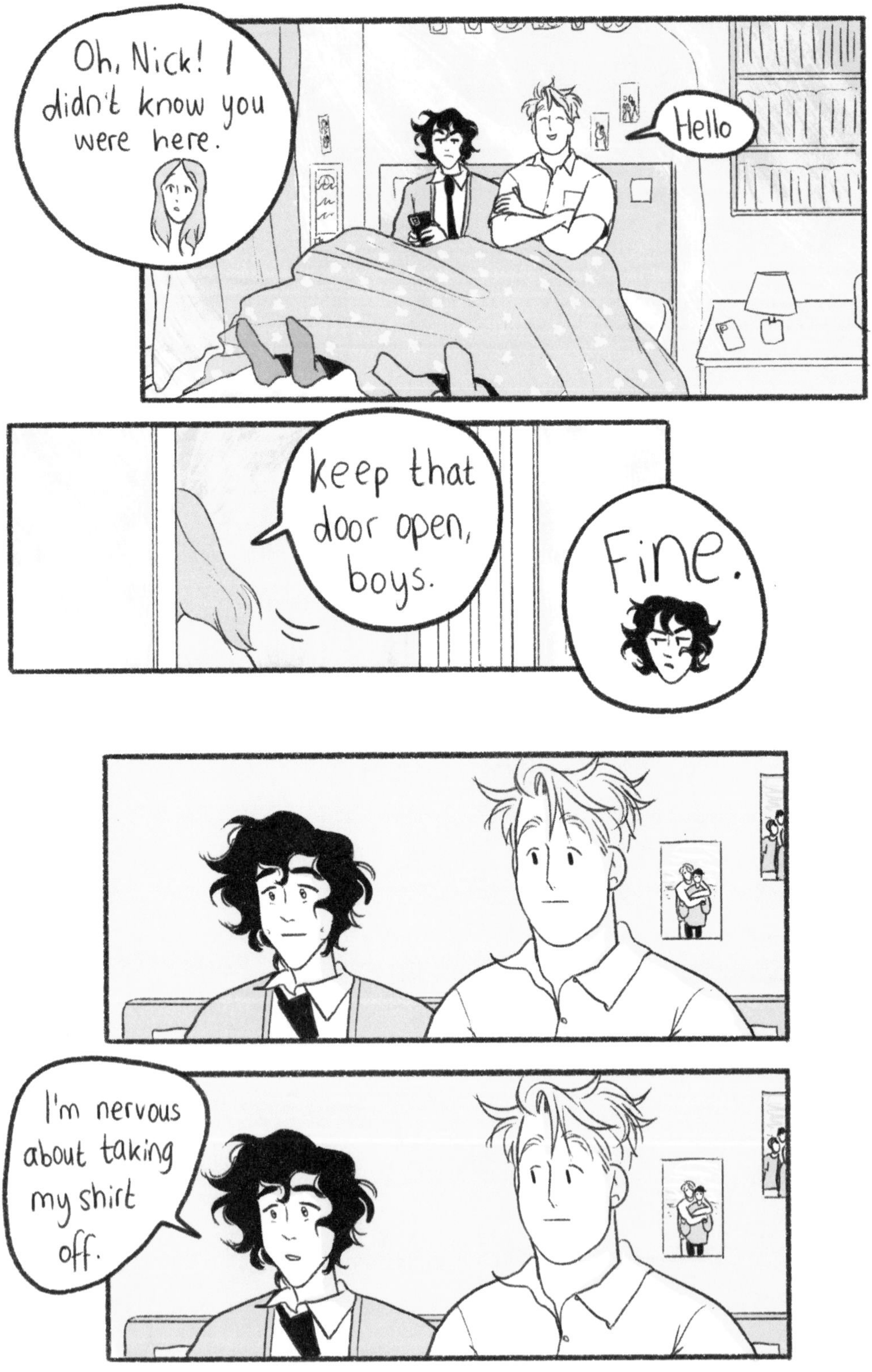
Oh, Nick! I didn't know you were here.
Hello
Keep that door open, boys.
Fine.
I'm nervous about taking my shirt off.

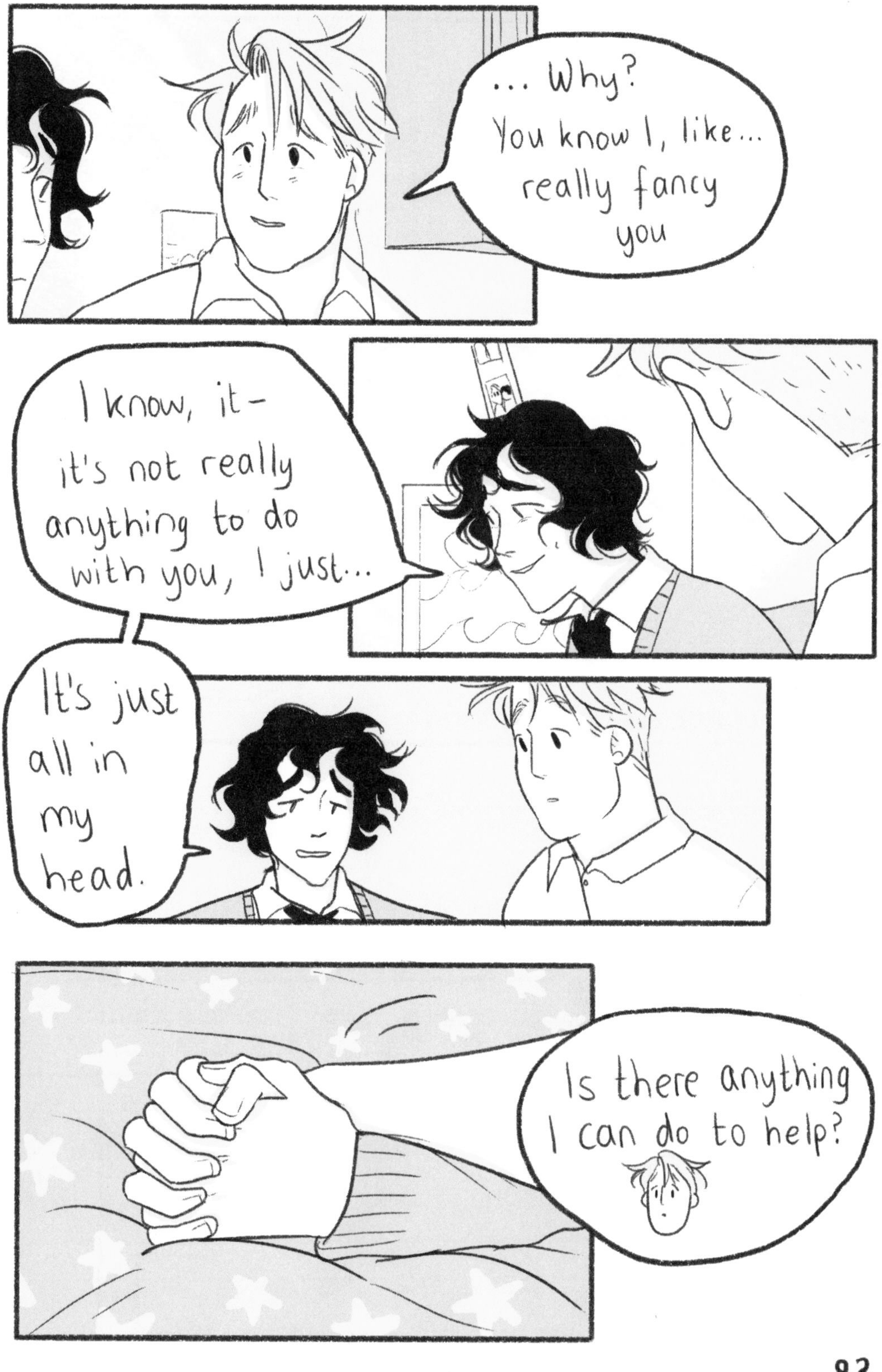
... Why?
You know I, like... really fancy you
I know, it- it's not really anything to do with you, I just...
It's just all in my head.
Is there anything I can do to help?

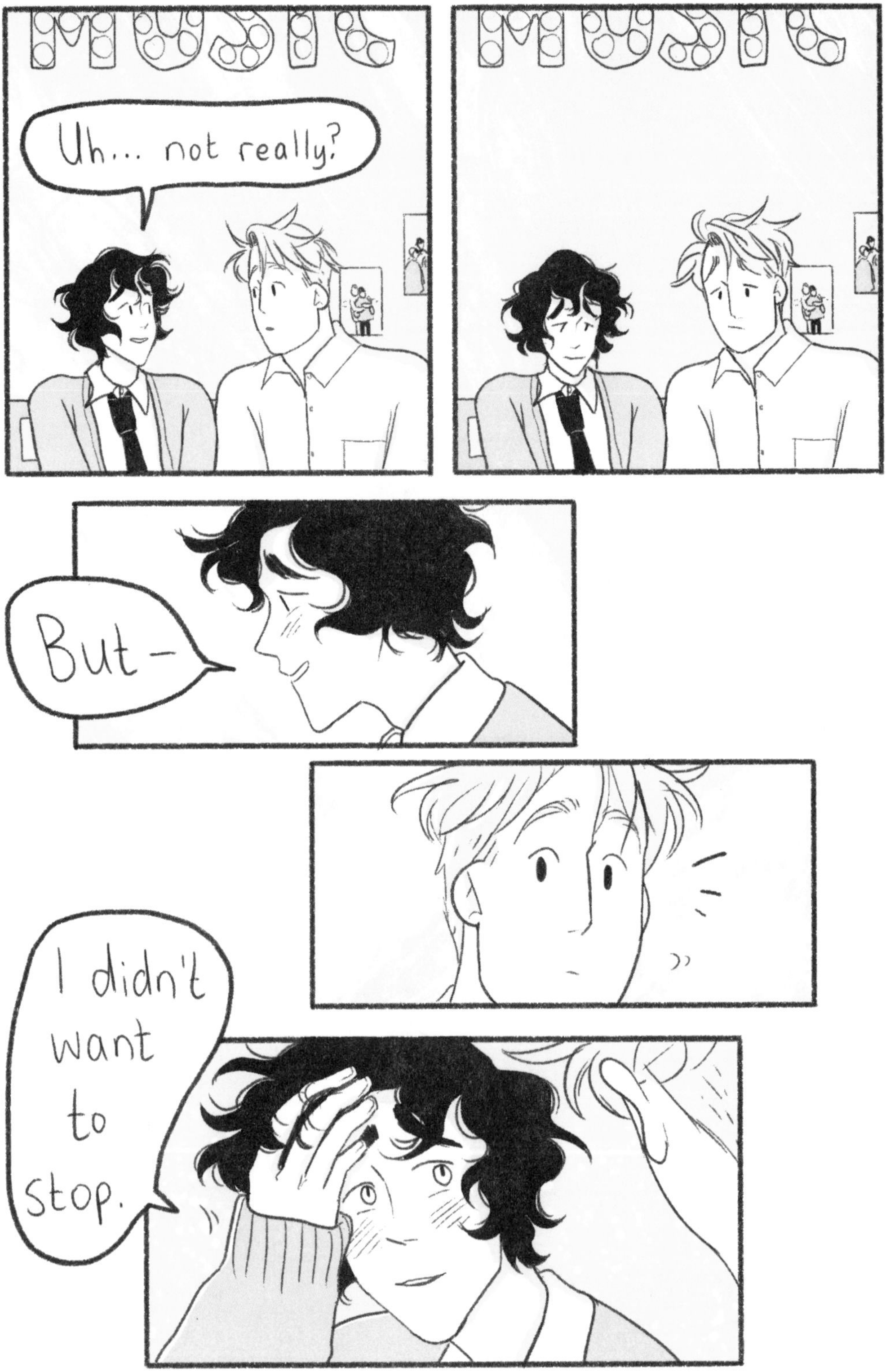
MUSIC
Uh... not really?
MUSIC
But-
I didn't want to stop.

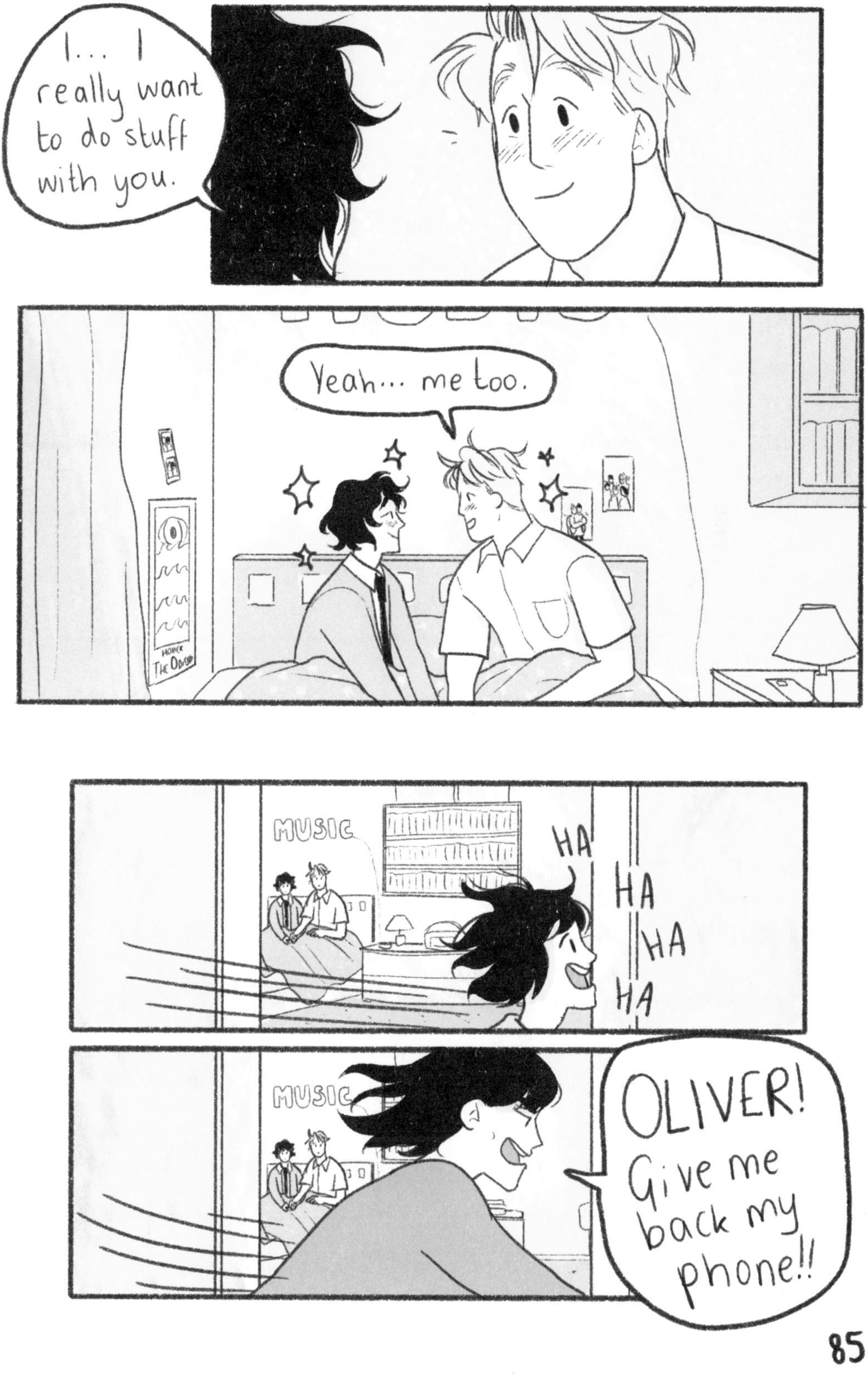
I… I really want to do stuff with you.
Yeah… me too.
MUSIC
HA
HA
HA
HA
MUSIC
OLIVER!
Give me back my phone!!

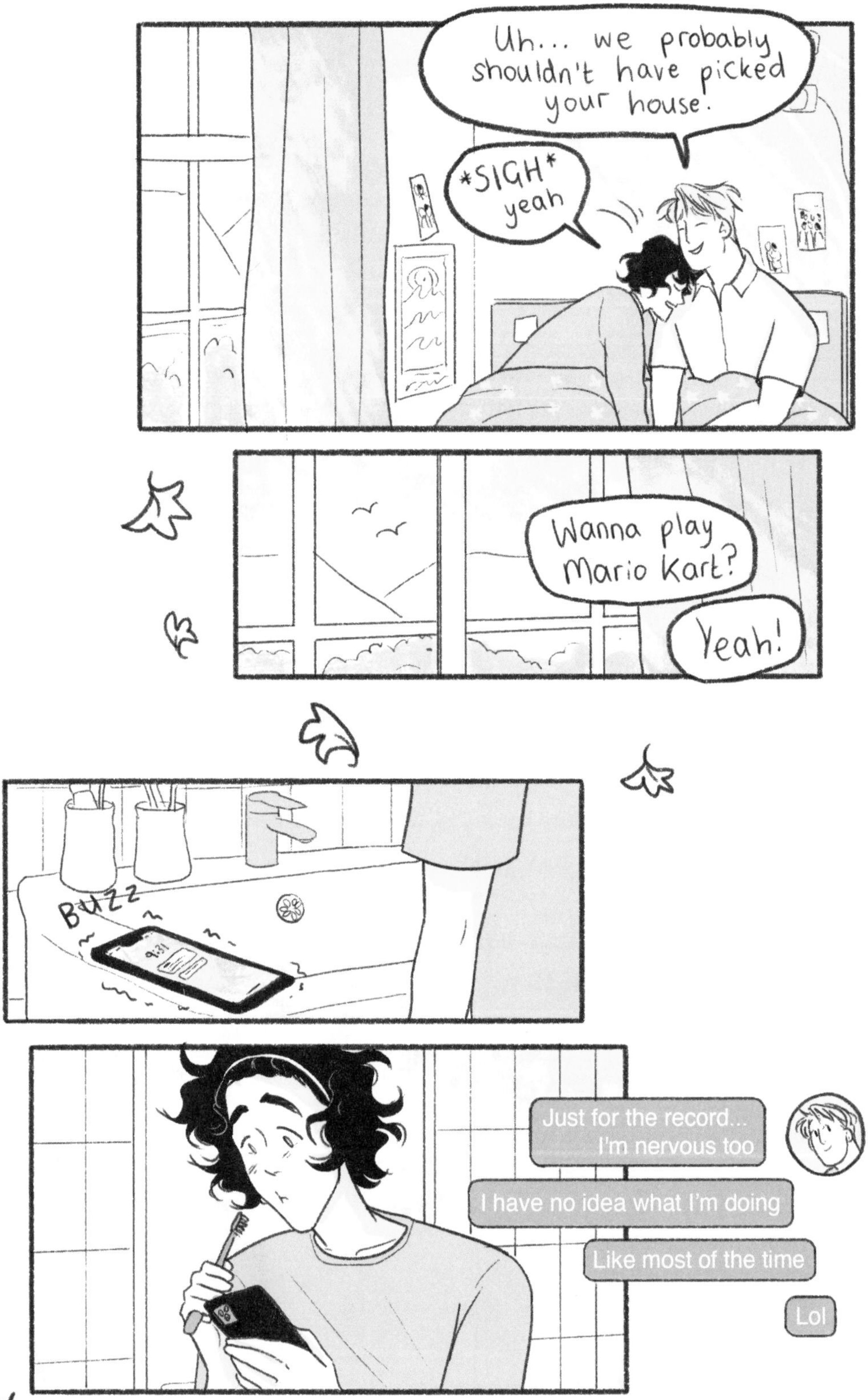
Uh... we probably shouldn't have picked your house.
SIGH yeah
Wanna play Mario Kart?
Yeah!
BUZZ
Just for the record... I'm nervous too
I have no idea what I'm doing
Like most of the time
Lol

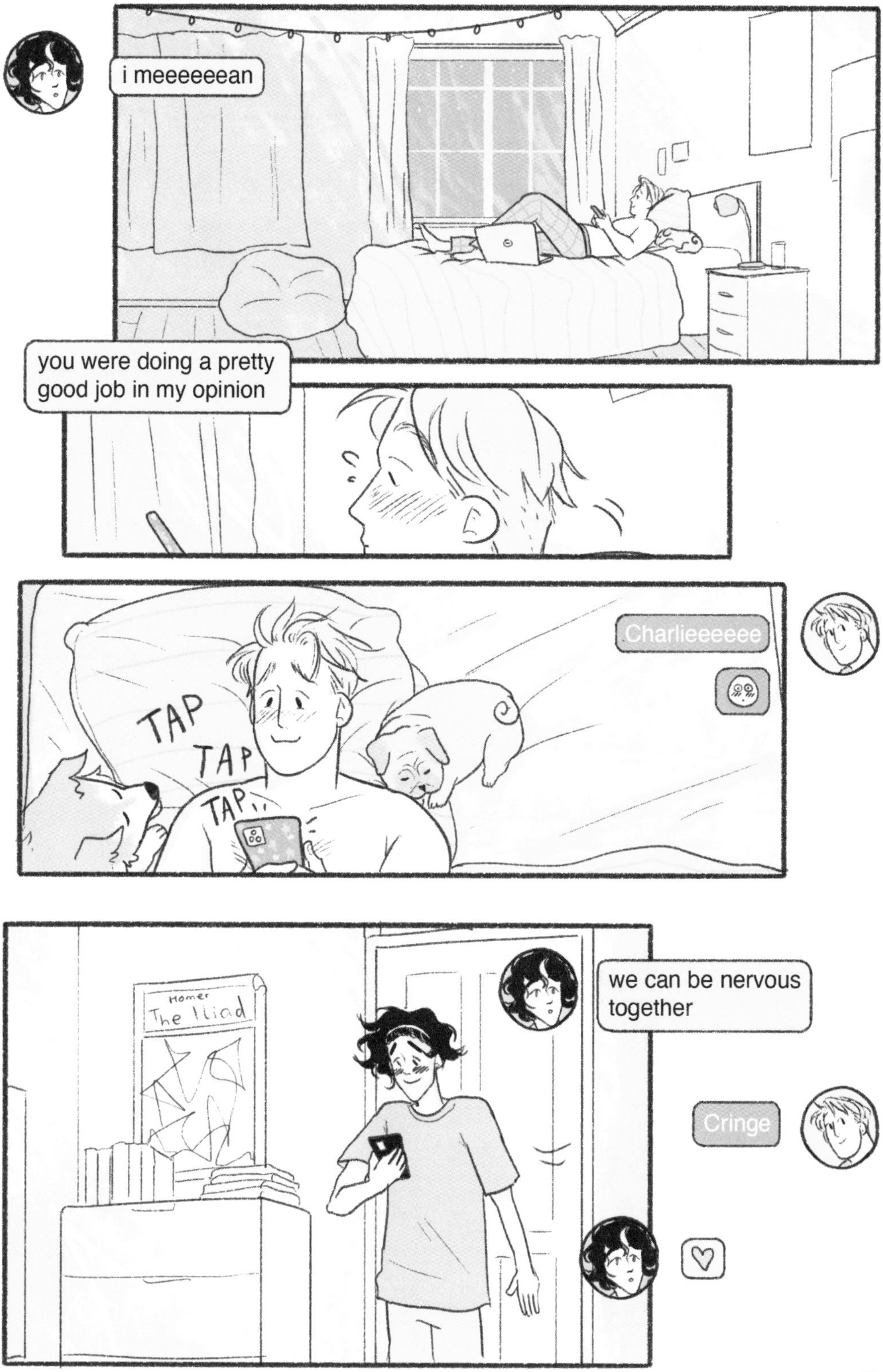
i meeeeeean
you were doing a pretty good job in my opinion
Charlieeeeee
TAP
TAP
TAP
Homer
The Iliad
we can be nervous together
Cringe

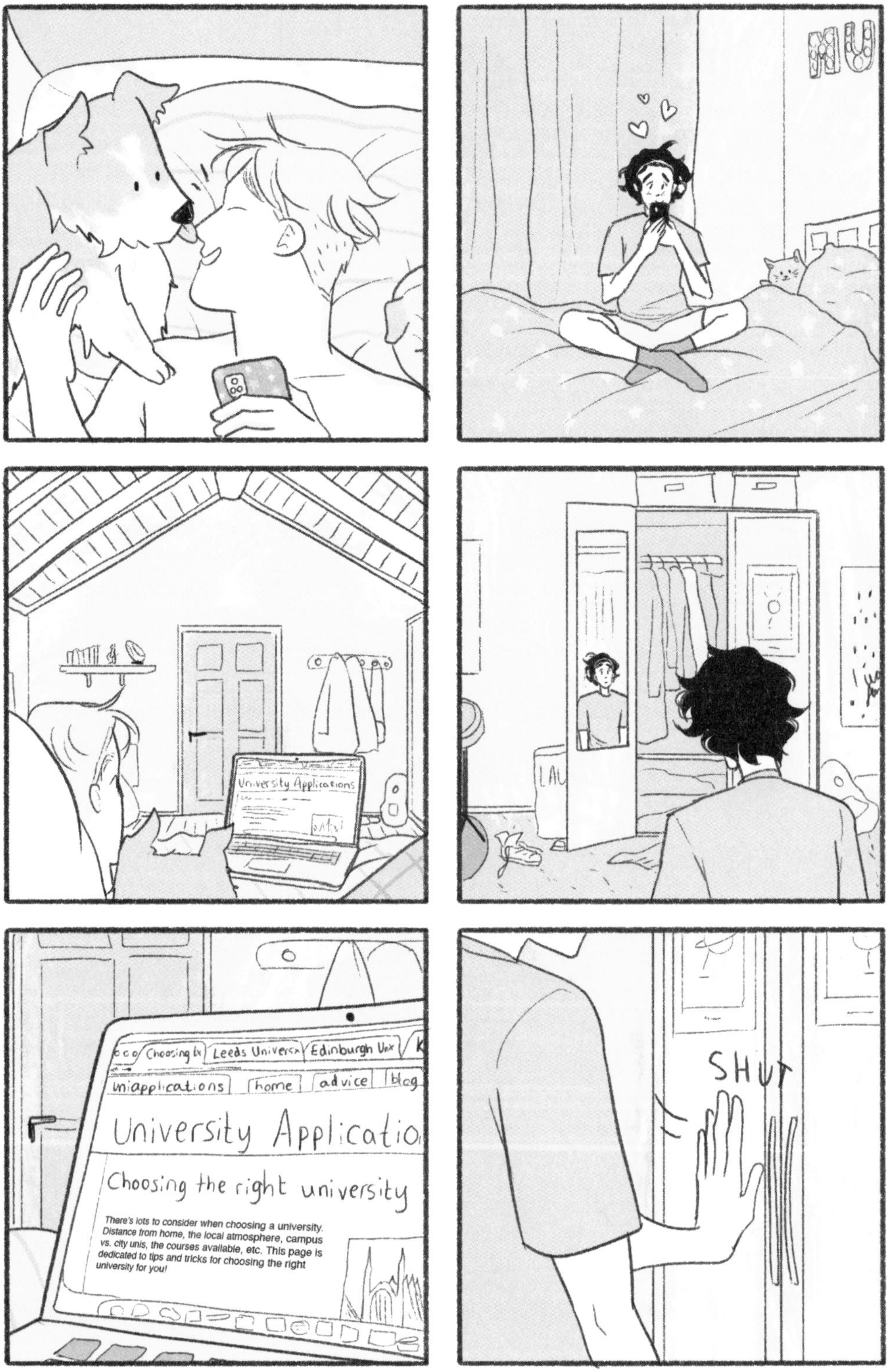
University Applications
uniapplications
home
advice
Choosing the right university
There's lots to consider when choosing a university. Distance from home, the local atmosphere, campus vs. city unis, the courses available, etc. This page is dedicated to tips and tricks for choosing the right university for you!
SHUT

MUSE
I was Born for This
BUZZ
21:47

Sahar Zahid

Hey Charlie!! So I needed to ask you a big favor

I'm in a band and we're playing at the summer fete in town in June

I know you play the drums and we really need a drummer

Would you be up for it?

hi!! ooh i don't know, i get nervous about being on stage...

like i've done school orchestra but not an actual proper band

i normally just play by myself haha

Well you can think about it! Let me know!

how many people will be in the audience?

It's an outdoor stage, so... everyone at the fete??

aah yeah wow haha

i'll think about it!! xx

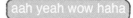

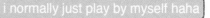

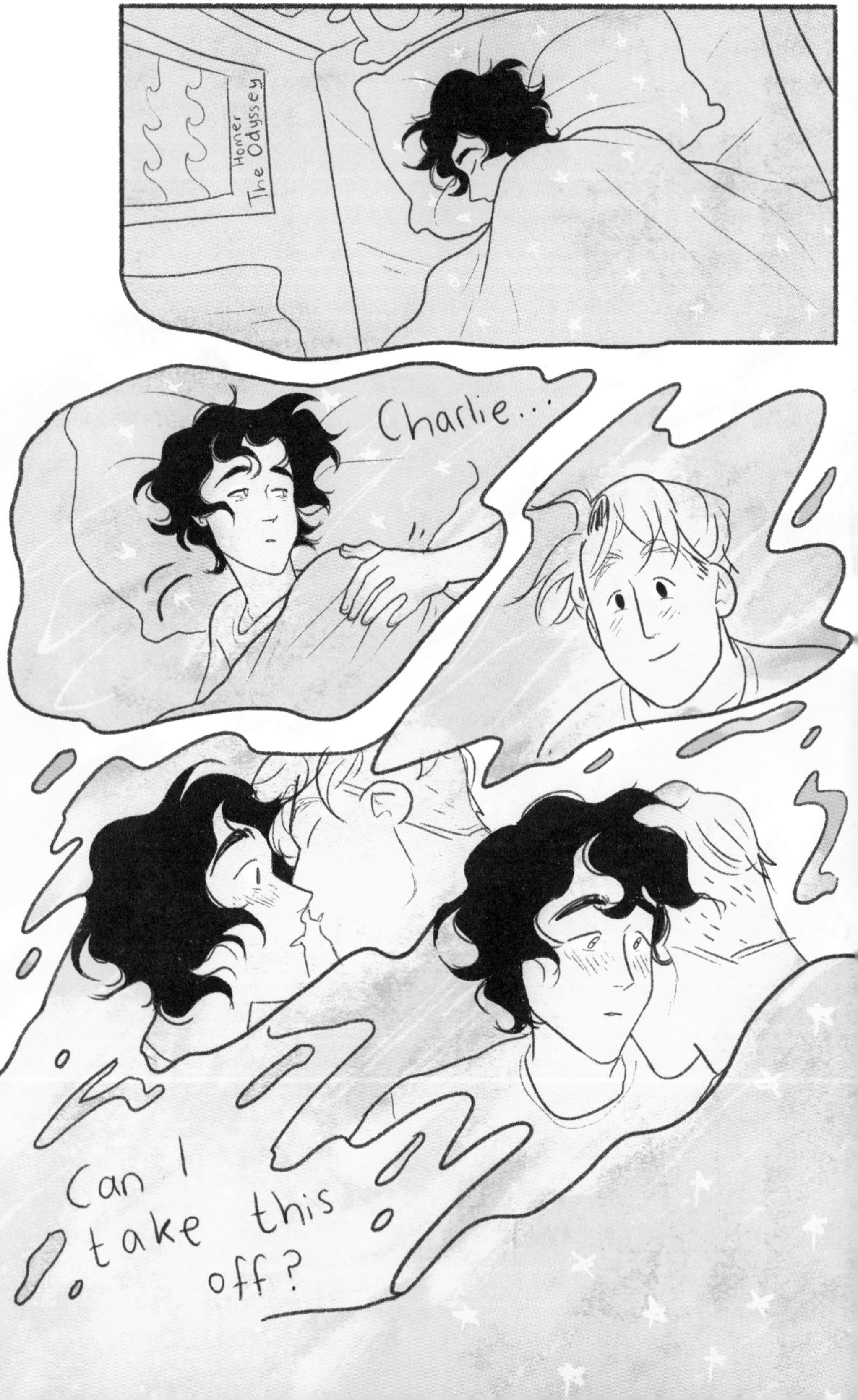
Homer
The Odyssey
Charlie...
Can I take this off?

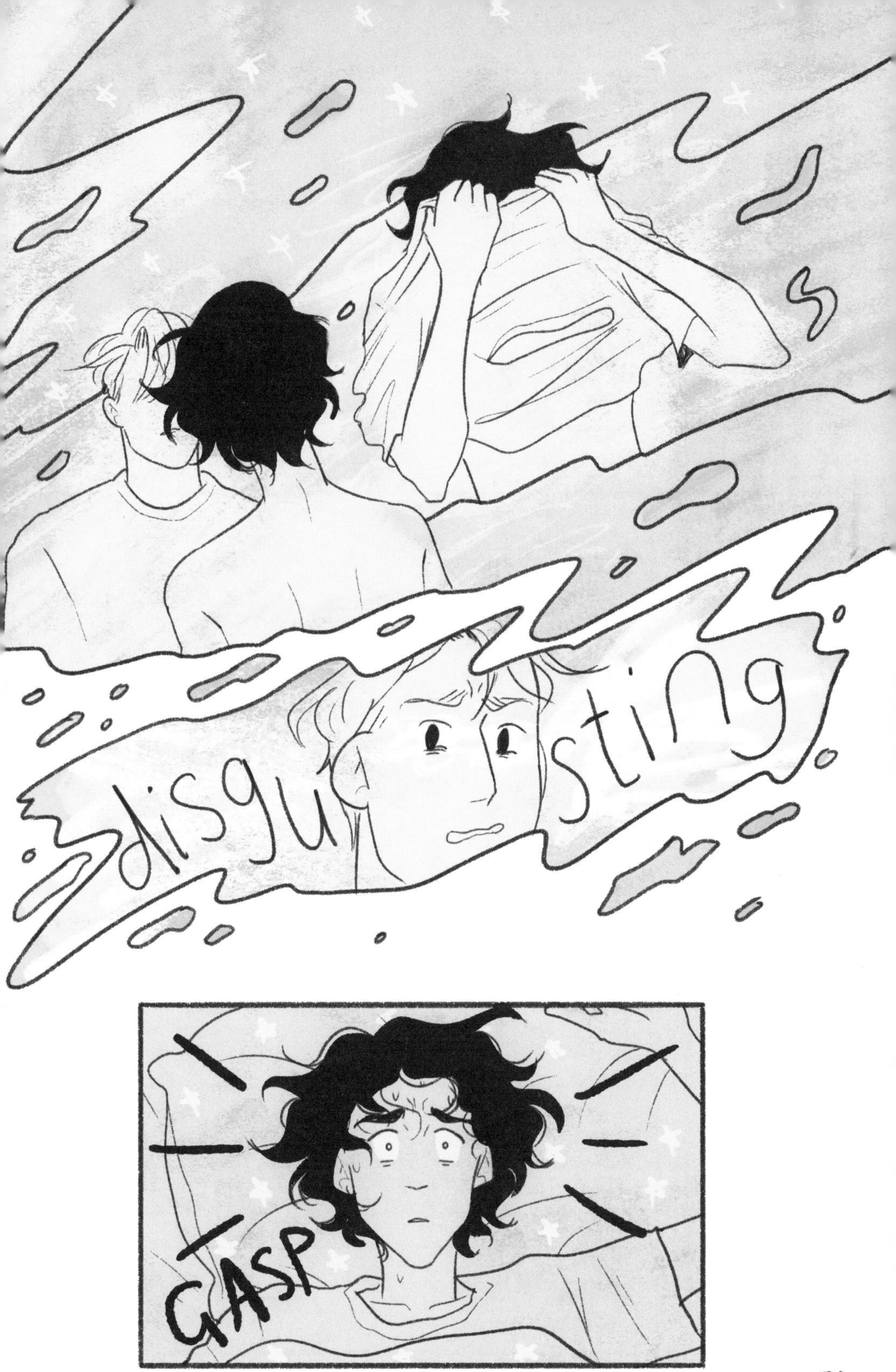
disgusting
GASP

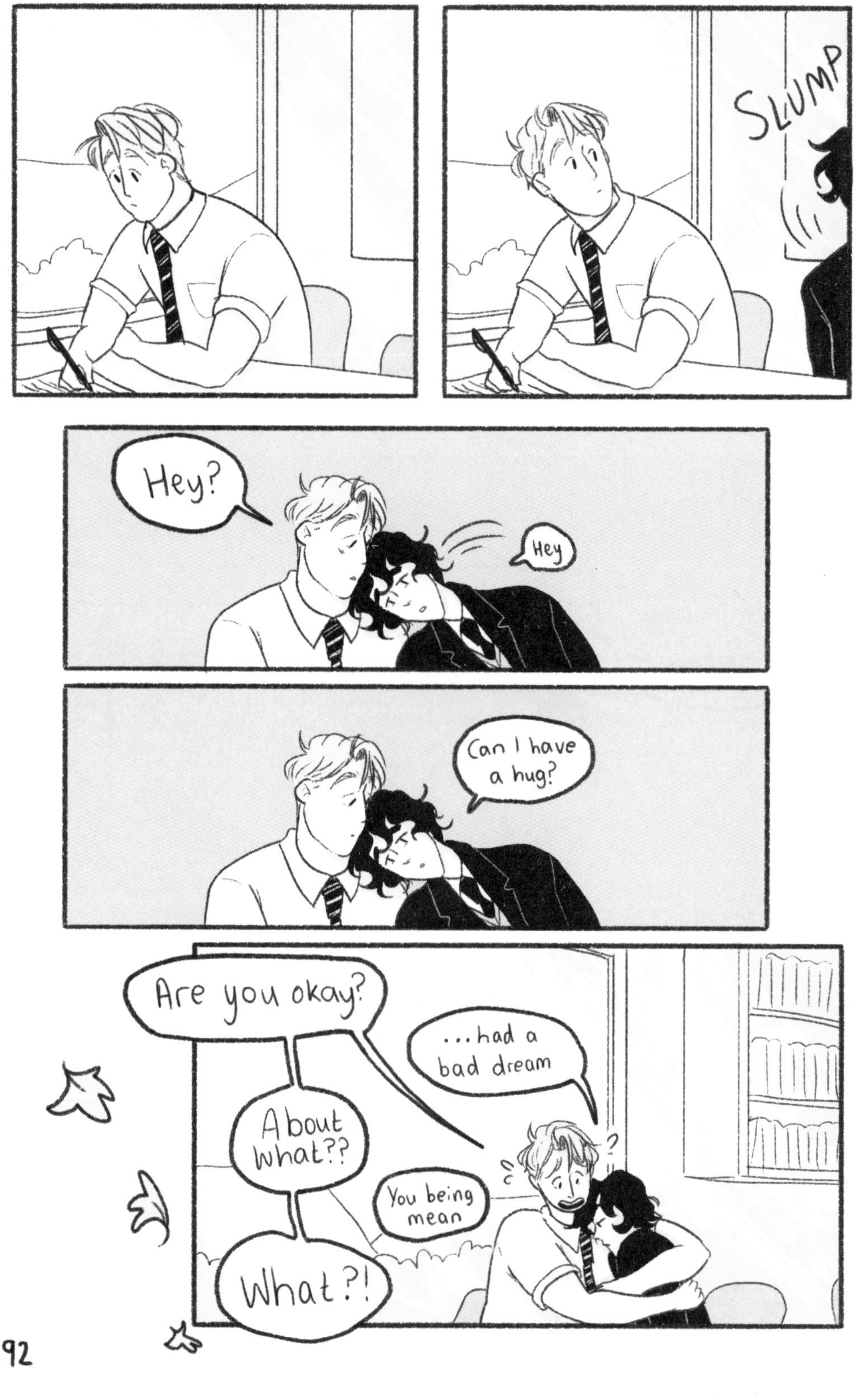
SLUMP
Hey?
Hey
Can I have a hug?
Are you okay?
...had a bad dream
About what??
You being mean
What?!

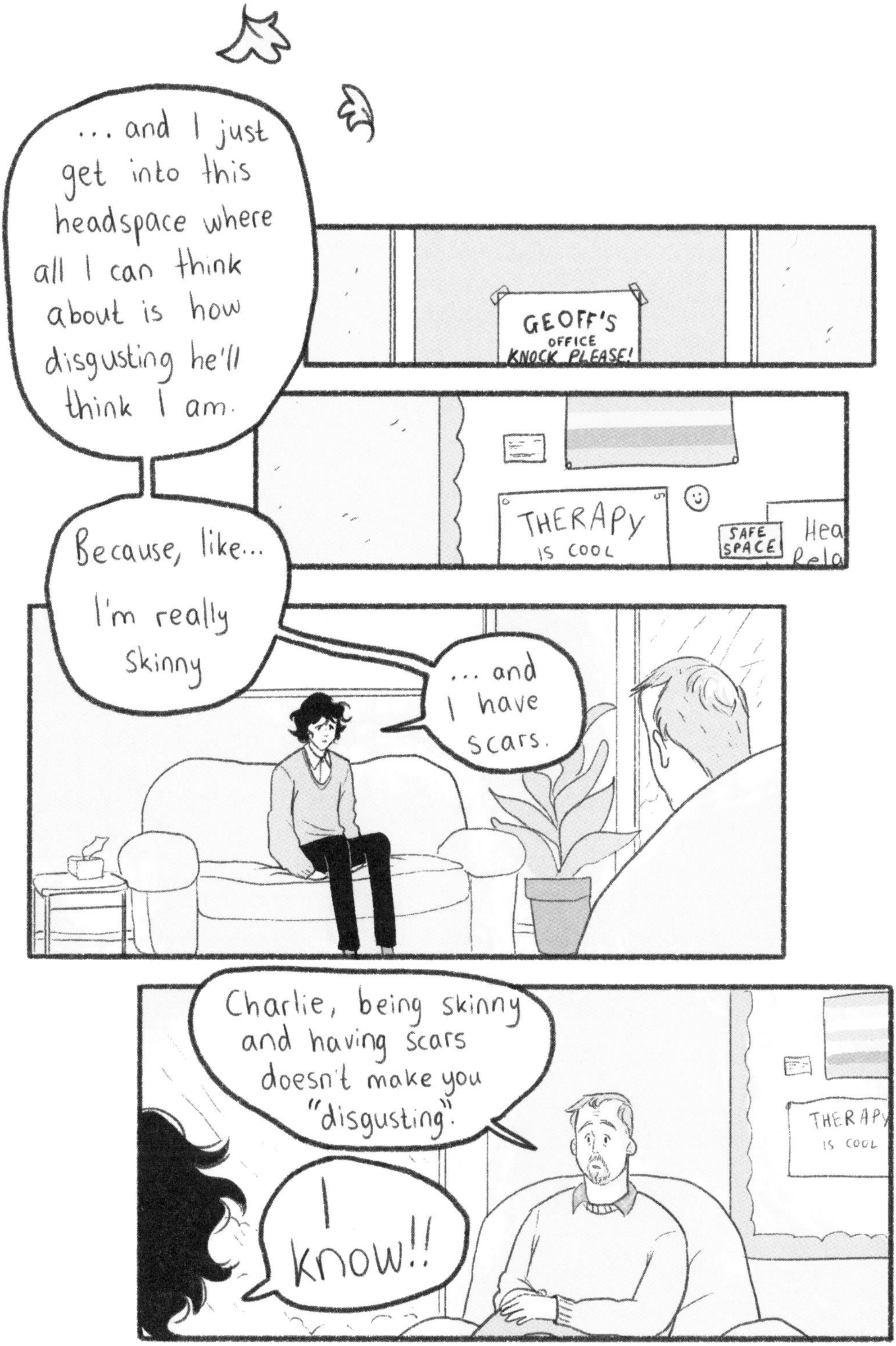
… and I just get into this headspace where all I can think about is how disgusting he'll think I am.
GEOFF'S OFFICE KNOCK PLEASE!
THERAPY IS COOL
SAFE SPACE
Because, like… I'm really skinny
… and I have scars.
Charlie, being skinny and having scars doesn't make you "disgusting".
THERAPY IS COOL
I know!!

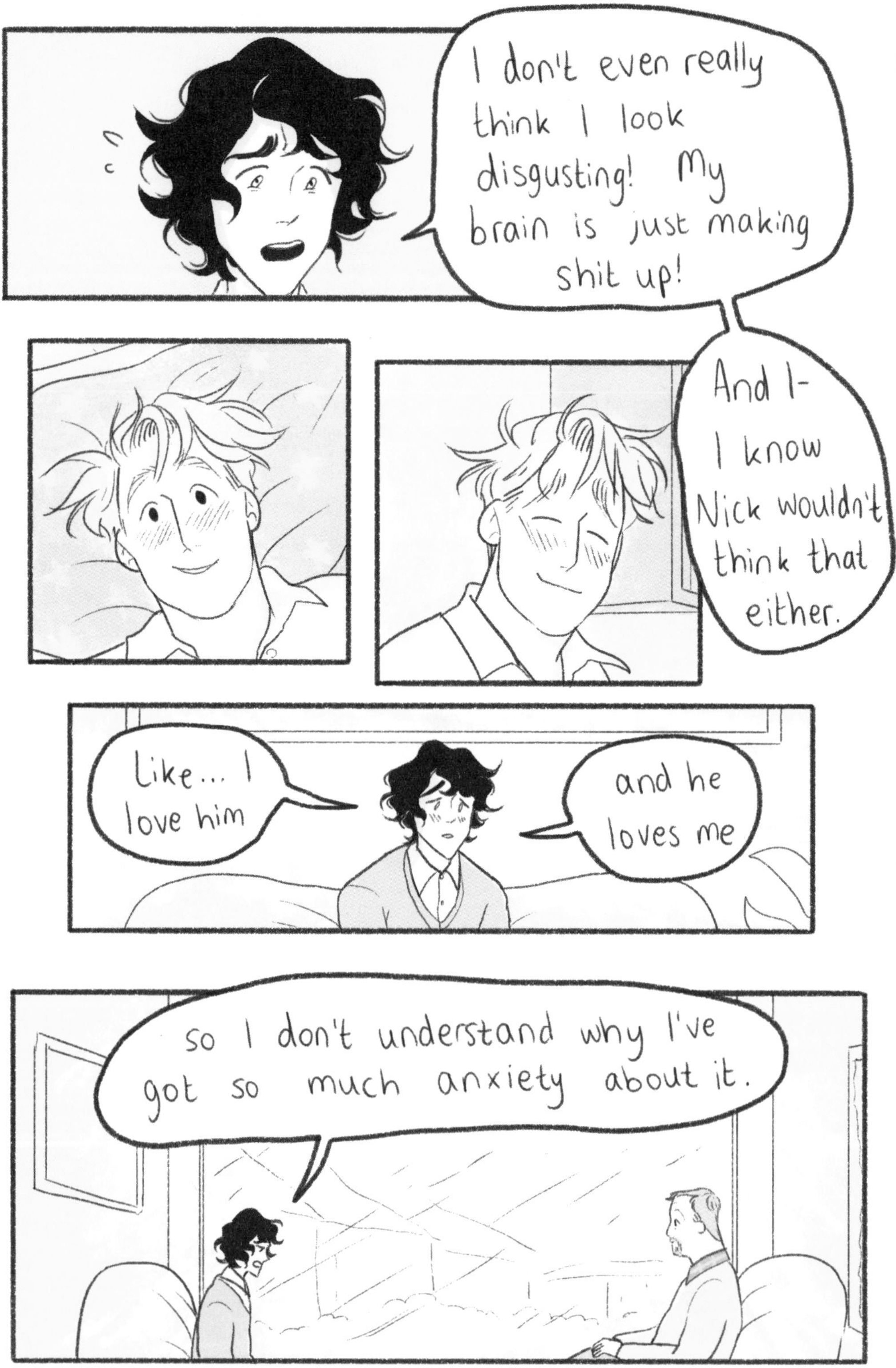
I don't even really think I look disgusting! My brain is just making shit up!
And I-
I know Nick wouldn't think that either.
Like... I love him
and he loves me
so I don't understand why I've got so much anxiety about it.

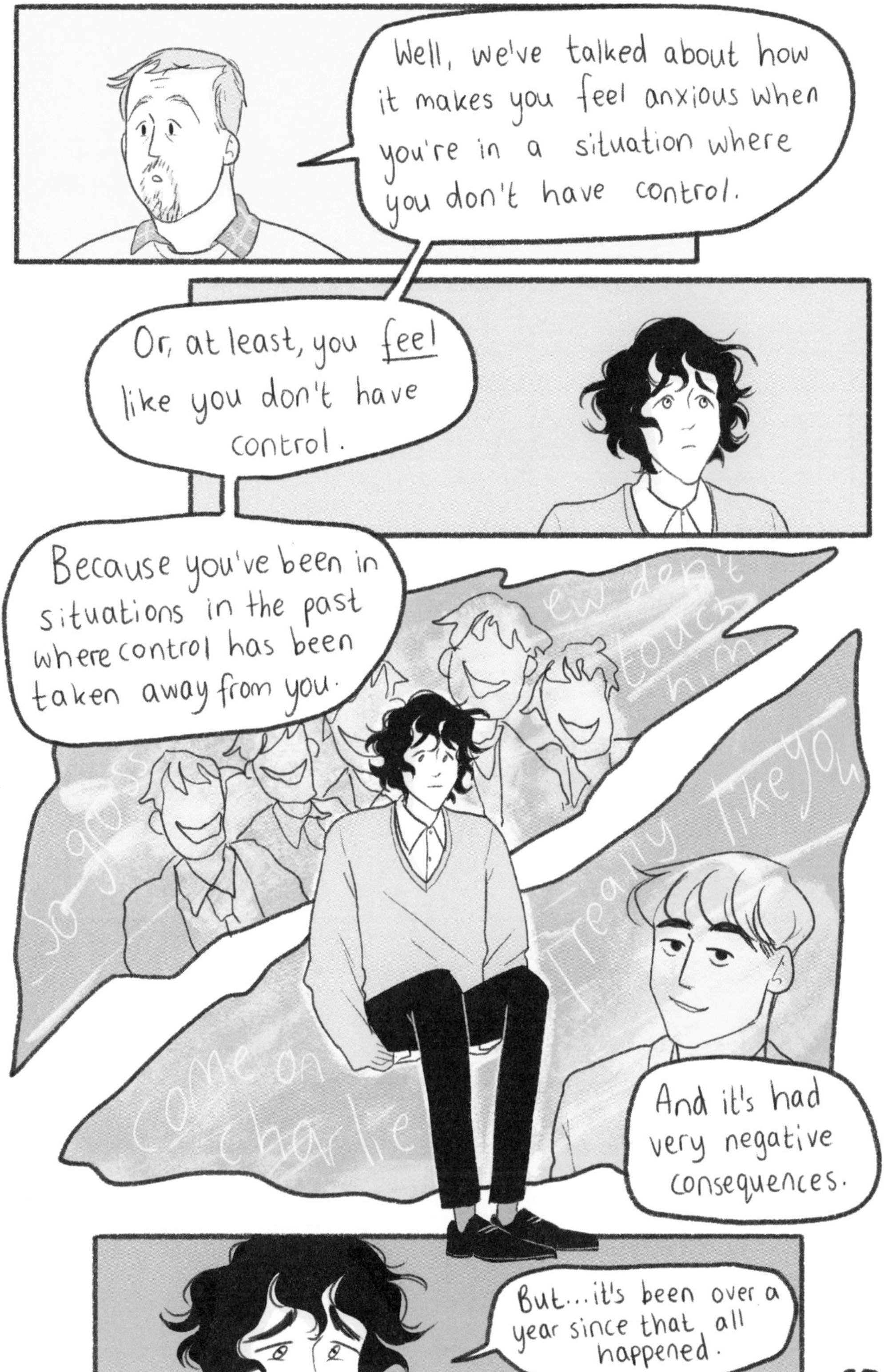
Well, we've talked about how it makes you feel anxious when you're in a situation where you don't have control.
Or, at least, you feel like you don't have control.
Because you've been in situations in the past where control has been taken away from you.
ew don't touch him
So gross
I really like you
come on Charlie
And it's had very negative consequences.
But...it's been over a year since that all happened.

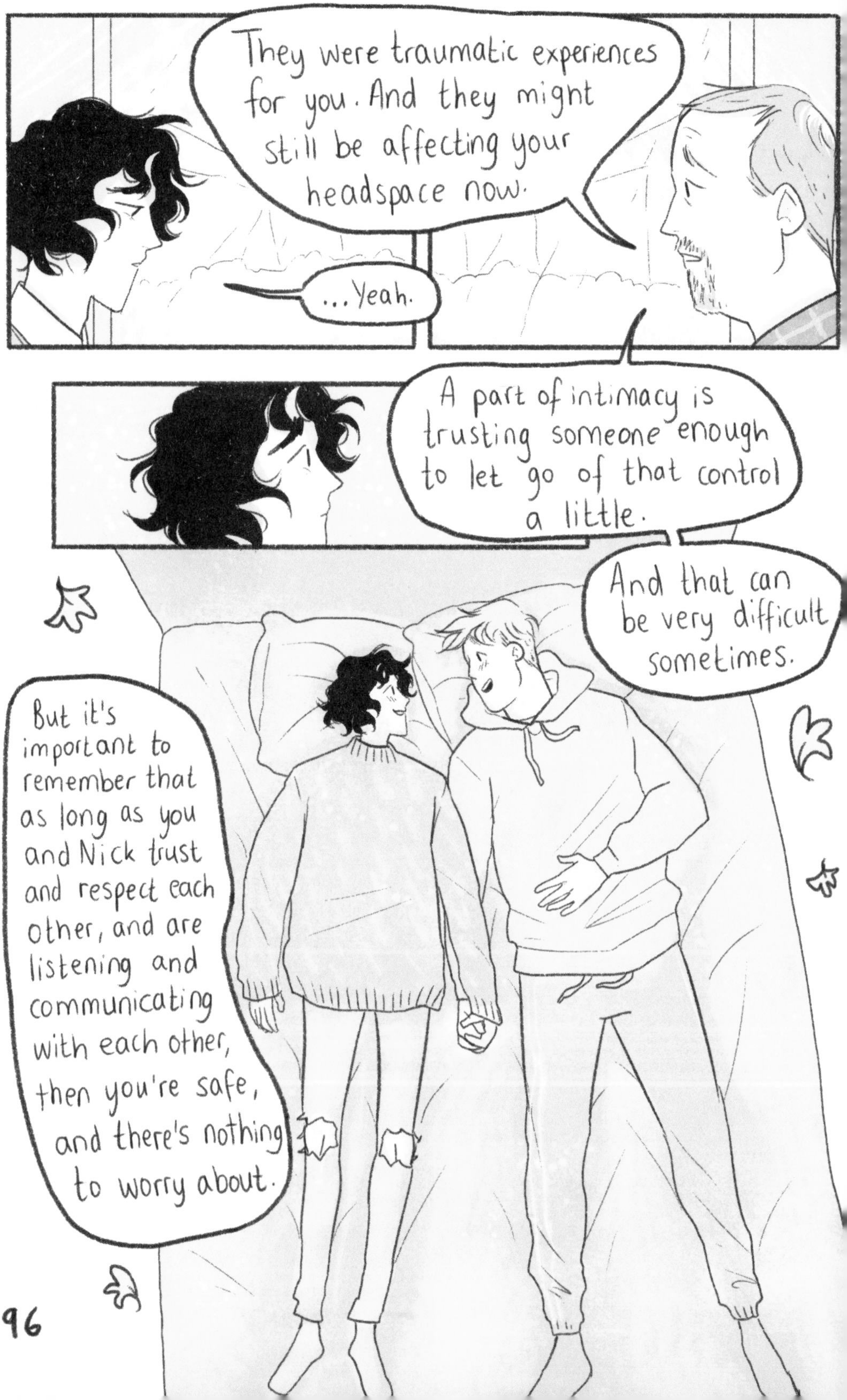
They were traumatic experiences for you. And they might still be affecting your headspace now.
...Yeah.
A part of intimacy is trusting someone enough to let go of that control a little.
And that can be very difficult sometimes.
But it's important to remember that as long as you and Nick trust and respect each other, and are listening and communicating with each other, then you're safe, and there's nothing to worry about.

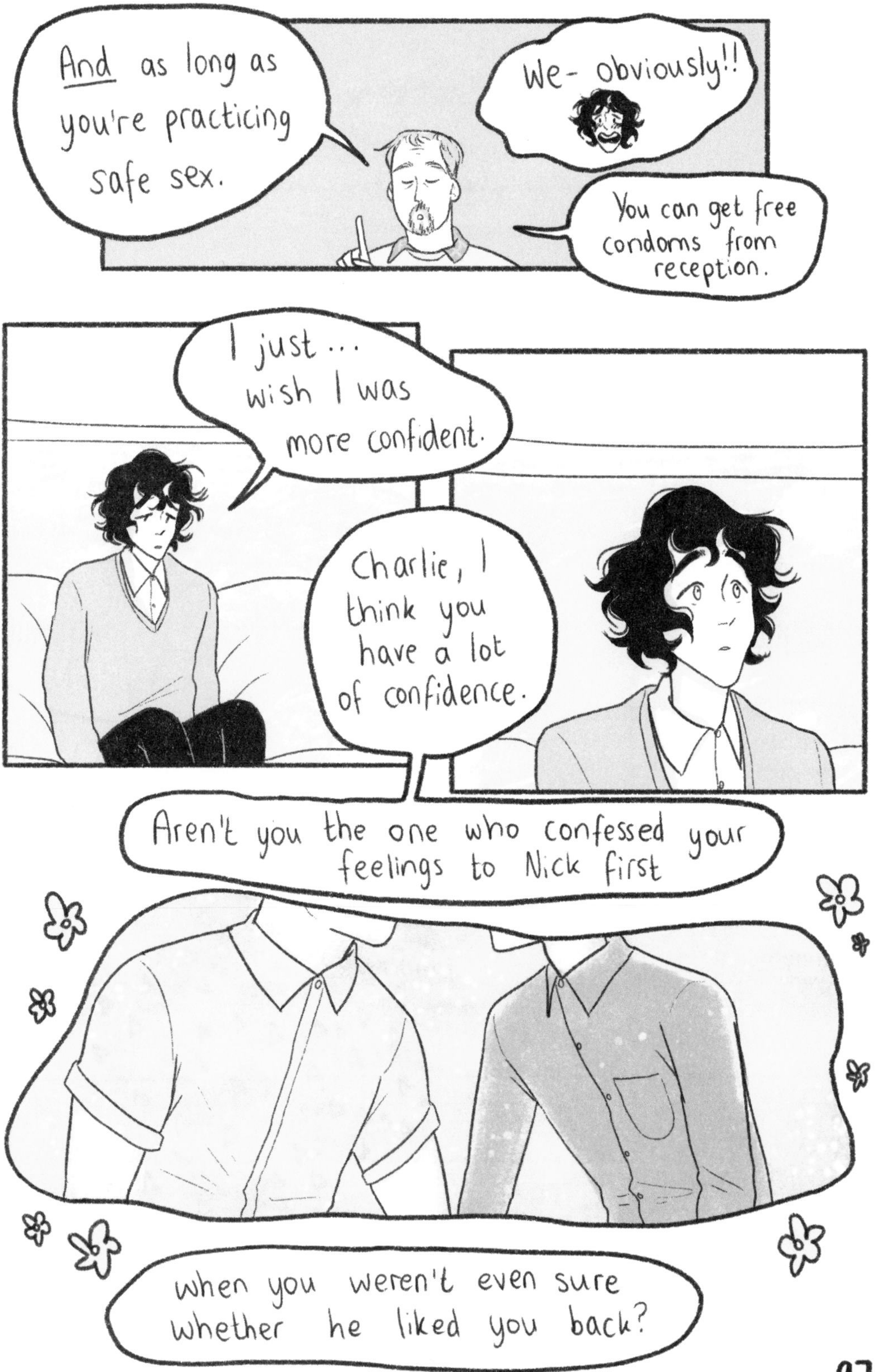
And as long as you're practicing safe sex.
We- obviously!!
You can get free condoms from reception.
I just... wish I was more confident.
Charlie, I think you have a lot of confidence.
Aren't you the one who confessed your feelings to Nick first
when you weren't even sure whether he liked you back?

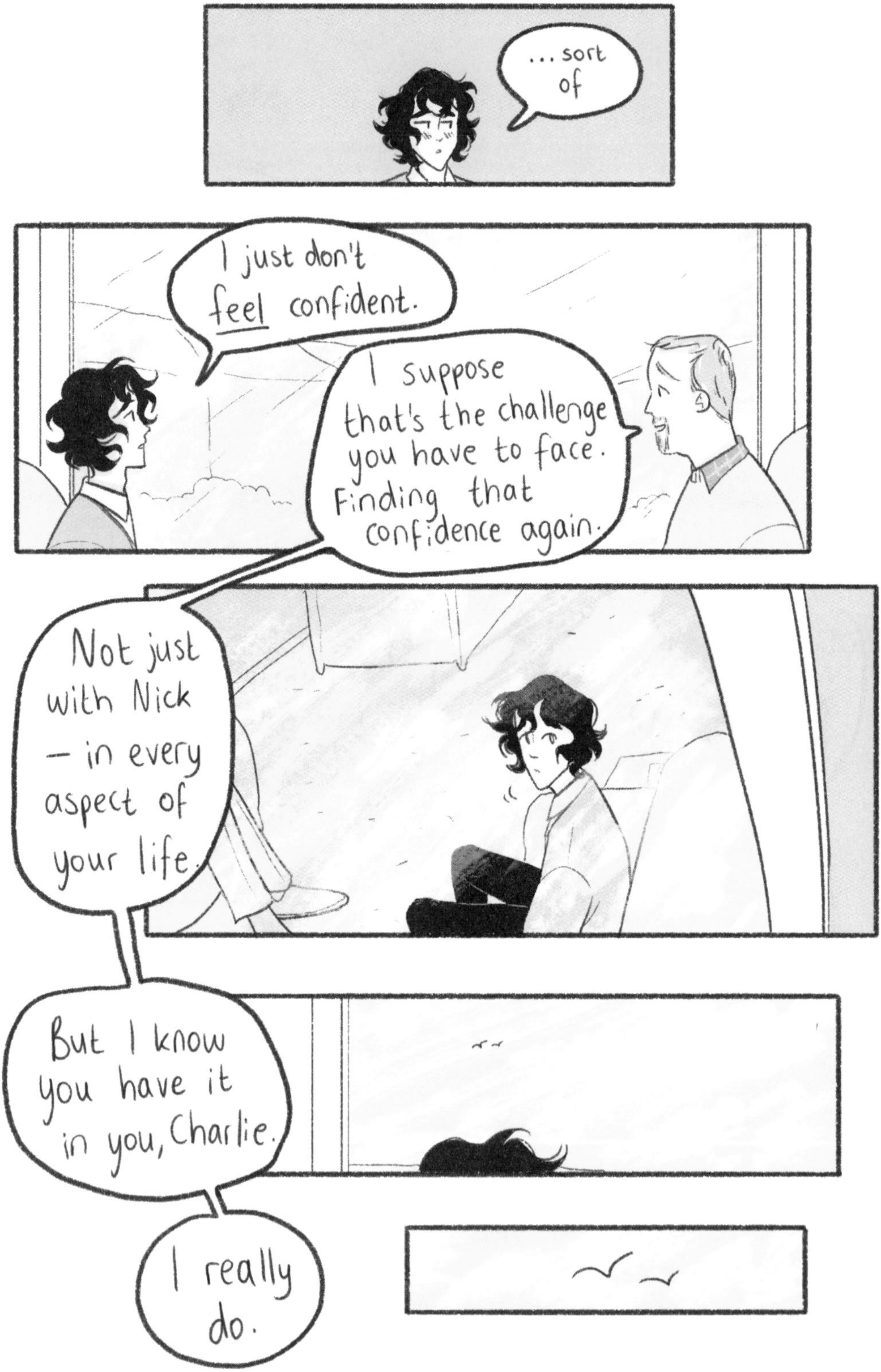
... sort of
I just don't feel confident.
I suppose that's the challenge you have to face. Finding that confidence again.
Not just with Nick – in every aspect of your life.
But I know you have it in you, Charlie.
I really do.

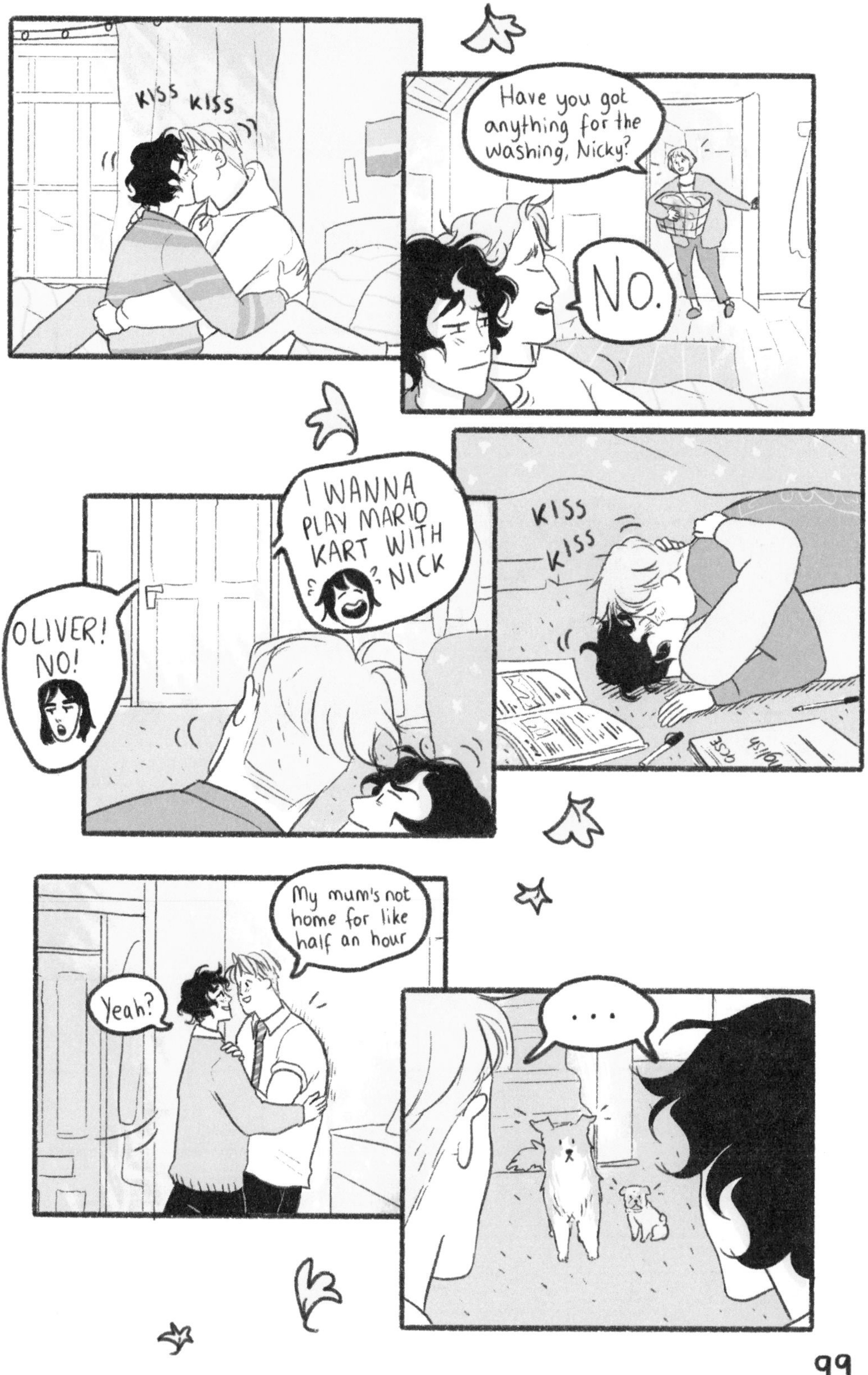
KISS KISS
Have you got anything for the washing, Nicky?
NO.
I WANNA PLAY MARIO KART WITH NICK
OLIVER! NO!
KISS KISS
My mum's not home for like half an hour
Yeah?
. . .

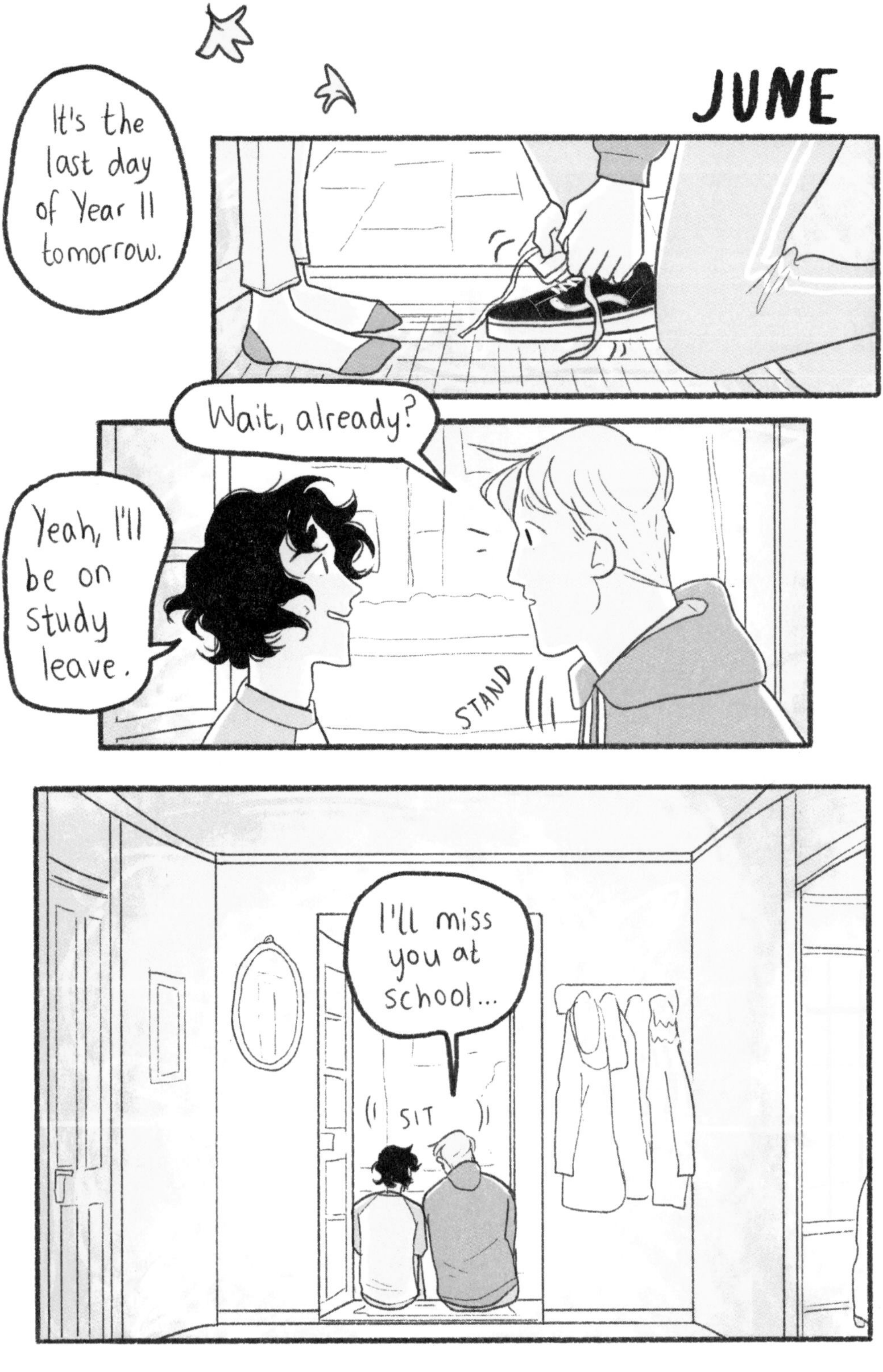
JUNE
It's the last day of Year 11 tomorrow.
Wait, already?
Yeah, I'll be on study leave.
STAND
I'll miss you at school...
SIT

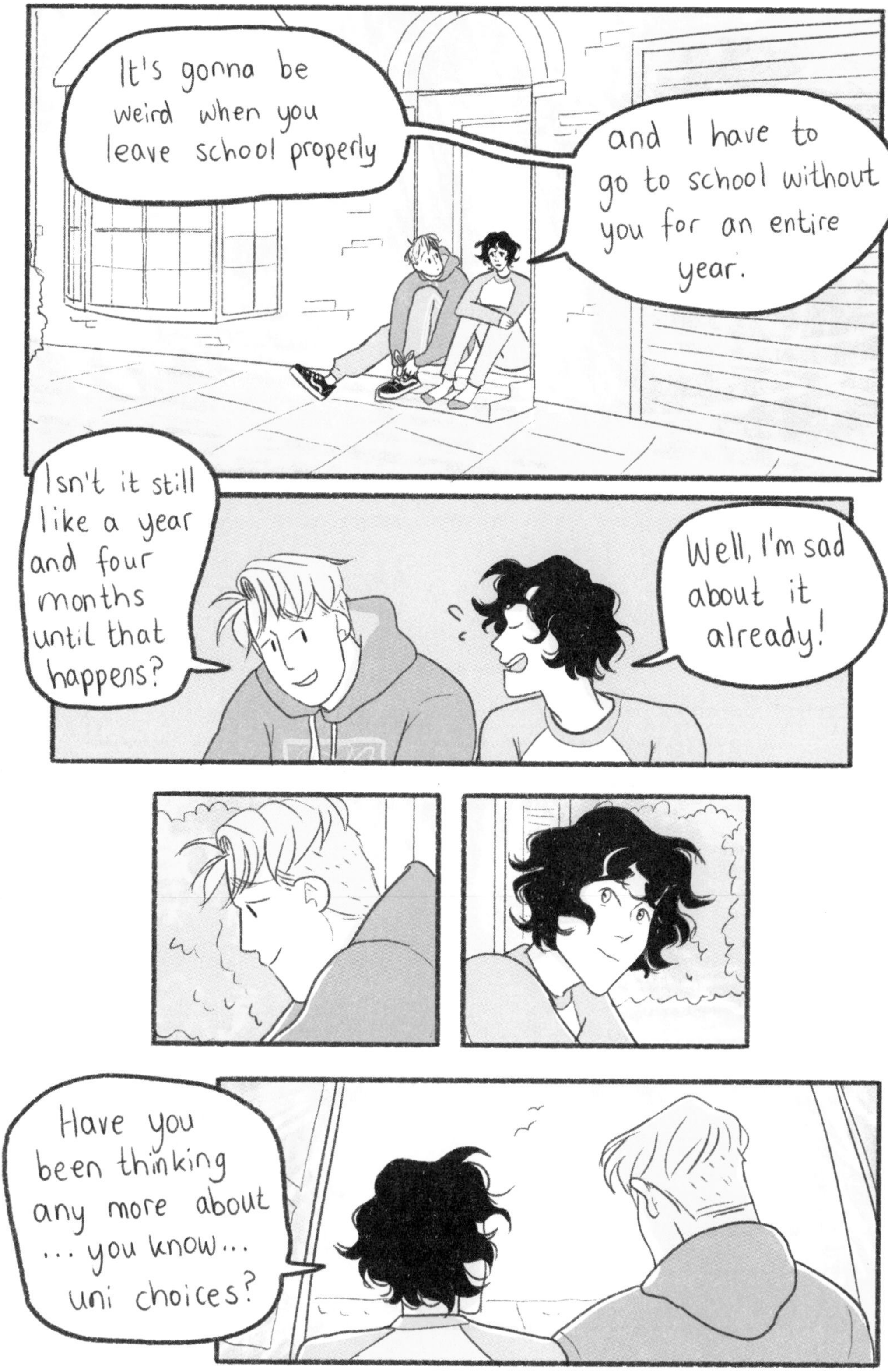
It's gonna be weird when you leave school properly
and I have to go to school without you for an entire year.
Isn't it still like a year and four months until that happens?
Well, I'm sad about it already!
Have you been thinking any more about ... you know... uni choices?

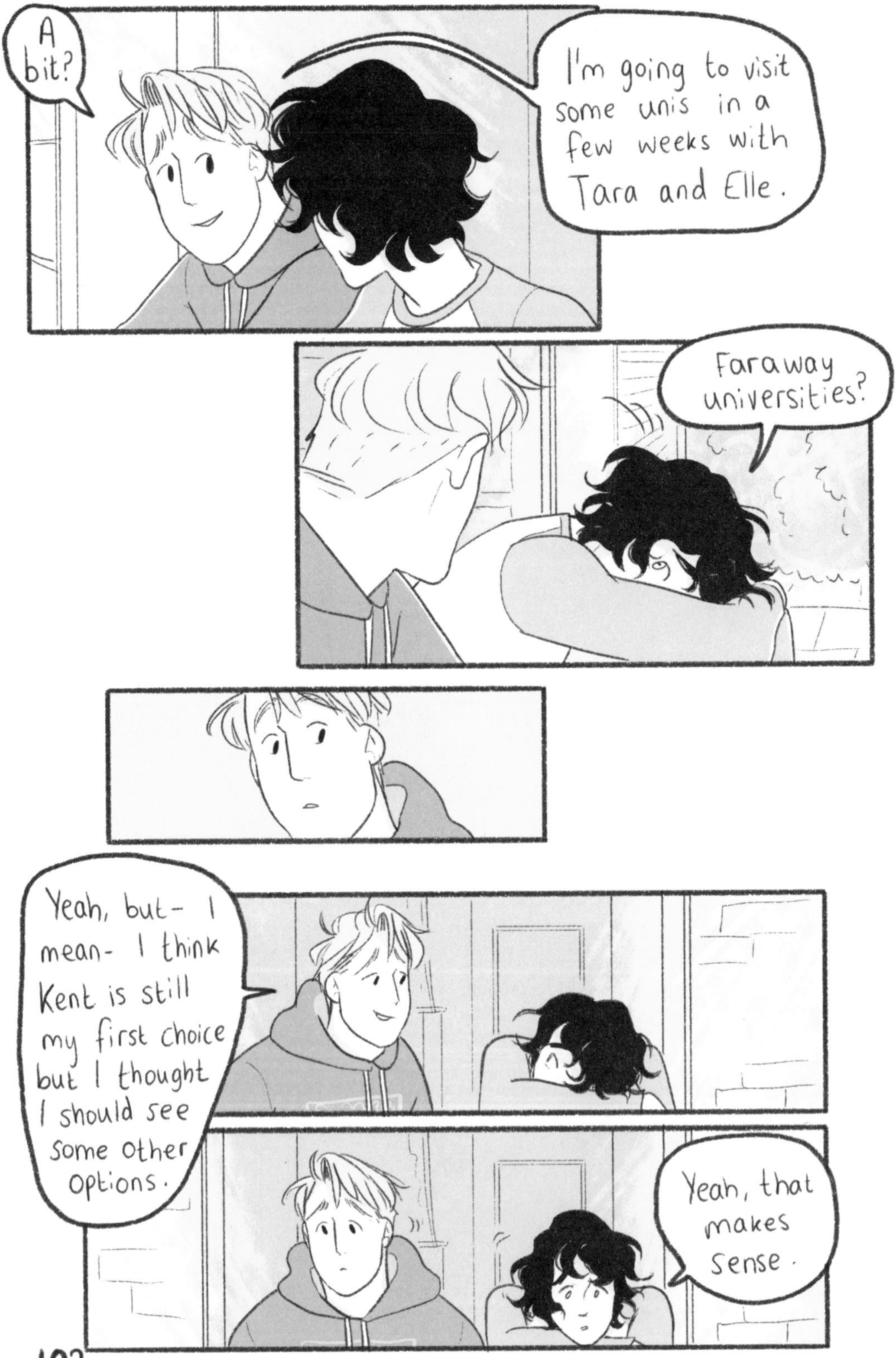
A bit?
I'm going to visit some unis in a few weeks with Tara and Elle.
Faraway universities?
Yeah, but- I mean- I think Kent is still my first choice but I thought I should see some other options.
Yeah, that makes sense.

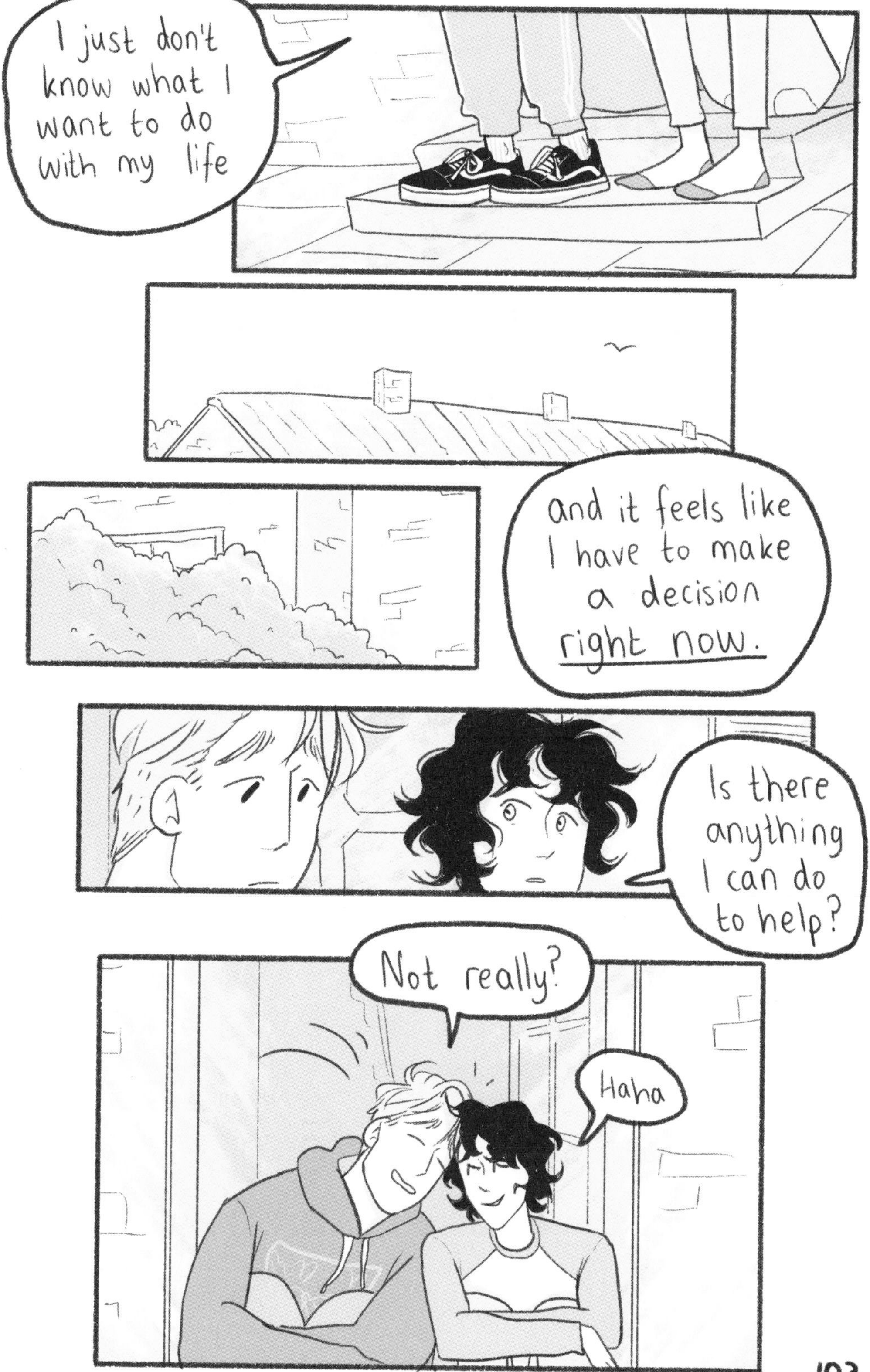
I just don't know what I want to do with my life
and it feels like I have to make a decision right now.
Is there anything I can do to help?
Not really?
Haha

STAND

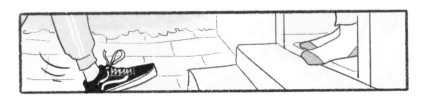

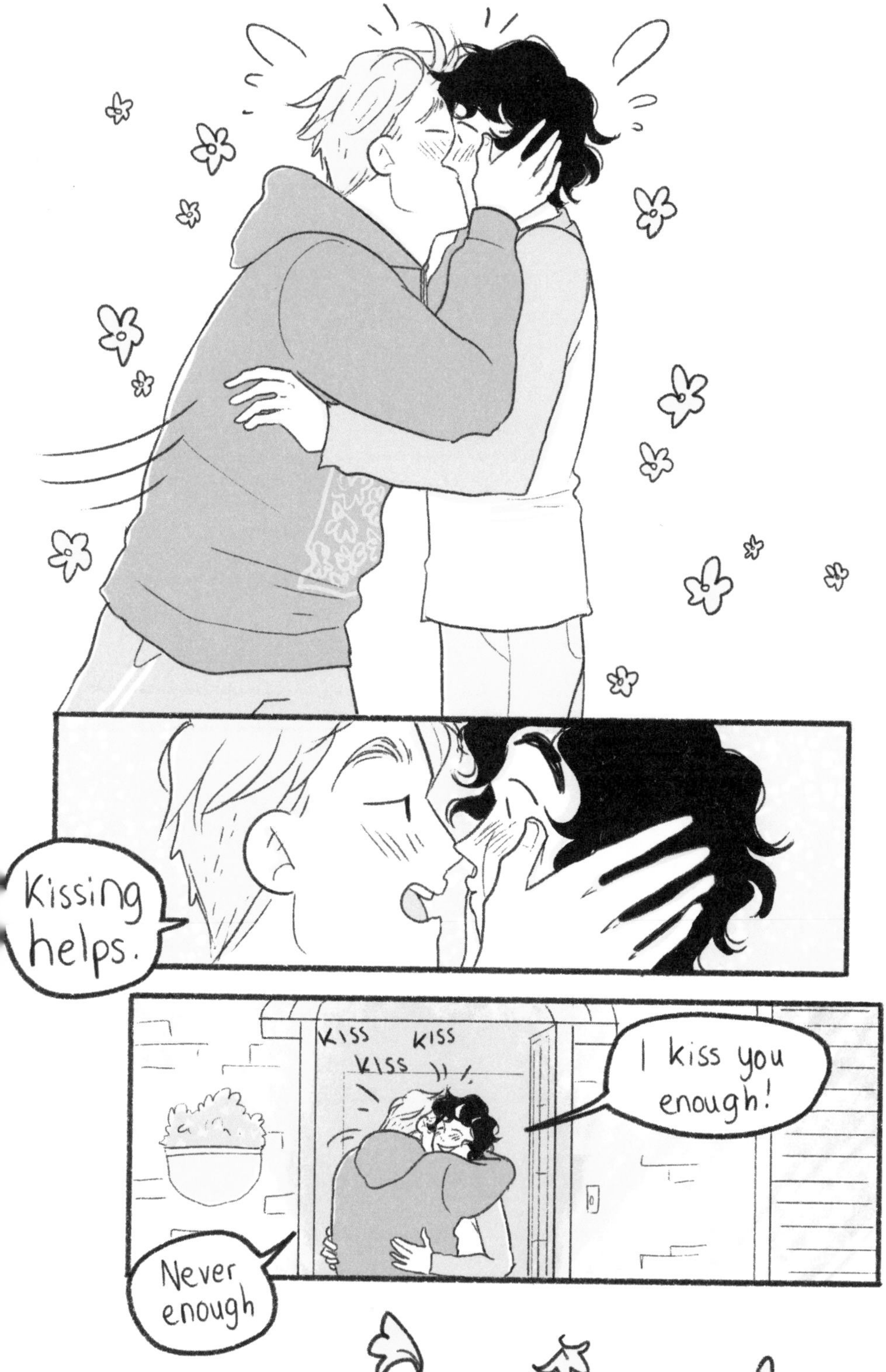
Kissing helps.
KISS
KISS
KISS
I kiss you enough!
Never enough

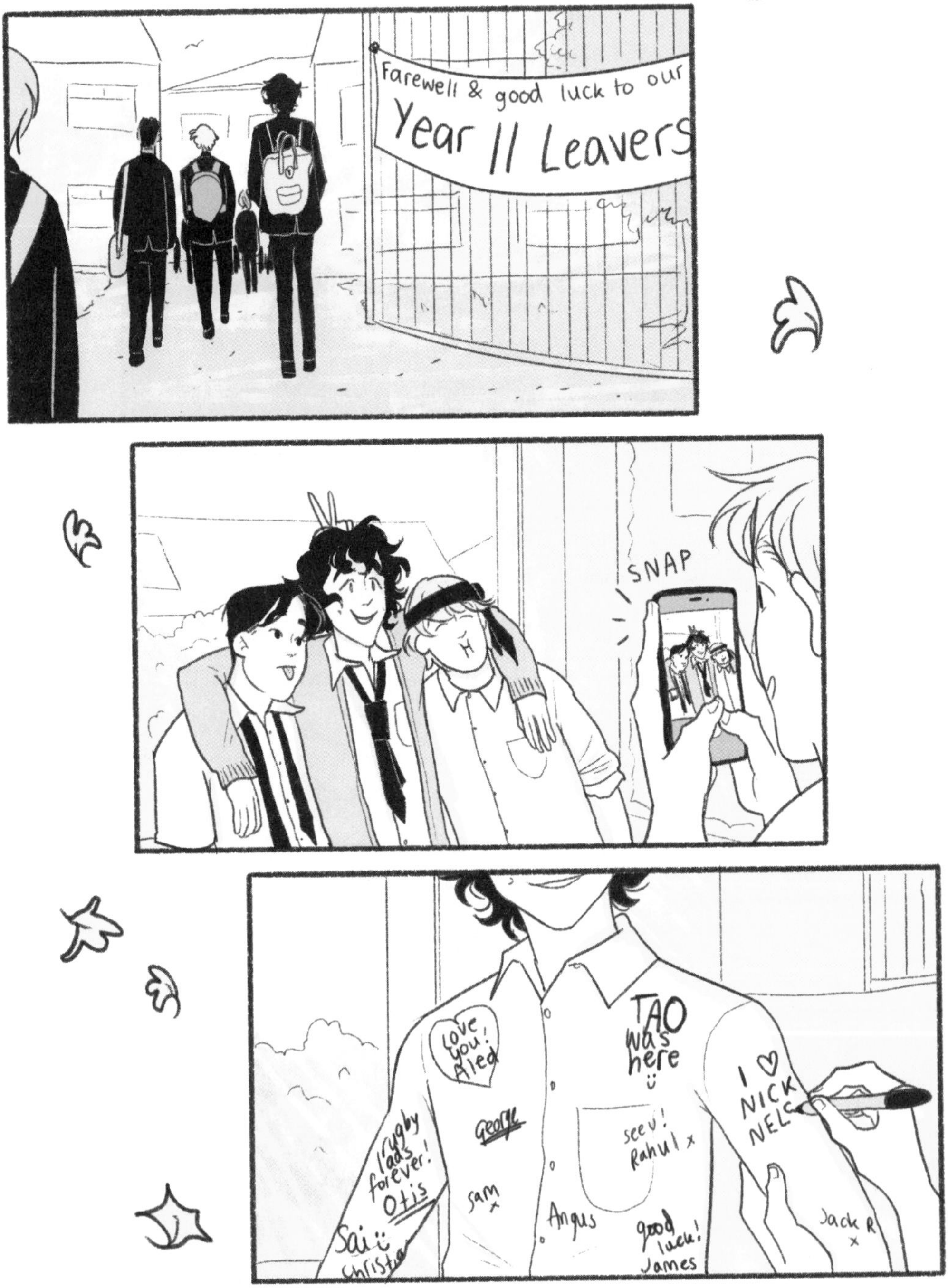
Farewell & good luck to our
Year 11 Leavers
SNAP
love you! Aled
TAO was here :)
I ♡ NICK NEL
George
see u! Rahul x
rugby lads forever! Otis
Sam x
Angus
good luck! James
Jack R x
Sai :)

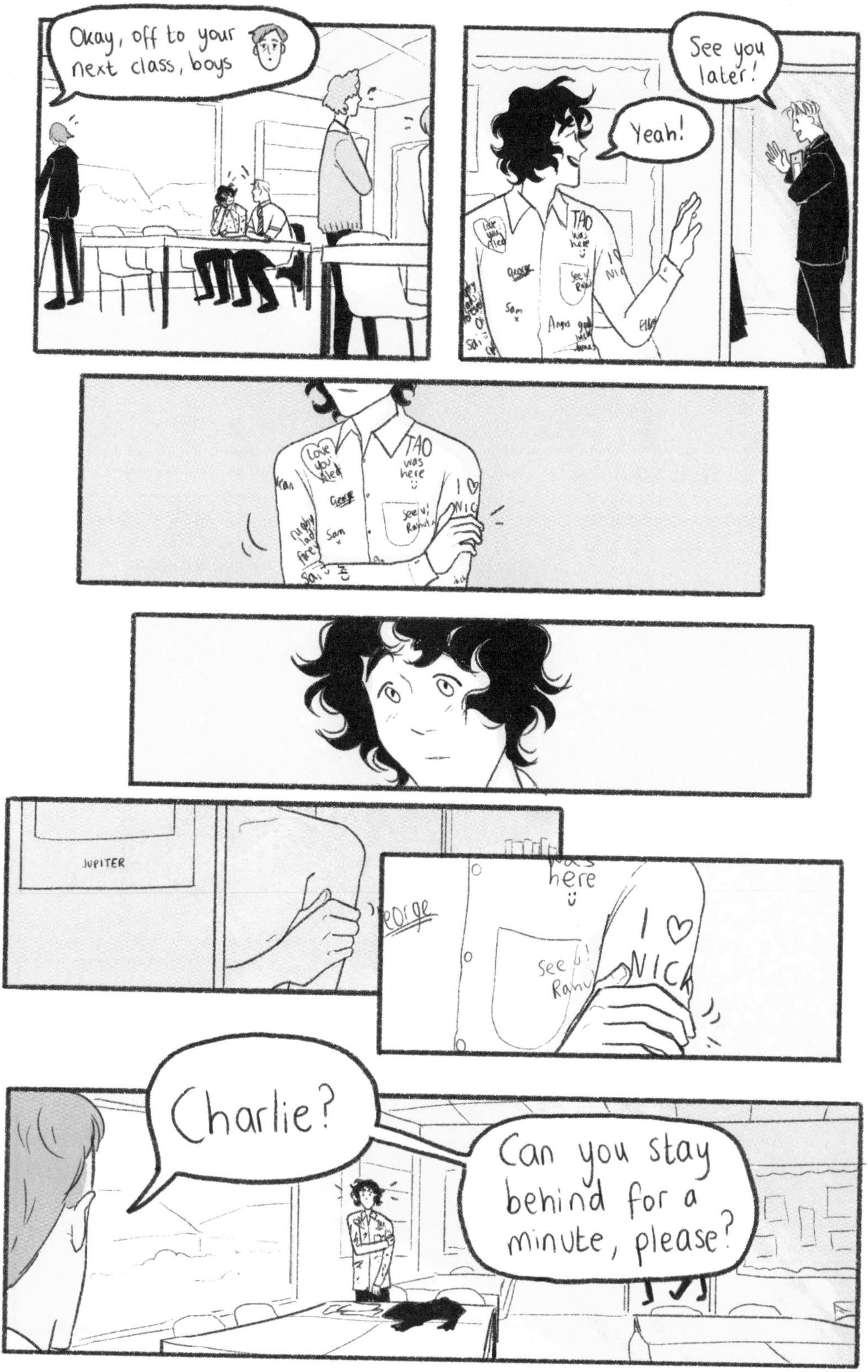
Okay, off to your next class, boys
See you later!
Yeah!
TAO was here
I ♡ NICK
See u! Rahul
Sam x
Angus
JUPITER
Charlie?
Can you stay behind for a minute, please?

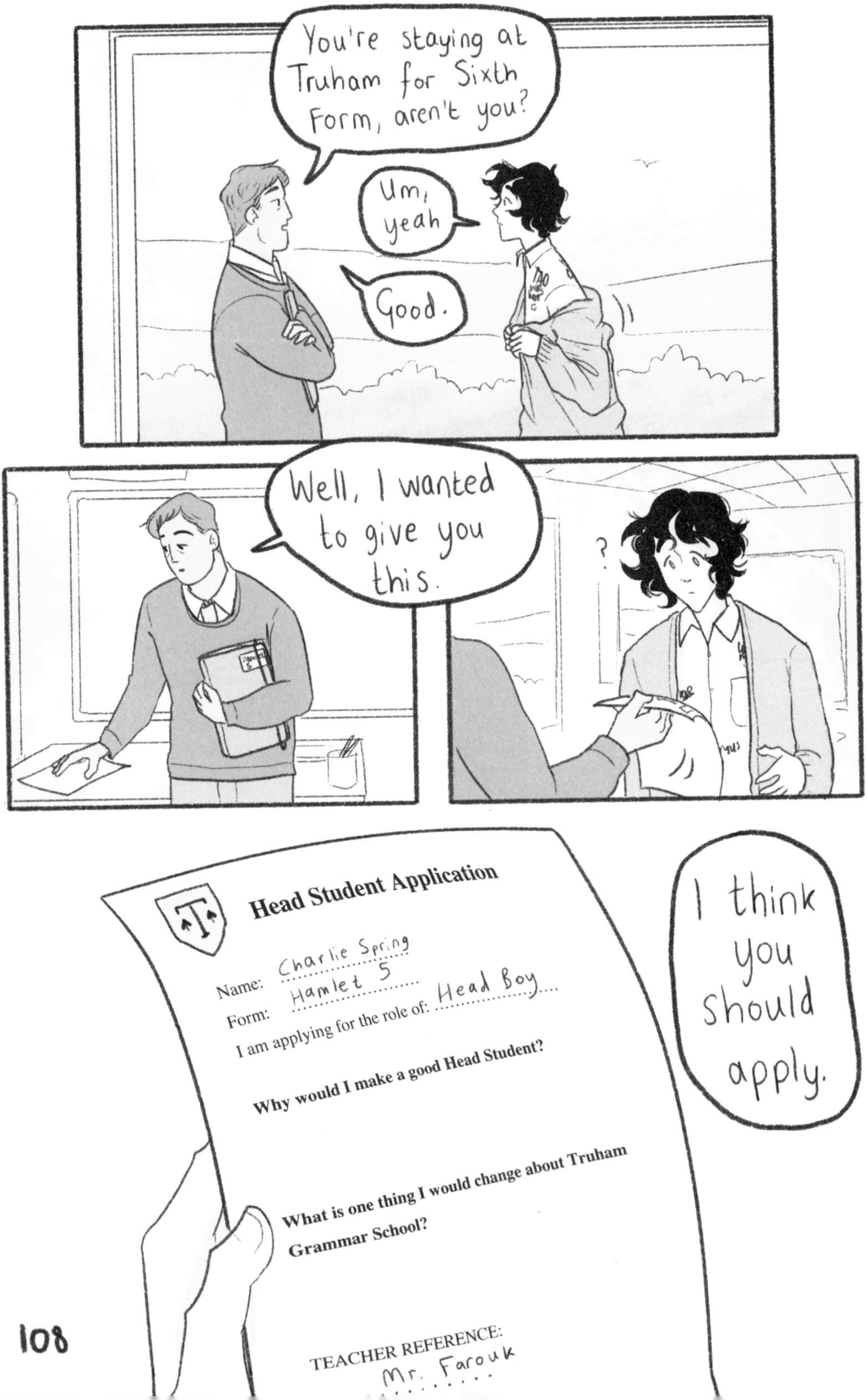
You're staying at Truham for Sixth Form, aren't you?
Um, yeah
Good.
Well, I wanted to give you this.
?
Head Student Application
Name: Charlie Spring
Form: Hamlet 5
I am applying for the role of: Head Boy
Why would I make a good Head Student?
What is one thing I would change about Truham Grammar School?
TEACHER REFERENCE: Mr. Farouk
I think you should apply.

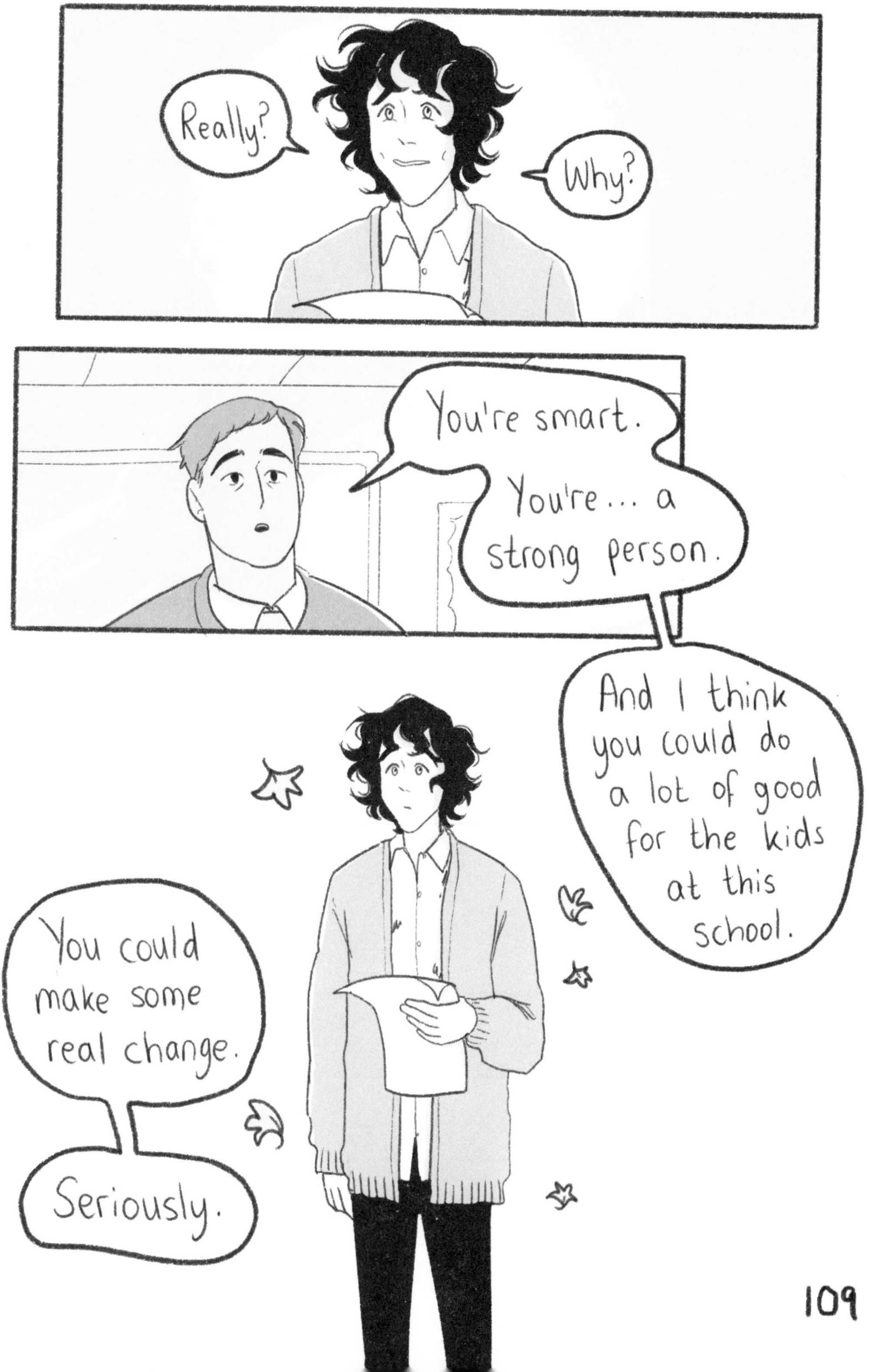
Really?
Why?
You're smart.
You're... a strong person.
And I think you could do a lot of good for the kids at this school.
You could make some real change.
Seriously.

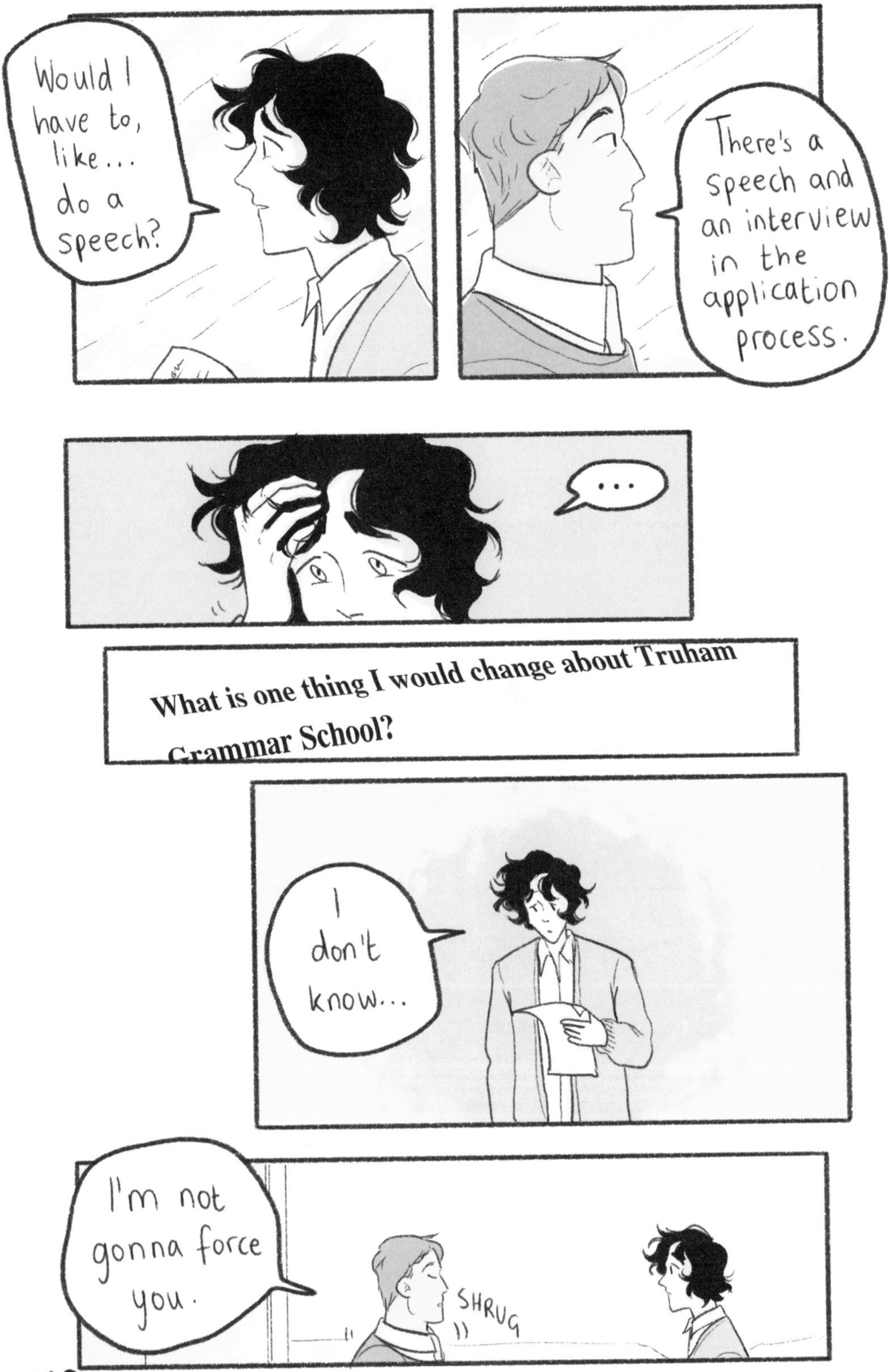
Would I have to, like... do a speech?
There's a speech and an interview in the application process.
...
What is one thing I would change about Truham Grammar School?
I don't know...
I'm not gonna force you.
SHRUG

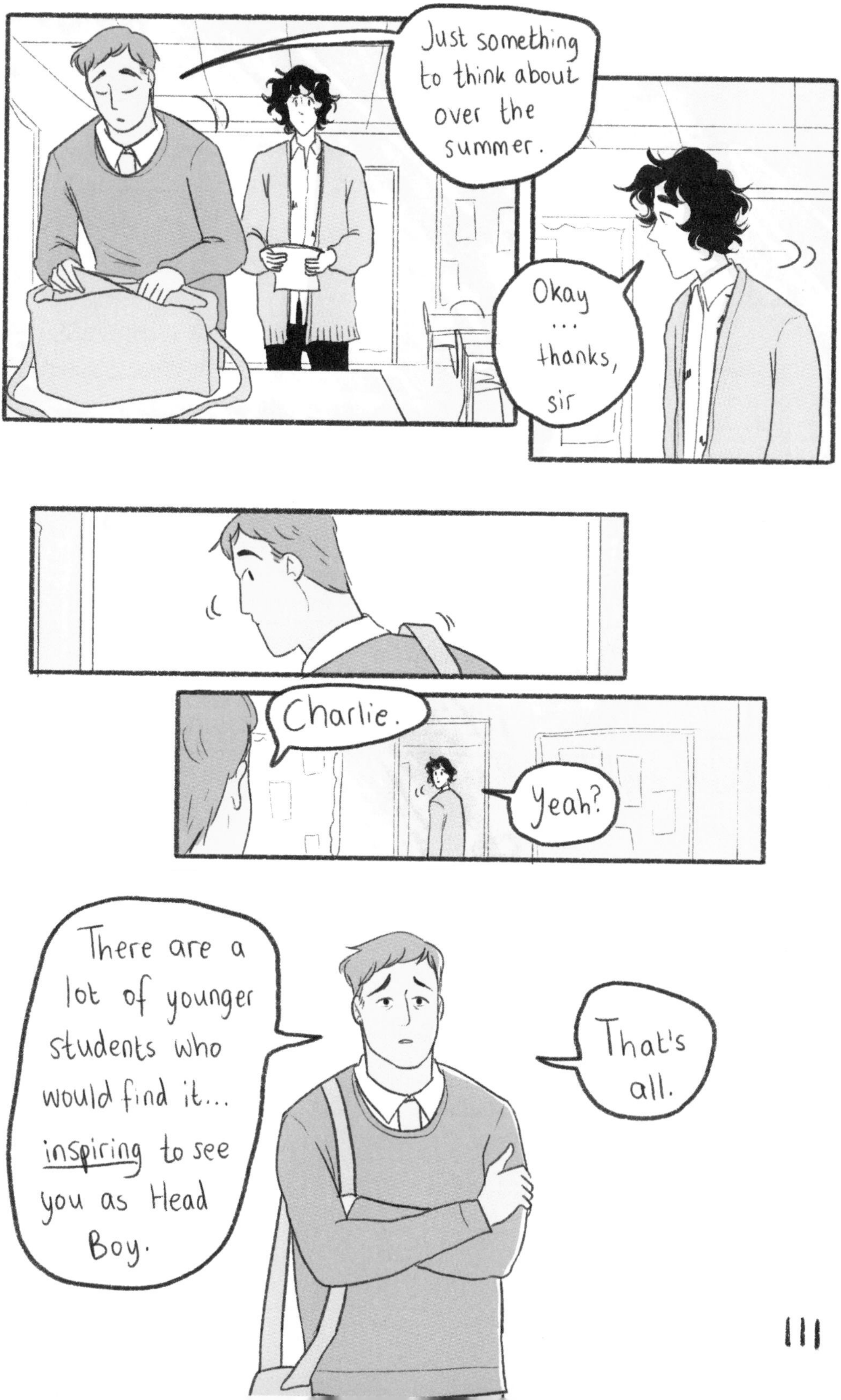
Just something to think about over the summer.
Okay ... thanks, sir
Charlie.
Yeah?
There are a lot of younger students who would find it... inspiring to see you as Head Boy.
That's all.

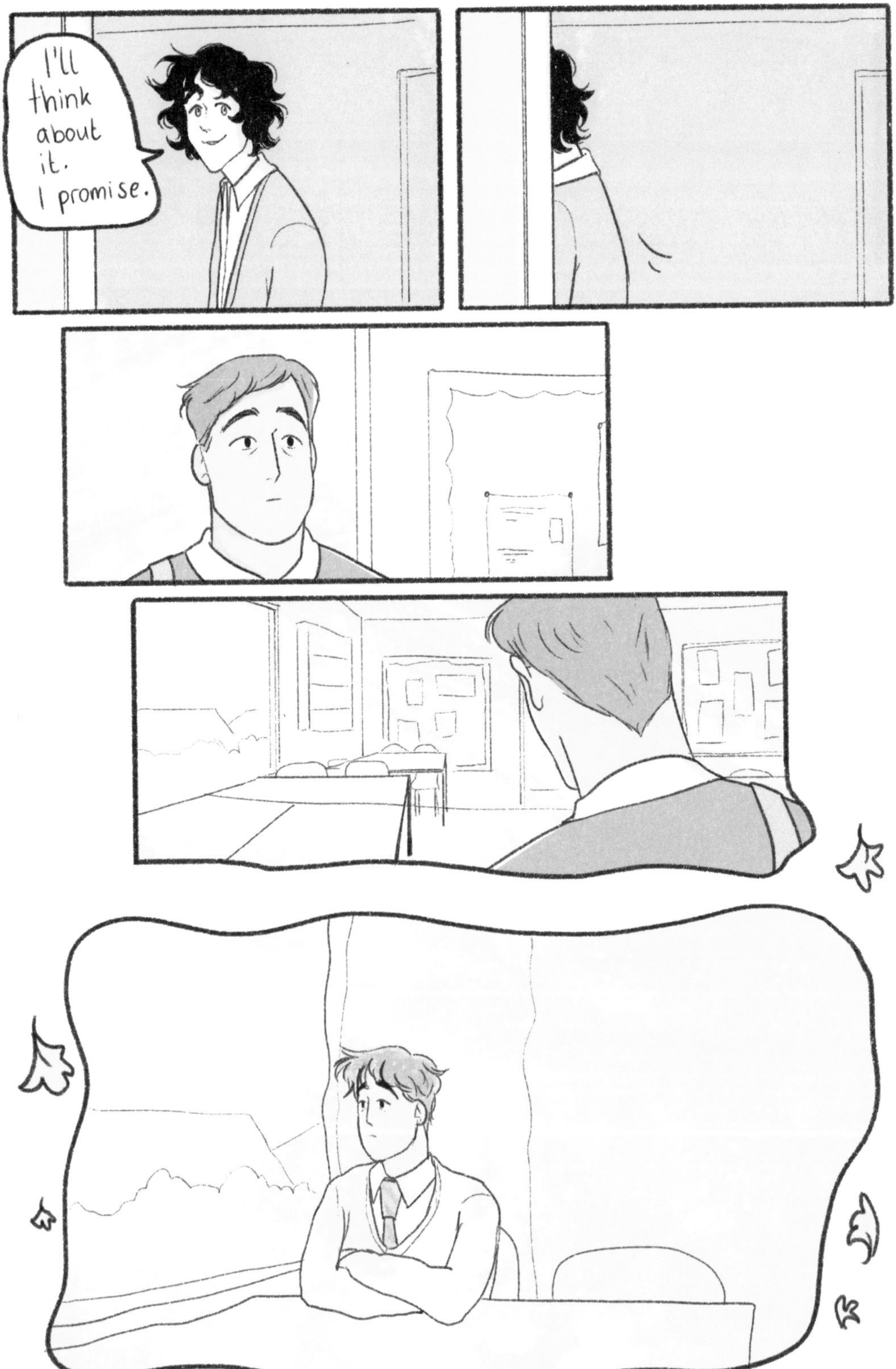
I'll think about it. I promise.

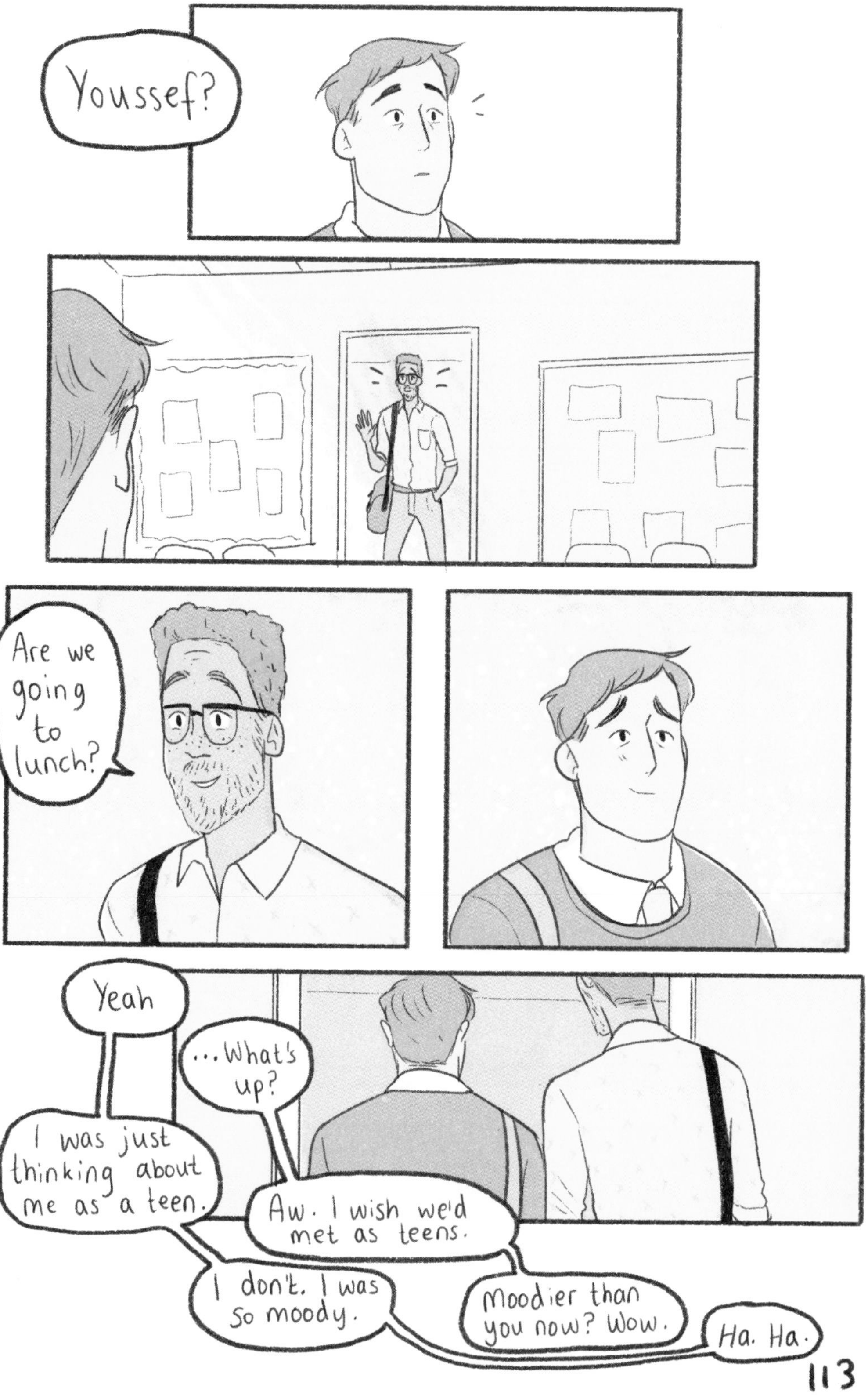
Youssef?
Are we going to lunch?
Yeah
...What's up?
I was just thinking about me as a teen.
Aw. I wish we'd met as teens.
I don't. I was so moody.
Moodier than you now? Wow.
Ha. Ha.

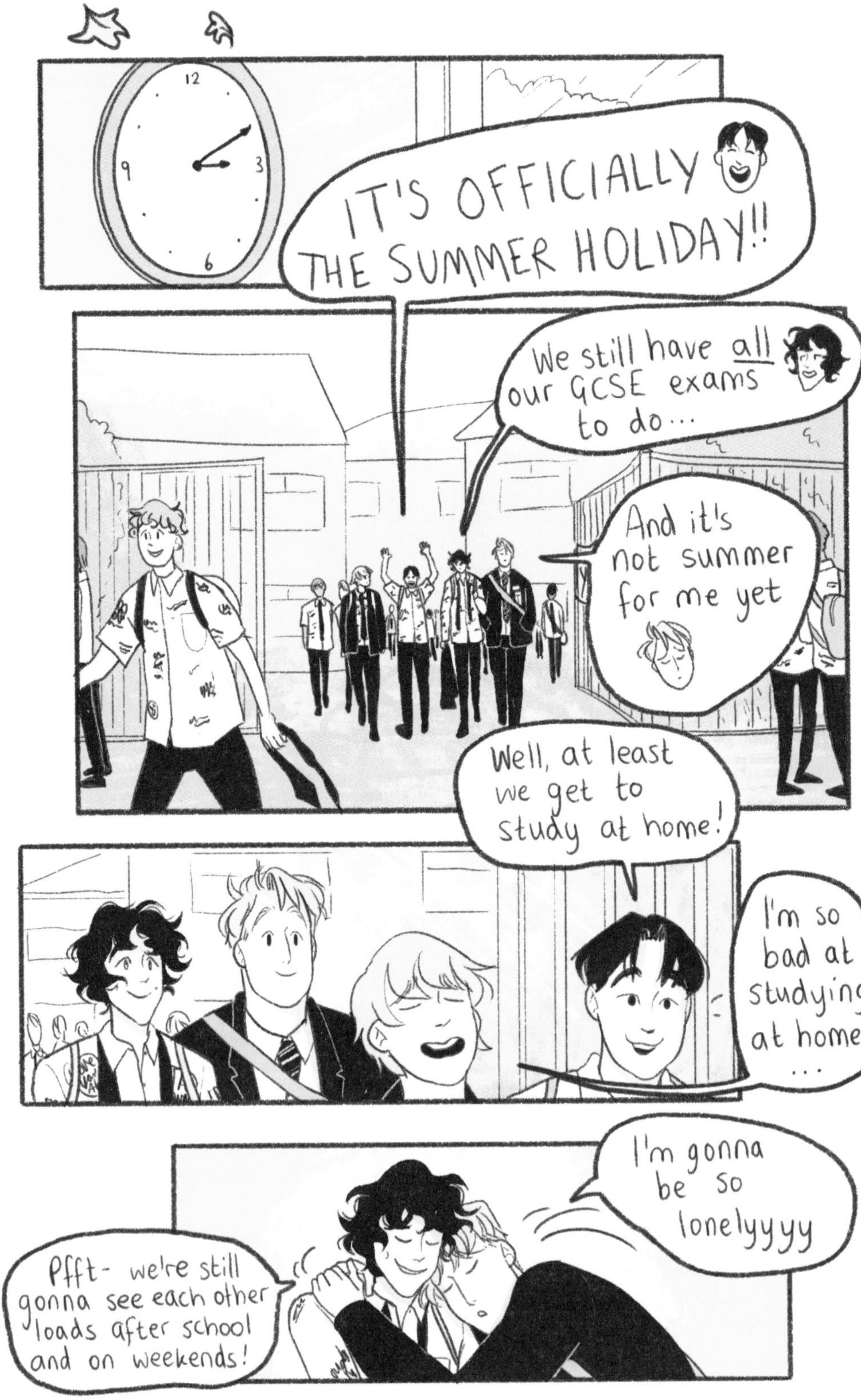
IT'S OFFICIALLY THE SUMMER HOLIDAY!!
We still have all our GCSE exams to do...
And it's not summer for me yet
Well, at least we get to study at home!
I'm so bad at studying at home...
I'm gonna be so lonelyyyy
Pfft- we're still gonna see each other loads after school and on weekends!

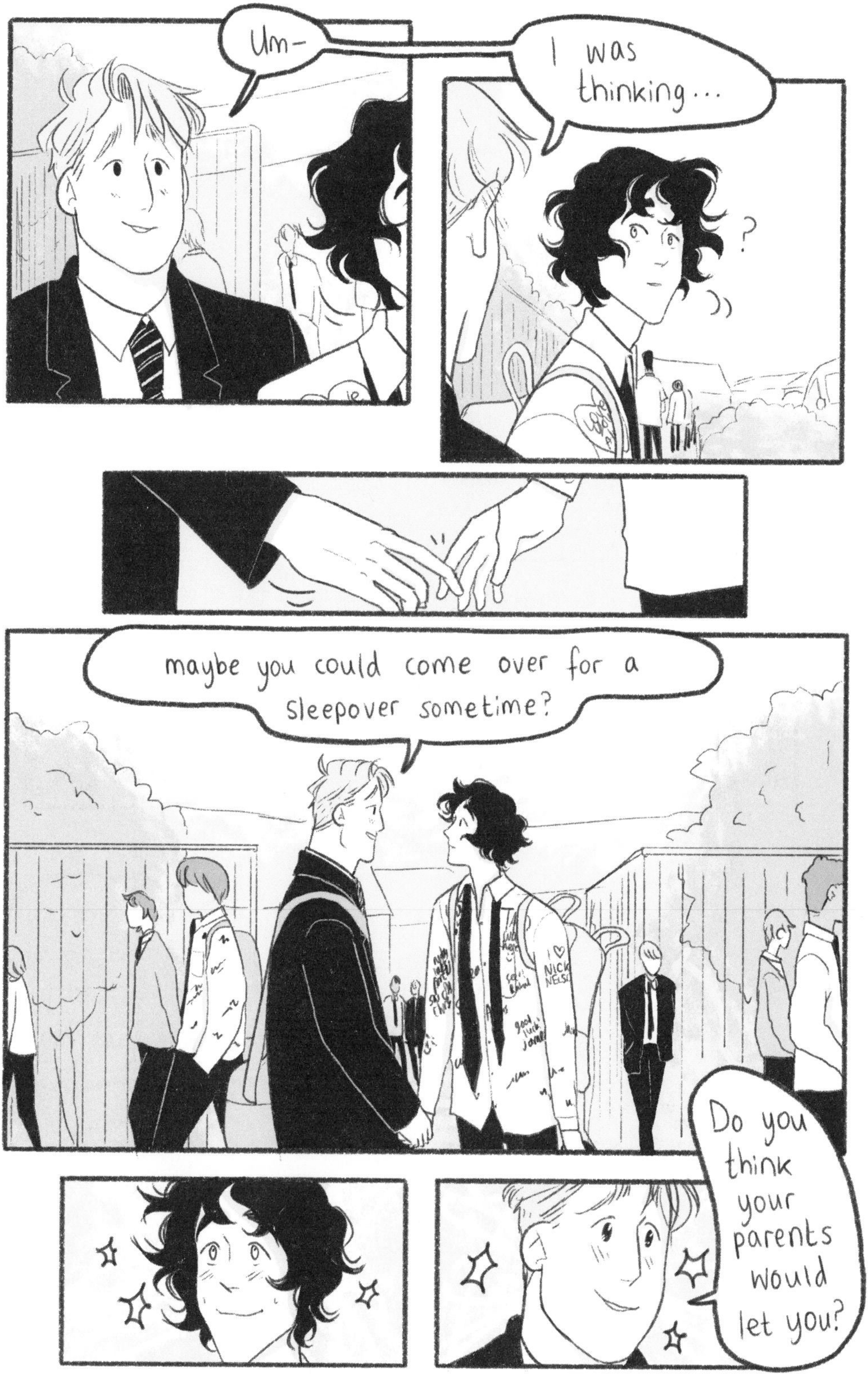
Um-
I was thinking...
maybe you could come over for a sleepover sometime?
Do you think your parents would let you?

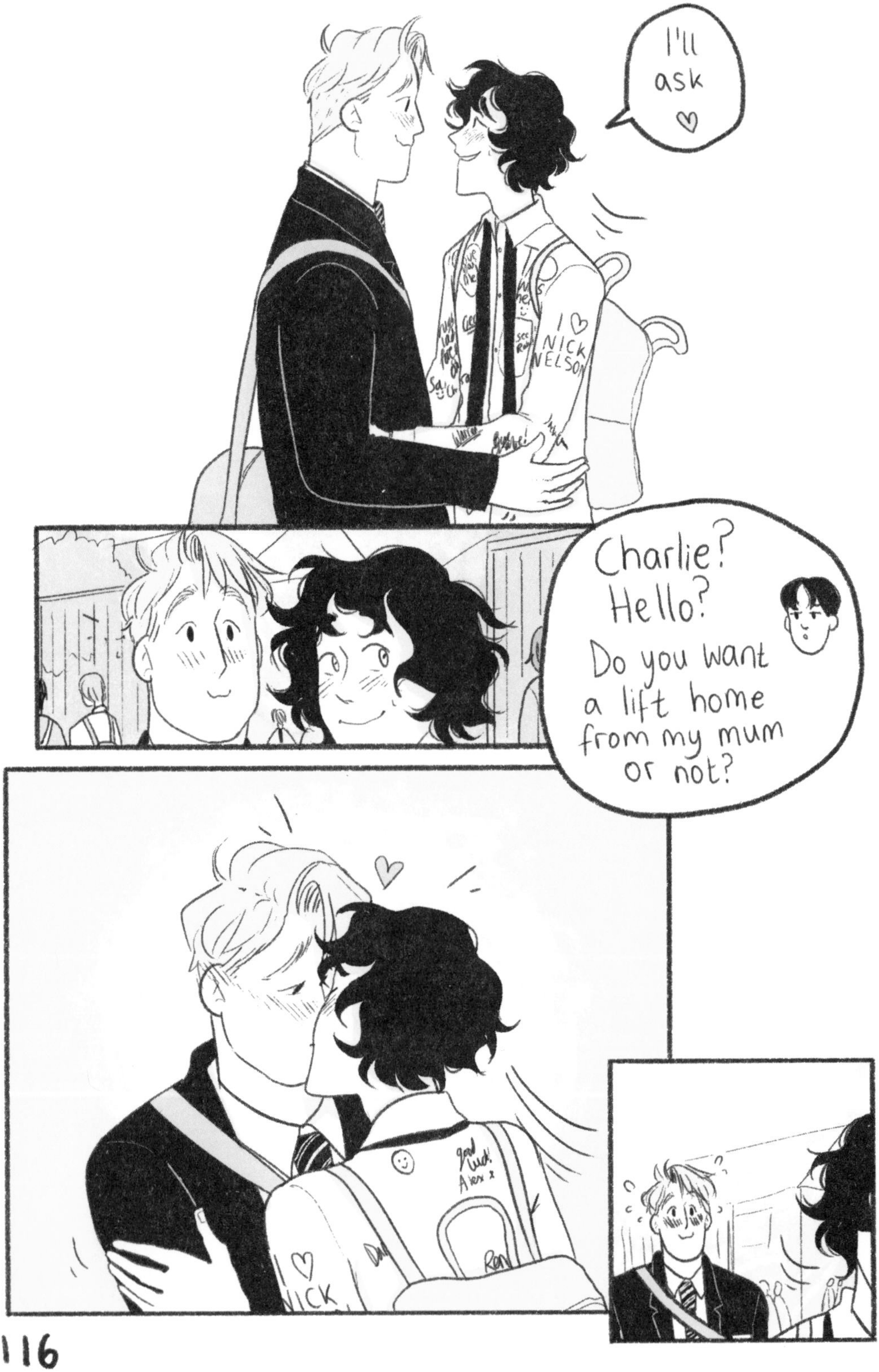
I'll ask ♥
I ♥ NICK NELSON
Charlie? Hello? Do you want a lift home from my mum or not?

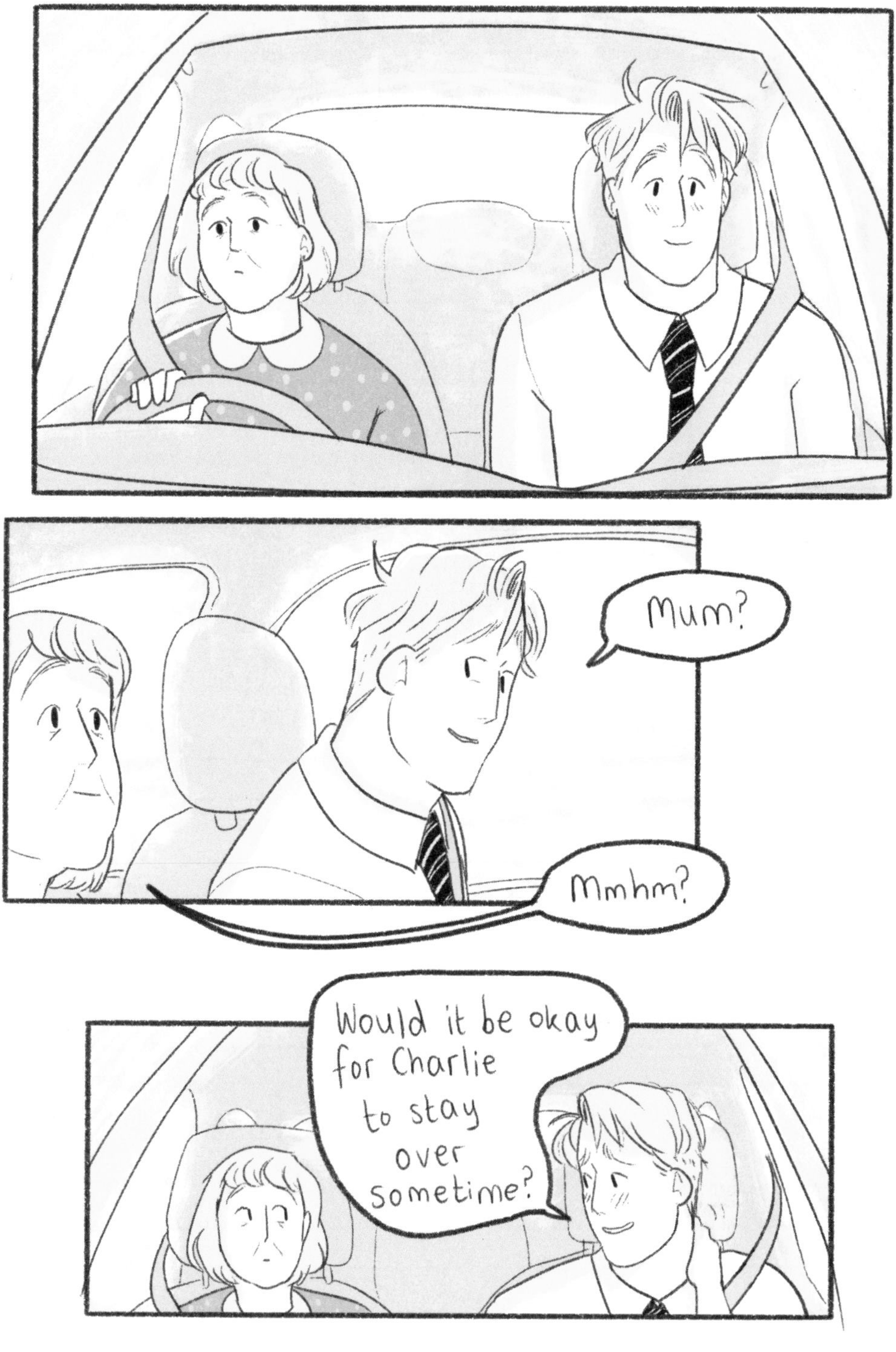
Mum?
Mmhm?
Would it be okay for Charlie to stay over sometime?

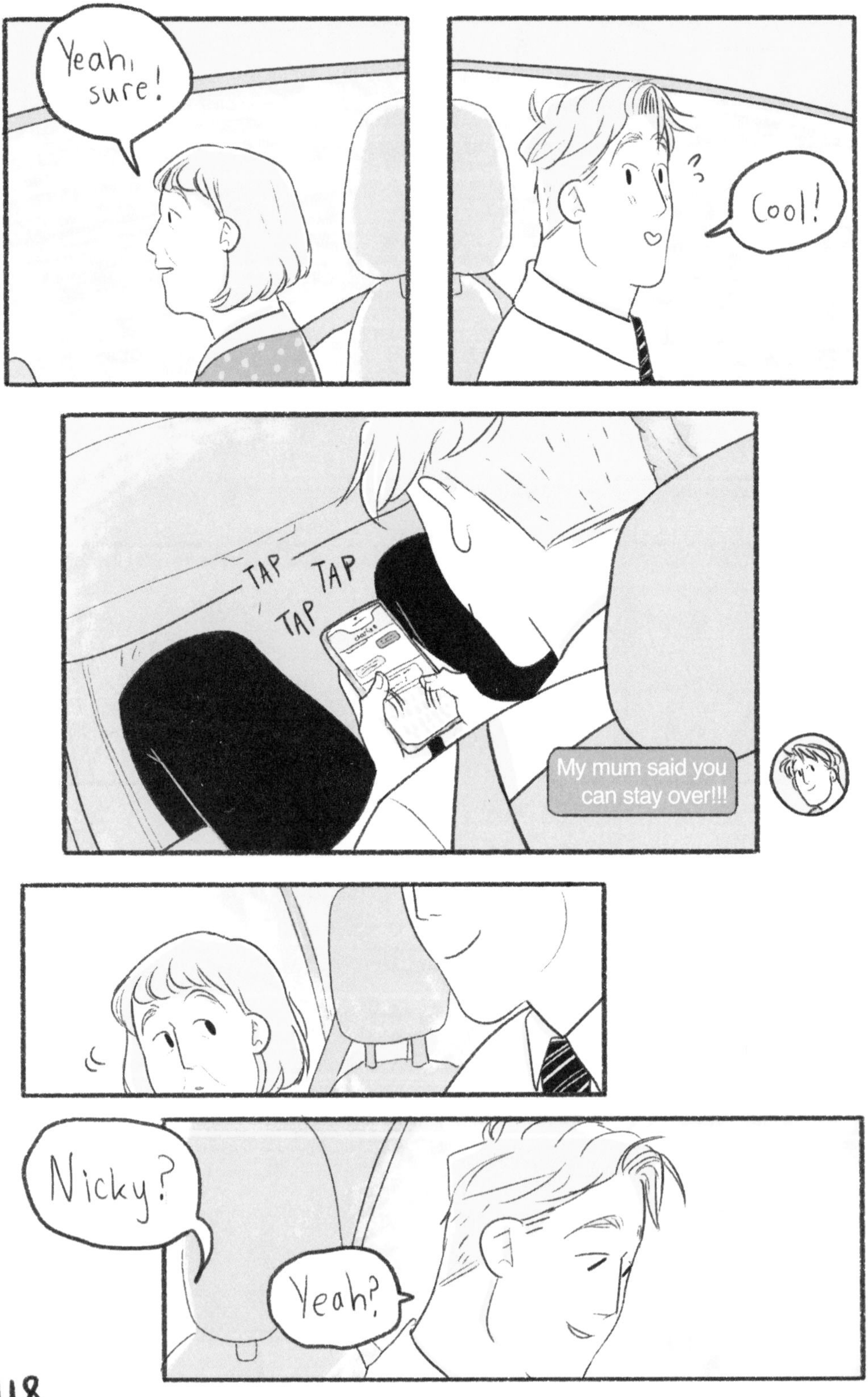
Yeah, sure!
Cool!
TAP TAP TAP
My mum said you can stay over!!!
Nicky?
Yeah?

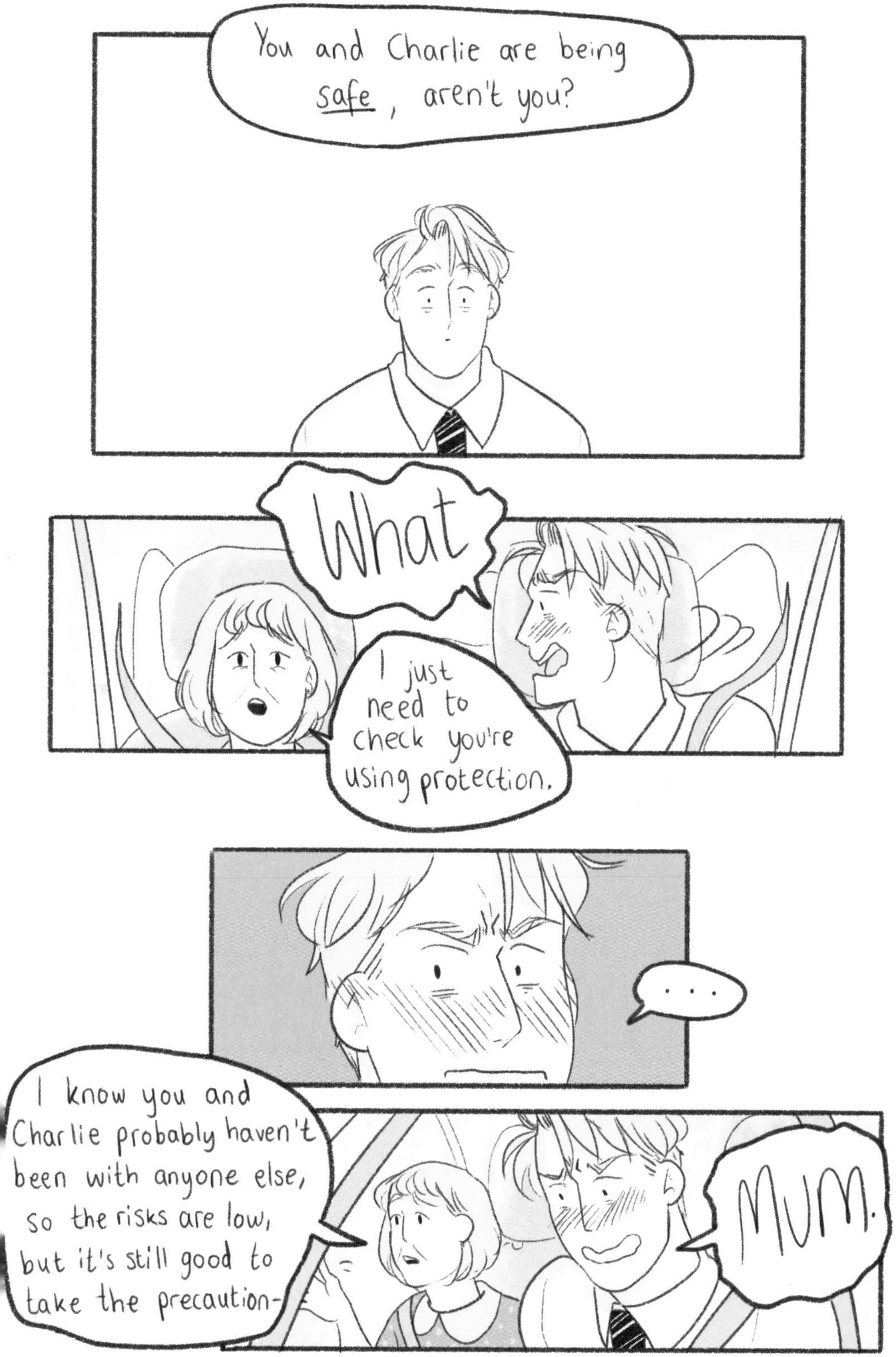
You and Charlie are being safe, aren't you?
What
I just need to check you're using protection.
...
I know you and Charlie probably haven't been with anyone else, so the risks are low, but it's still good to take the precaution-
MUM.

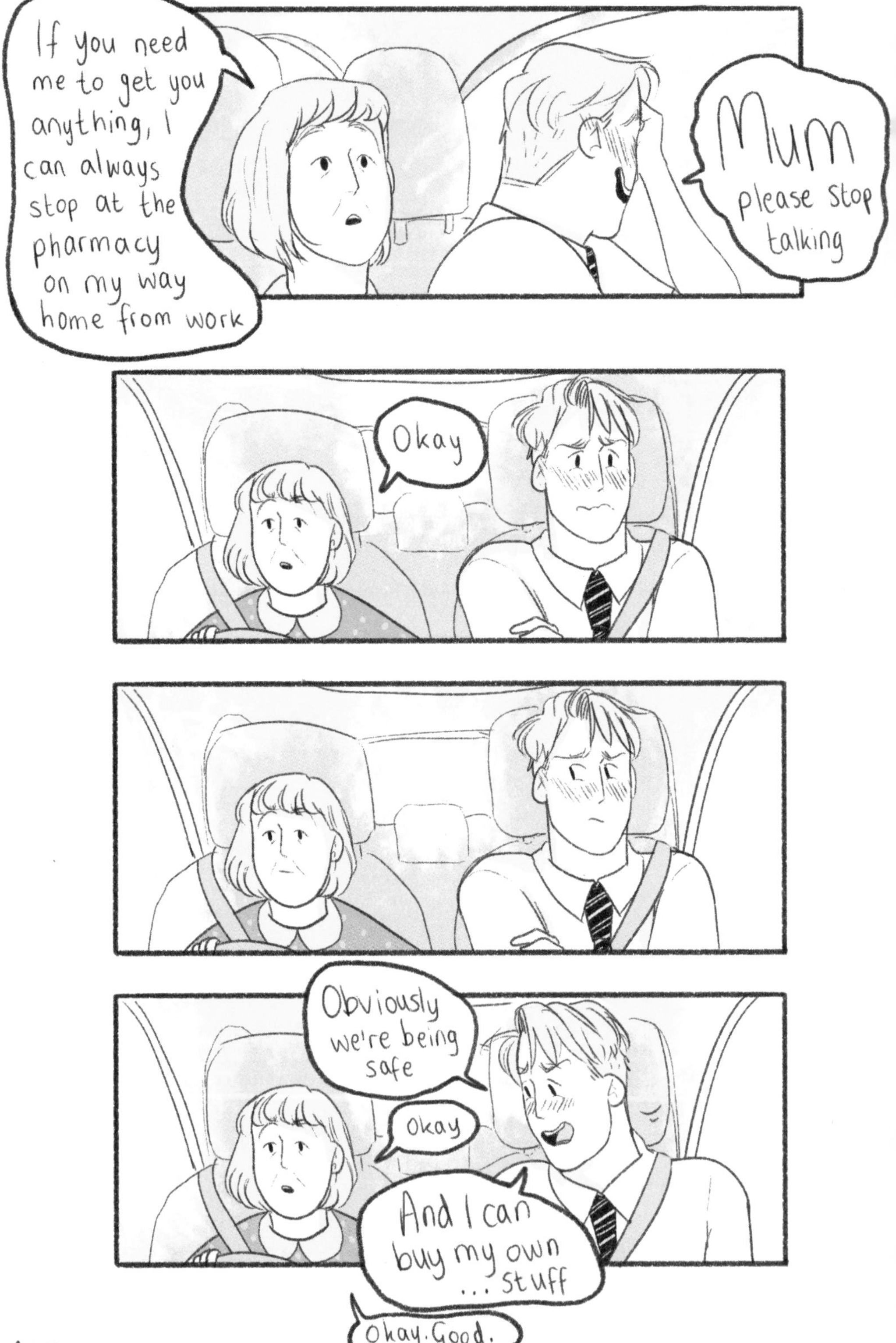
If you need me to get you anything, I can always stop at the pharmacy on my way home from work
Mum
please stop talking
Okay
Obviously we're being safe
Okay
And I can buy my own ... stuff
Okay. Good.

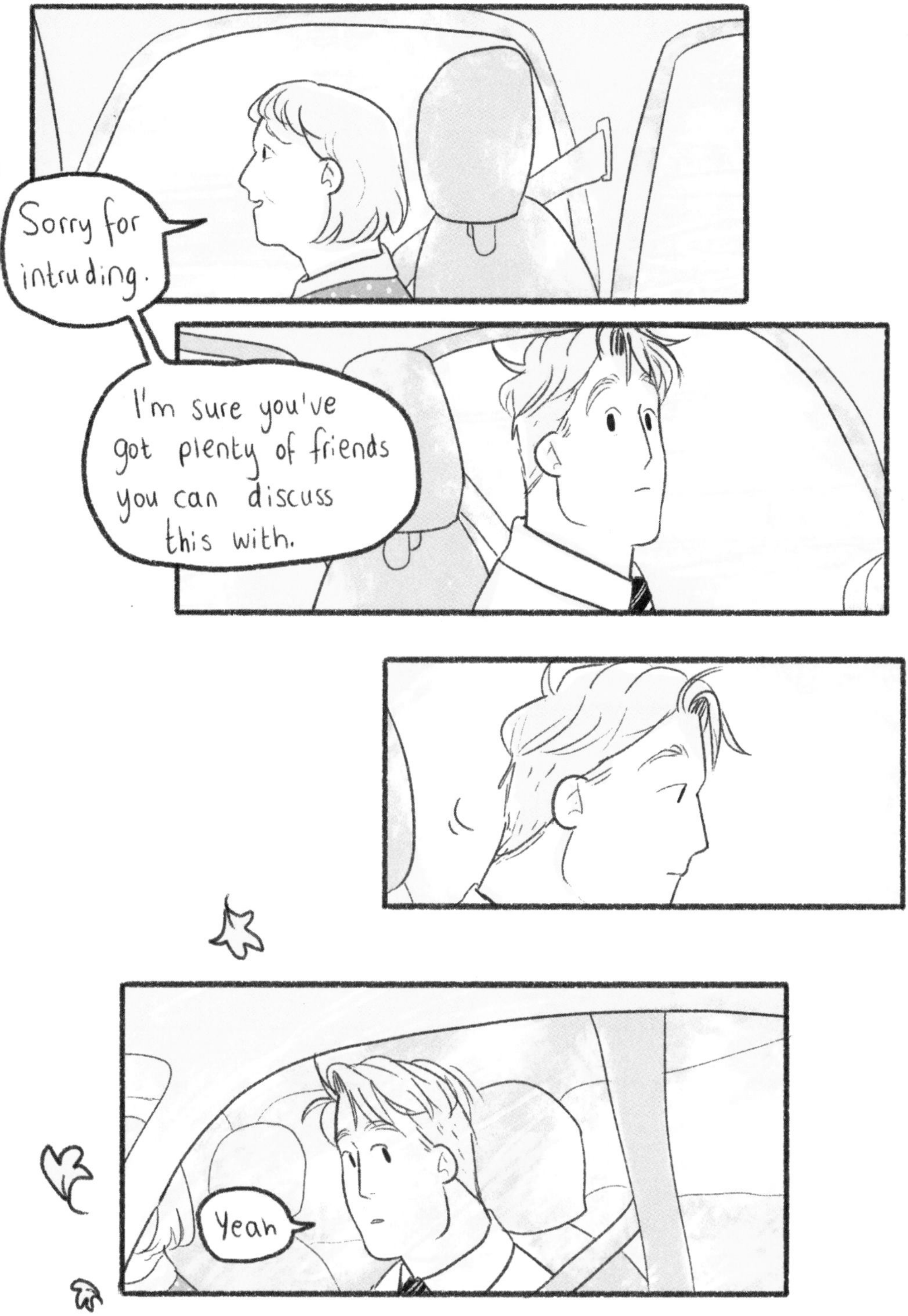
Sorry for intruding.
I'm sure you've got plenty of friends you can discuss this with.
Yeah

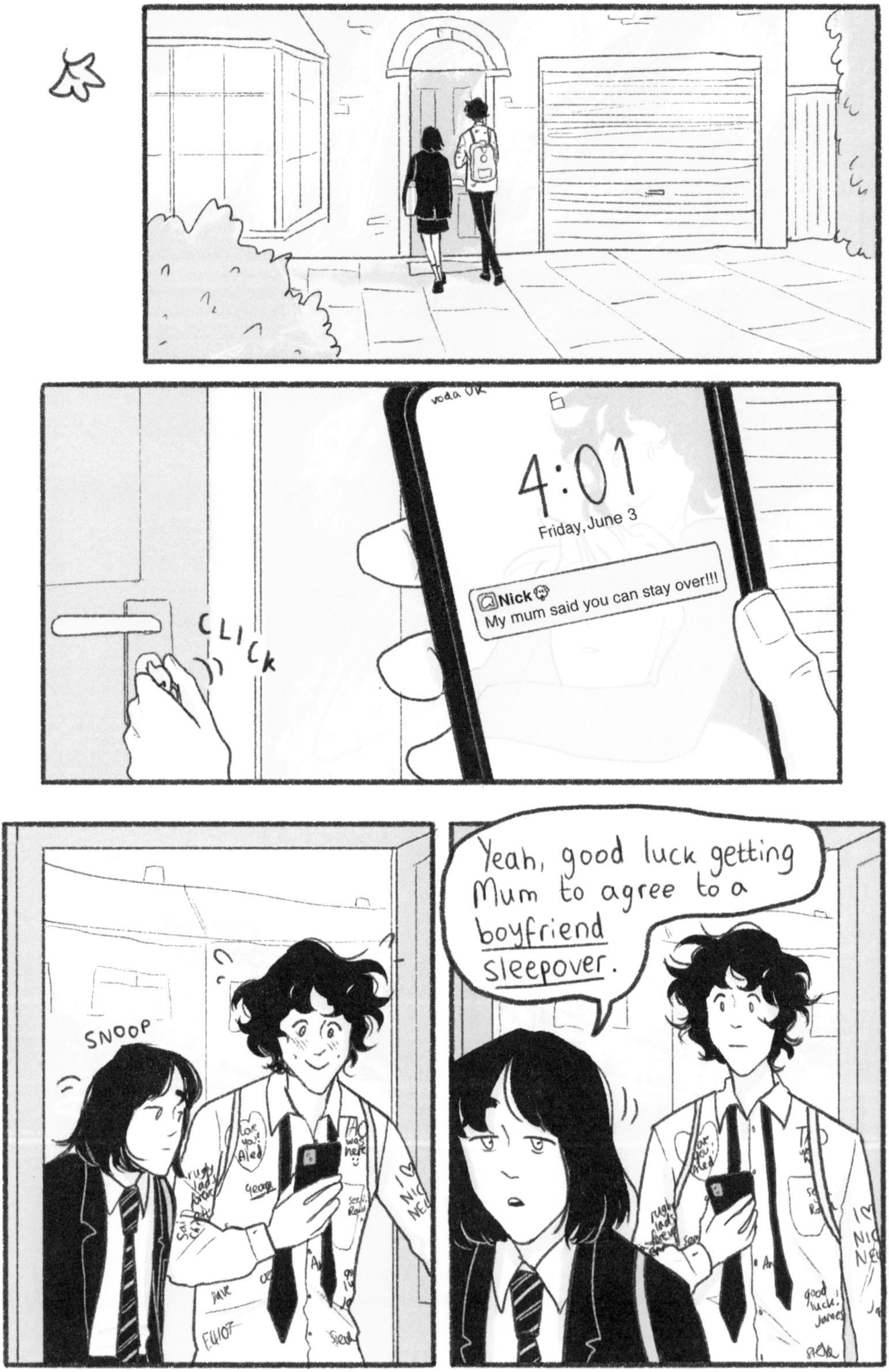
voda UK
4:01
Friday, June 3
Nick
My mum said you can stay over!!!
CLICK
SNOOP
Yeah, good luck getting Mum to agree to a boyfriend sleepover.

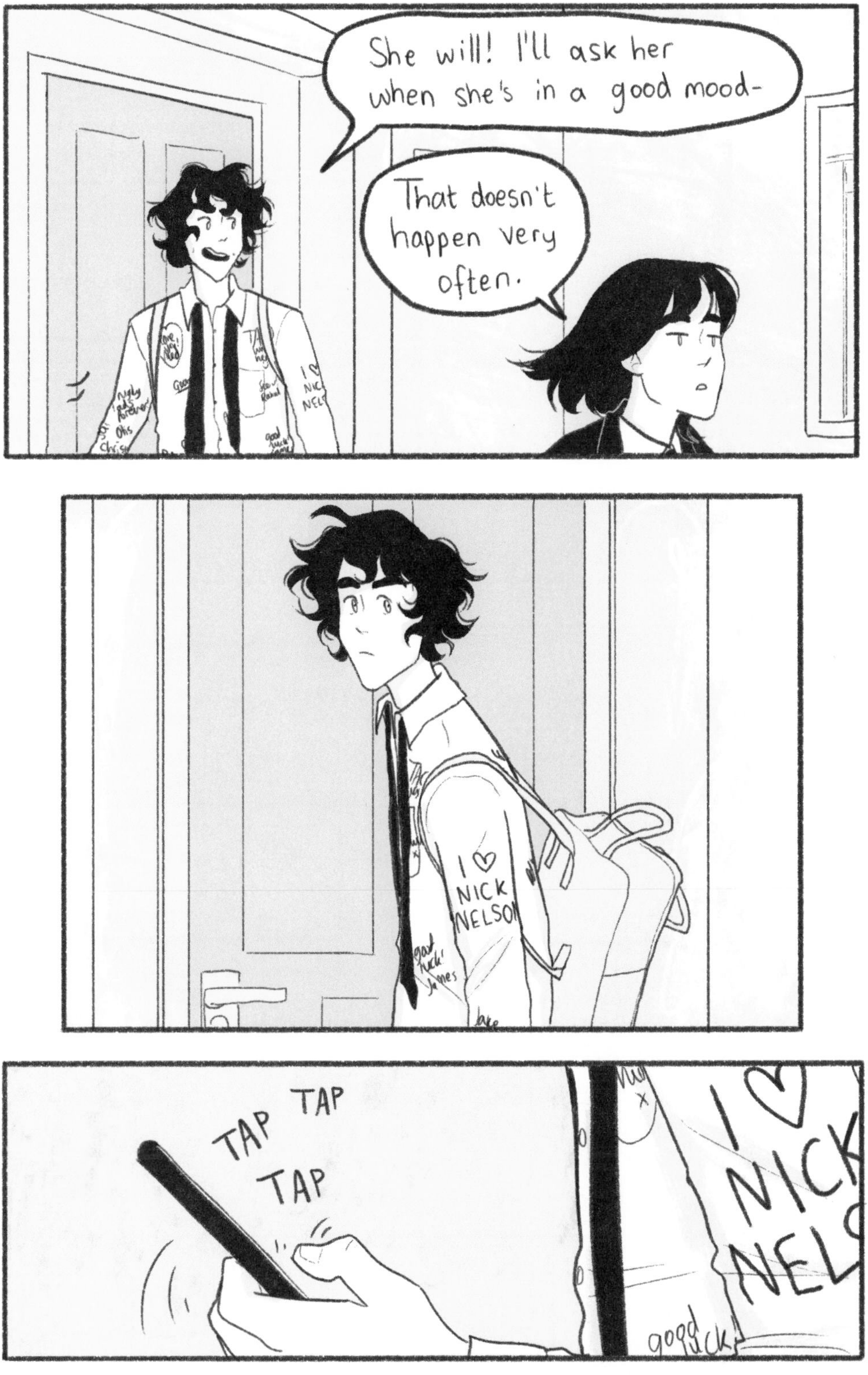
She will! I'll ask her when she's in a good mood-
That doesn't happen very often.
I ♡ NICK NELSON
TAP TAP
TAP

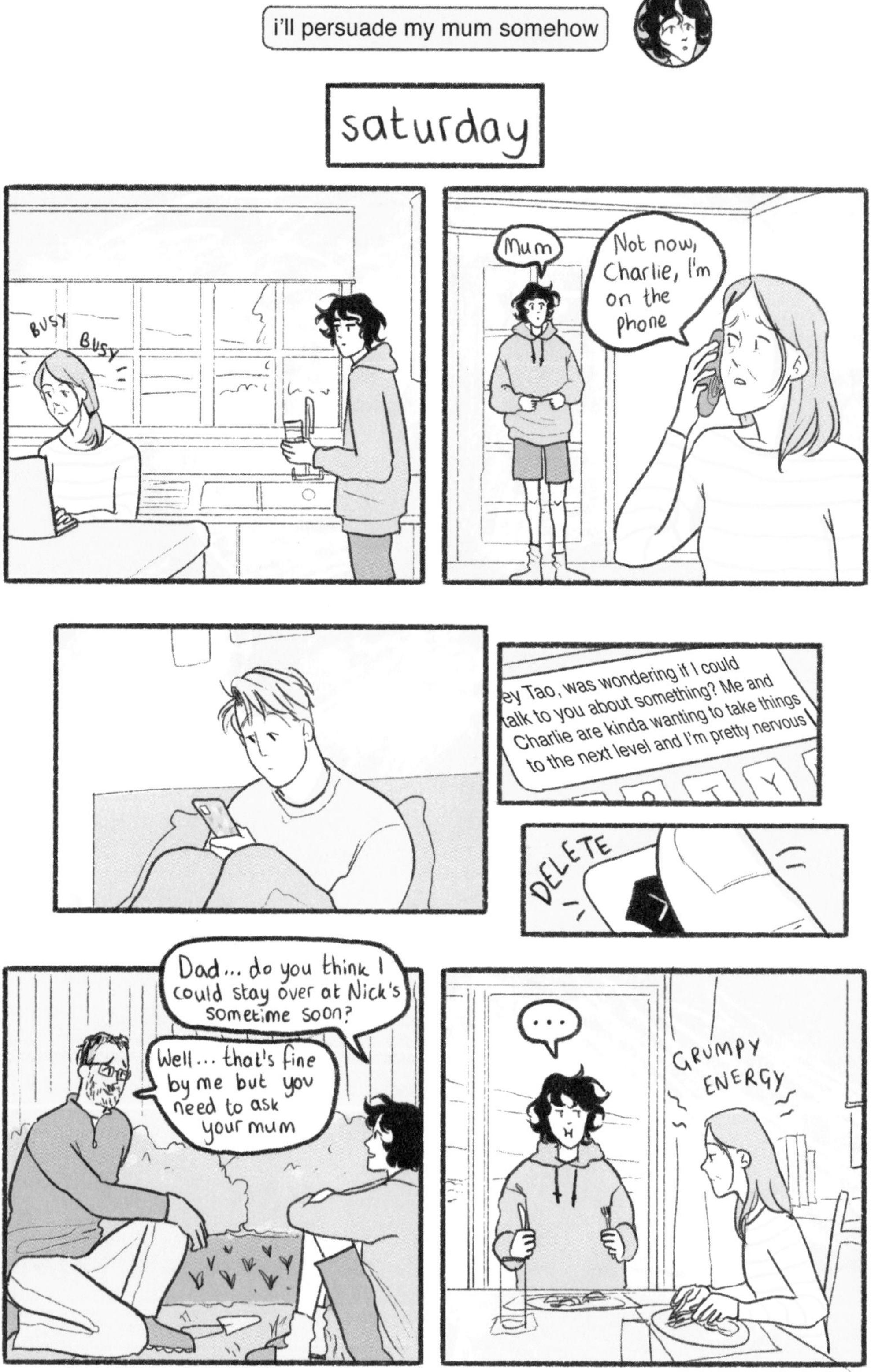
i'll persuade my mum somehow
saturday
BUSY
BUSY
Mum
Not now, Charlie, I'm on the phone
ey Tao, was wondering if I could
talk to you about something? Me and
Charlie are kinda wanting to take things
to the next level and I'm pretty nervous
DELETE
Dad... do you think I could stay over at Nick's sometime soon?
Well... that's fine by me but you need to ask your mum
...
GRUMPY ENERGY

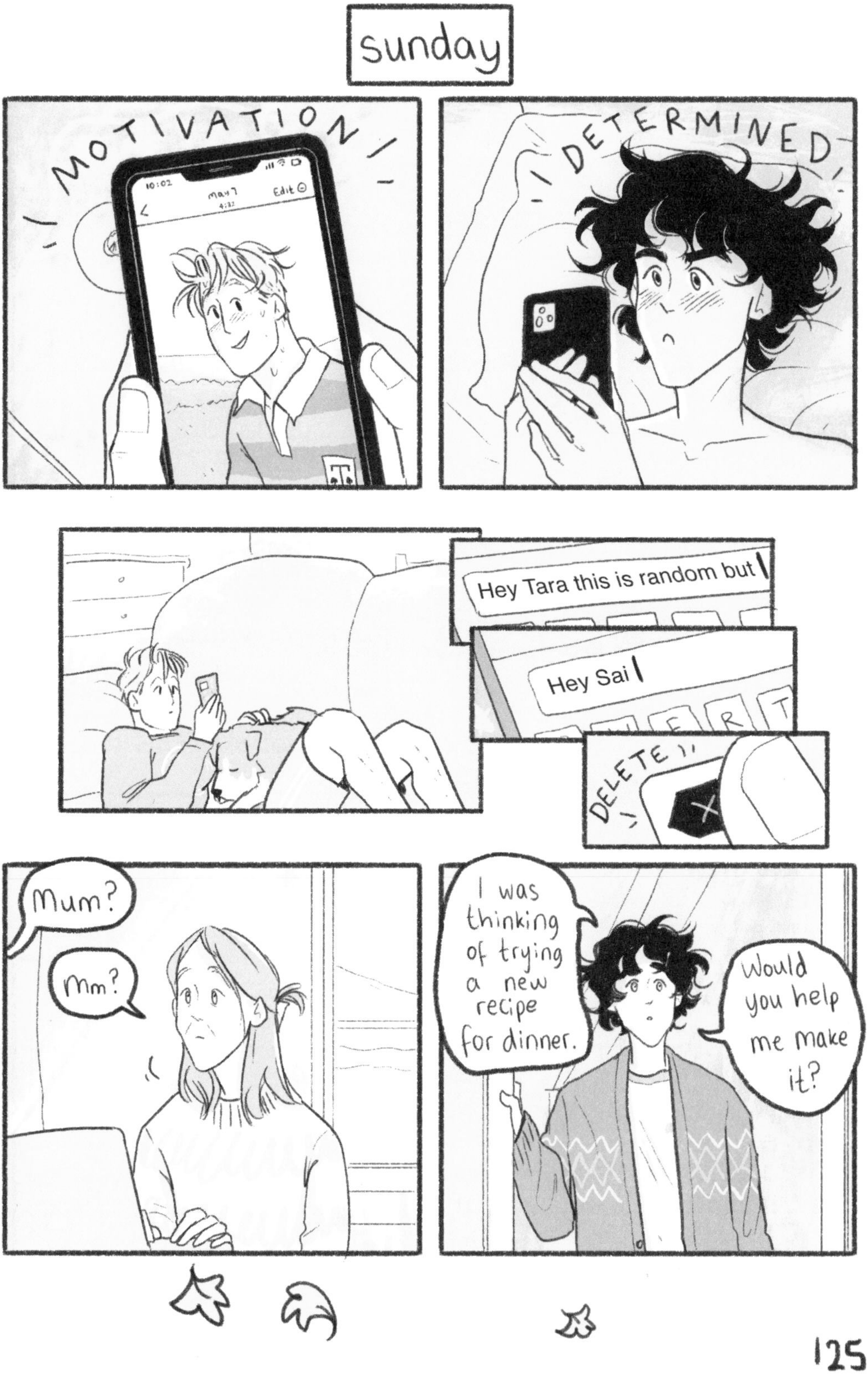
sunday
MOTIVATION
DETERMINED
Hey Tara this is random but
Hey Sai
DELETE
Mum?
Mm?
I was thinking of trying a new recipe for dinner.
Would you help me make it?

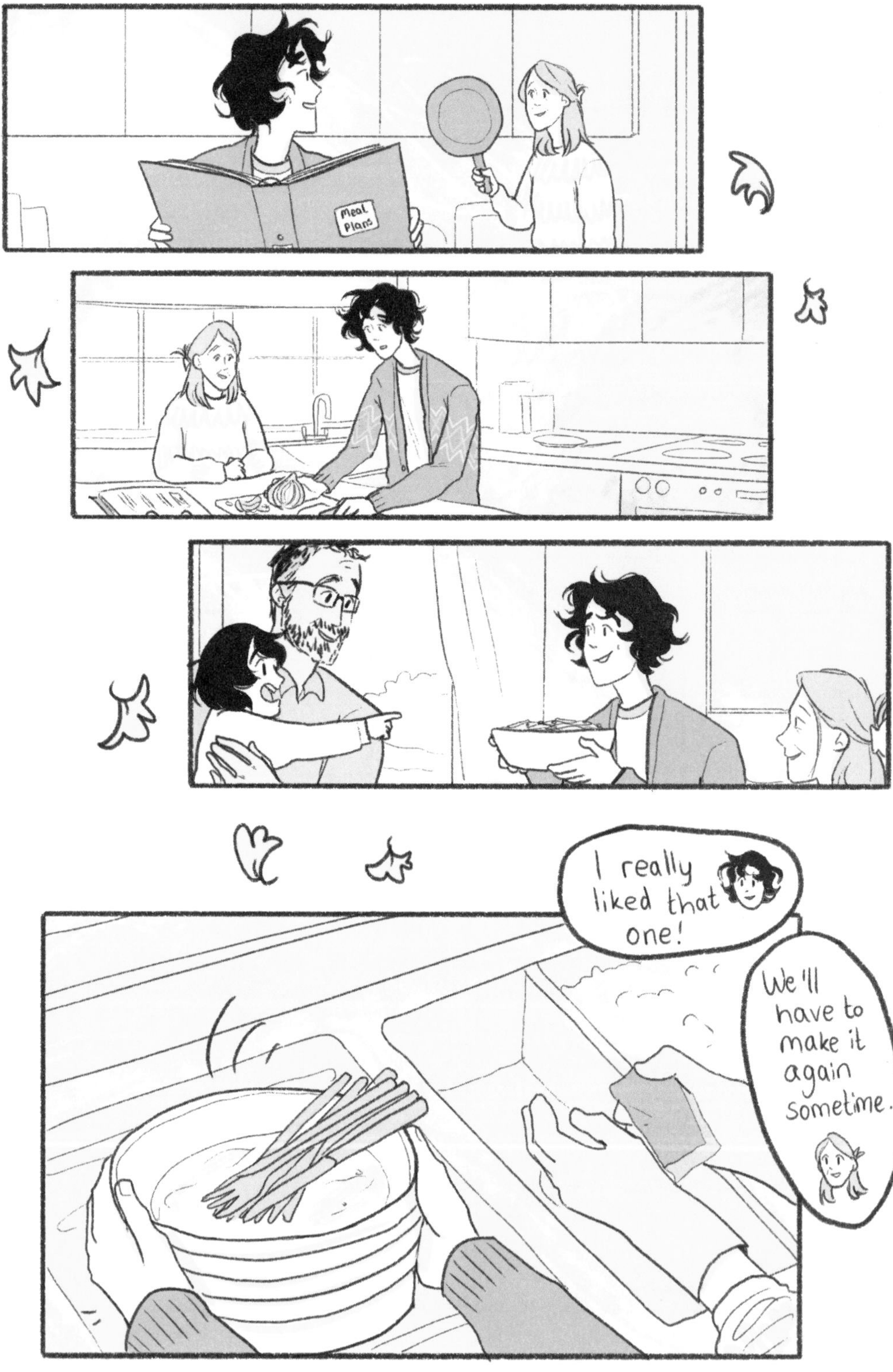
Meal Plans
I really liked that one!
We'll have to make it again sometime.

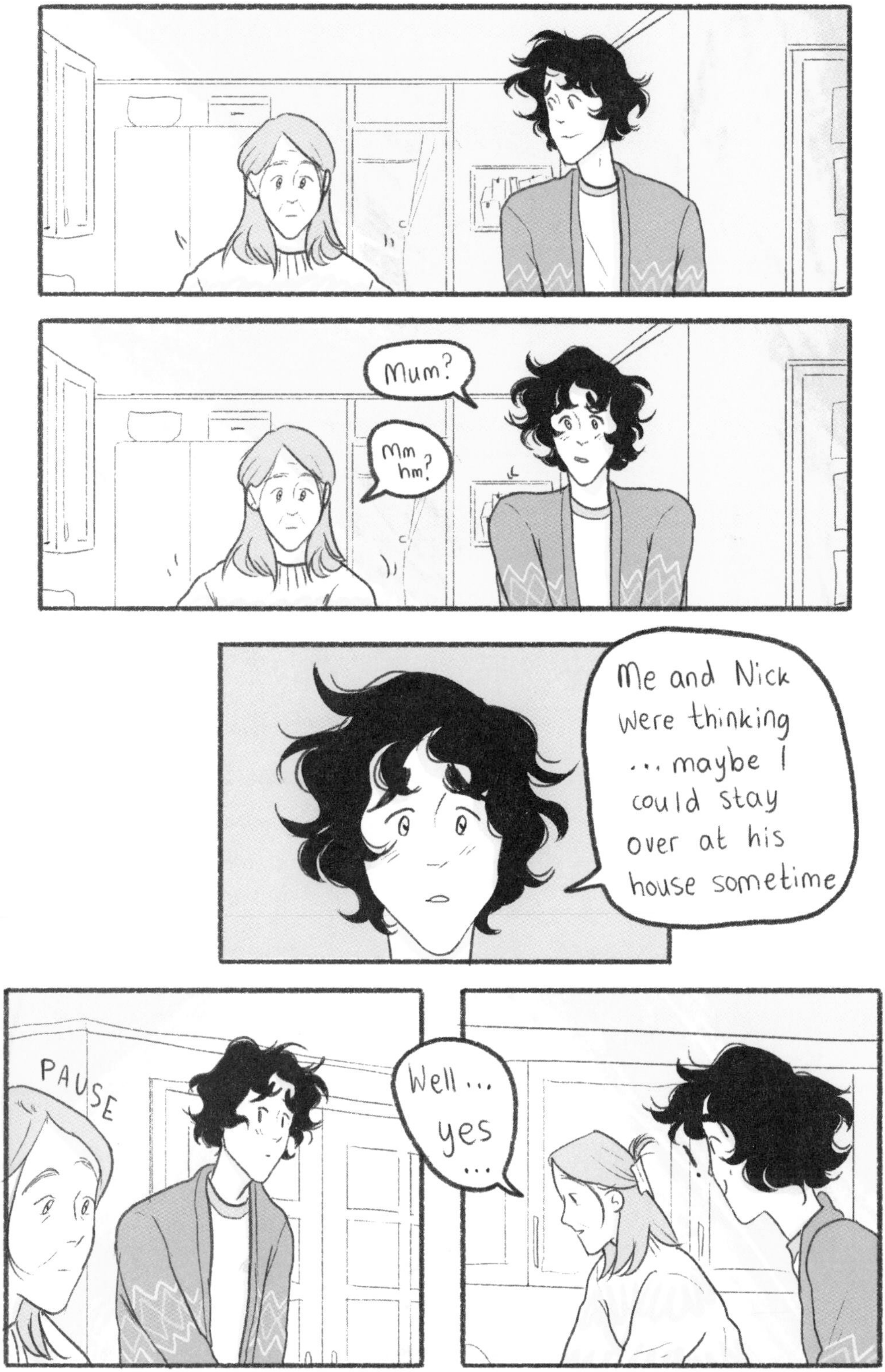

Mum?
Mm hm?
Me and Nick were thinking ... maybe I could stay over at his house sometime
PAUSE
Well ... yes ...

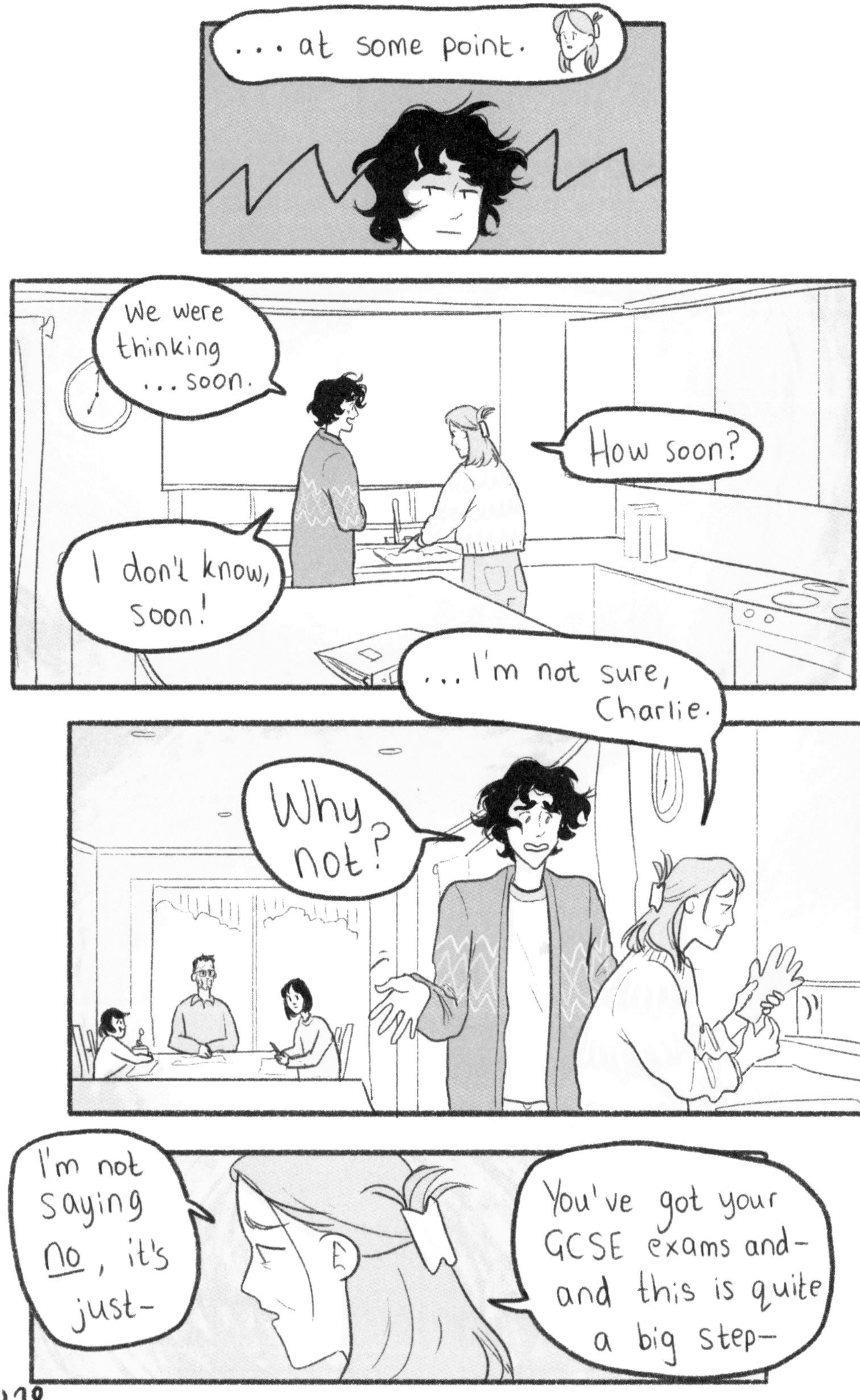
...at some point.
We were thinking ...soon.
How soon?
I don't know, soon!
...I'm not sure, Charlie.
Why not?
I'm not saying no, it's just-
You've got your GCSE exams and- and this is quite a big step-

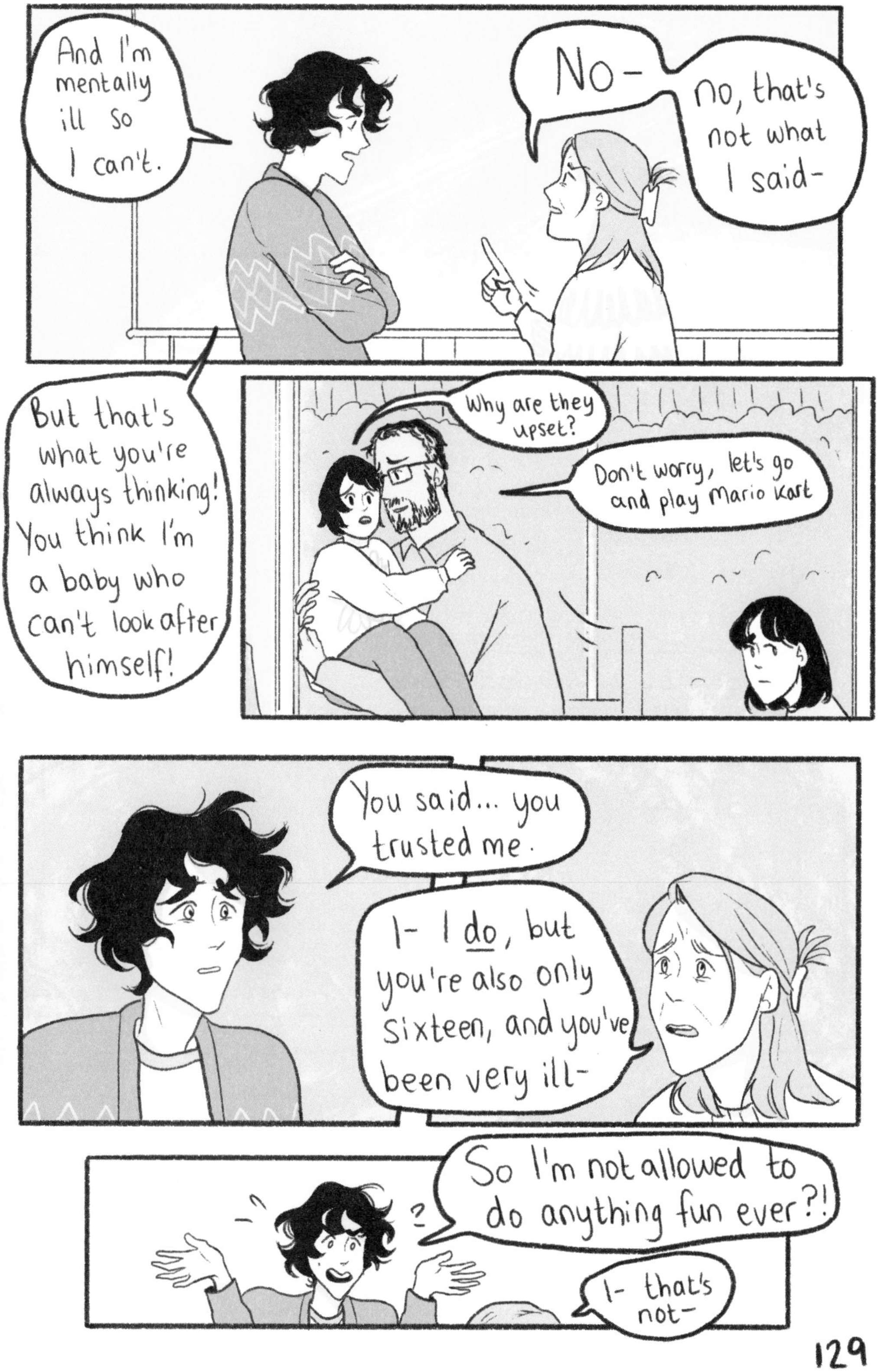
And I'm mentally ill so I can't.
No-
no, that's not what I said-
But that's what you're always thinking! You think I'm a baby who can't look after himself!
Why are they upset?
Don't worry, let's go and play Mario Kart
You said... you trusted me.
I- I do, but you're also only sixteen, and you've been very ill-
So I'm not allowed to do anything fun ever?!
?
I- that's not-

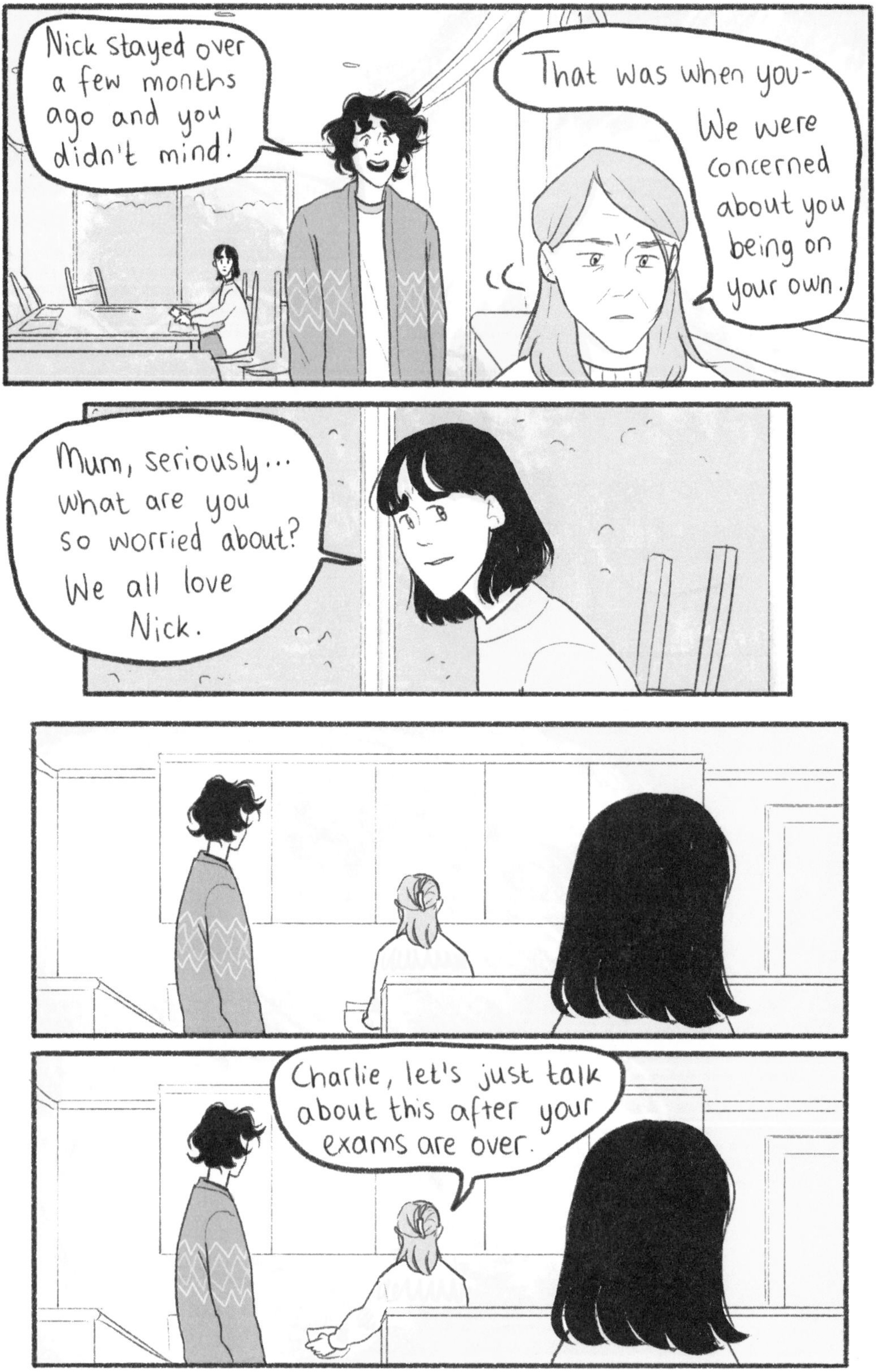
Nick stayed over a few months ago and you didn't mind!
That was when you- We were concerned about you being on your own.
Mum, seriously... what are you so worried about? We all love Nick.
Charlie, let's just talk about this after your exams are over.

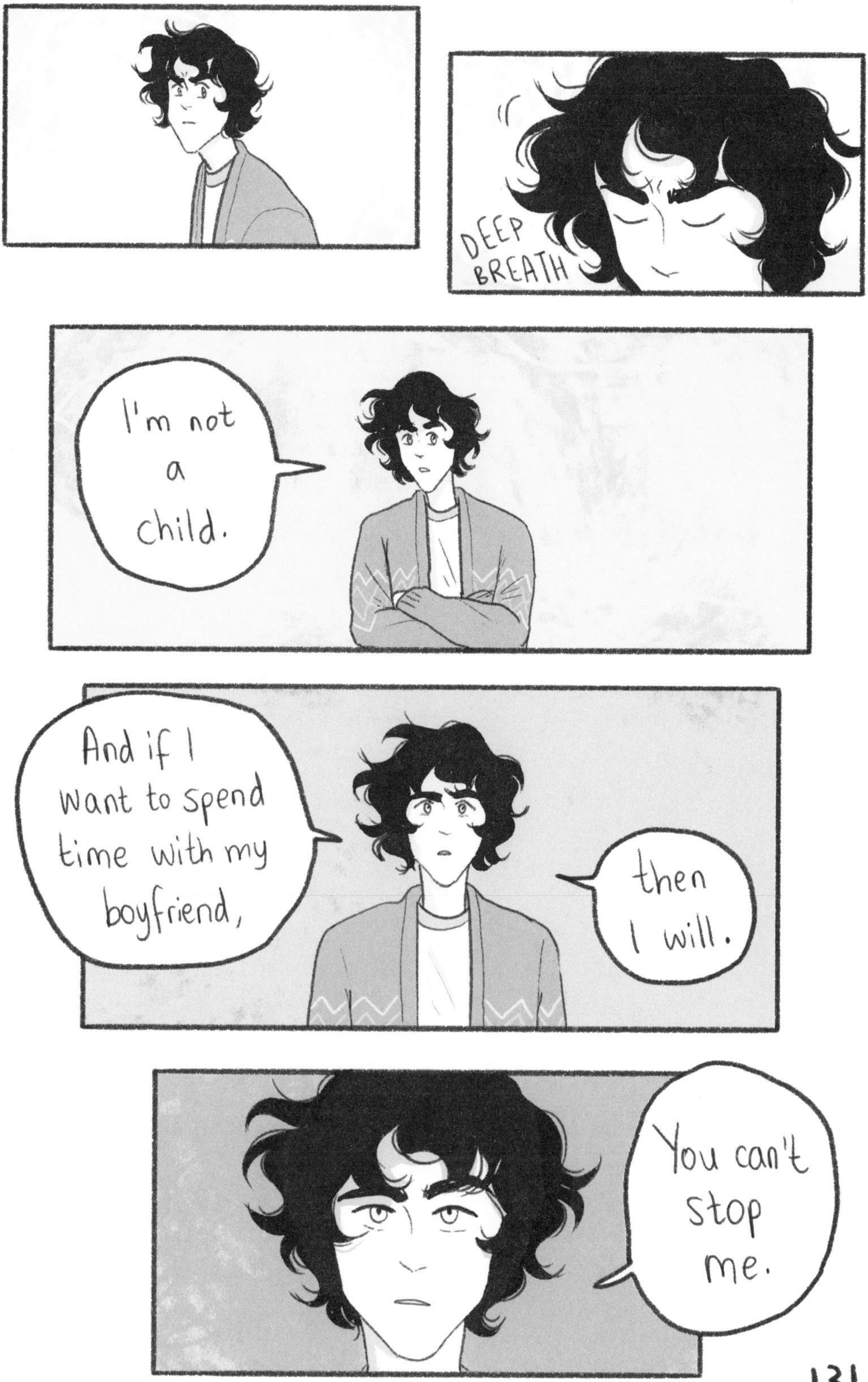
DEEP BREATH
I'm not a child.
And if I want to spend time with my boyfriend,
then I will.
You can't stop me.

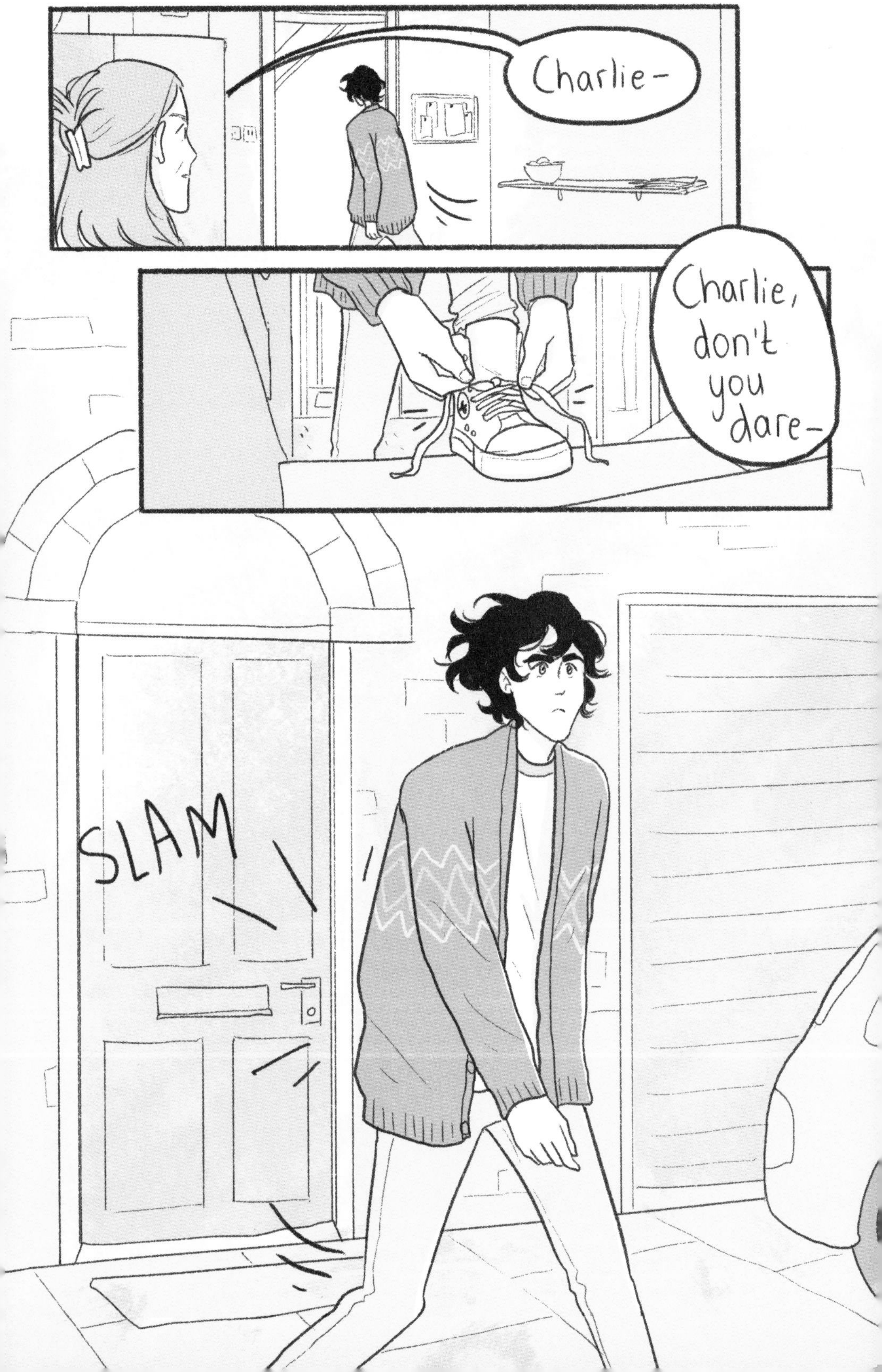
Charlie-
Charlie, don't you dare-
SLAM

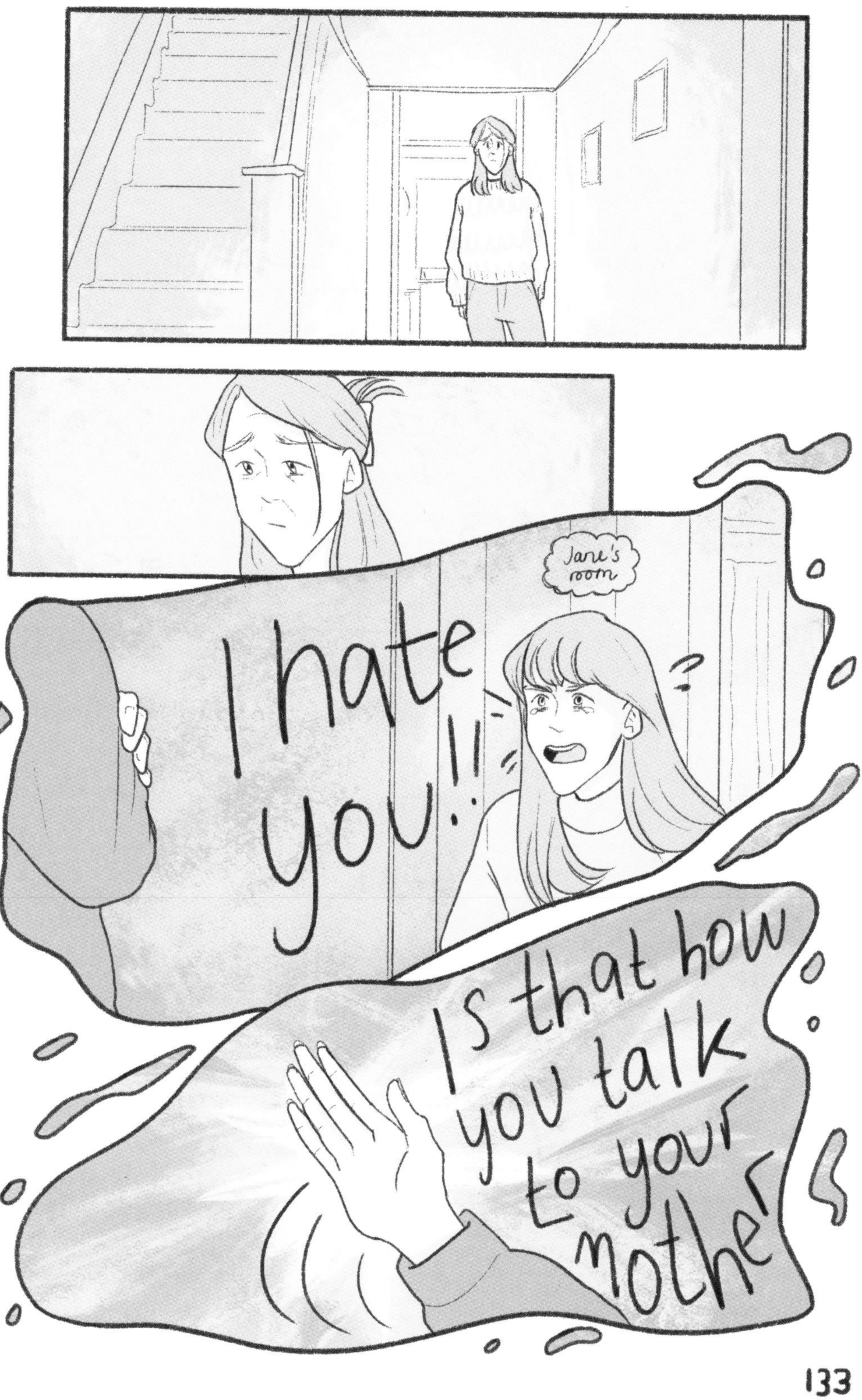
Jane's room
I hate you!!
?
Is that how you talk to your mother

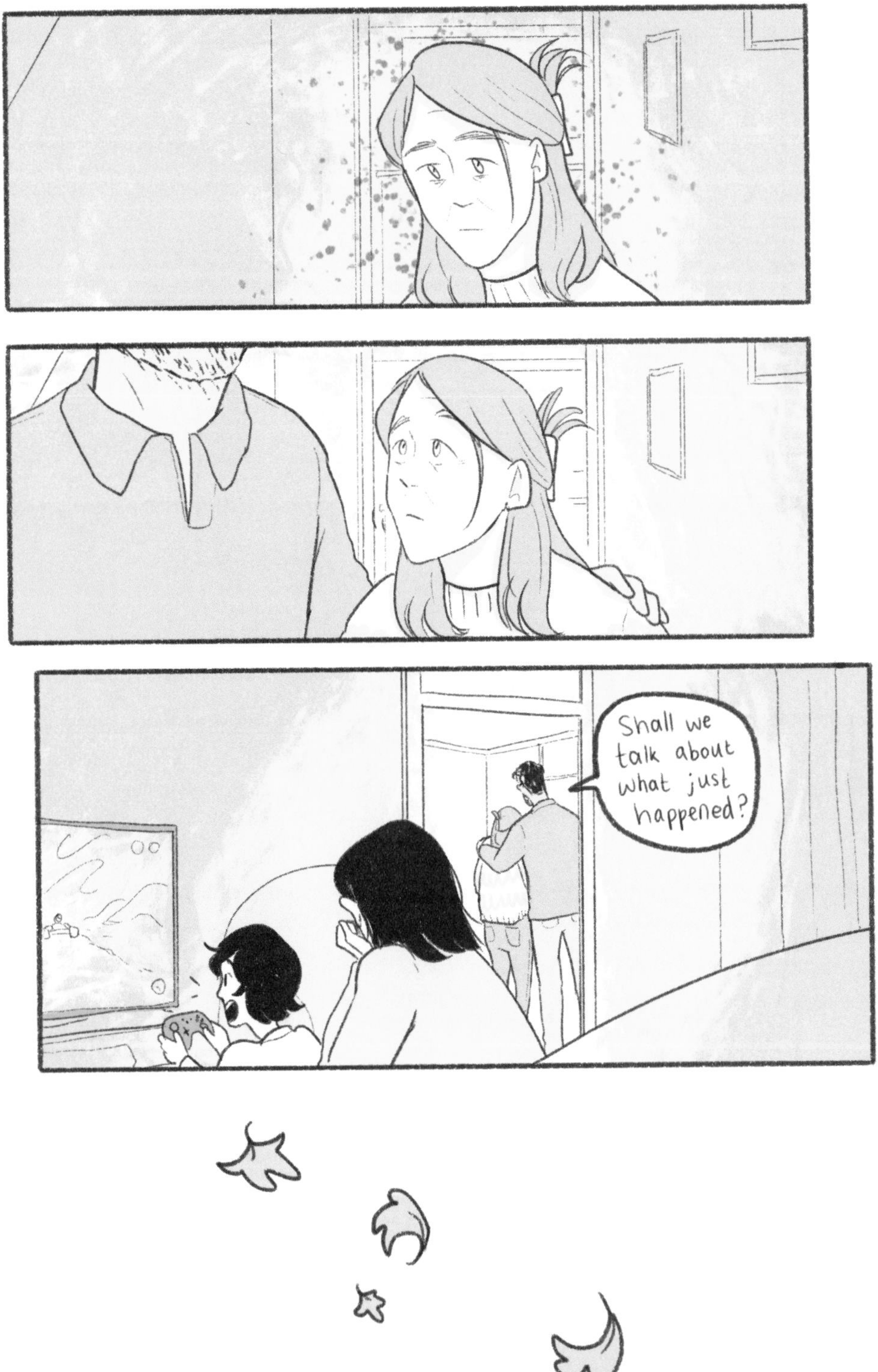
Shall we talk about what just happened?

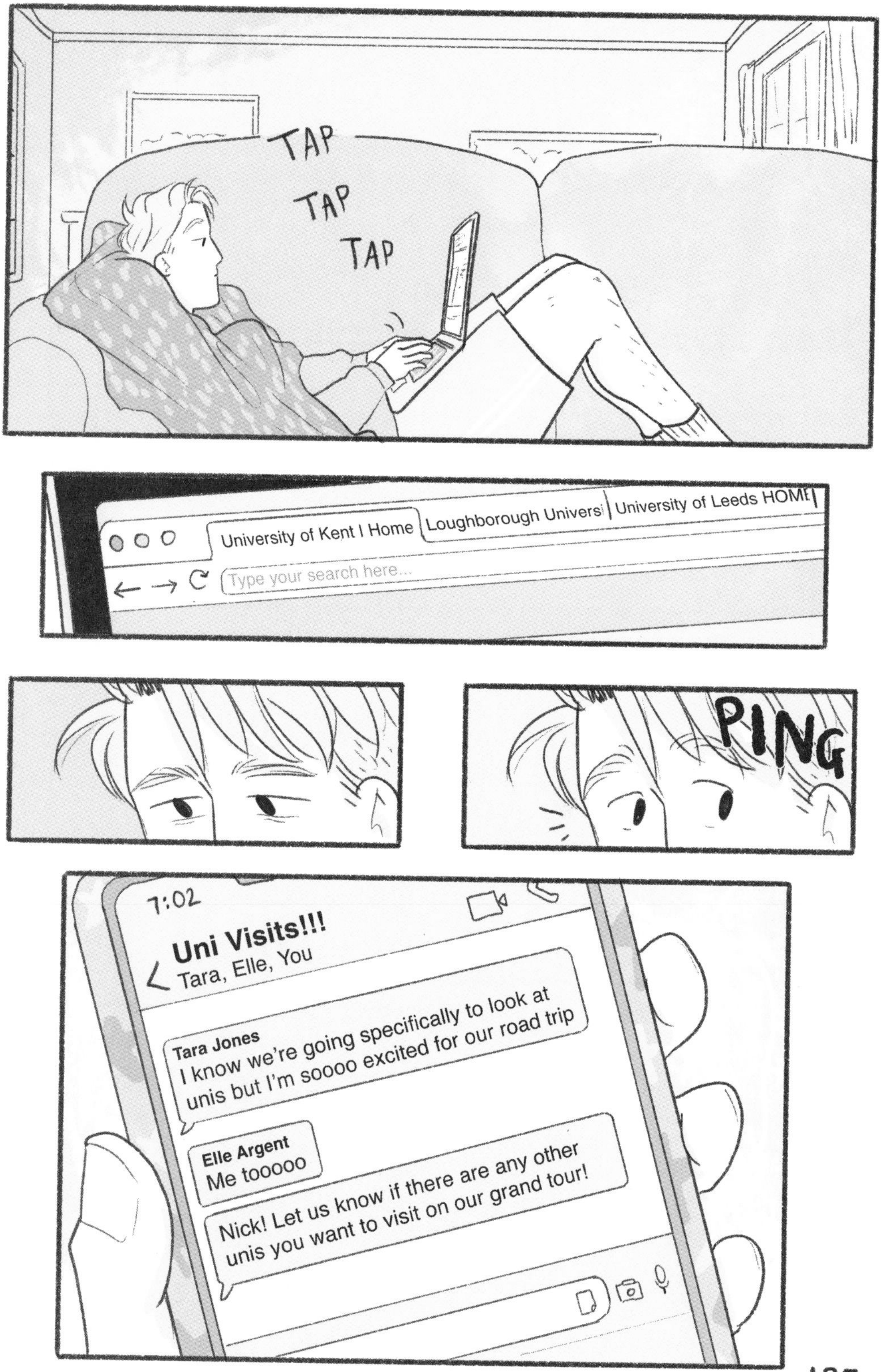
TAP
TAP
TAP
University of Kent I Home
Loughborough Universi
University of Leeds HOME
Type your search here...
PING
7:02
Uni Visits!!!
Tara, Elle, You
Tara Jones
I know we're going specifically to look at unis but I'm soooo excited for our road trip
Elle Argent
Me tooooo
Nick! Let us know if there are any other unis you want to visit on our grand tour!

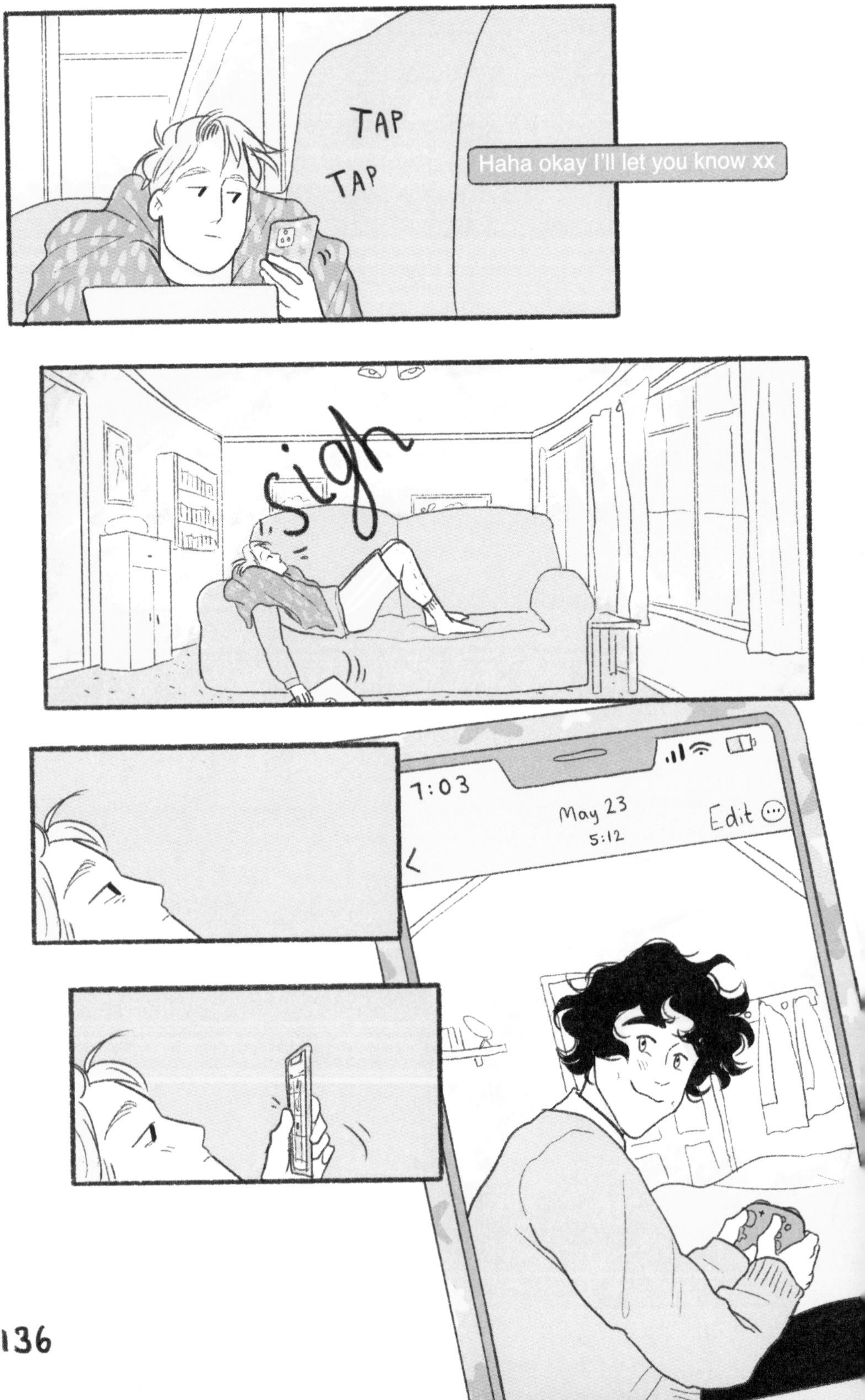
TAP
TAP
Haha okay I'll let you know xx
sigh
7:03
May 23
5:12
Edit

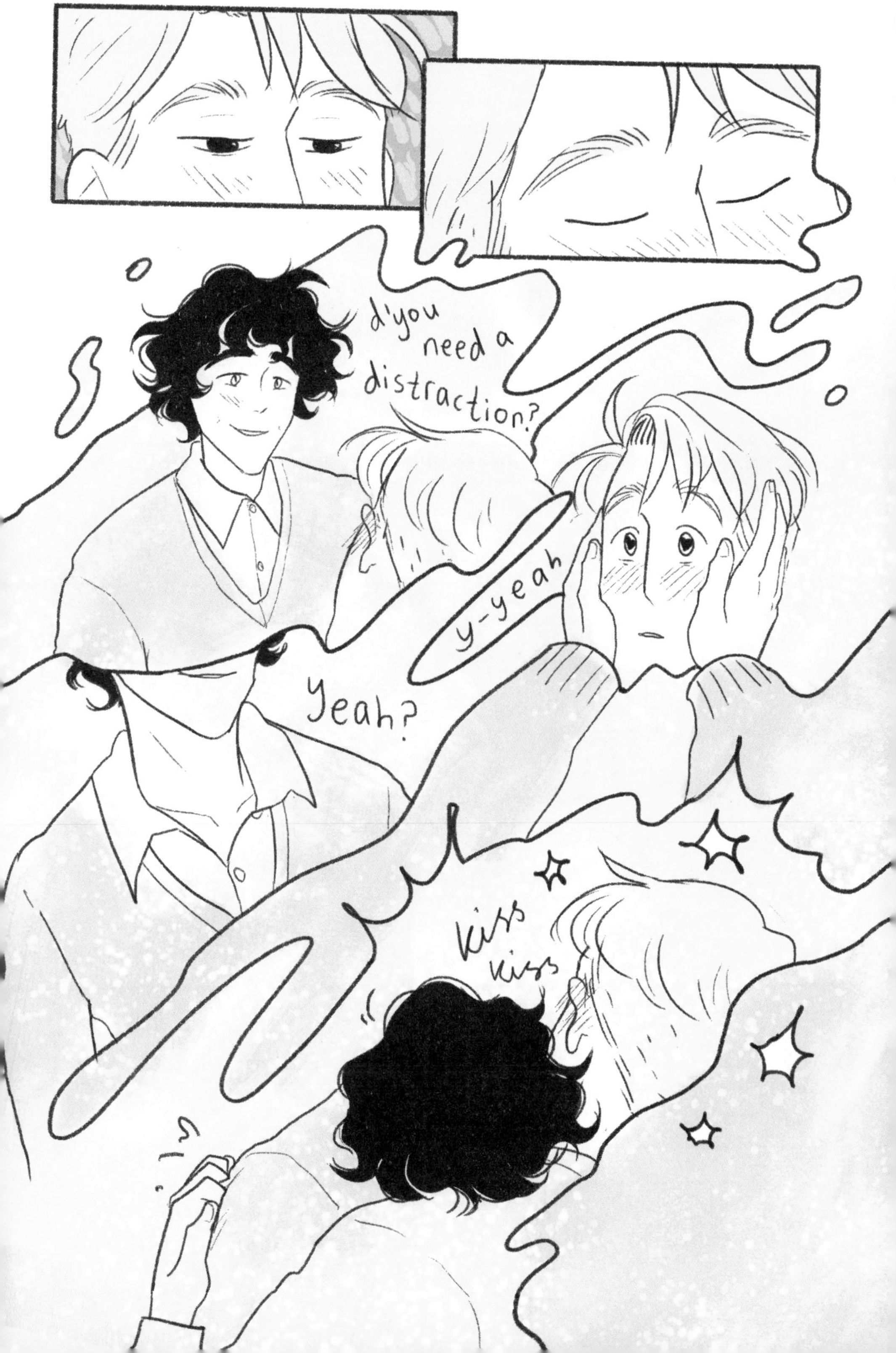
d'you need a distraction?
y-yeah
Yeah?
kiss kiss

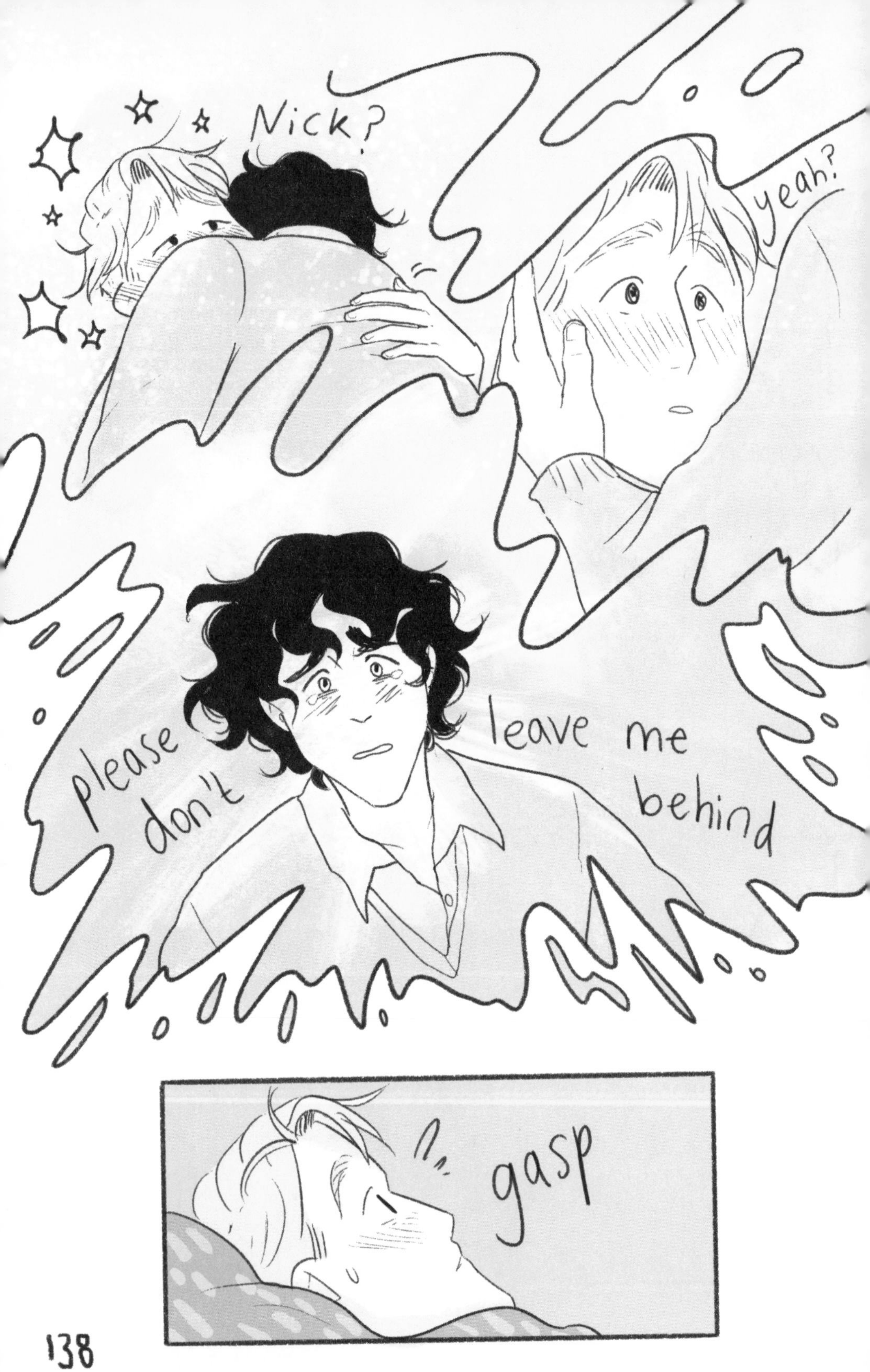
Nick?
yeah?
please don't leave me behind
gasp

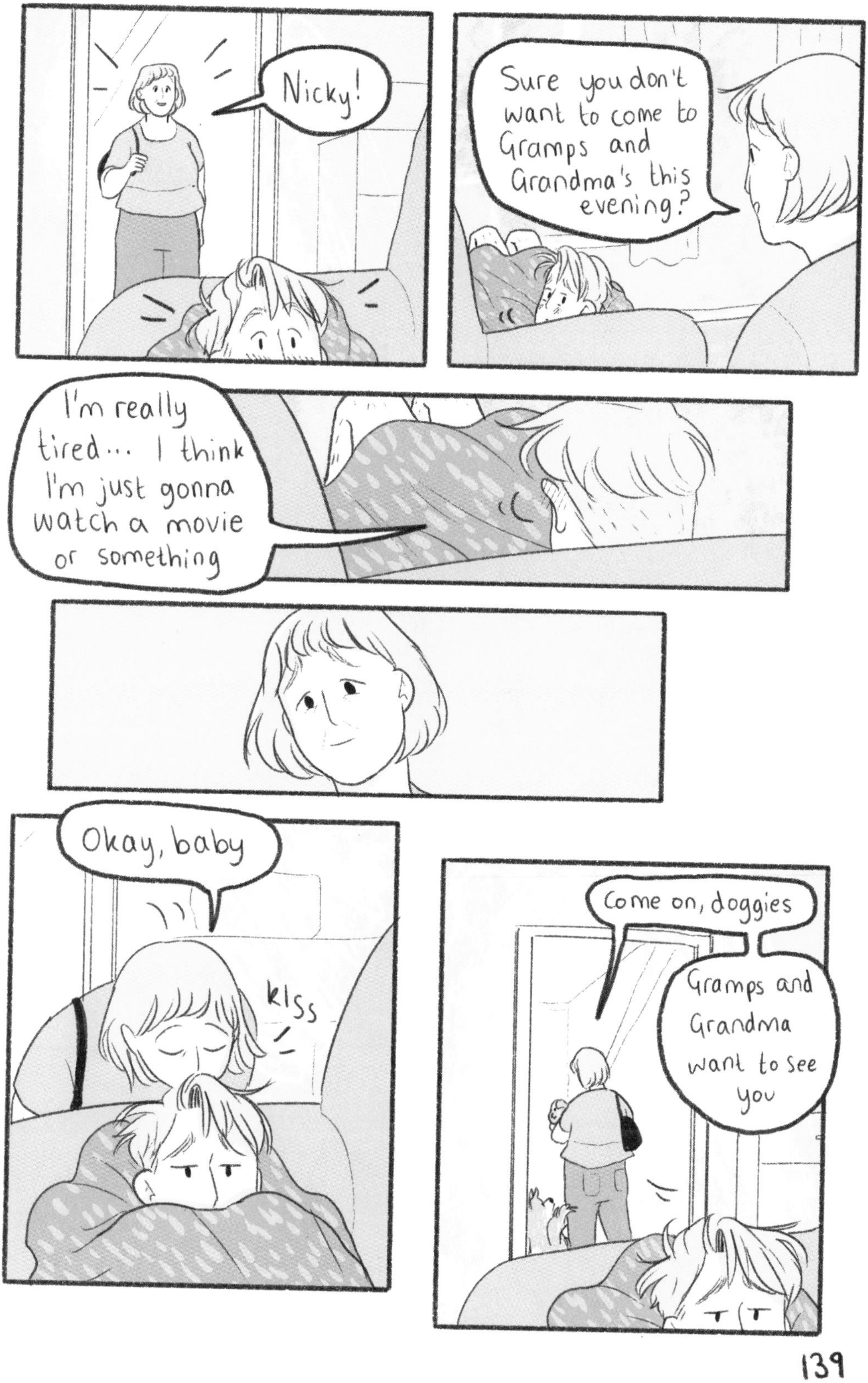

Nicky!
Sure you don't want to come to Gramps and Grandma's this evening?
I'm really tired... I think I'm just gonna watch a movie or something
Okay, baby
kiss
Come on, doggies
Gramps and Grandma want to see you

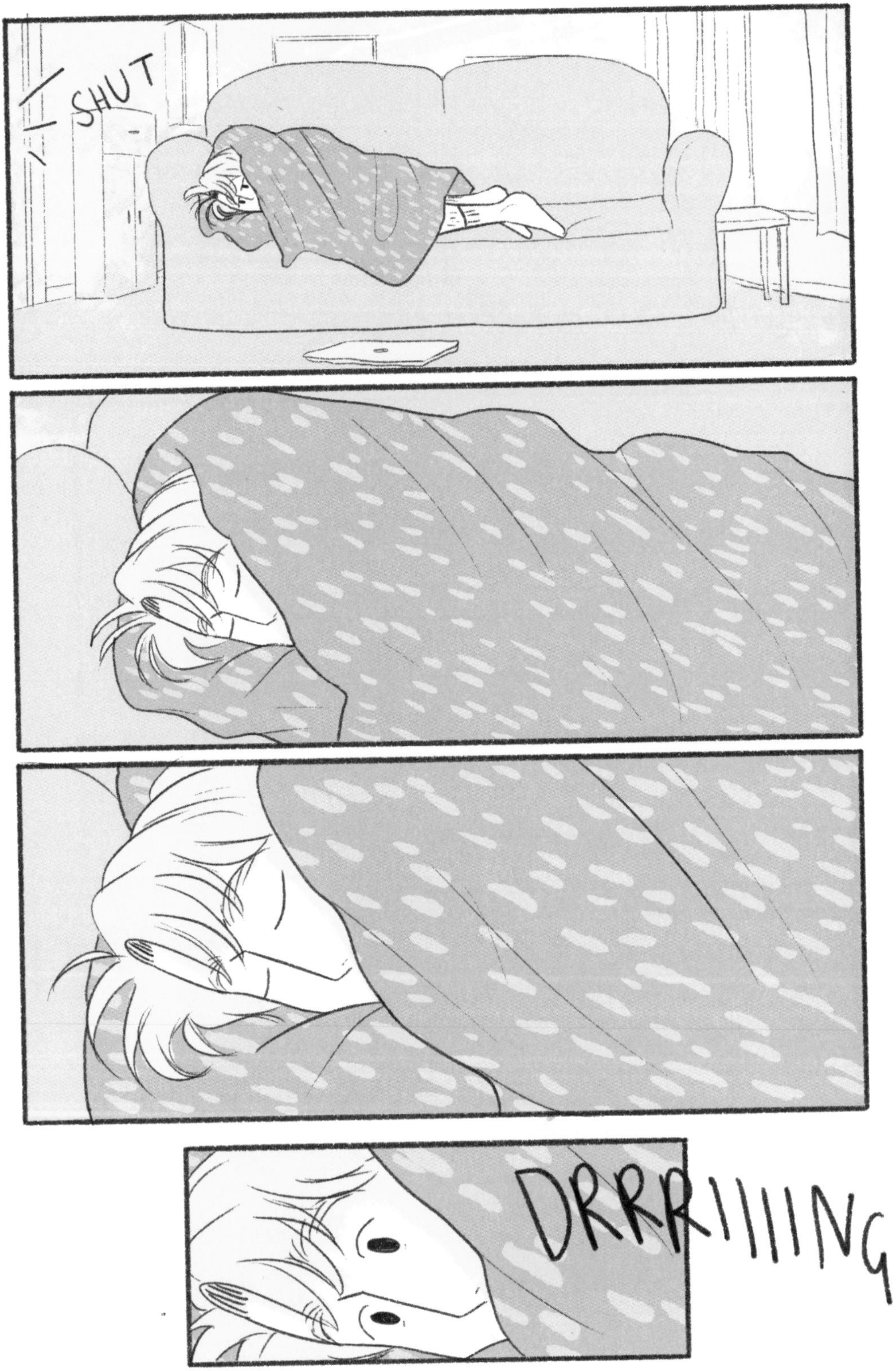
SHUT
DRRRIIIING

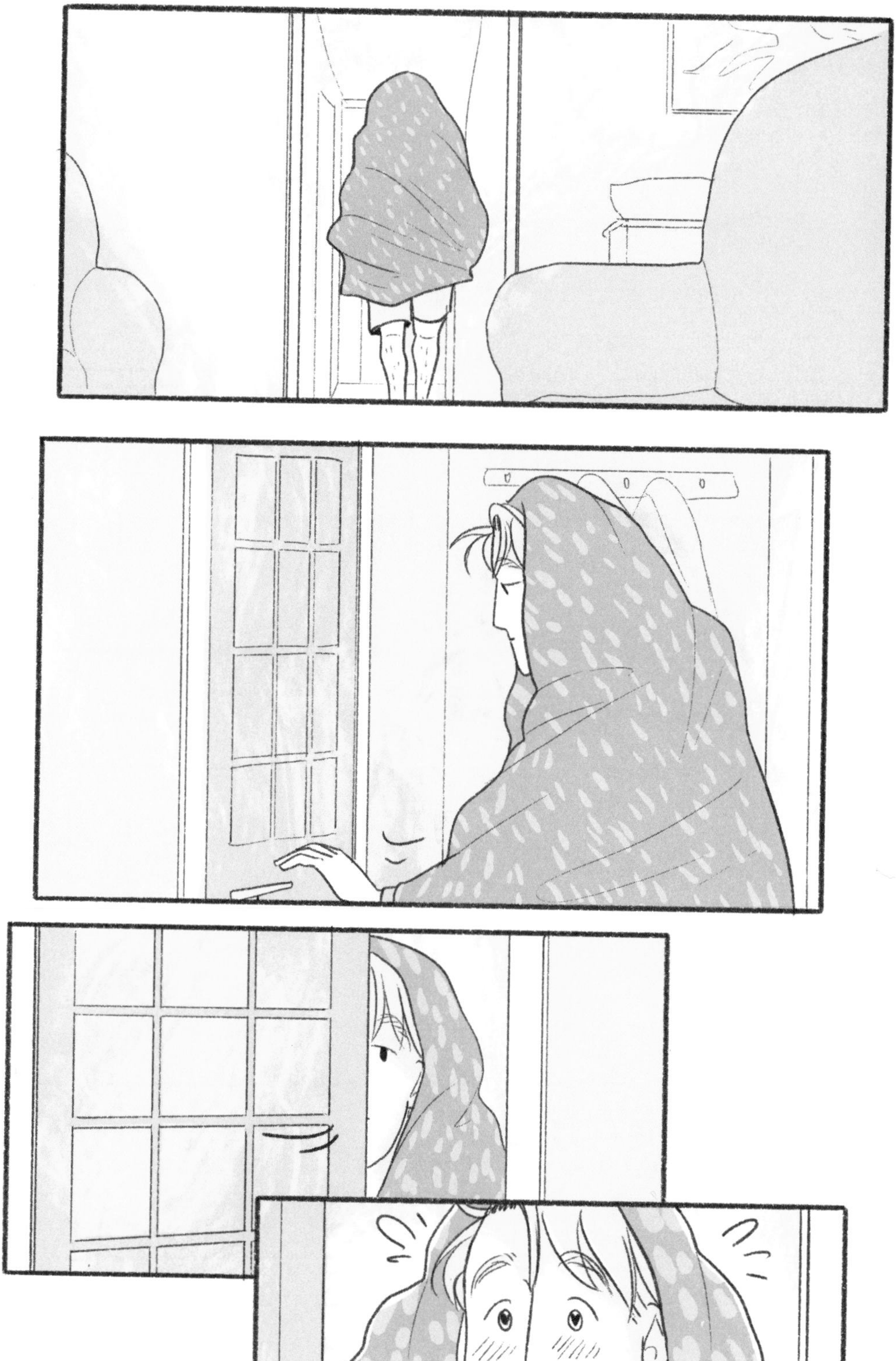

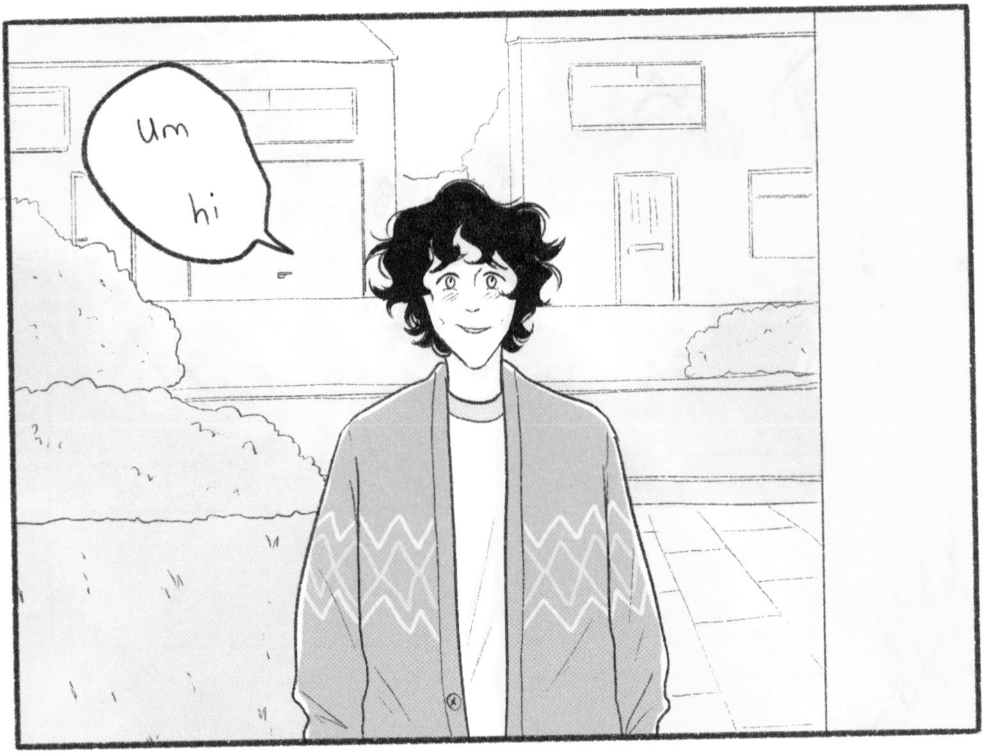
Um
hi

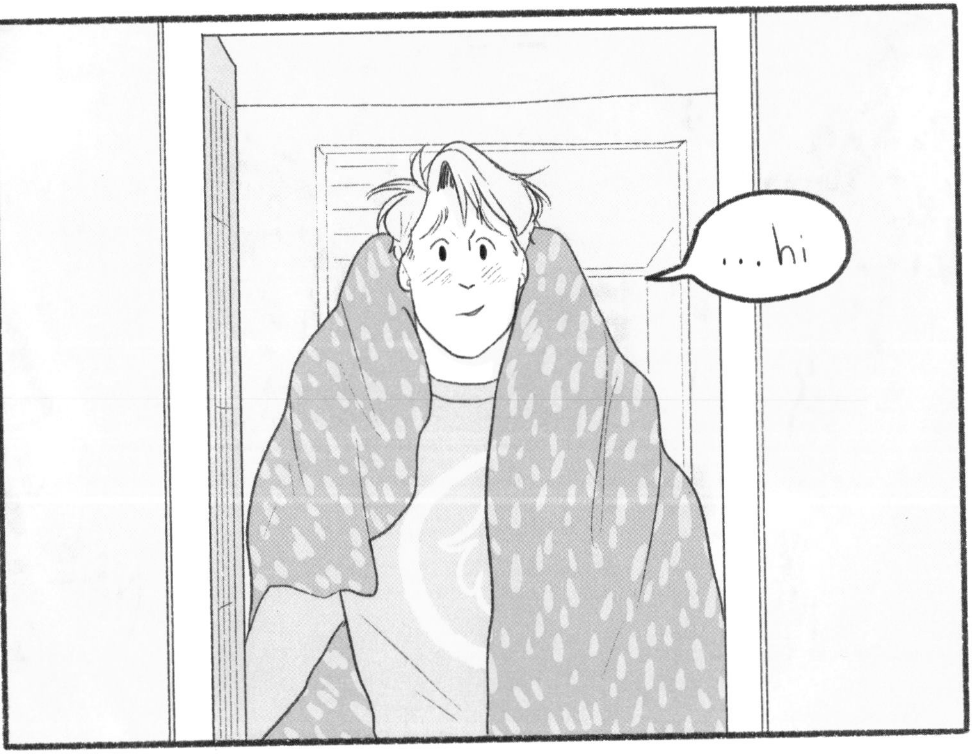
...hi

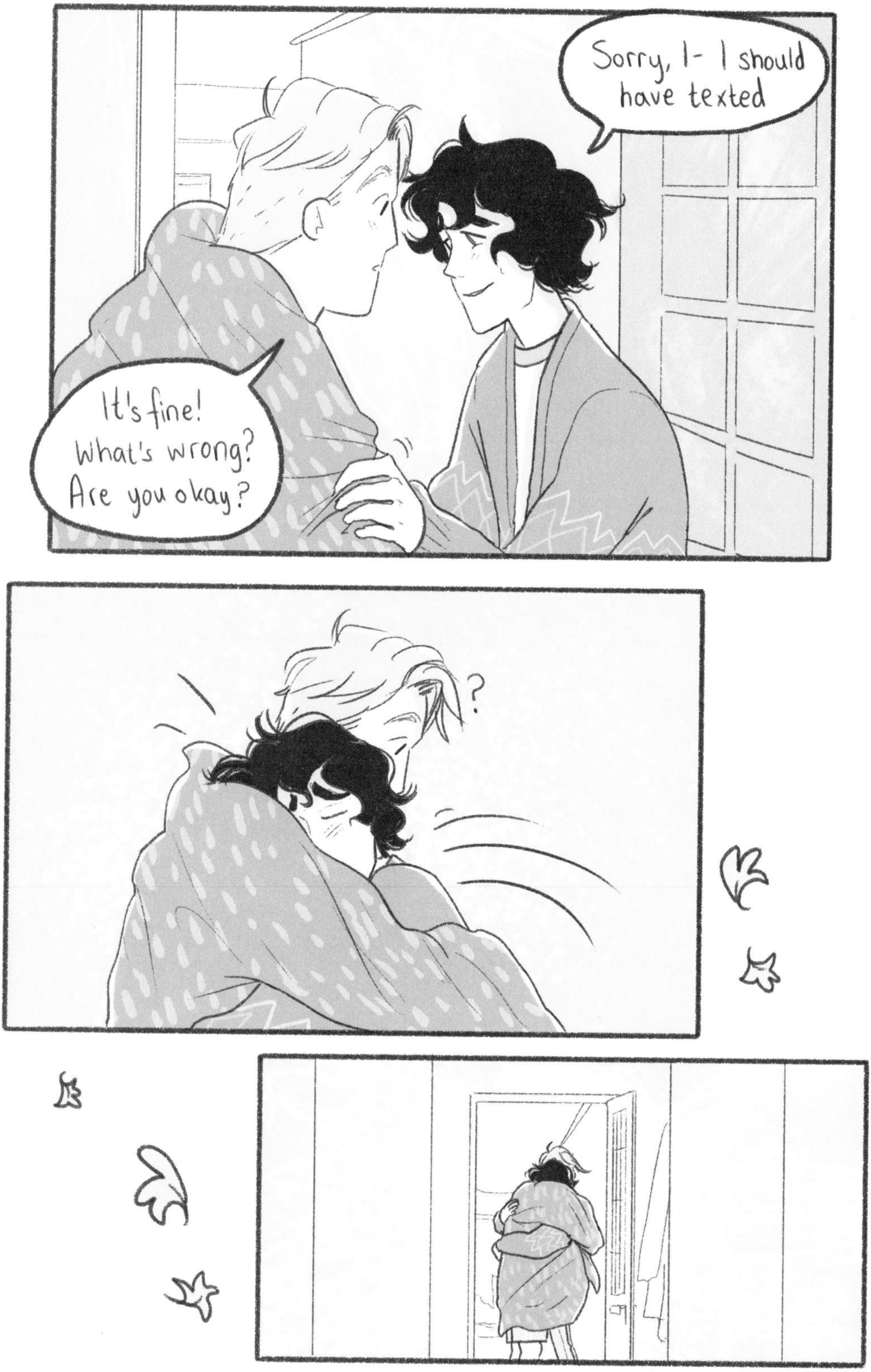
Sorry, I- I should have texted
It's fine! What's wrong? Are you okay?
?

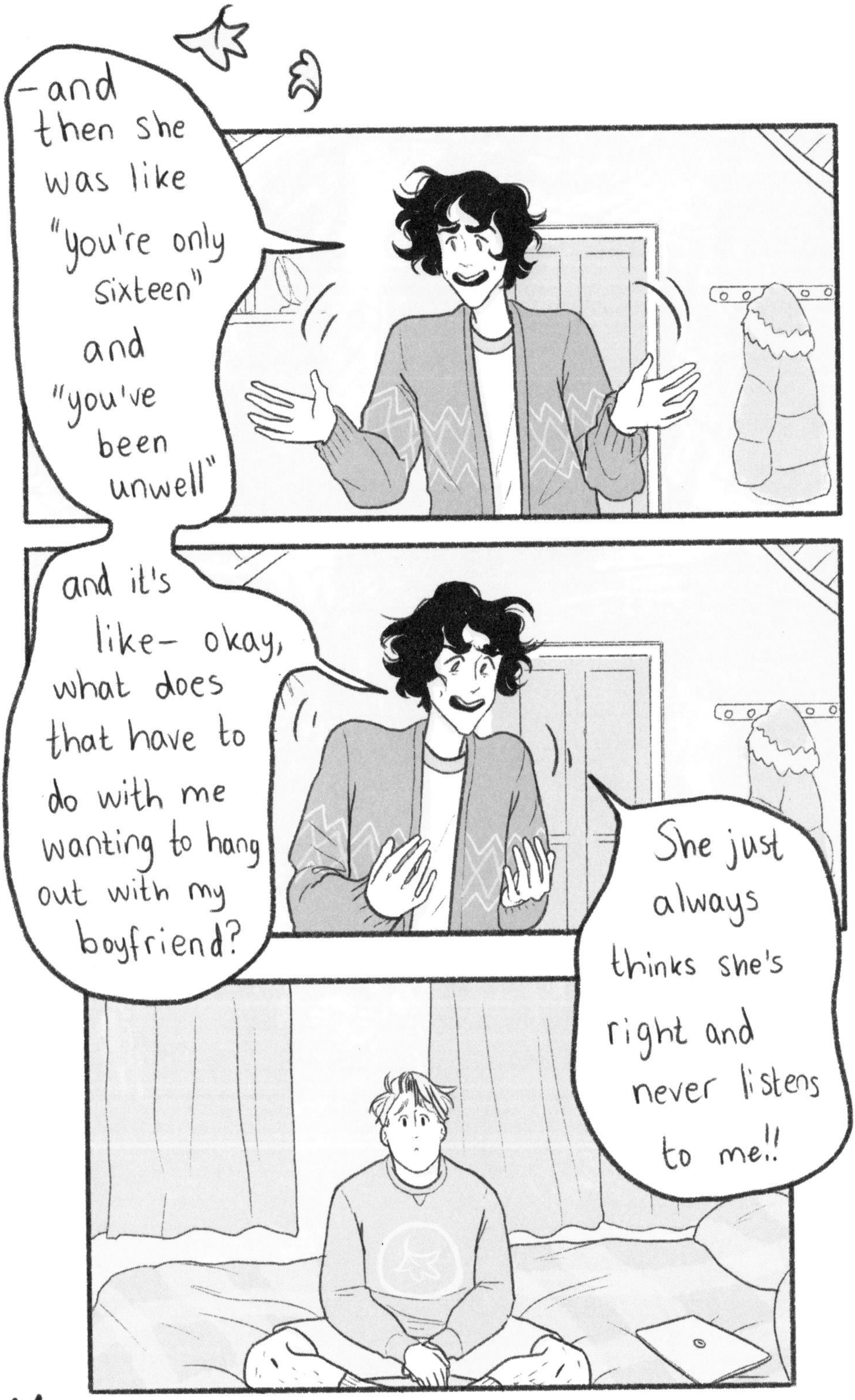
-and then she was like "you're only sixteen" and "you've been unwell"
and it's like- okay, what does that have to do with me wanting to hang out with my boyfriend?
She just always thinks she's right and never listens to me!!

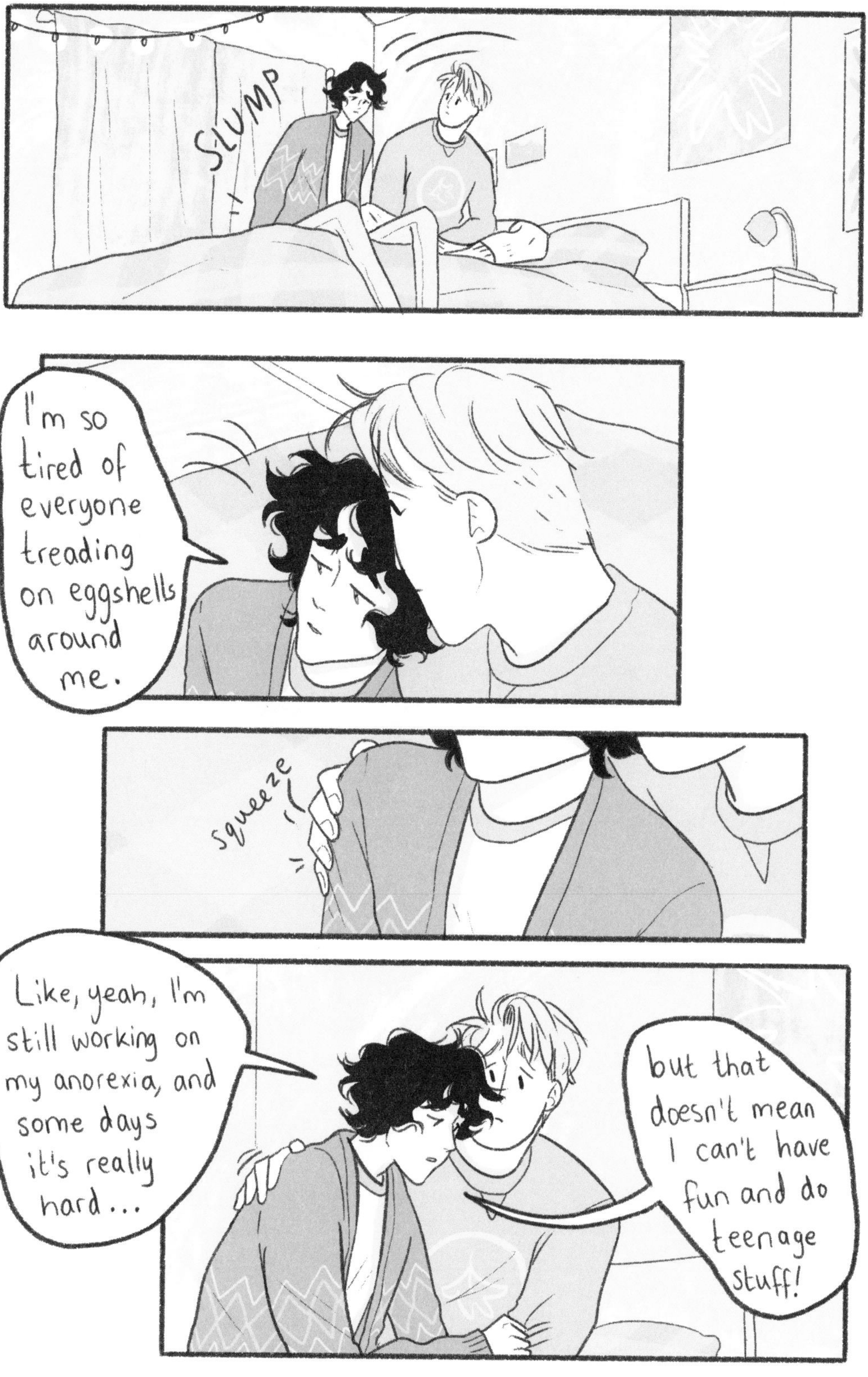
SLUMP
I'm so tired of everyone treading on eggshells around me.
squeeze
Like, yeah, I'm still working on my anorexia, and some days it's really hard...
but that doesn't mean I can't have fun and do teenage stuff!

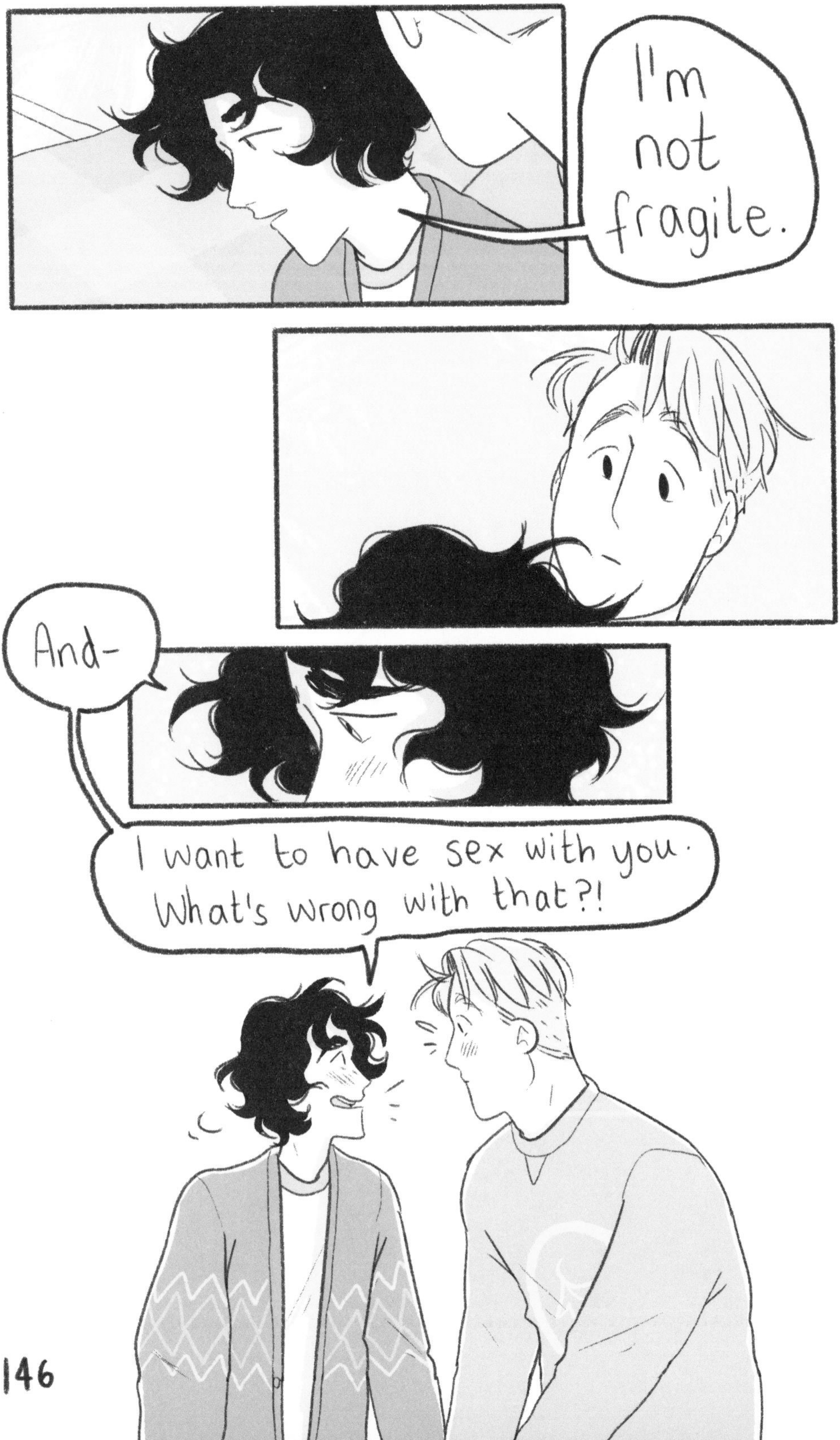
I'm not fragile.
And-
I want to have sex with you. What's wrong with that?!

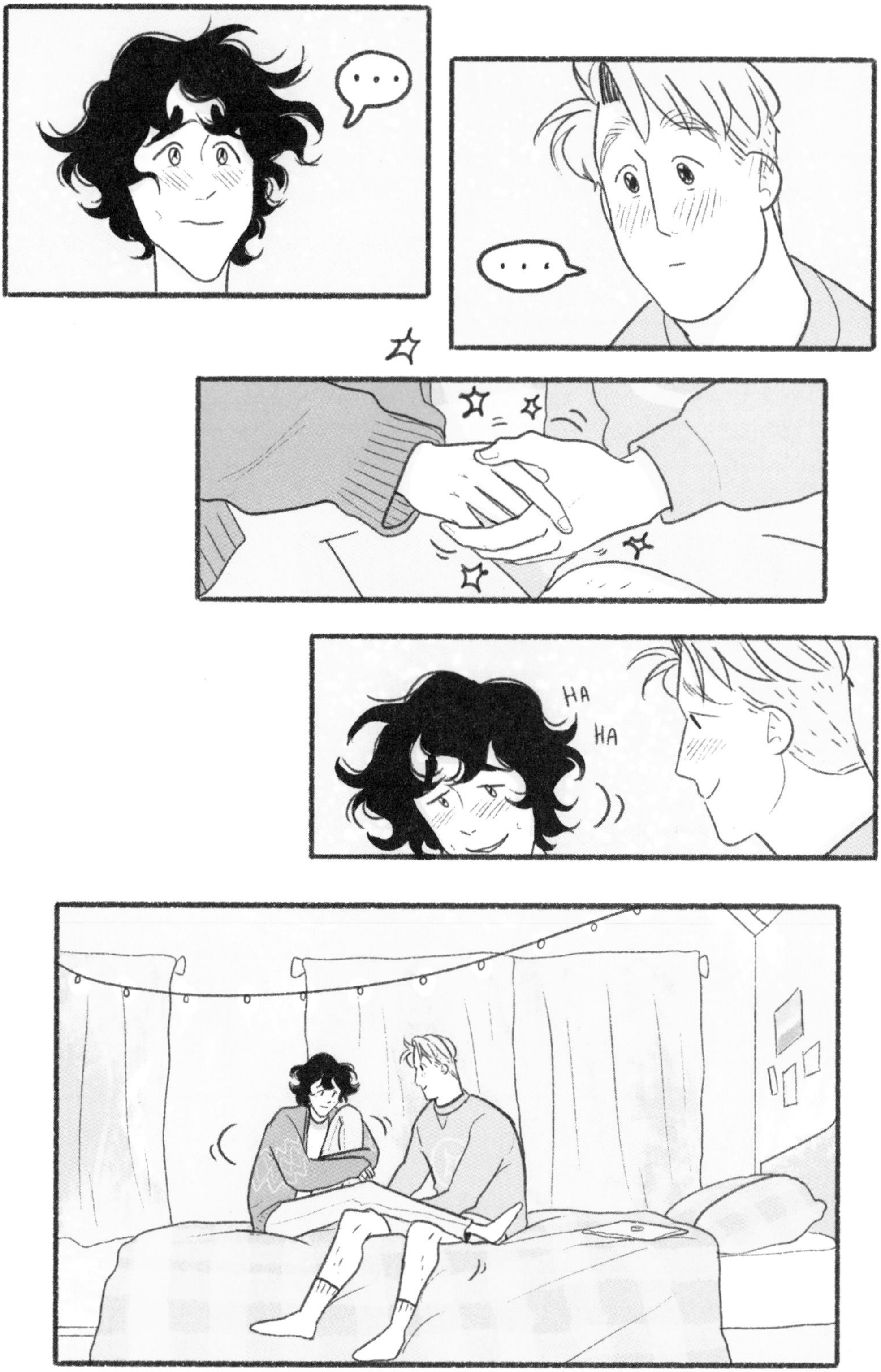
...
...
HA
HA

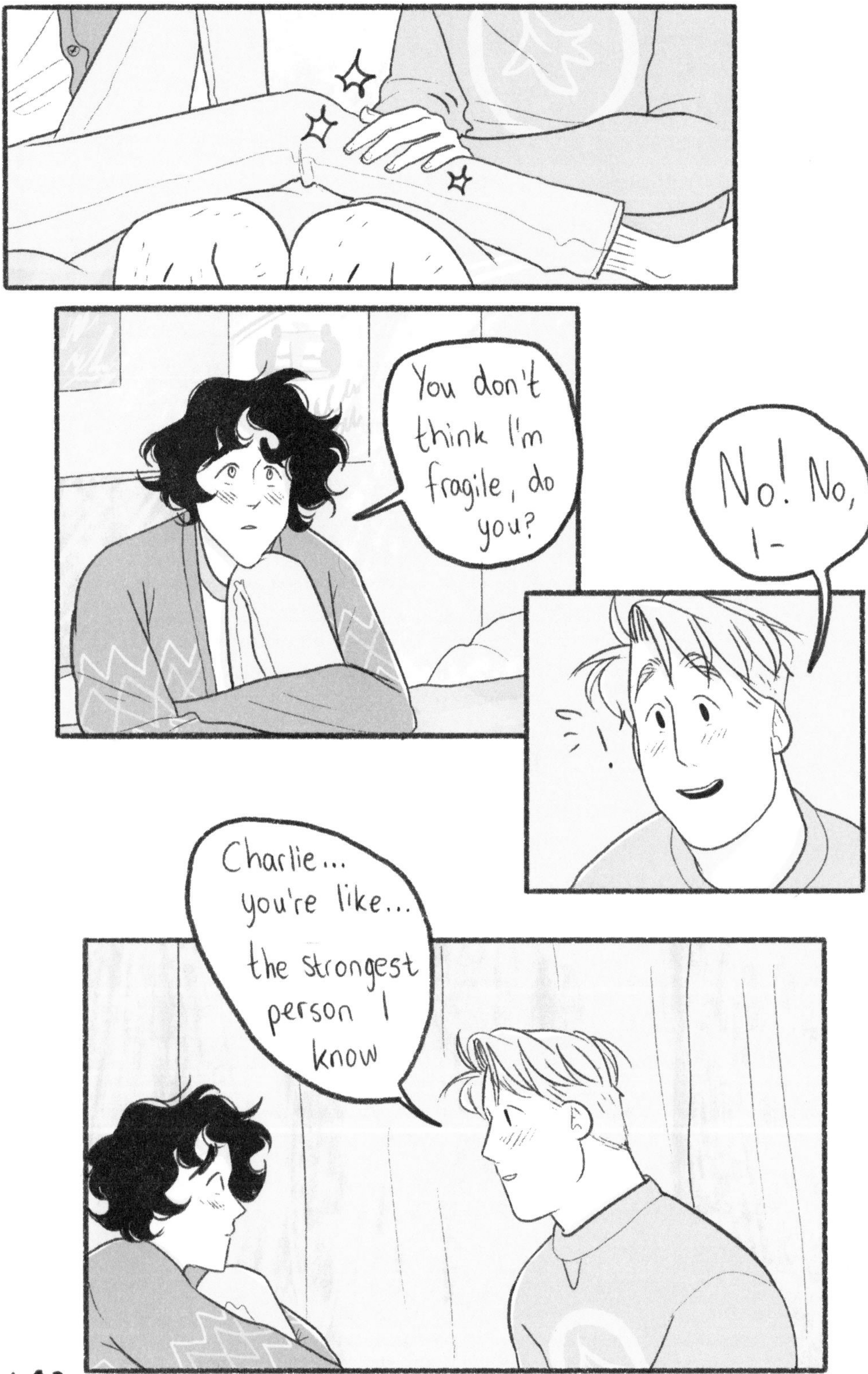
You don't think I'm fragile, do you?
No! No, I-
Charlie... you're like... the strongest person I know

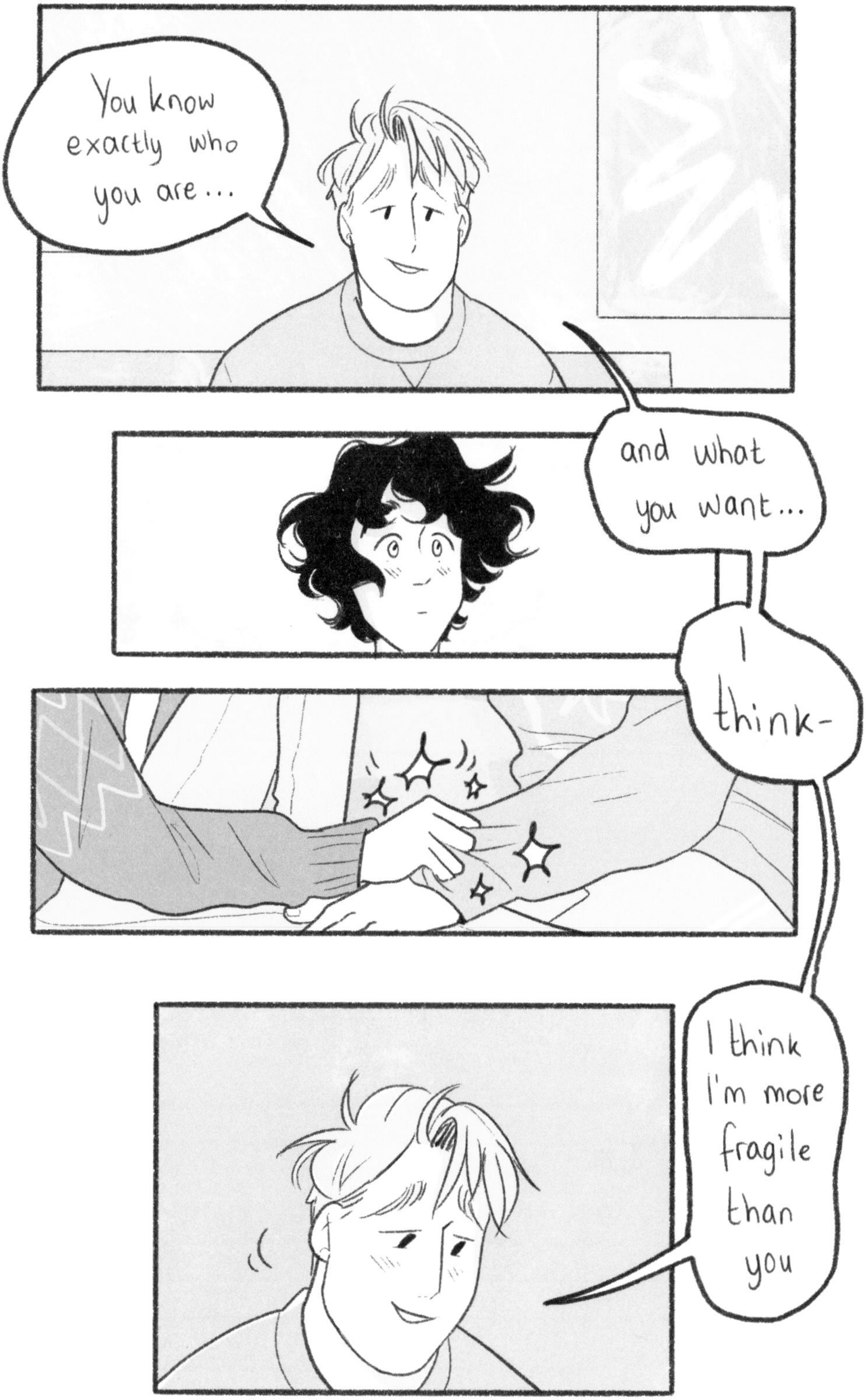
You know exactly who you are...
and what you want...
I think-
I think I'm more fragile than you

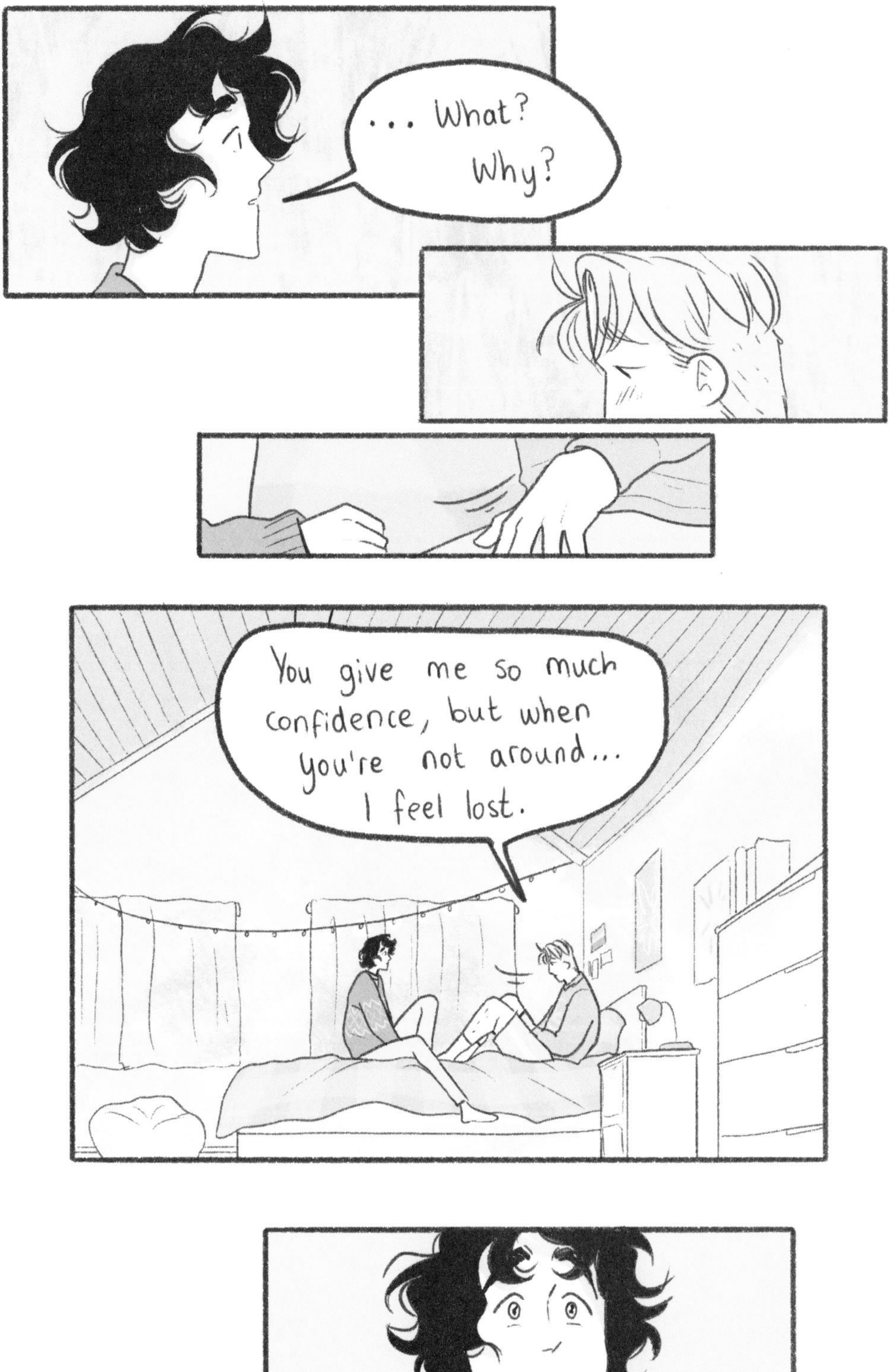
... What? Why?
You give me so much confidence, but when you're not around... I feel lost.

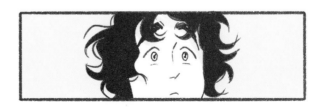

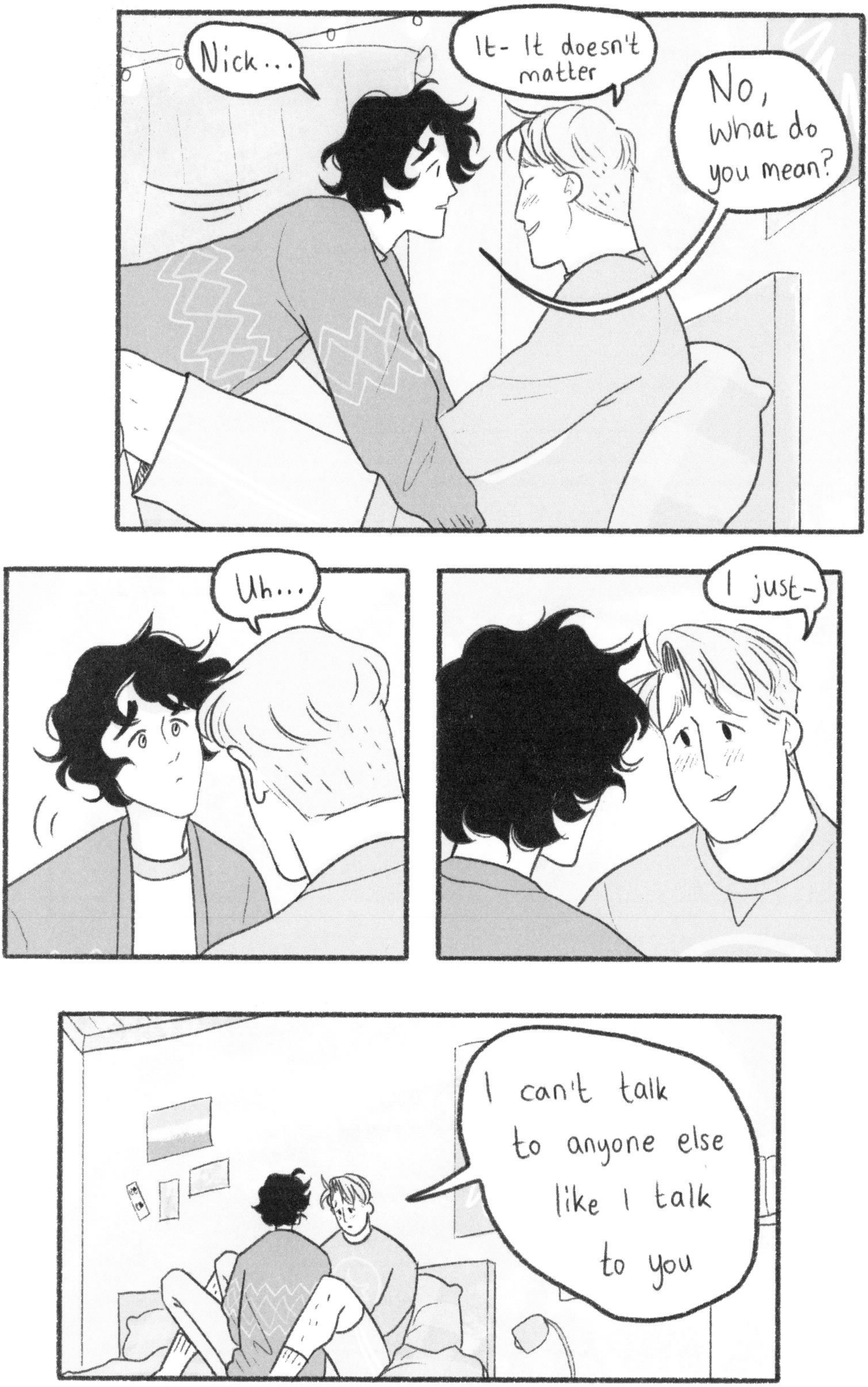
Nick...
It- It doesn't matter
No, what do you mean?
Uh...
I just-
I can't talk to anyone else like I talk to you

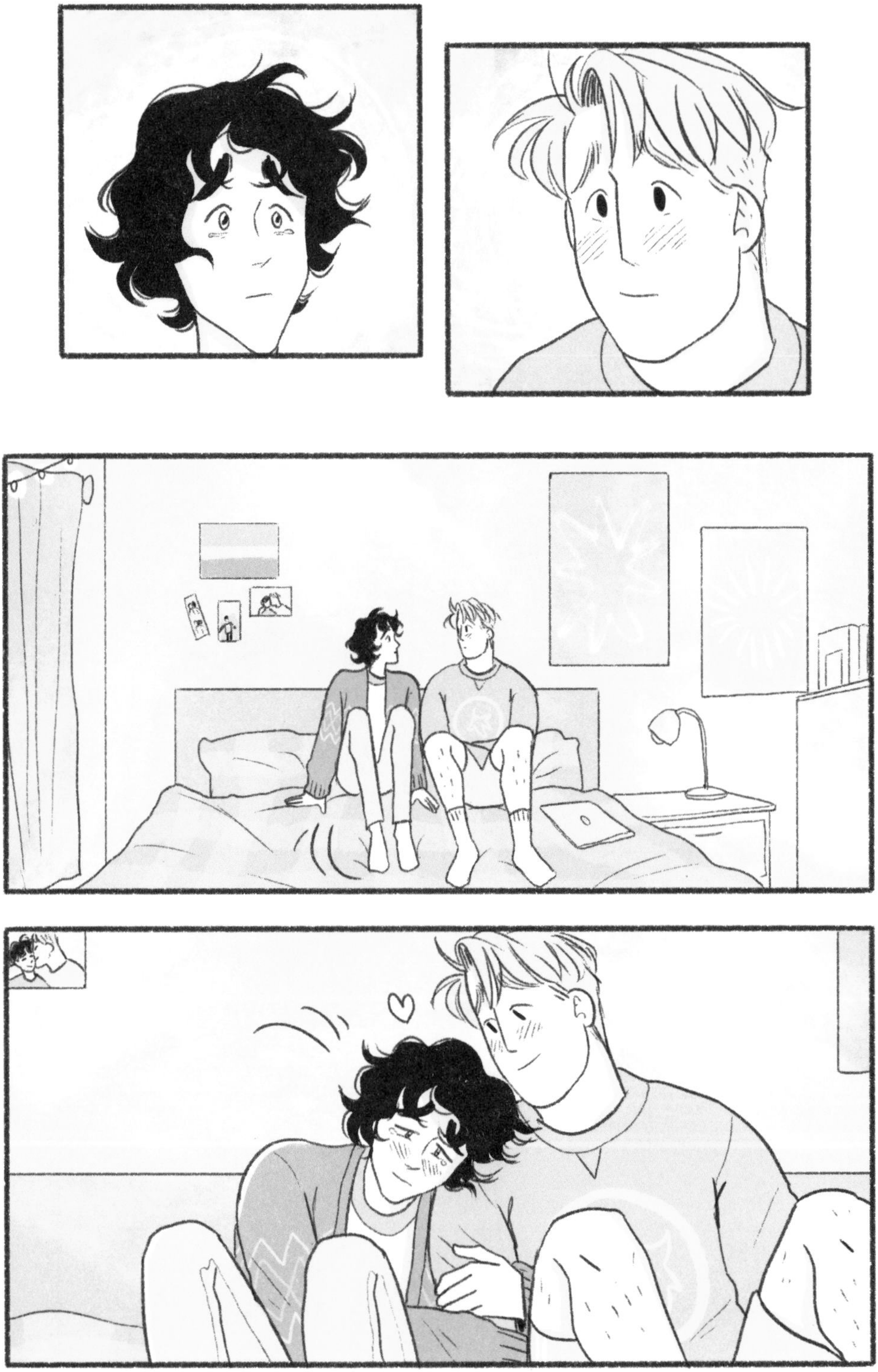

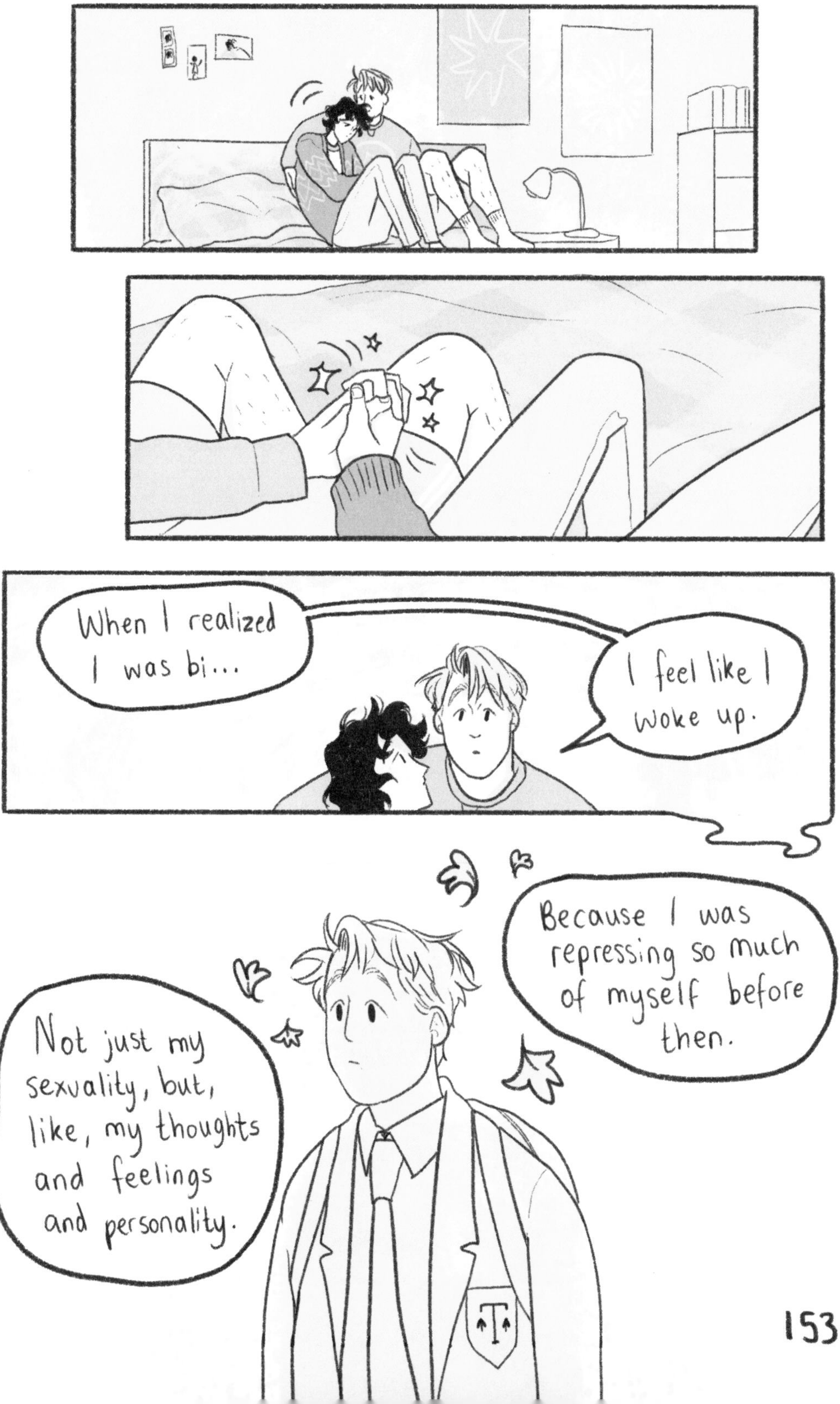
When I realized I was bi...
I feel like I woke up.
Because I was repressing so much of myself before then.
Not just my sexuality, but, like, my thoughts and feelings and personality.

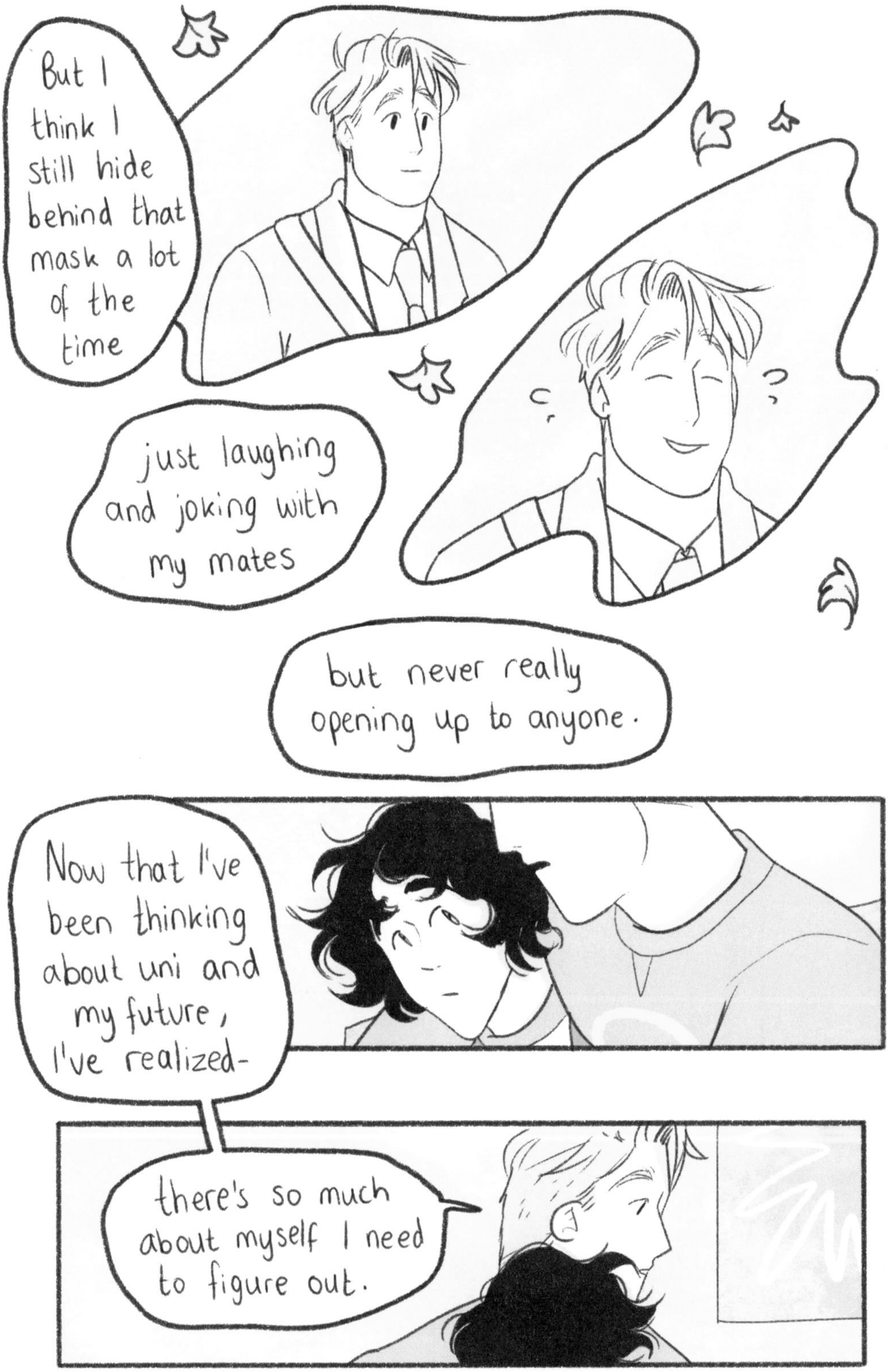
But I think I still hide behind that mask a lot of the time
just laughing and joking with my mates
but never really opening up to anyone.
Now that I've been thinking about uni and my future, I've realized-
there's so much about myself I need to figure out.

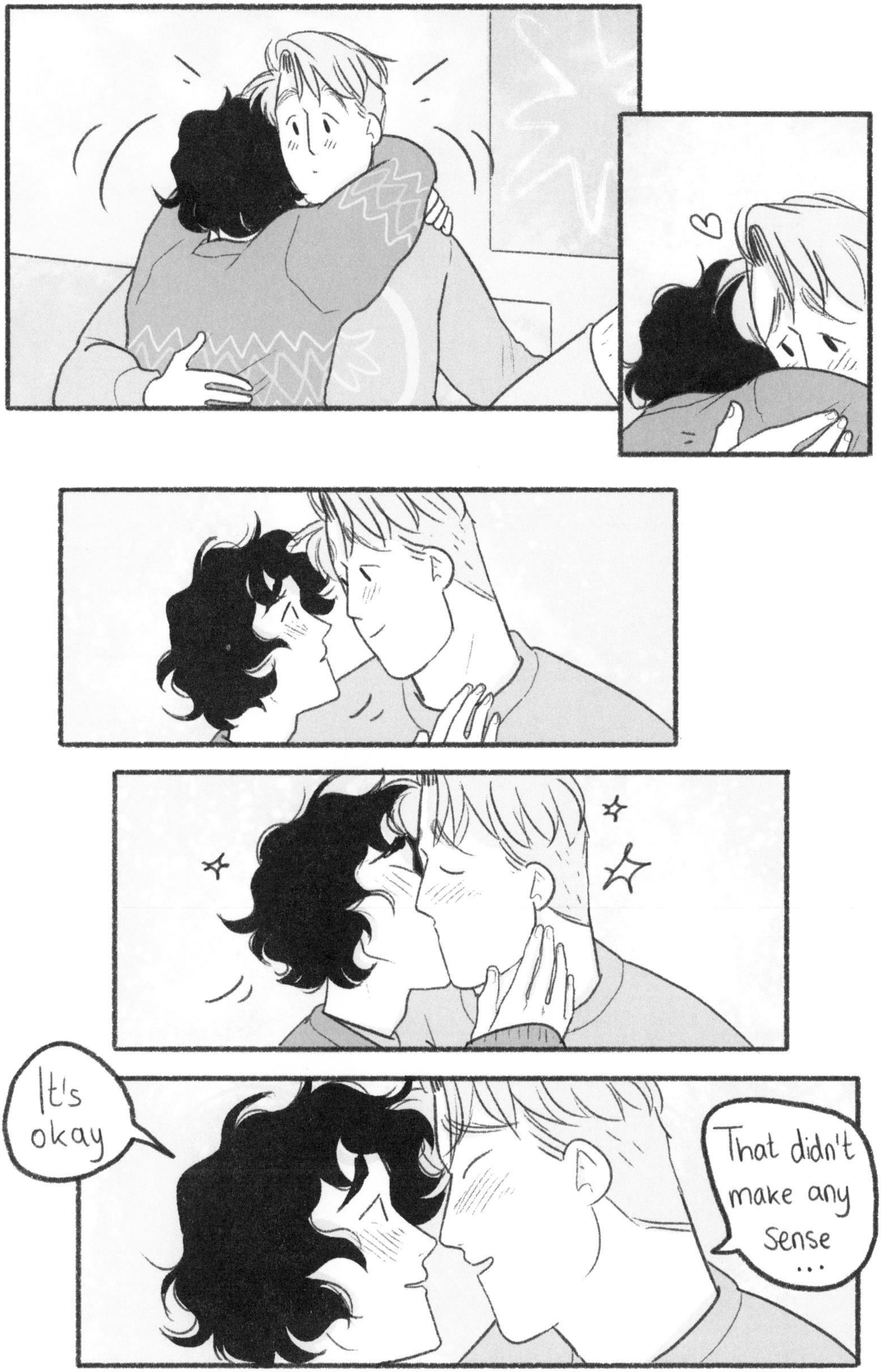
It's okay
That didn't make any sense ...

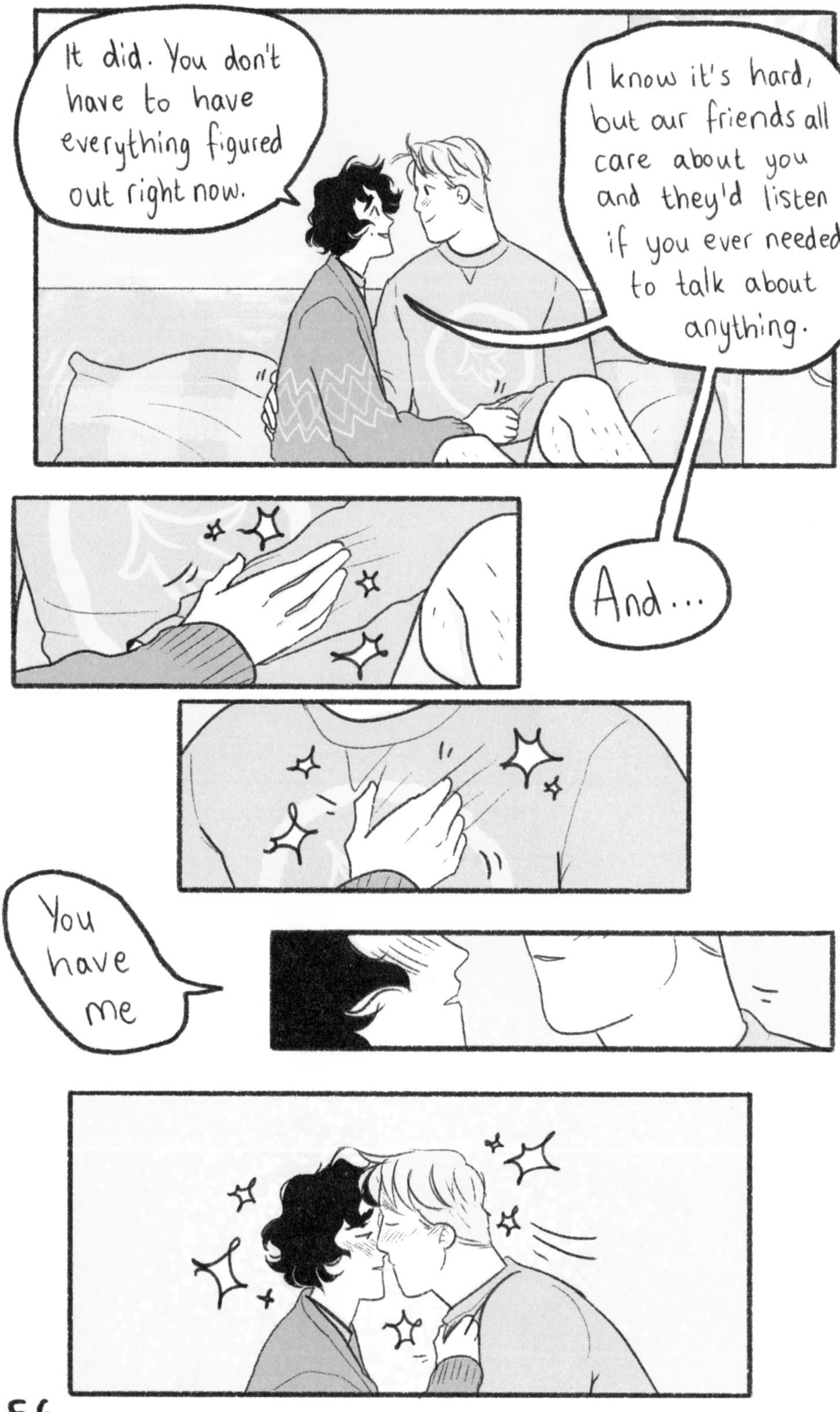
It did. You don't have to have everything figured out right now.
I know it's hard, but our friends all care about you and they'd listen if you ever needed to talk about anything.
And...
You have me

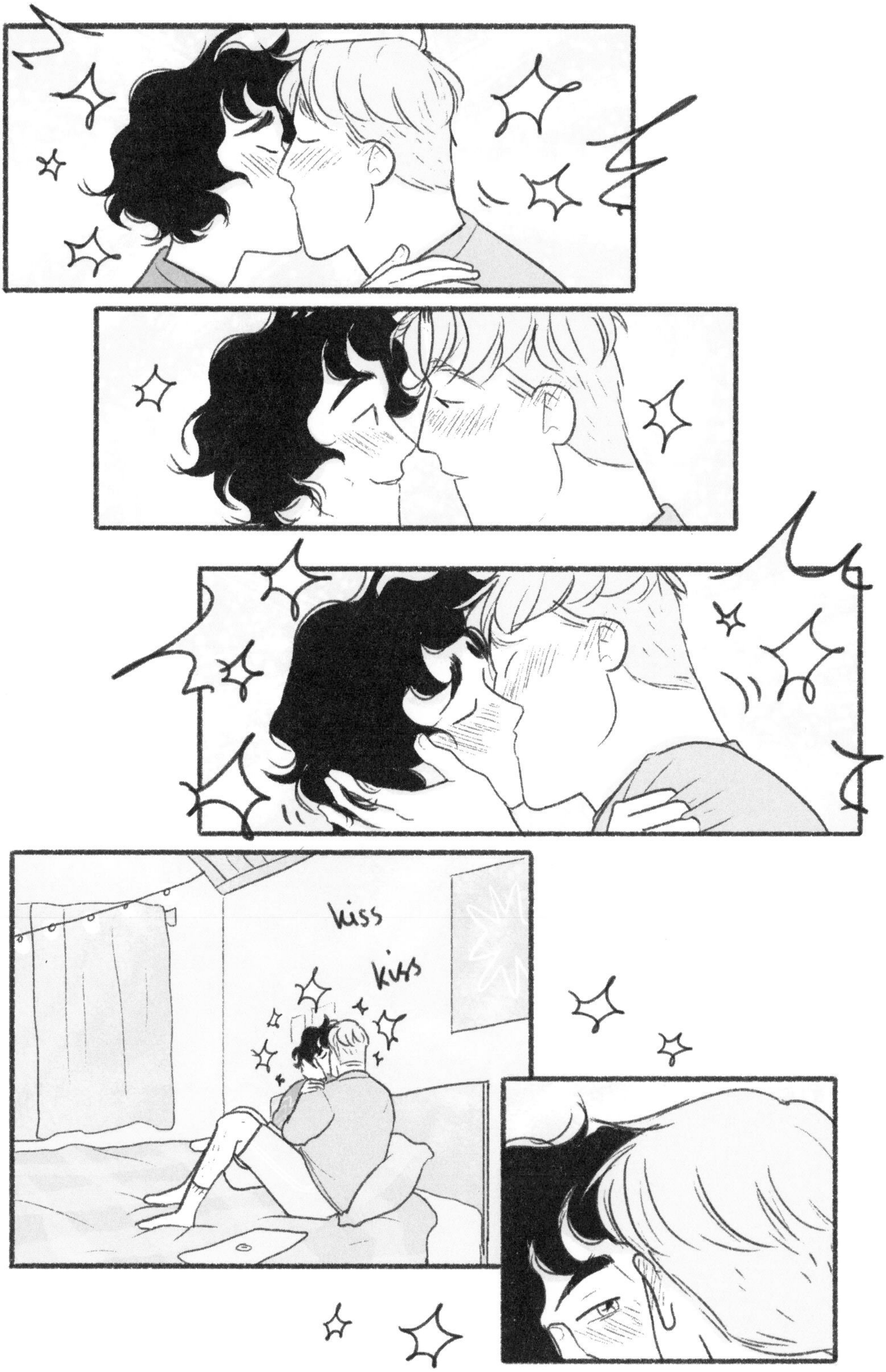
kiss
kiss

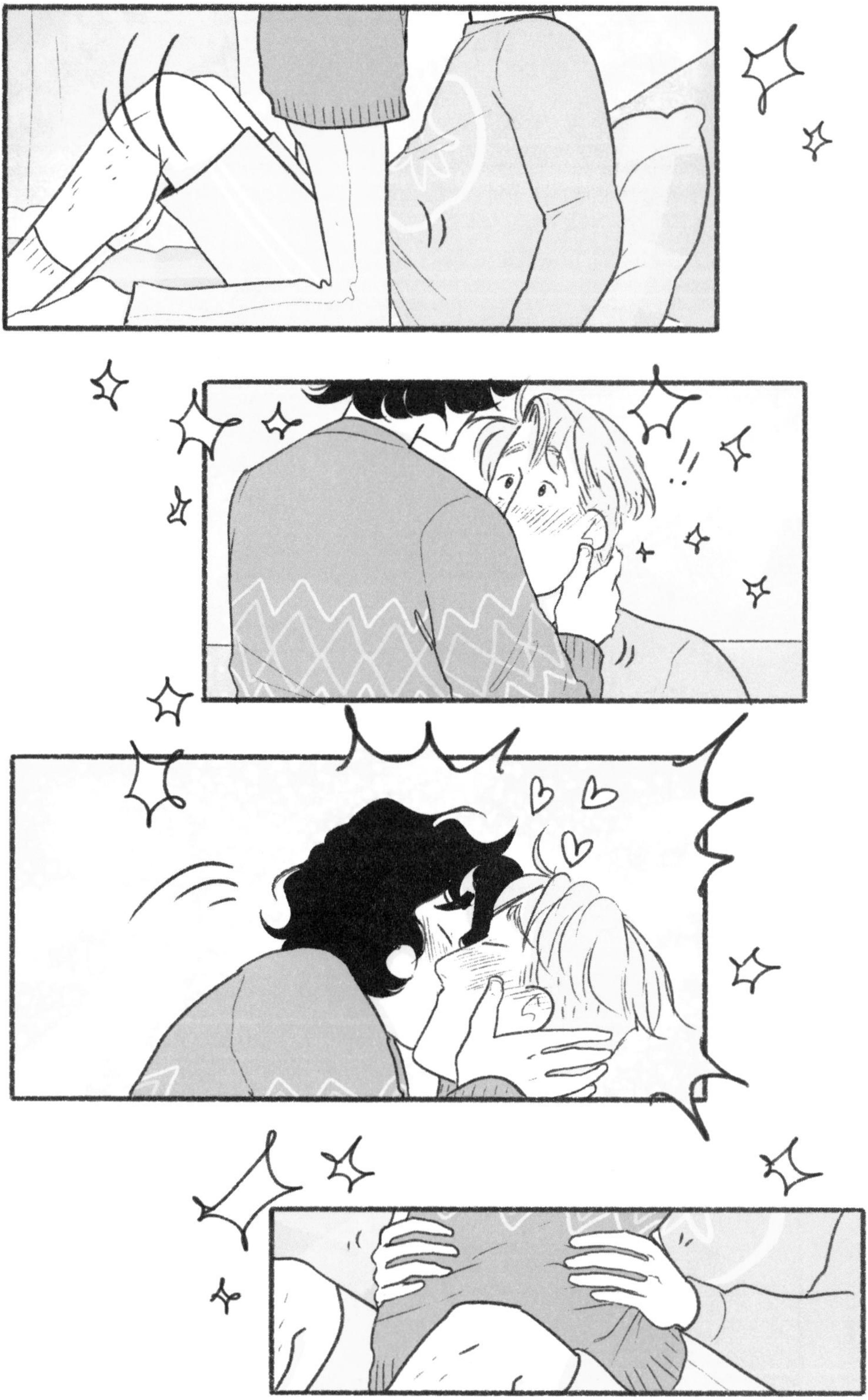
!!

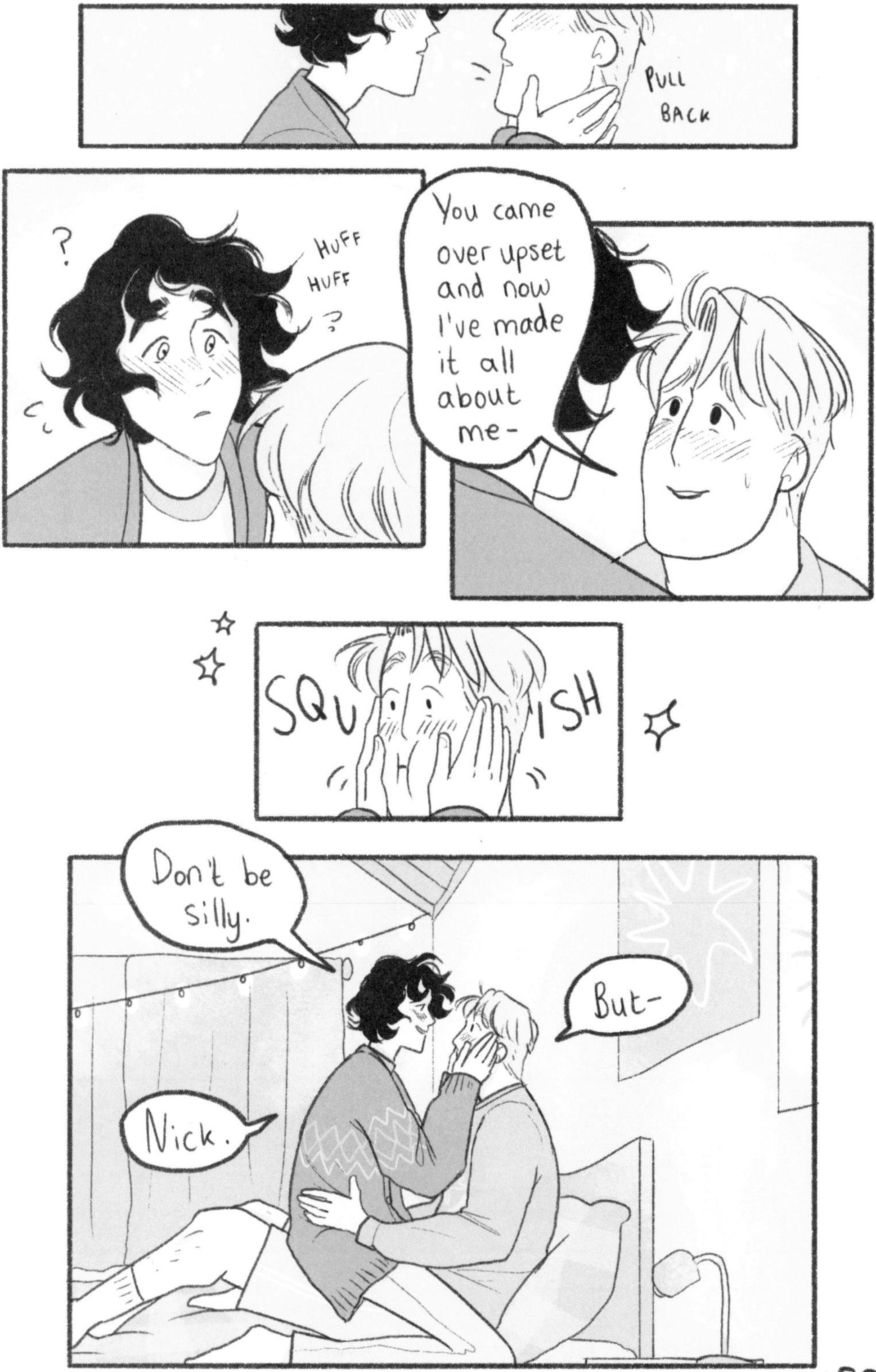
PULL BACK
?
HUFF HUFF
You came over upset and now I've made it all about me-
SQUISH
Don't be silly.
But-
Nick.

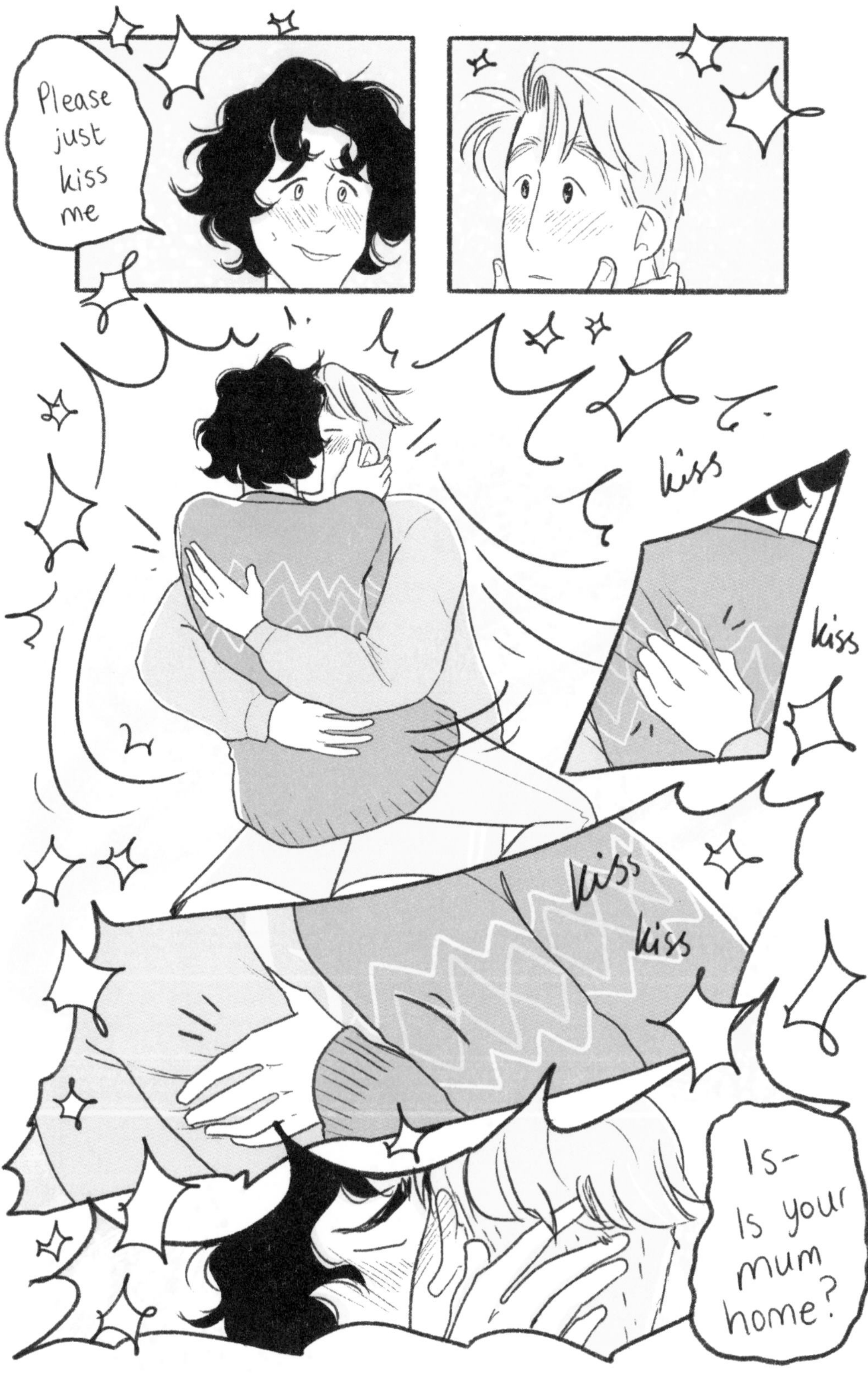
Please just kiss me
kiss
kiss
kiss
kiss
Is- Is your mum home?

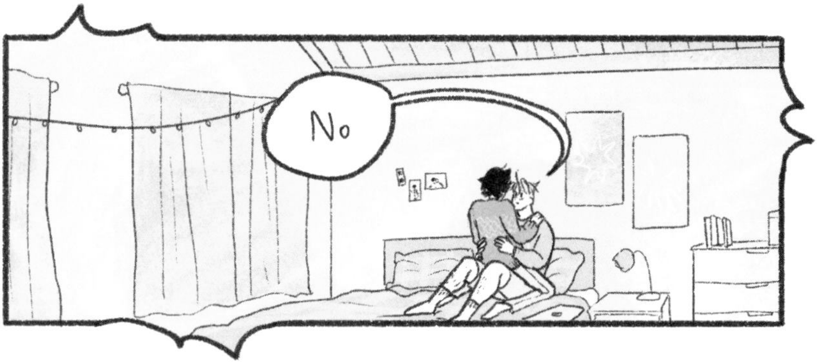
No

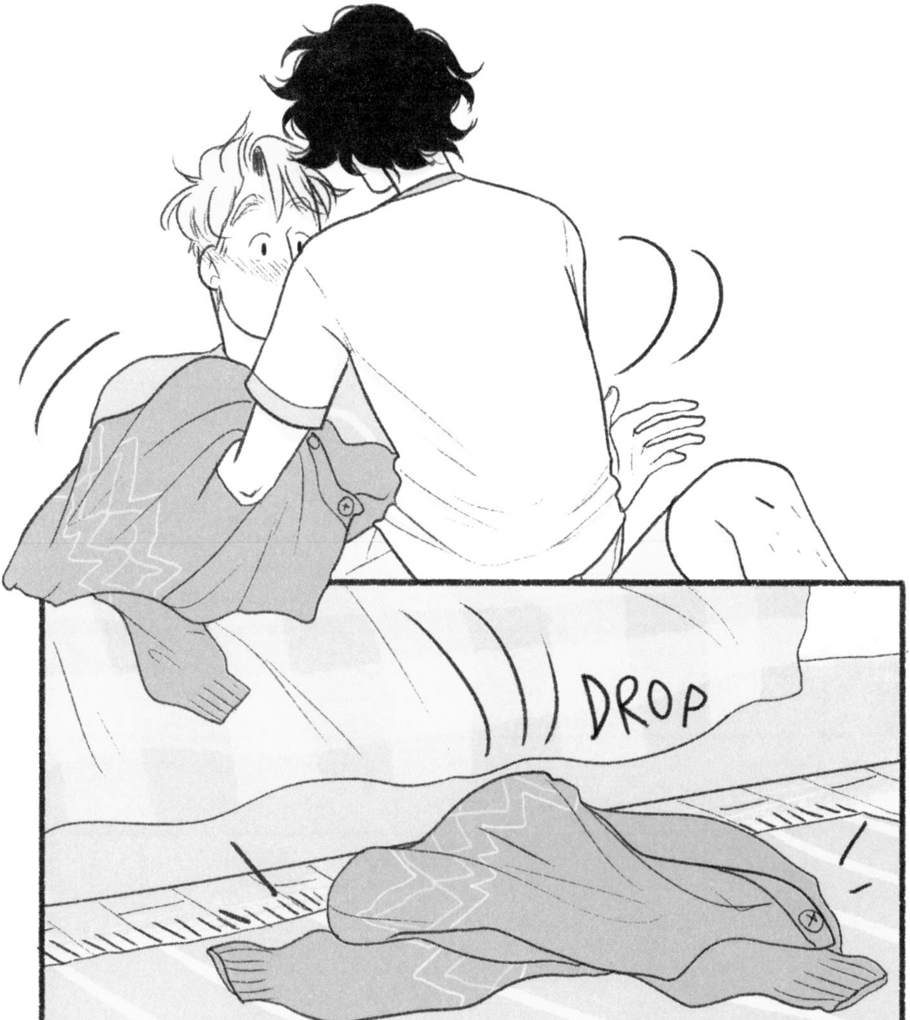
DROP

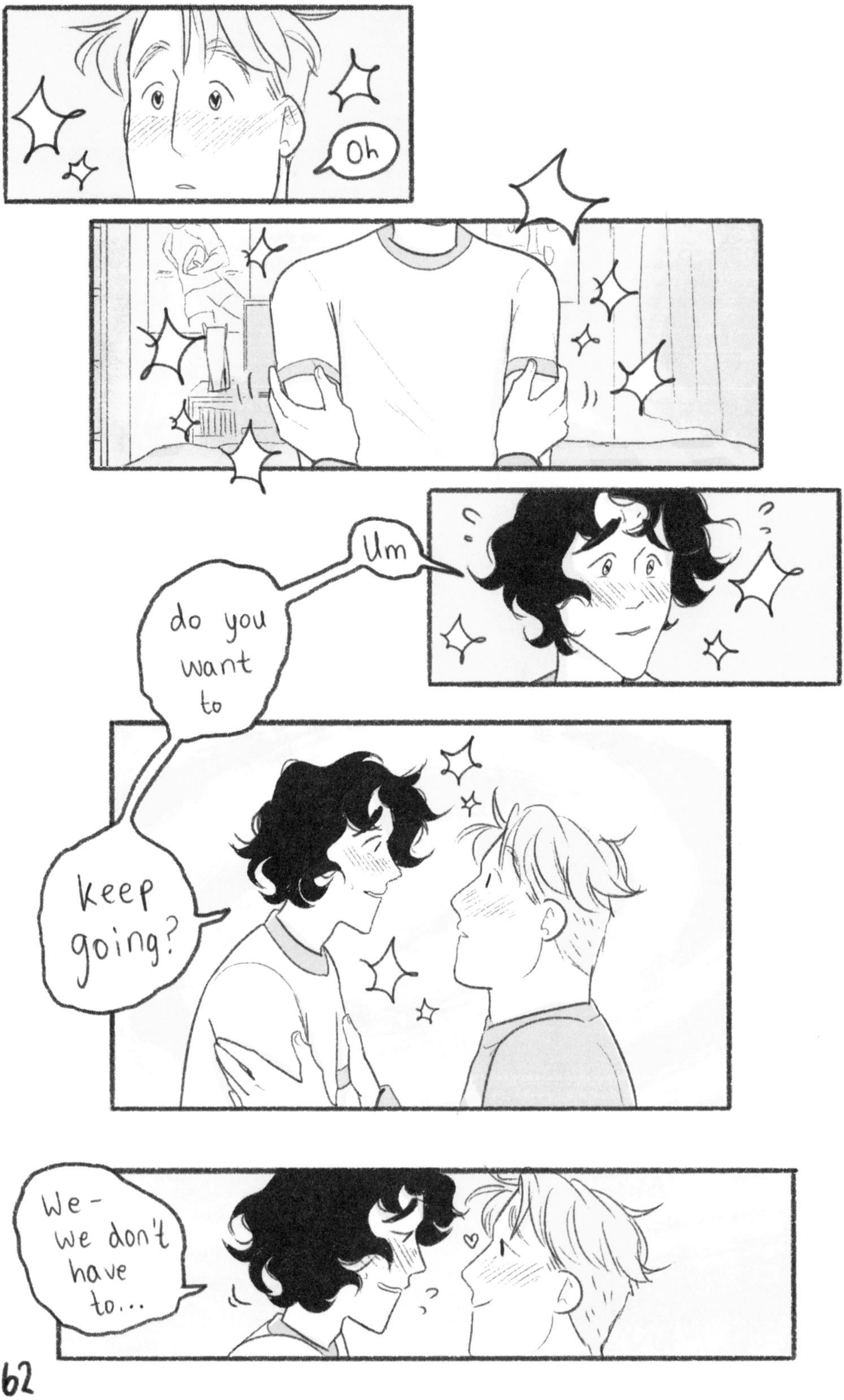
Oh
Um
do you want to
keep going?
We-
we don't have to...

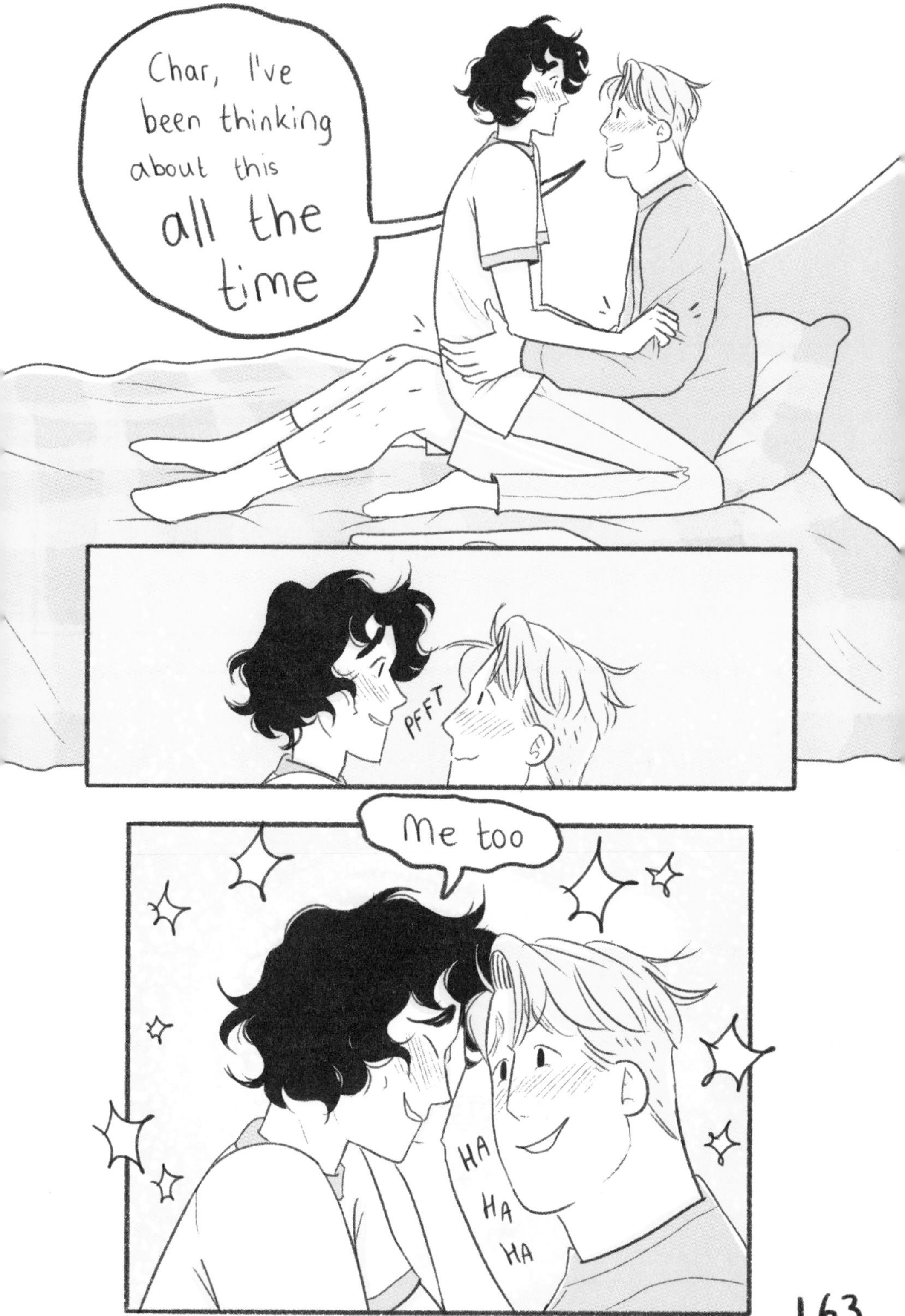
Char, I've been thinking about this all the time
PFFT
Me too
HA HA HA

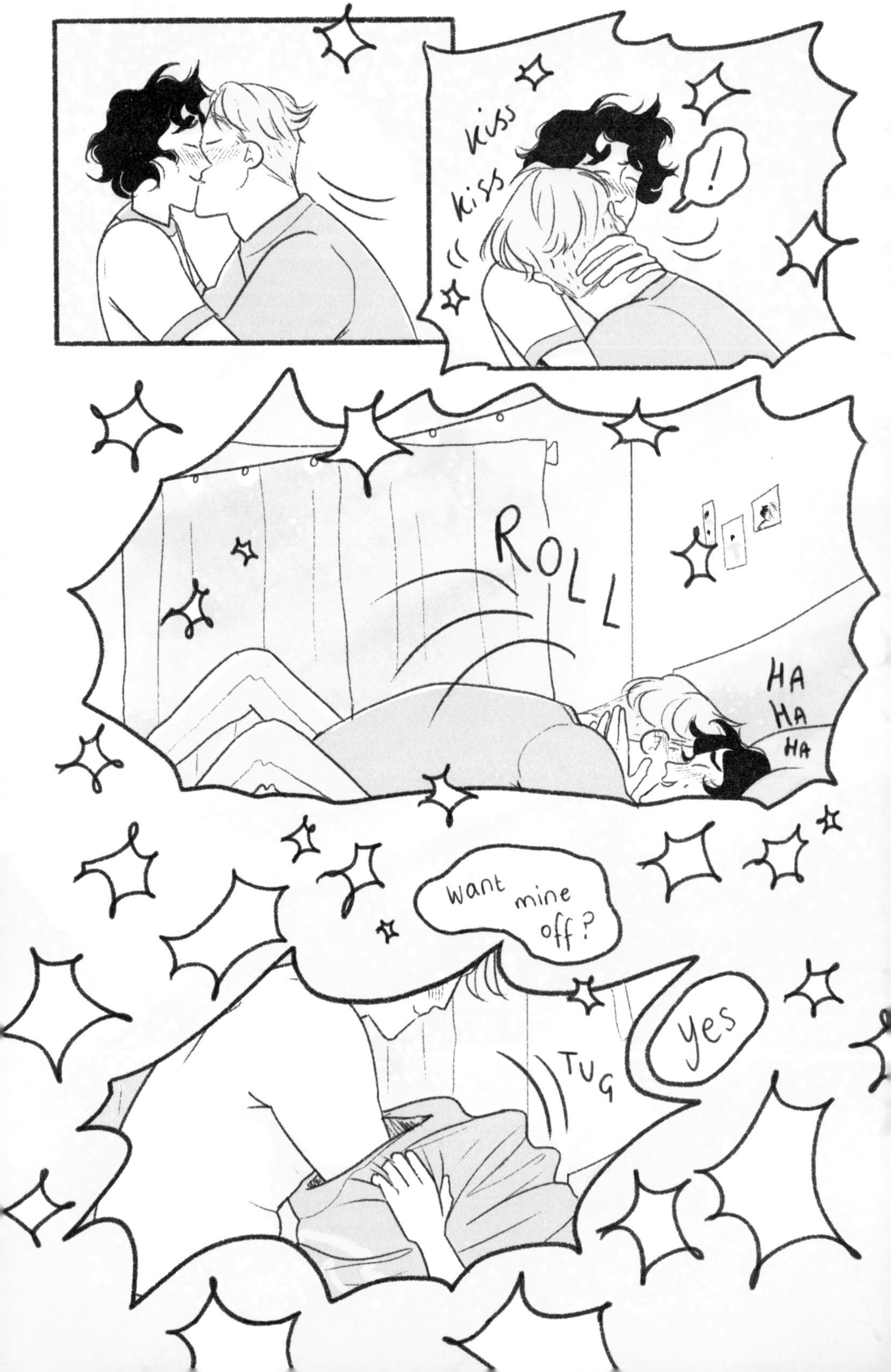
kiss
kiss
!
ROLL
HA
HA
HA
want mine off?
yes
TUG

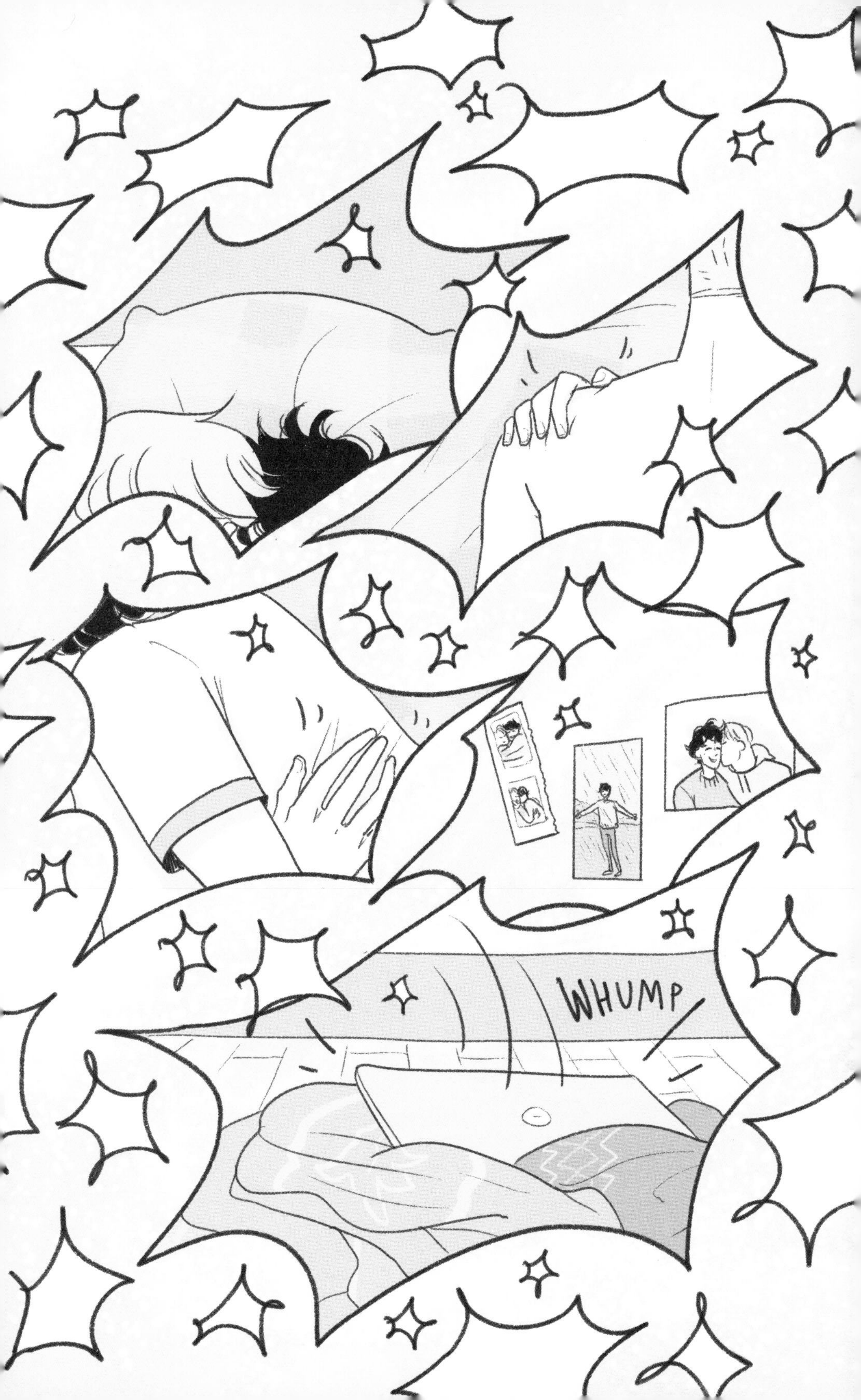
WHUMP

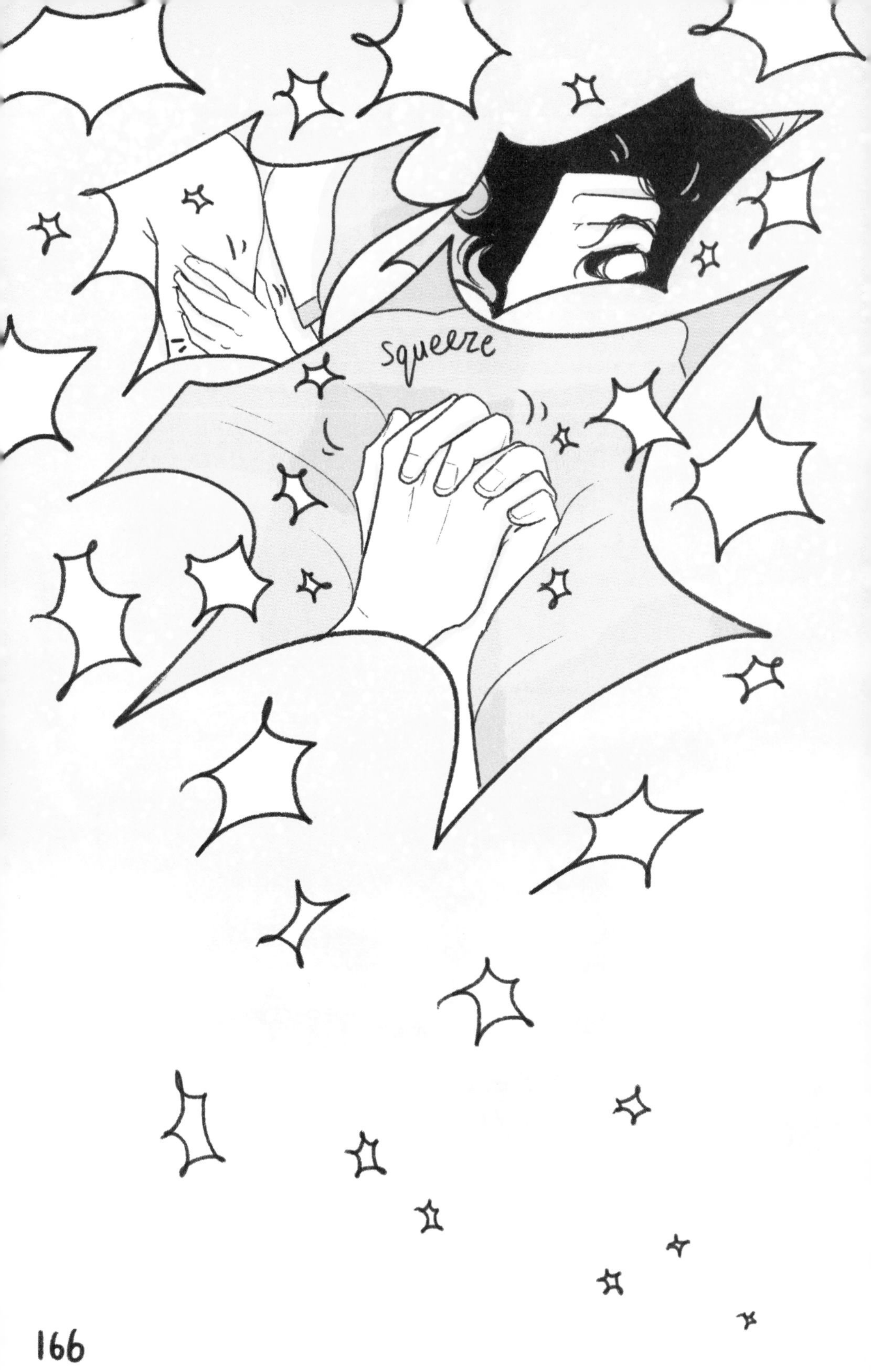
squeeze

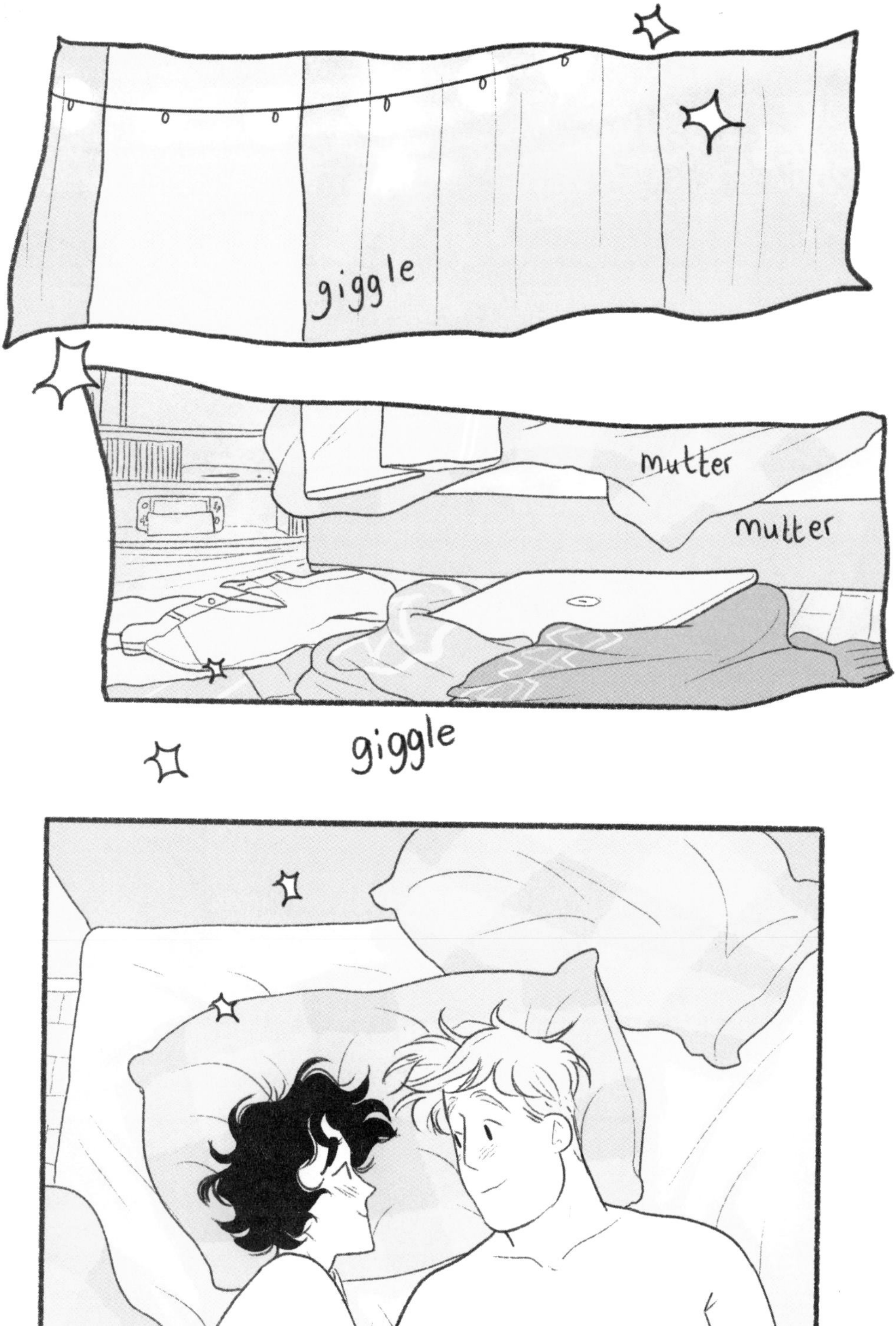
giggle
mutter
mutter
giggle

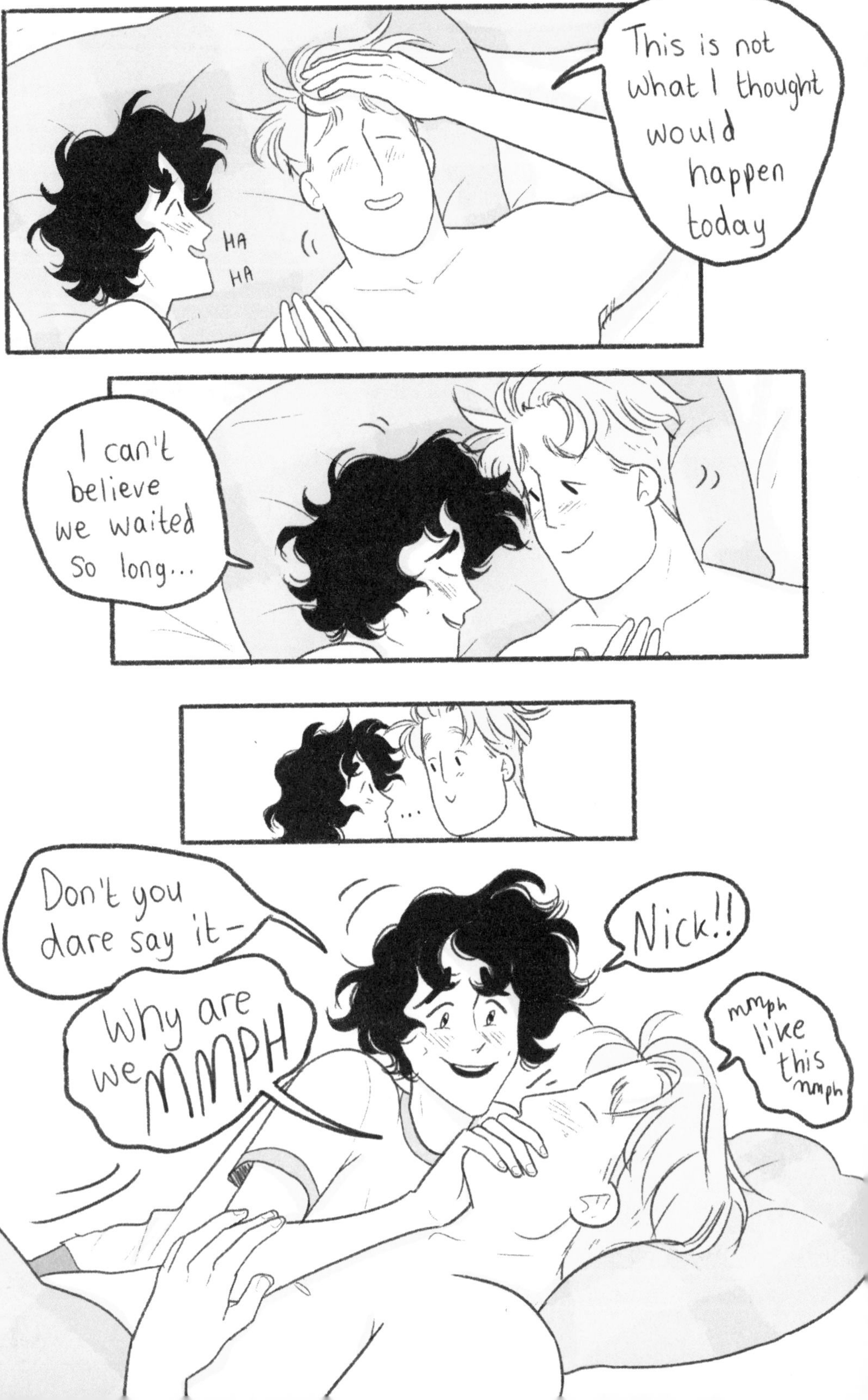
HA
HA
This is not what I thought would happen today
I can't believe we waited so long...
...
Don't you dare say it–
Nick!!
Why are we MMPH
mmph like this mmph

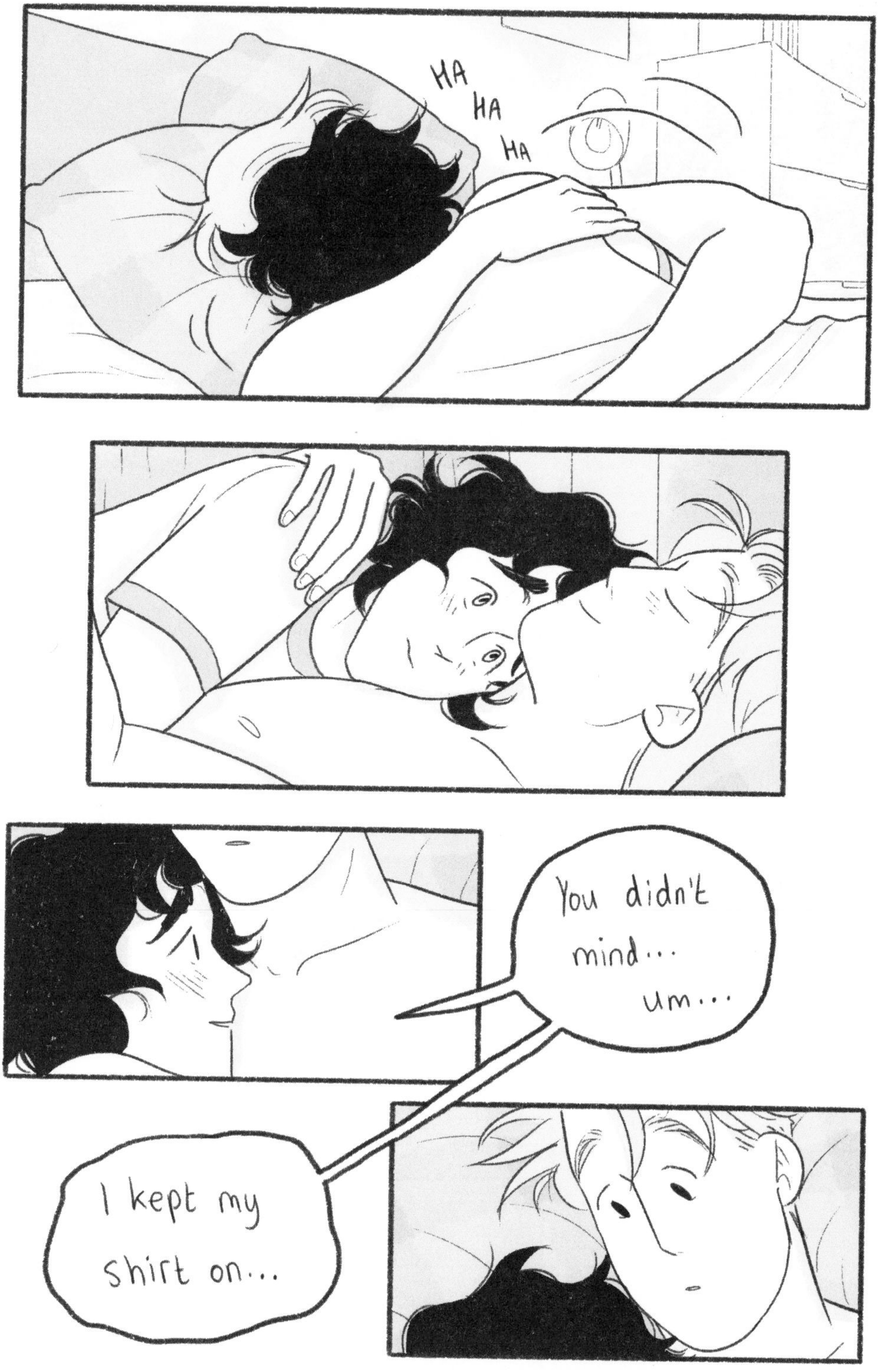
HA
HA
HA
You didn't mind... um...
I kept my shirt on...

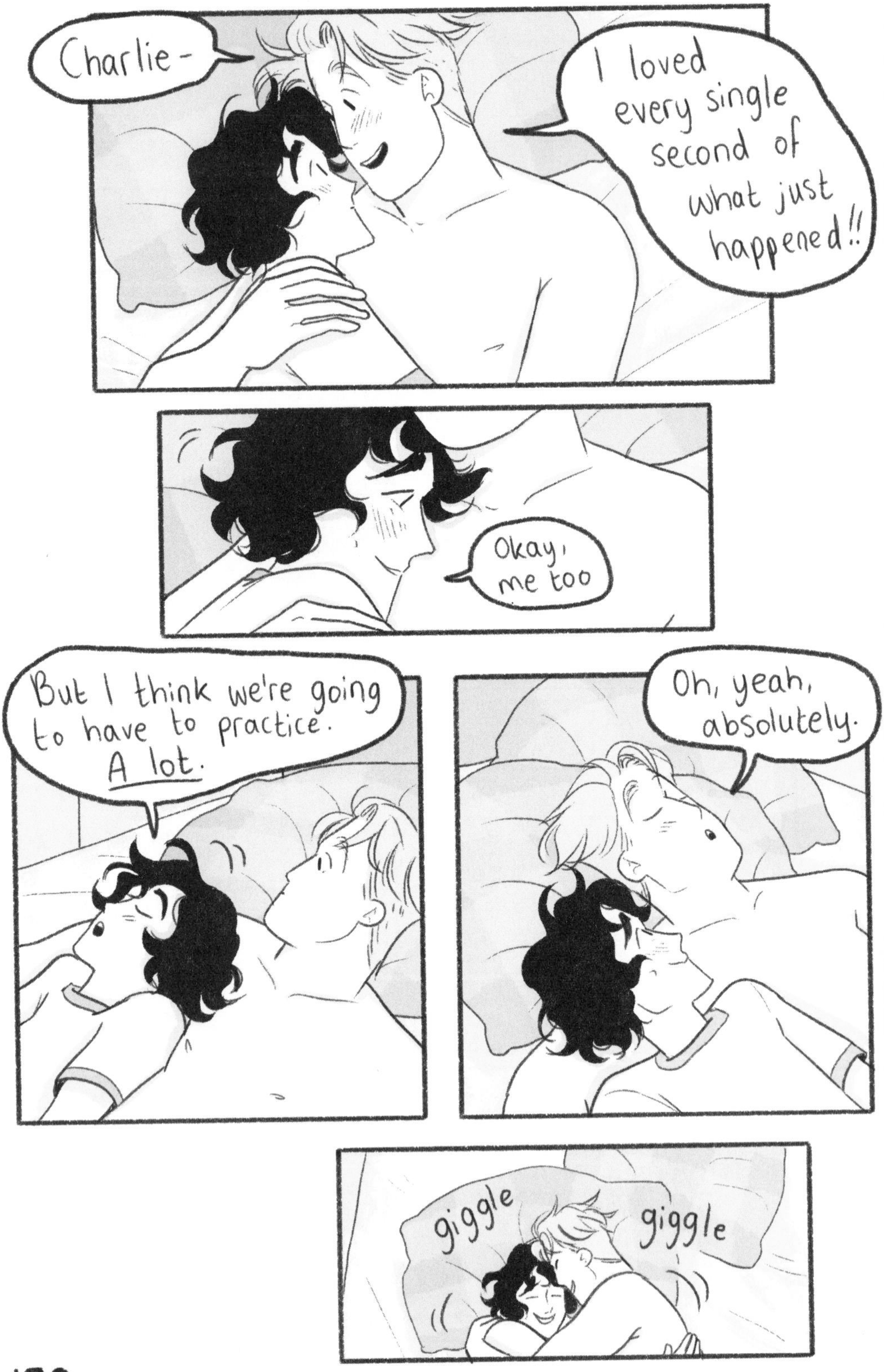
Charlie-
I loved every single second of what just happened!!
Okay, me too
But I think we're going to have to practice. A lot.
Oh, yeah, absolutely.
giggle
giggle

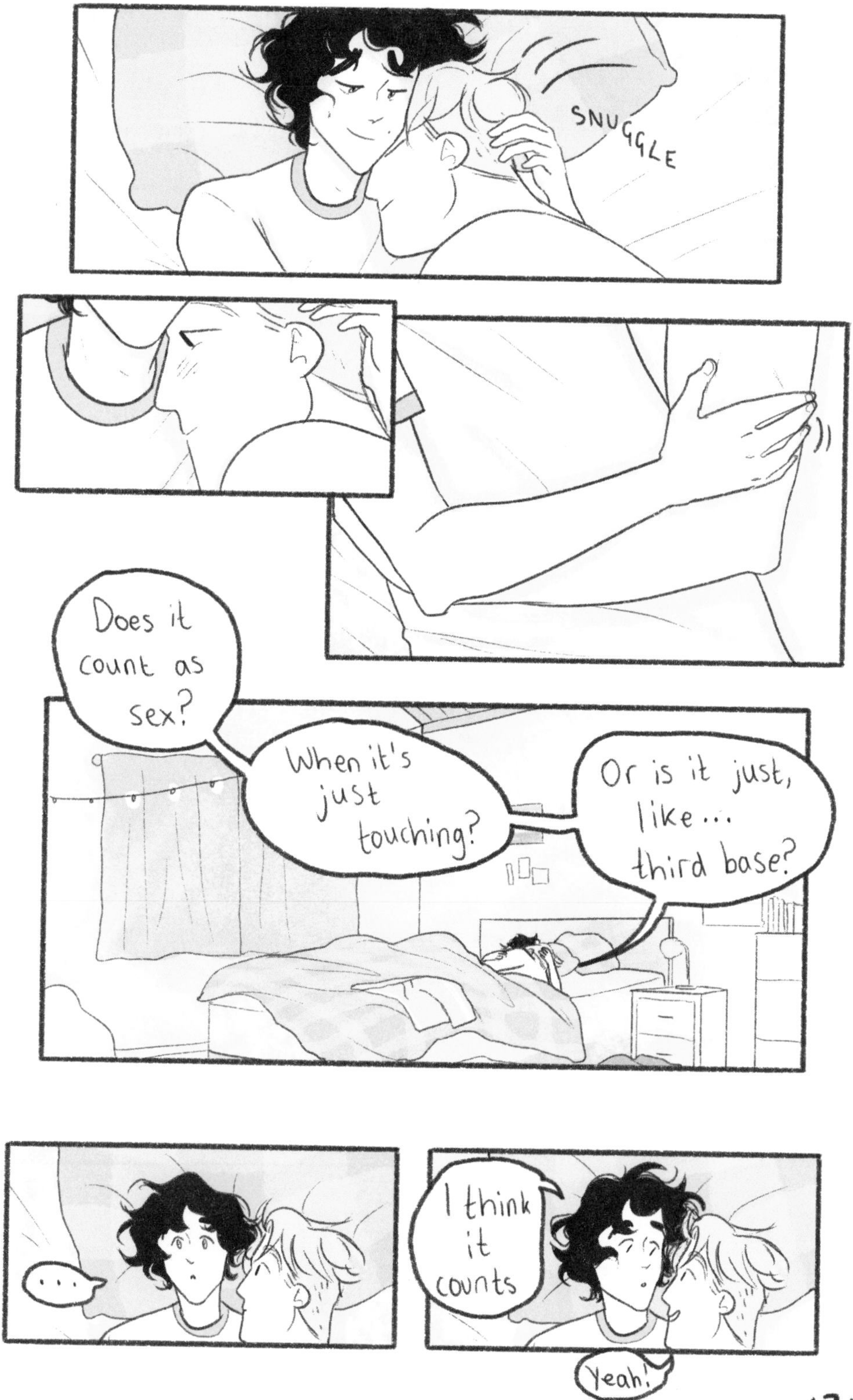
SNUGGLE
Does it count as sex?
When it's just touching?
Or is it just, like... third base?
...
I think it counts
Yeah!

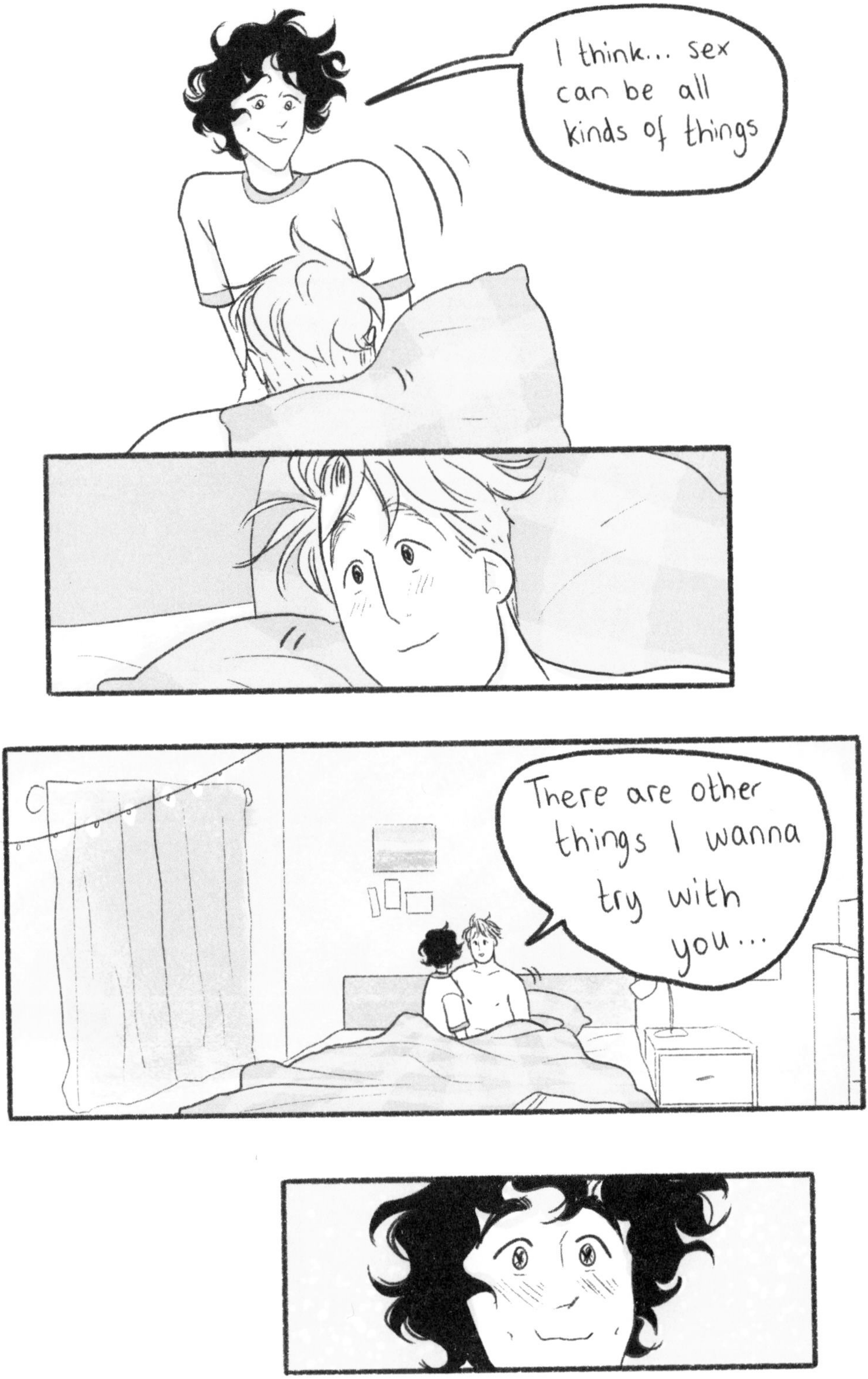
I think... sex can be all kinds of things
There are other things I wanna try with you...

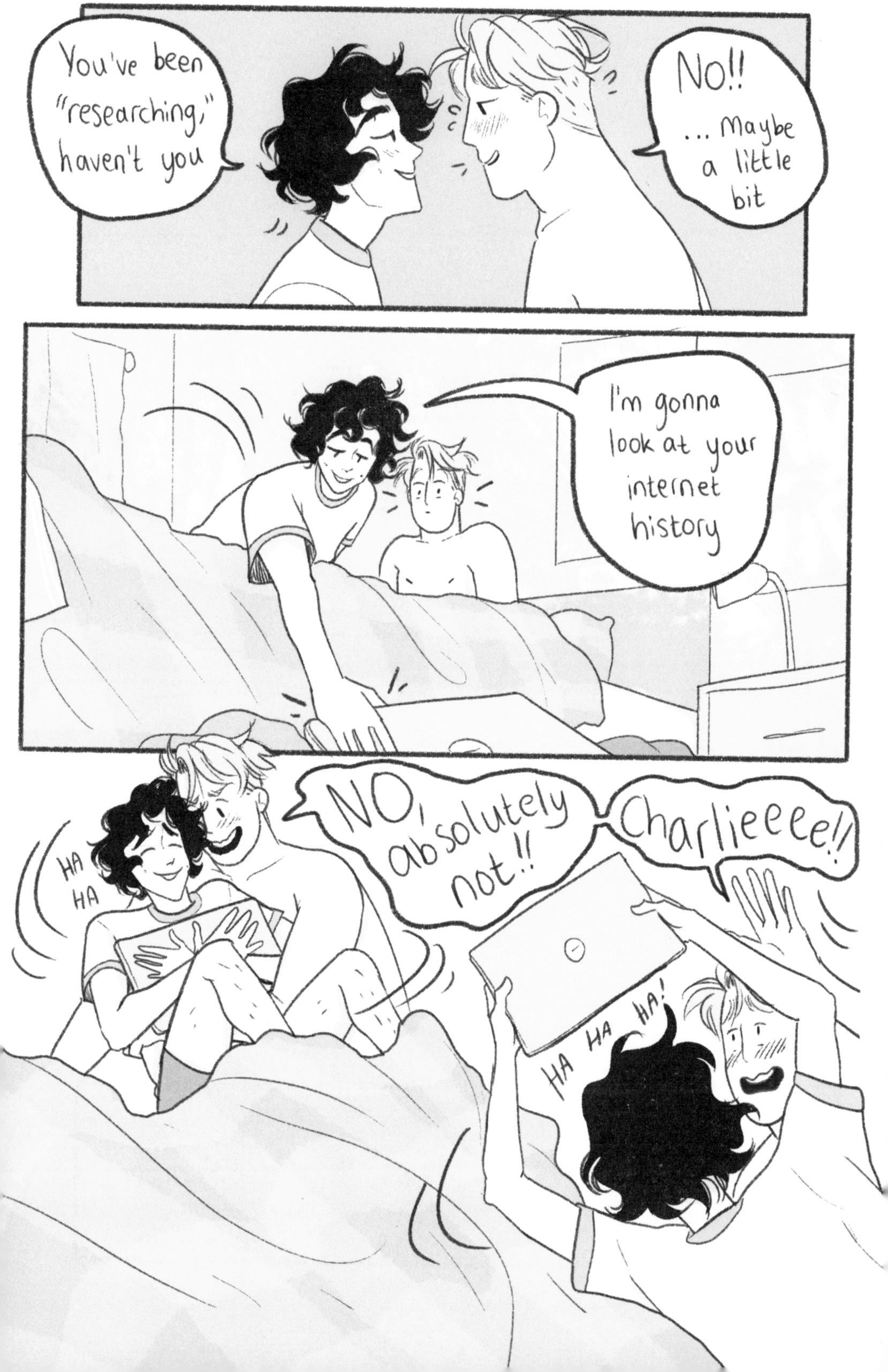
You've been "researching," haven't you
No!! ...Maybe a little bit
I'm gonna look at your internet history
HA HA
NO, absolutely not!!
Charlieeee!!
HA HA HA!

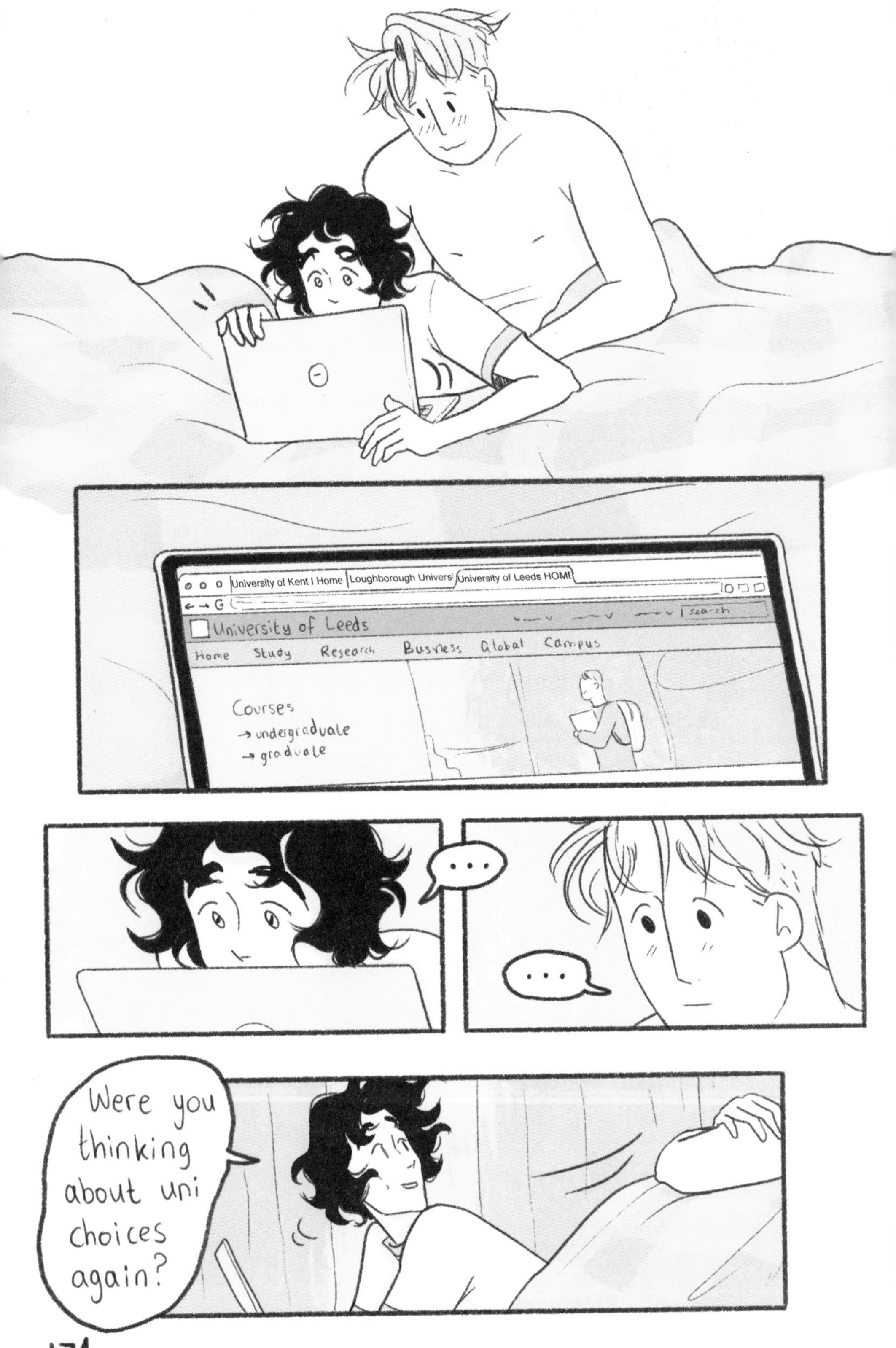
University of Kent I Home
Loughborough Univers
University of Leeds HOME
University of Leeds
Home
Study
Research
Busness
Global
Campus
Courses
→ undergraduate
→ graduate
...
...
Were you thinking about uni choices again?

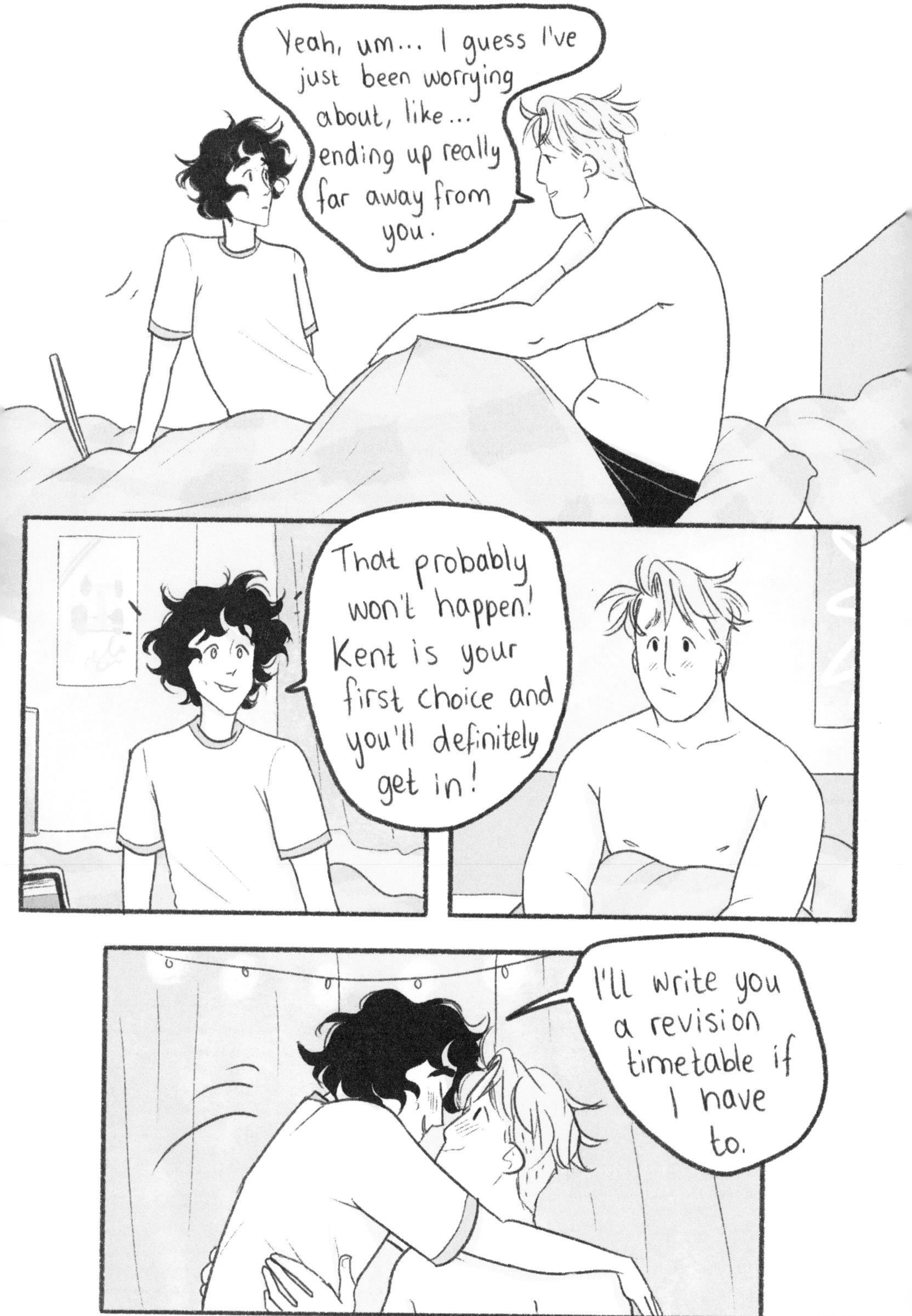
Yeah, um... I guess I've just been worrying about, like... ending up really far away from you.
That probably won't happen! Kent is your first choice and you'll definitely get in!
I'll write you a revision timetable if I have to.

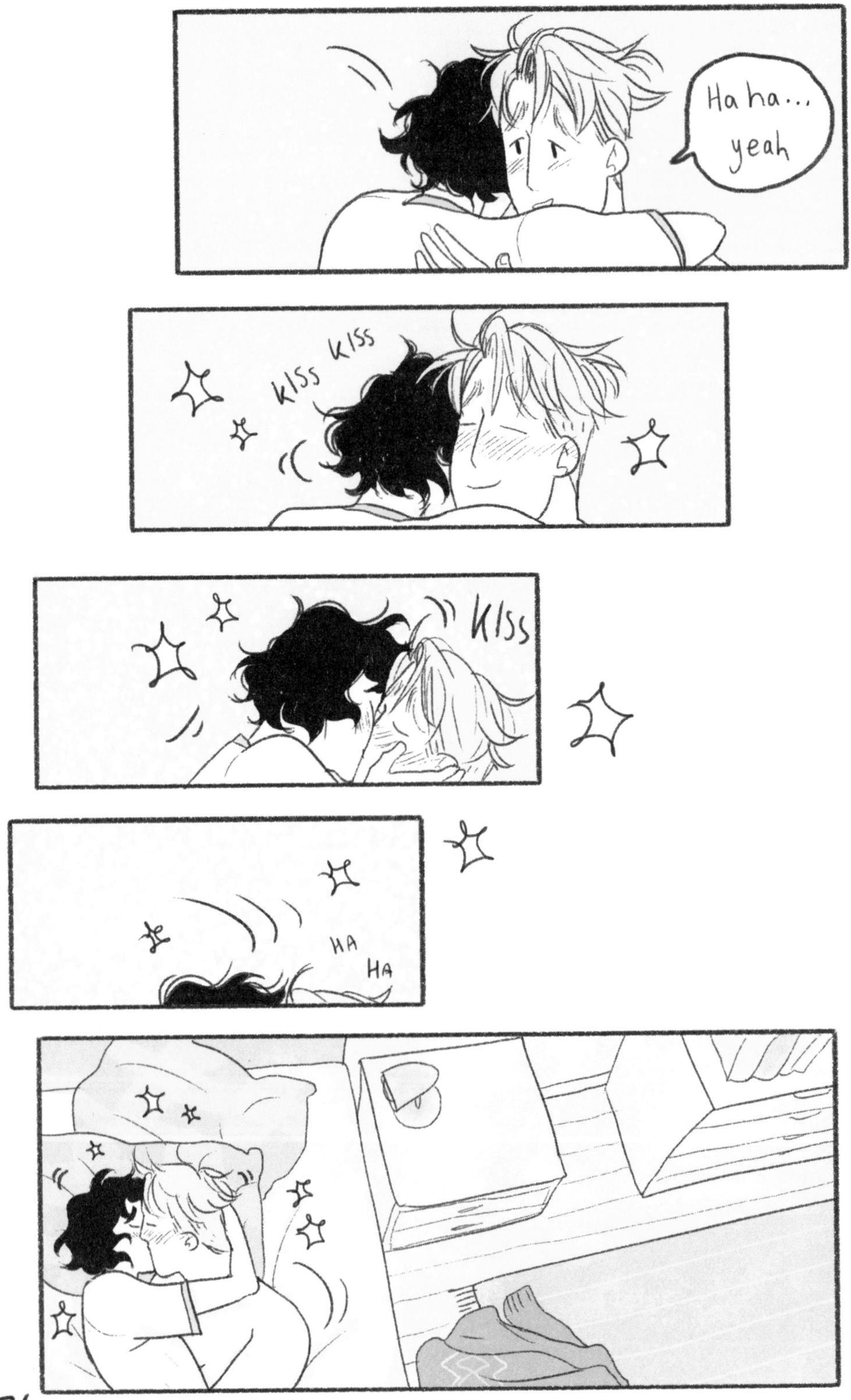
Haha... yeah
KISS KISS
KISS
HA HA

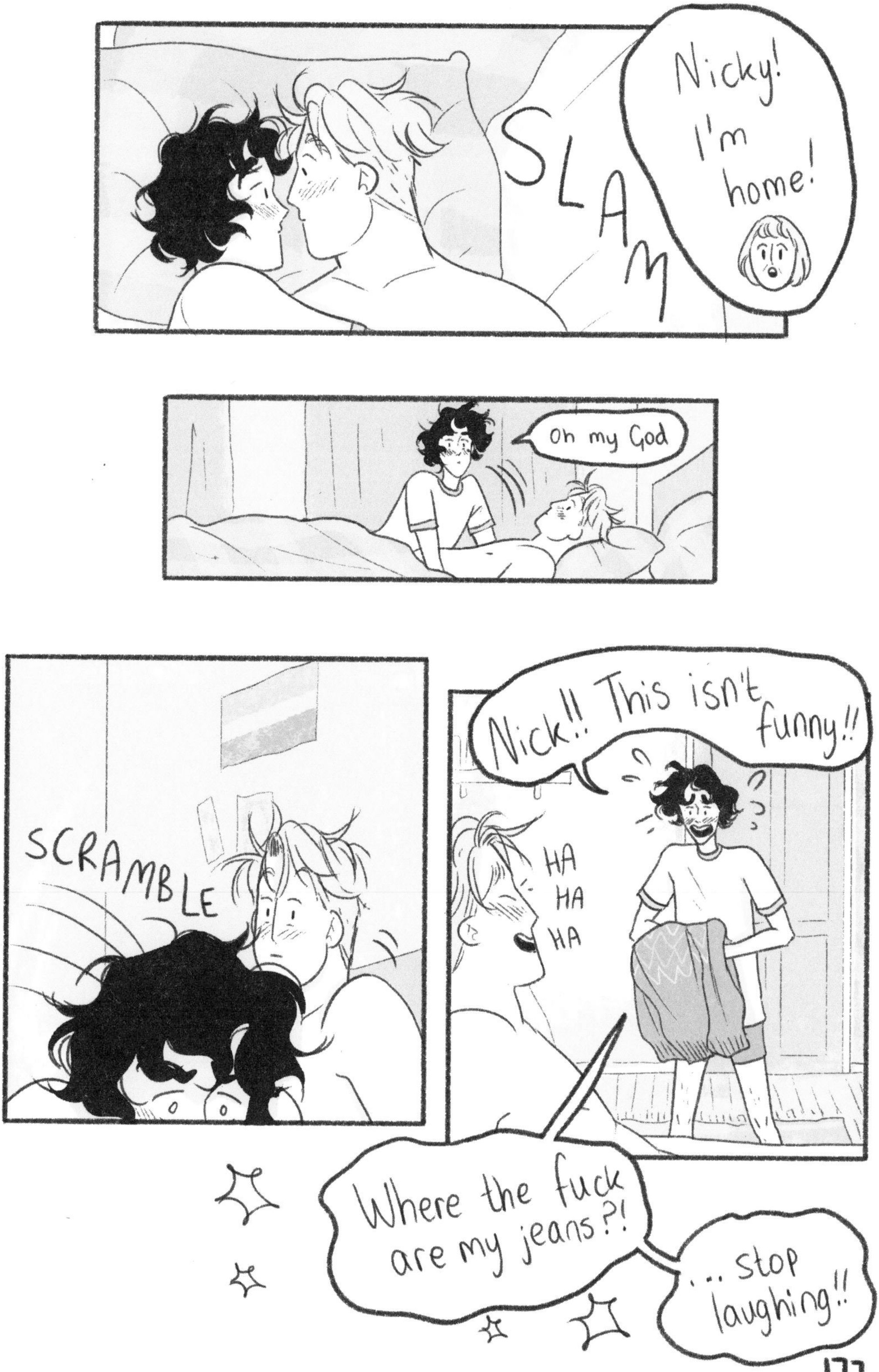
SLAM
Nicky! I'm home!
Oh my God
SCRAMBLE
Nick!! This isn't funny!!
HA HA HA
Where the fuck are my jeans?!
... stop laughing!!

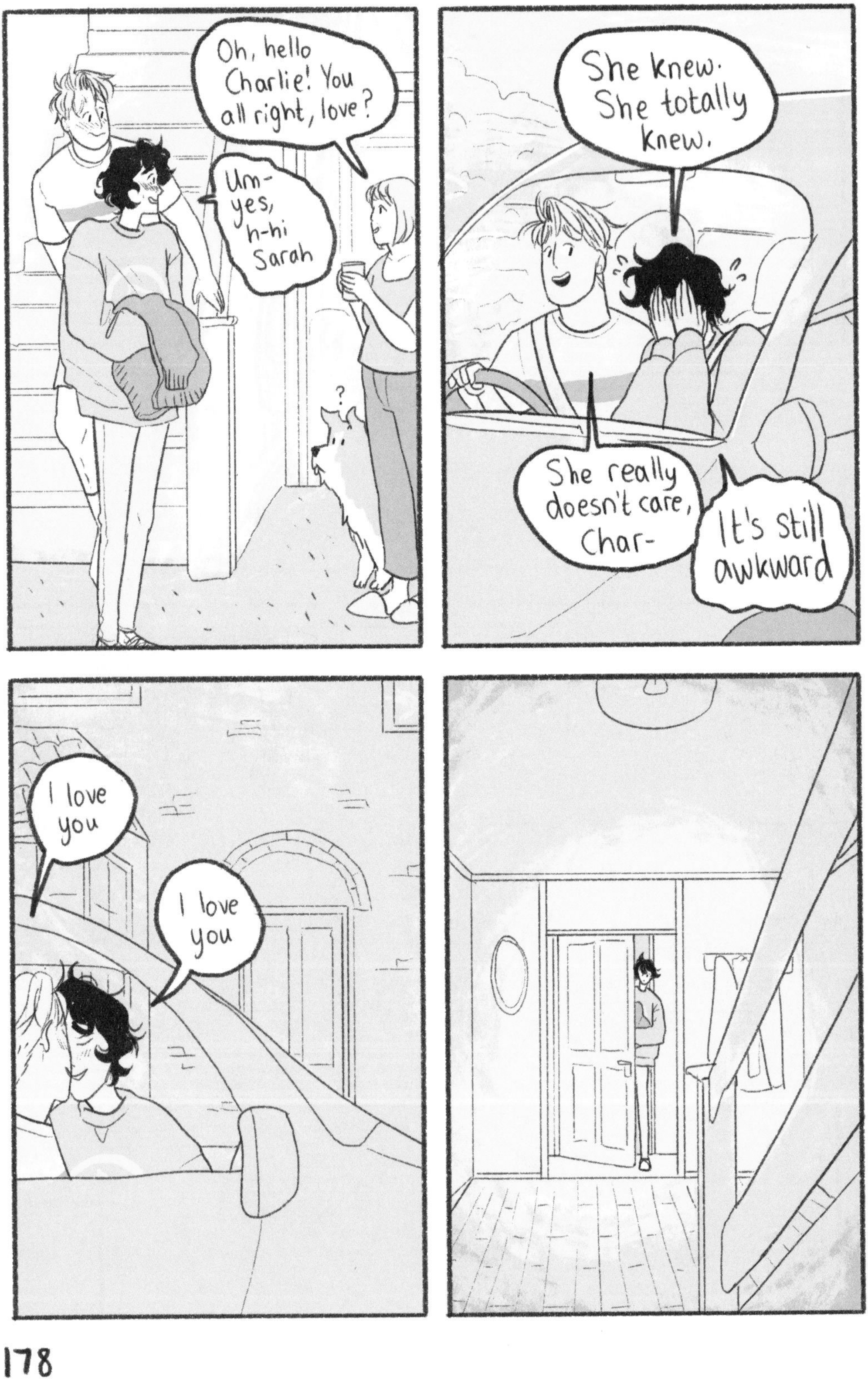
Oh, hello Charlie! You all right, love?
Um- yes, h-hi Sarah
?
She knew. She totally knew.
She really doesn't care, Char-
It's still awkward
I love you
I love you

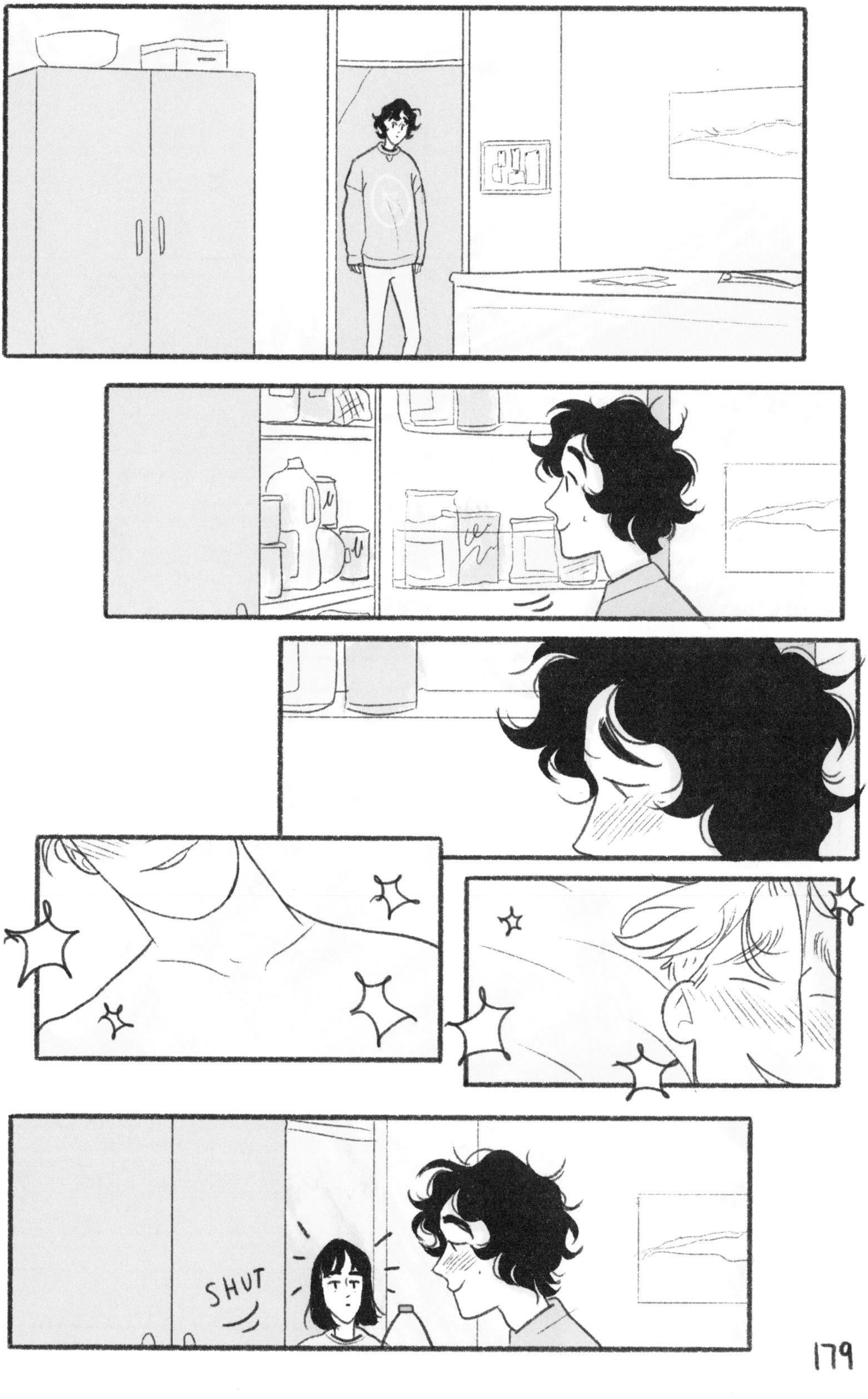
SHUT

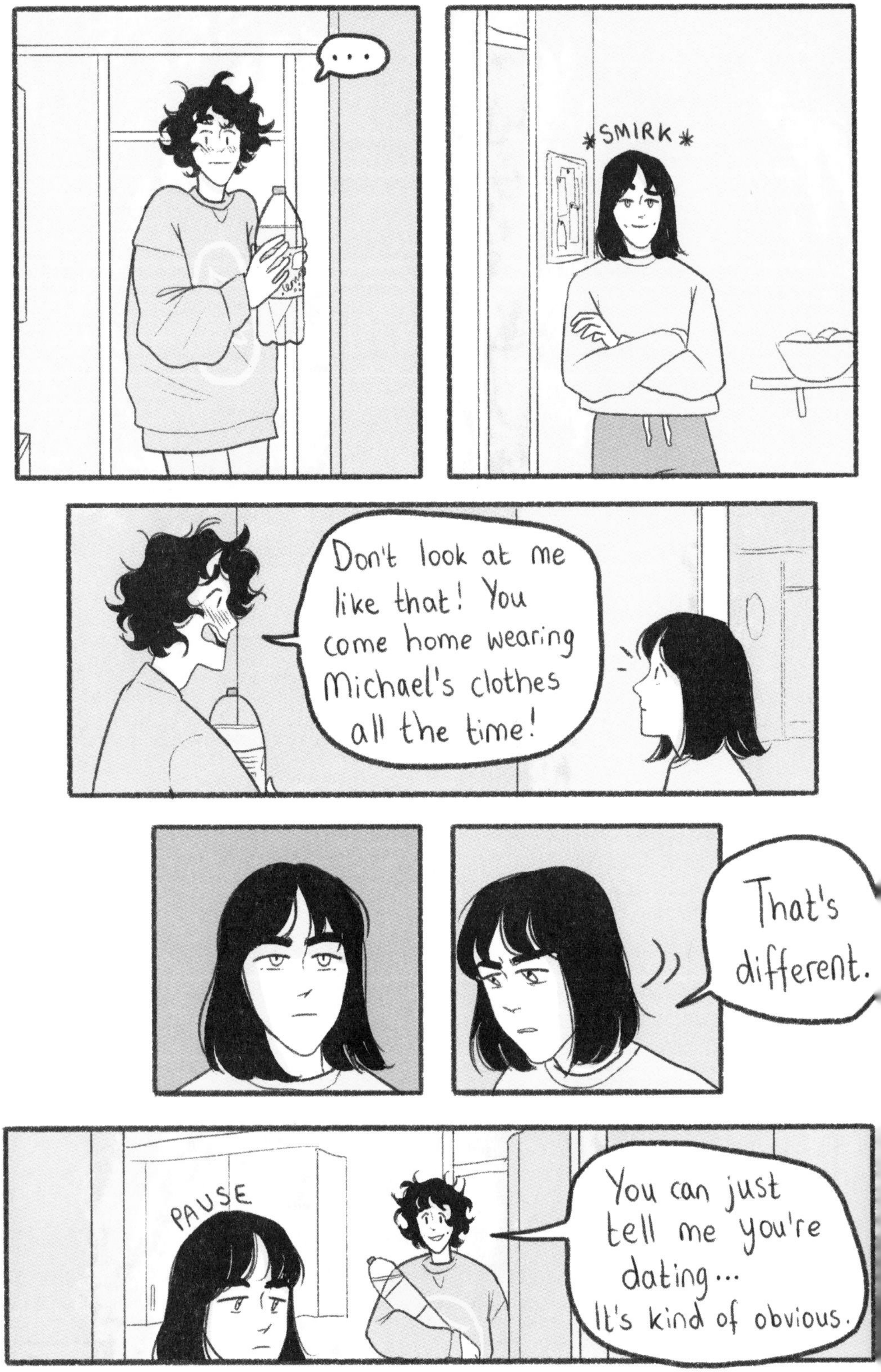
...
SMIRK
Don't look at me like that! You come home wearing Michael's clothes all the time!
That's different.
PAUSE
You can just tell me you're dating... It's kind of obvious.

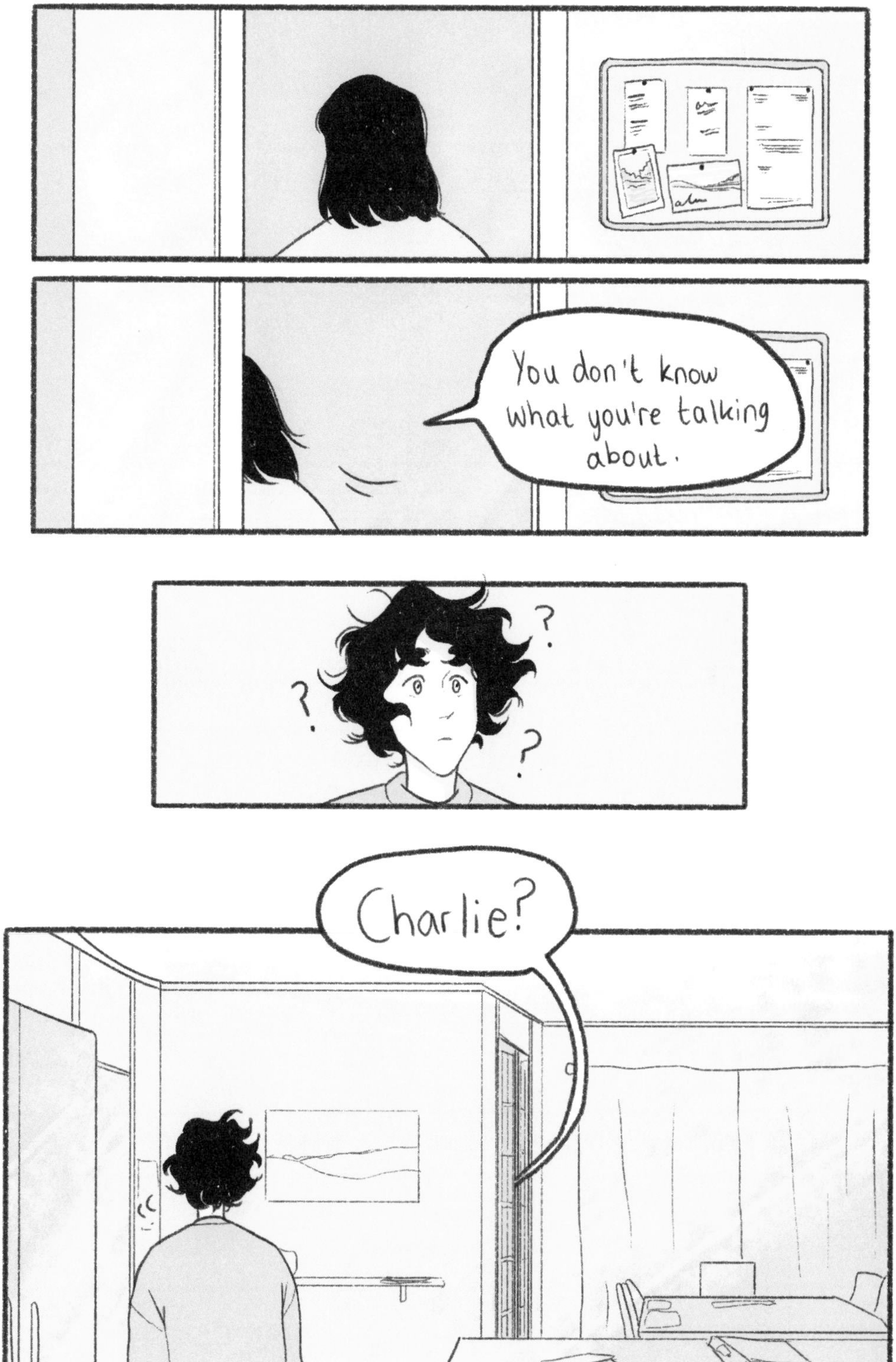
You don't know what you're talking about.
? ? ?
Charlie?

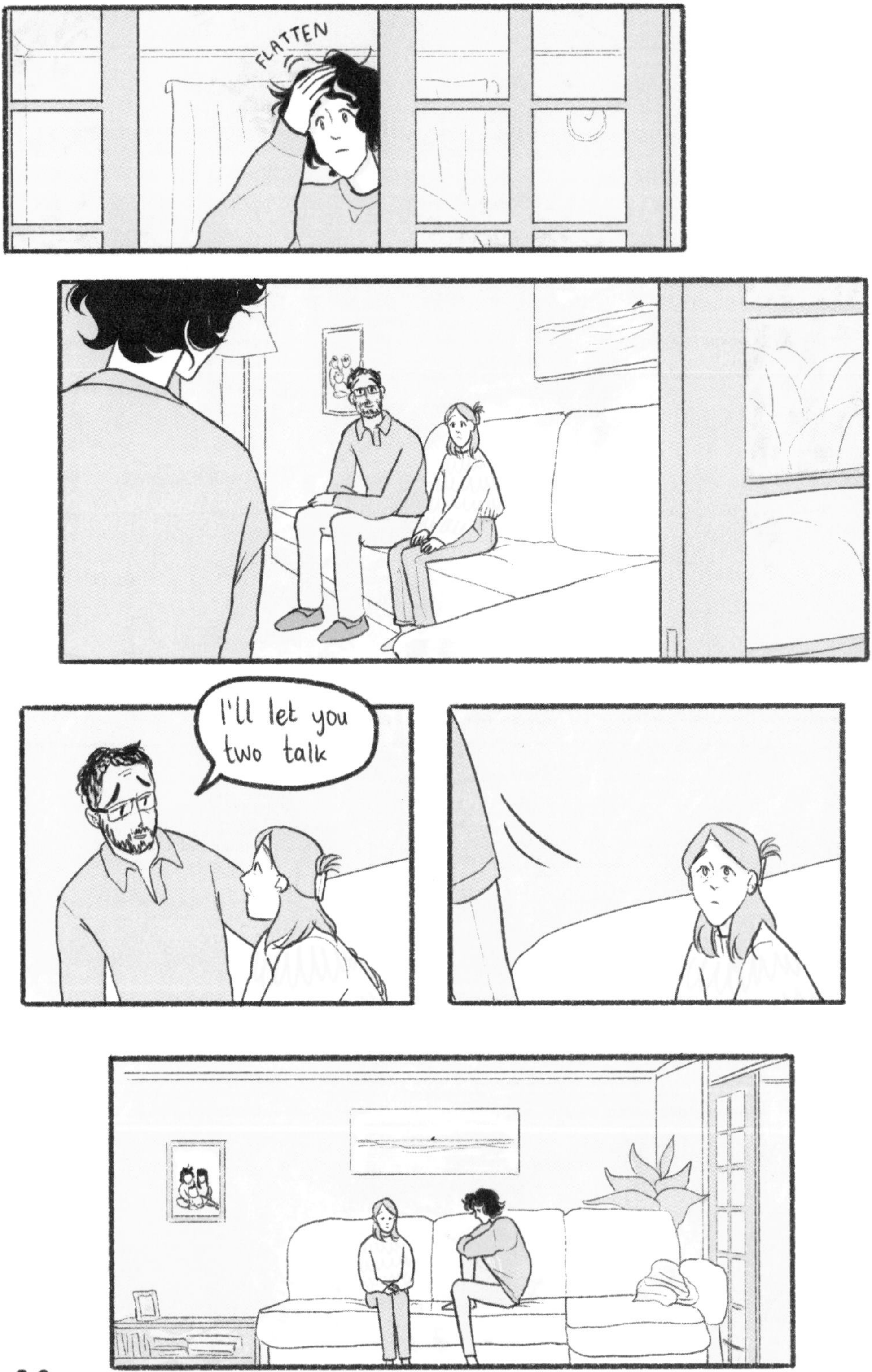
FLATTEN
I'll let you two talk

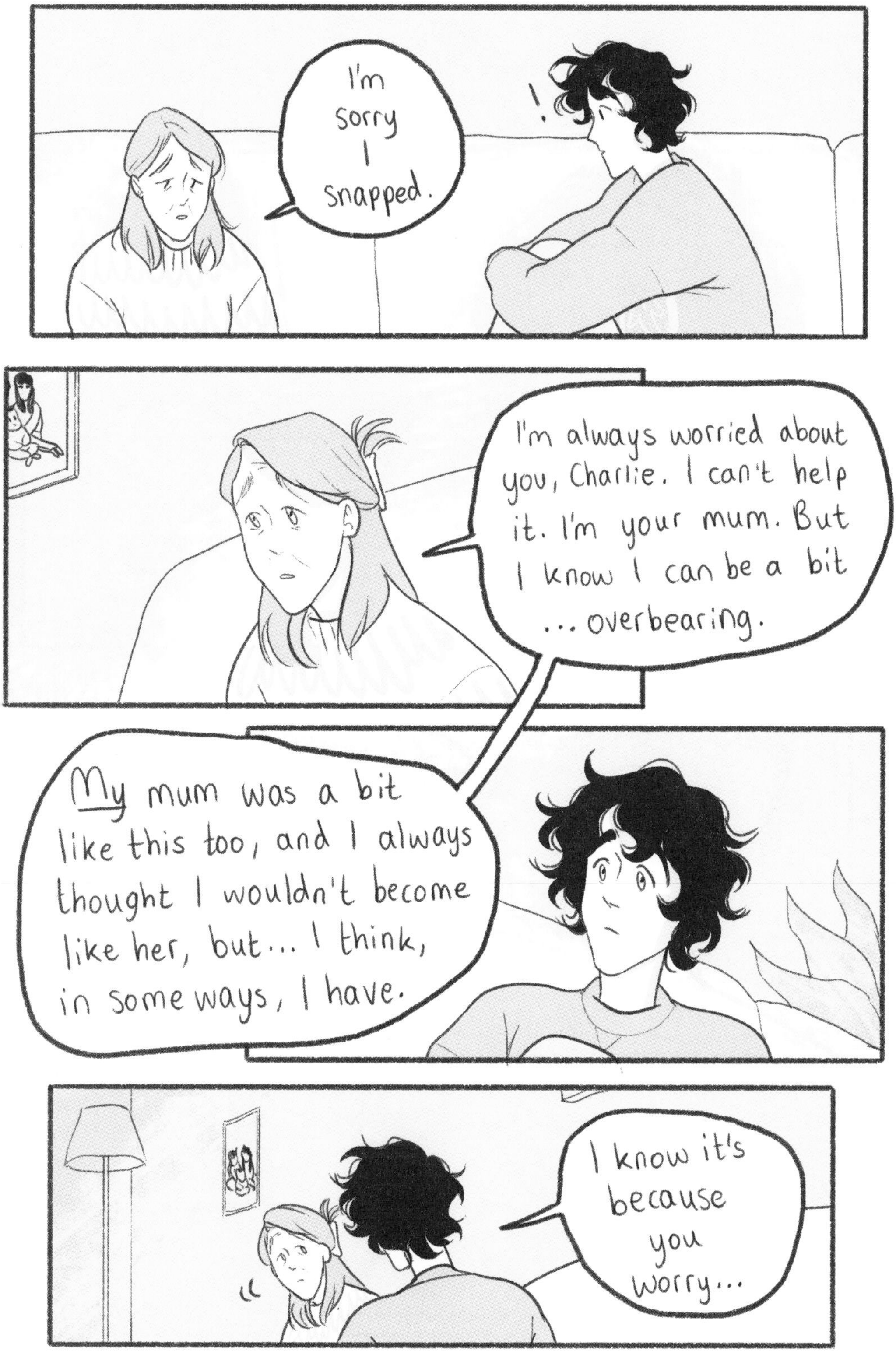
I'm sorry I snapped.
!
I'm always worried about you, Charlie. I can't help it. I'm your mum. But I know I can be a bit ...overbearing.
My mum was a bit like this too, and I always thought I wouldn't become like her, but... I think, in some ways, I have.
I know it's because you worry...

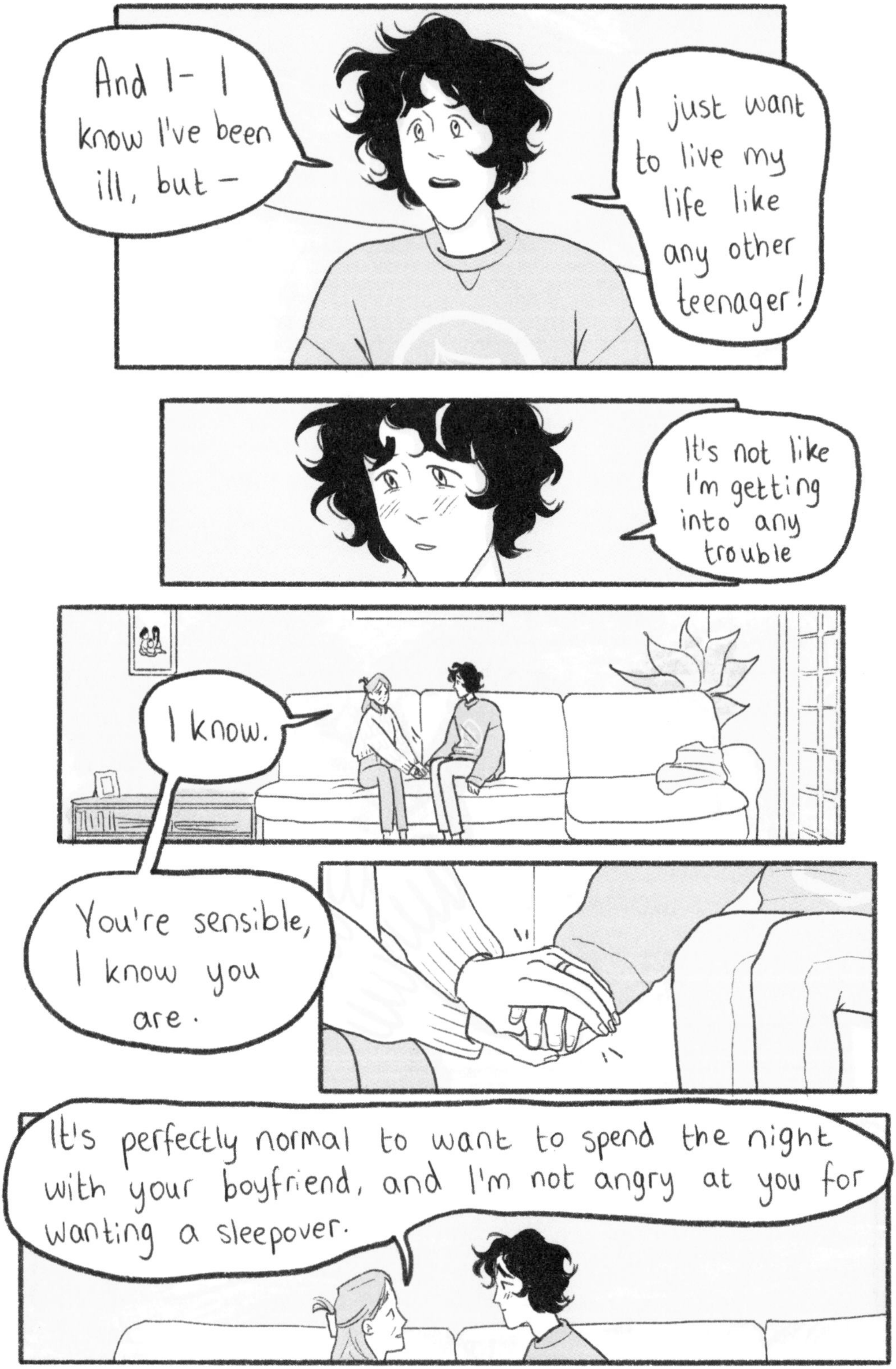
And I- I know I've been ill, but -
I just want to live my life like any other teenager!
It's not like I'm getting into any trouble
I know.
You're sensible, I know you are.
It's perfectly normal to want to spend the night with your boyfriend, and I'm not angry at you for wanting a sleepover.

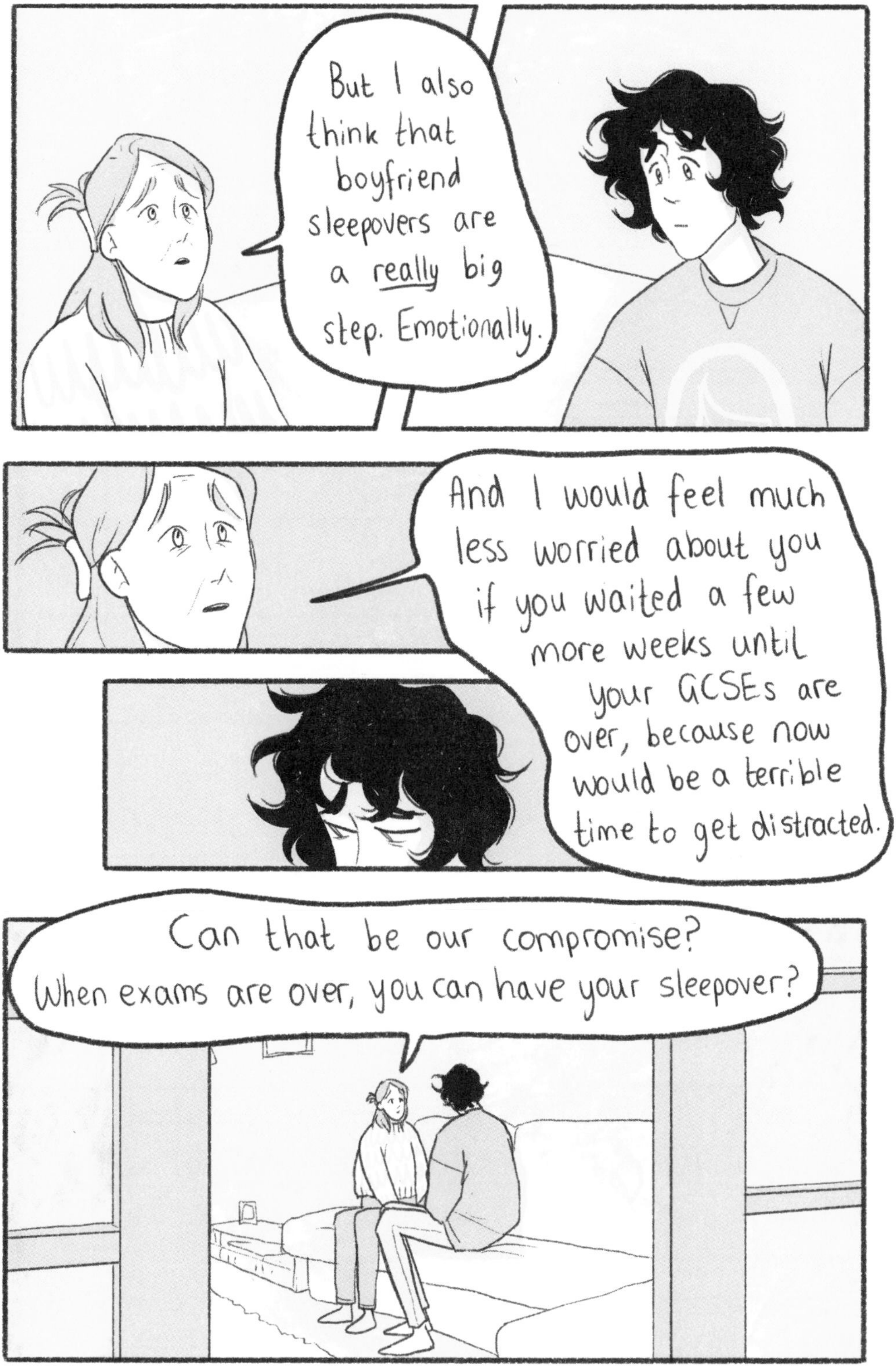
But I also think that boyfriend sleepovers are a really big step. Emotionally.
And I would feel much less worried about you if you waited a few more weeks until your GCSEs are over, because now would be a terrible time to get distracted.
Can that be our compromise?
When exams are over, you can have your sleepover?

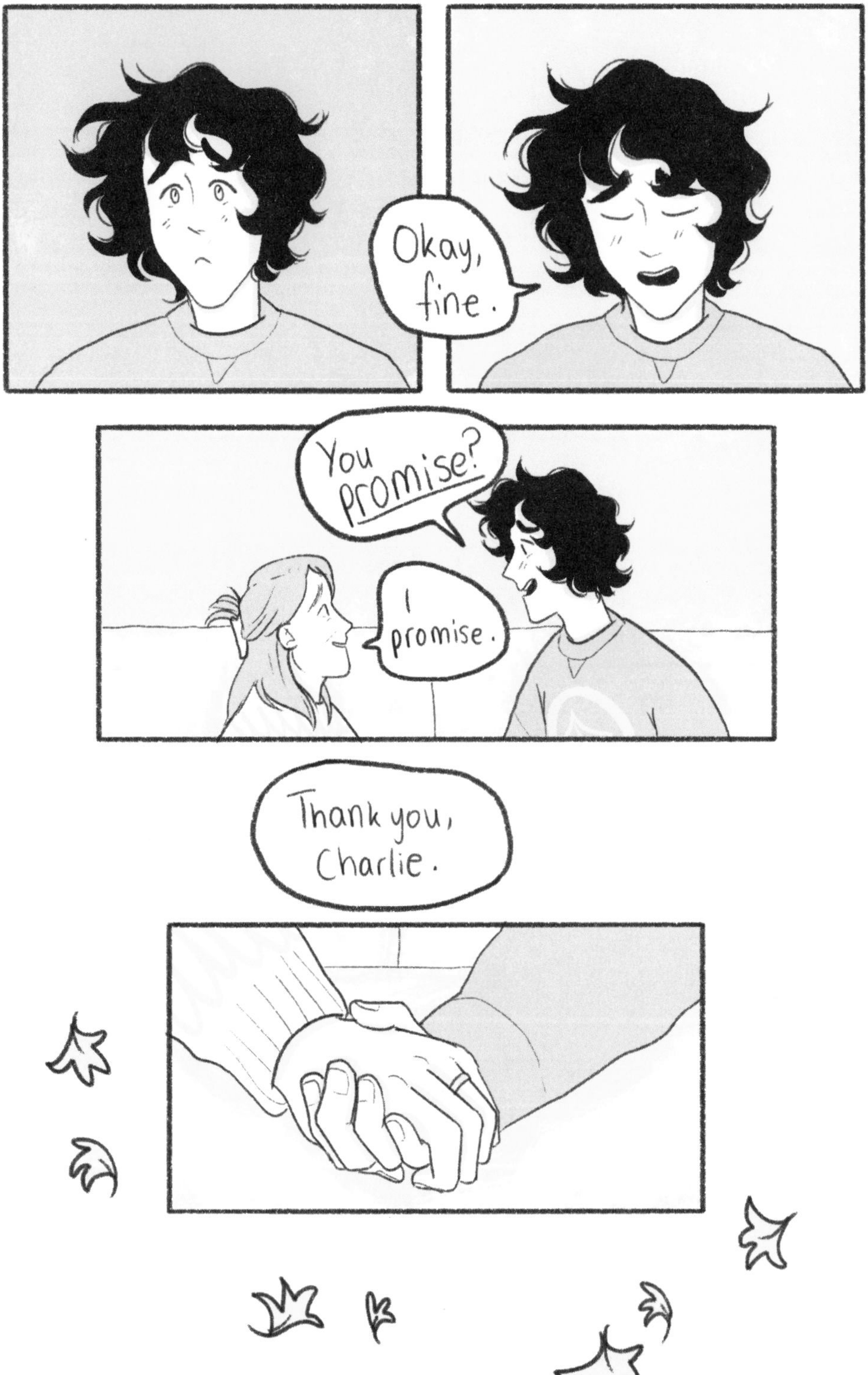
Okay, fine.
You promise?
I promise.
Thank you, Charlie.

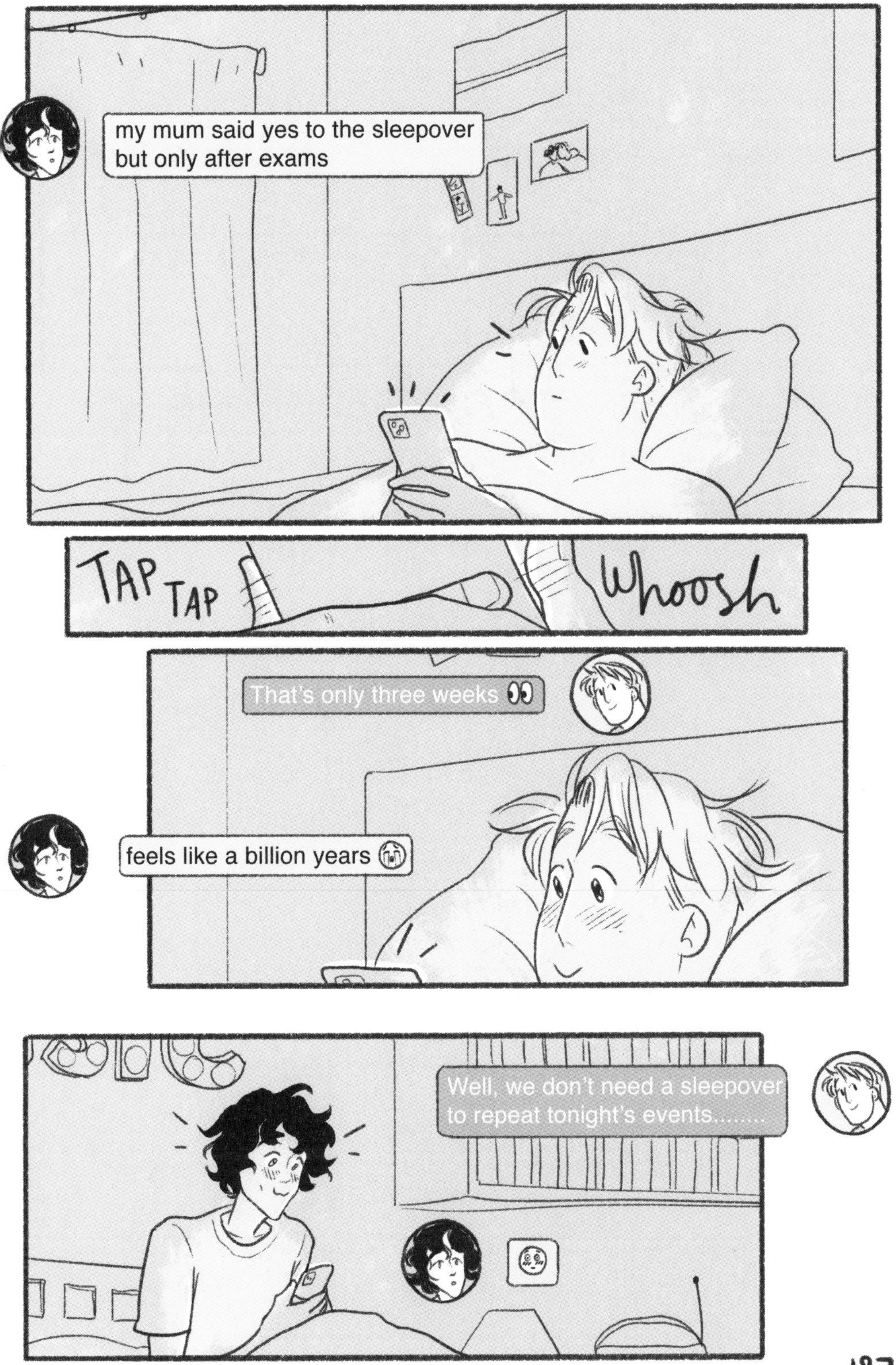
my mum said yes to the sleepover
but only after exams
TAP TAP
Whoosh
That's only three weeks
feels like a billion years
Well, we don't need a sleepover
to repeat tonight's events........

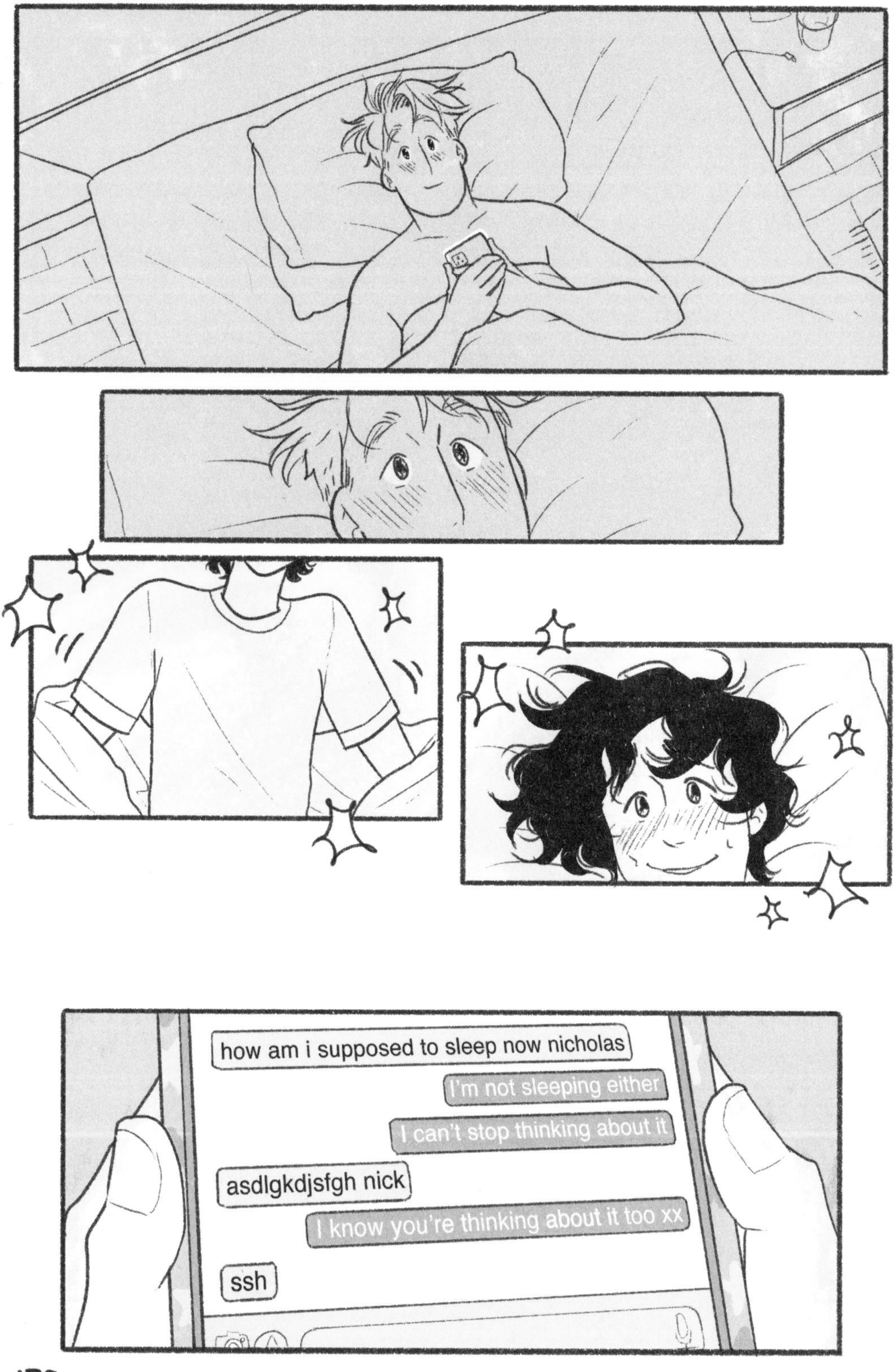
how am i supposed to sleep now nicholas
I'm not sleeping either
I can't stop thinking about it
asdlgkdjsfgh nick
I know you're thinking about it too xx
ssh

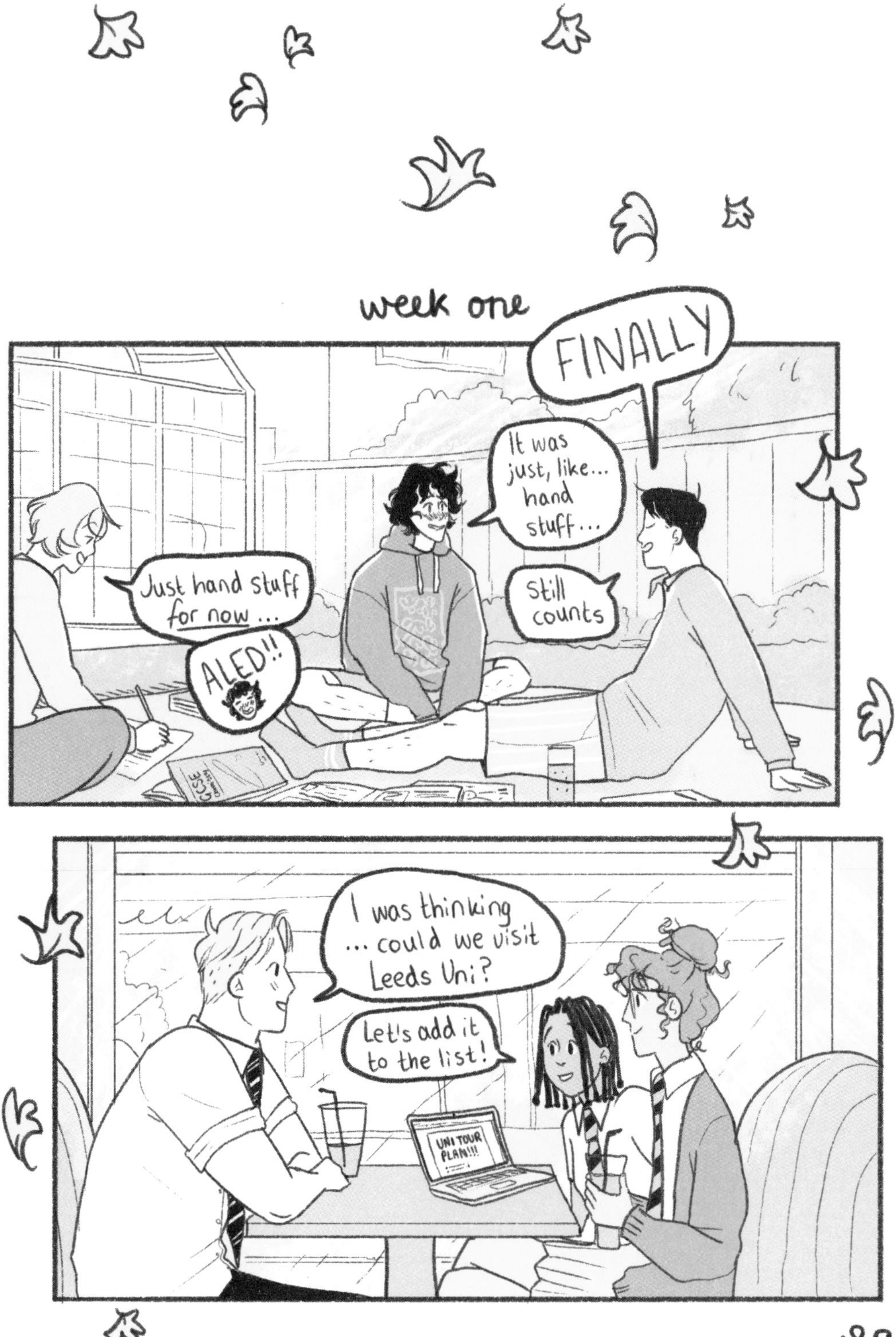
week one
FINALLY
It was just, like... hand stuff...
Still counts
Just hand stuff for now...
ALED!!
GCSE
I was thinking ... could we visit Leeds Uni?
Let's add it to the list!
UNI TOUR PLAN!!!

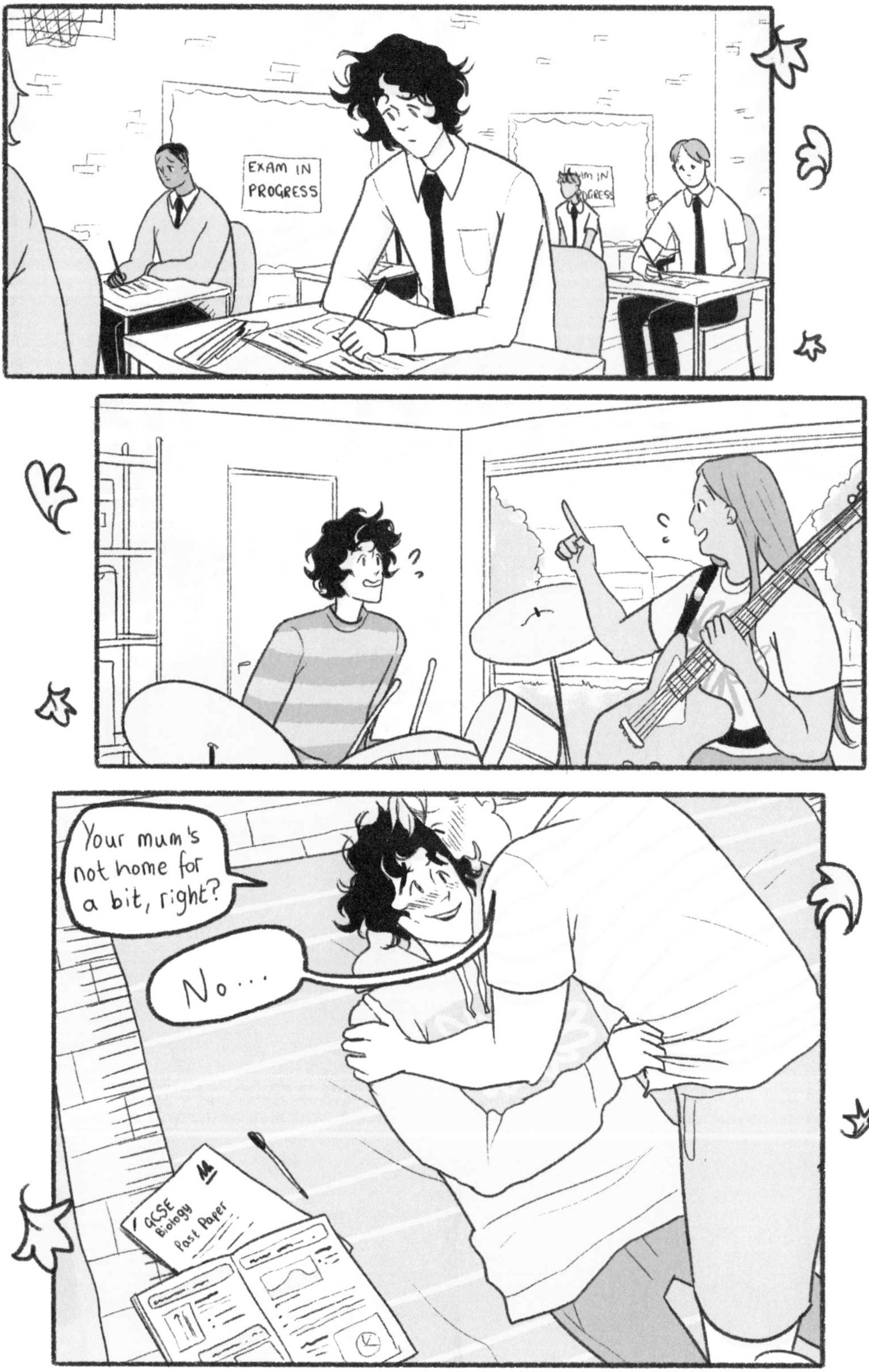
EXAM IN PROGRESS
Your mum's not home for a bit, right?
No...
GCSE Biology Past Paper

week two

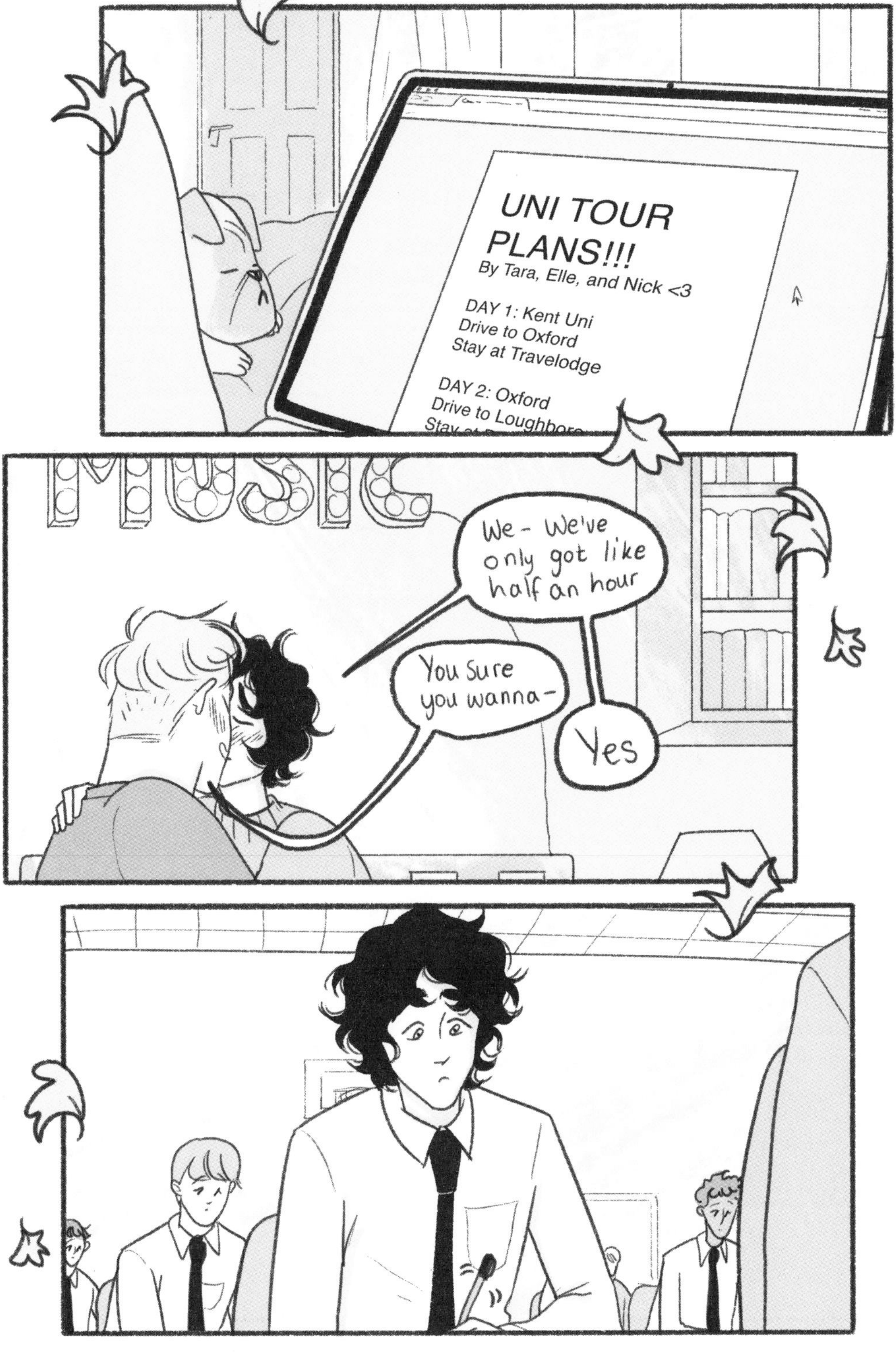
UNI TOUR PLANS!!!
By Tara, Elle, and Nick <3
DAY 1: Kent Uni
Drive to Oxford
Stay at Travelodge
DAY 2: Oxford
MUSIC
We - We've only got like half an hour
You sure you wanna-
Yes

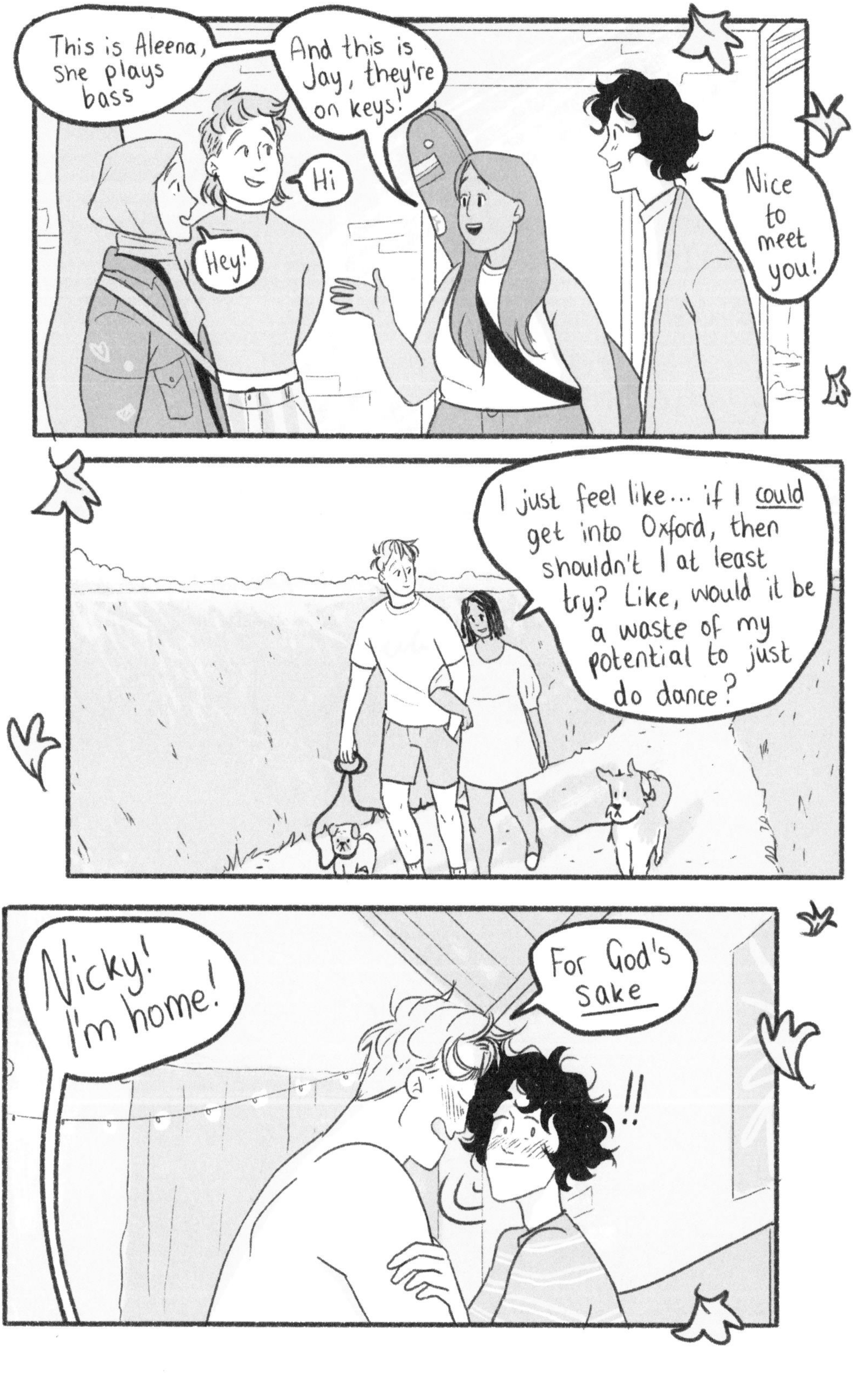
This is Aleena, she plays bass
And this is Jay, they're on keys!
Hey!
Hi
Nice to meet you!
I just feel like... if I could get into Oxford, then shouldn't I at least try? Like, would it be a waste of my potential to just do dance?
Nicky! I'm home!
For God's sake
!!

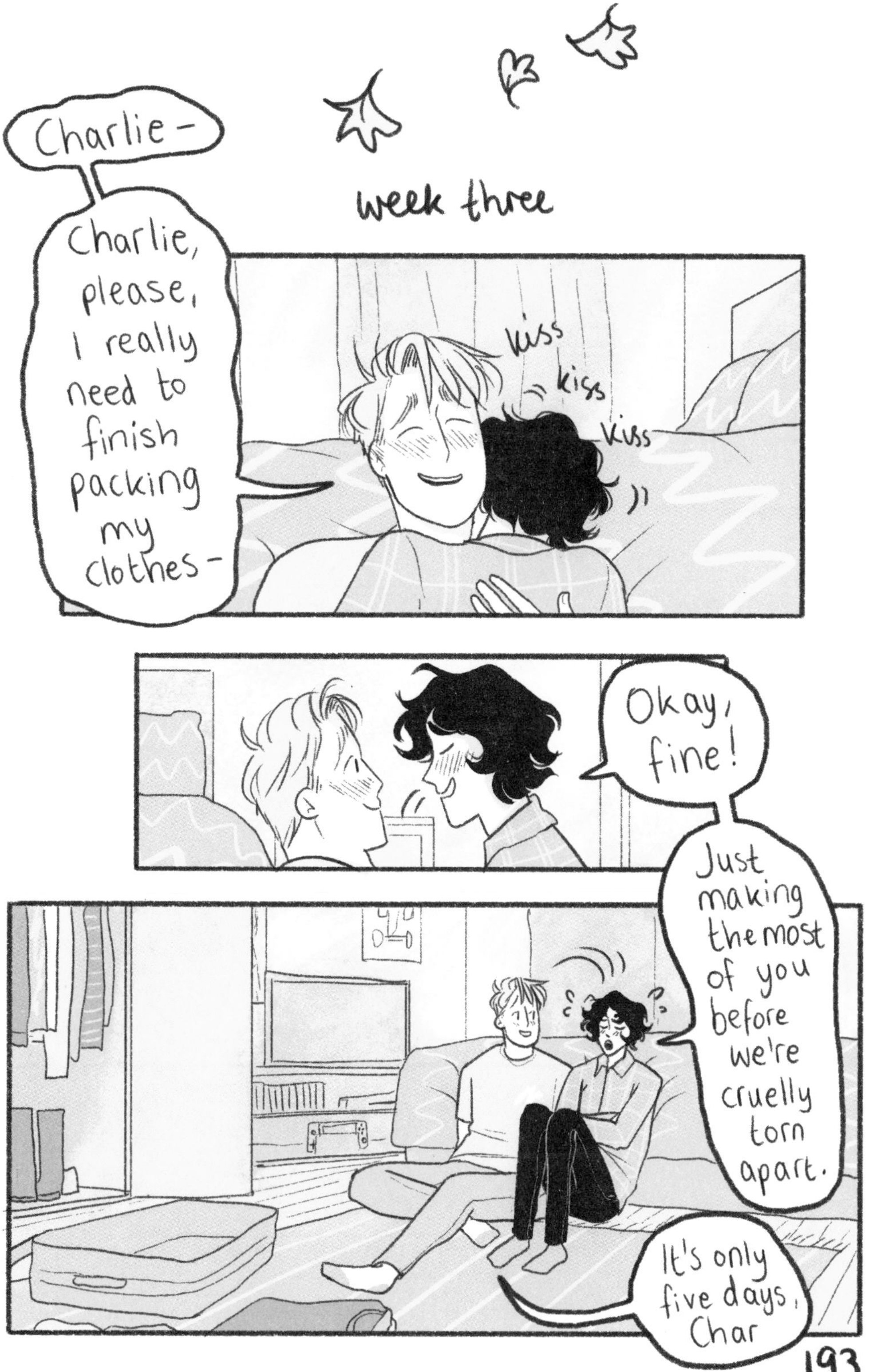
week three
Charlie-
Charlie, please, I really need to finish packing my clothes-
kiss
kiss
kiss
Okay, fine!
Just making the most of you before we're cruelly torn apart.
It's only five days, Char

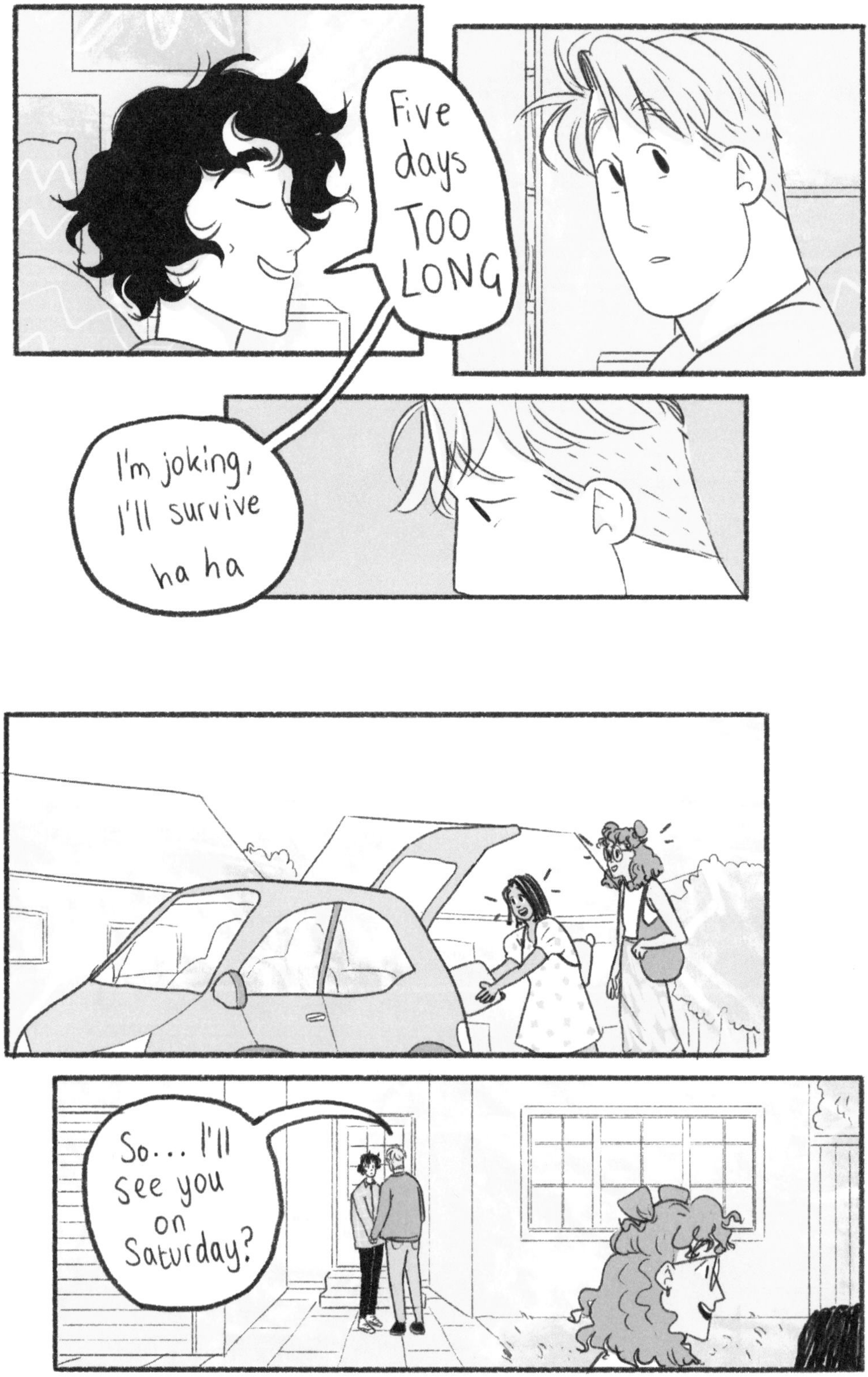
Five days TOO LONG
I'm joking, I'll survive ha ha
So... I'll see you on Saturday?

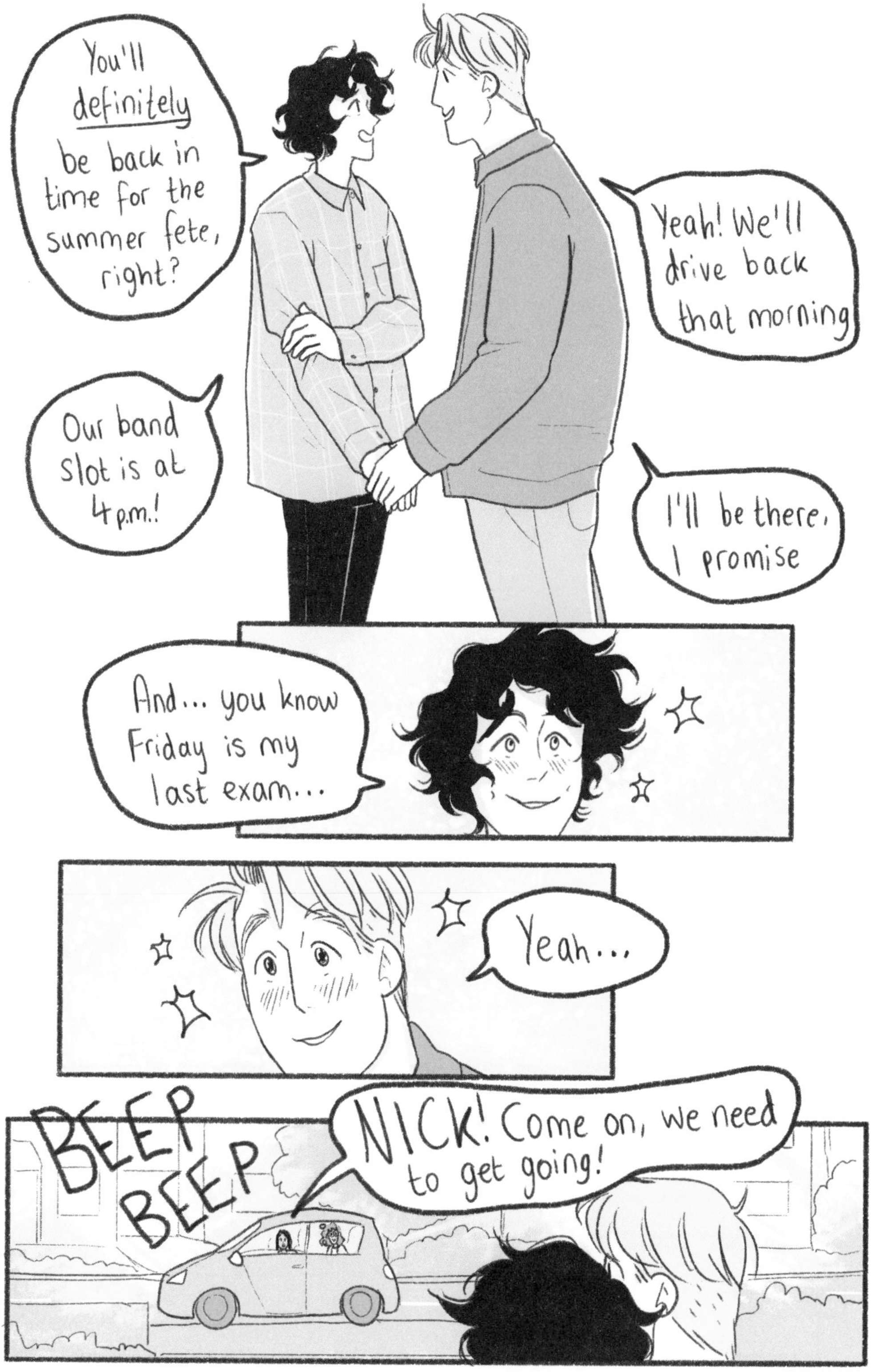
You'll definitely be back in time for the summer fete, right?
Yeah! We'll drive back that morning
Our band slot is at 4 p.m.!
I'll be there, I promise
And... you know Friday is my last exam...
Yeah...
BEEP BEEP
NICK! Come on, we need to get going!

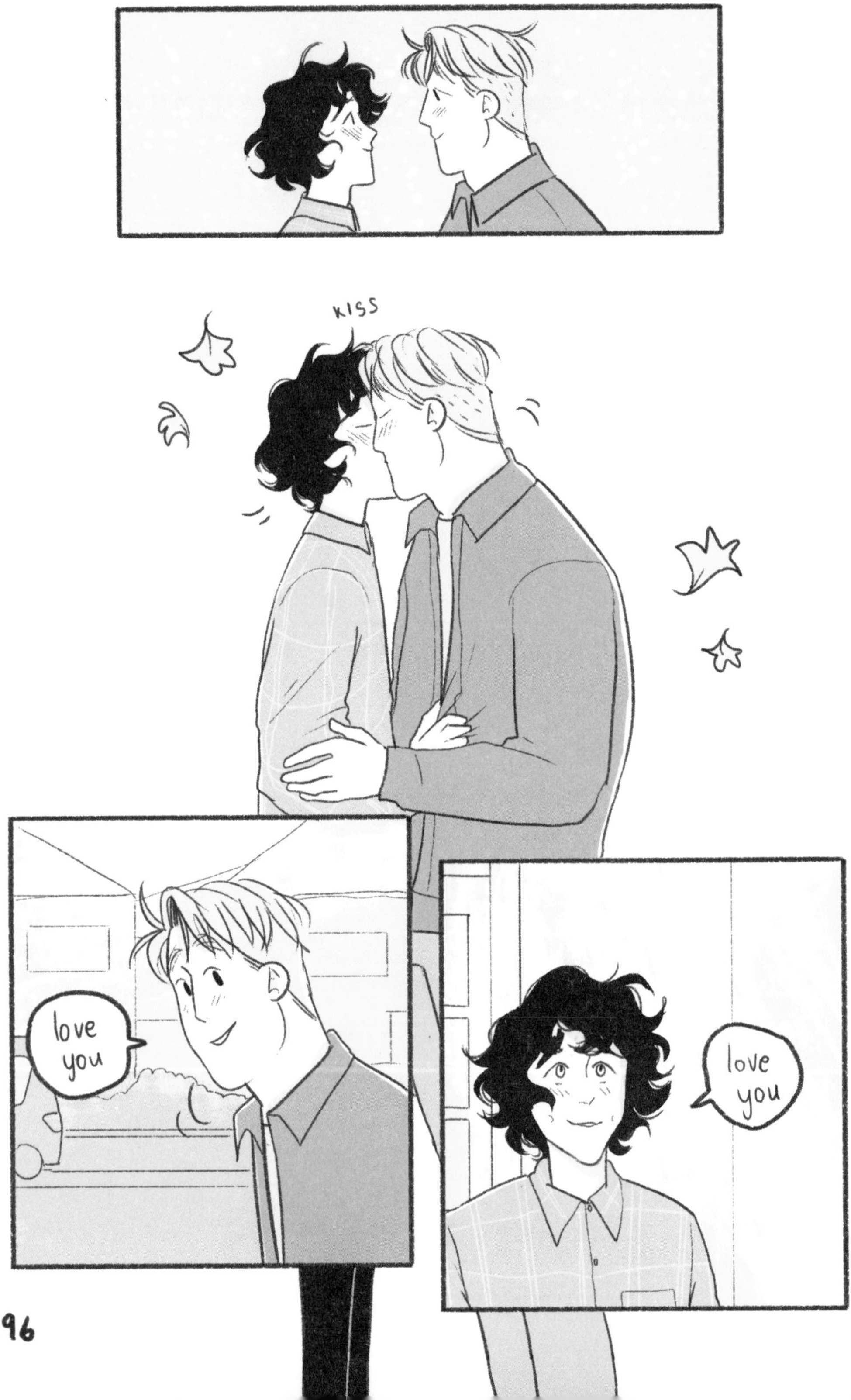
KISS
love you
love you

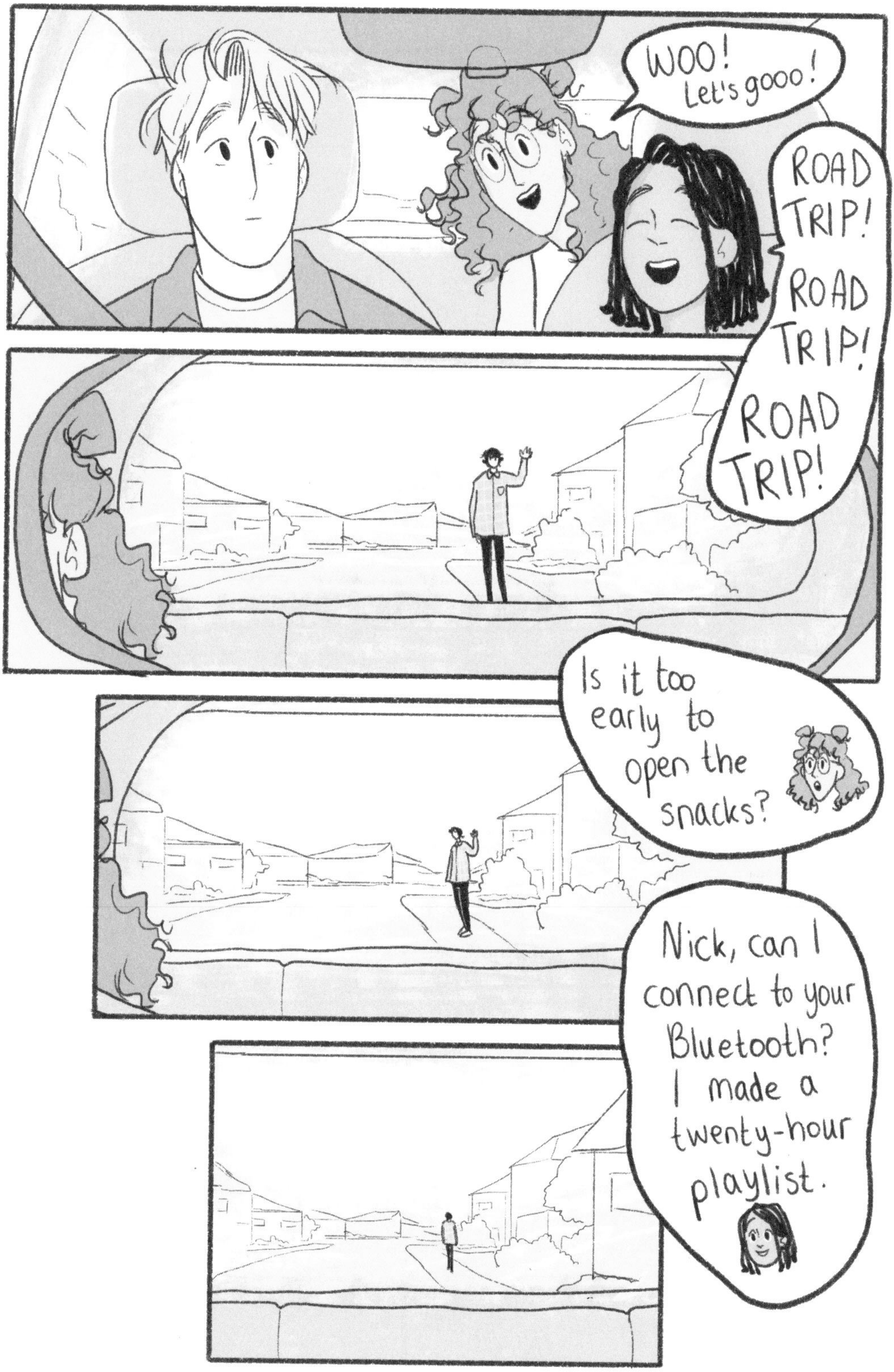
WOO! Let's gooo!
ROAD TRIP! ROAD TRIP! ROAD TRIP!
Is it too early to open the snacks?
Nick, can I connect to your Bluetooth? I made a twenty-hour playlist.

15 MINUTES LATER

UNIVERSITY OF KENT
(day 1)

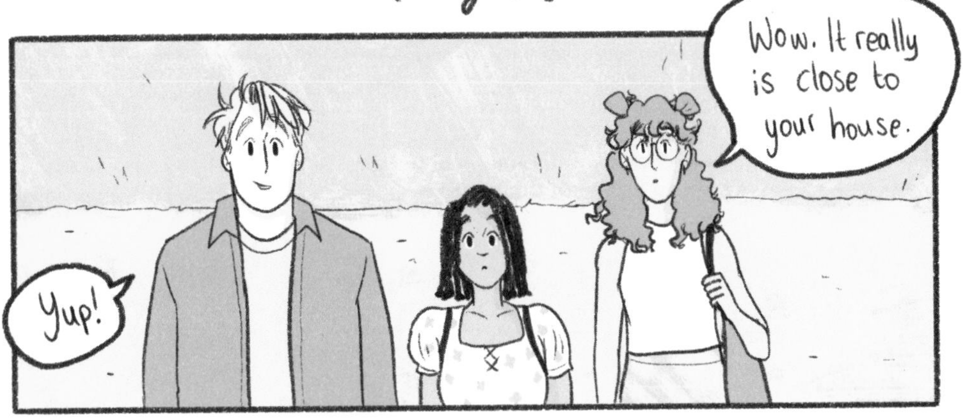
Wow. It really is close to your house.
Yup!

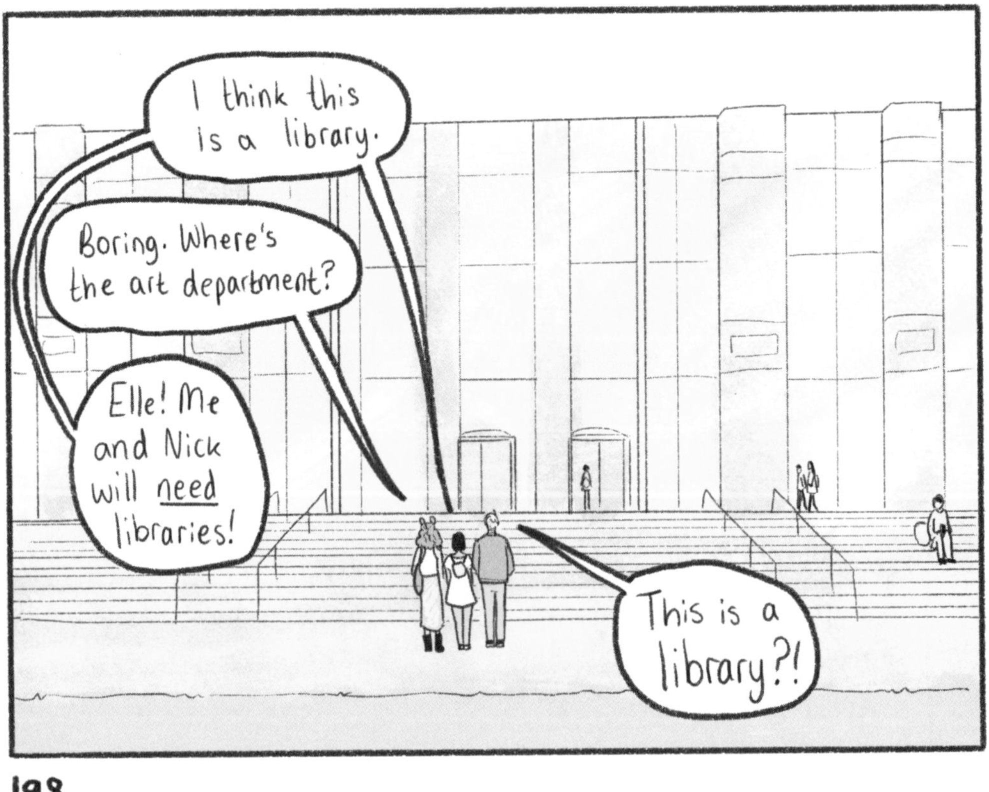
I think this is a library.
Boring. Where's the art department?
Elle! Me and Nick will need libraries!
This is a library?!

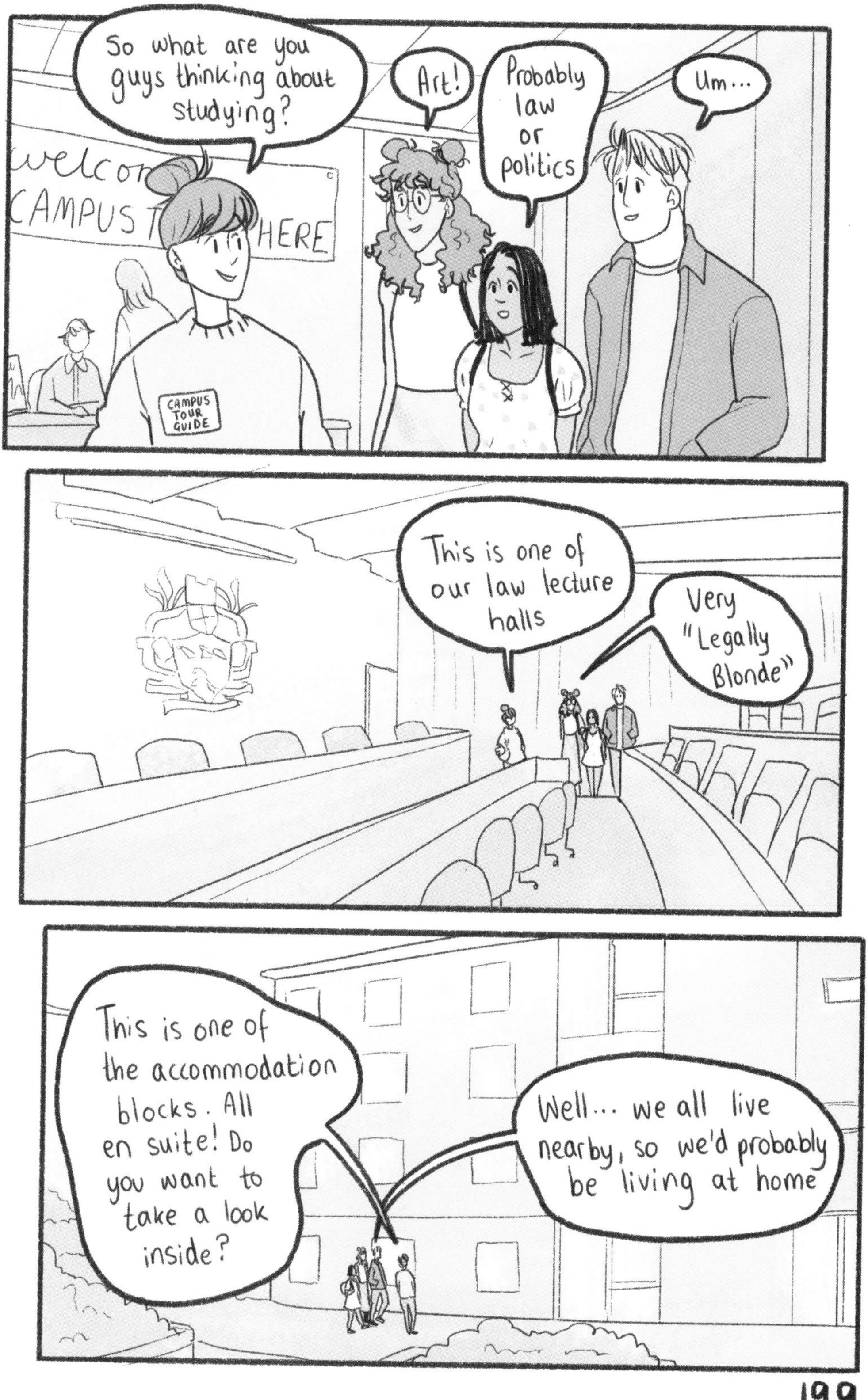
So what are you guys thinking about studying?
Art!
Probably law or politics
Um...
welcom
CAMPUS T
HERE
CAMPUS TOUR GUIDE
This is one of our law lecture halls
Very "Legally Blonde"
This is one of the accommodation blocks. All en suite! Do you want to take a look inside?
Well... we all live nearby, so we'd probably be living at home

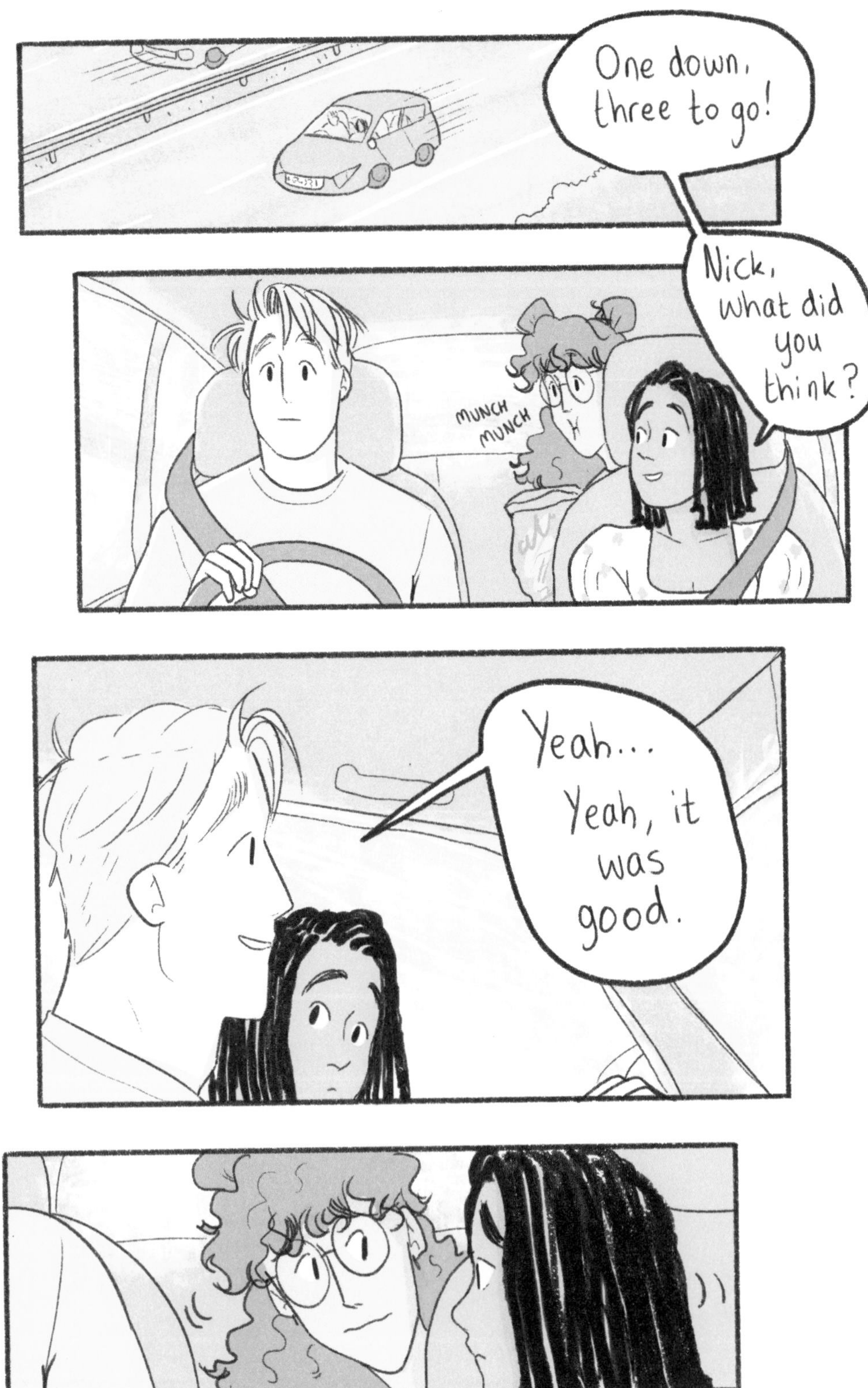
One down, three to go!
Nick, what did you think?
MUNCH MUNCH
Yeah... Yeah, it was good.

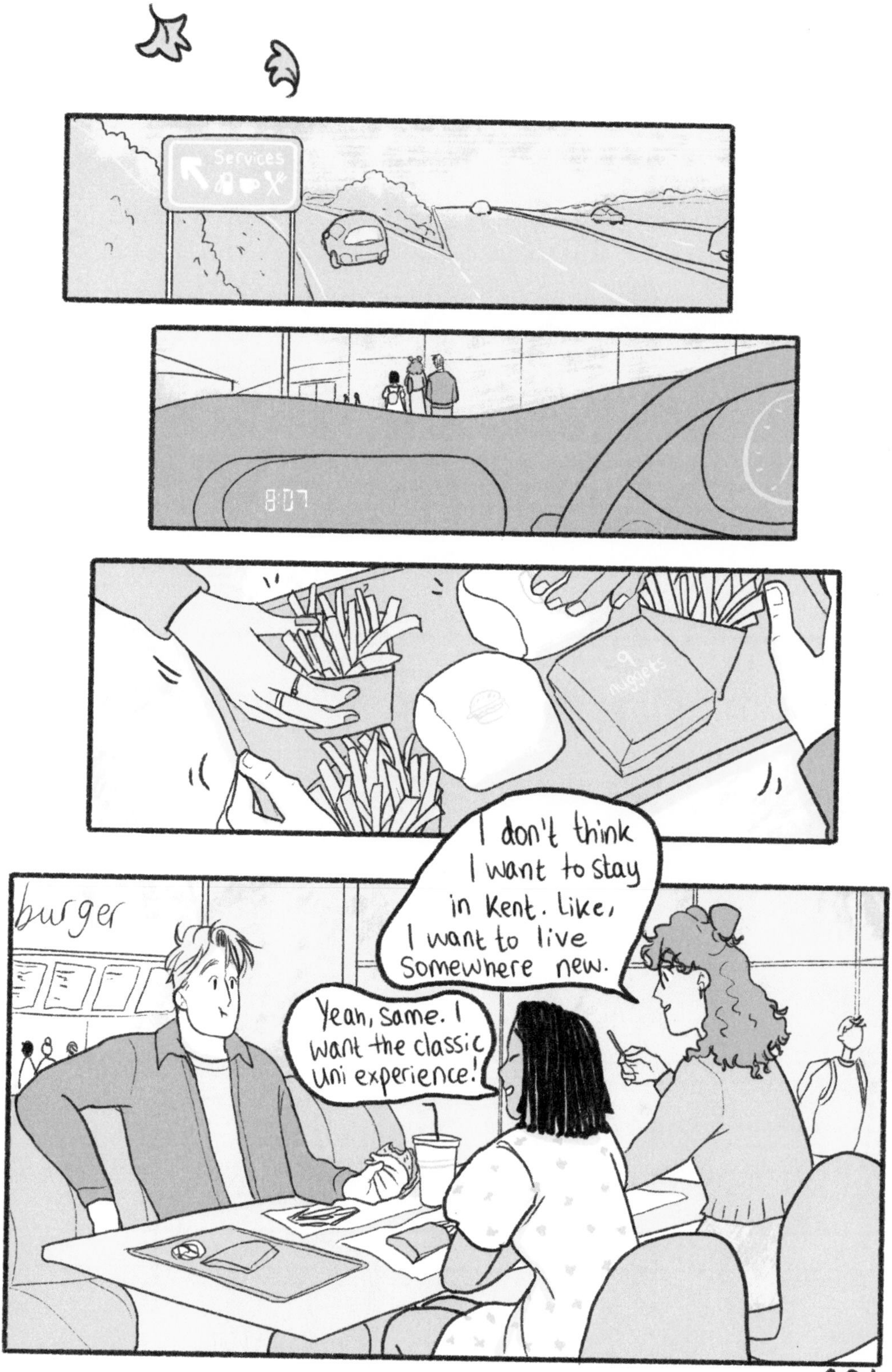
Services
8:07
9 nuggets
burger
I don't think I want to stay in Kent. Like, I want to live somewhere new.
Yeah, same. I want the classic uni experience!

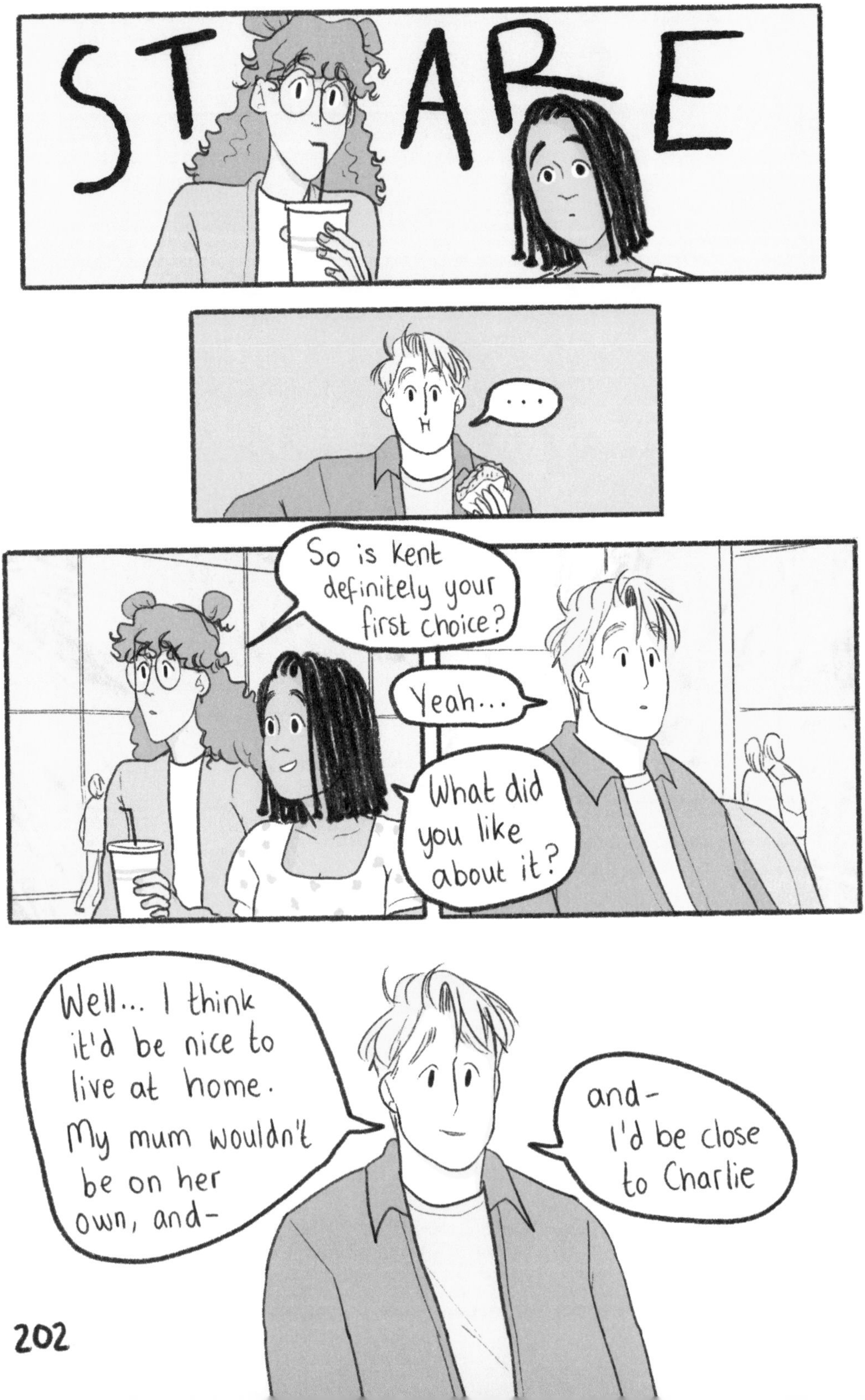
STARE
...
So is Kent definitely your first choice?
Yeah...
What did you like about it?
Well... I think it'd be nice to live at home. My mum wouldn't be on her own, and-
and-
I'd be close to Charlie

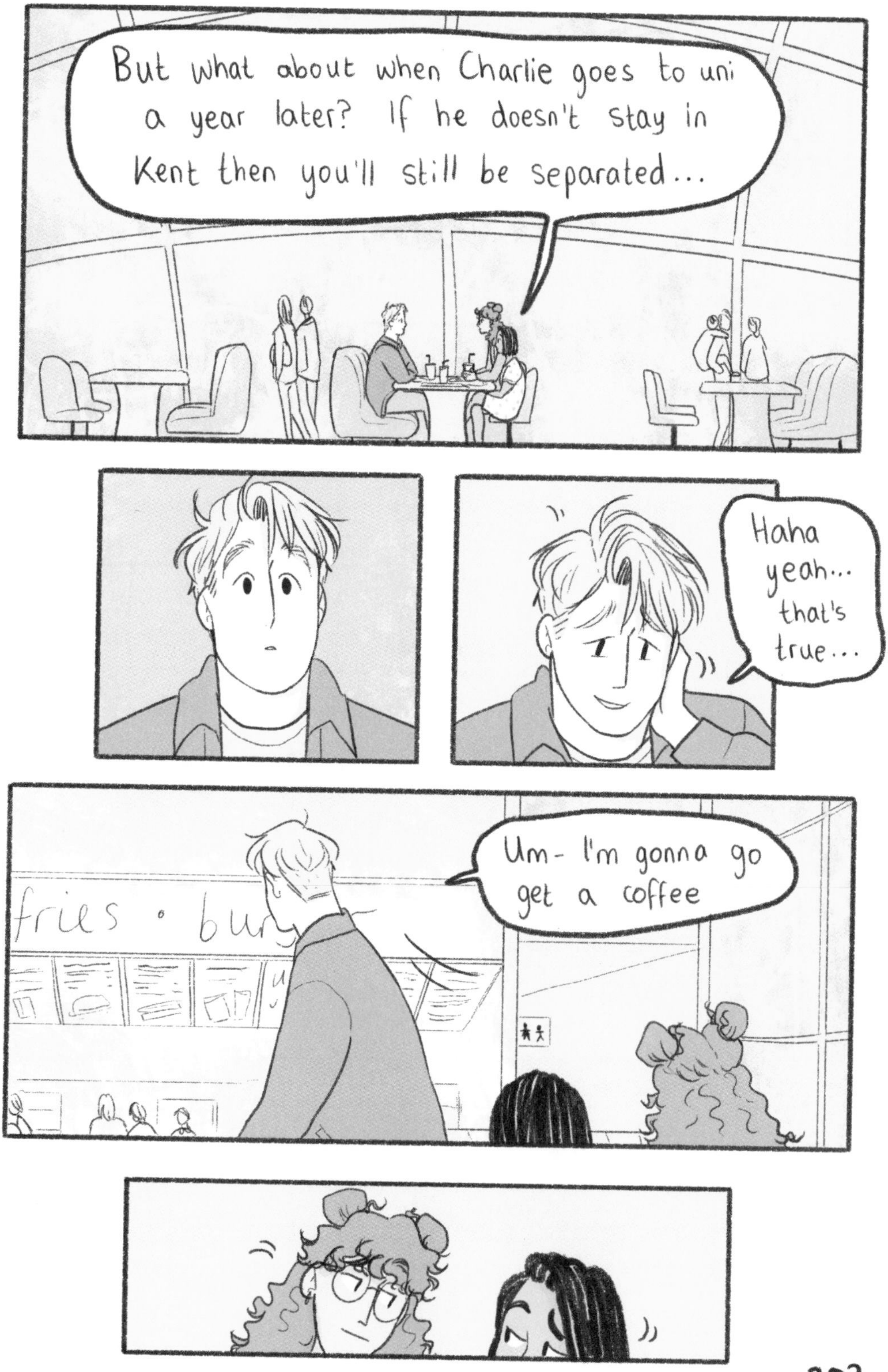
But what about when Charlie goes to uni a year later? If he doesn't stay in Kent then you'll still be separated...
Haha yeah... that's true...
fries • bur
Um- I'm gonna go get a coffee

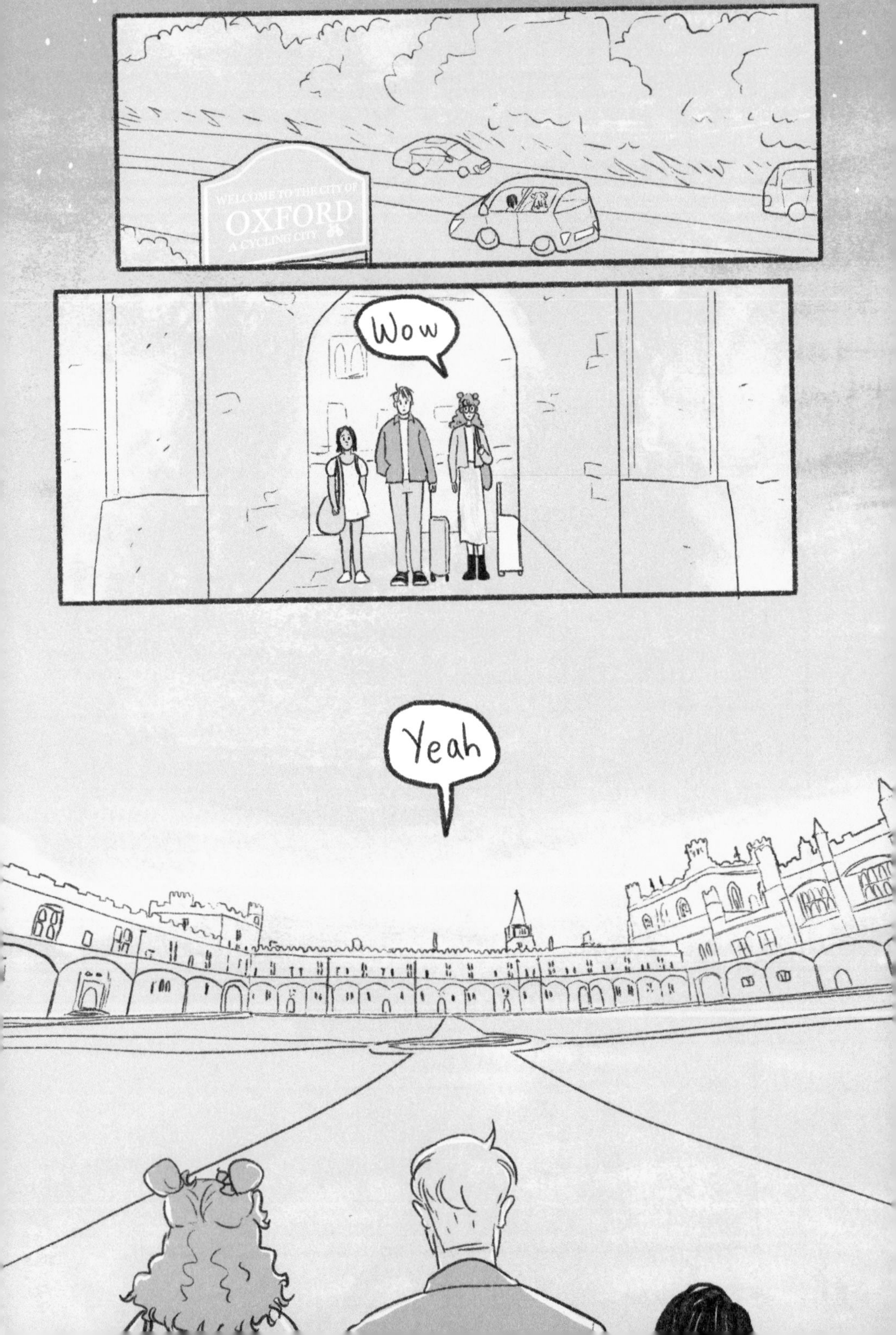
WELCOME TO THE CITY OF
OXFORD
A CYCLING CITY
Wow
Yeah

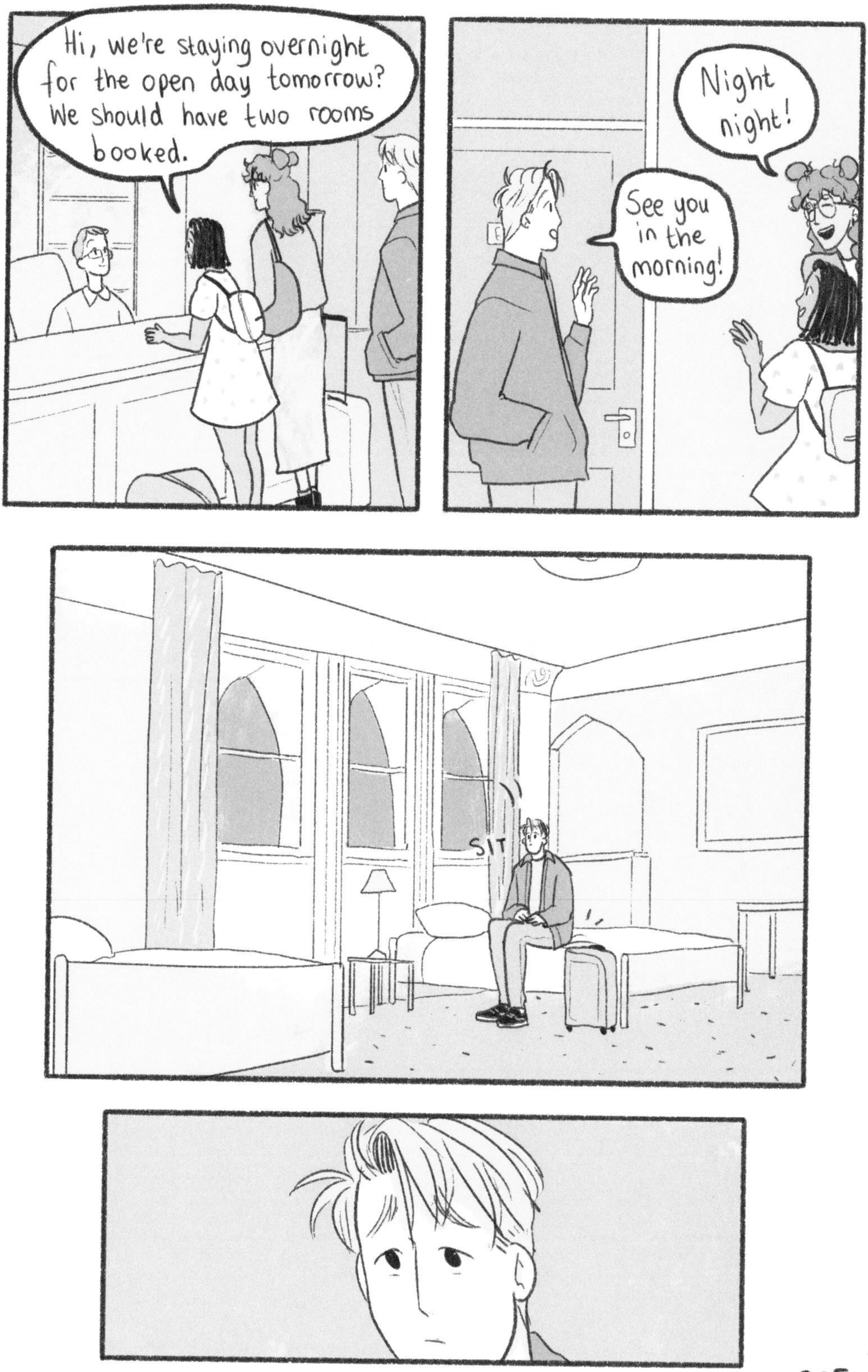
Hi, we're staying overnight for the open day tomorrow? We should have two rooms booked.
Night night!
See you in the morning!
SIT

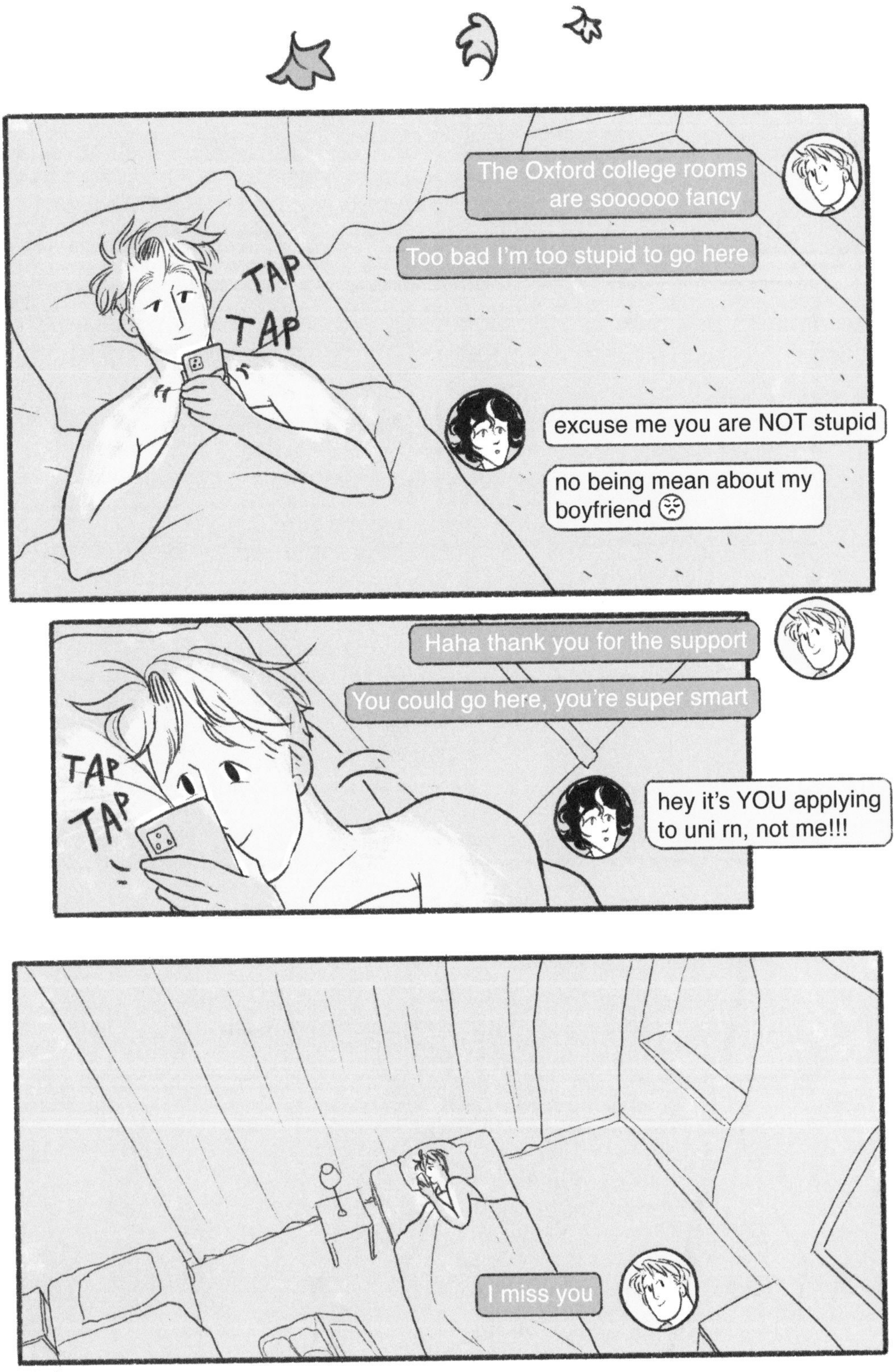
The Oxford college rooms are soooooo fancy
Too bad I'm too stupid to go here
TAP TAP
excuse me you are NOT stupid
no being mean about my boyfriend 😠
Haha thank you for the support
You could go here, you're super smart
TAP TAP
hey it's YOU applying to uni rn, not me!!!
I miss you

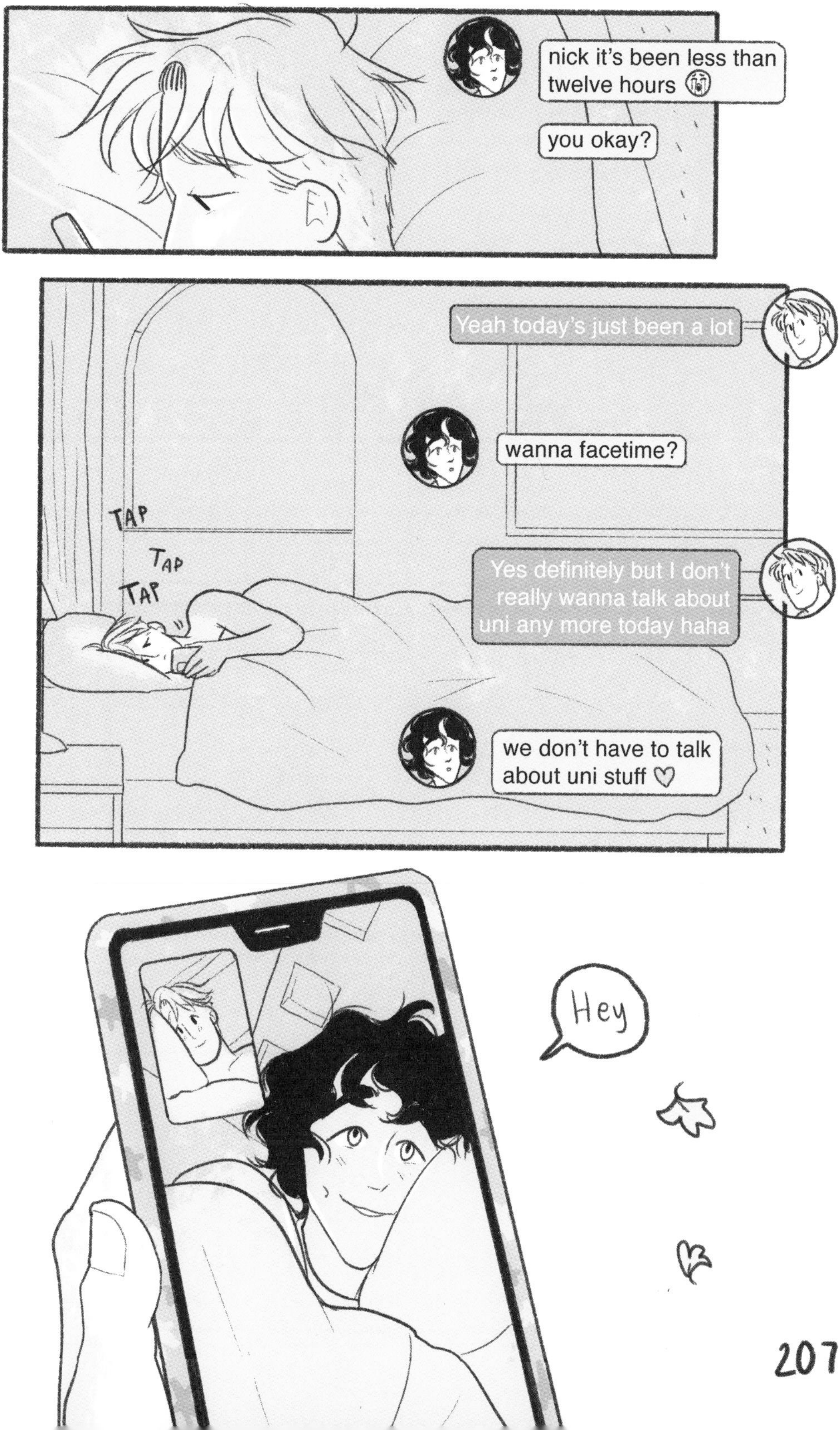
nick it's been less than twelve hours 😭
you okay?
Yeah today's just been a lot
wanna facetime?
TAP
TAP
TAP
Yes definitely but I don't really wanna talk about uni any more today haha
we don't have to talk about uni stuff ♡
Hey

day 2

UNIVERSITY OF OXFORD

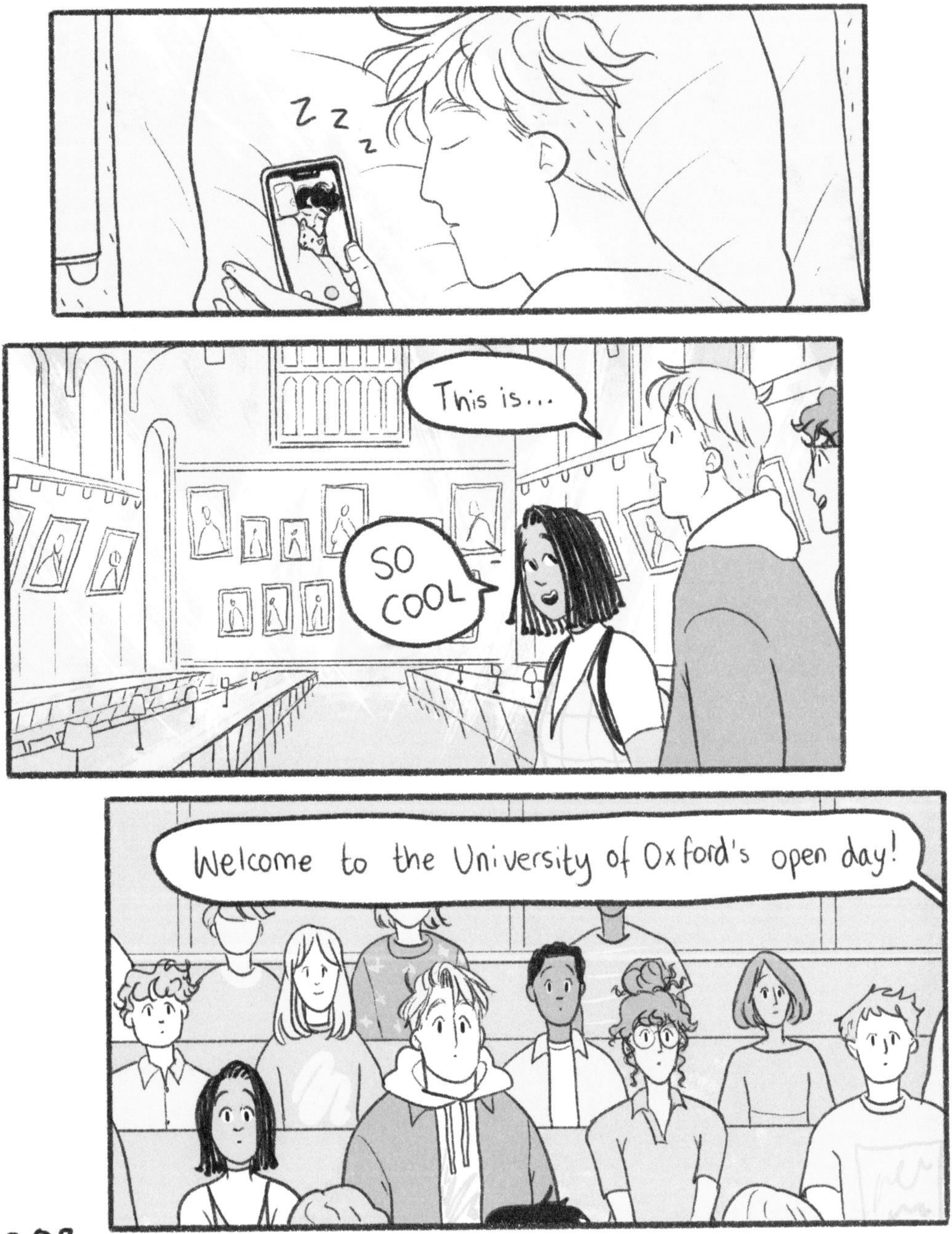

Z z z
This is...
SO COOL
Welcome to the University of Oxford's open day!

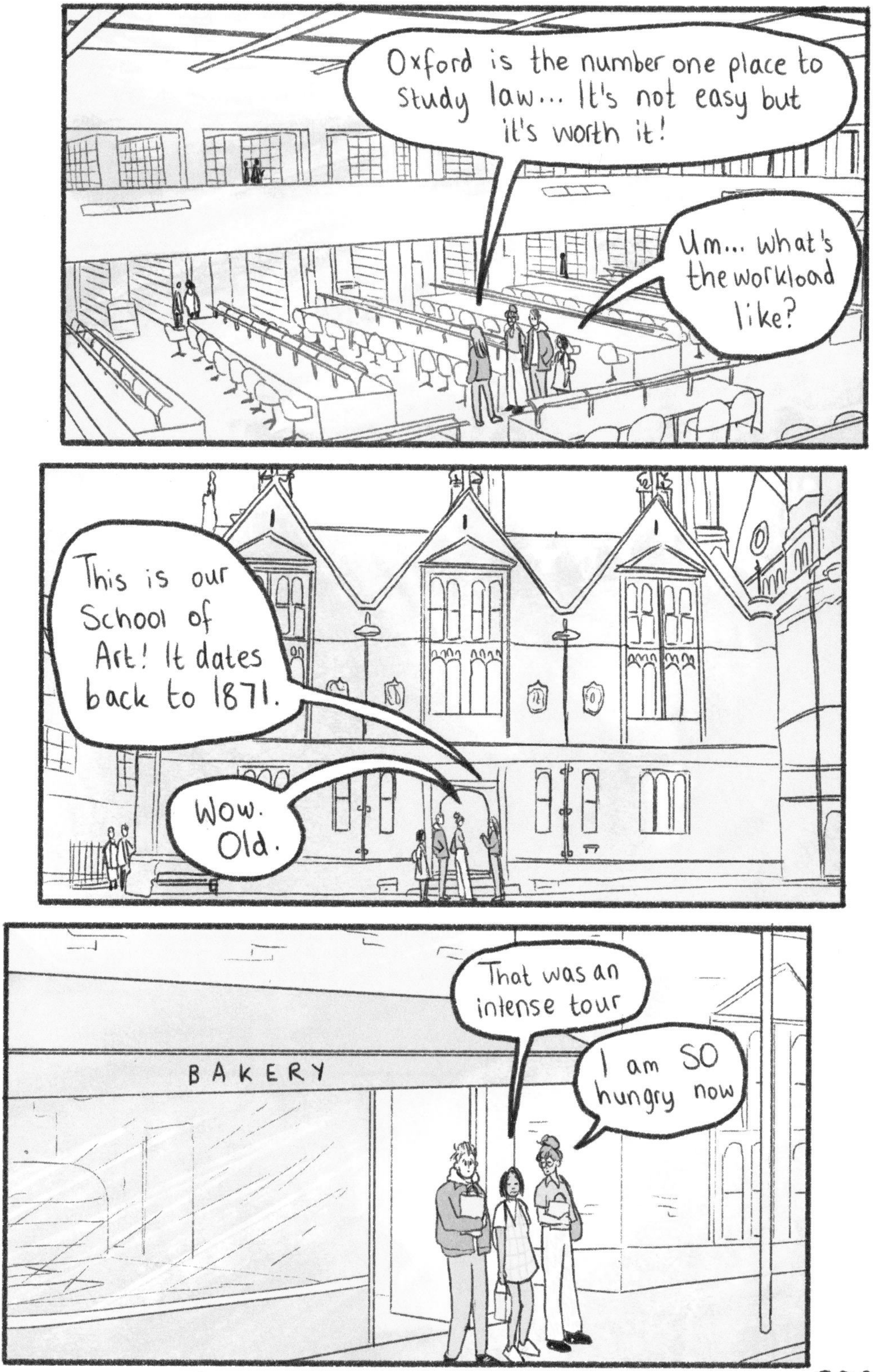
Oxford is the number one place to study law... It's not easy but it's worth it!
Um... what's the workload like?
This is our School of Art! It dates back to 1871.
Wow. Old.
BAKERY
That was an intense tour
I am SO hungry now

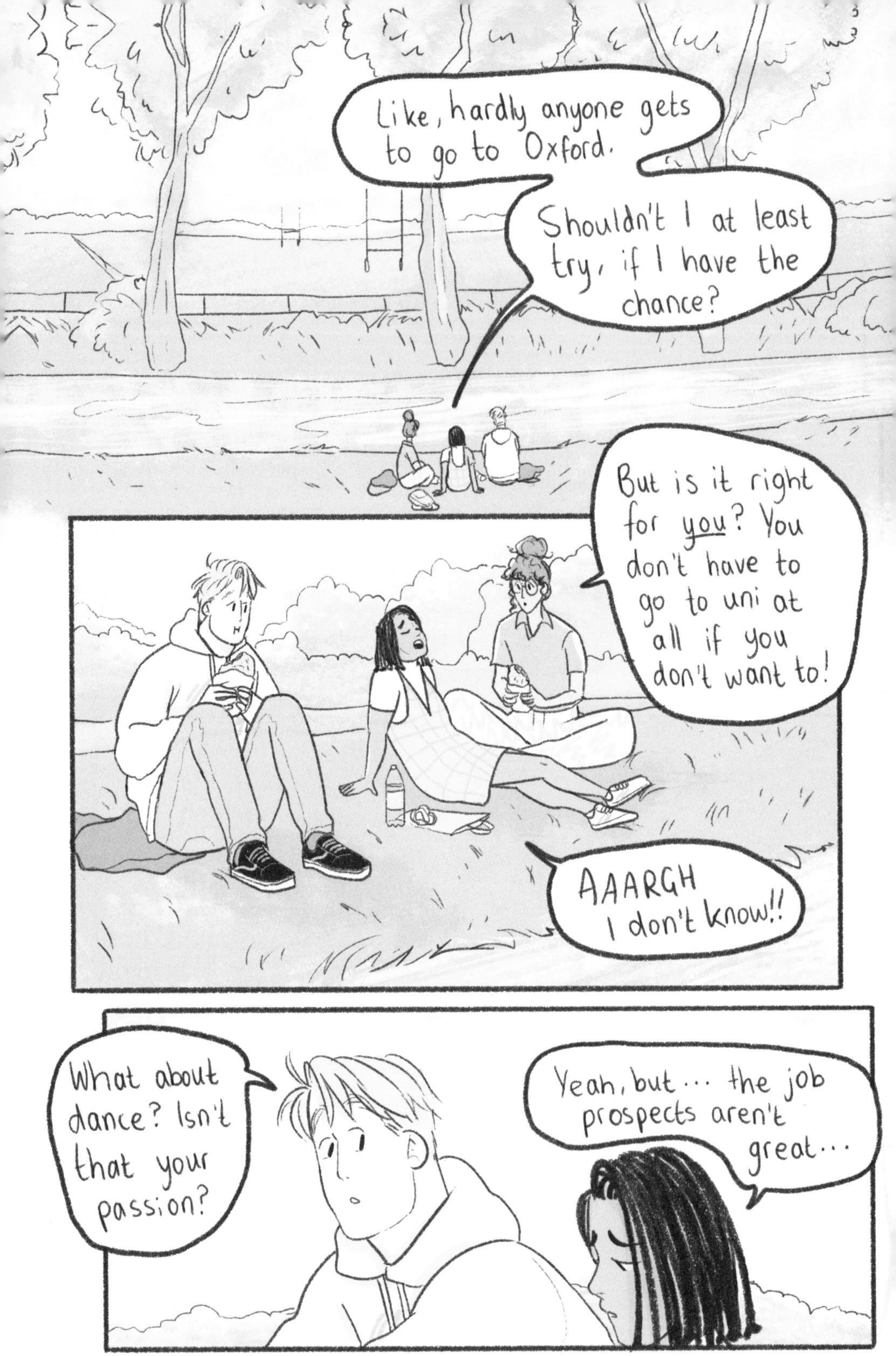
Like, hardly anyone gets to go to Oxford.
Shouldn't I at least try, if I have the chance?
But is it right for you? You don't have to go to uni at all if you don't want to!
AAARGH I don't know!!
What about dance? Isn't that your passion?
Yeah, but... the job prospects aren't great...

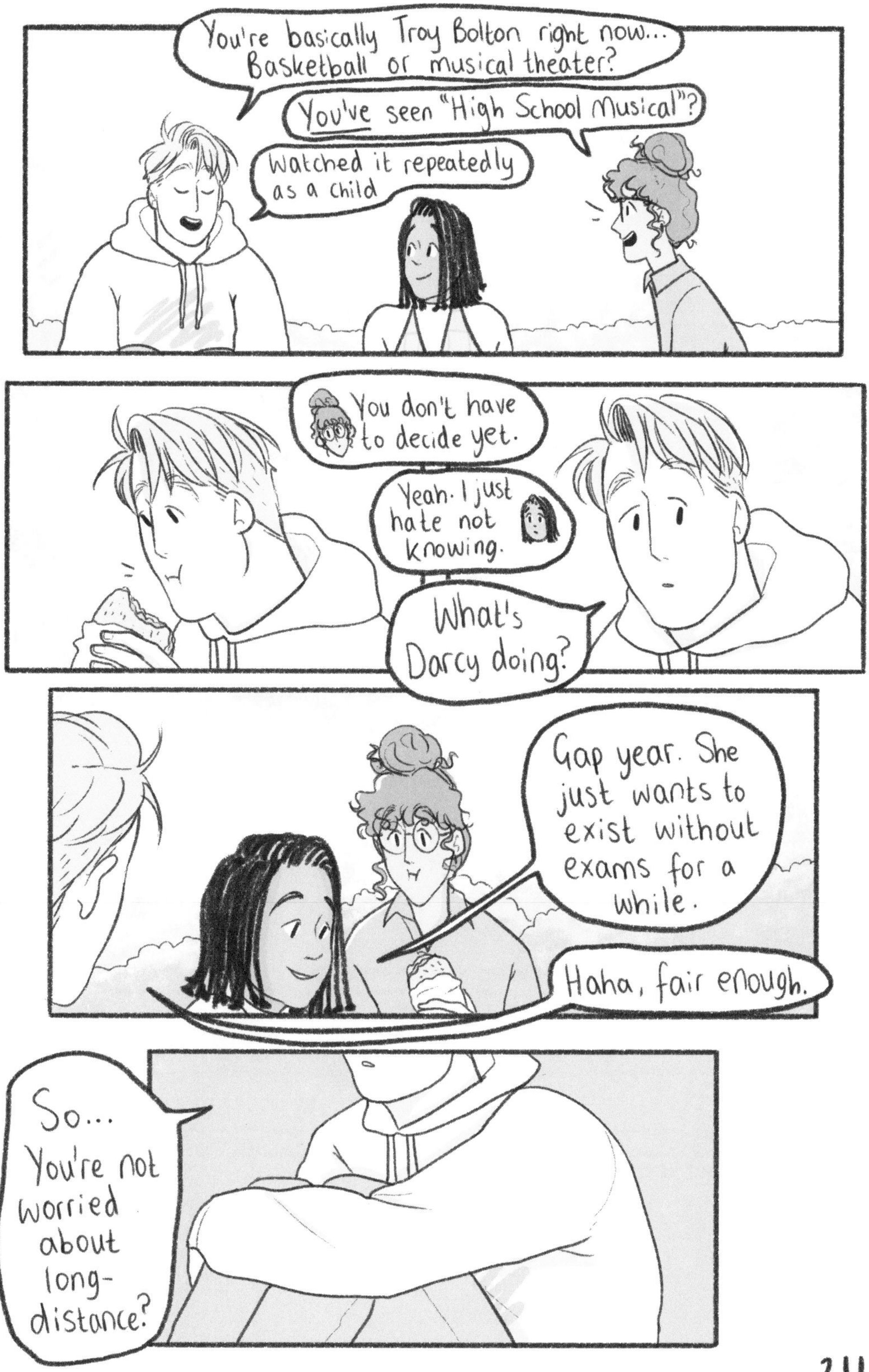
You're basically Troy Bolton right now... Basketball or musical theater?
You've seen "High School Musical"?
Watched it repeatedly as a child
You don't have to decide yet.
Yeah. I just hate not knowing.
What's Darcy doing?
Gap year. She just wants to exist without exams for a while.
Haha, fair enough.
So... You're not worried about long-distance?

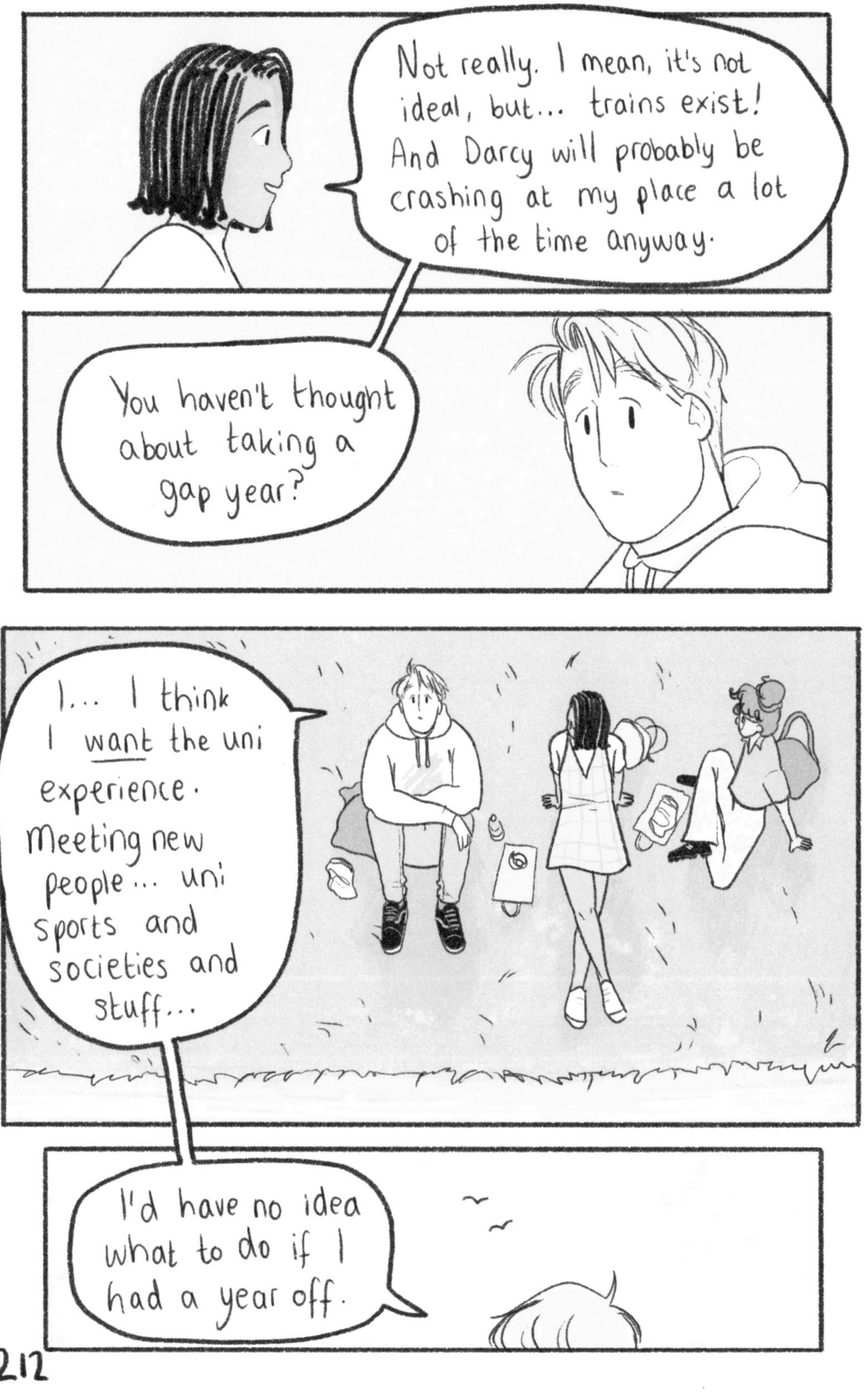
Not really. I mean, it's not ideal, but... trains exist! And Darcy will probably be crashing at my place a lot of the time anyway.
You haven't thought about taking a gap year?
I... I think I want the uni experience. Meeting new people... uni sports and societies and stuff...
I'd have no idea what to do if I had a year off.

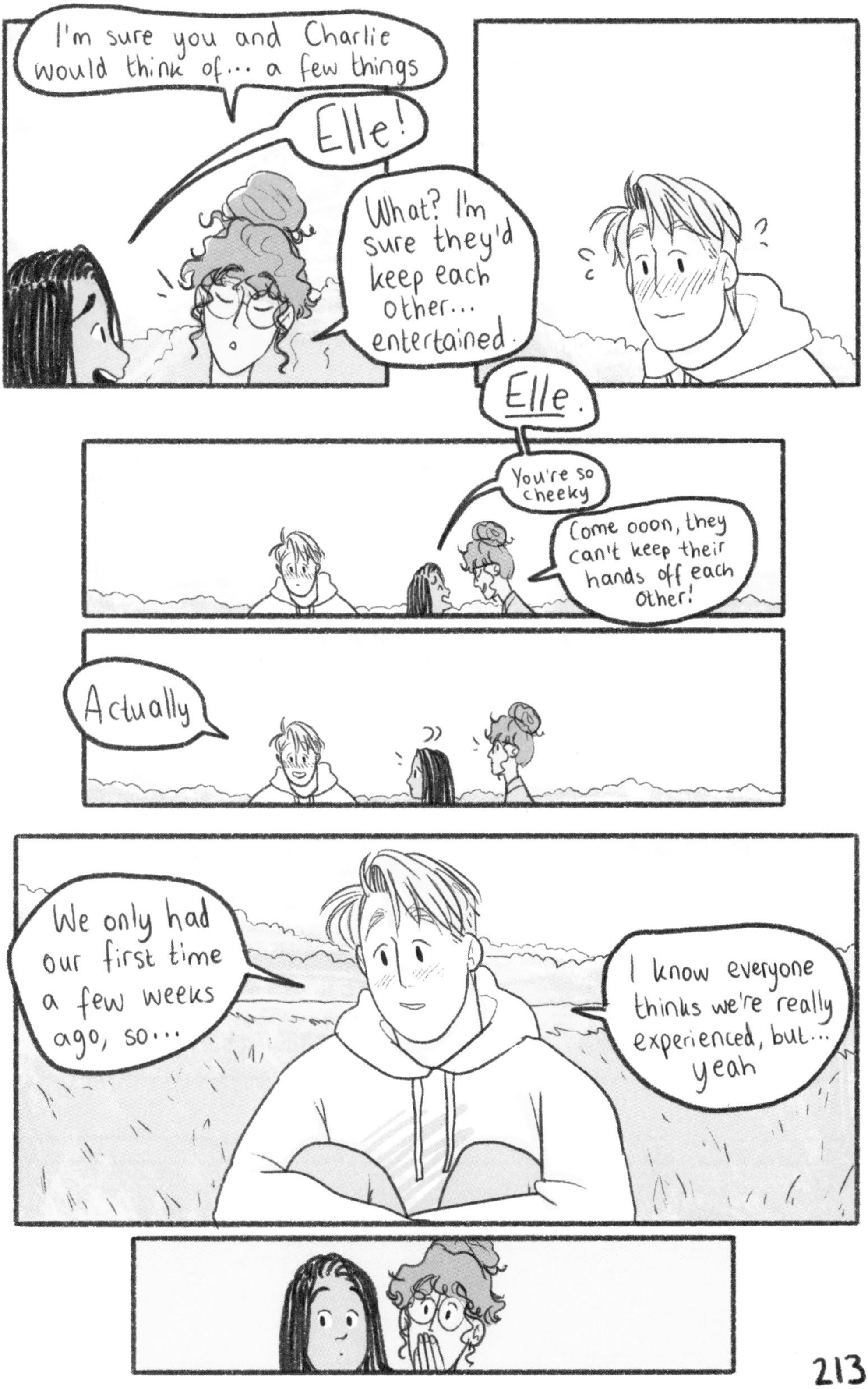

I'm sure you and Charlie would think of... a few things
Elle!
What? I'm sure they'd keep each other... entertained.
Elle.
You're so cheeky
Come ooon, they can't keep their hands off each other!
Actually
We only had our first time a few weeks ago, so...
I know everyone thinks we're really experienced, but... yeah

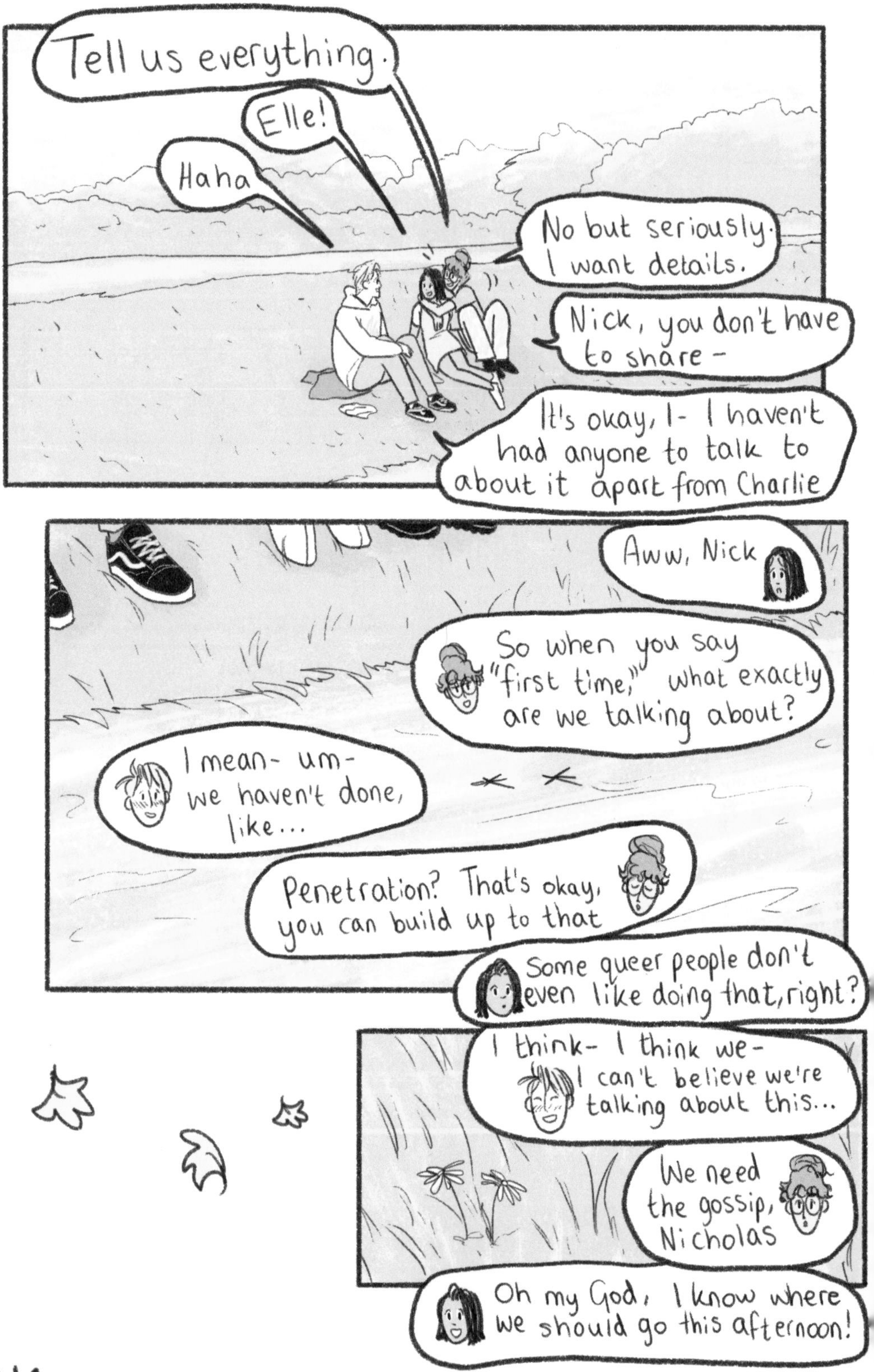
Tell us everything.
Elle!
Haha
No but seriously. I want details.
Nick, you don't have to share-
It's okay, I- I haven't had anyone to talk to about it apart from Charlie
Aww, Nick
So when you say "first time," what exactly are we talking about?
I mean- um- we haven't done, like...
Penetration? That's okay, you can build up to that
Some queer people don't even like doing that, right?
I think- I think we- I can't believe we're talking about this...
We need the gossip, Nicholas
Oh my God, I know where we should go this afternoon!

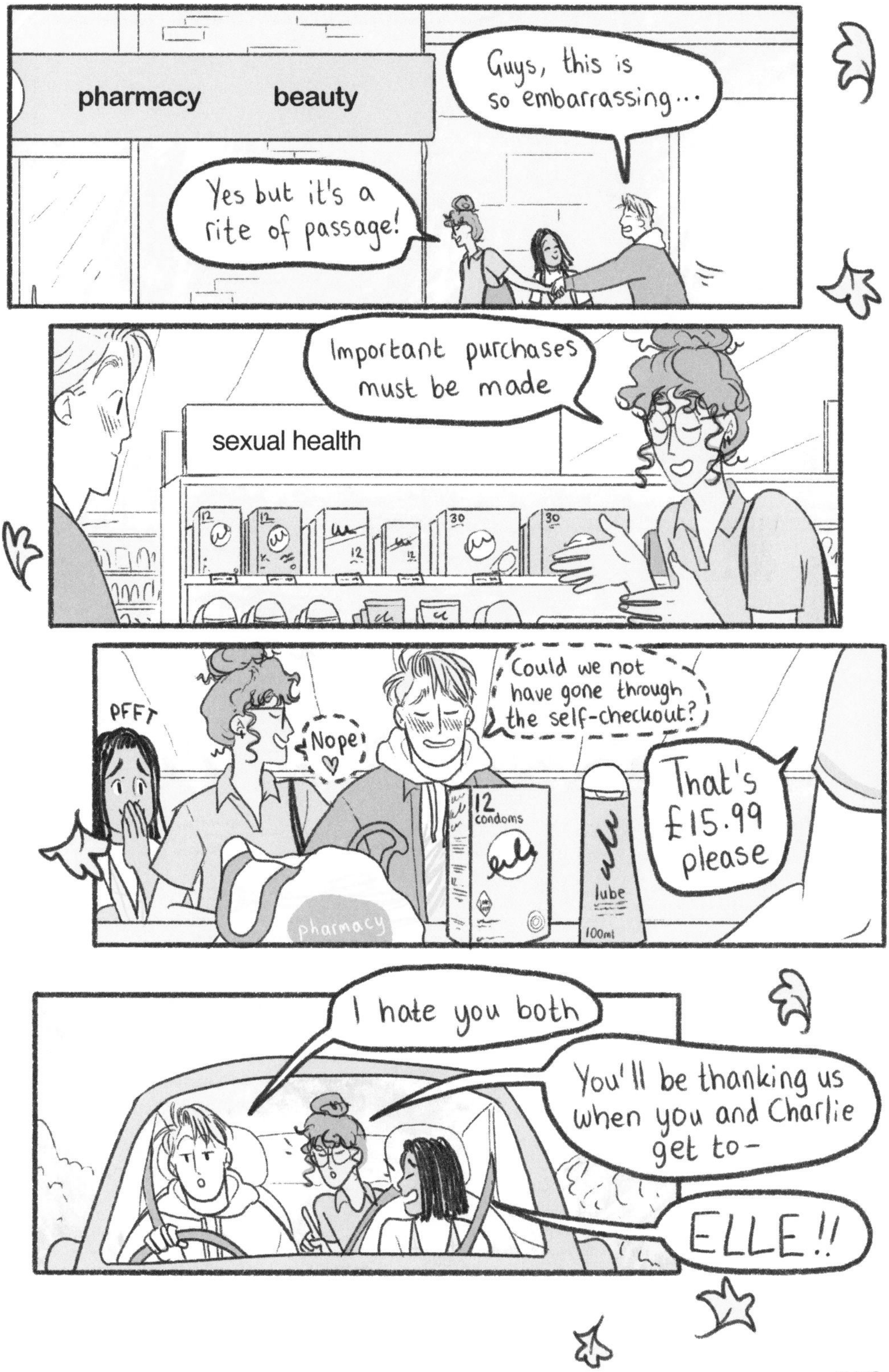
pharmacy
beauty
Guys, this is so embarrassing...
Yes but it's a rite of passage!
Important purchases must be made
sexual health
PFFT
Nope ♡
Could we not have gone through the self-checkout?
12 condoms
lube
100ml
That's £15.99 please
pharmacy
I hate you both
You'll be thanking us when you and Charlie get to–
ELLE!!

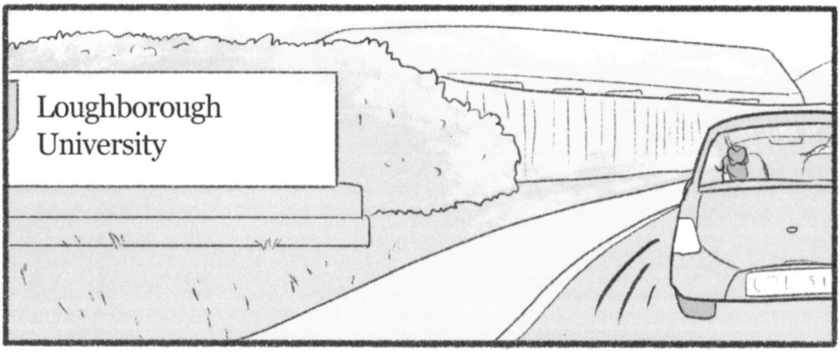
Loughborough
University

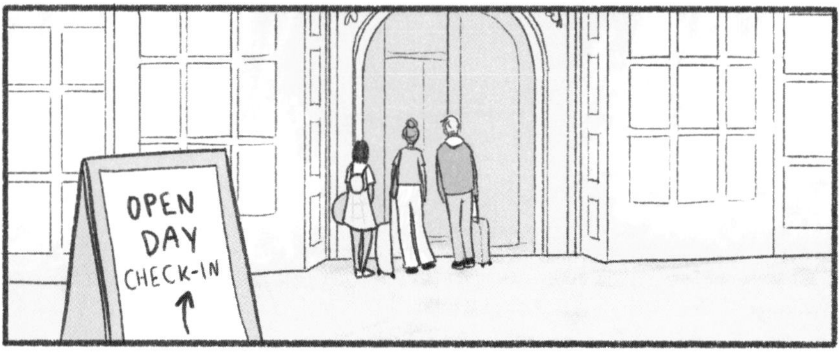
OPEN
DAY
CHECK-IN

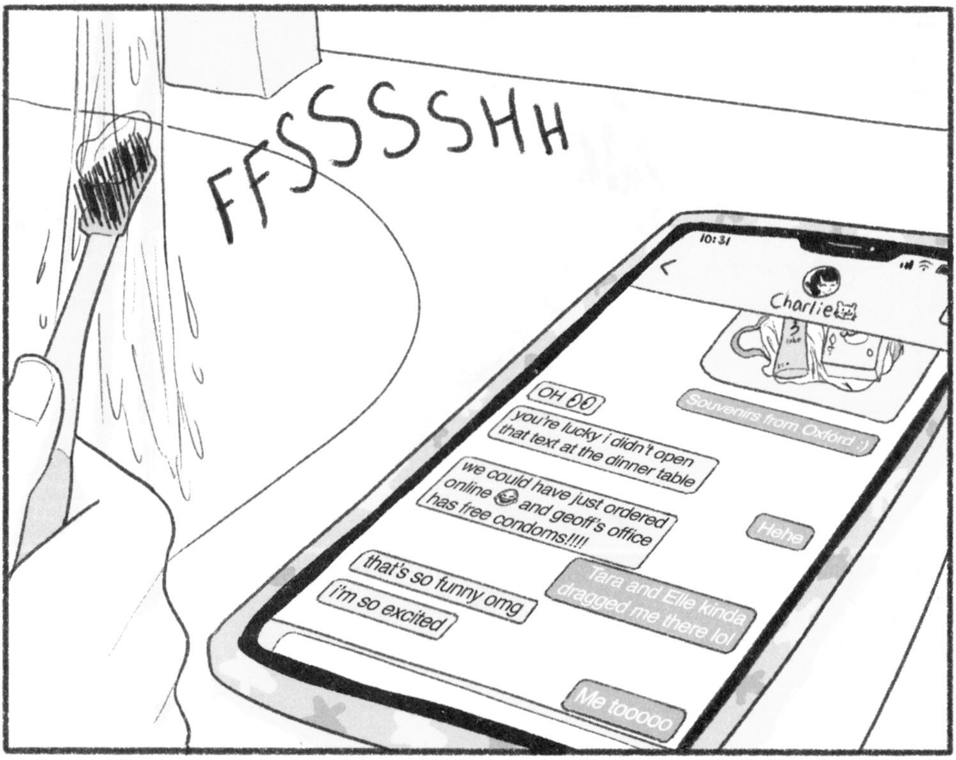
FFSSSSHH
10:31
Charlie
Souvenirs from Oxford :)
OH
you're lucky i didn't open
that text at the dinner table
we could have just ordered
online and geoff's office
has free condoms!!!!
Hehe
that's so funny omg
i'm so excited
Tara and Elle kinda
dragged me there lol
Me tooooo

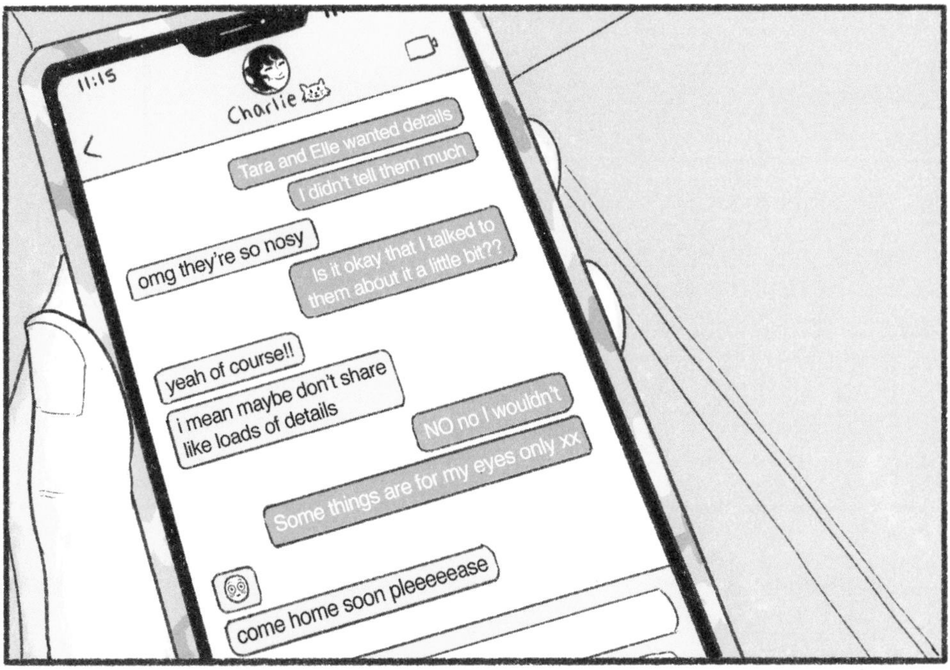
11:15
Charlie
Tara and Elle wanted details
I didn't tell them much
omg they're so nosy
Is it okay that I talked to them about it a little bit??
yeah of course!!
i mean maybe don't share like loads of details
NO no I wouldn't
Some things are for my eyes only xx
come home soon pleeeeease

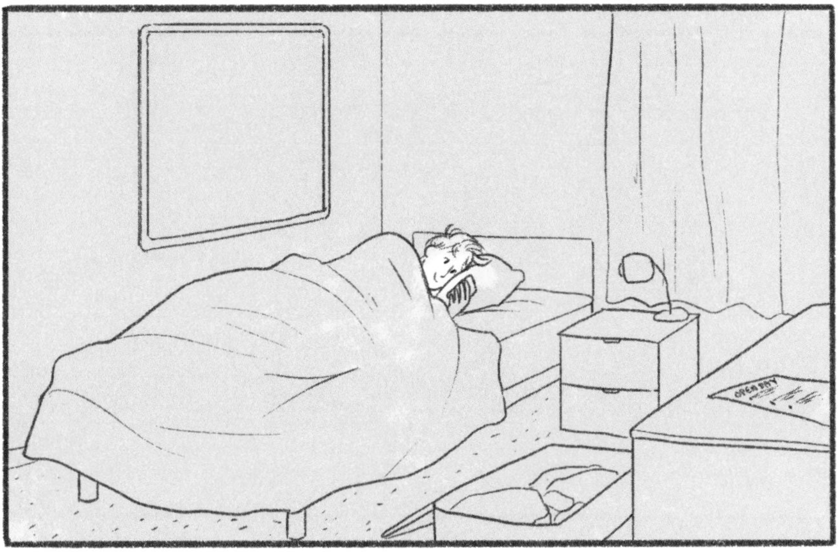

day 3

LOUGHBOROUGH UNIVERSITY

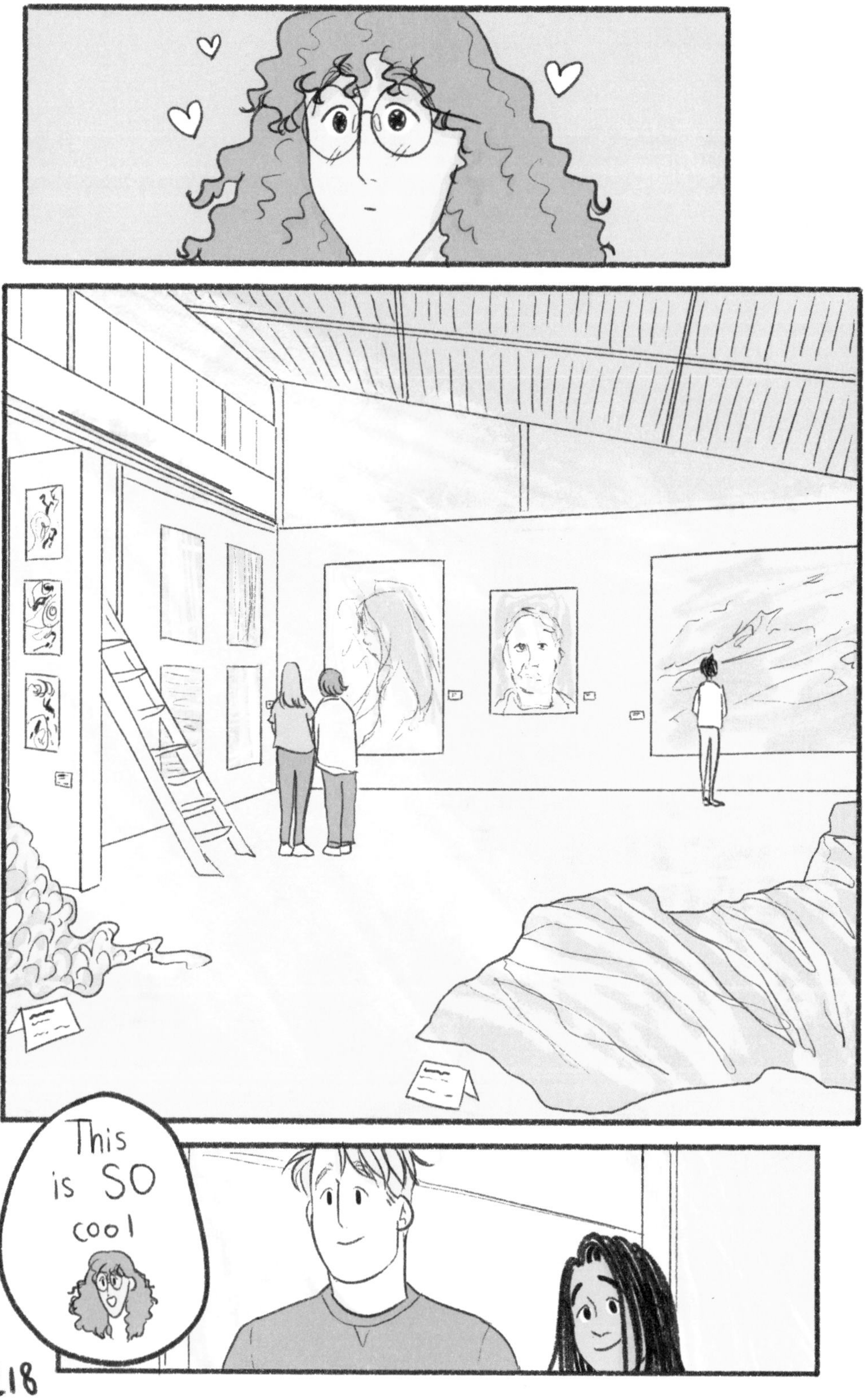
This is SO cool

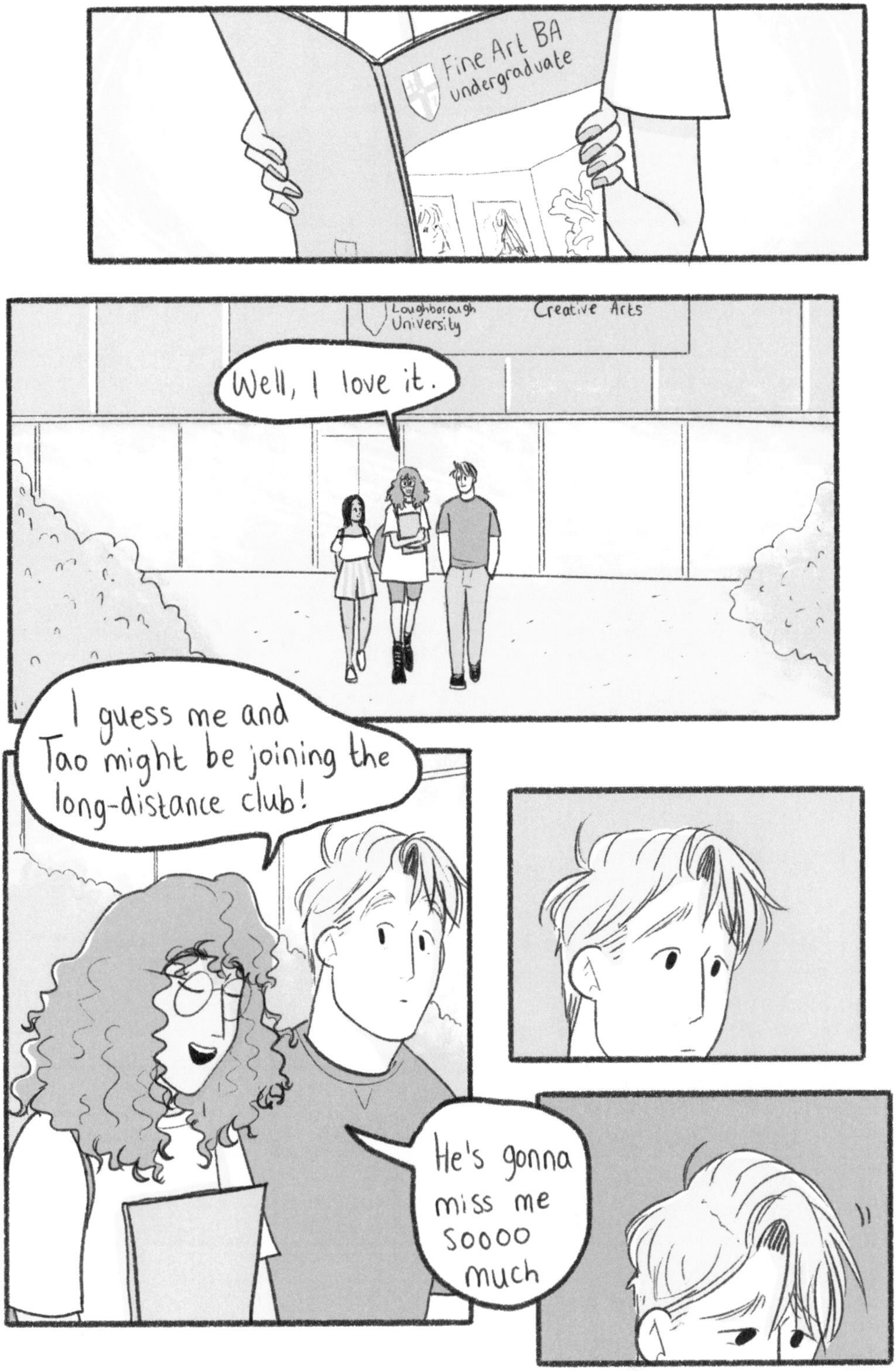

Fine Art BA
undergraduate
Loughborough University
Creative Arts
Well, I love it.
I guess me and Tao might be joining the long-distance club!
He's gonna miss me soooo much

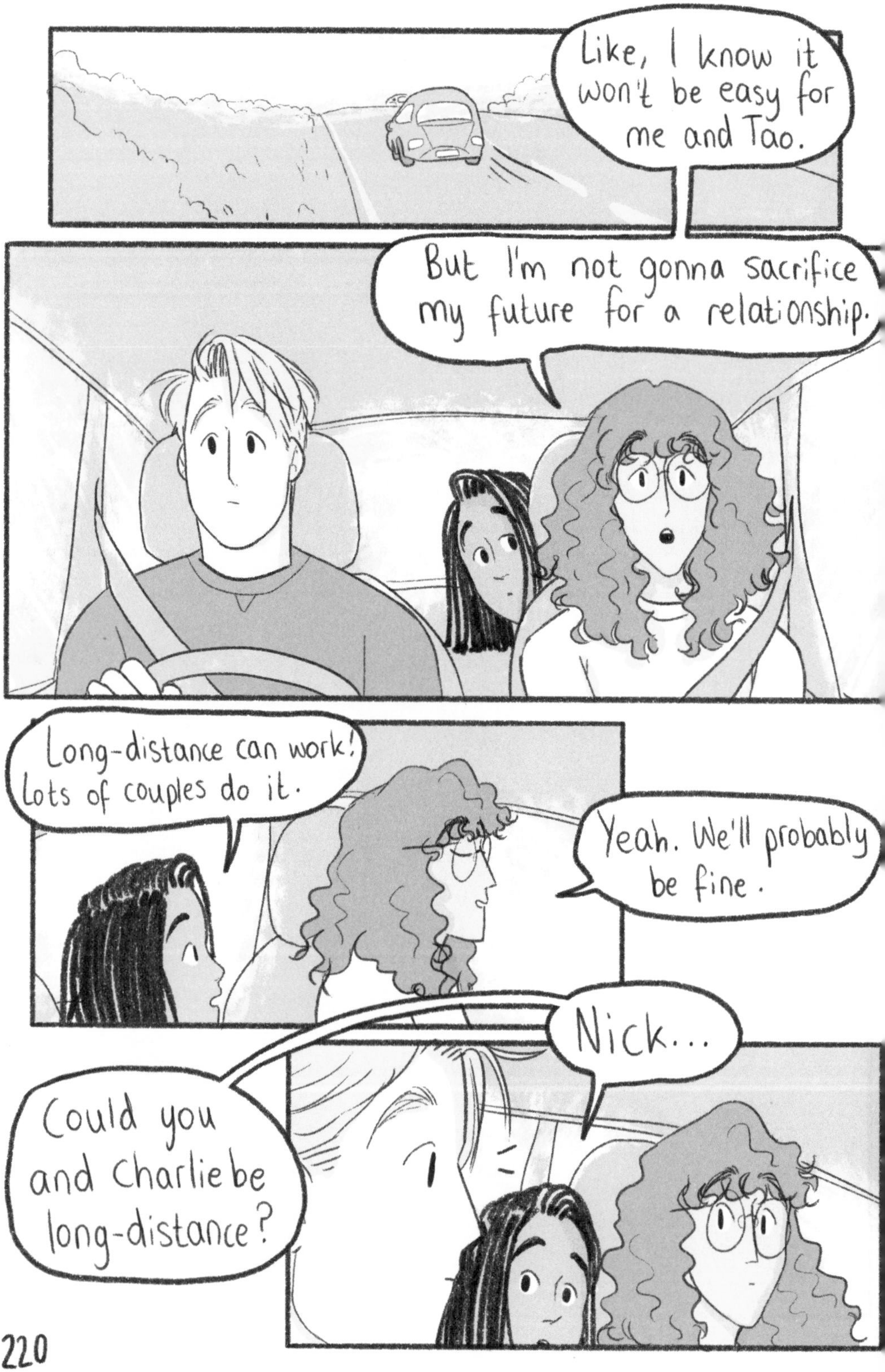
Like, I know it won't be easy for me and Tao.
But I'm not gonna sacrifice my future for a relationship.
Long-distance can work! Lots of couples do it.
Yeah. We'll probably be fine.
Nick...
Could you and Charlie be long-distance?

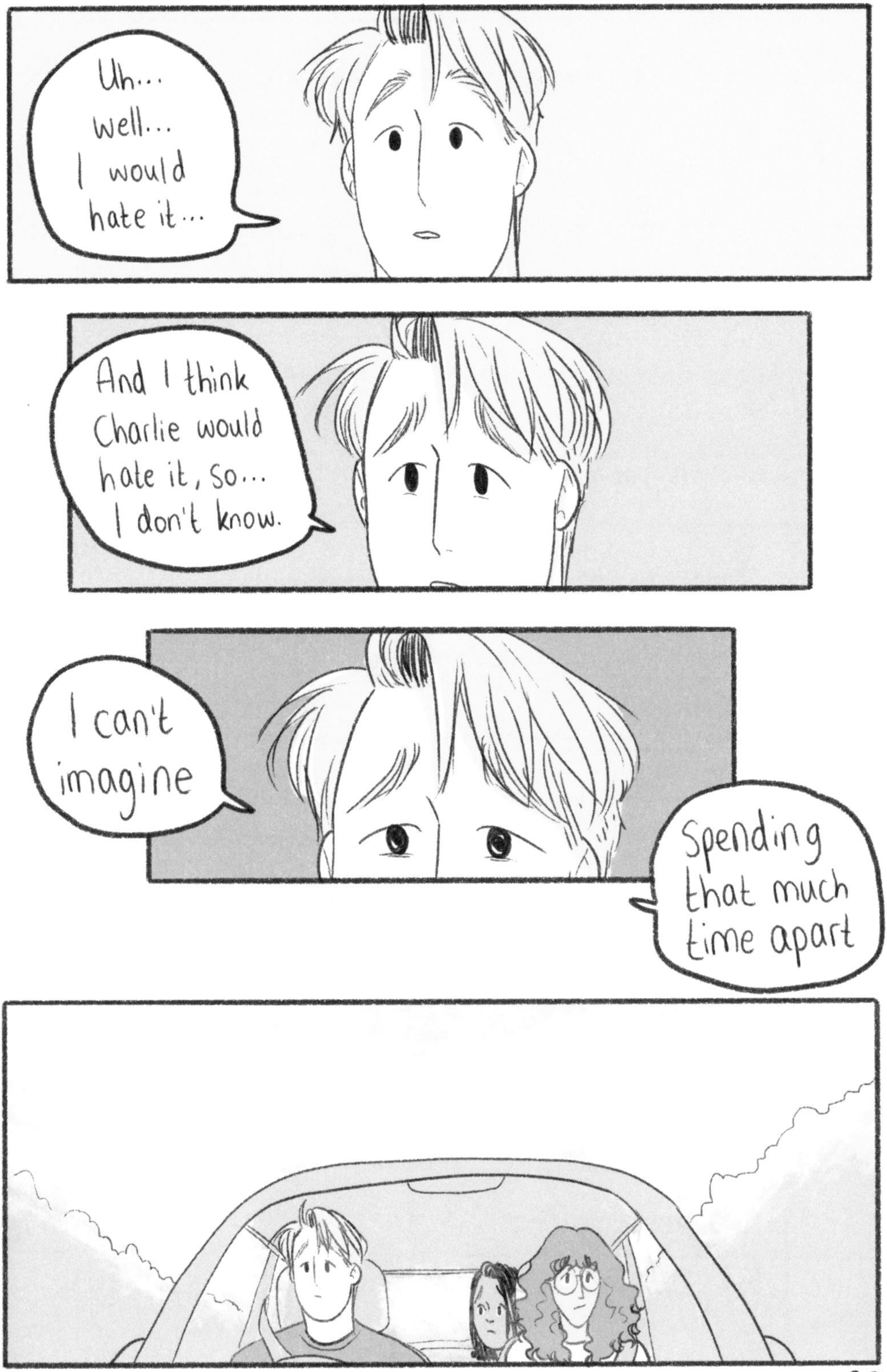
Uh... well... I would hate it...
And I think Charlie would hate it, so... I don't know.
I can't imagine
Spending that much time apart

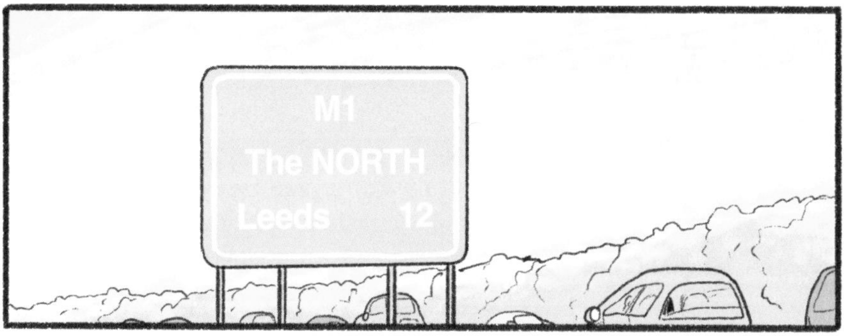
M1
The NORTH
Leeds 12

day 4

UNIVERSITY OF LEEDS

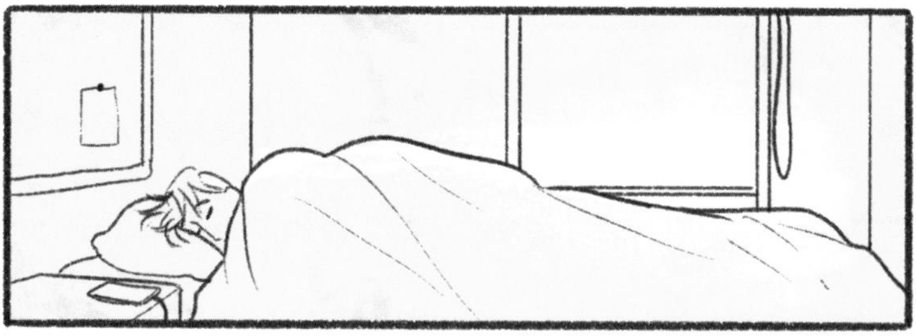

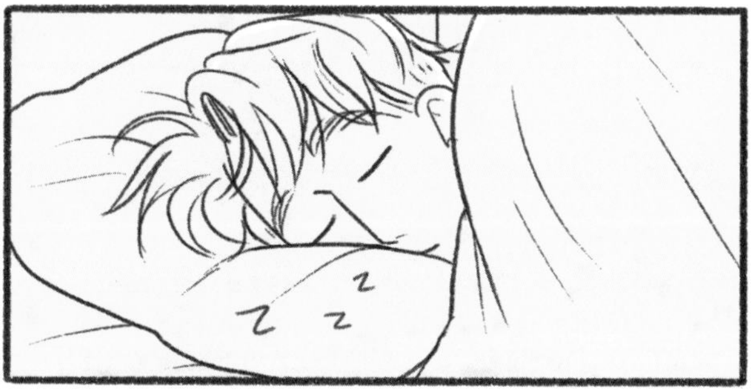
Z Z Z

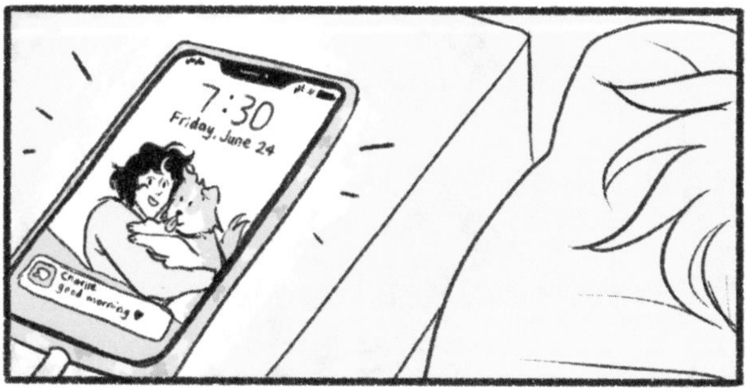
7:30
Friday, June 24
Charlie
good morning ♥

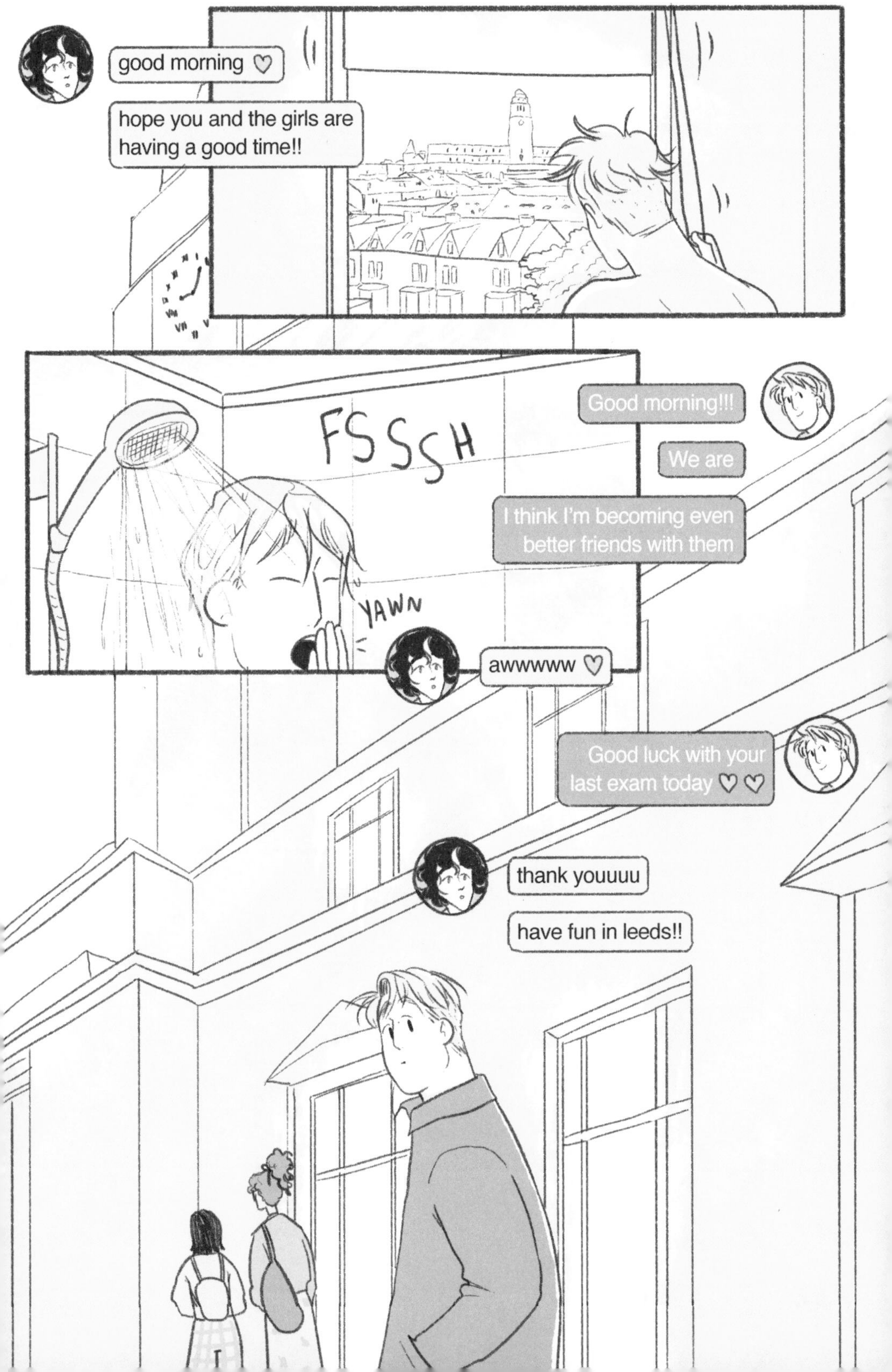
good morning ♡
hope you and the girls are having a good time!!
FSSSH
Good morning!!!
We are
I think I'm becoming even better friends with them
YAWN
awwwww ♡
Good luck with your last exam today ♡ ♡
thank youuuu
have fun in leeds!!

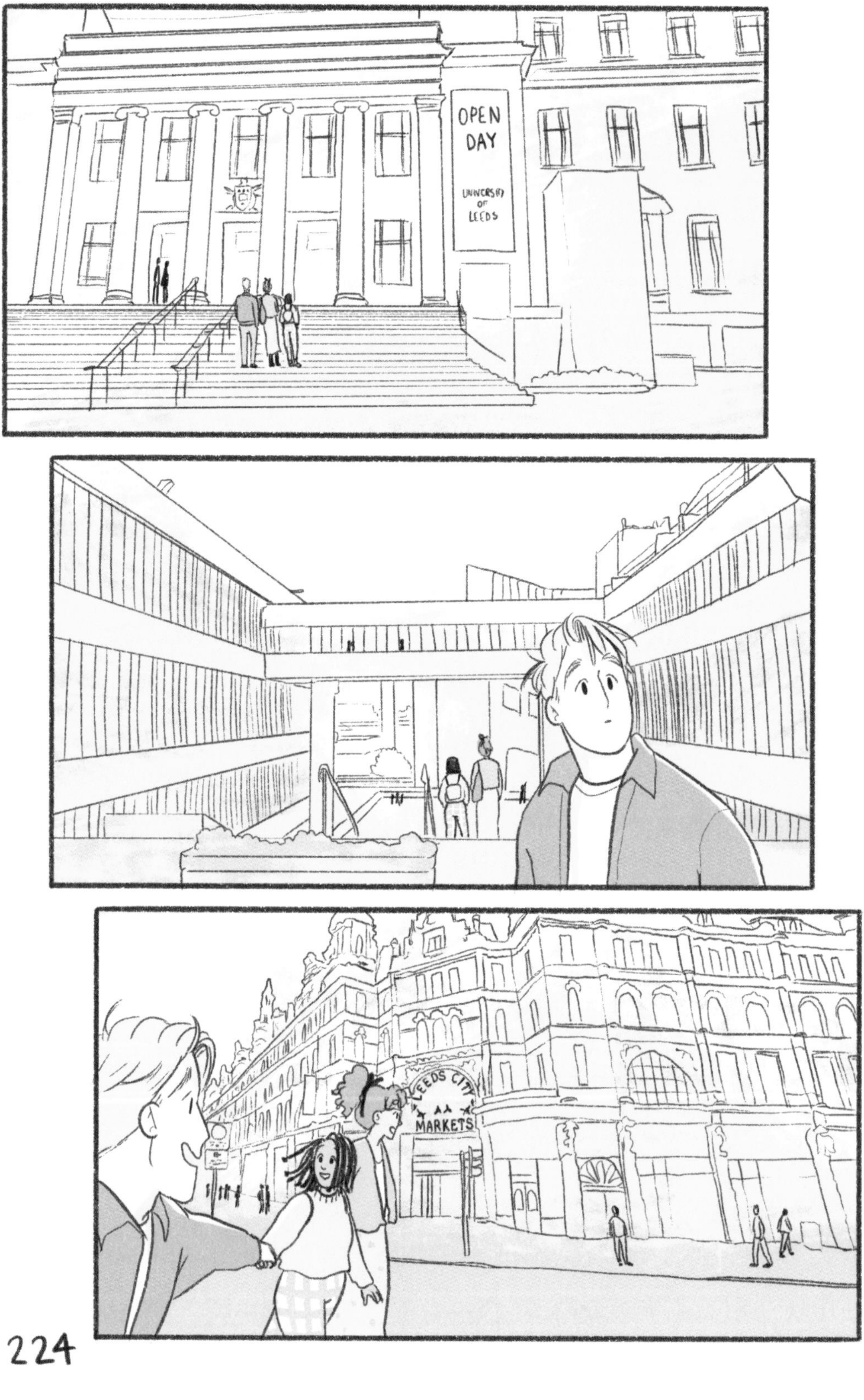
OPEN DAY
UNIVERSITY OF LEEDS
LEEDS CITY MARKETS

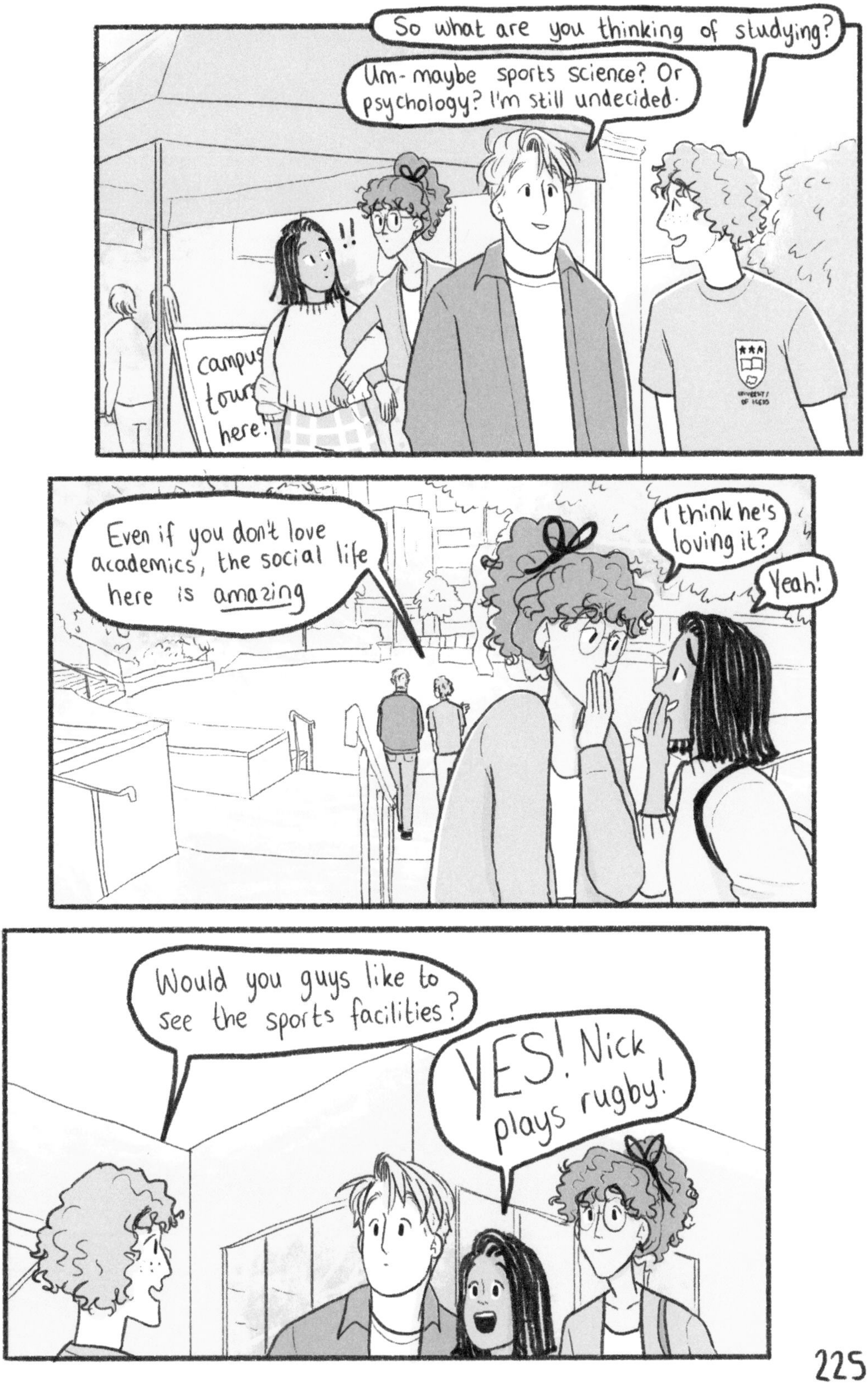
So what are you thinking of studying?
Um- maybe sports science? Or psychology? I'm still undecided.
!!
campus tours here!
Even if you don't love academics, the social life here is amazing
I think he's loving it?
Yeah!
Would you guys like to see the sports facilities?
YES! Nick plays rugby!

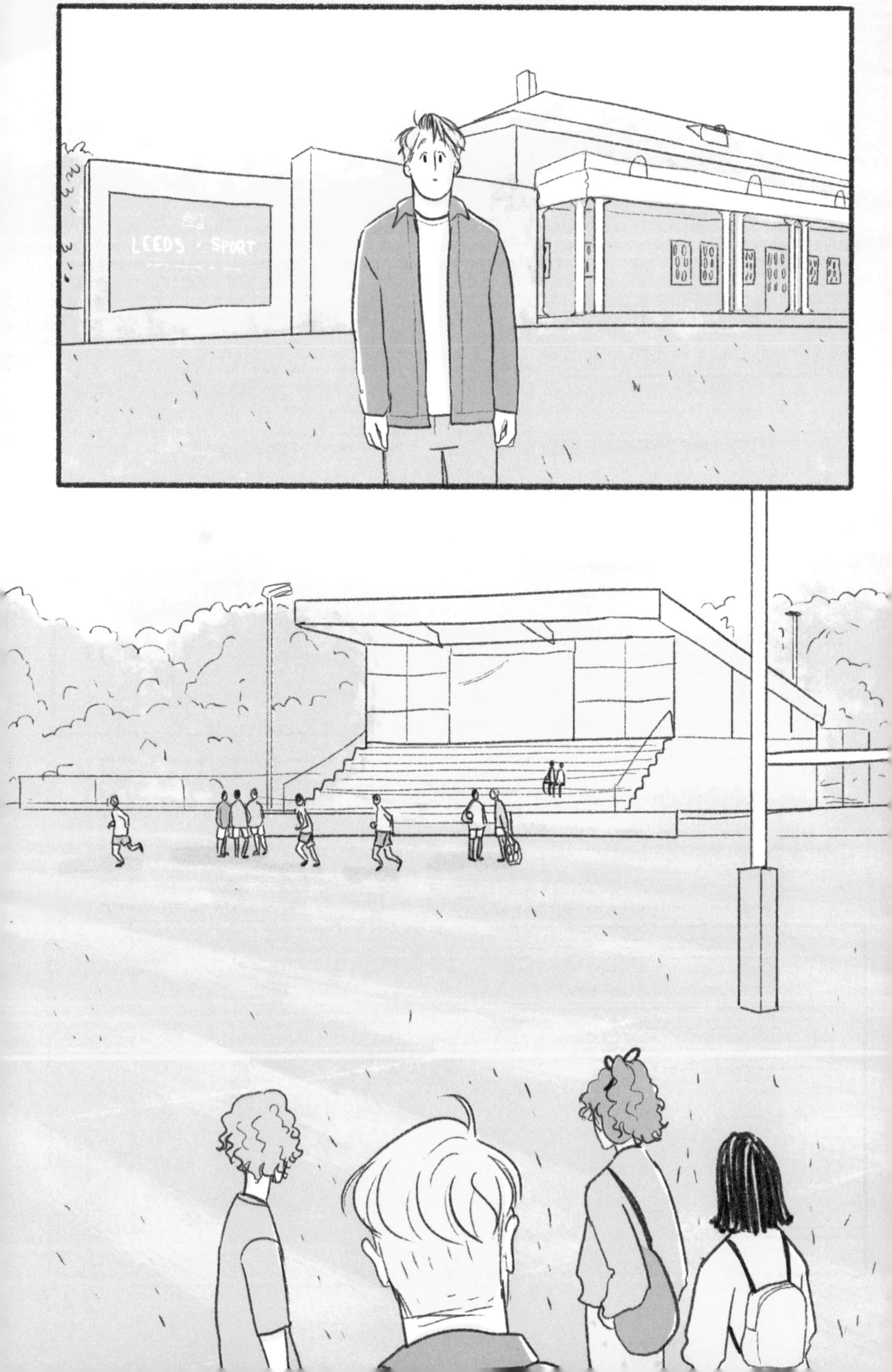
LEEDS · SPORT

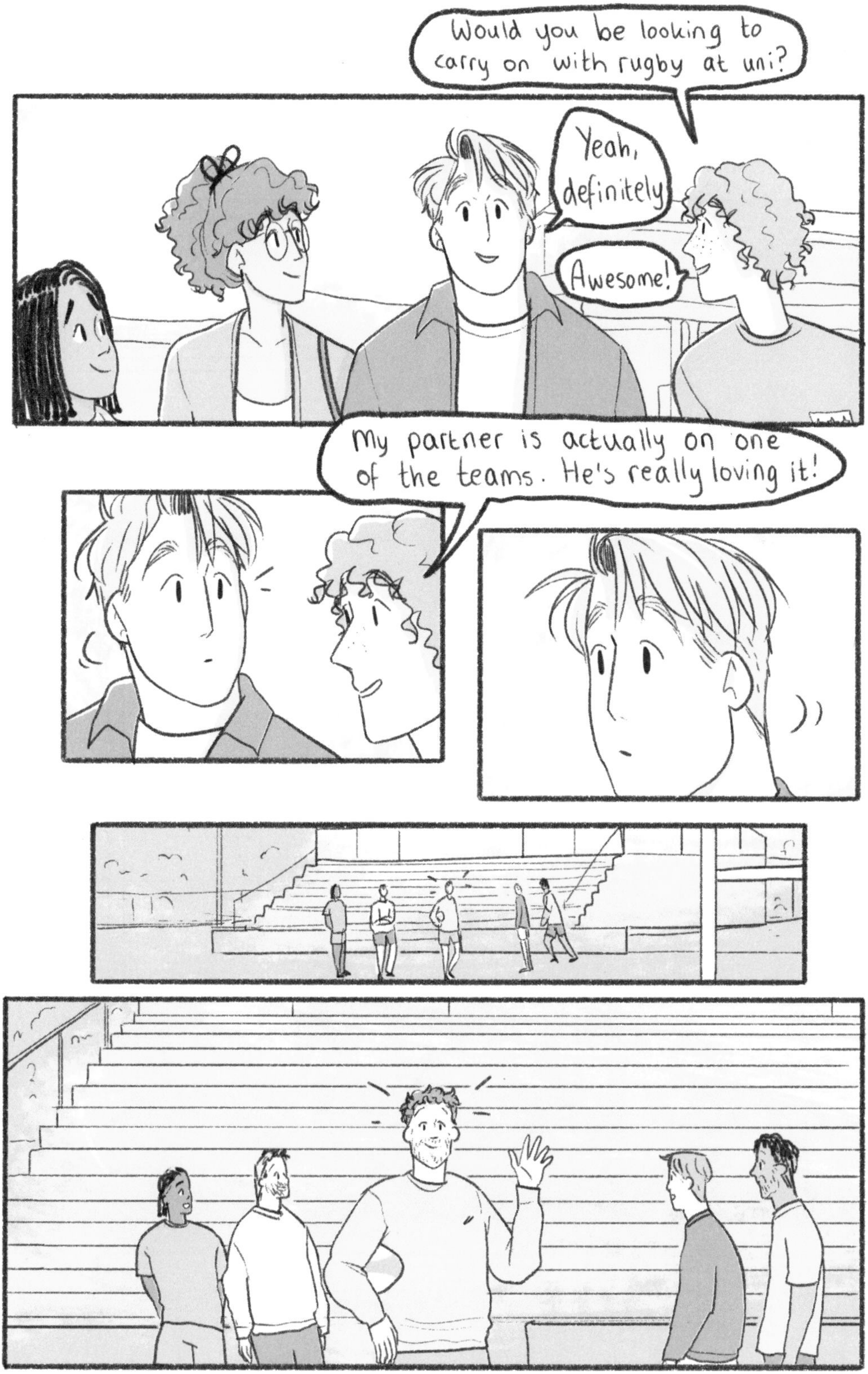
Would you be looking to carry on with rugby at uni?
Yeah, definitely
Awesome!
My partner is actually on one of the teams. He's really loving it!

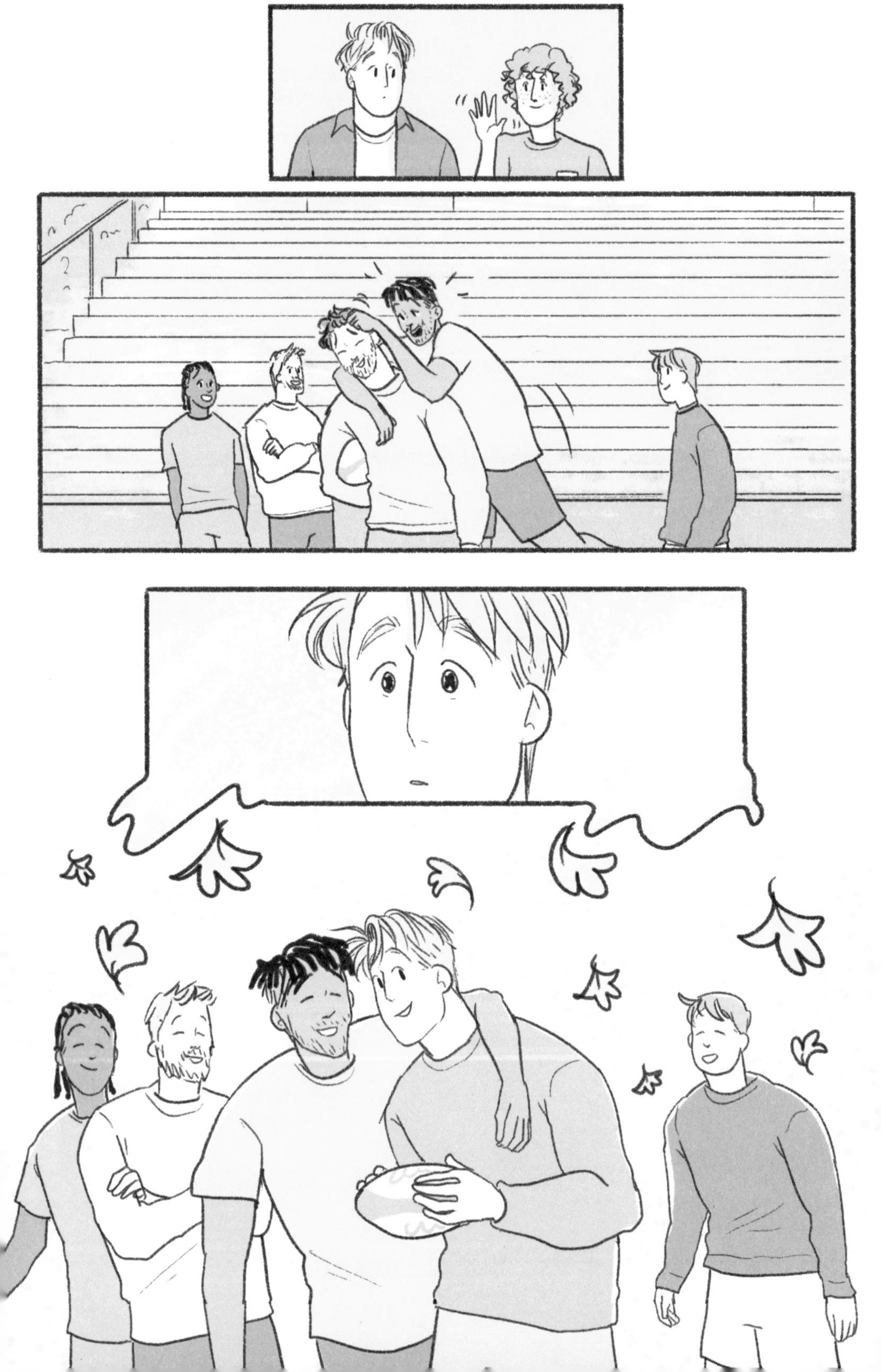

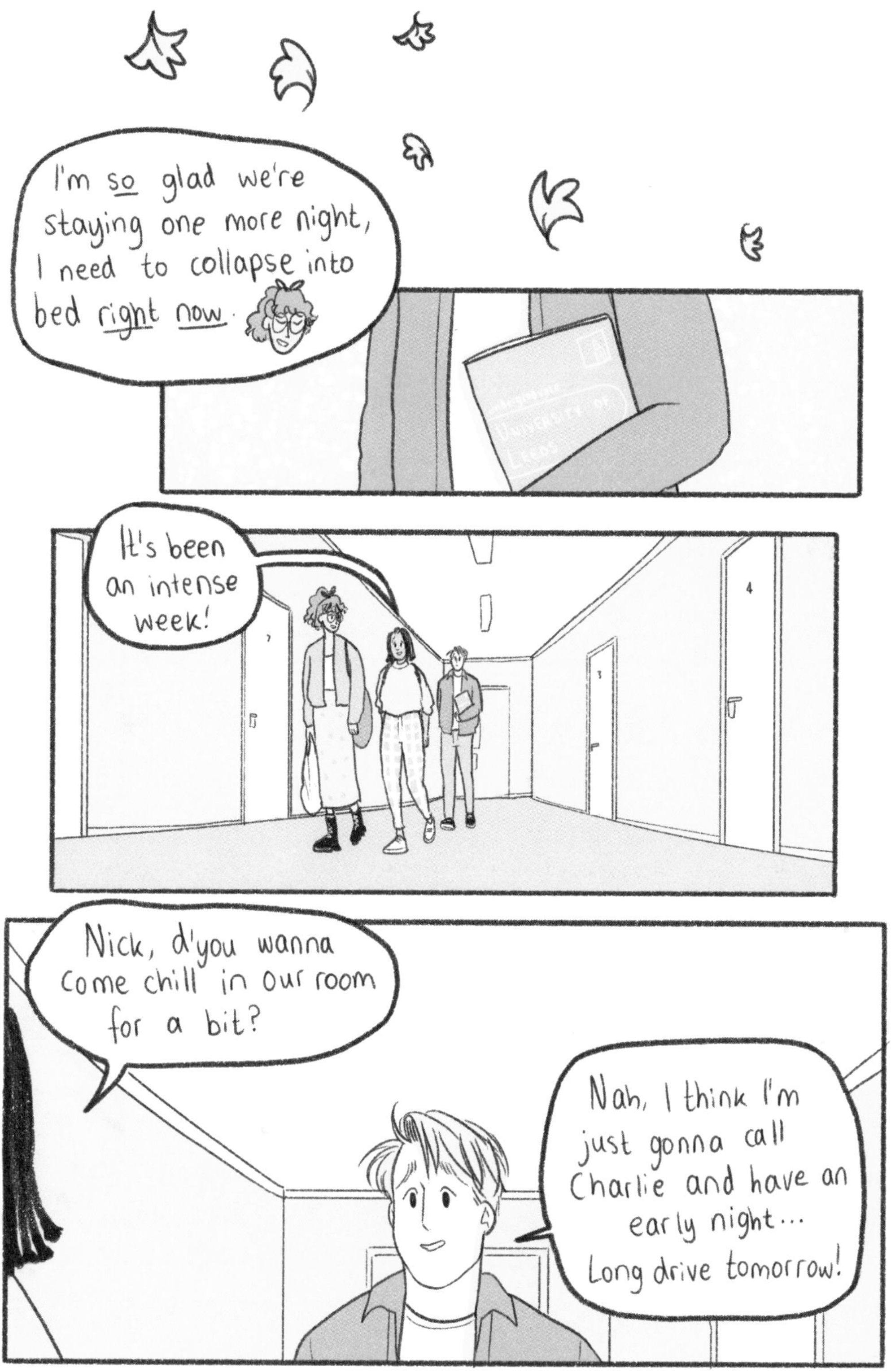
I'm so glad we're staying one more night, I need to collapse into bed right now.
UNIVERSITY OF LEEDS
It's been an intense week!
Nick, d'you wanna come chill in our room for a bit?
Nah, I think I'm just gonna call Charlie and have an early night... Long drive tomorrow!

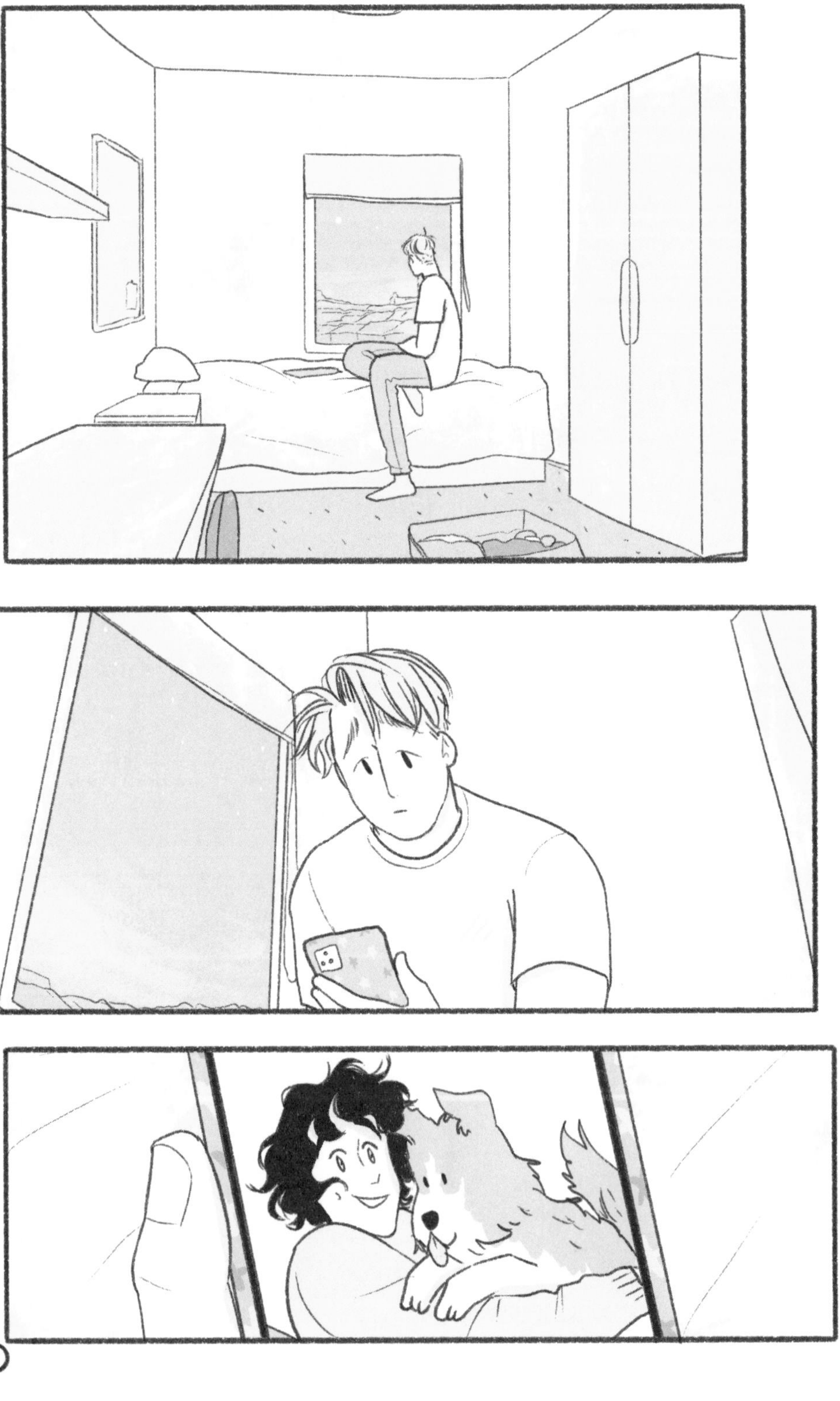

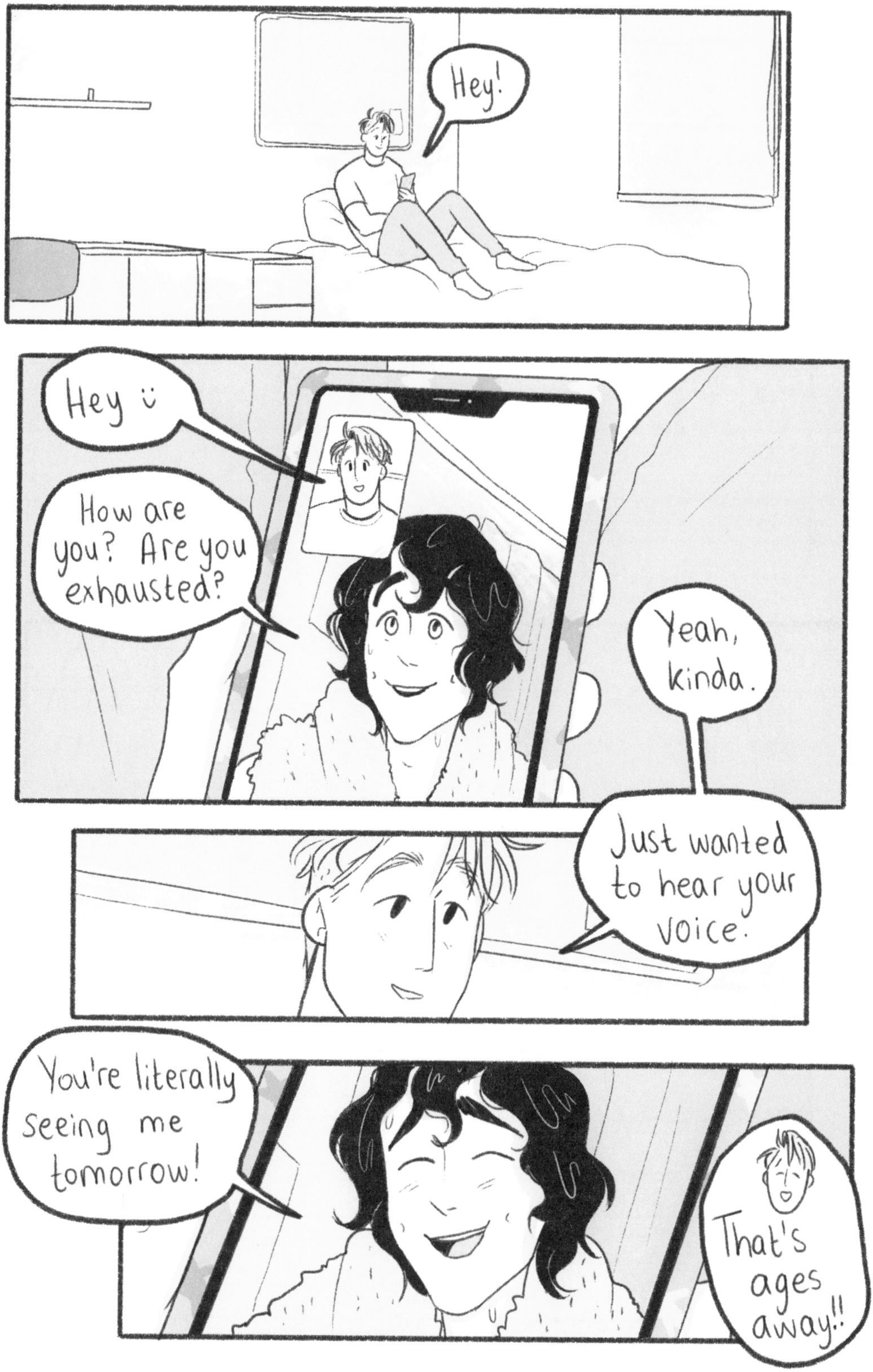
Hey!
Hey ☺
How are you? Are you exhausted?
Yeah, kinda.
Just wanted to hear your voice.
You're literally seeing me tomorrow!
That's ages away!!

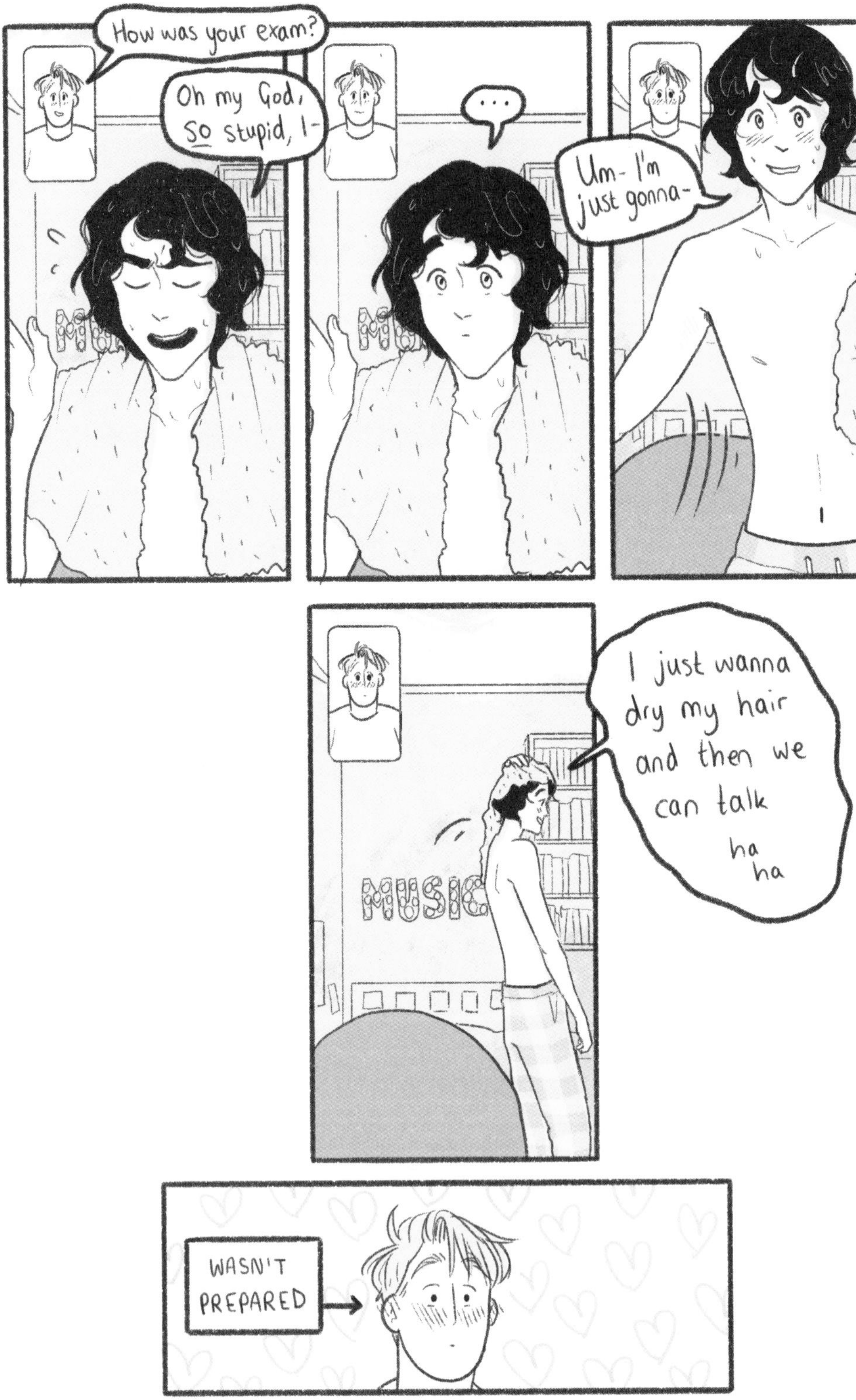
How was your exam?
Oh my God, so stupid, I-
...
Um- I'm just gonna-
I just wanna dry my hair and then we can talk
ha ha
MUSIC
WASN'T PREPARED

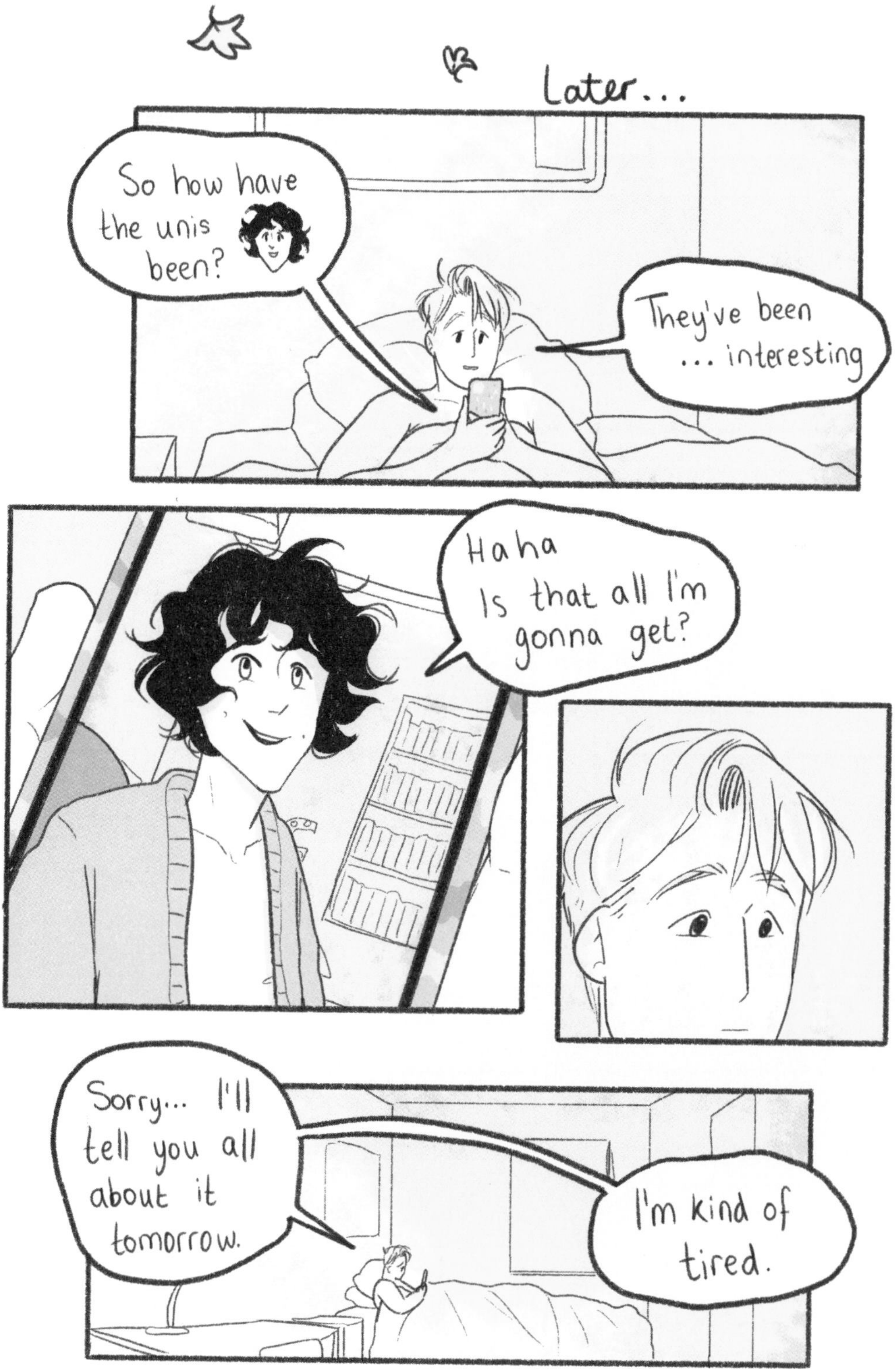
Later...
So how have the unis been?
They've been ... interesting
Haha Is that all I'm gonna get?
Sorry... I'll tell you all about it tomorrow.
I'm kind of tired.

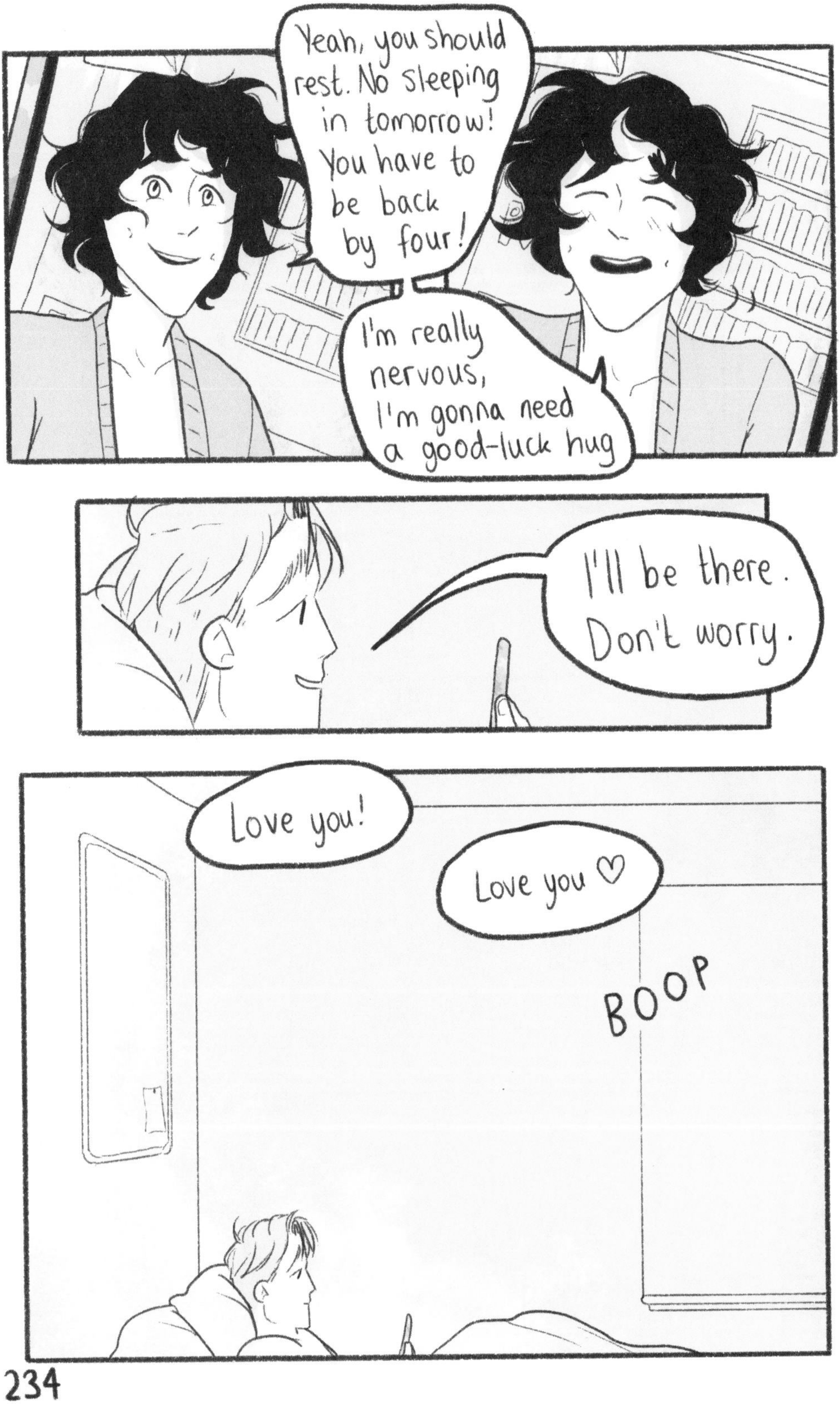
Yeah, you should rest. No sleeping in tomorrow! You have to be back by four!
I'm really nervous, I'm gonna need a good-luck hug
I'll be there. Don't worry.
Love you!
Love you ♡
BOOP

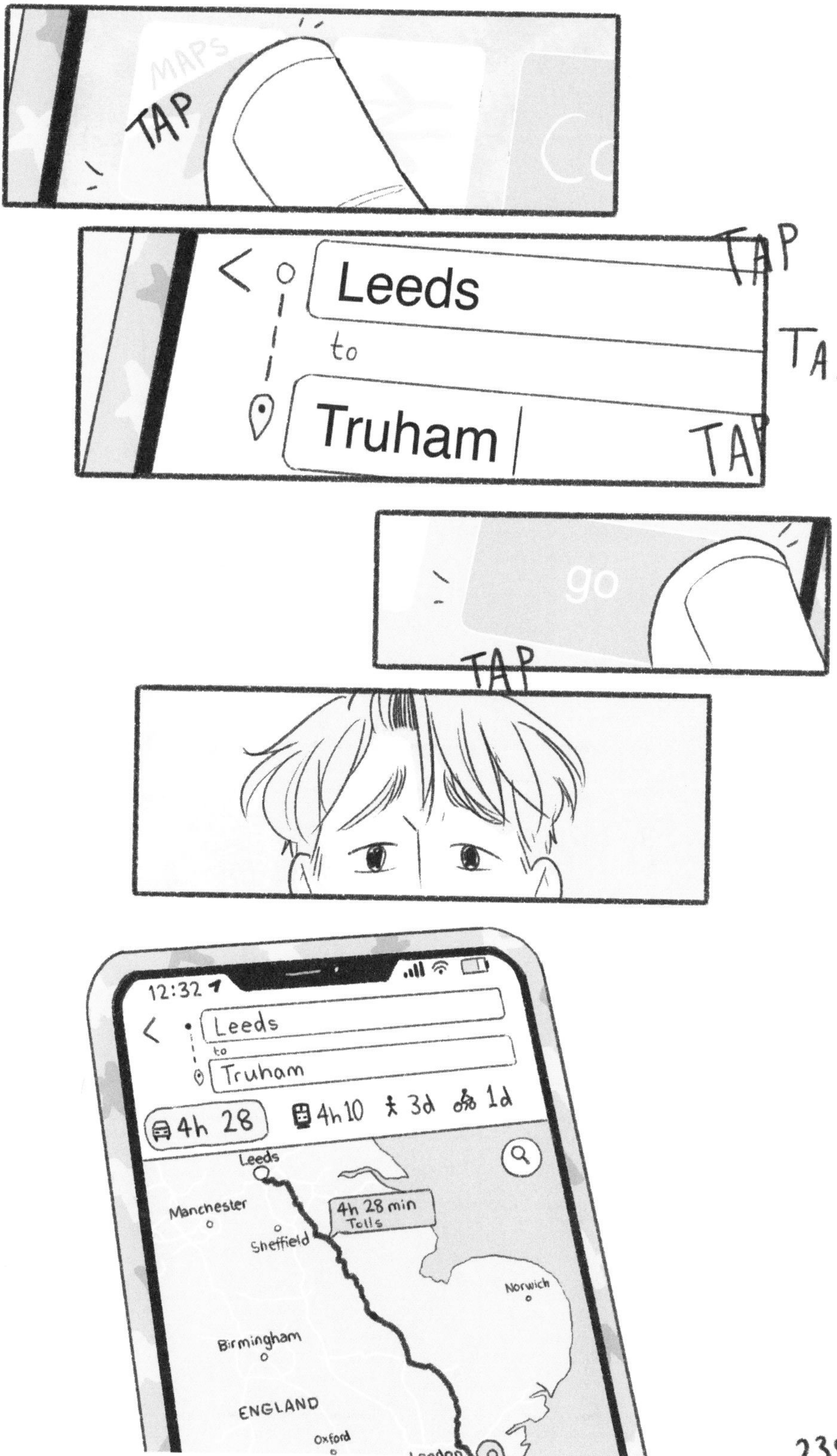
MAPS
TAP
Leeds
to
Truham
TAP
TAP
TAP
go
TAP
12:32
Leeds
to
Truham
4h 28
4h 10
3d
1d
Leeds
Manchester
4h 28 min
Tolls
Sheffield
Norwich
Birmingham
ENGLAND
Oxford

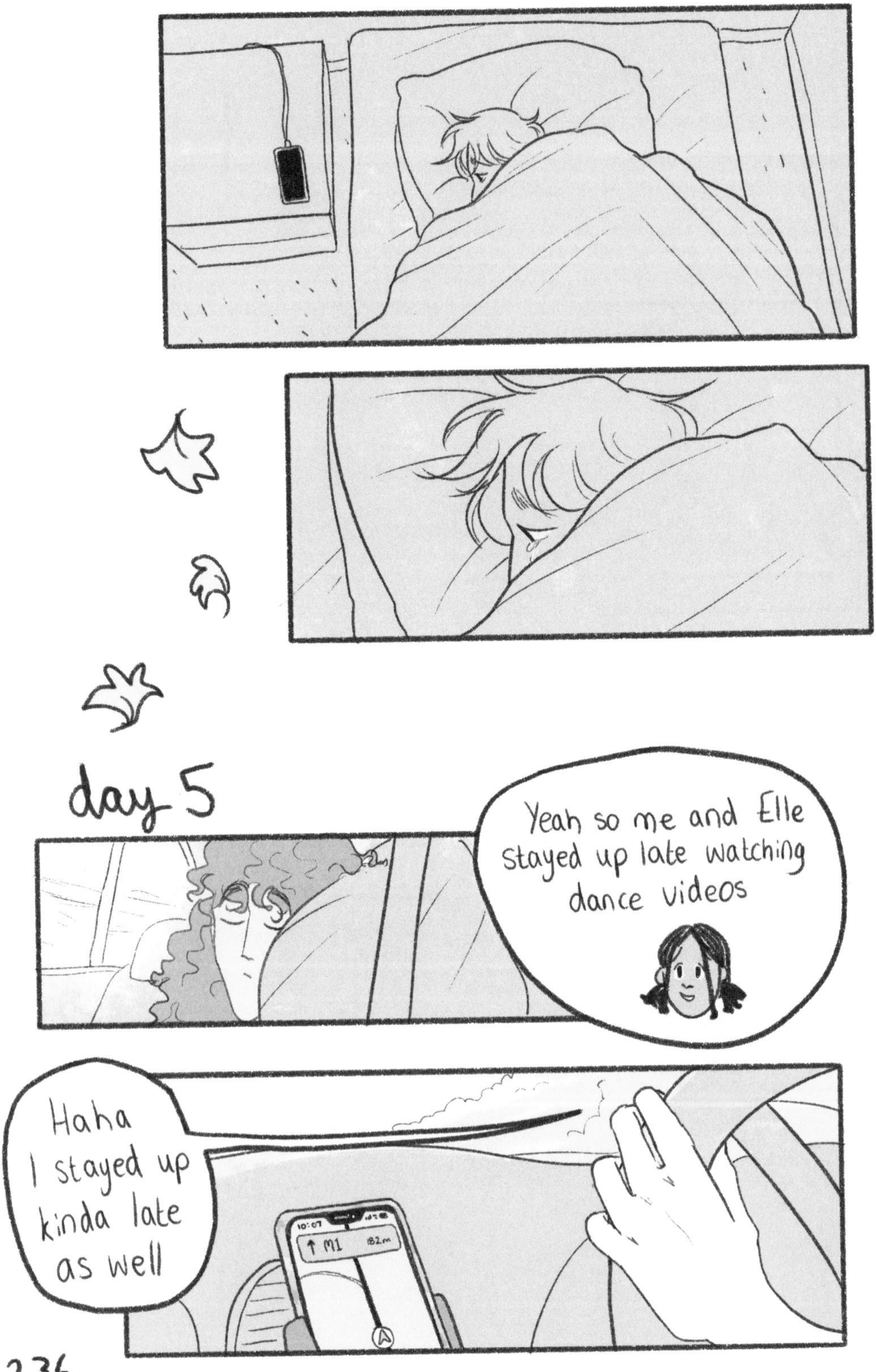
day 5
Yeah so me and Elle stayed up late watching dance videos
Haha I stayed up kinda late as well

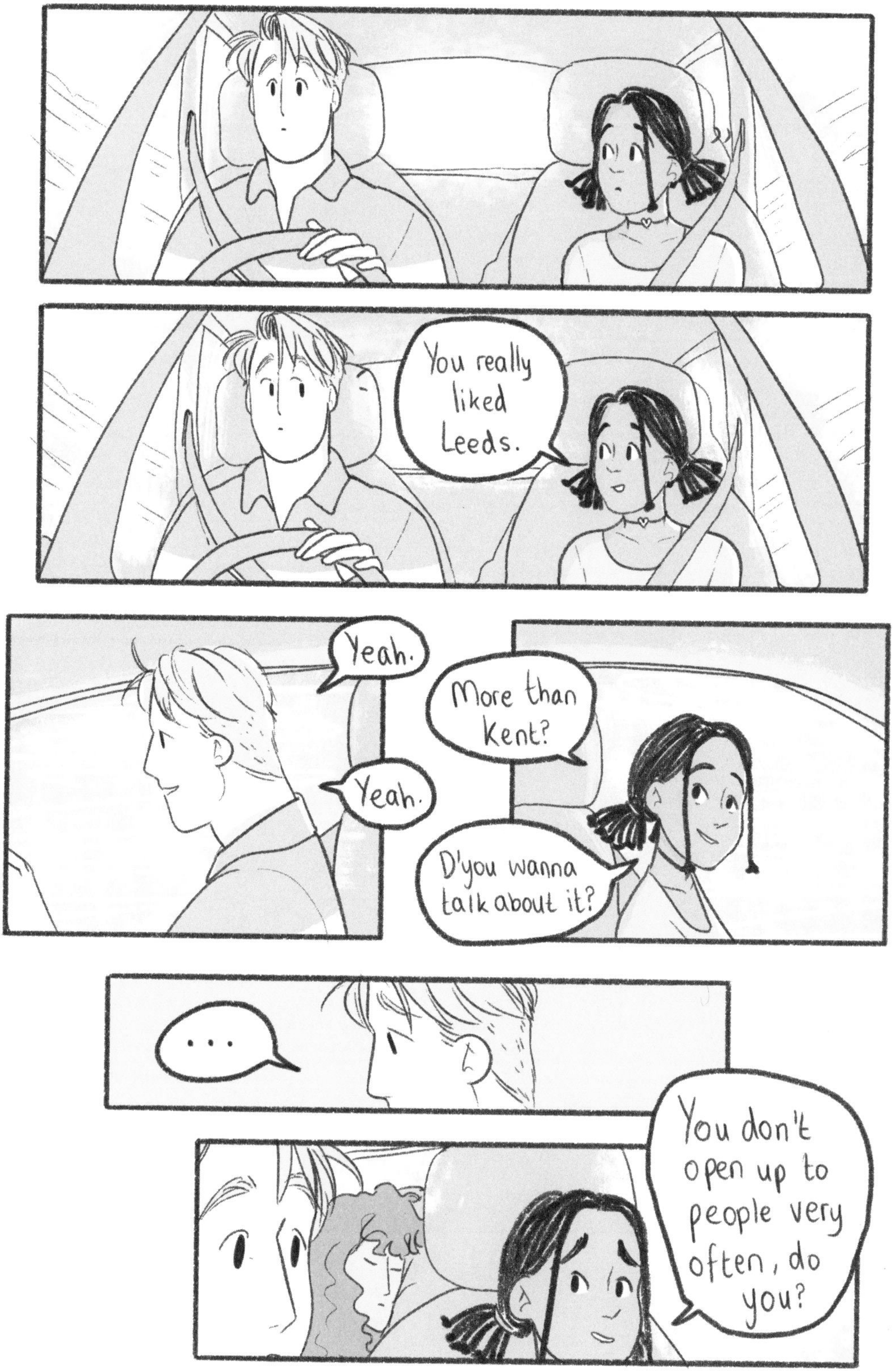
You really liked Leeds.
Yeah.
More than Kent?
Yeah.
D'you wanna talk about it?
...
You don't open up to people very often, do you?

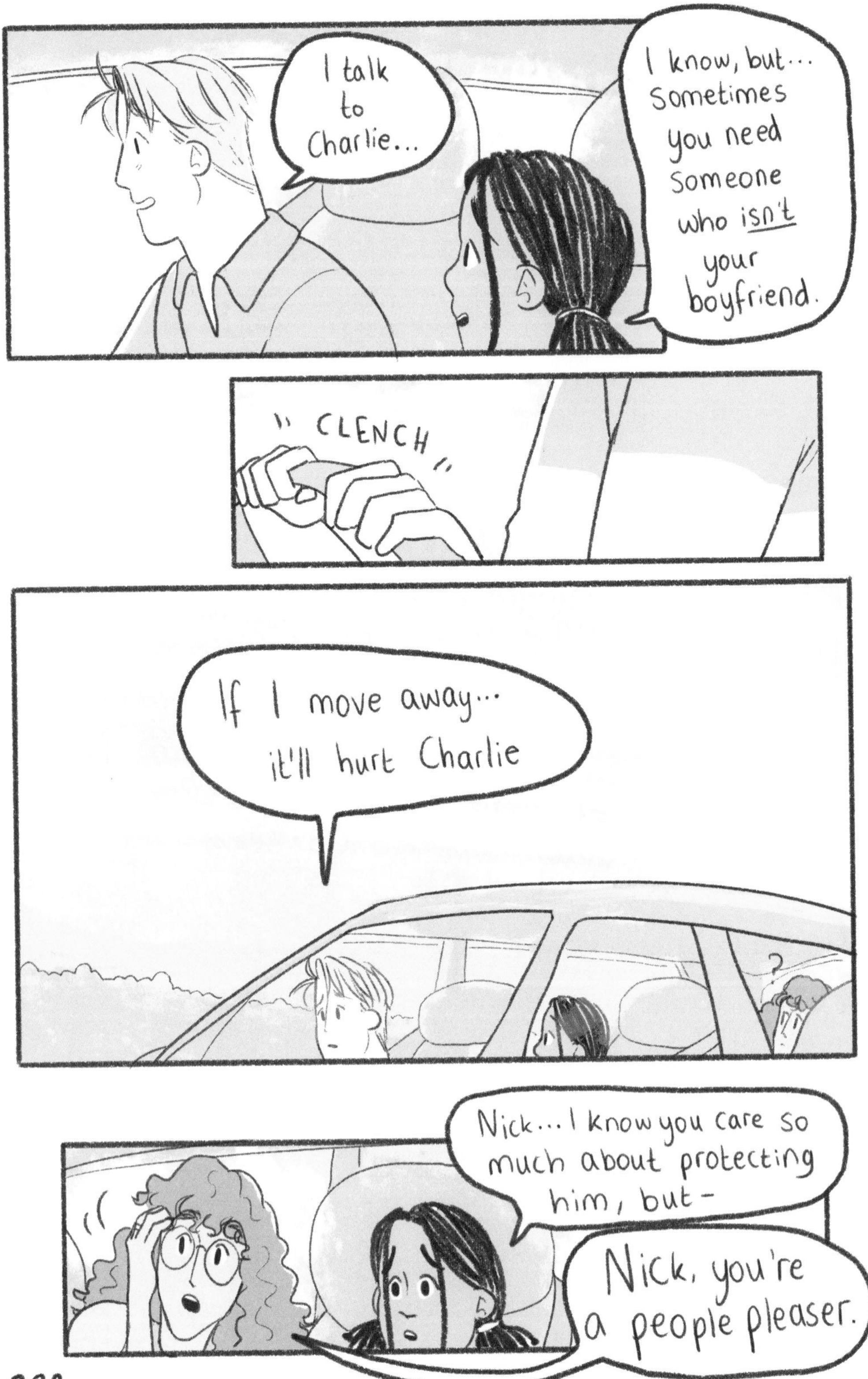
I talk to Charlie...
I know, but... Sometimes you need someone who isn't your boyfriend.
CLENCH
If I move away... it'll hurt Charlie
?
Nick... I know you care so much about protecting him, but-
Nick, you're a people pleaser.

Elle—

No, he needs to hear this!

Nick, you always put everyone else's feelings above your own. And I know you and Charlie love each other, but this is *your* future.

Like, I know how you feel. I'm in the same boat. But... I have to put myself first right now.

Charlie would support you! He wants you to be happy! Putting yourself first for once wouldn't make him hate you!

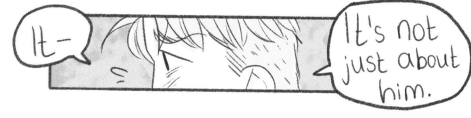

It—

It's not just about him.

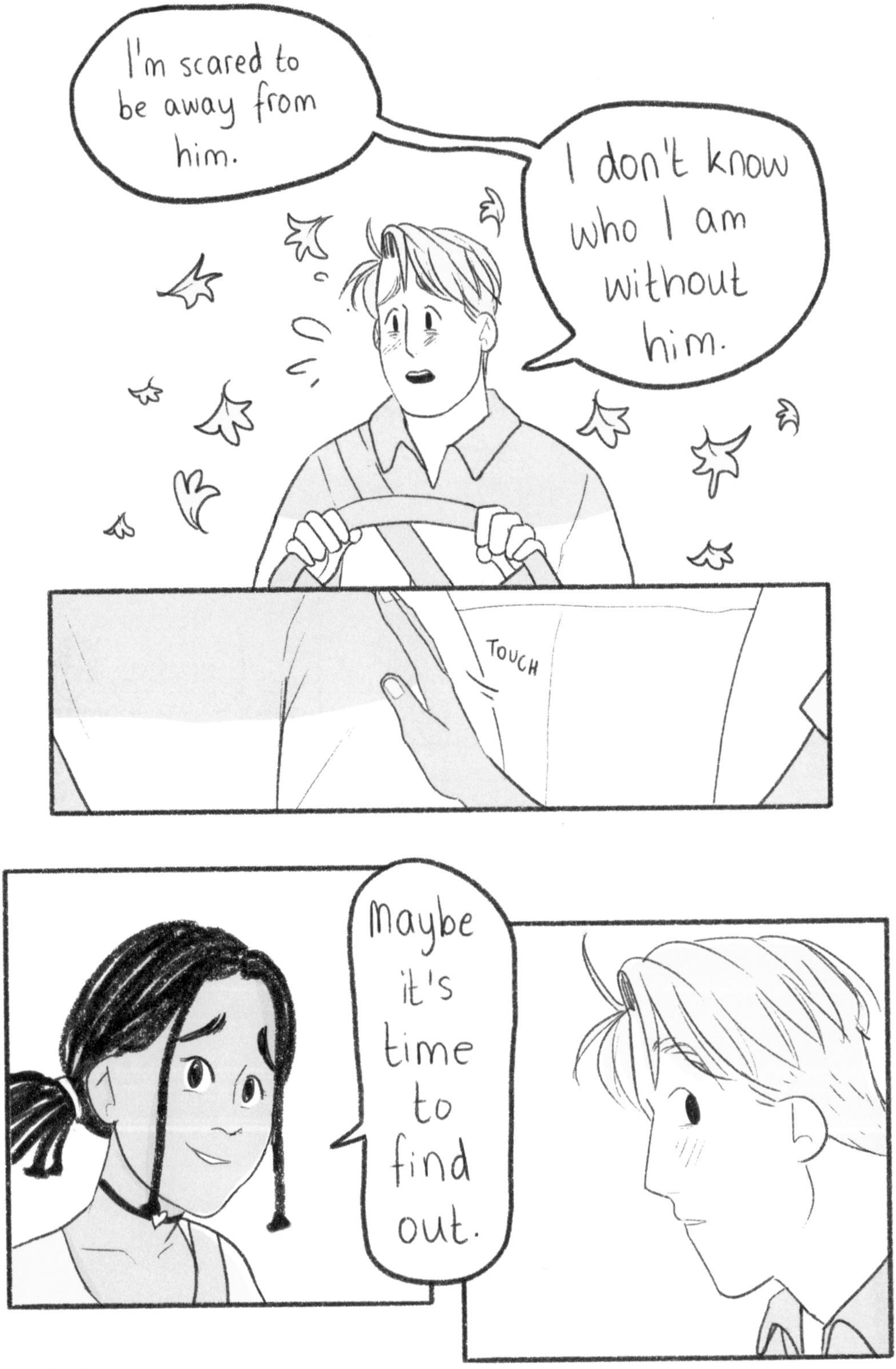
I'm scared to be away from him.
I don't know who I am without him.
TOUCH
Maybe it's time to find out.

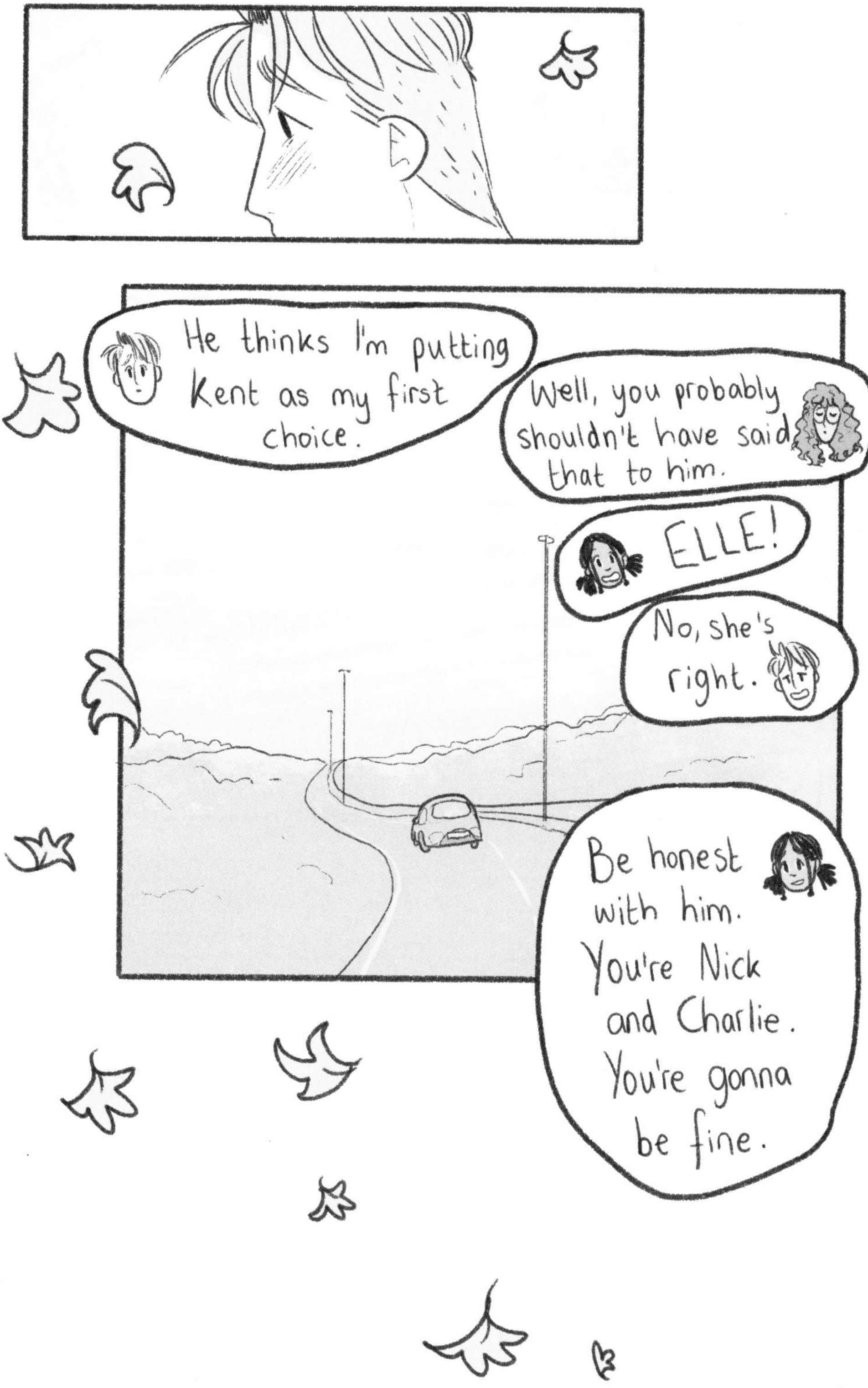
He thinks I'm putting Kent as my first choice.
Well, you probably shouldn't have said that to him.
ELLE!
No, she's right.
Be honest with him. You're Nick and Charlie. You're gonna be fine.

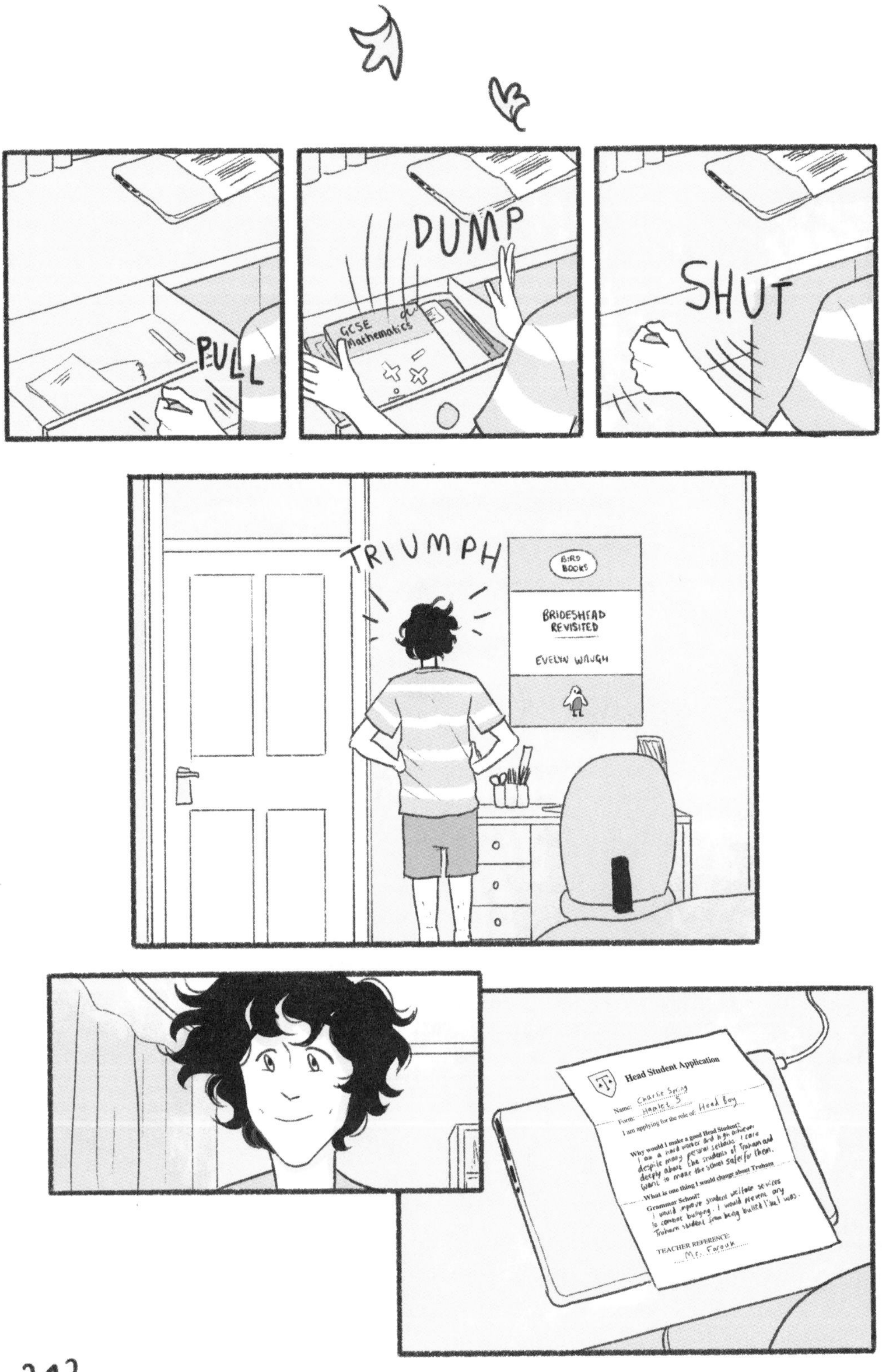
PULL
GCSE Mathematics
DUMP
SHUT
TRIUMPH
BIRD BOOKS
BRIDESHEAD REVISITED
EVELYN WAUGH
Head Student Application
Name: Charlie Spring
Form: Hamlet 5
I am applying for the role of: Head Boy
Why would I make a good Head Student?
I am a hard worker and high achiever despite many personal setbacks. I care deeply about the students of Truham and want to make the school safer for them.
What is one thing I would change about Truham Grammar School?
I would improve student welfare services to combat bullying. I would prevent any Truham student from being bullied like I was.
TEACHER REFERENCE:
Mr. Farouk

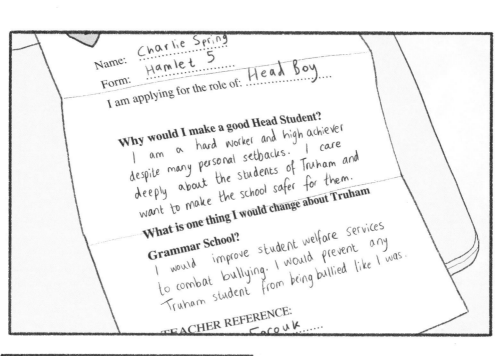

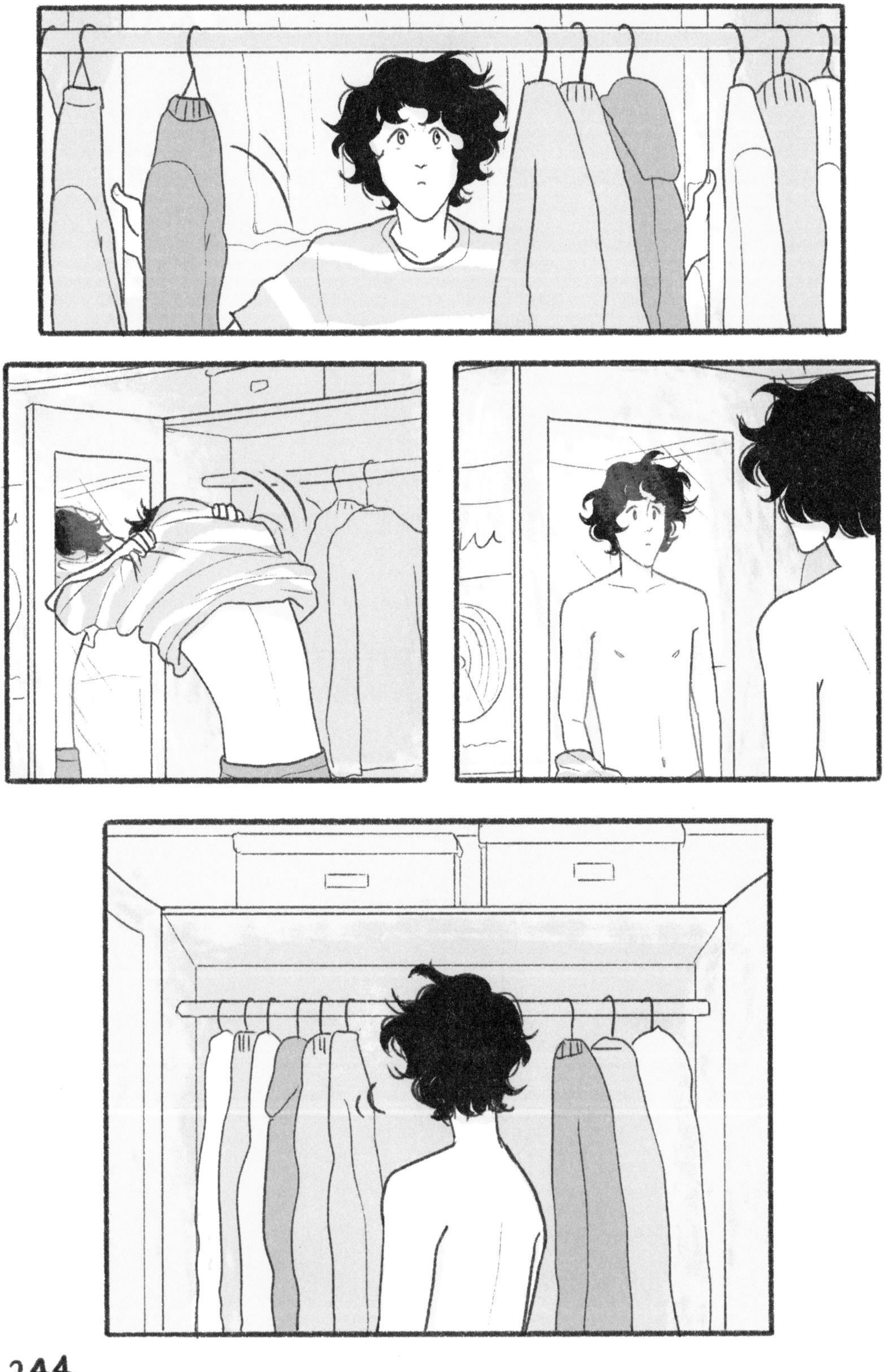

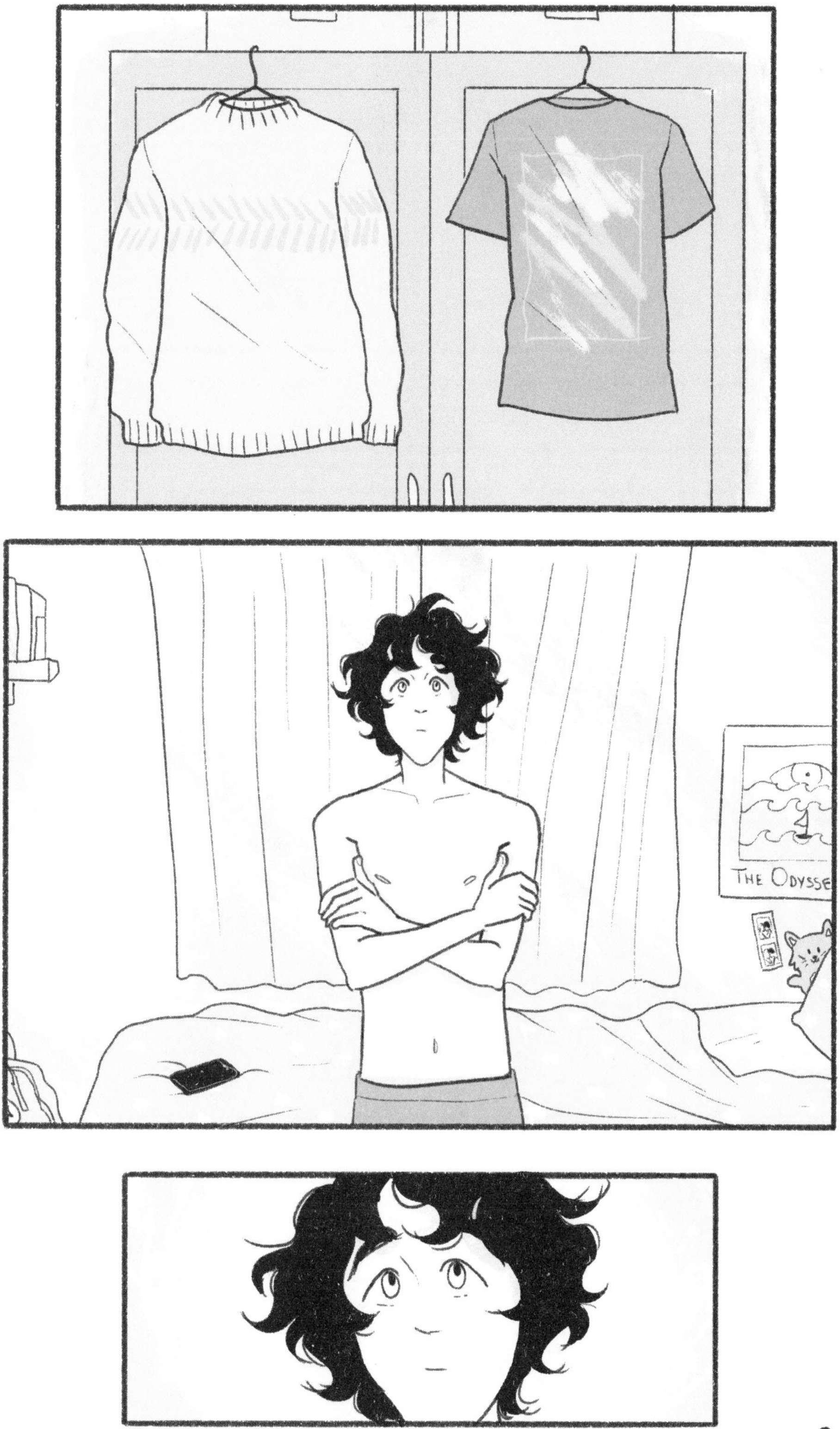
THE ODYSSE

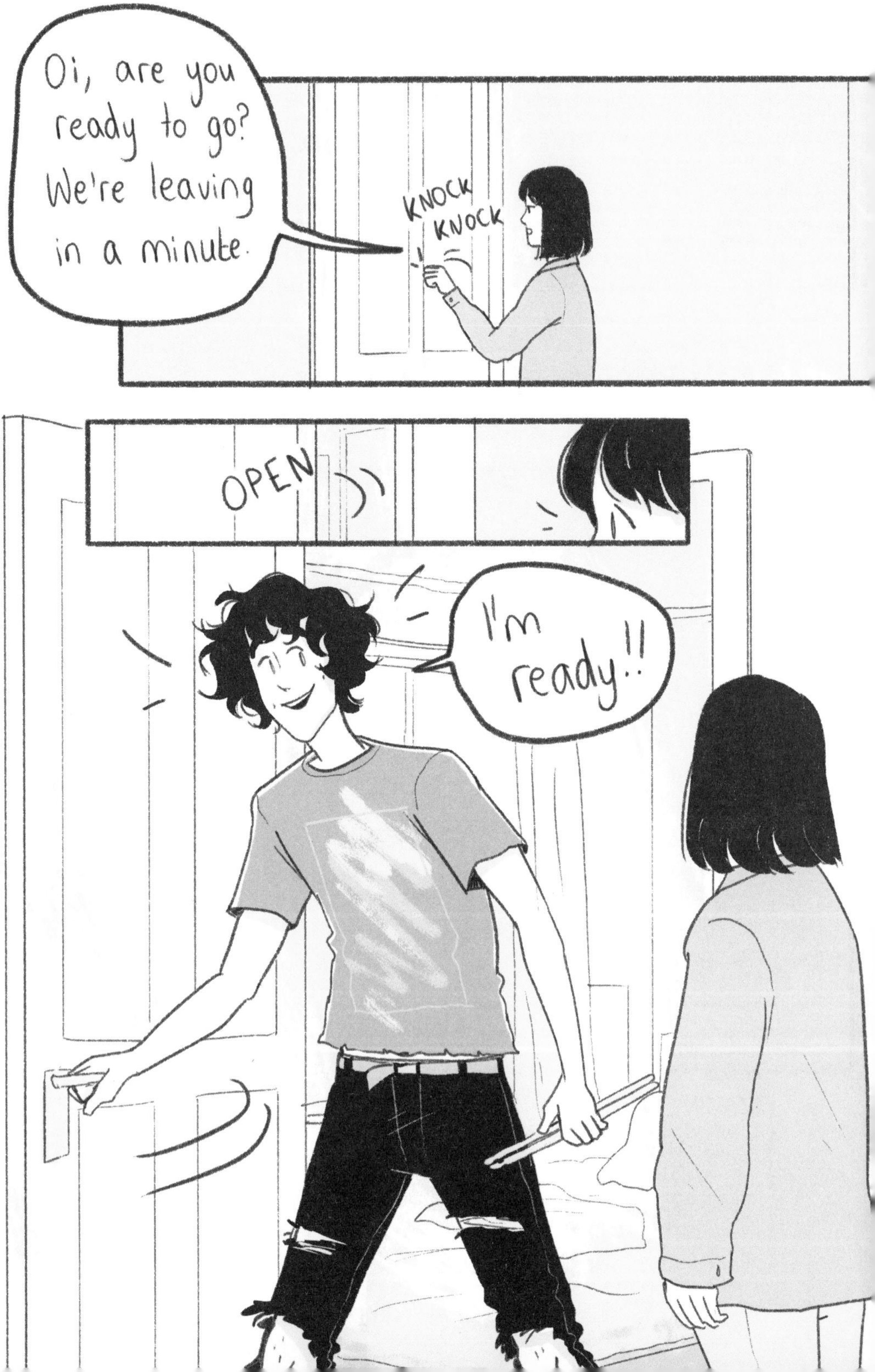
Oi, are you ready to go? We're leaving in a minute.
KNOCK KNOCK
OPEN
I'm ready!!

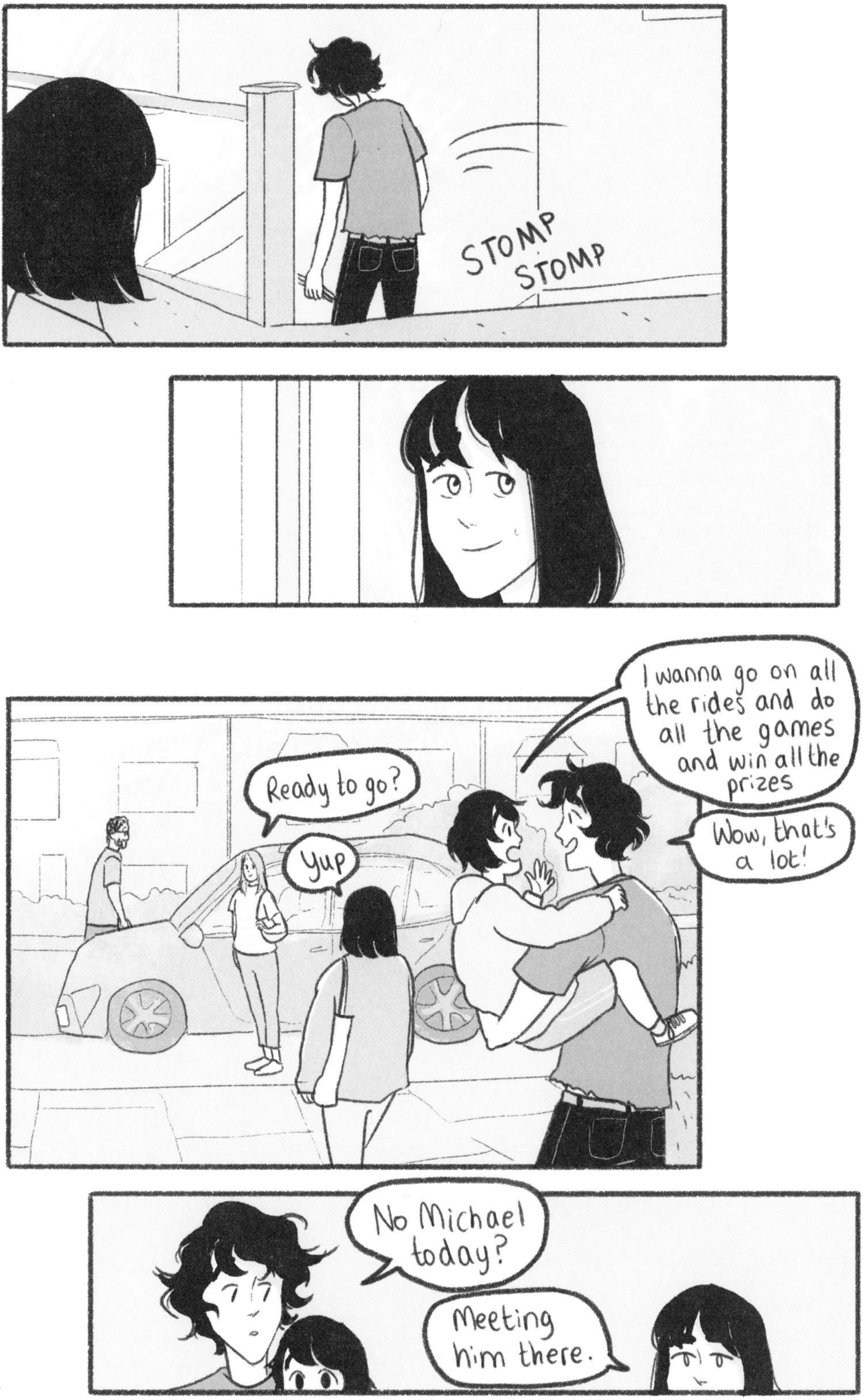
STOMP
STOMP
Ready to go?
Yup
I wanna go on all the rides and do all the games and win all the prizes
Wow, that's a lot!
No Michael today?
Meeting him there.

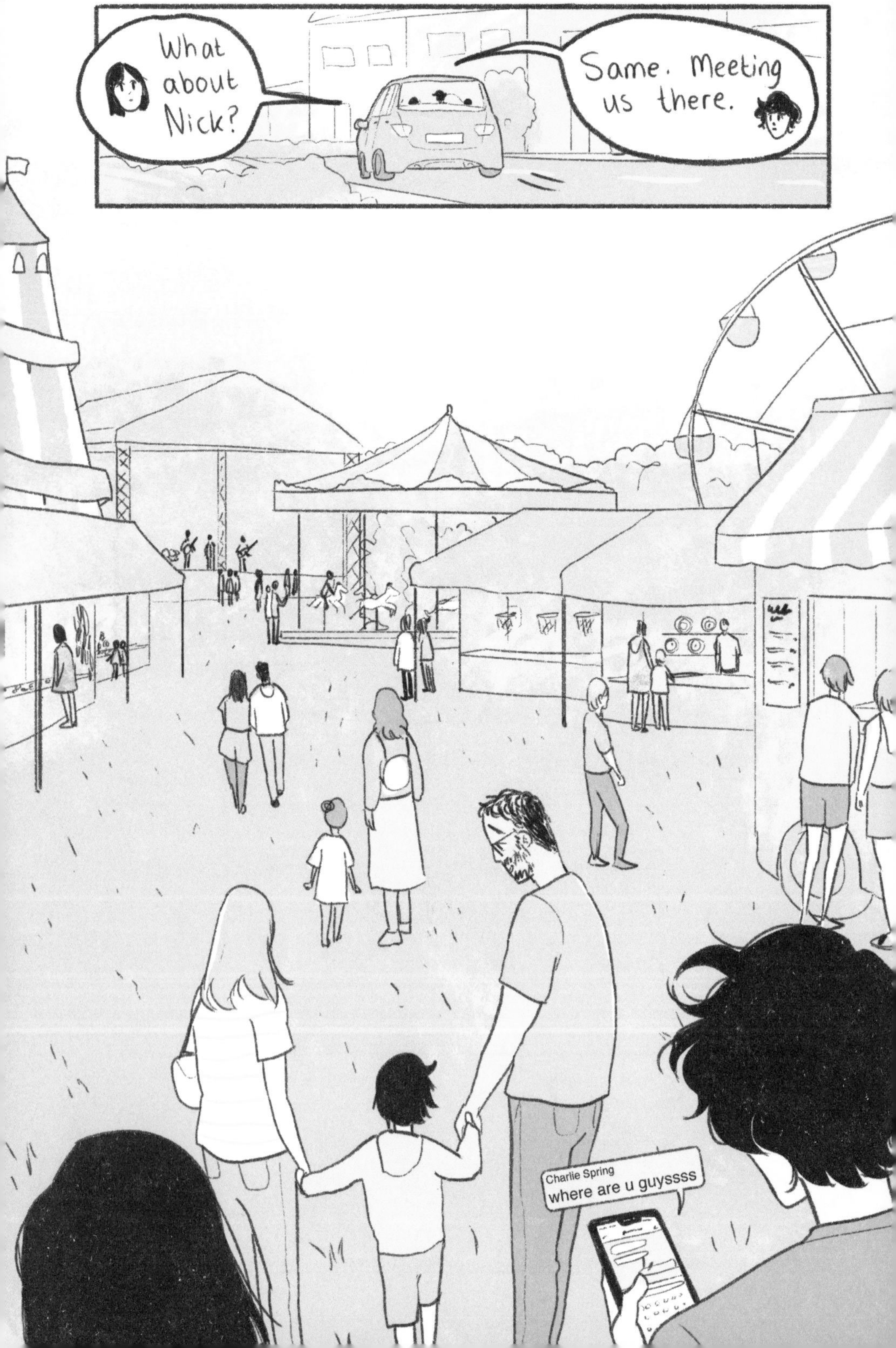
What about Nick?
Same. Meeting us there.
Charlie Spring
where are u guyssss

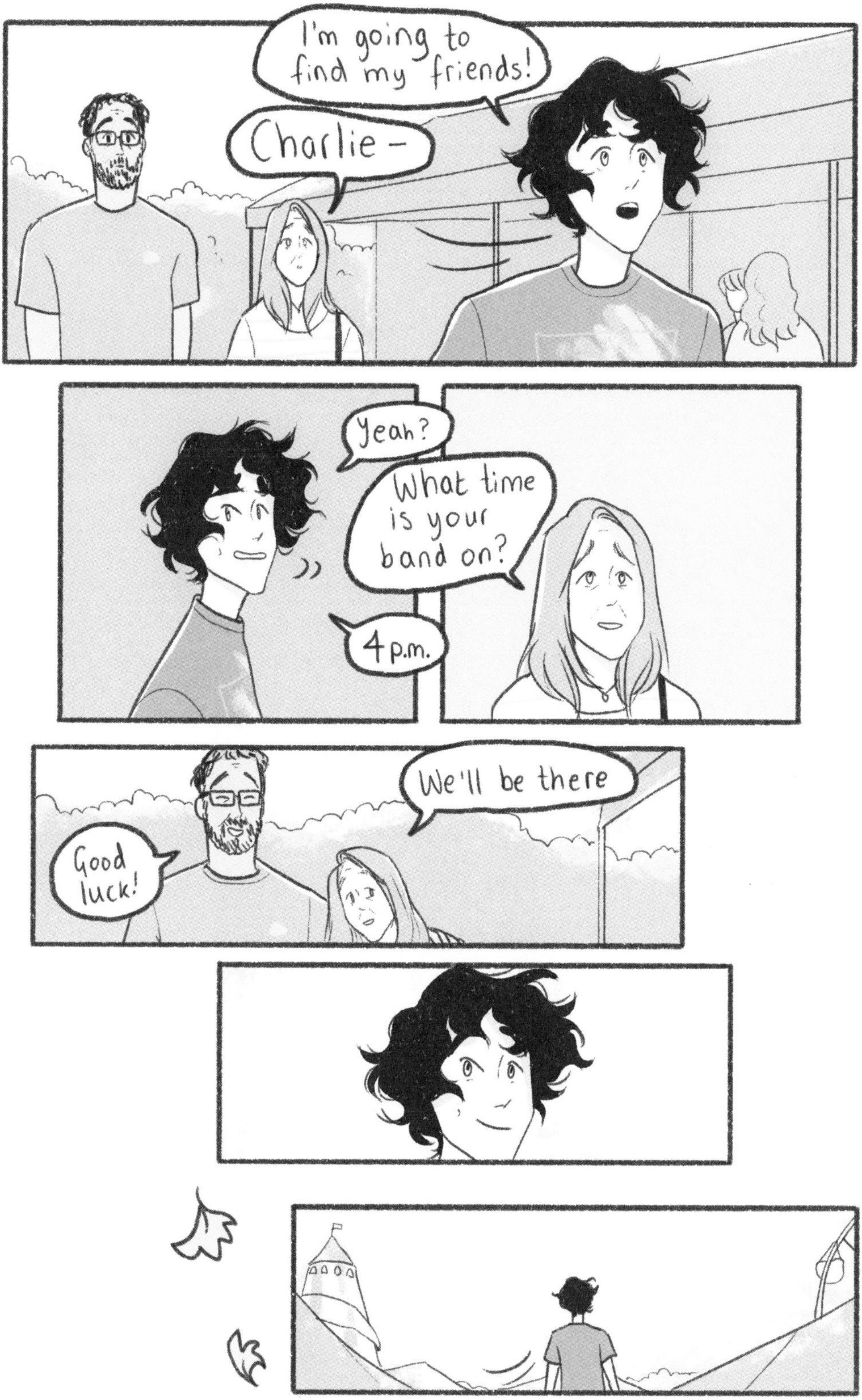
I'm going to find my friends!
Charlie -
Yeah?
What time is your band on?
4 p.m.
We'll be there
Good luck!

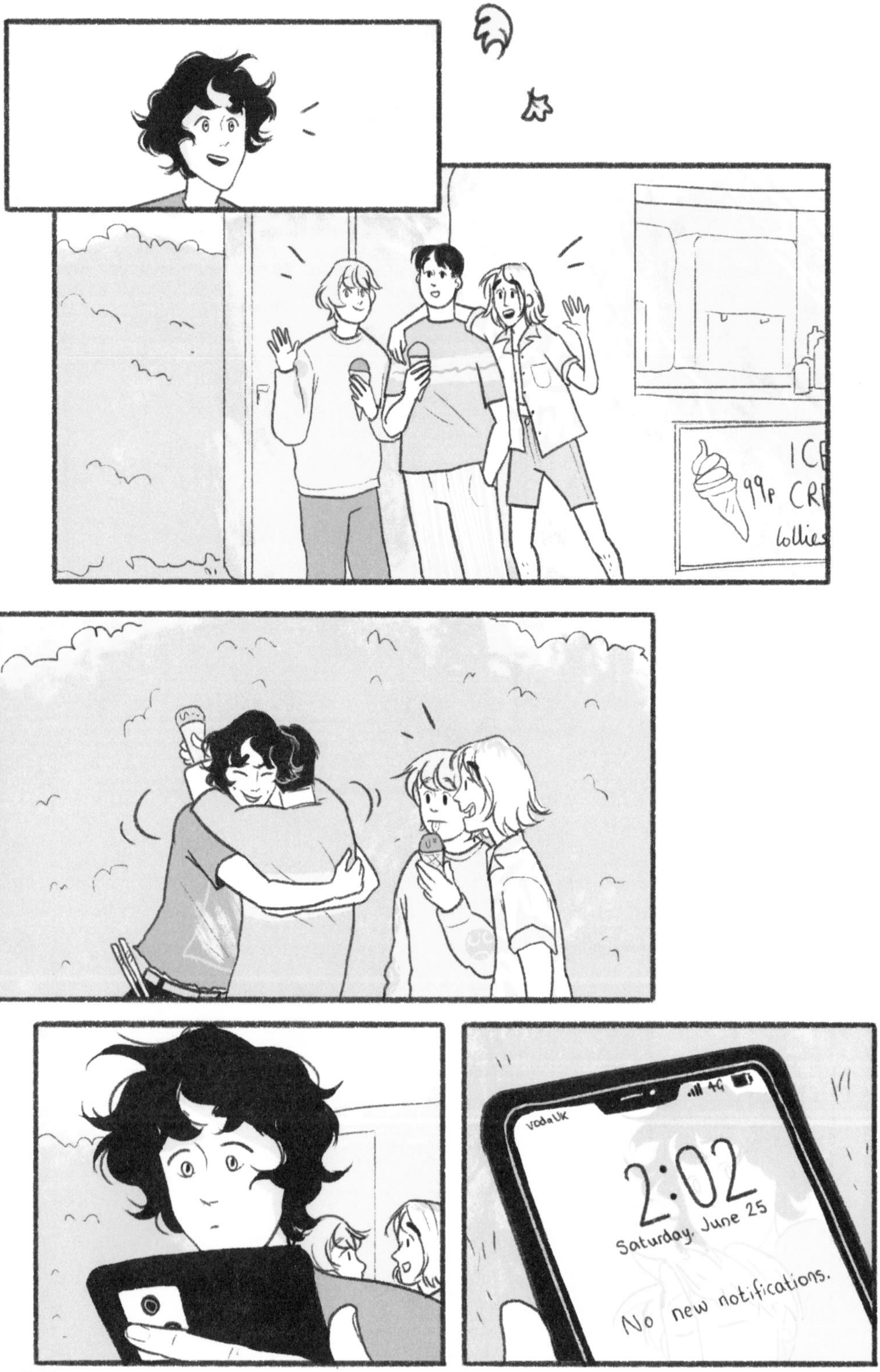
99p
VodaUK
4G
2:02
Saturday, June 25
No new notifications.

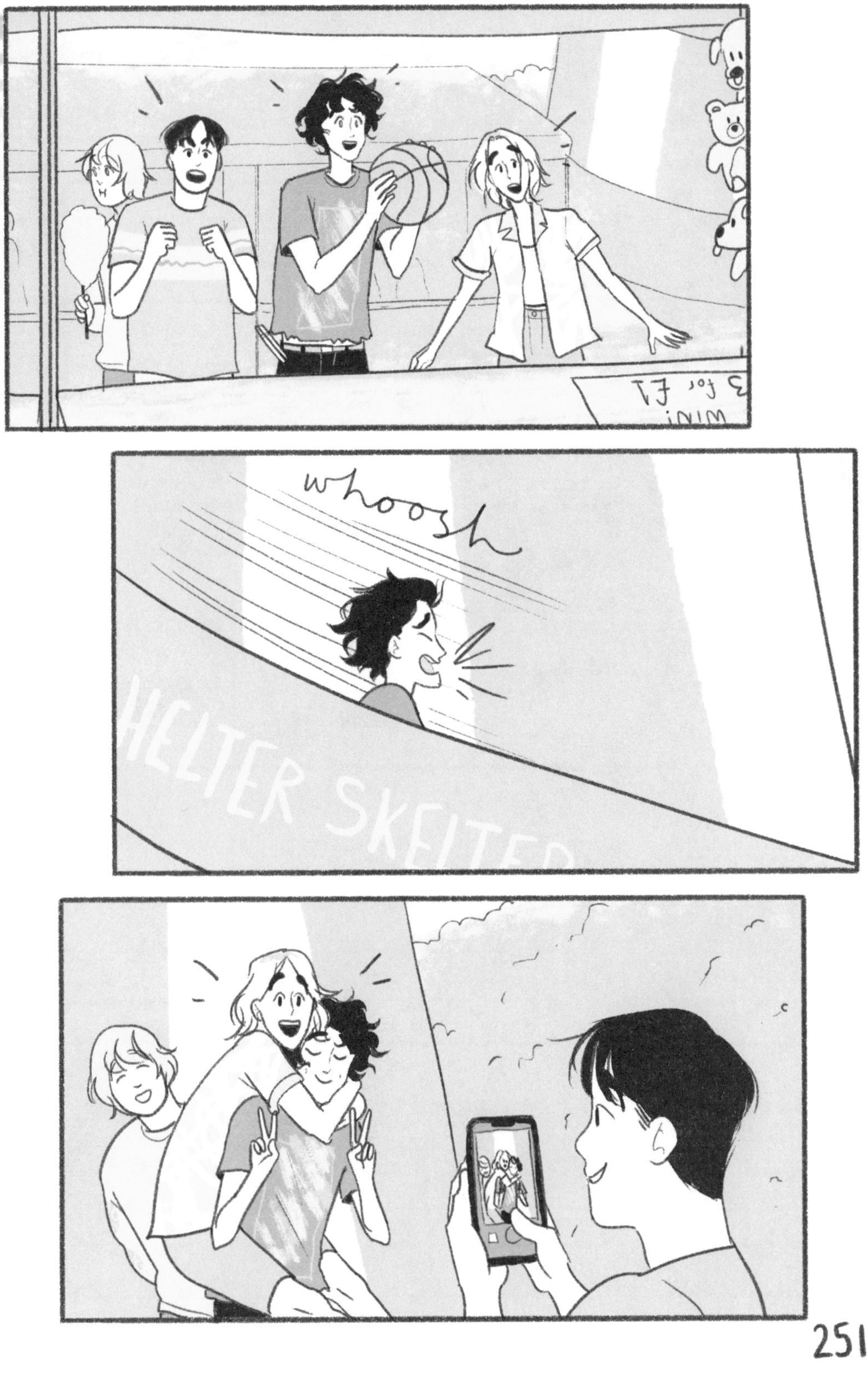
whoosh
HELTER SKELTE

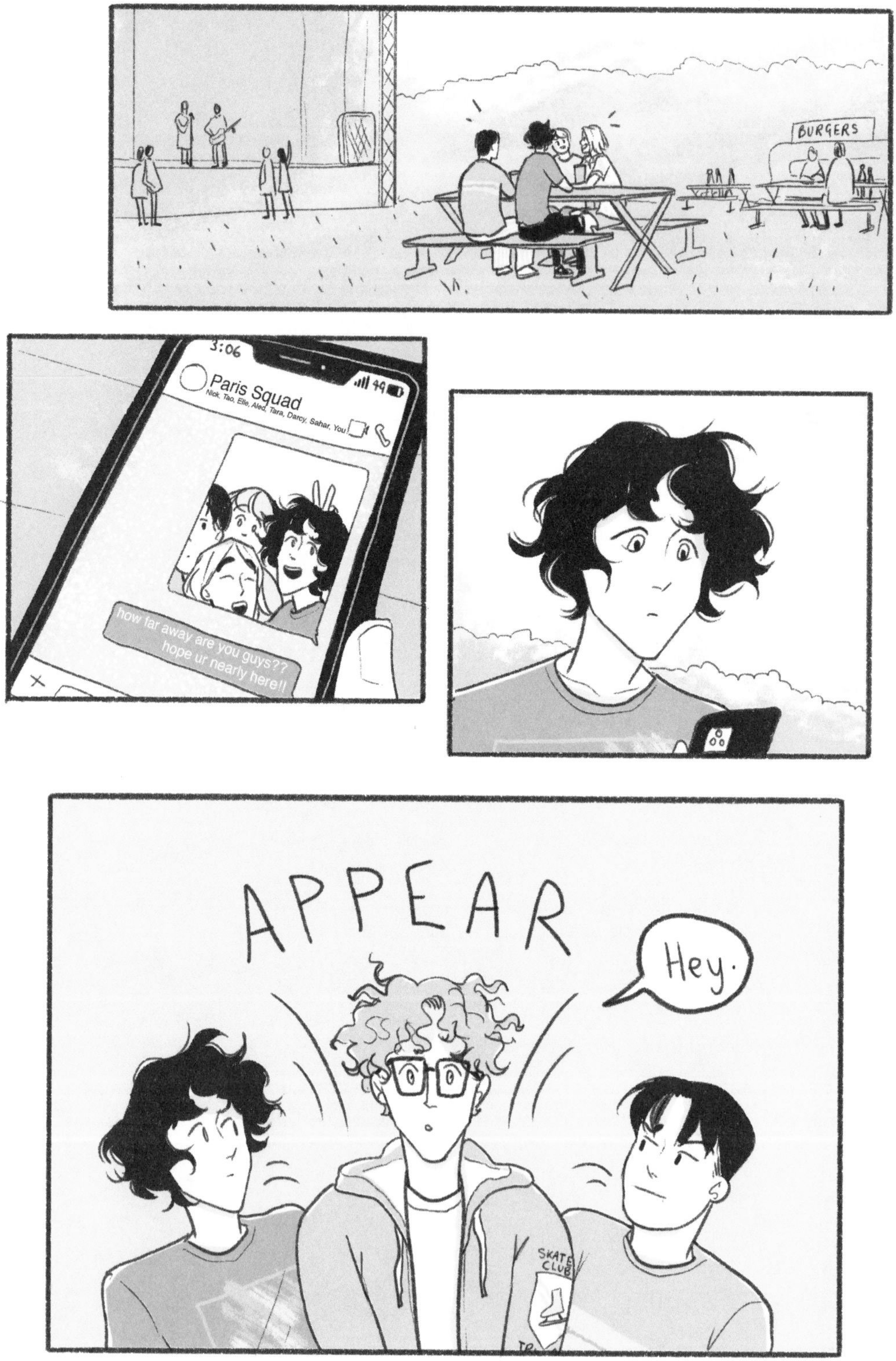
BURGERS
3:06
Paris Squad
Nick, Tao, Elle, Aled, Tara, Darcy, Sahar, You
how far away are you guys??
hope ur nearly here!!
APPEAR
Hey.
SKATE CLUB

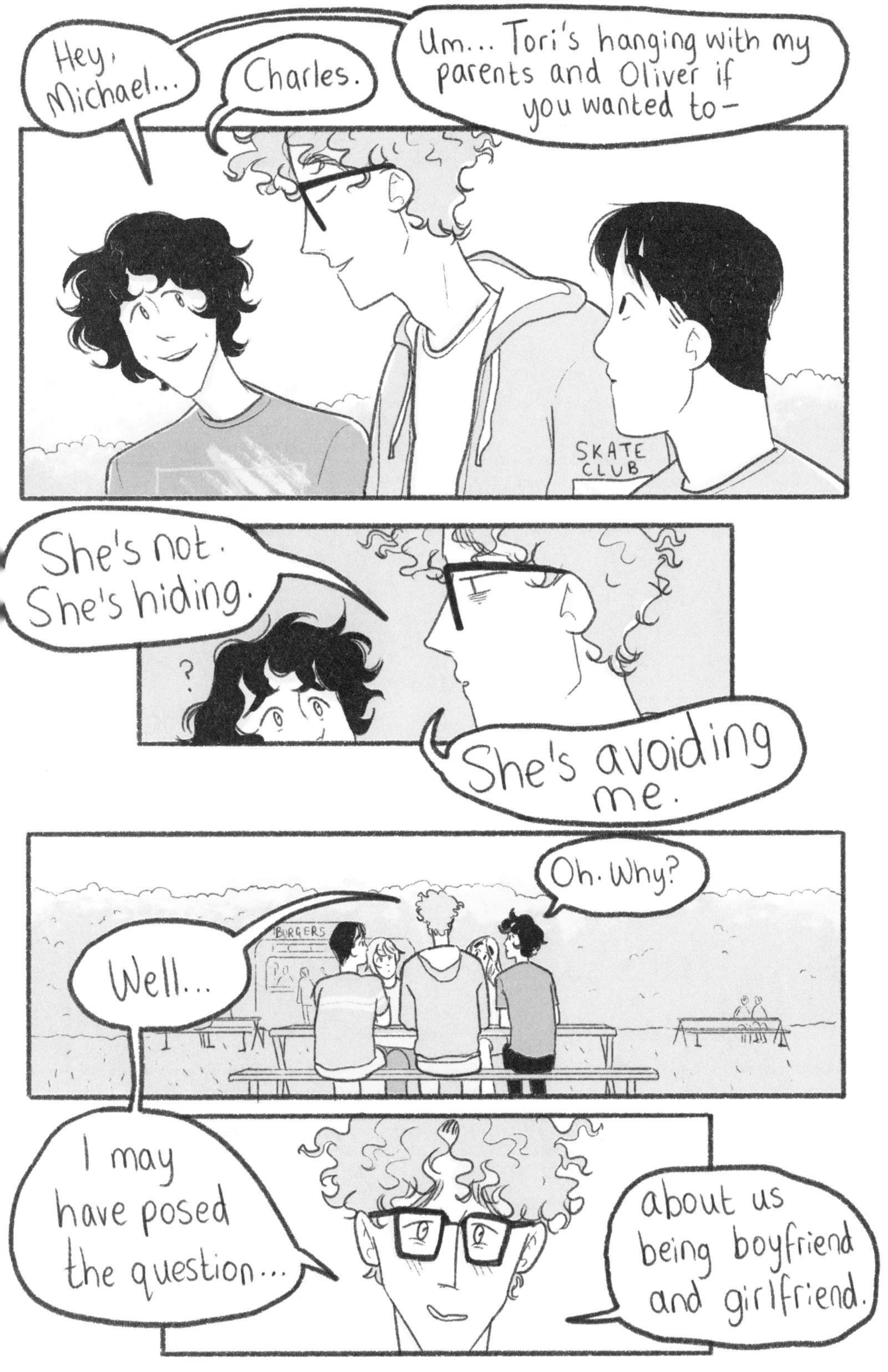
Hey, Michael...
Charles.
Um... Tori's hanging with my parents and Oliver if you wanted to-
SKATE CLUB
She's not. She's hiding.
?
She's avoiding me.
Oh. Why?
BURGERS
Well...
I may have posed the question...
about us being boyfriend and girlfriend.

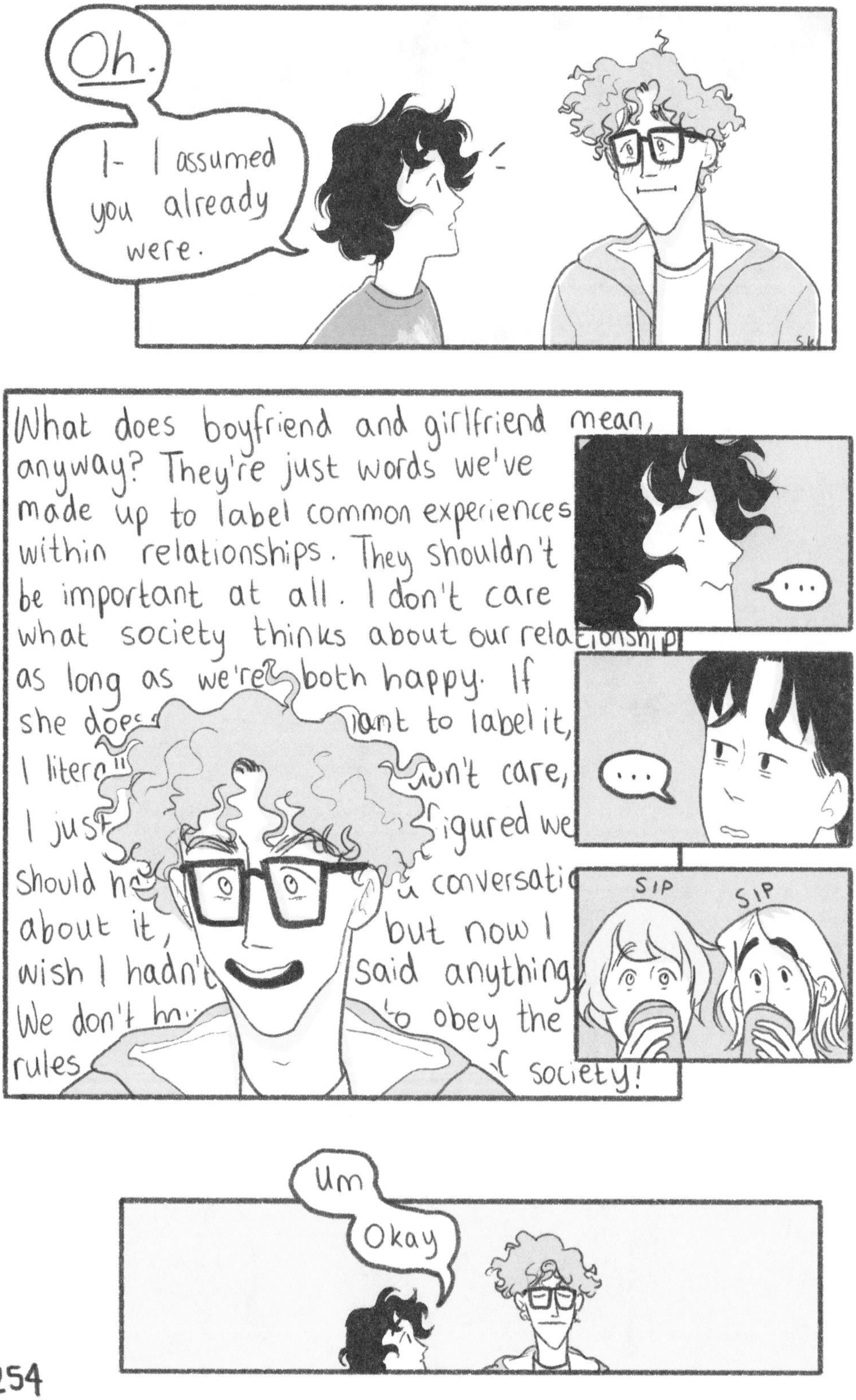
Oh.
I- I assumed you already were.
What does boyfriend and girlfriend mean, anyway? They're just words we've made up to label common experiences within relationships. They shouldn't be important at all. I don't care what society thinks about our relationship as long as we're both happy. If
she does
ant to label it,
I litera
n't care,
I just
figured we
should h
conversatio
about it,
but now I
wish I hadn't
said anything
We don't h
o obey the
rules
society!
...
...
SIP
SIP
Um
Okay

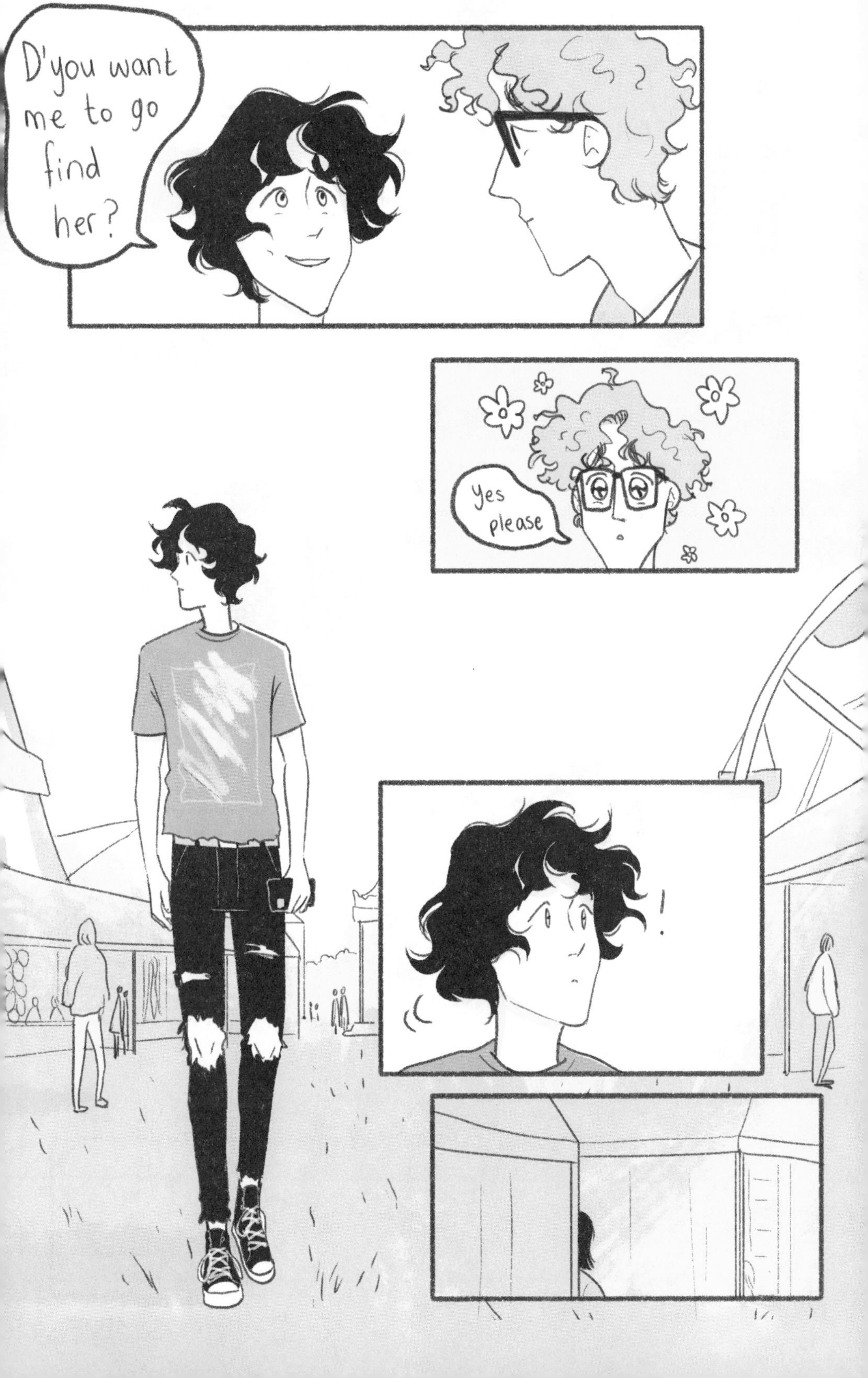
D'you want me to go find her?
Yes please
!

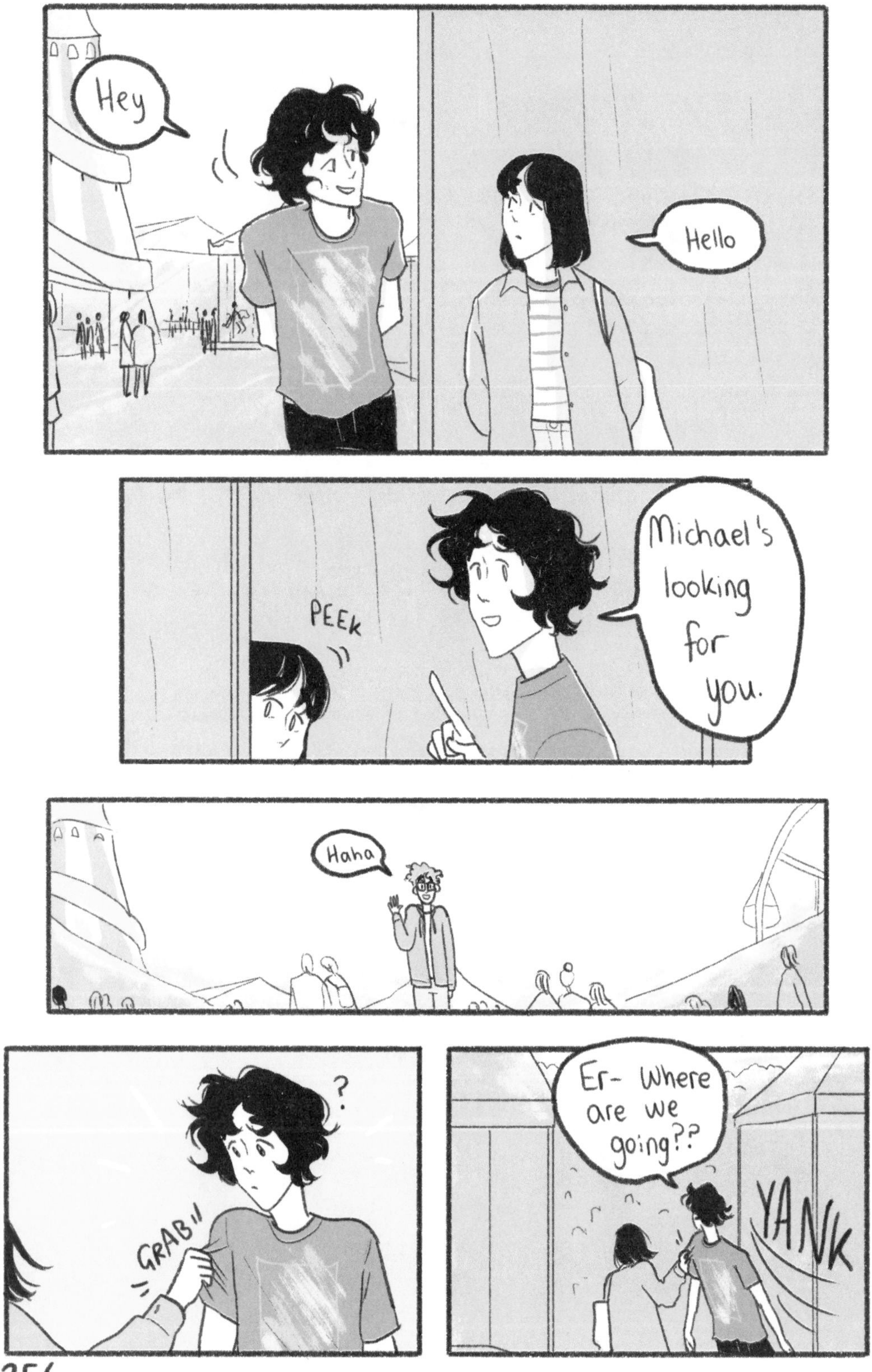
Hey
Hello
Michael's looking for you.
PEEK
Haha
?
GRAB
Er- Where are we going??
YANK

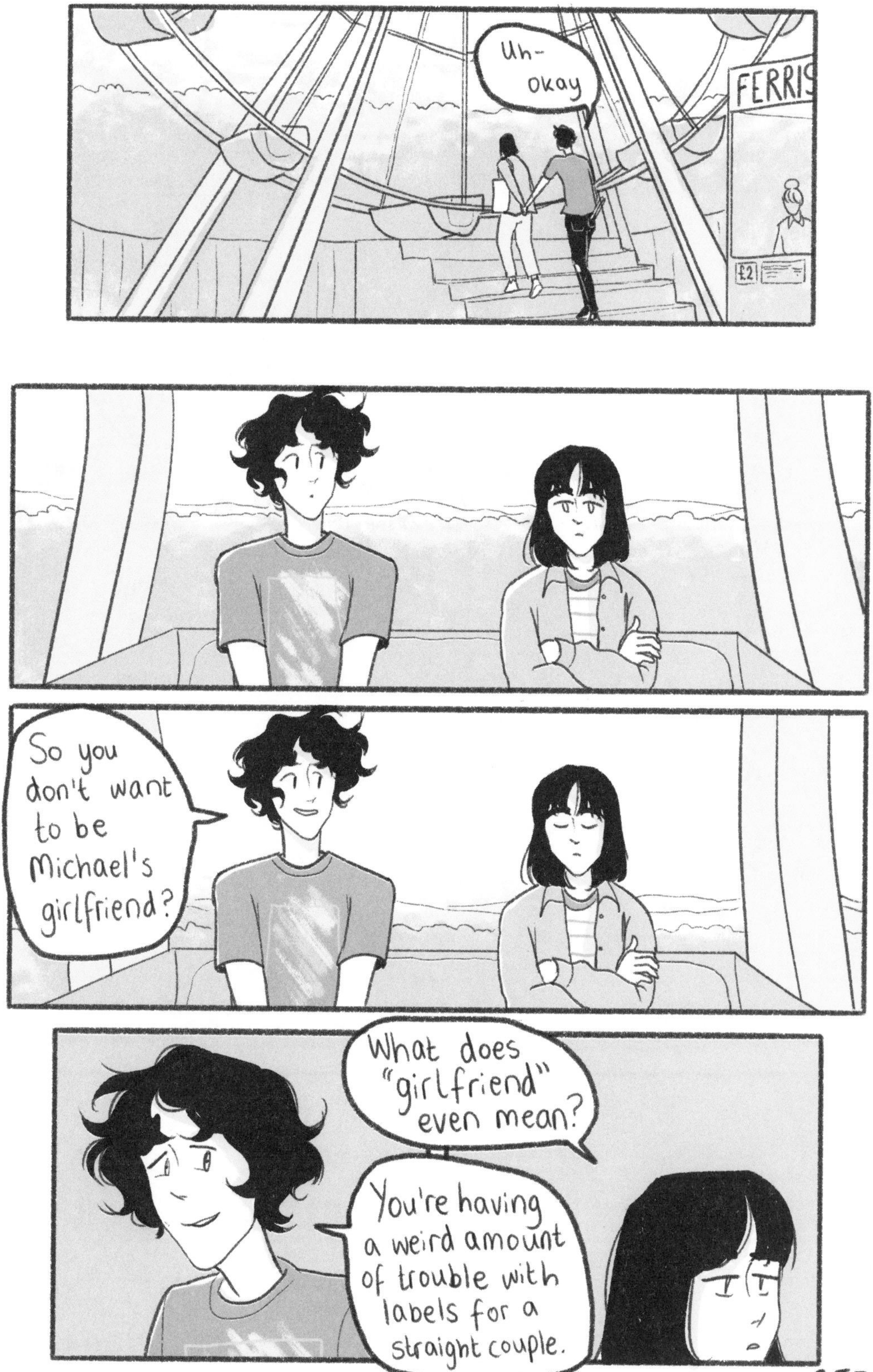
Uh-
okay
FERRIS
£2
So you don't want to be Michael's girlfriend?
What does "girlfriend" even mean?
You're having a weird amount of trouble with labels for a straight couple.

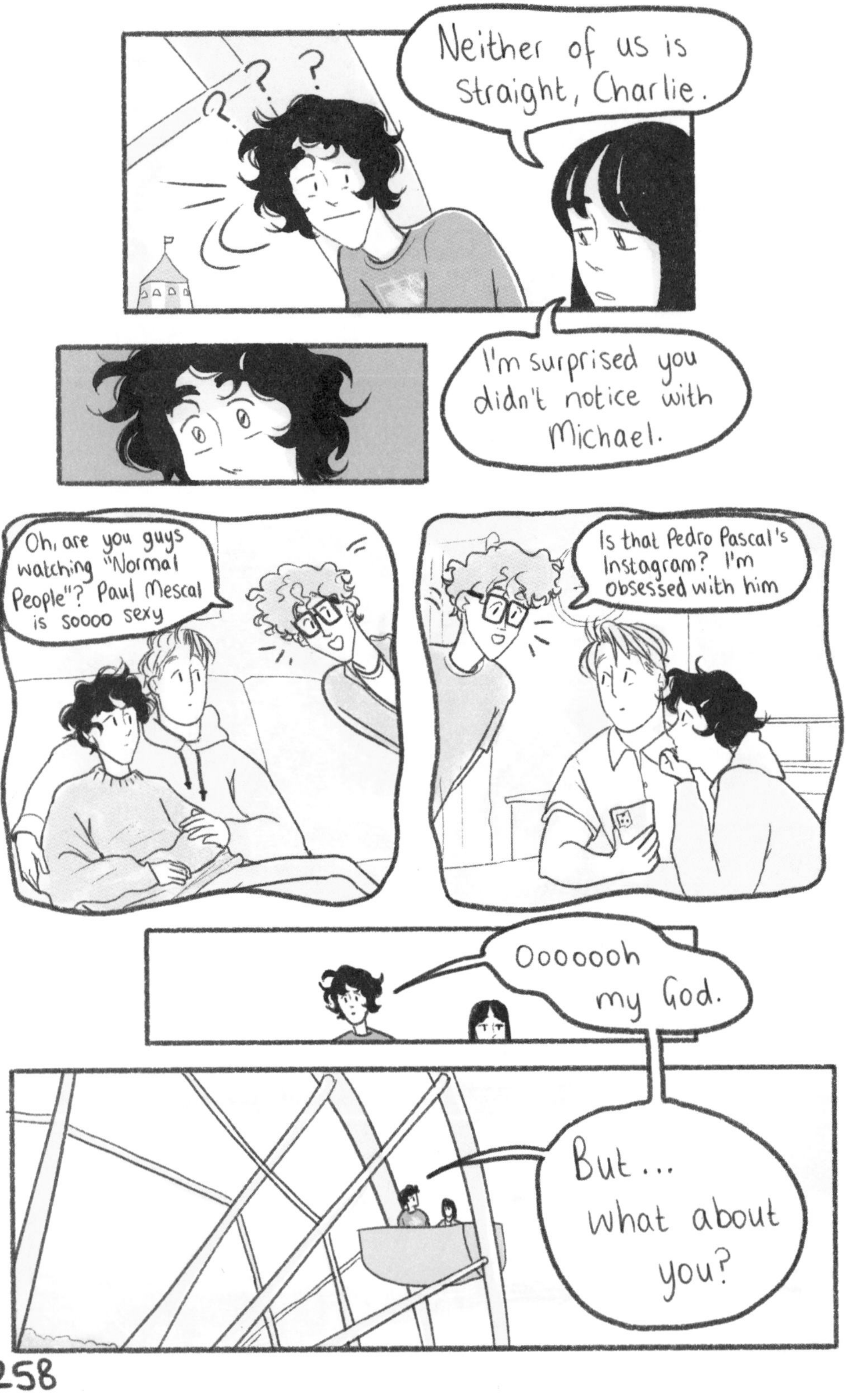
? ? ?
Neither of us is straight, Charlie.
I'm surprised you didn't notice with Michael.
Oh, are you guys watching "Normal People"? Paul Mescal is soooo sexy
Is that Pedro Pascal's Instagram? I'm obsessed with him
Ooooooh my God.
But... what about you?

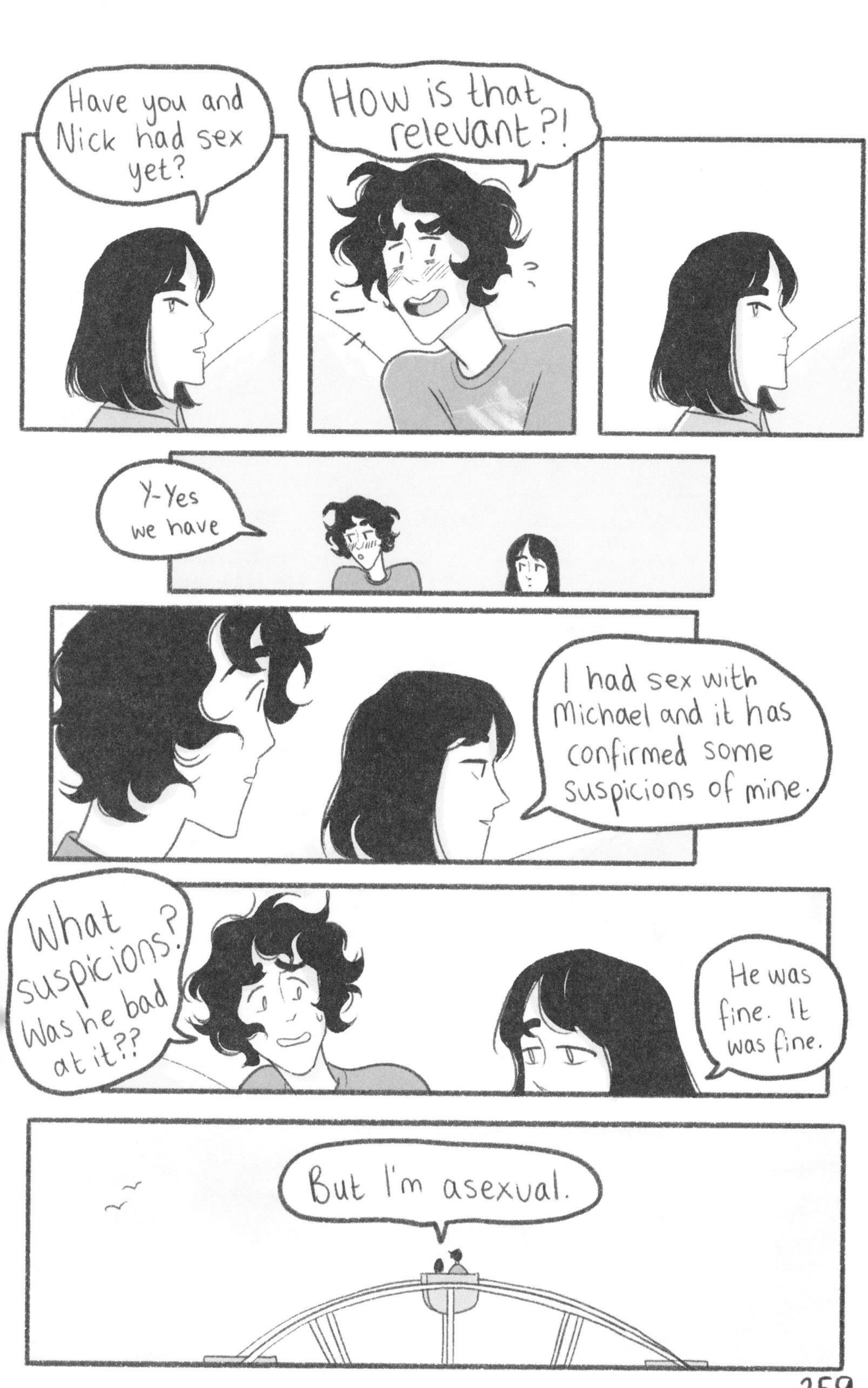
Have you and Nick had sex yet?
How is that relevant?!
Y-Yes we have
I had sex with Michael and it has confirmed some suspicions of mine.
What suspicions? Was he bad at it??
He was fine. It was fine.
But I'm asexual.

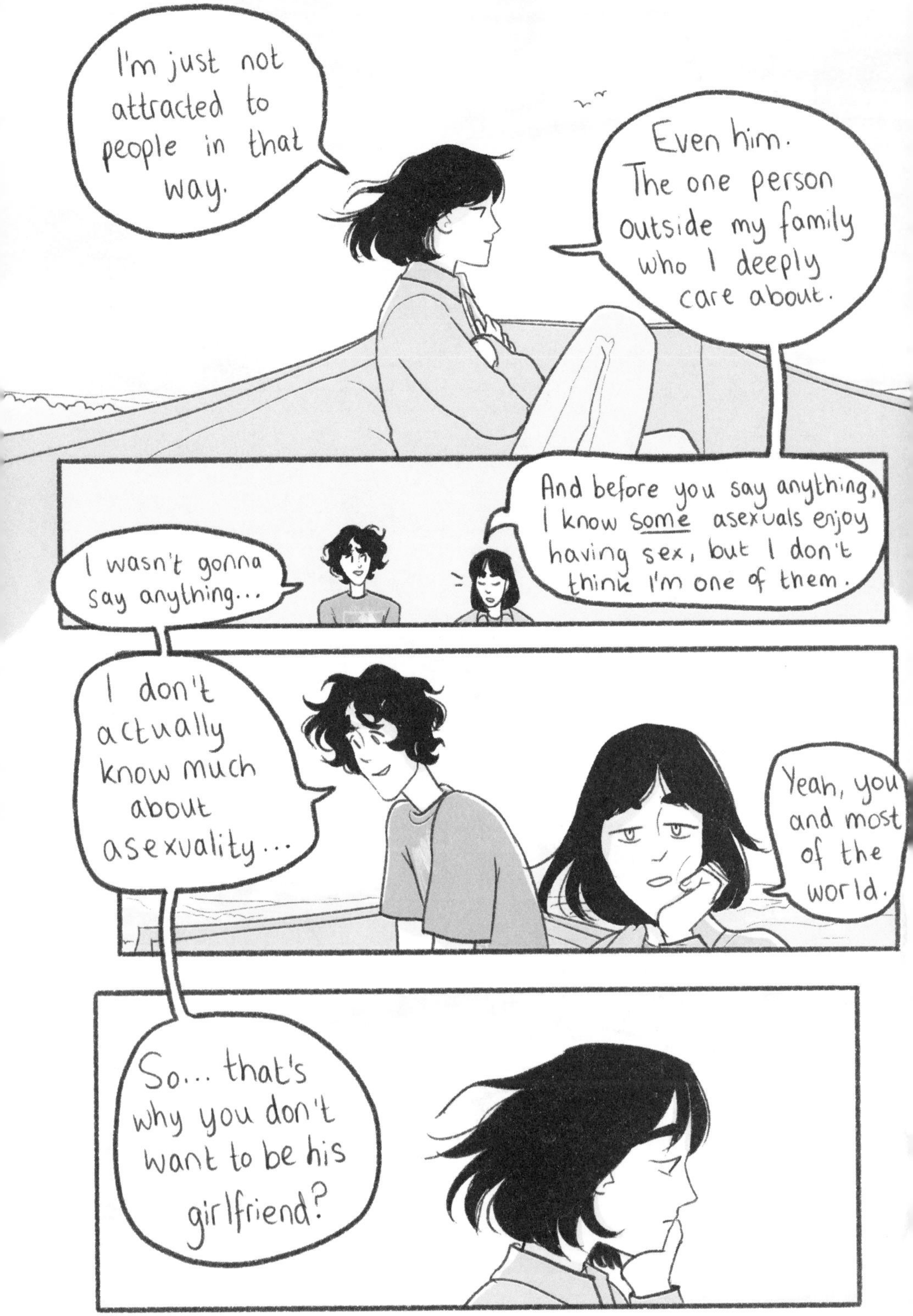
I'm just not attracted to people in that way.
Even him. The one person outside my family who I deeply care about.
And before you say anything, I know some asexuals enjoy having sex, but I don't think I'm one of them.
I wasn't gonna say anything...
I don't actually know much about asexuality...
Yeah, you and most of the world.
So... that's why you don't want to be his girlfriend?

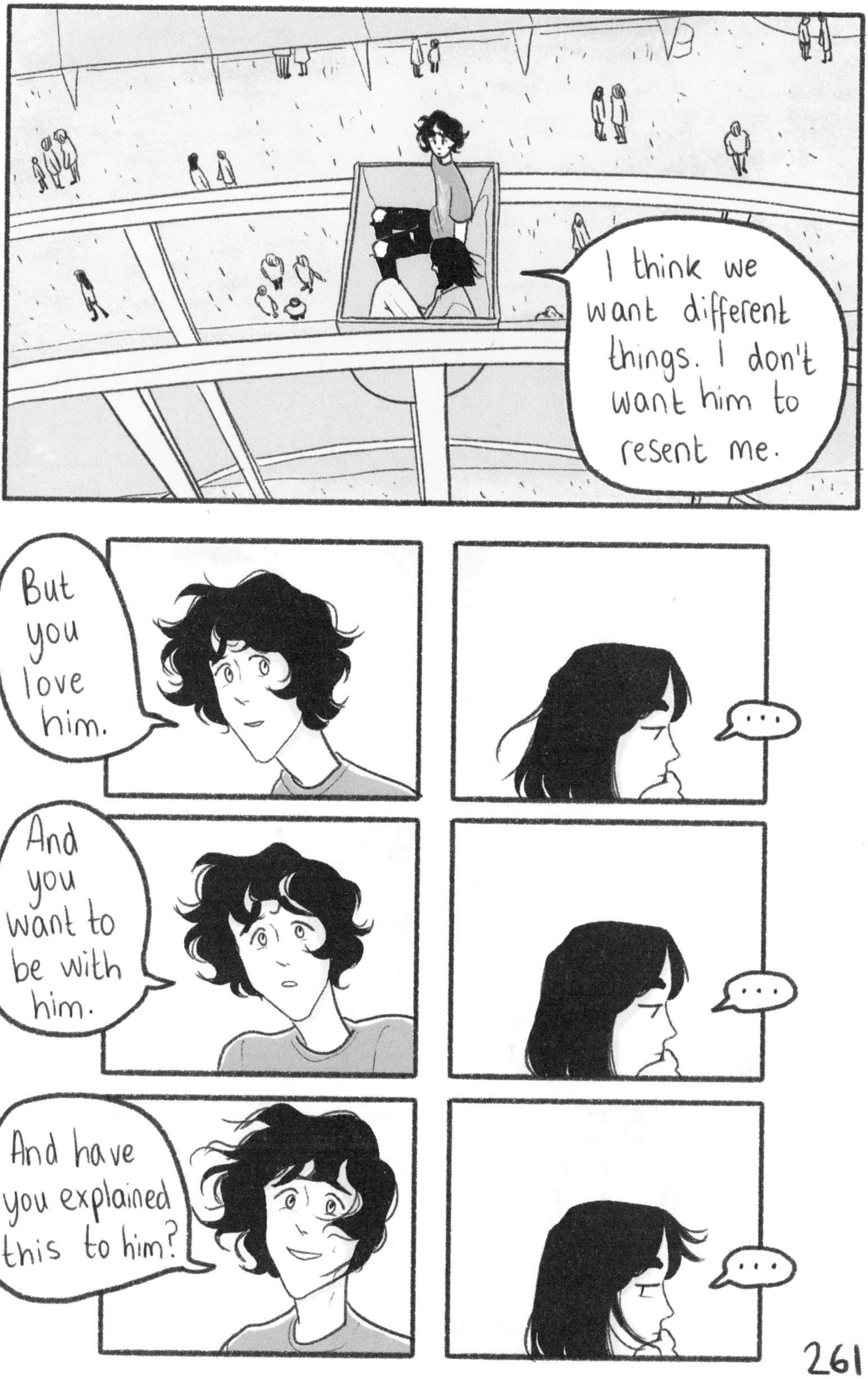
I think we want different things. I don't want him to resent me.
But you love him.
...
And you want to be with him.
...
And have you explained this to him?
...

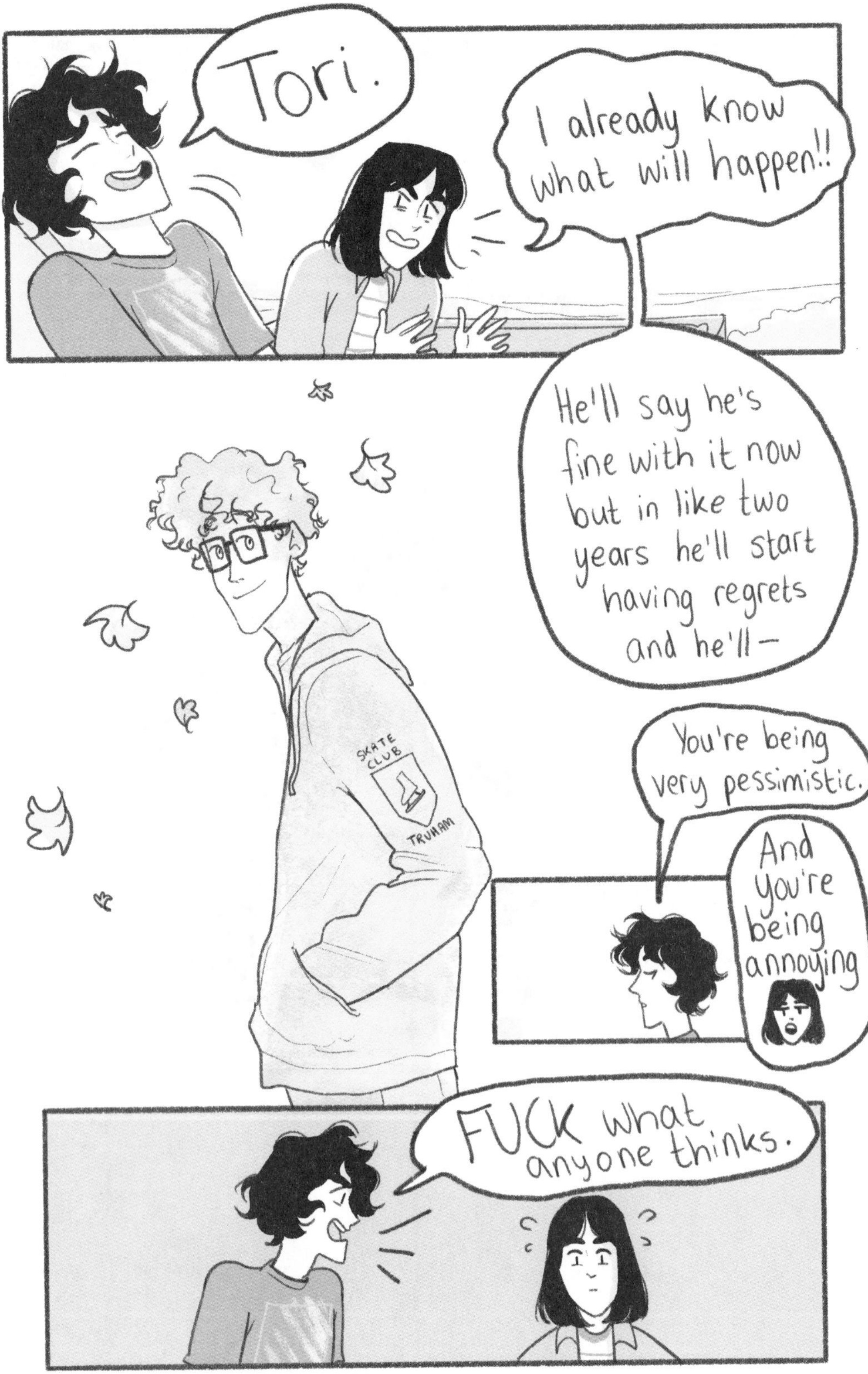
Tori.
I already know what will happen!!
He'll say he's fine with it now but in like two years he'll start having regrets and he'll–
SKATE CLUB
TRUHAM
You're being very pessimistic.
And you're being annoying
FUCK what anyone thinks.

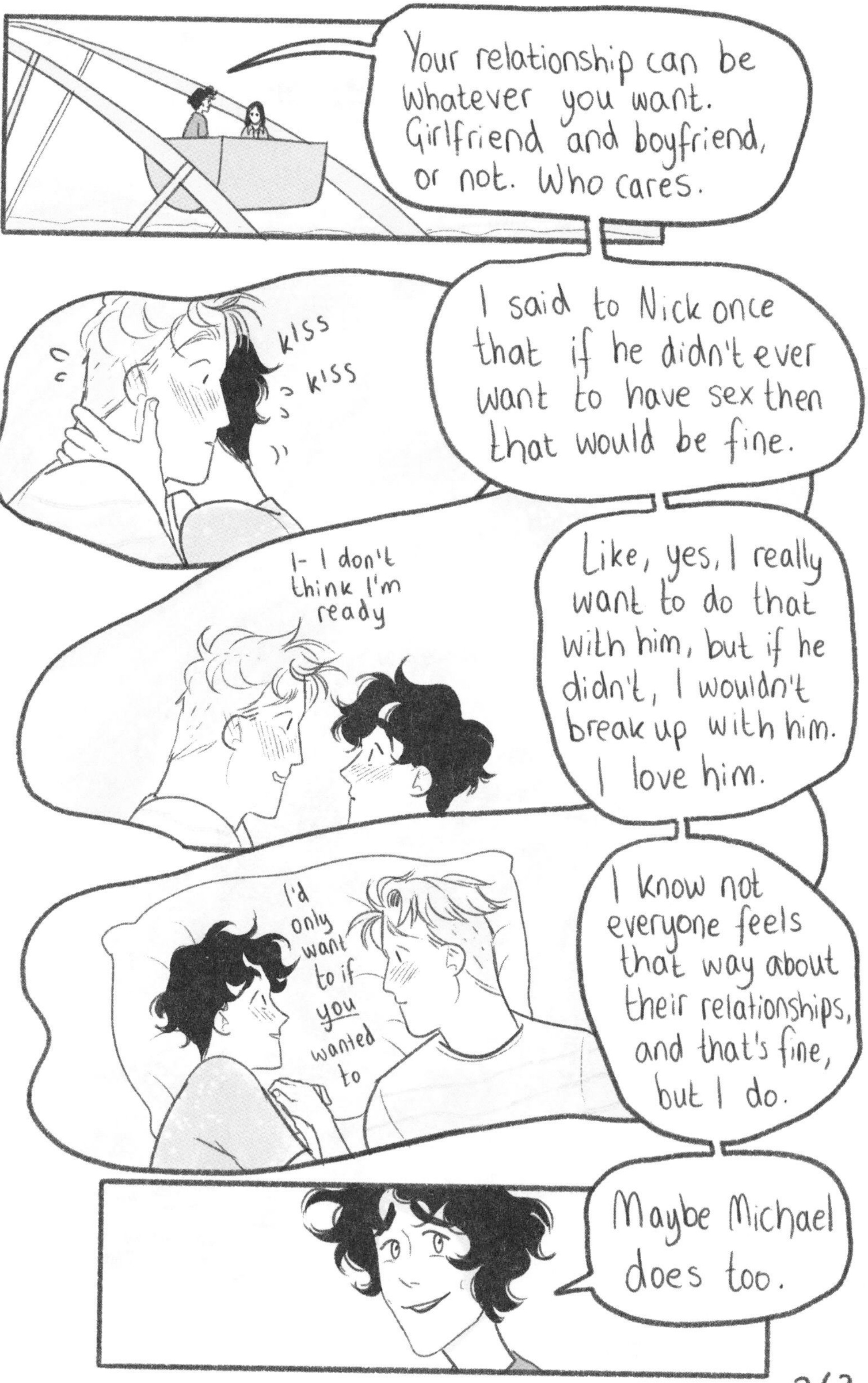

Your relationship can be whatever you want. Girlfriend and boyfriend, or not. Who cares.
I said to Nick once that if he didn't ever want to have sex then that would be fine.
kiss
kiss
Like, yes, I really want to do that with him, but if he didn't, I wouldn't break up with him. I love him.
I- I don't think I'm ready
I know not everyone feels that way about their relationships, and that's fine, but I do.
I'd only want to if you wanted to
Maybe Michael does too.

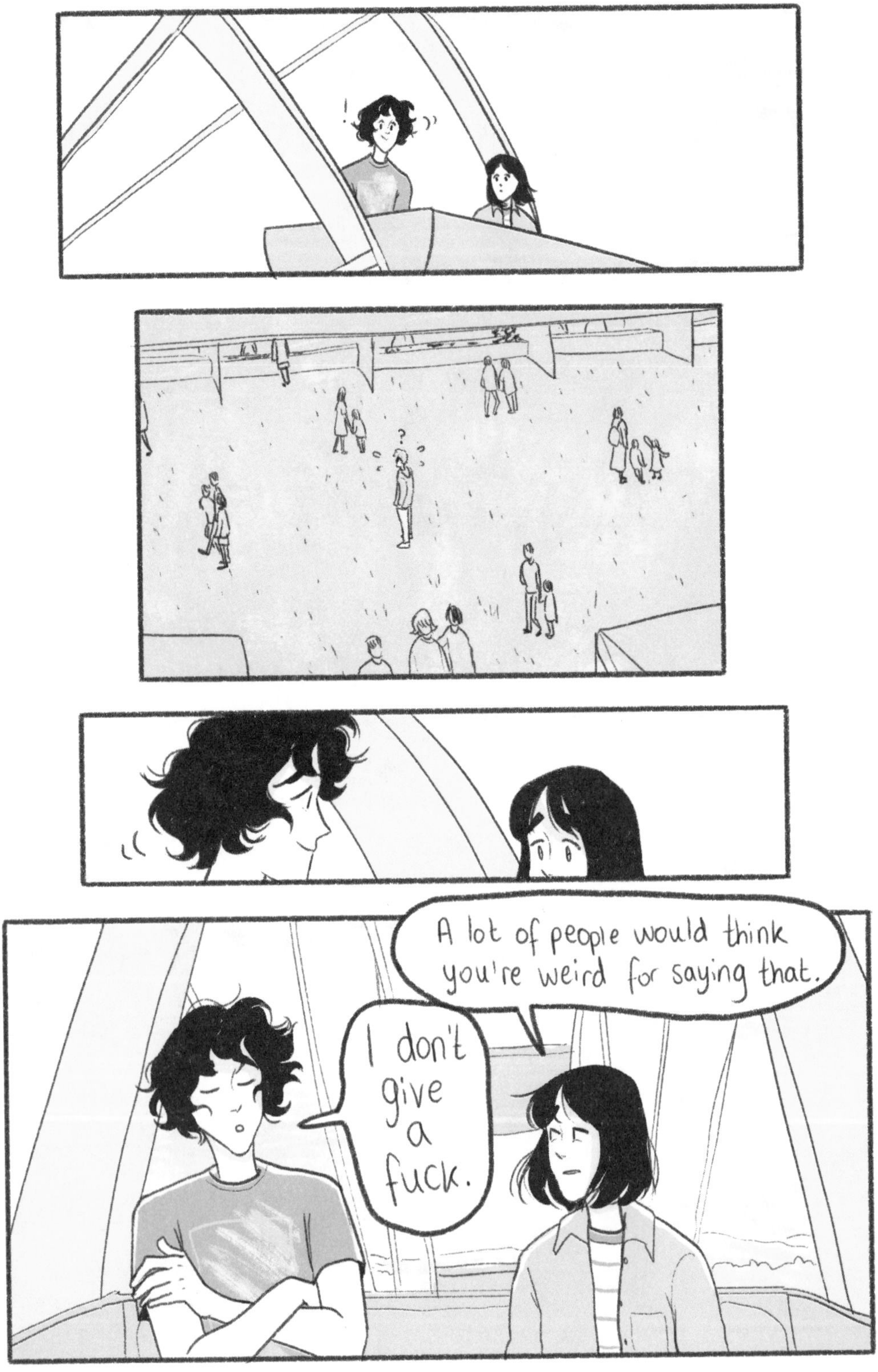
!
?
A lot of people would think you're weird for saying that.
I don't give a fuck.

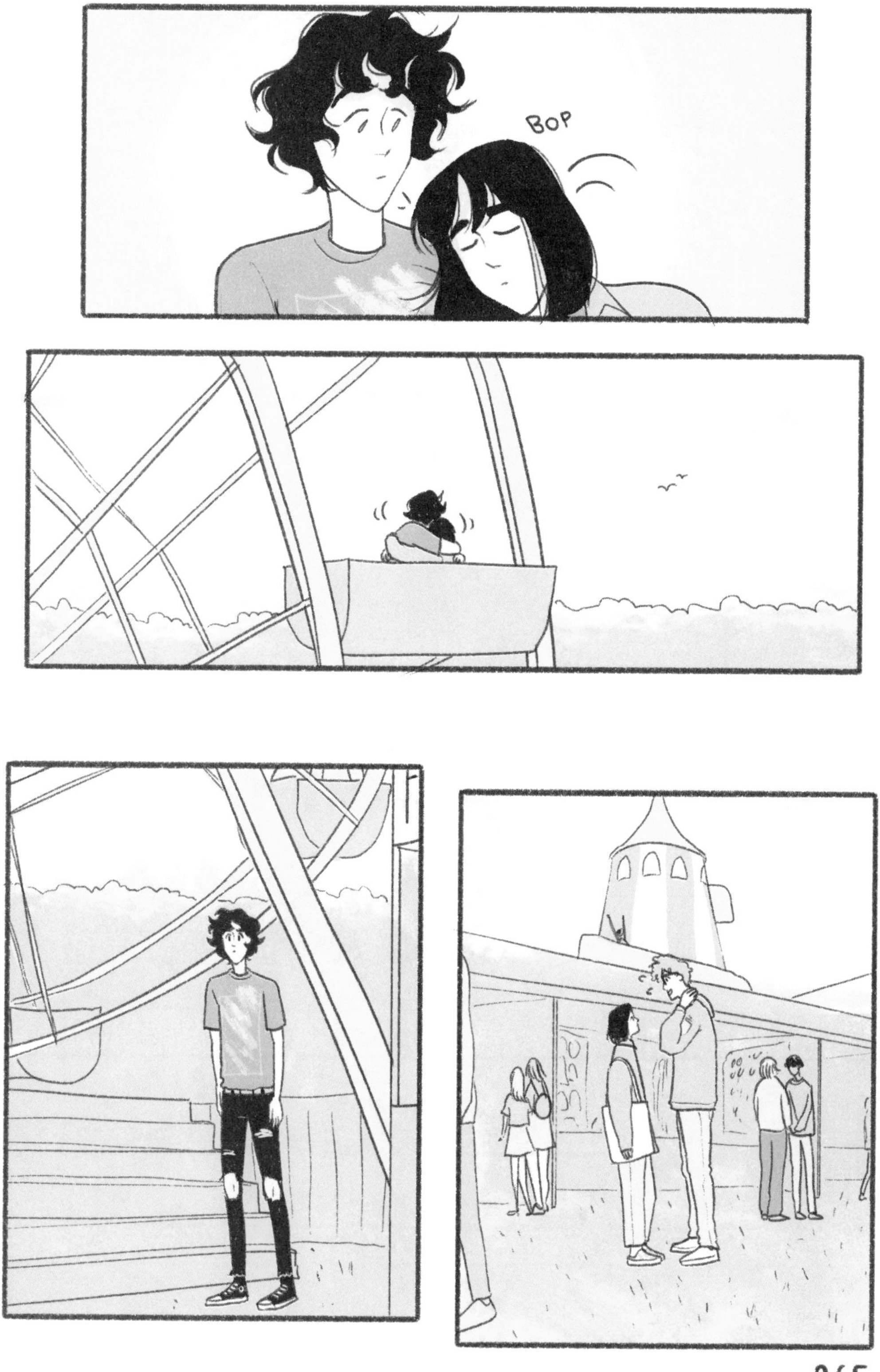
BOP

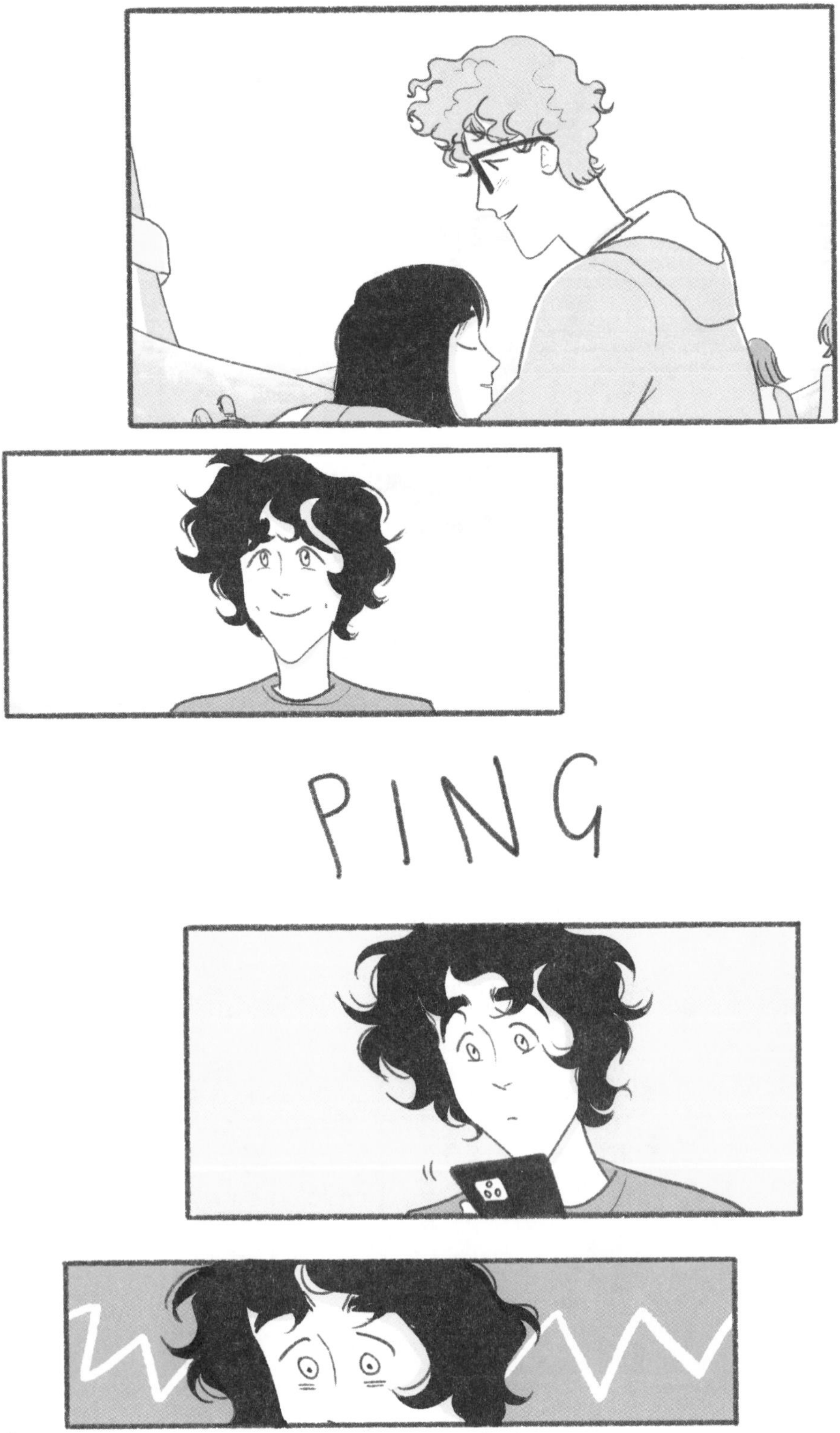
PING

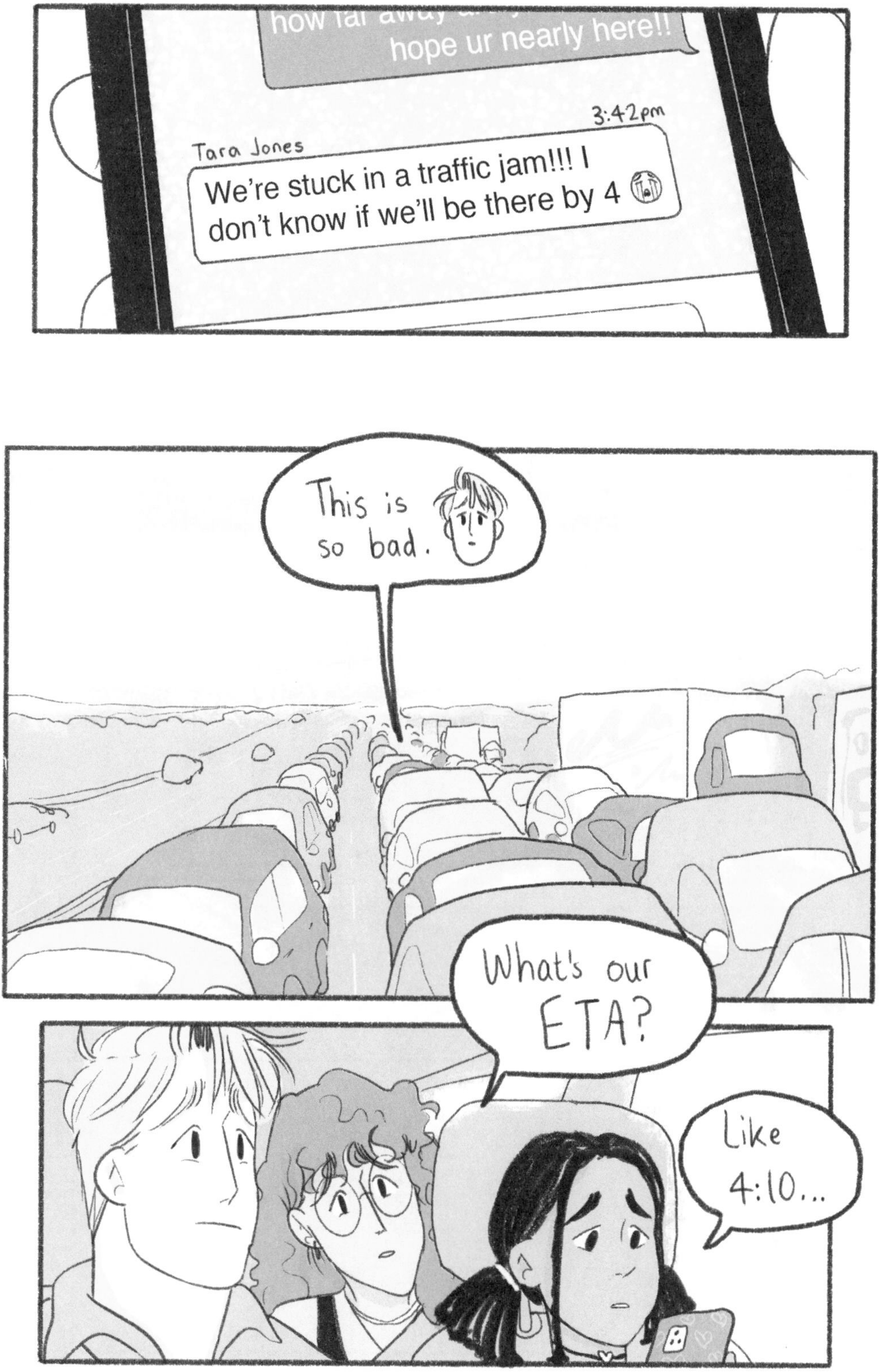

hope ur nearly here!!
3:42pm
Tara Jones
We're stuck in a traffic jam!!! I don't know if we'll be there by 4
This is so bad.
What's our ETA?
Like 4:10...

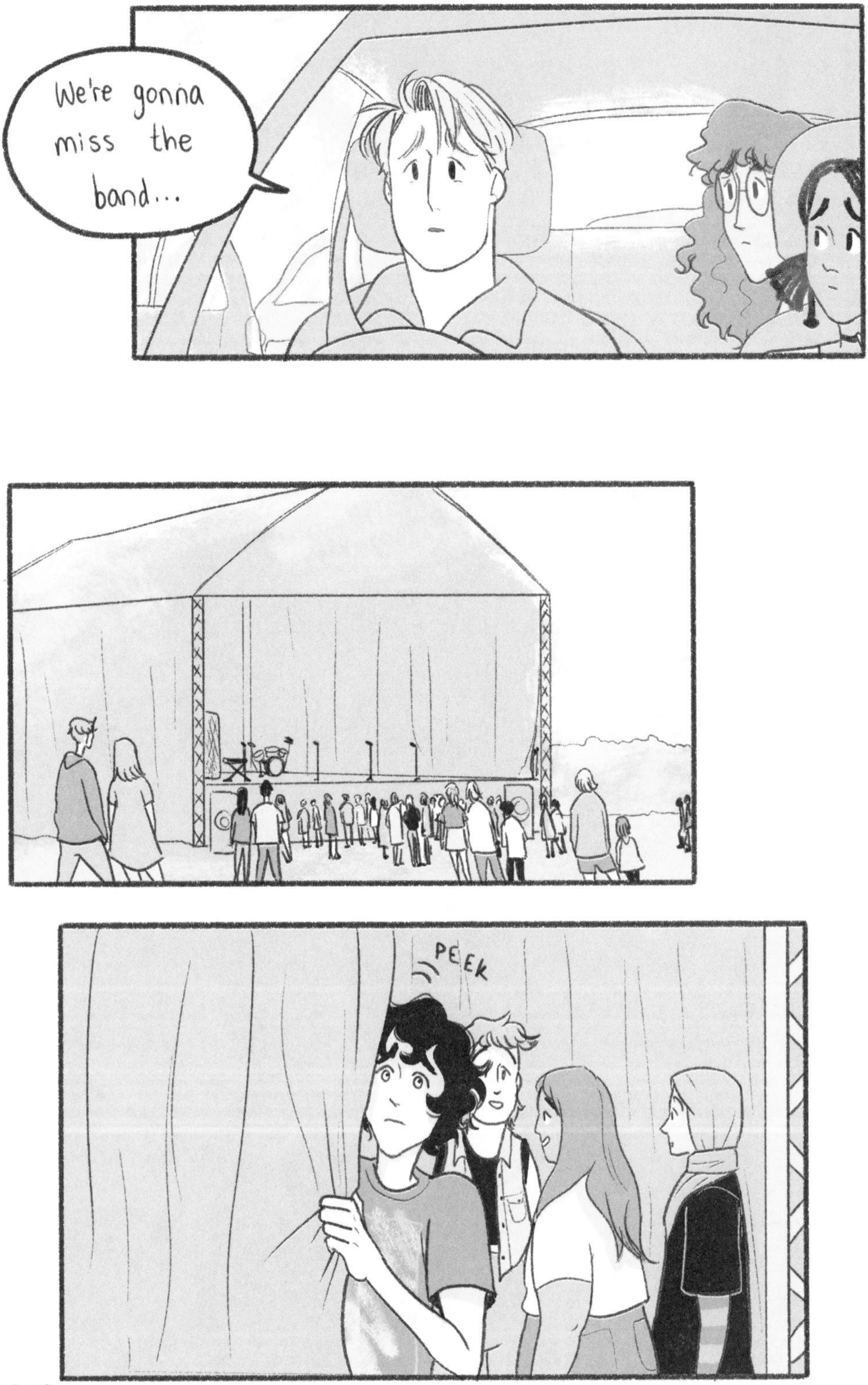
We're gonna miss the band...
PEEK

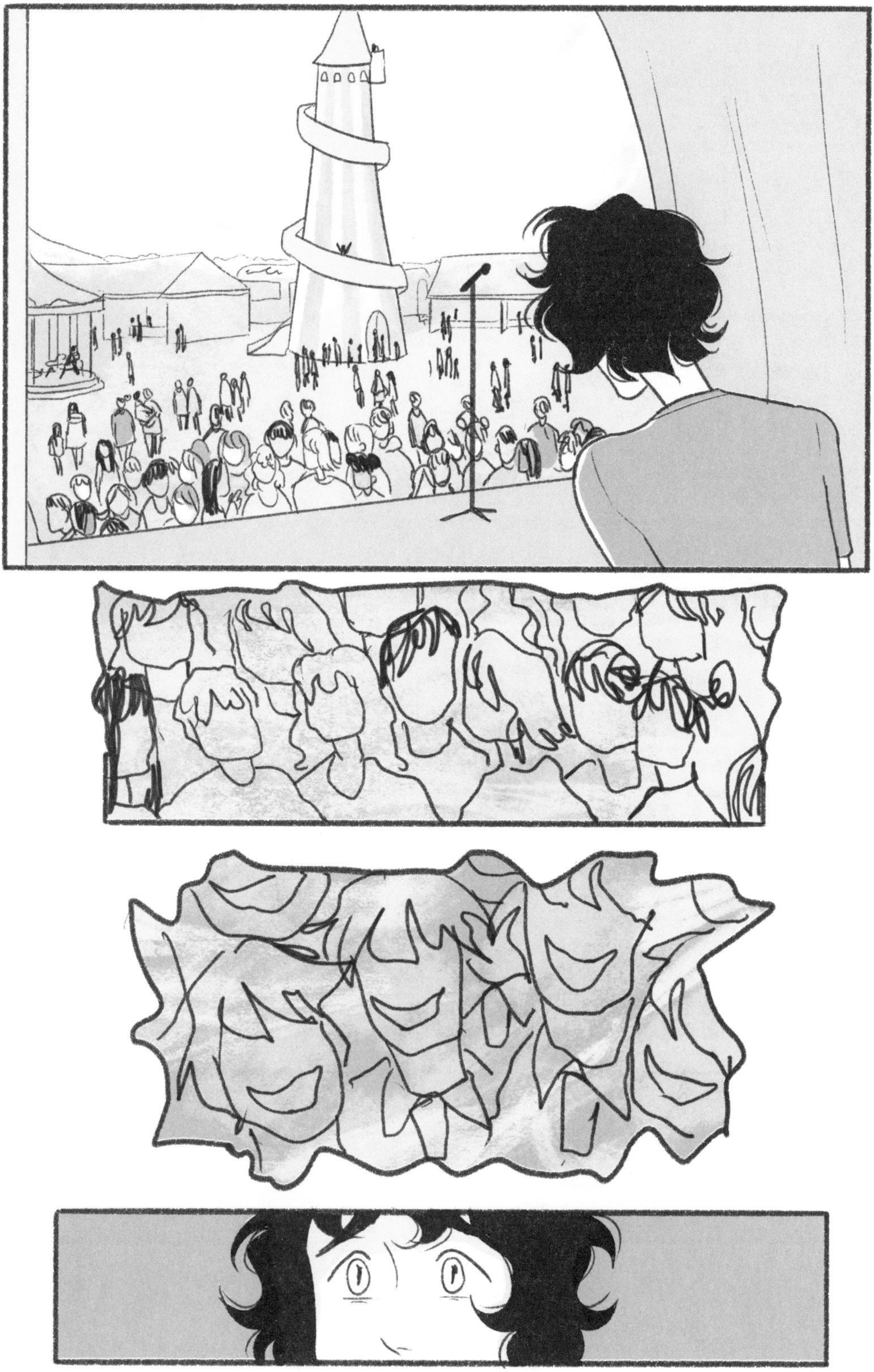

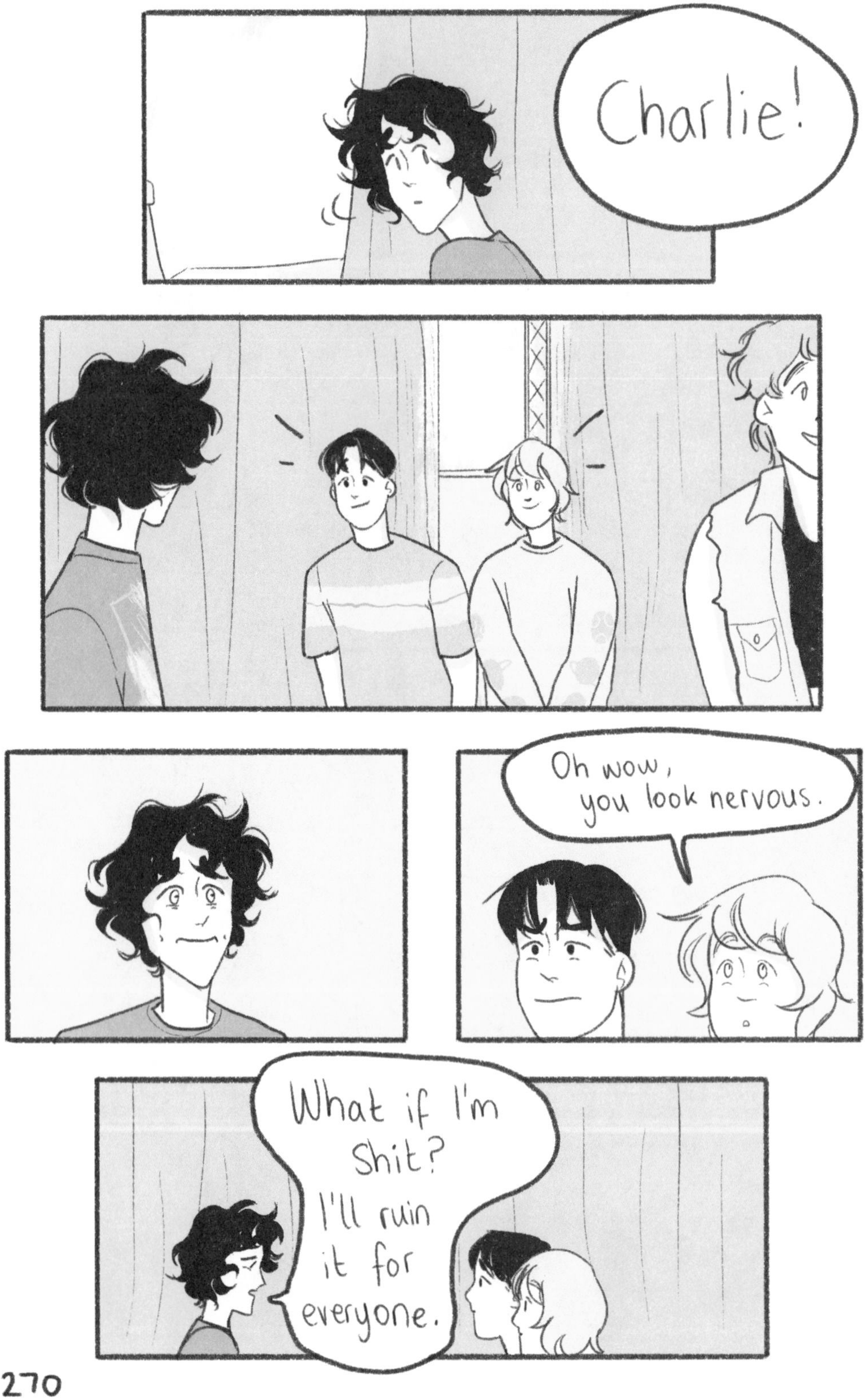
Charlie!
Oh wow, you look nervous.
What if I'm shit? I'll ruin it for everyone.

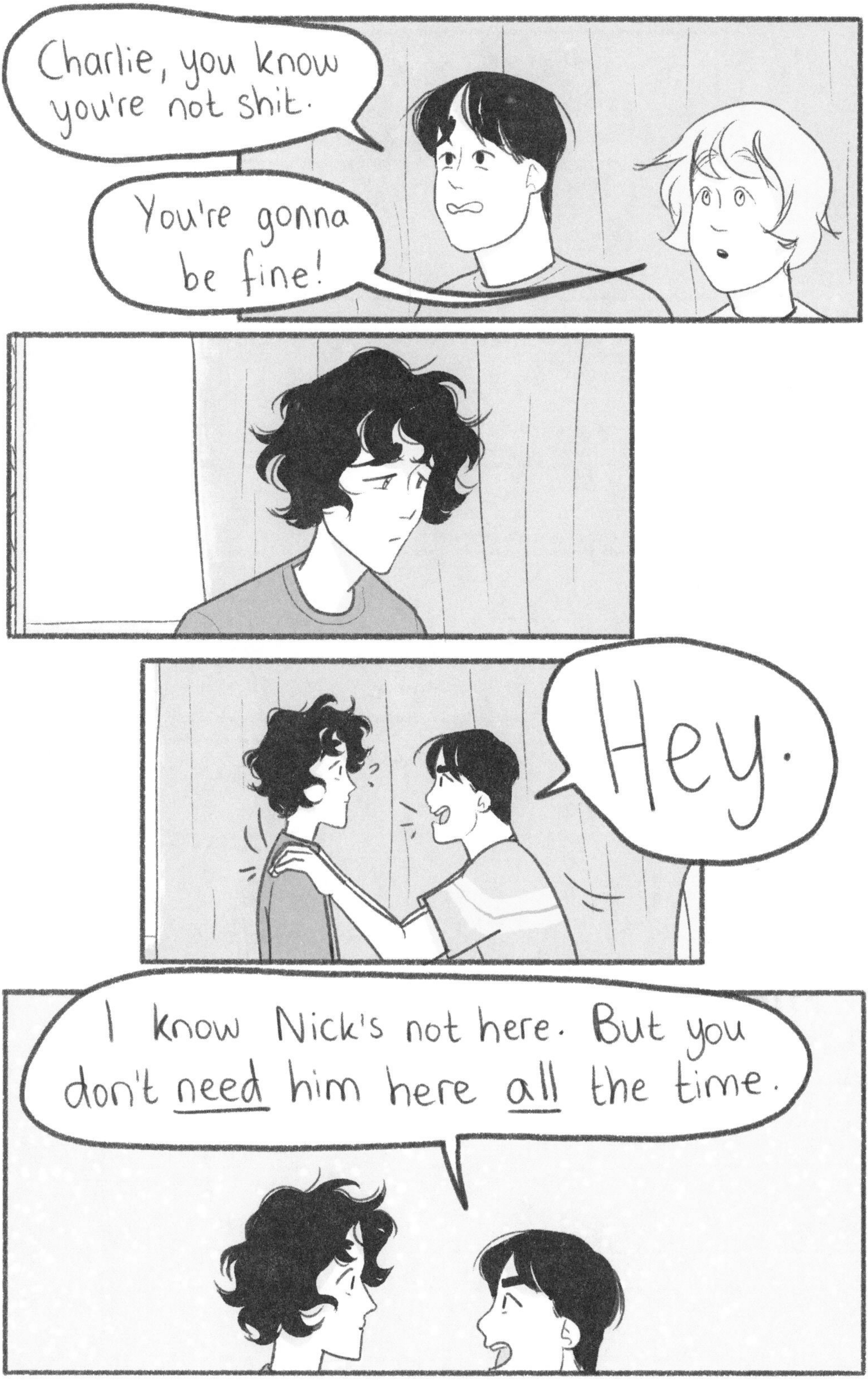
Charlie, you know you're not shit.
You're gonna be fine!
Hey.
I know Nick's not here. But you don't need him here all the time.

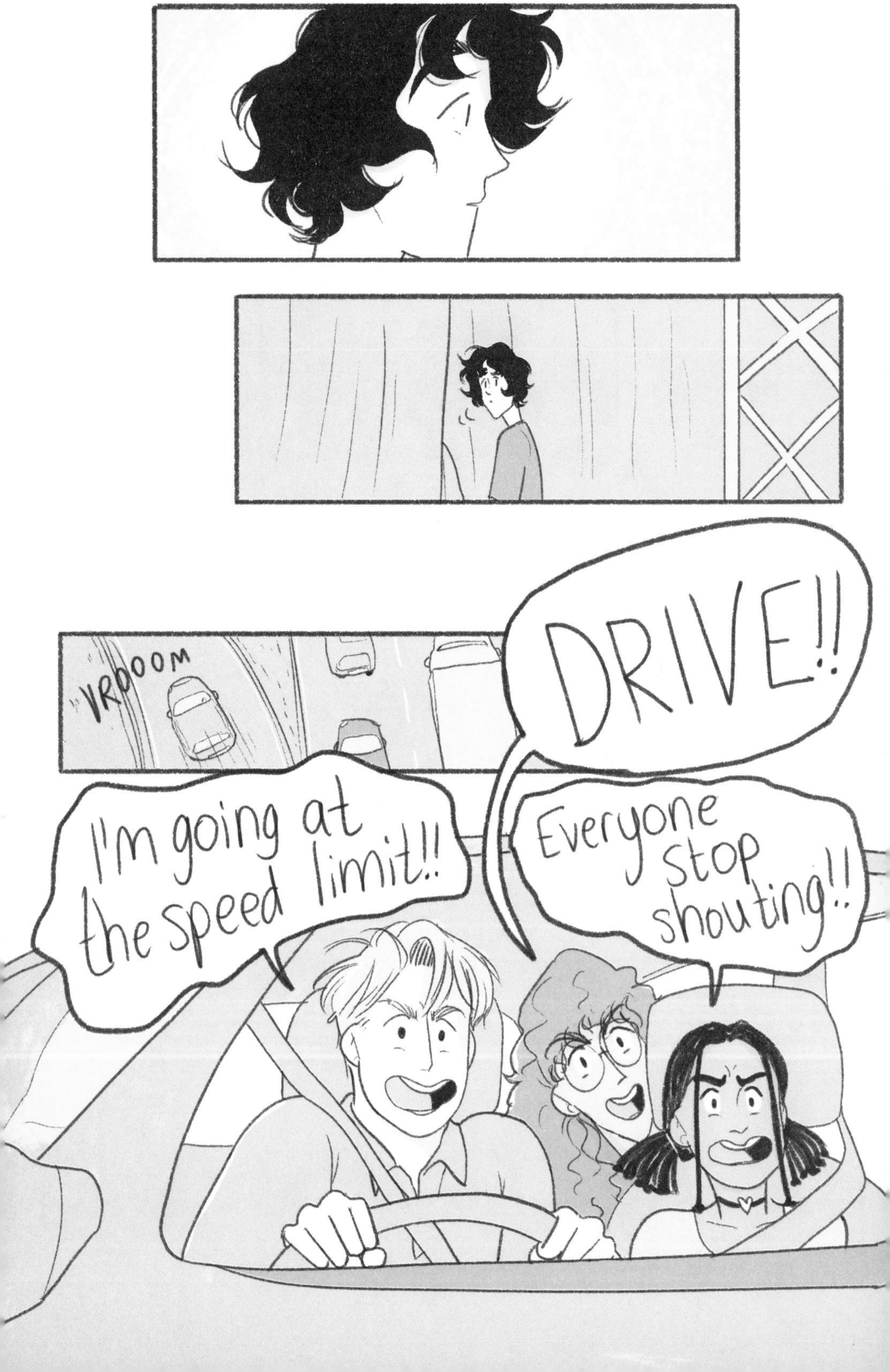
VROOOM
DRIVE!!
I'm going at the speed limit!!
Everyone stop shouting!!

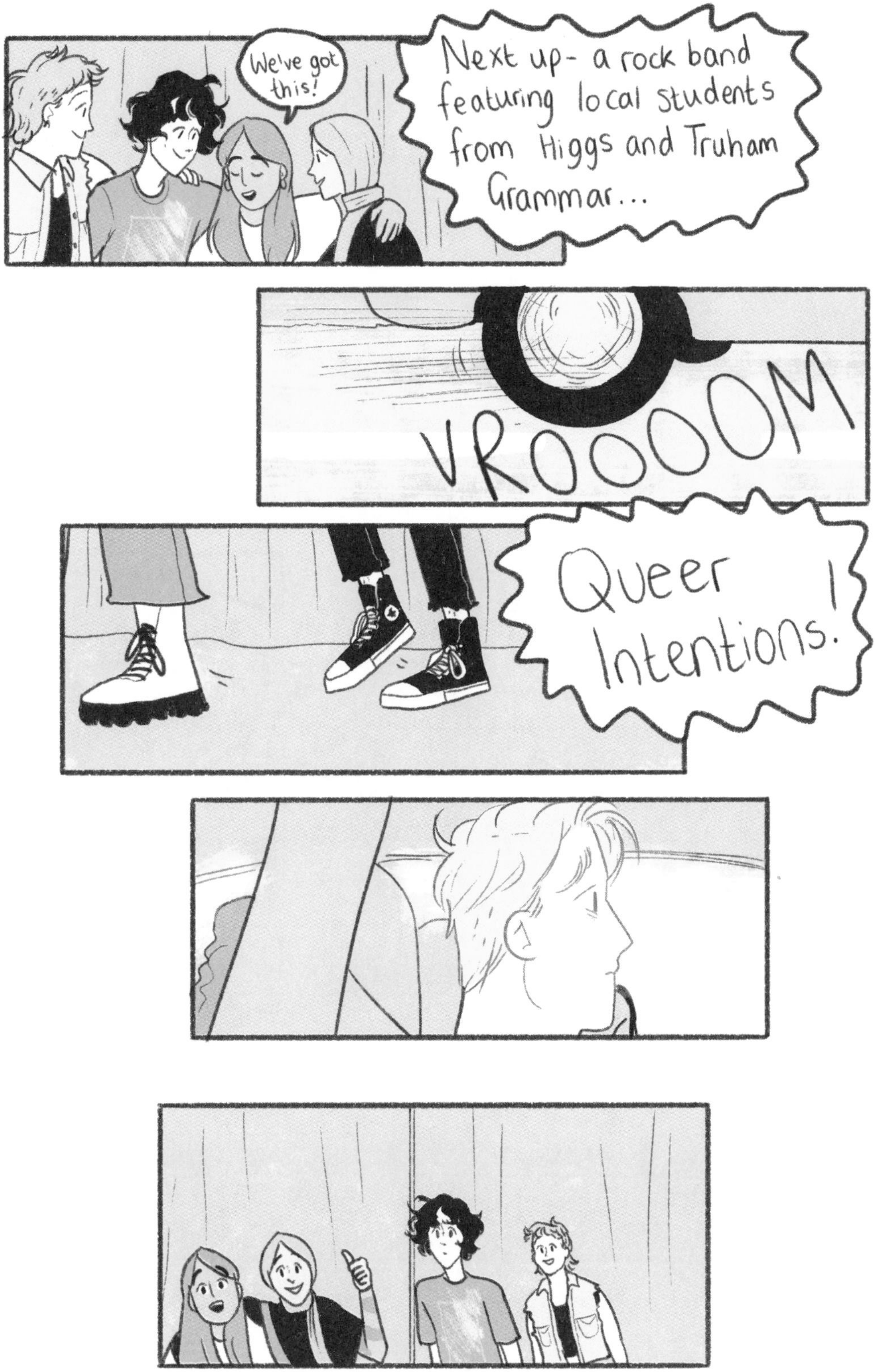
We've got this!
Next up- a rock band featuring local students from Higgs and Truham Grammar...
VROOOOM
Queer Intentions!

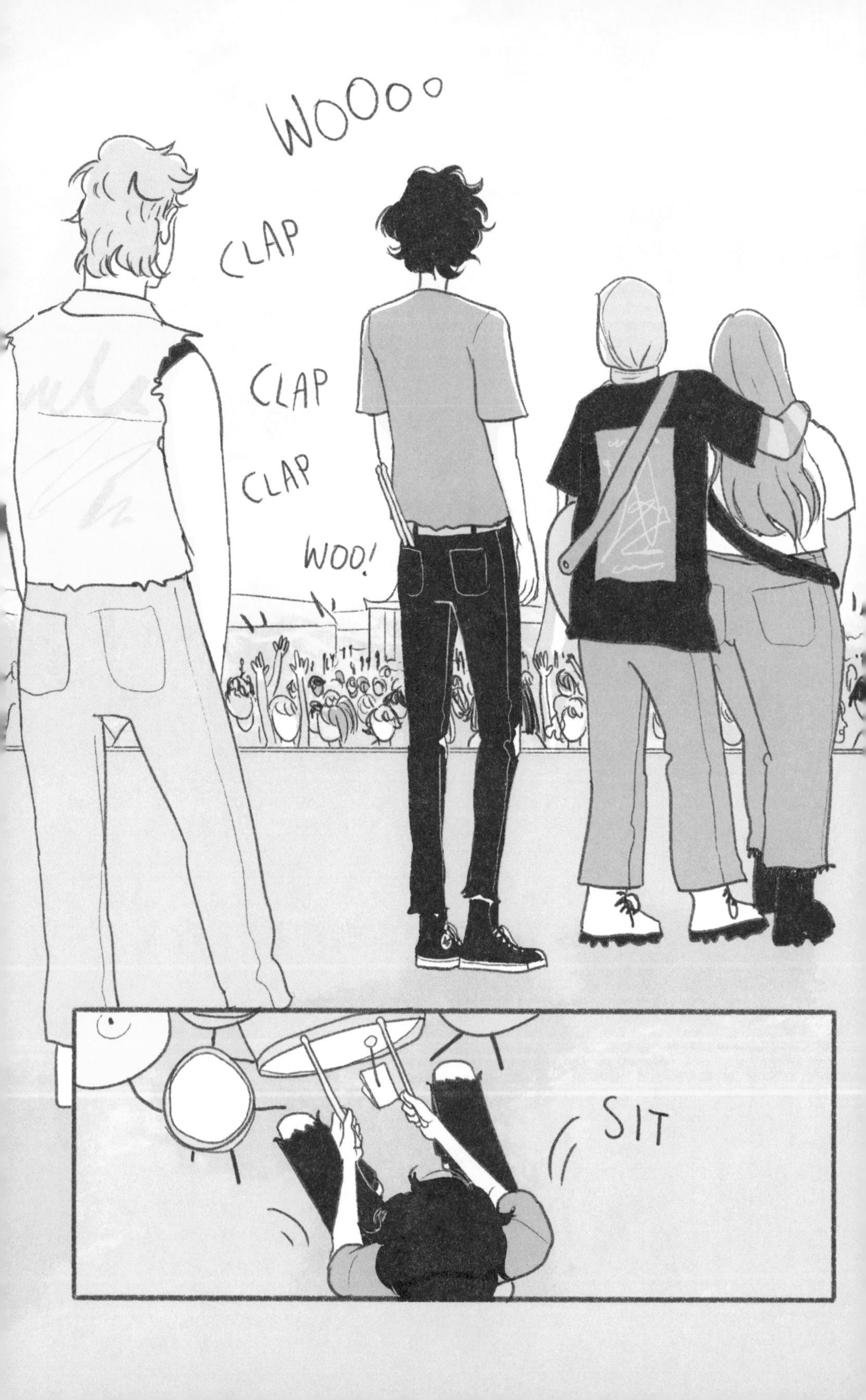
WOOoo
CLAP
CLAP
CLAP
WOO!
SIT

WOO!

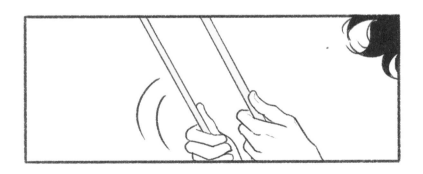

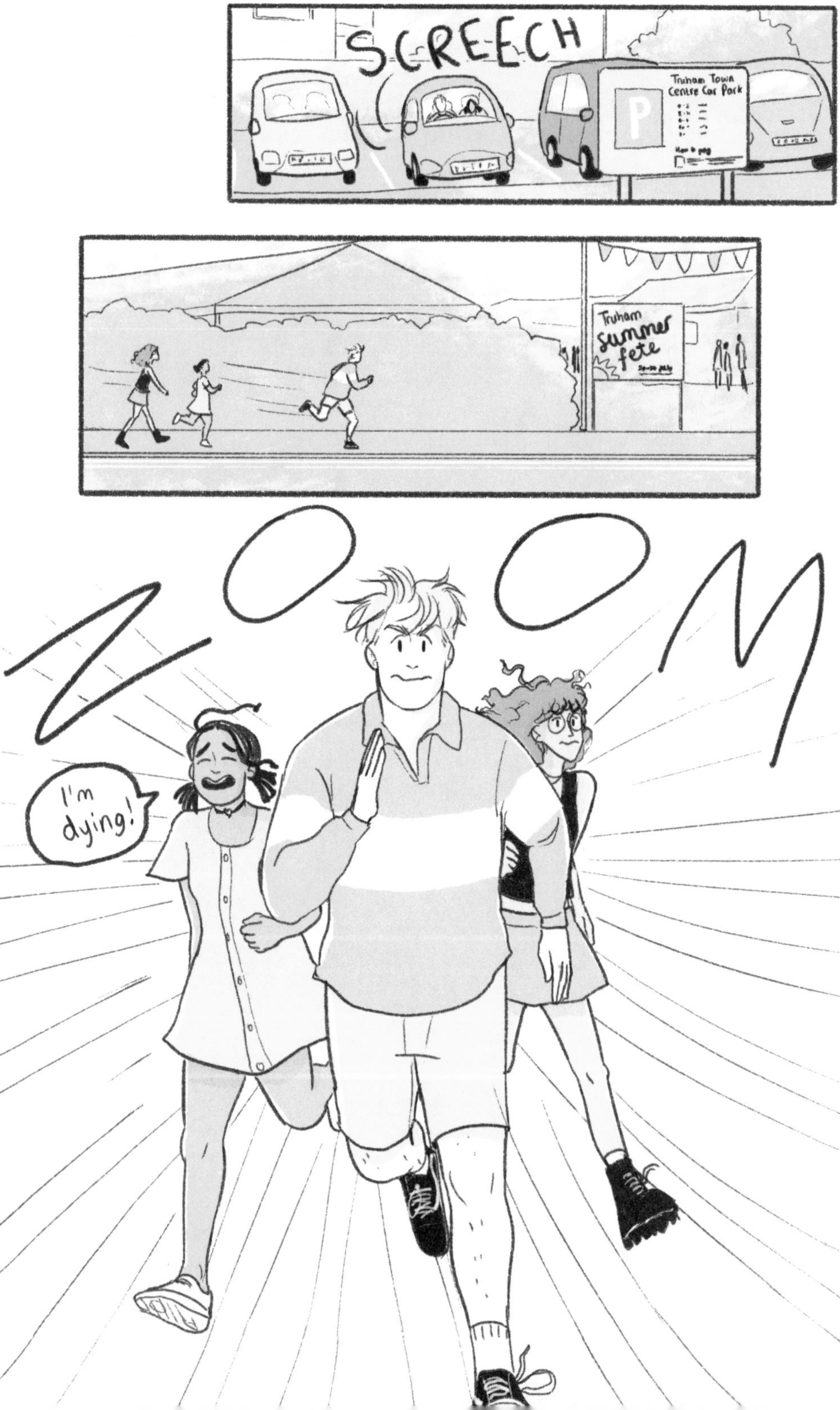
SCREECH
Truham Town Centre Car Park
Truham summer fete
ZOOM
I'm dying!

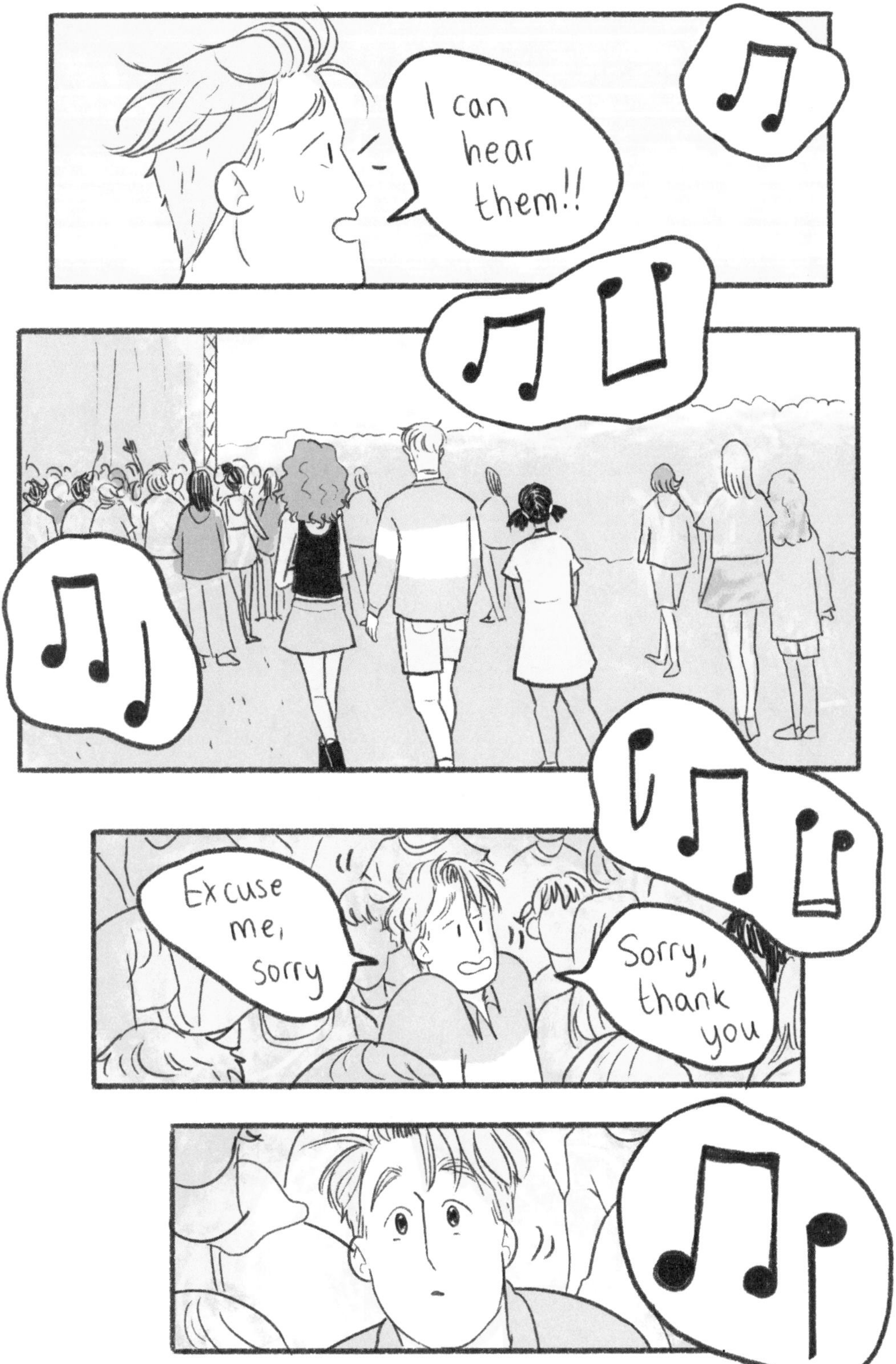
I can hear them!!
Excuse me, sorry
Sorry, thank you

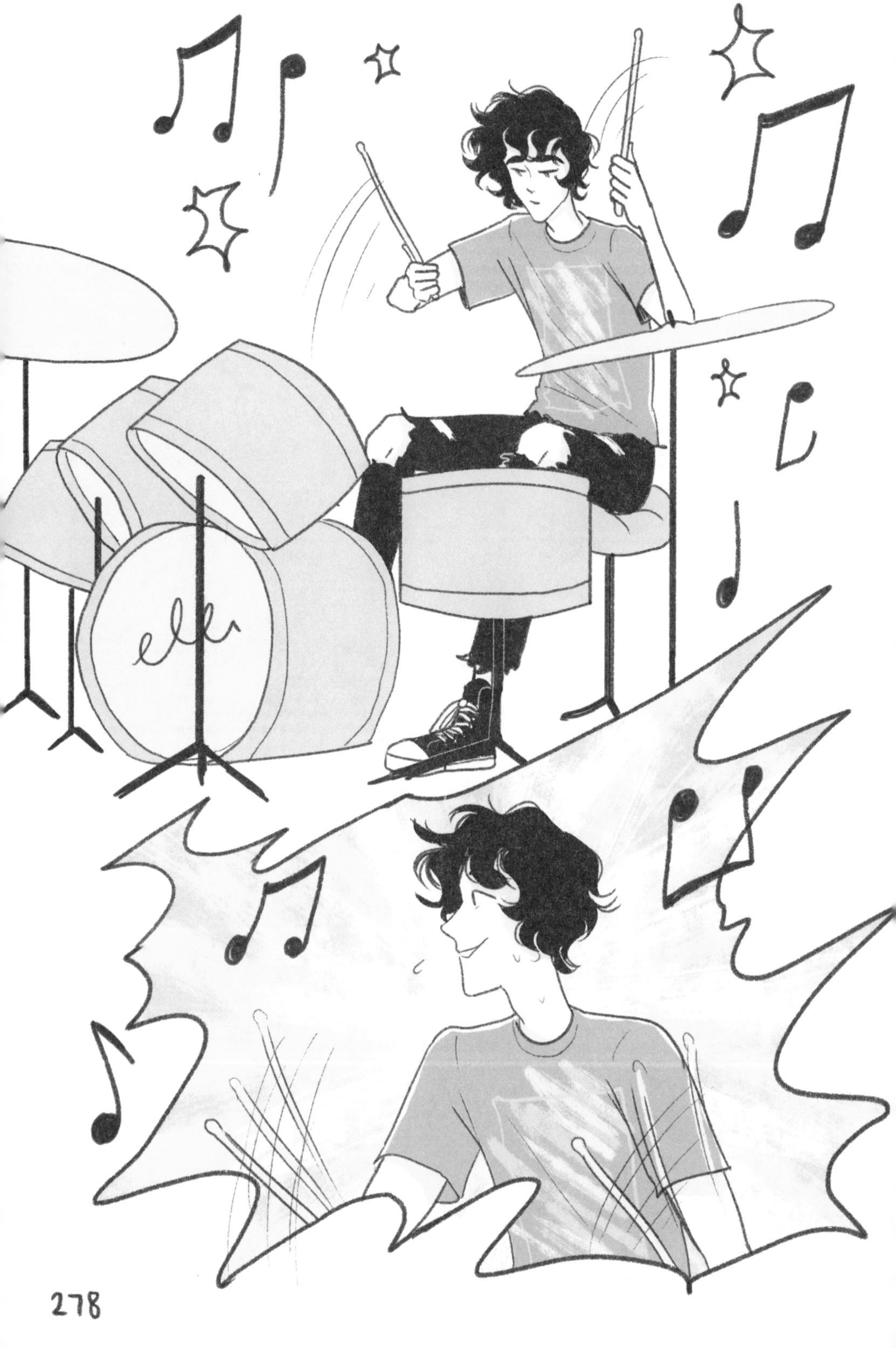

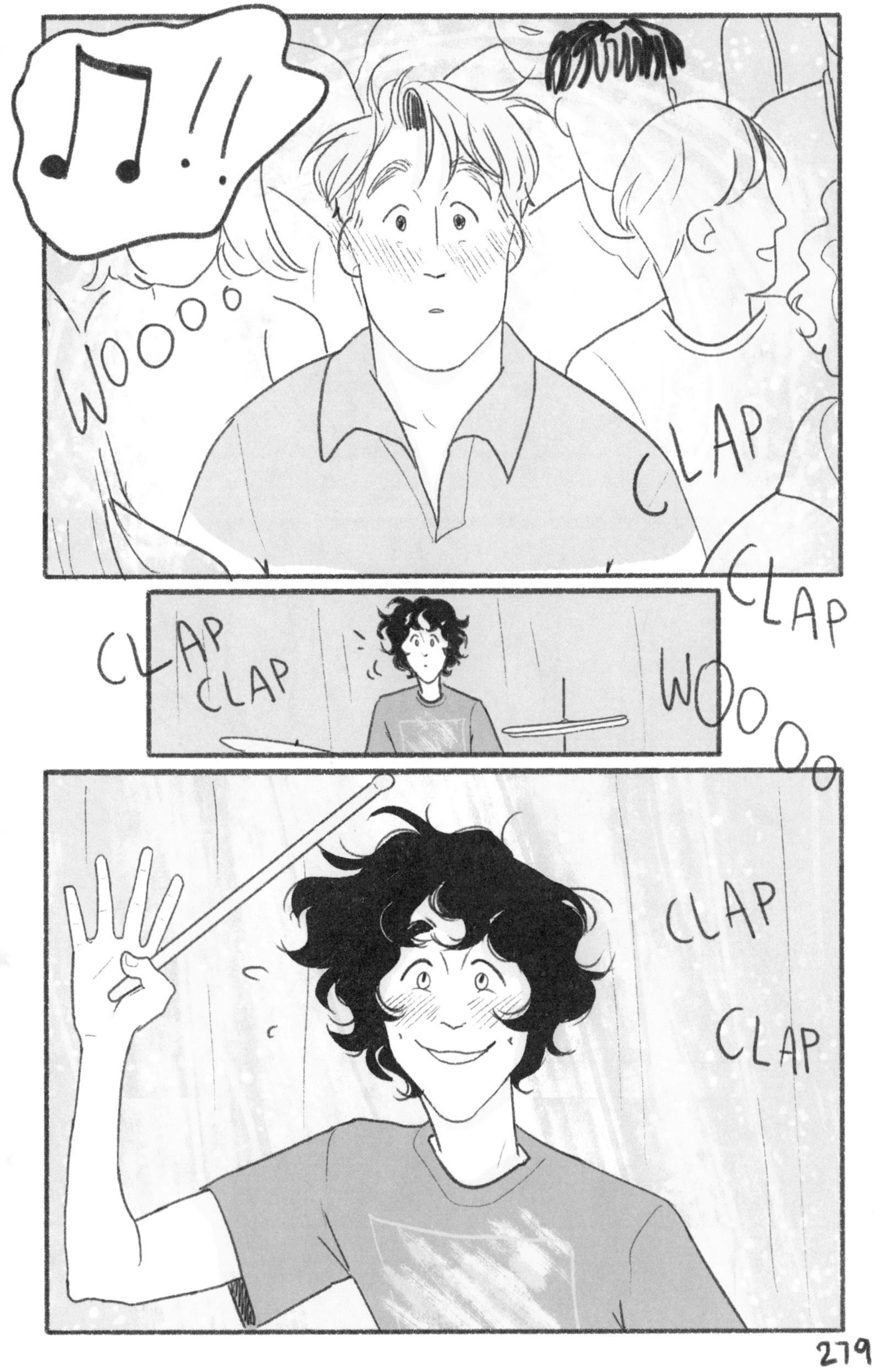

♫!!
WOOOOO
CLAP
CLAP
CLAP
CLAP
WOOOOO
CLAP
CLAP

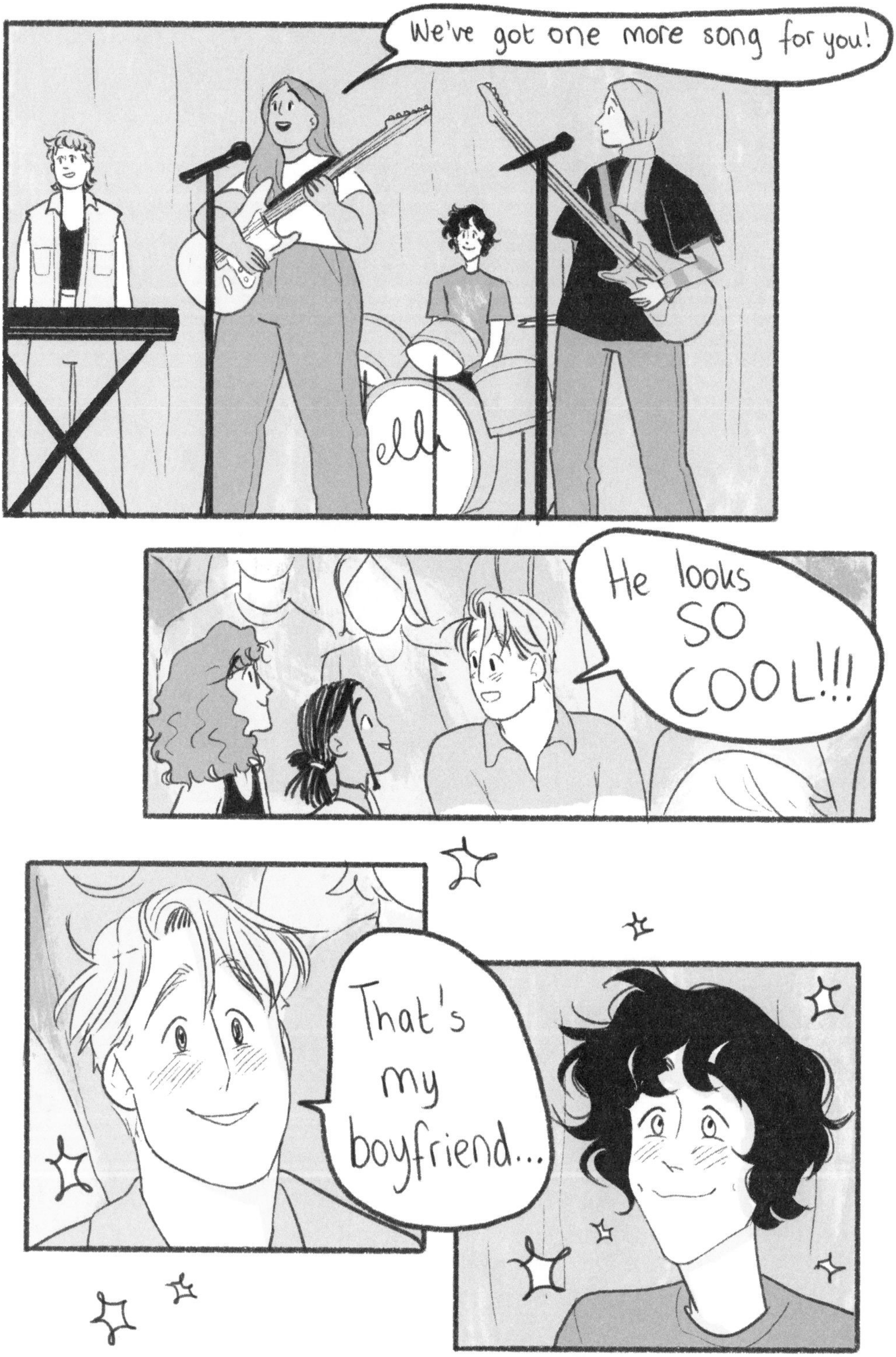
We've got one more song for you!
He looks SO COOL!!!
That's my boyfriend...

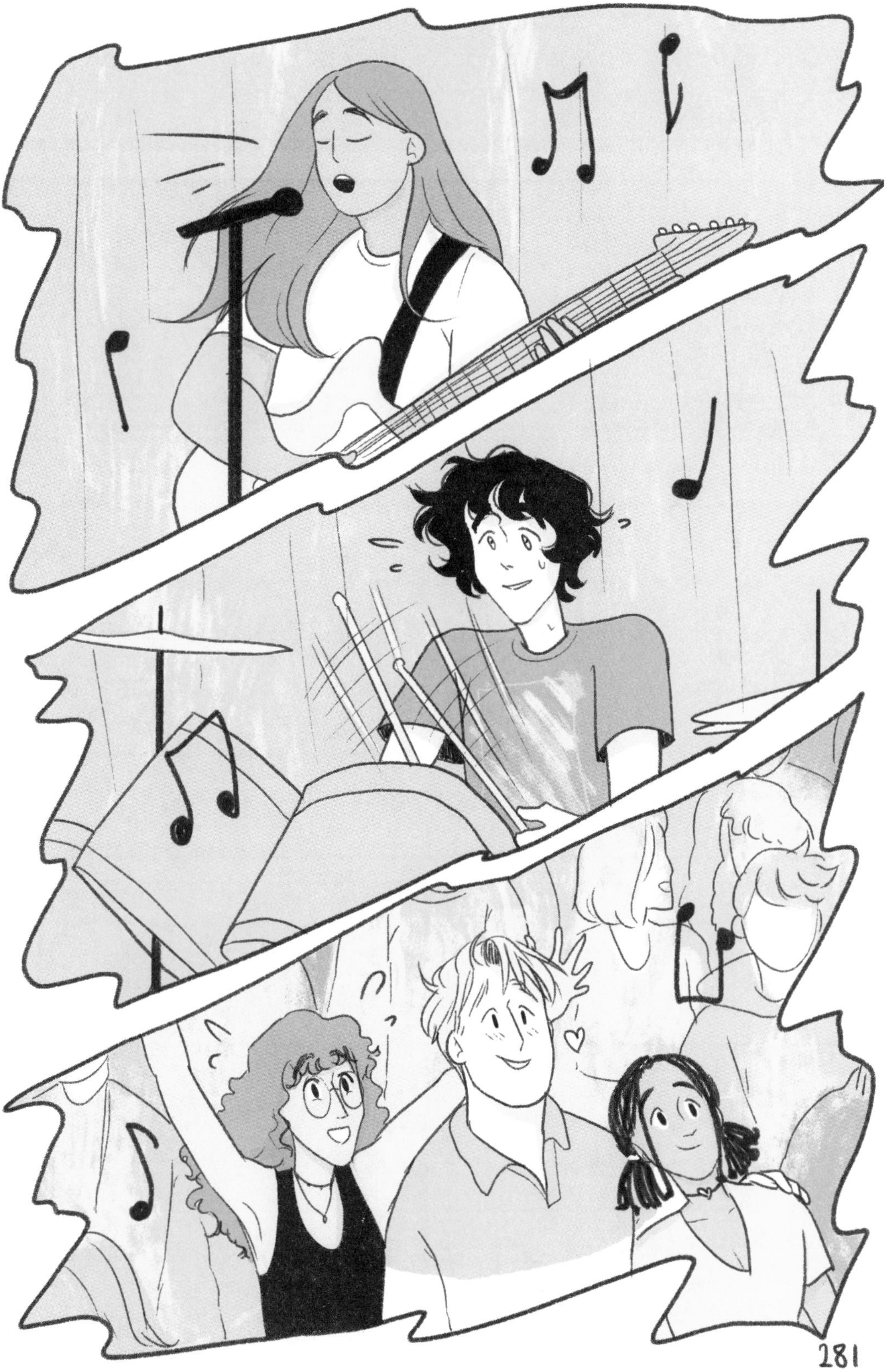

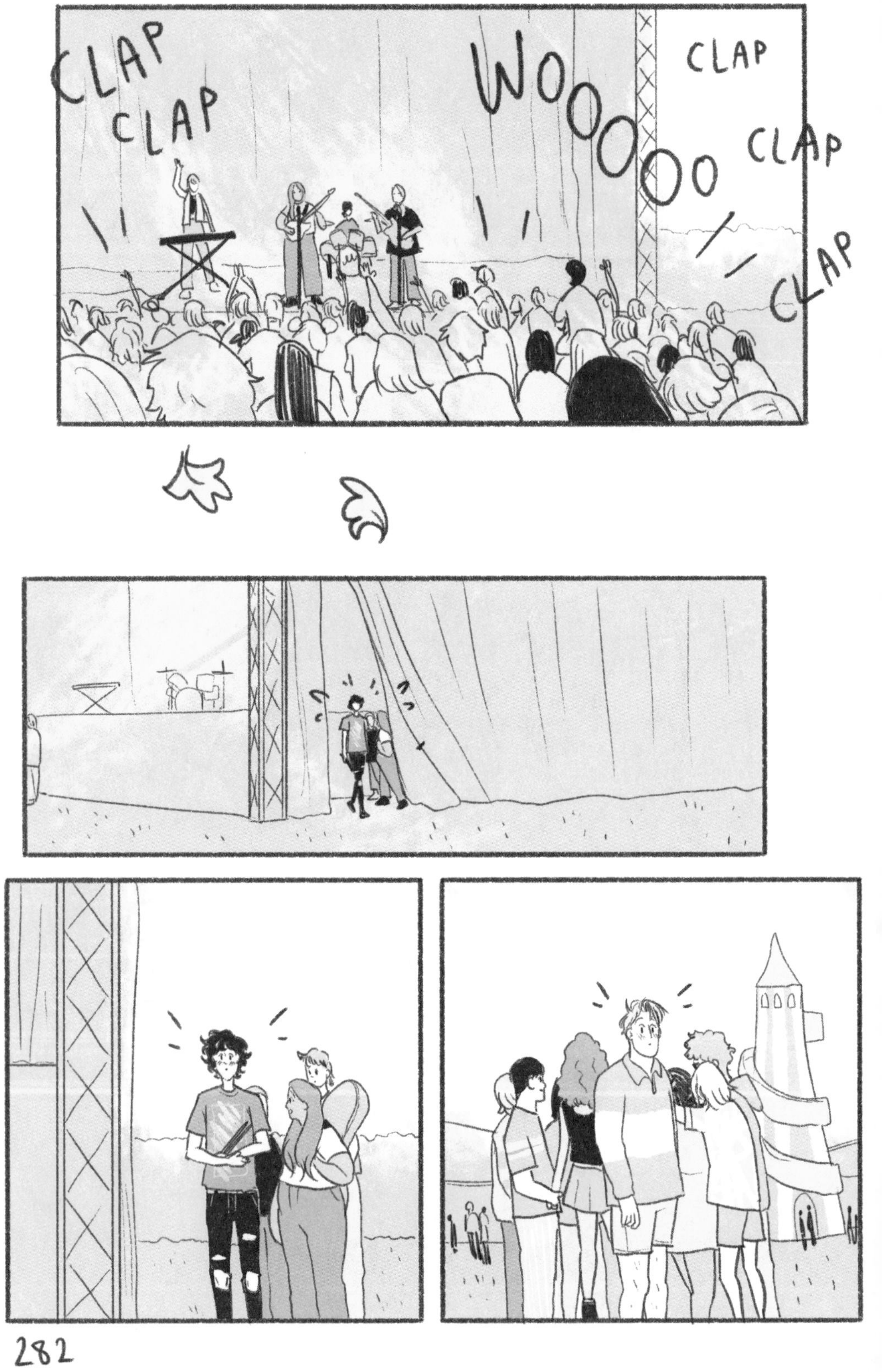
CLAP
CLAP
WOOOOO
CLAP
CLAP
CLAP

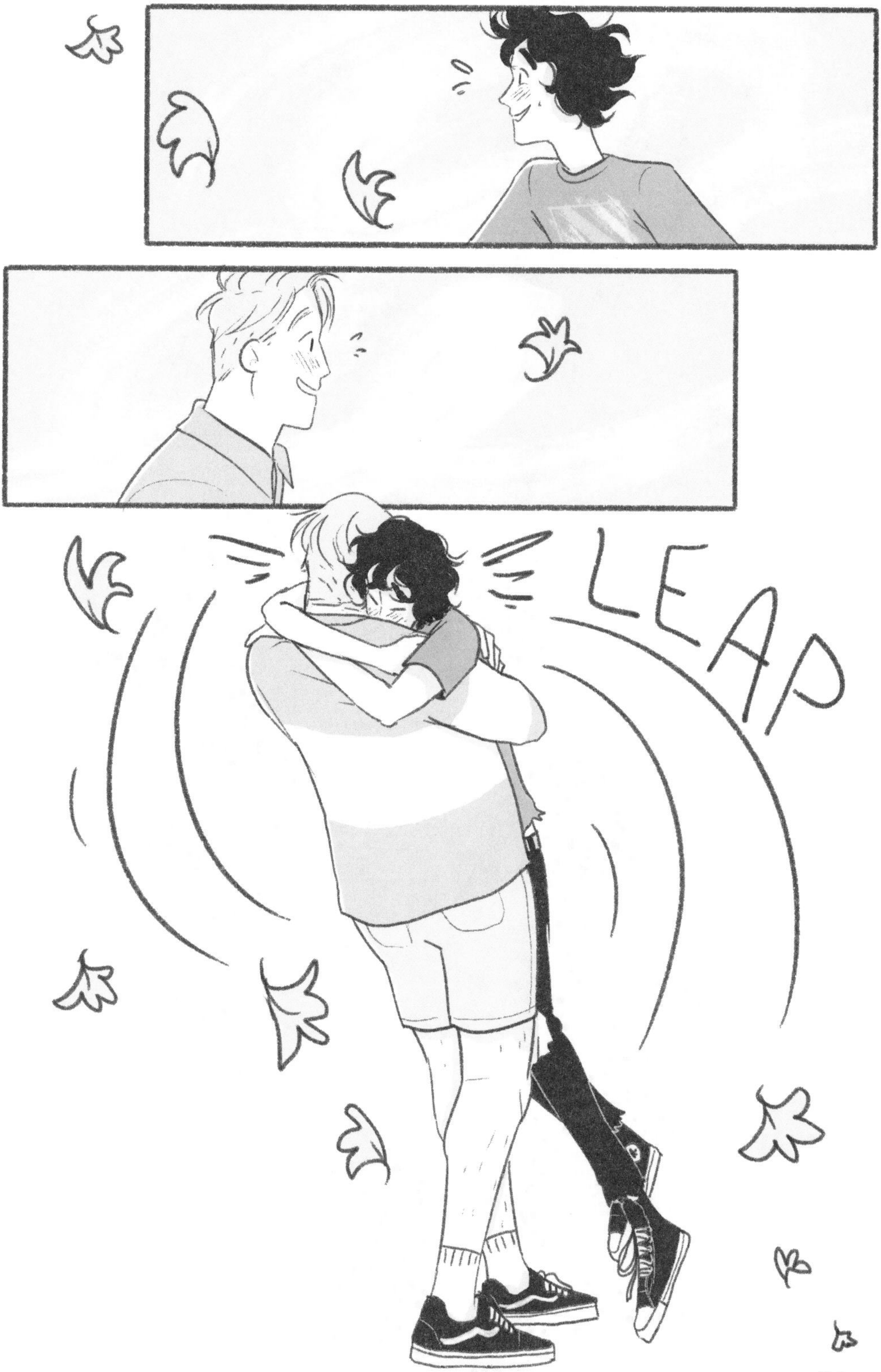
LEAP

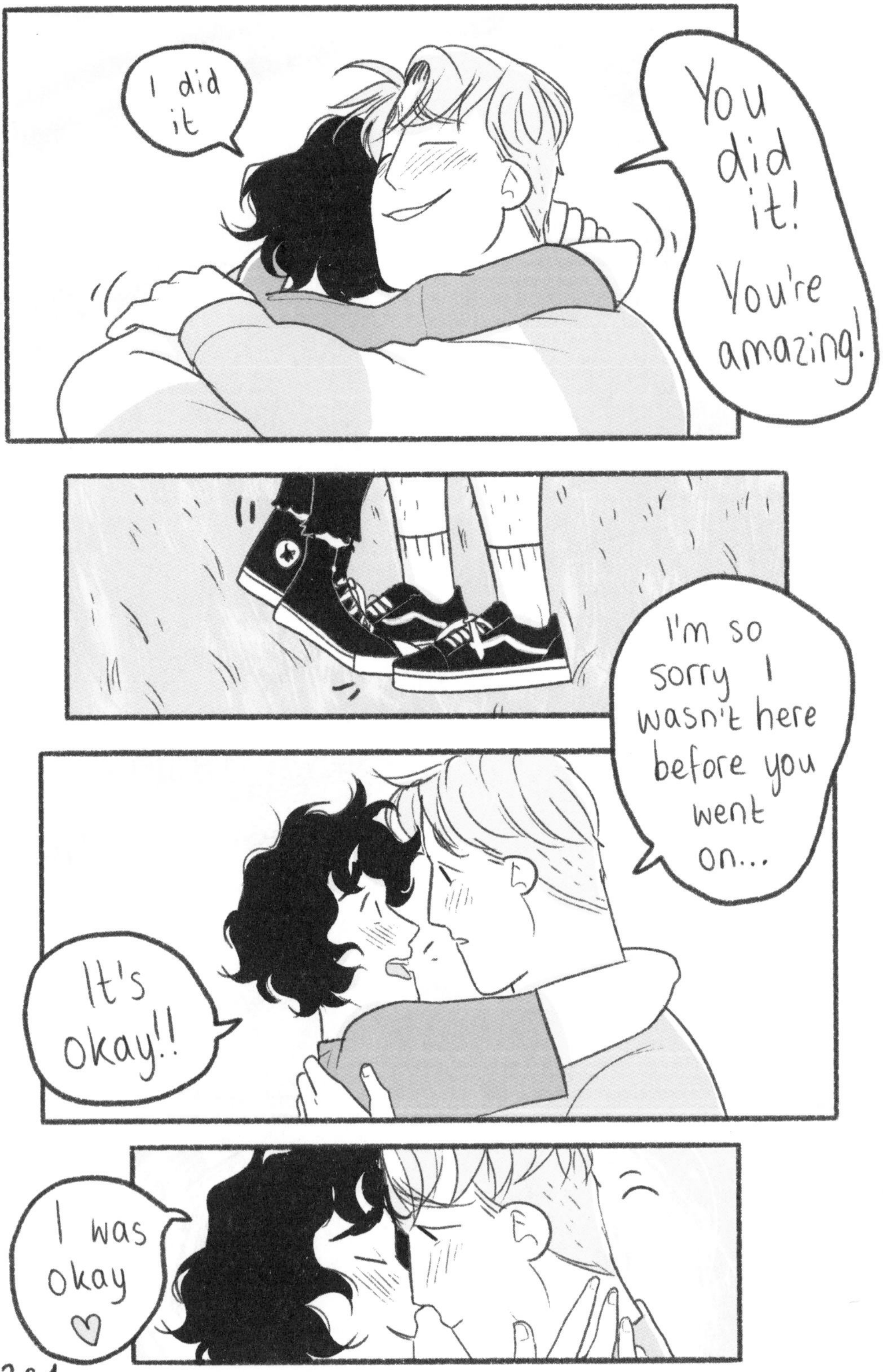
I did it
You did it! You're amazing!
I'm so sorry I wasn't here before you went on...
It's okay!!
I was okay ♡

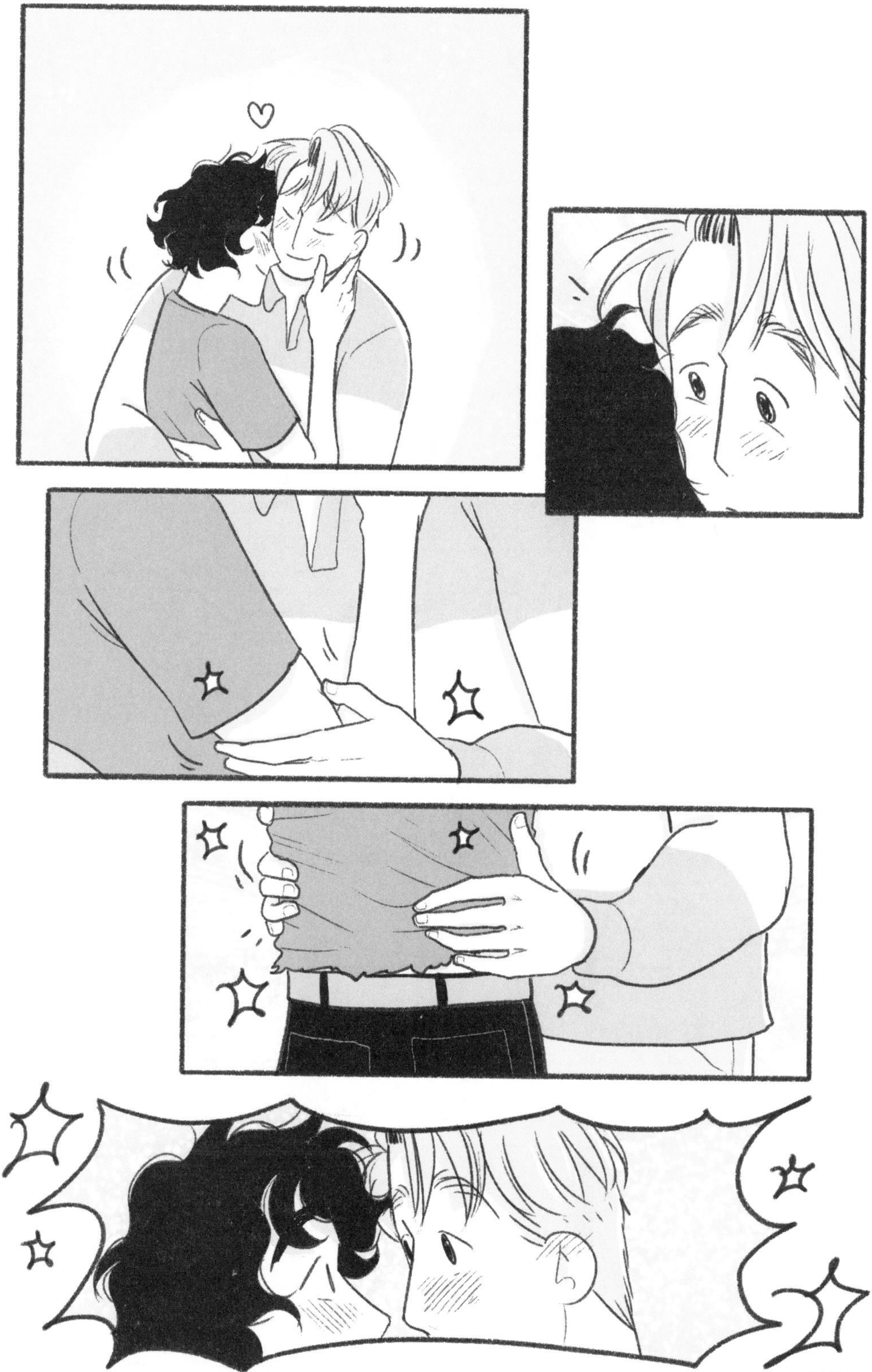

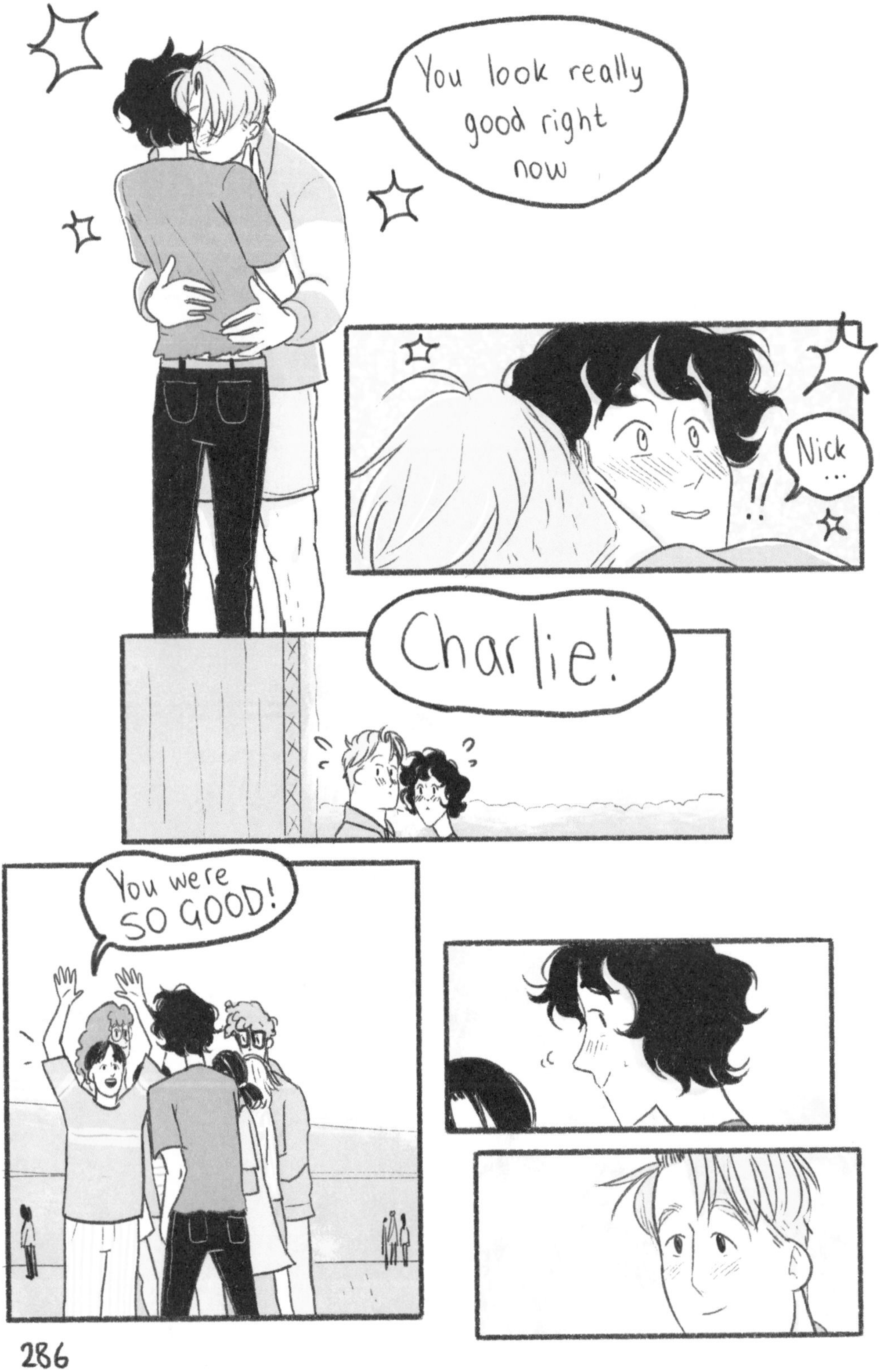
You look really good right now
Nick...
!!
Charlie!
You were SO GOOD!

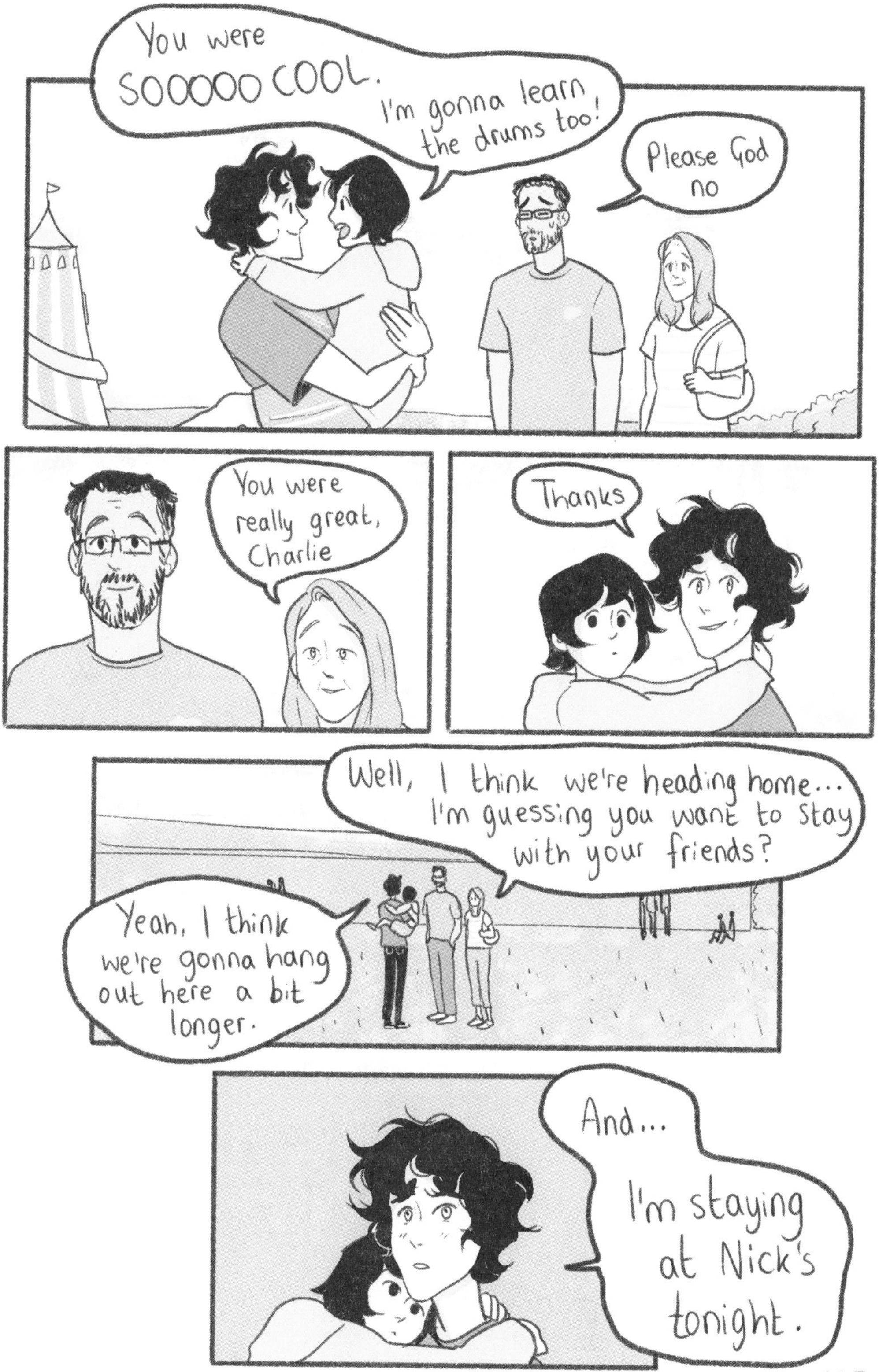
You were SOOOOO COOL.
I'm gonna learn the drums too!
Please God no
You were really great, Charlie
Thanks
Well, I think we're heading home... I'm guessing you want to stay with your friends?
Yeah, I think we're gonna hang out here a bit longer.
And...
I'm staying at Nick's tonight.

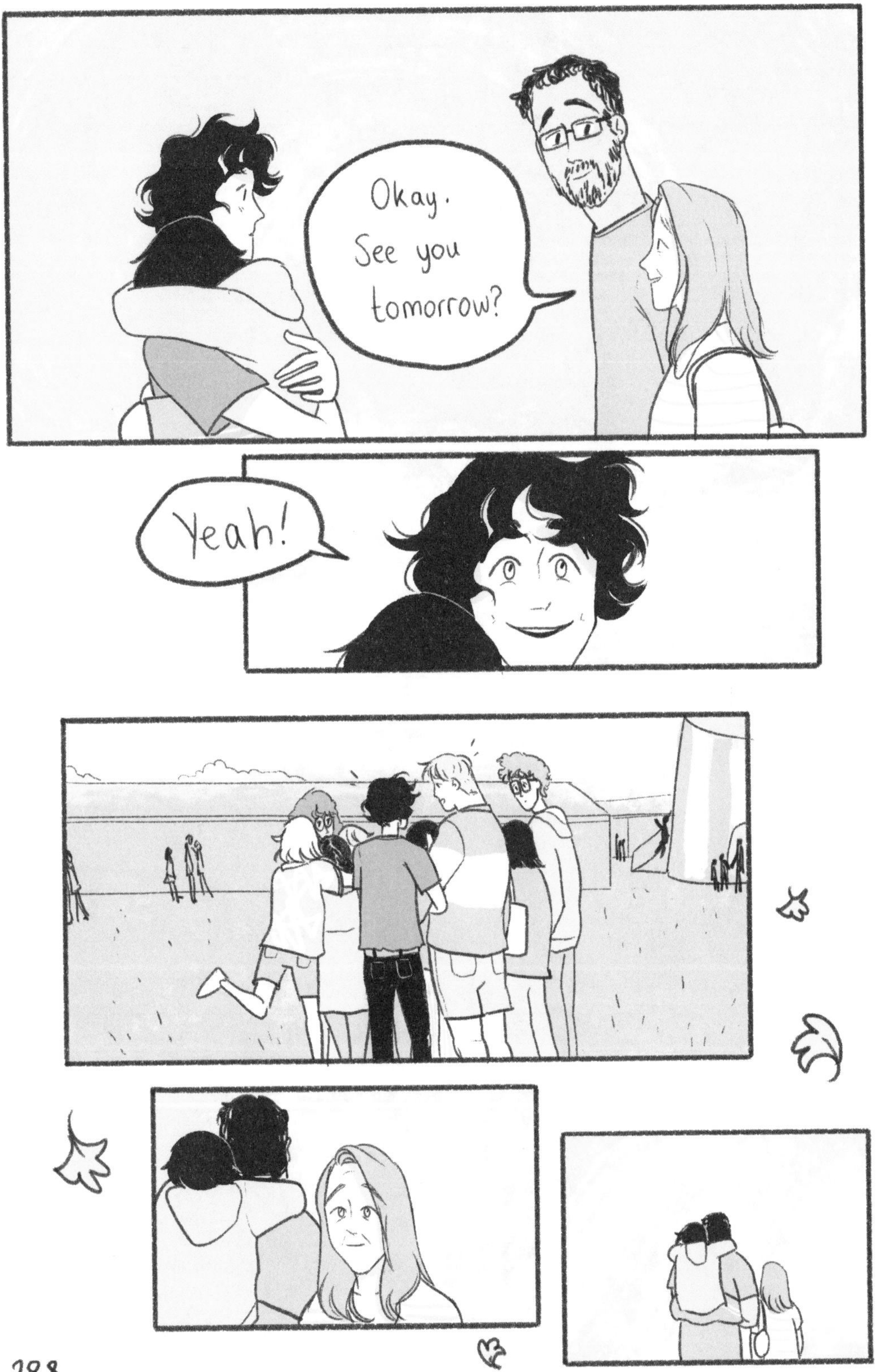
Okay. See you tomorrow?
Yeah!

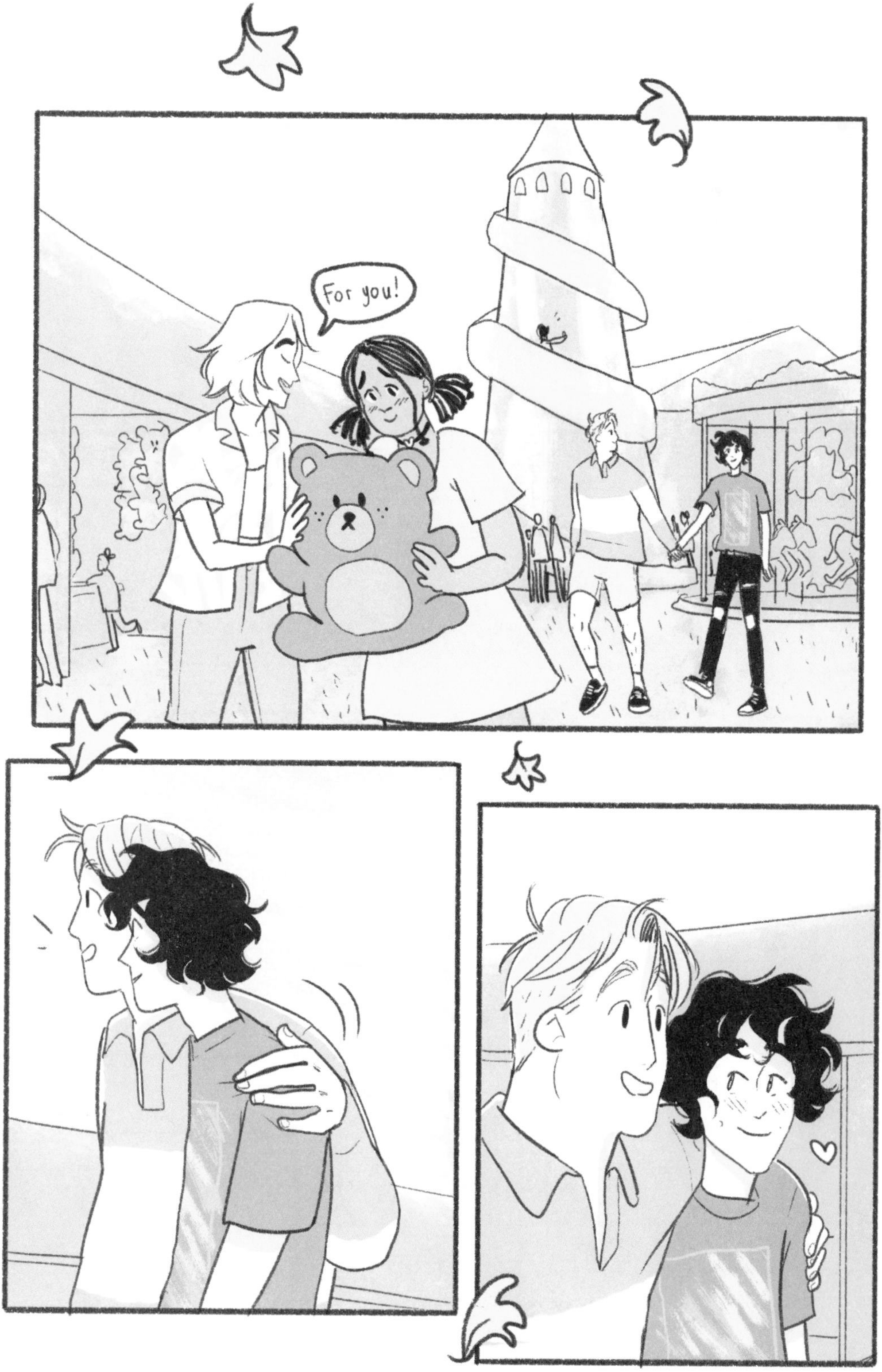
For you!

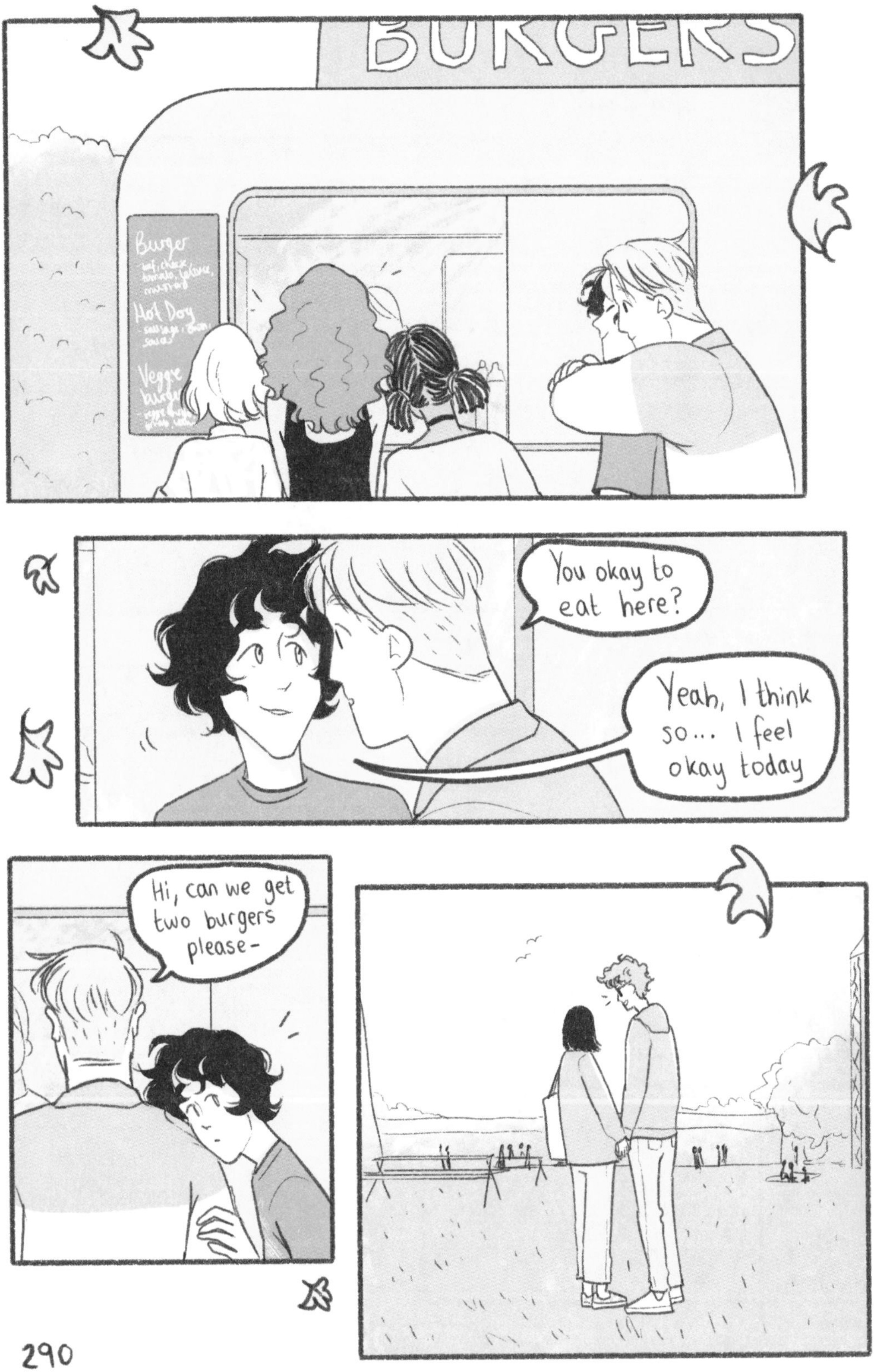
BURGERS
Burger
Hot Dog
You okay to eat here?
Yeah, I think so... I feel okay today
Hi, can we get two burgers please-

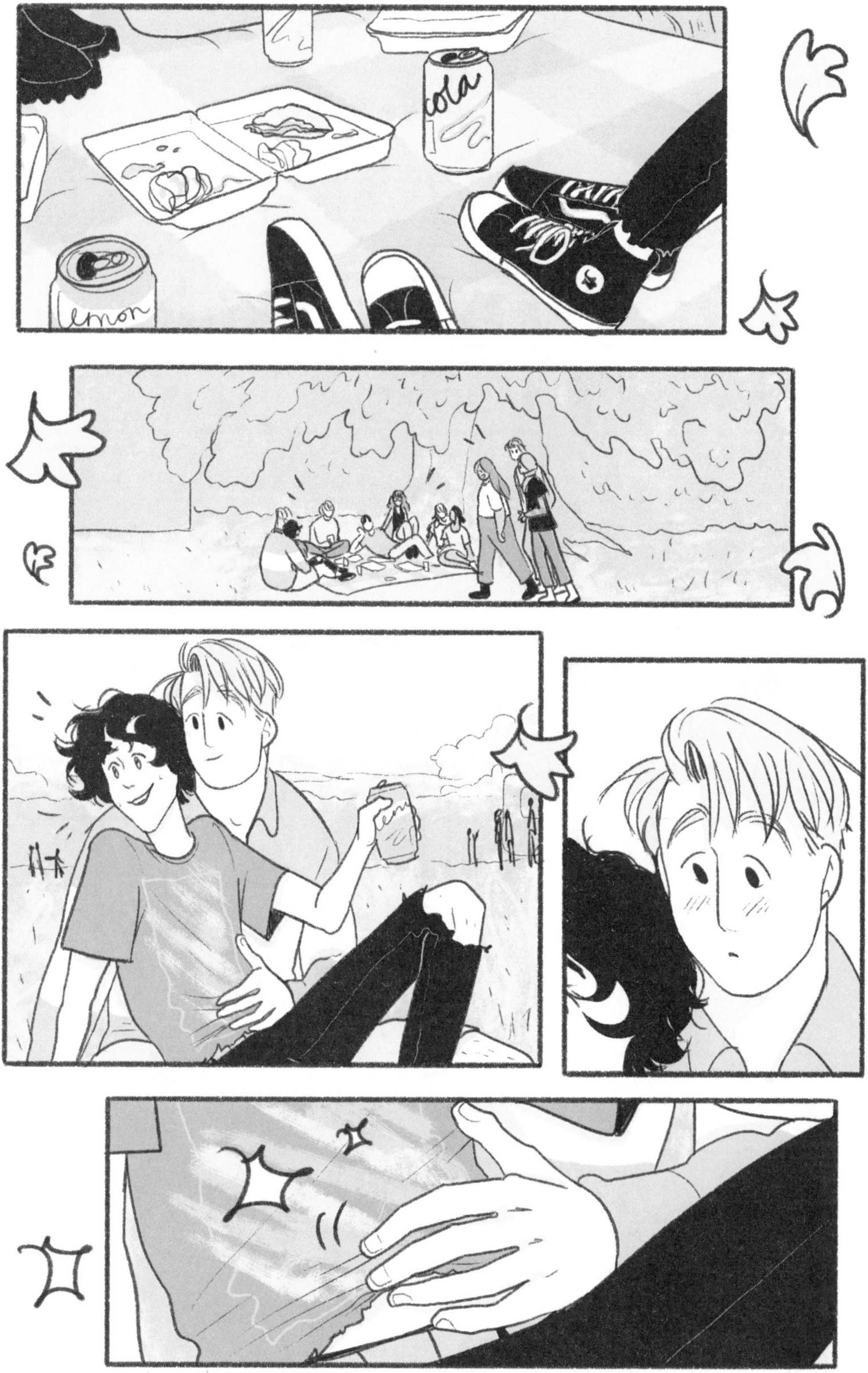
cola
lemon

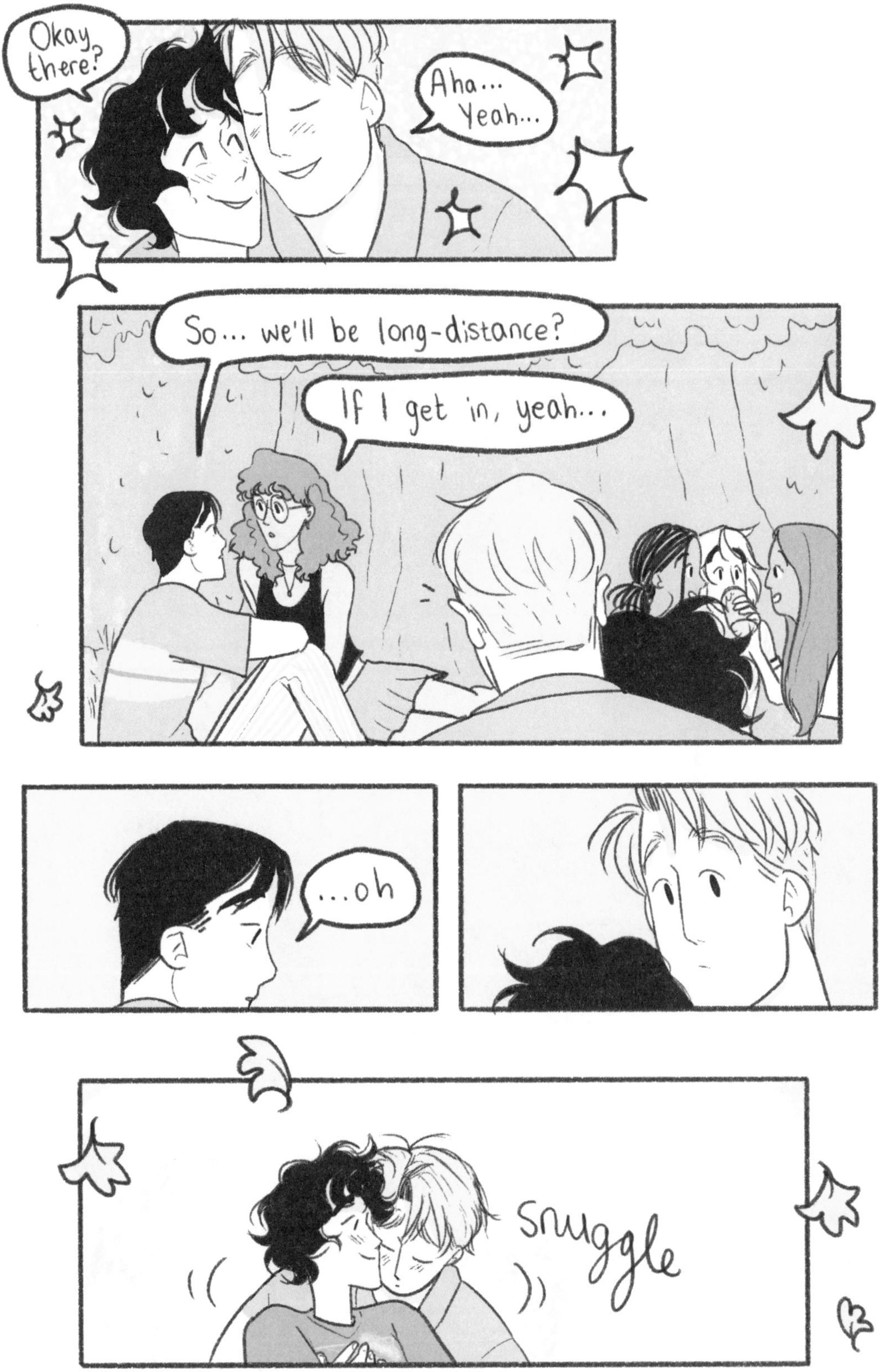
Okay there?
Aha... Yeah...
So... we'll be long-distance?
If I get in, yeah...
...oh
snuggle

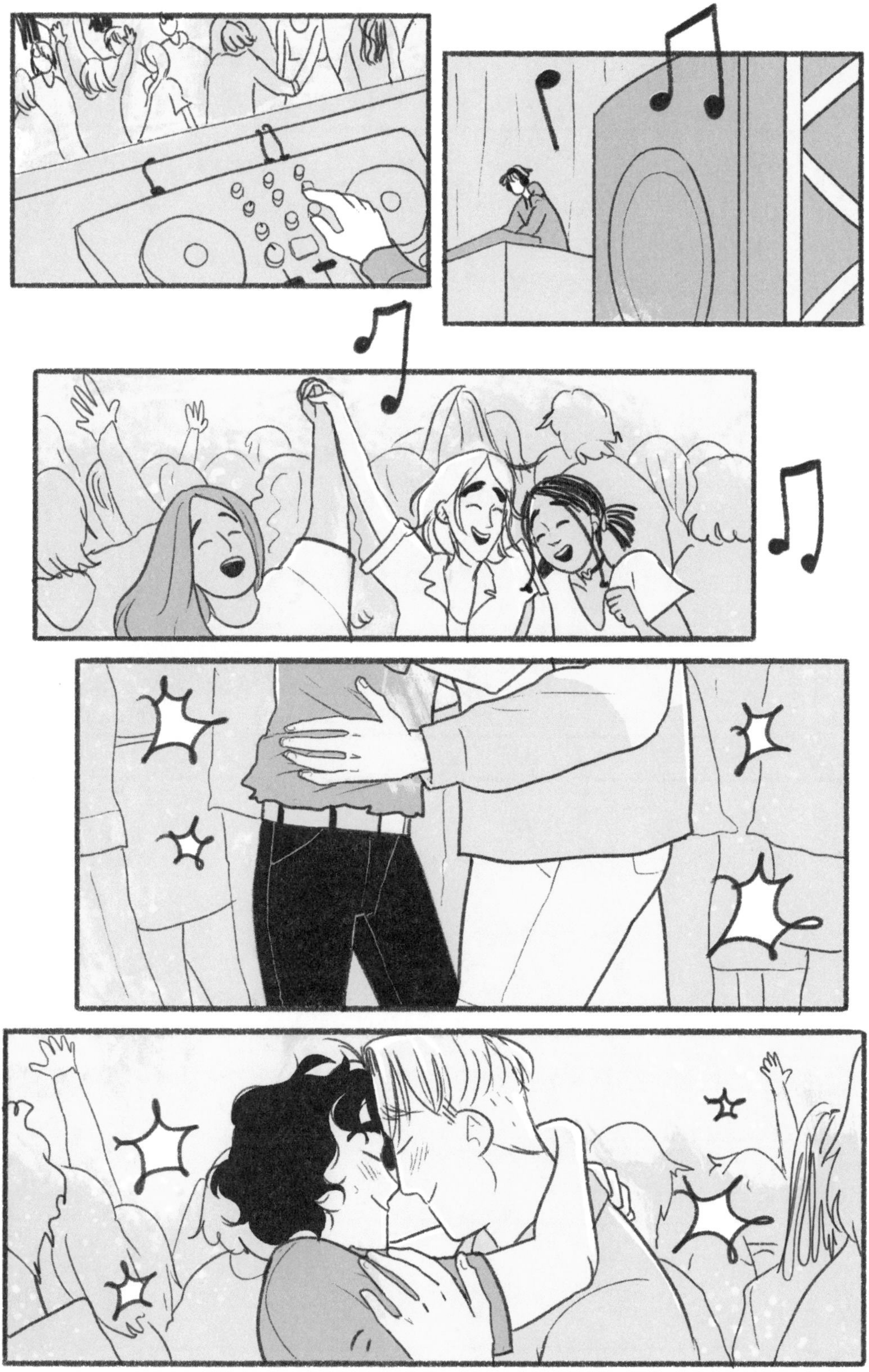

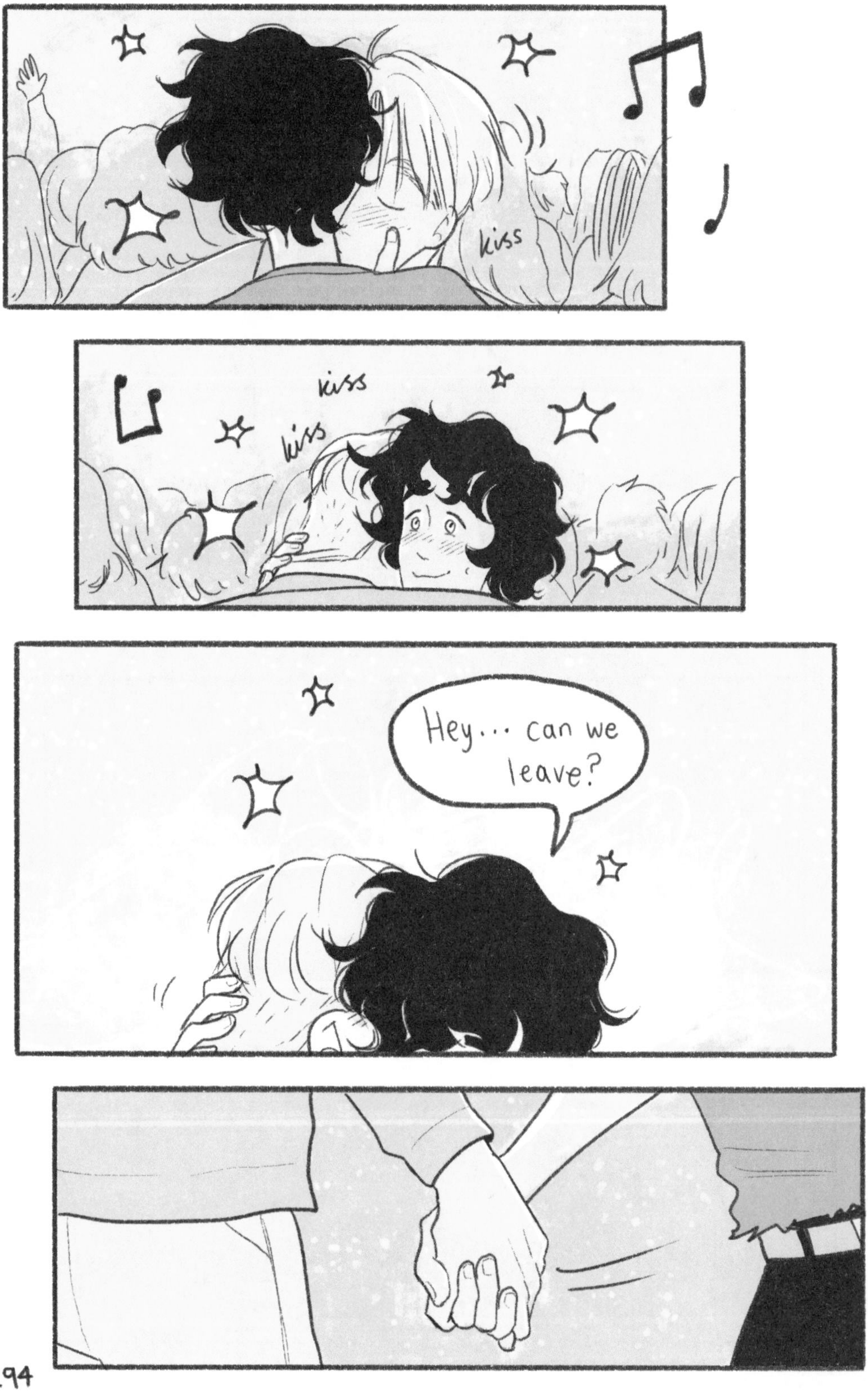
kiss
kiss
kiss
Hey... can we leave?

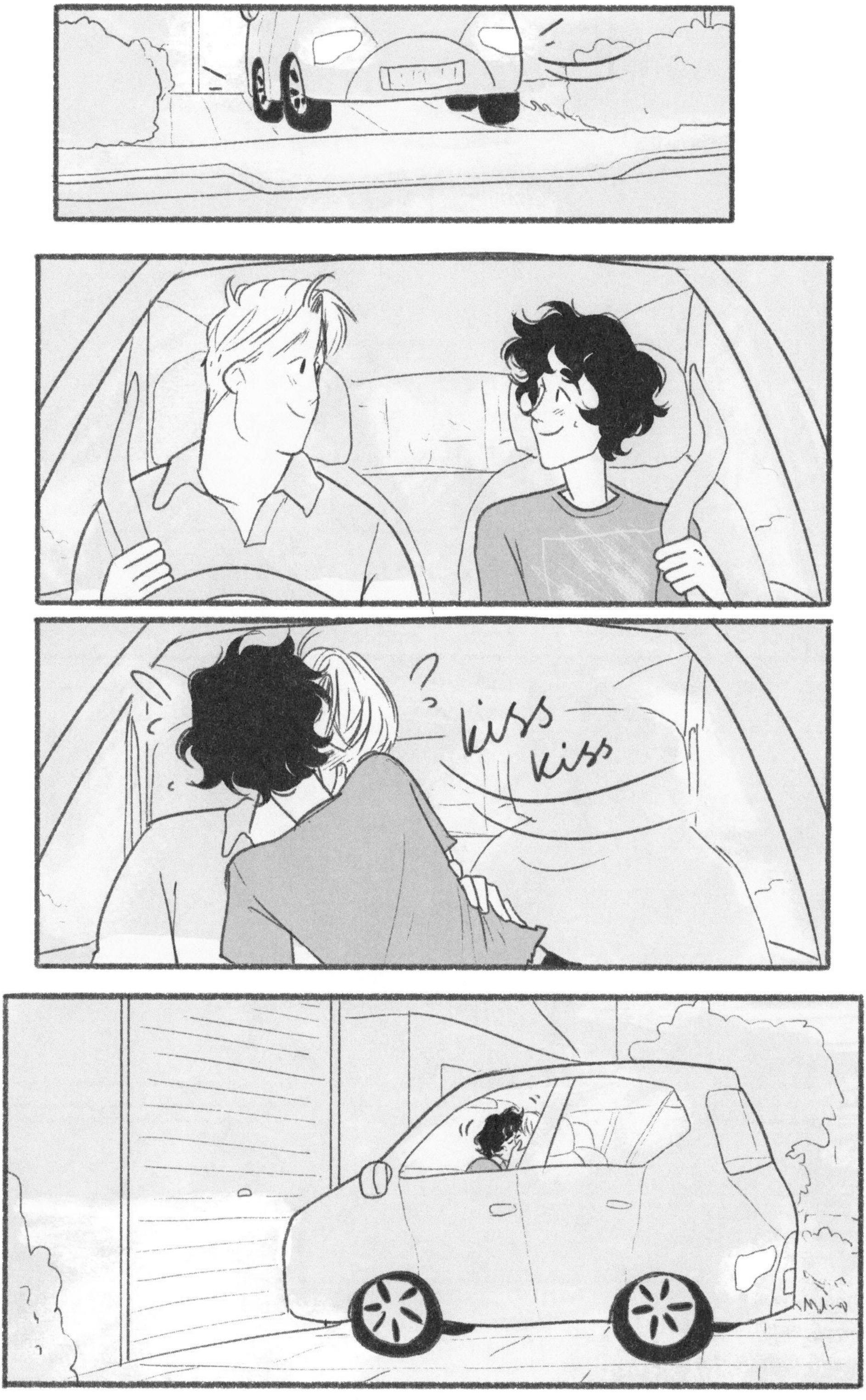
kiss
kiss

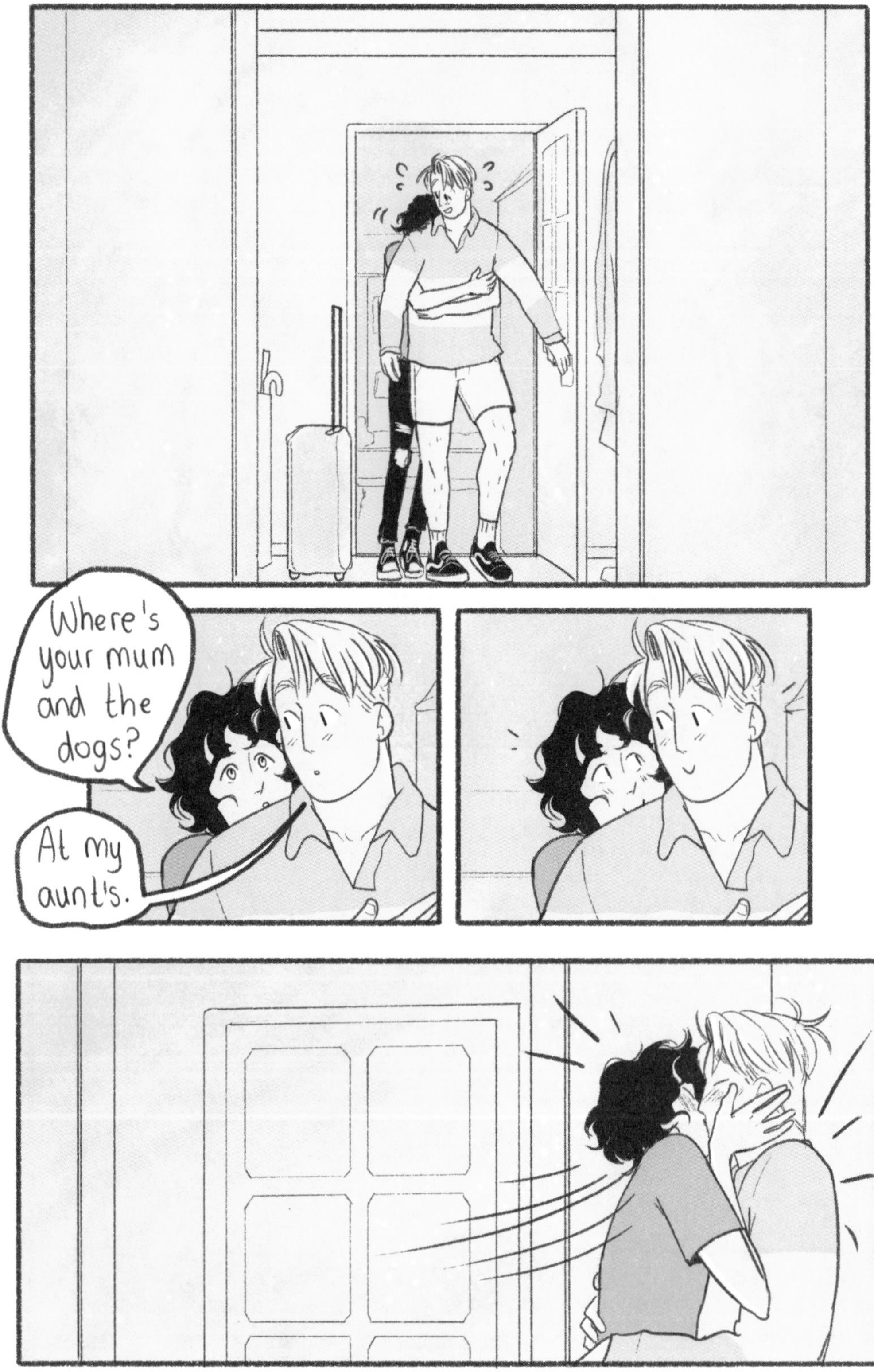
Where's your mum and the dogs?
At my aunt's.

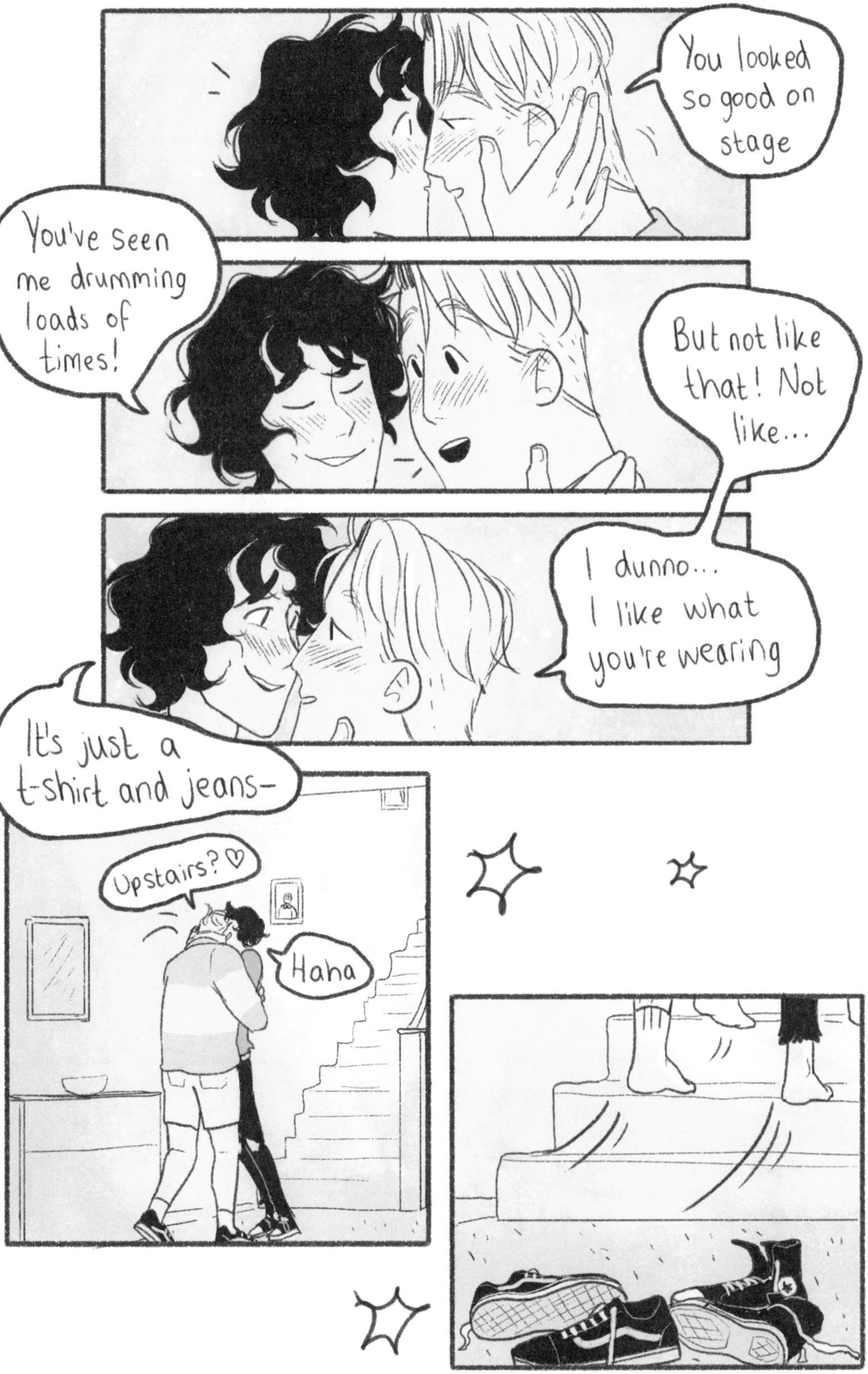
You looked so good on stage
You've seen me drumming loads of times!
But not like that! Not like...
I dunno... I like what you're wearing
It's just a t-shirt and jeans-
Upstairs? ♡
Haha

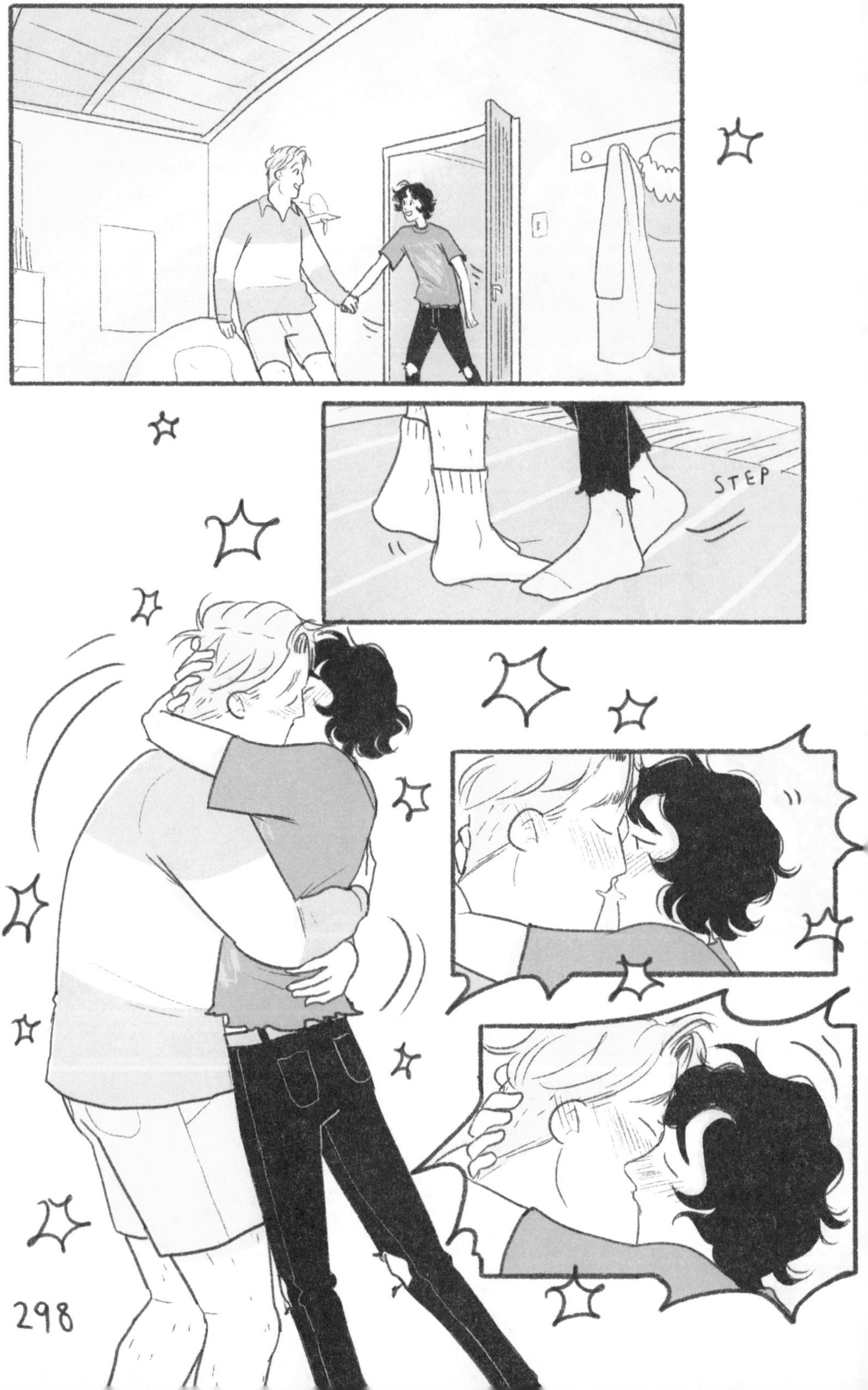
STEP

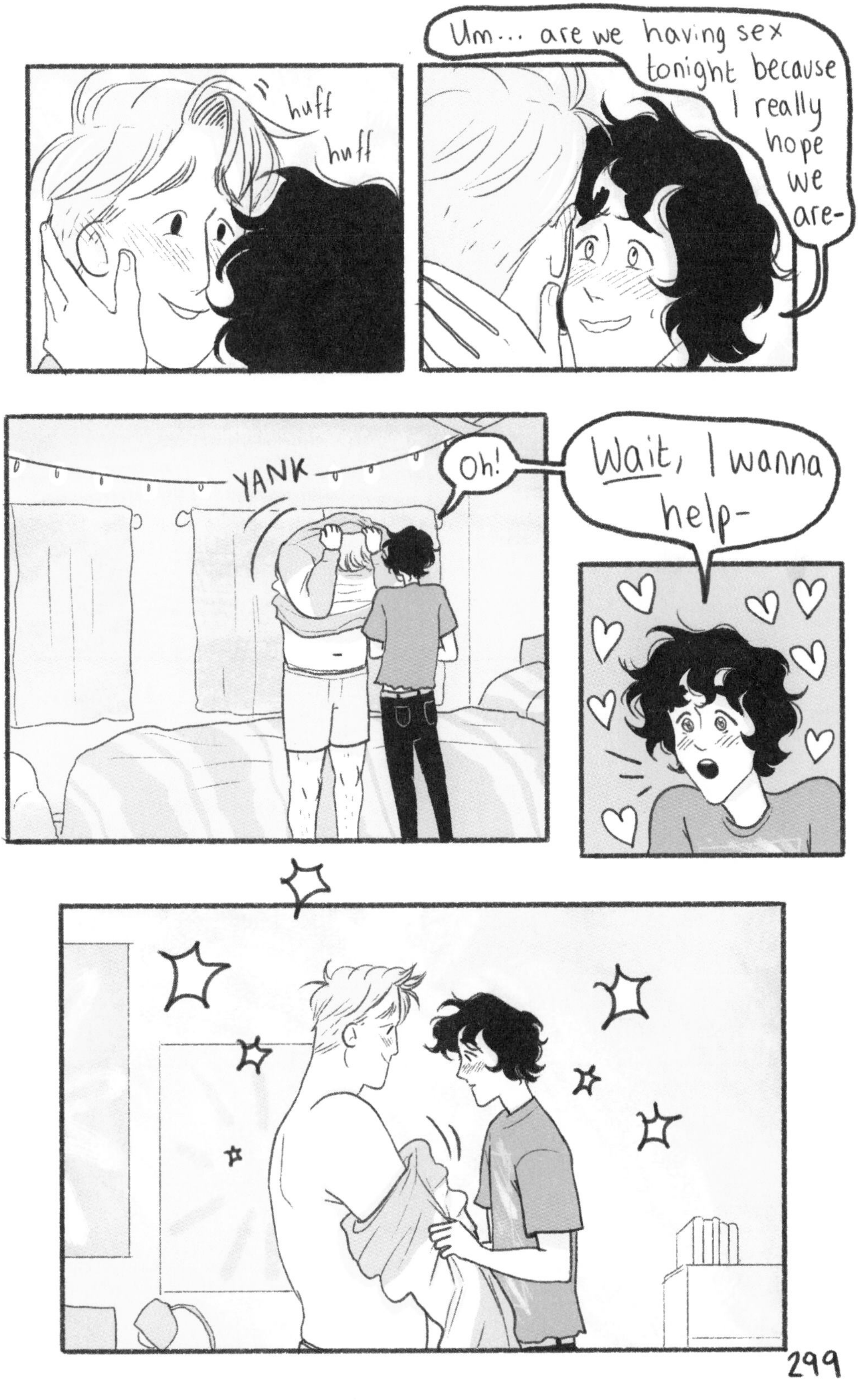
huff
huff
Um... are we having sex tonight because I really hope we are-
YANK
Oh!
Wait, I wanna help-

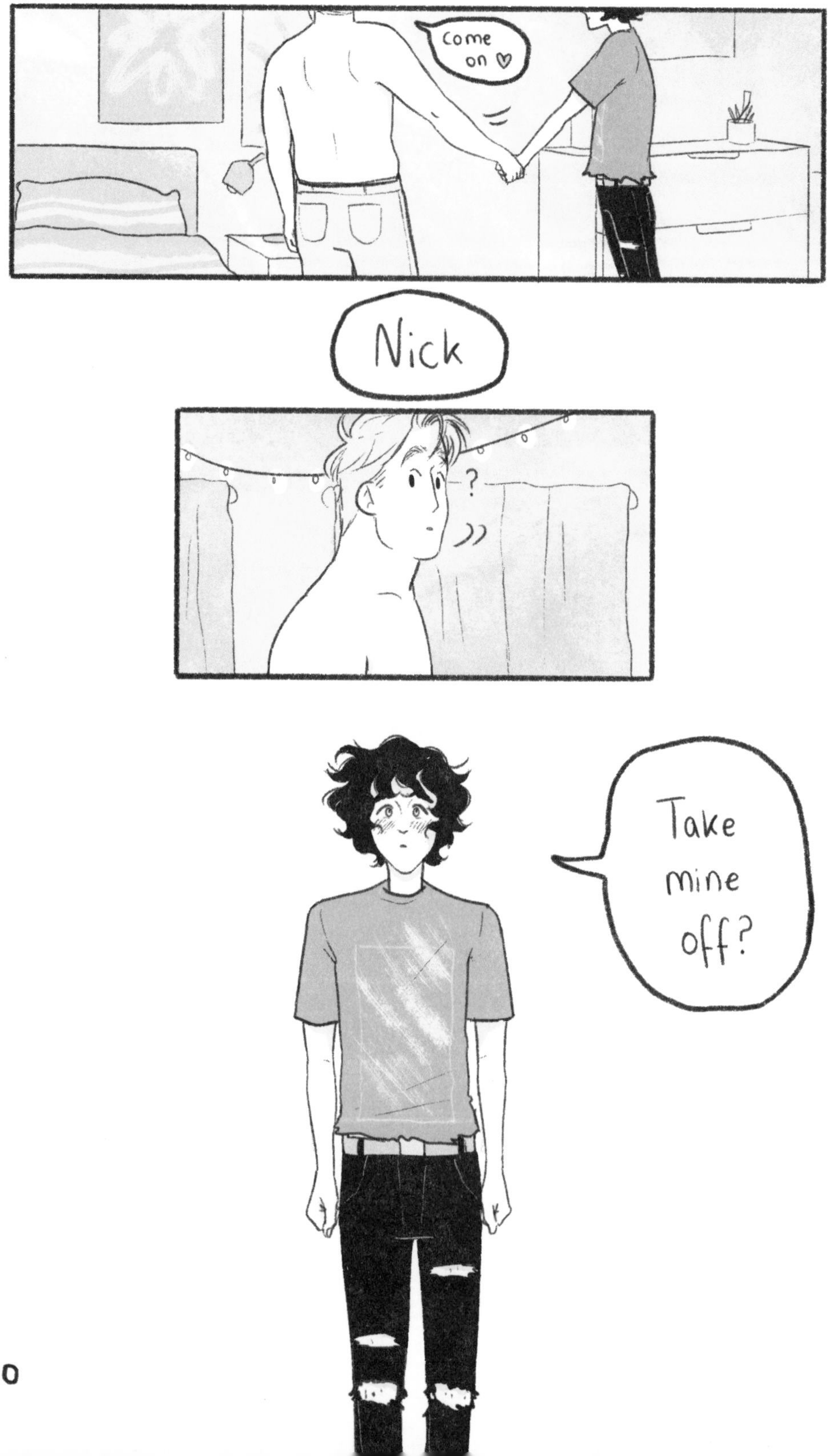
Come on ♡
Nick
Take mine off?

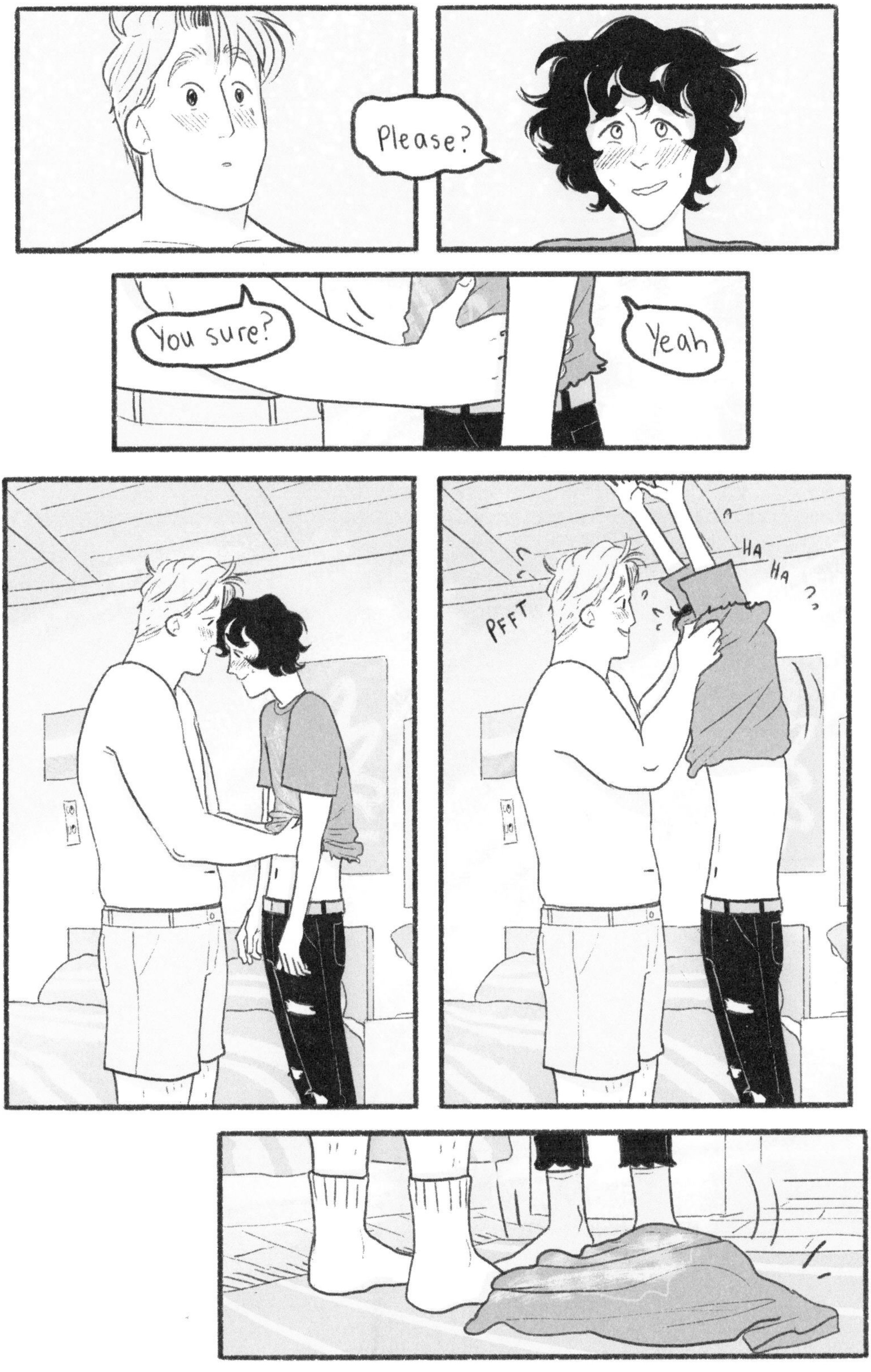
Please?
You sure?
Yeah
PFFT
HA
HA

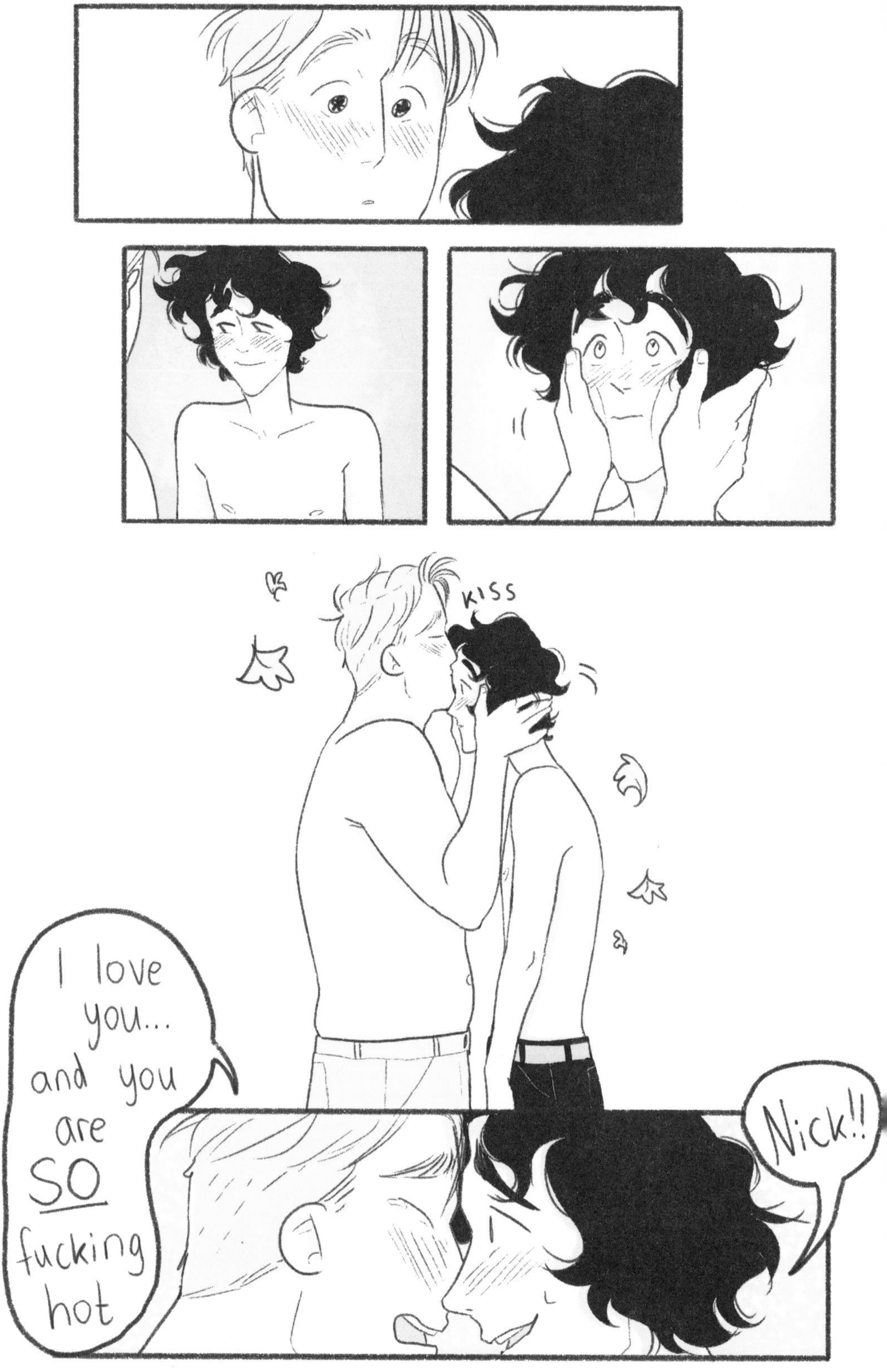
KISS
I love you... and you are SO fucking hot
Nick!!

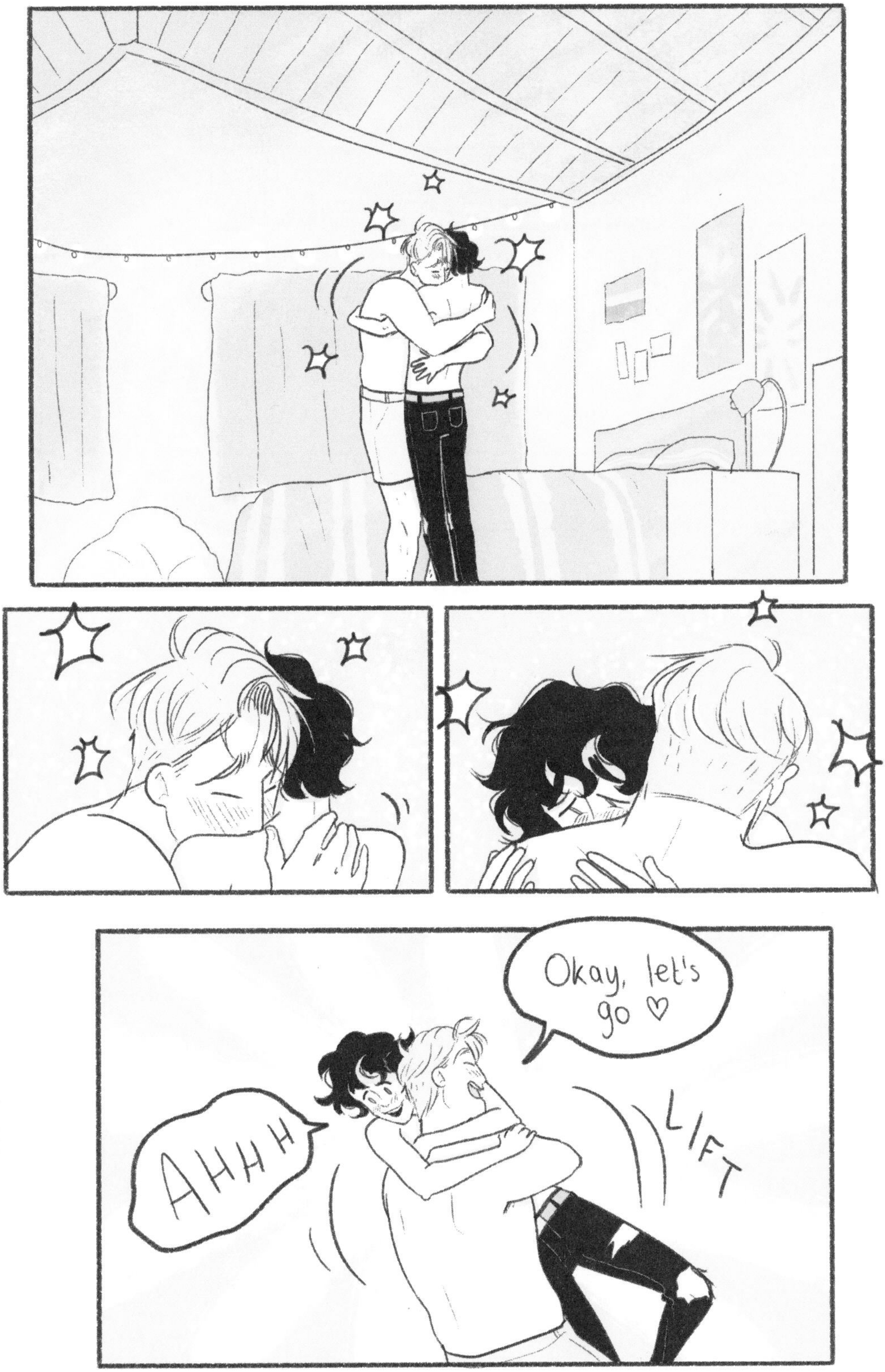
Okay, let's go ♡
AHHH
LIFT

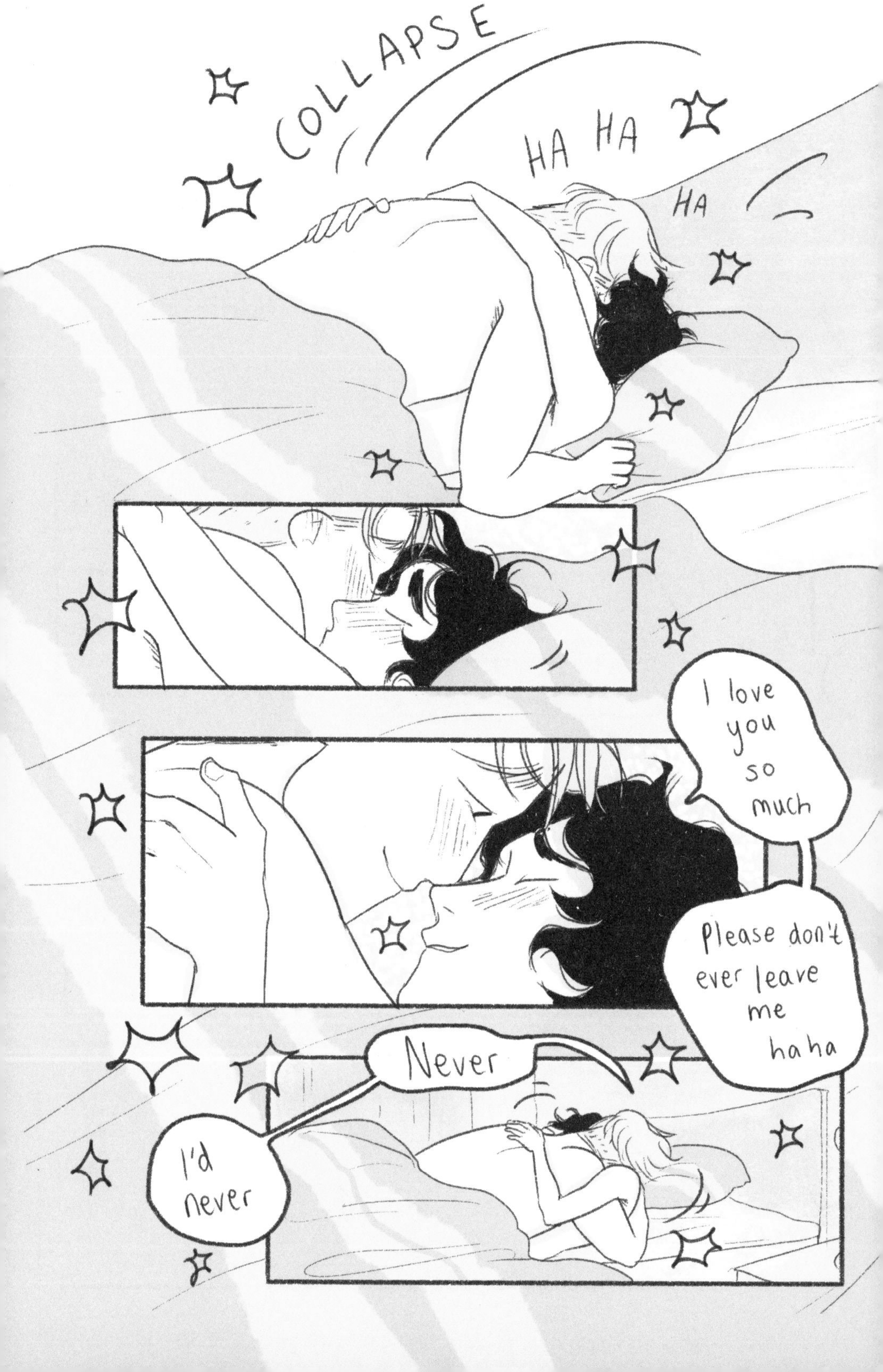
COLLAPSE
HA HA
HA
I love you so much
Please don't ever leave me haha
Never
I'd never

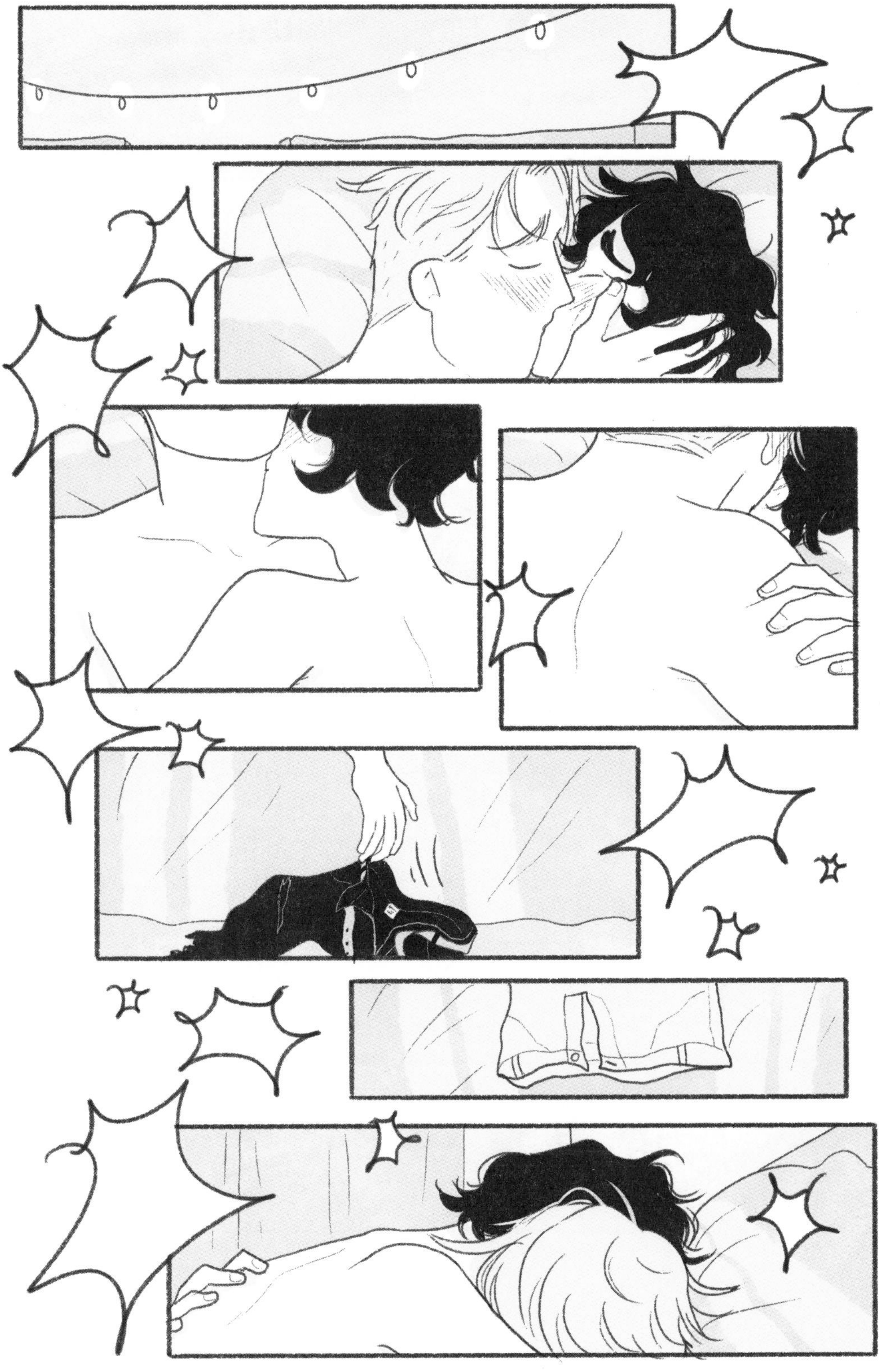

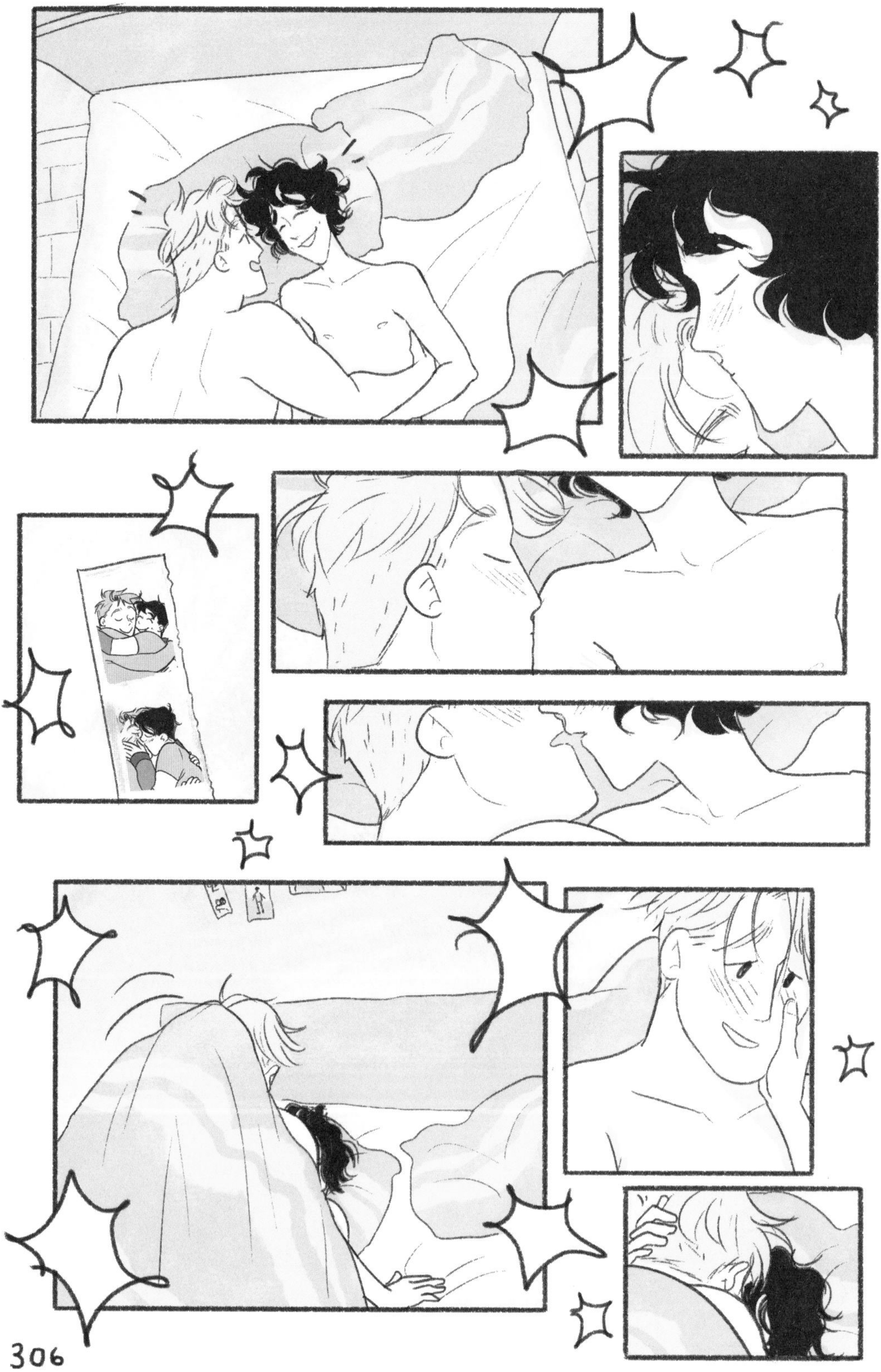

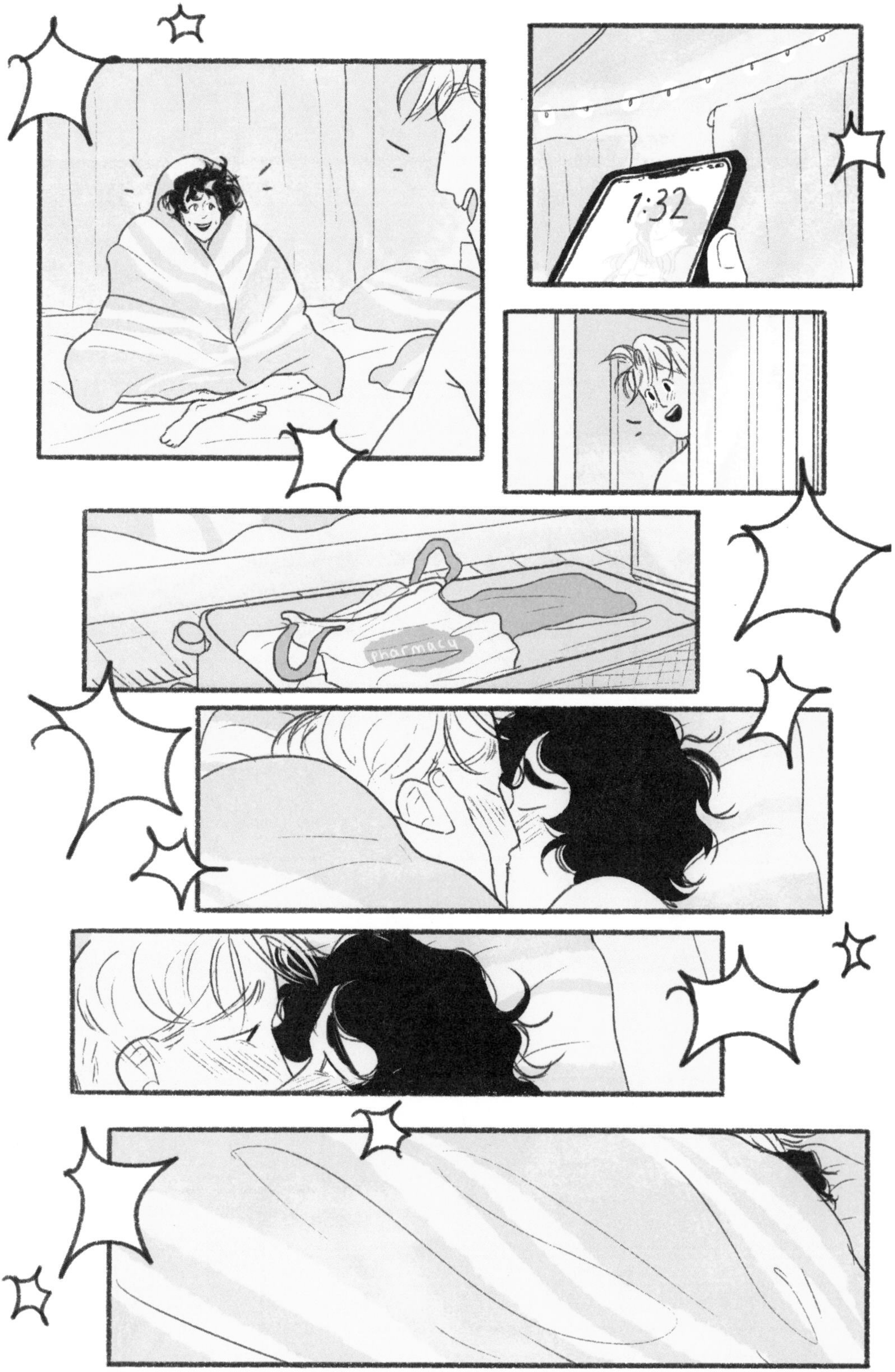
1:32
pharmacy

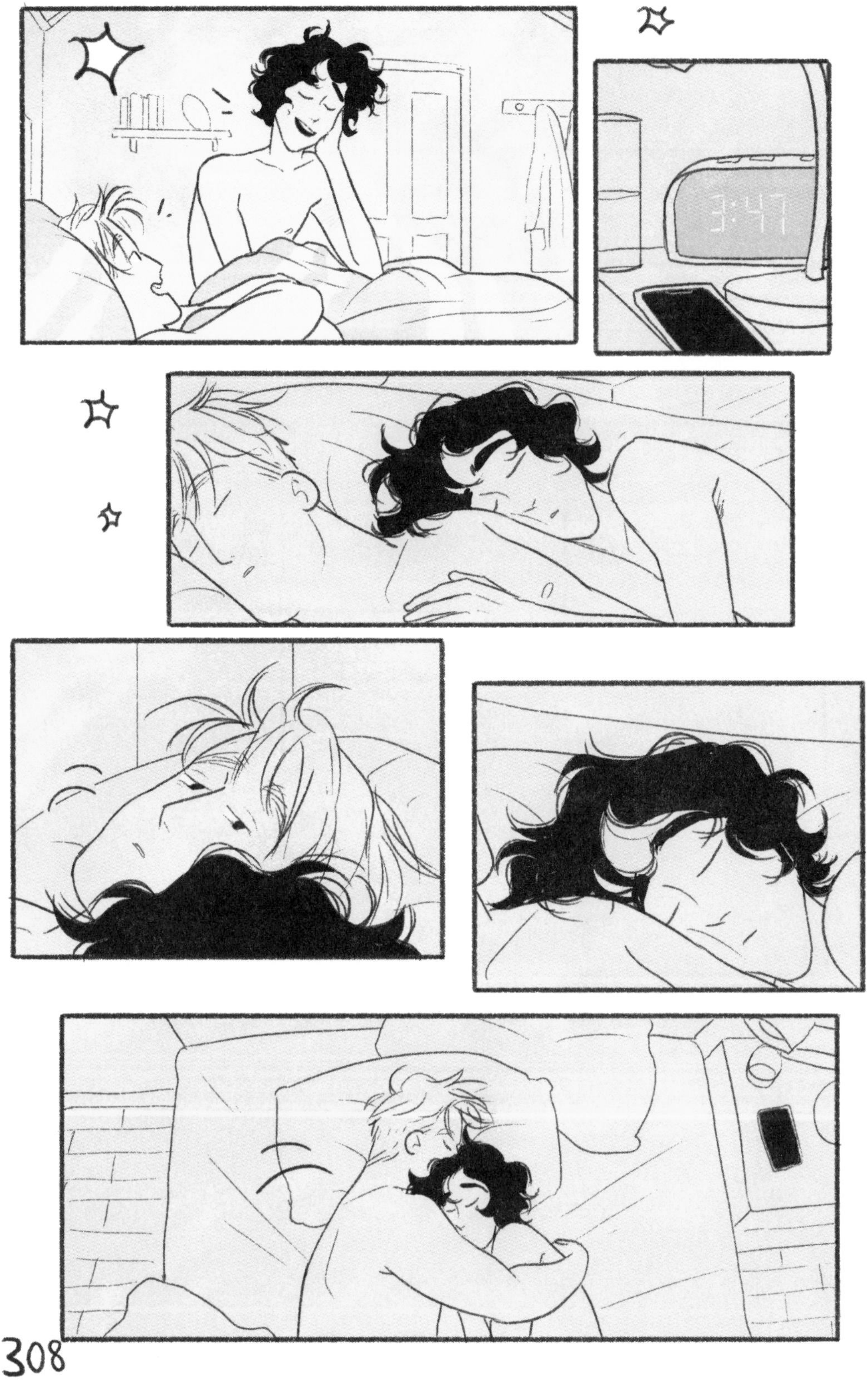
3:47

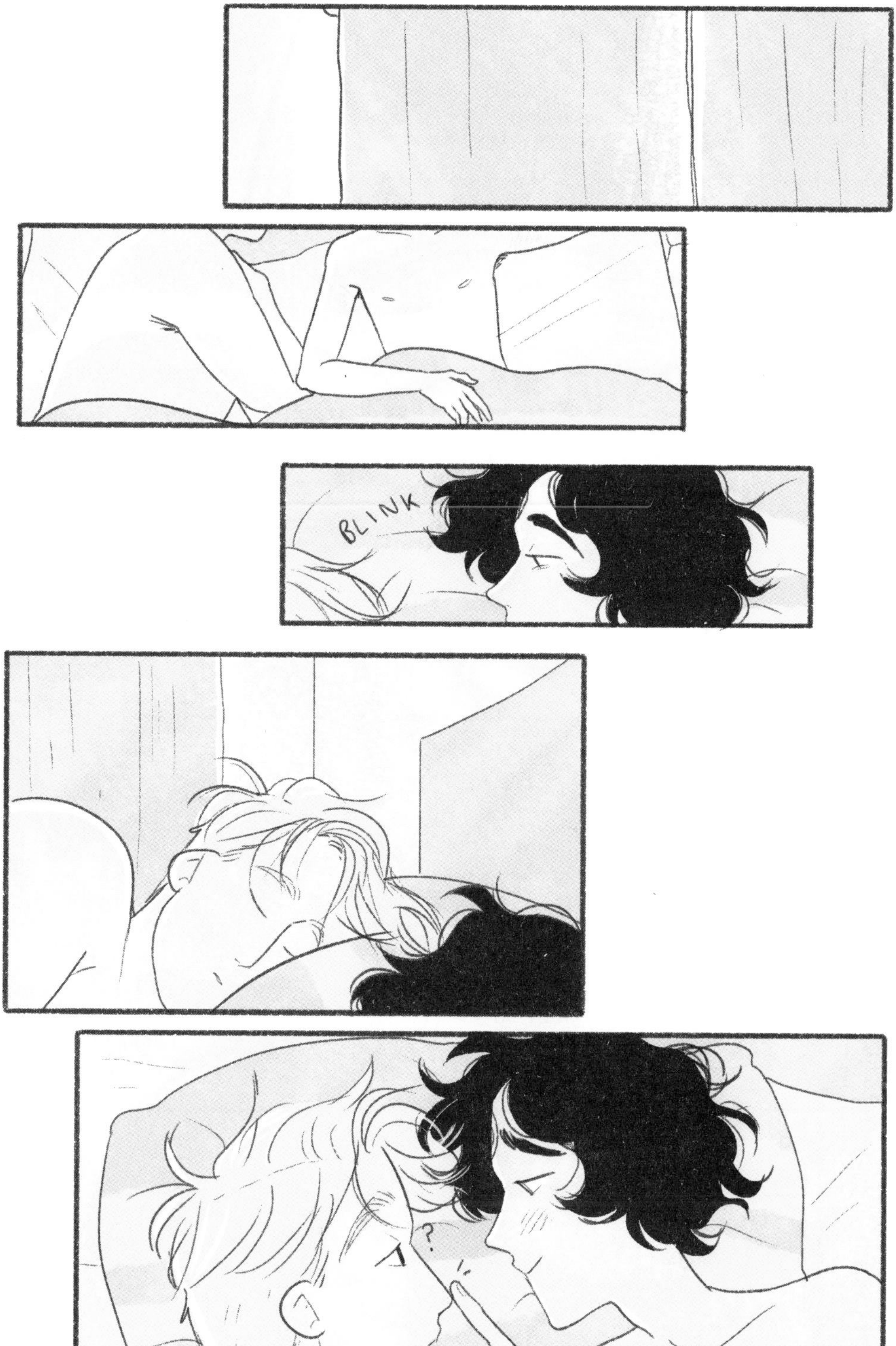
BLINK
?

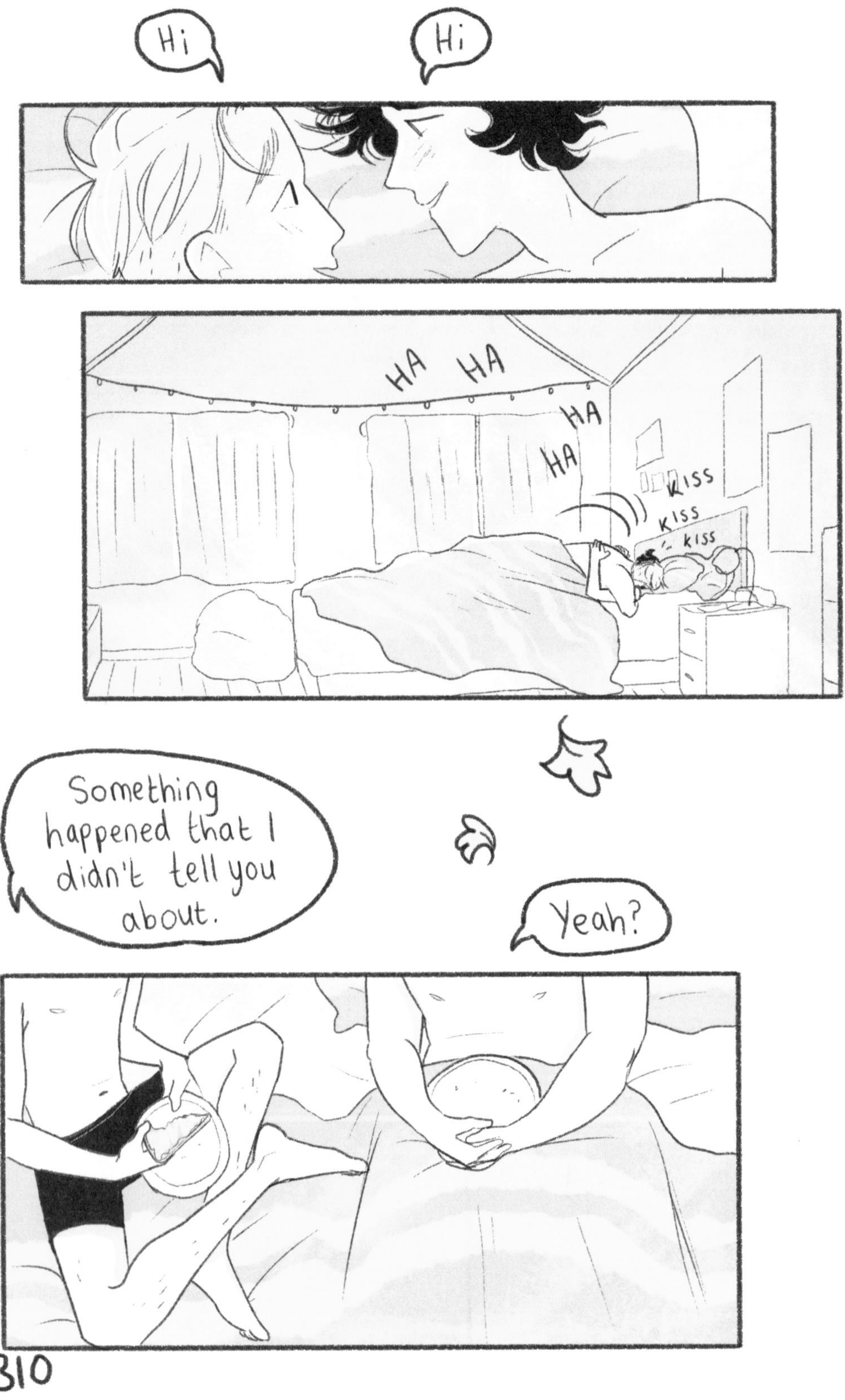
Hi
Hi
HA HA
HA
HA
KISS
KISS
KISS
Something happened that I didn't tell you about.
Yeah?

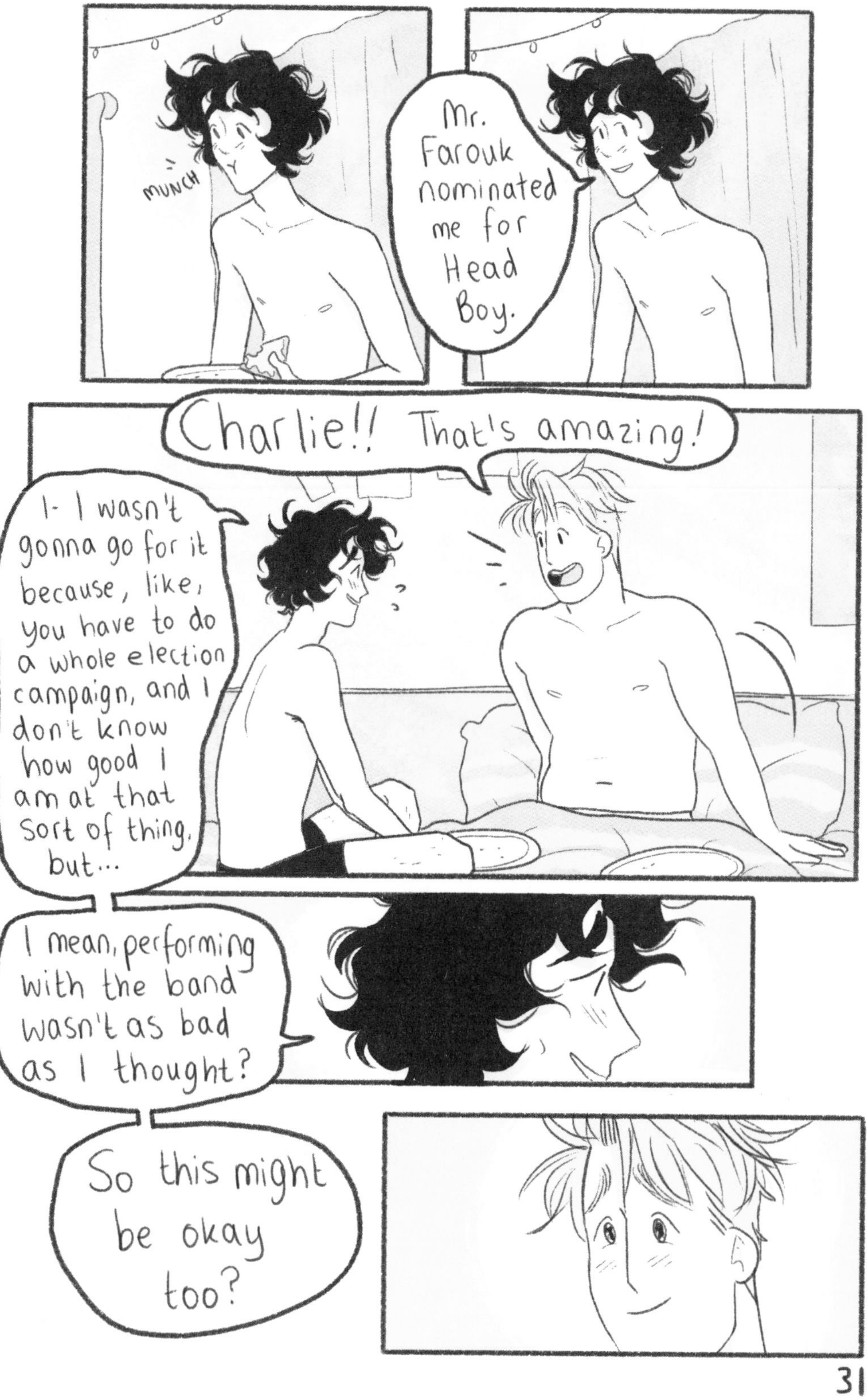
MUNCH
Mr. Farouk nominated me for Head Boy.
Charlie!! That's amazing!
I- I wasn't gonna go for it because, like, you have to do a whole election campaign, and I don't know how good I am at that sort of thing, but...
I mean, performing with the band wasn't as bad as I thought?
So this might be okay too?

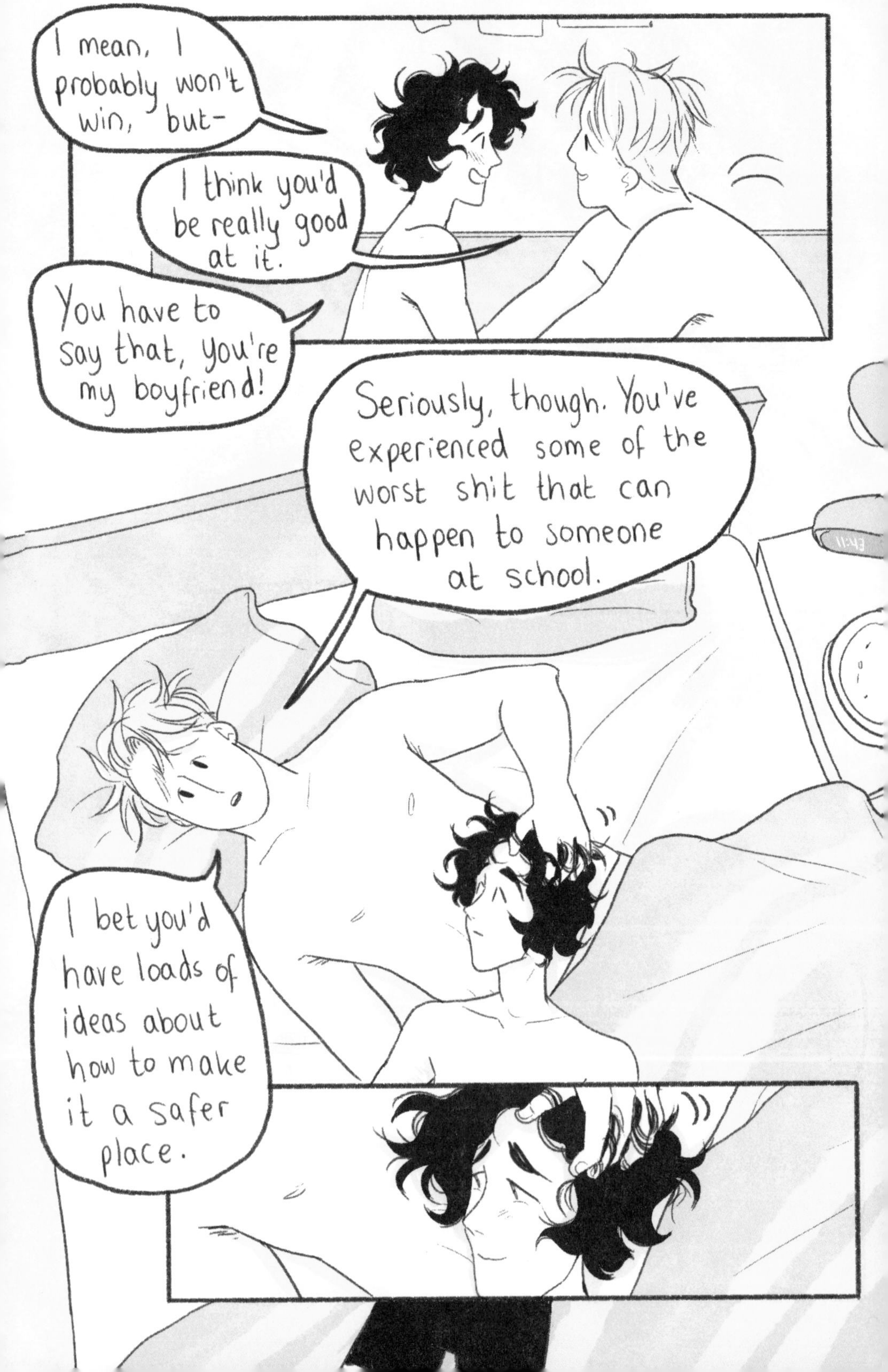

I mean, I probably won't win, but-
I think you'd be really good at it.
You have to say that, you're my boyfriend!
Seriously, though. You've experienced some of the worst shit that can happen to someone at school.
I bet you'd have loads of ideas about how to make it a safer place.

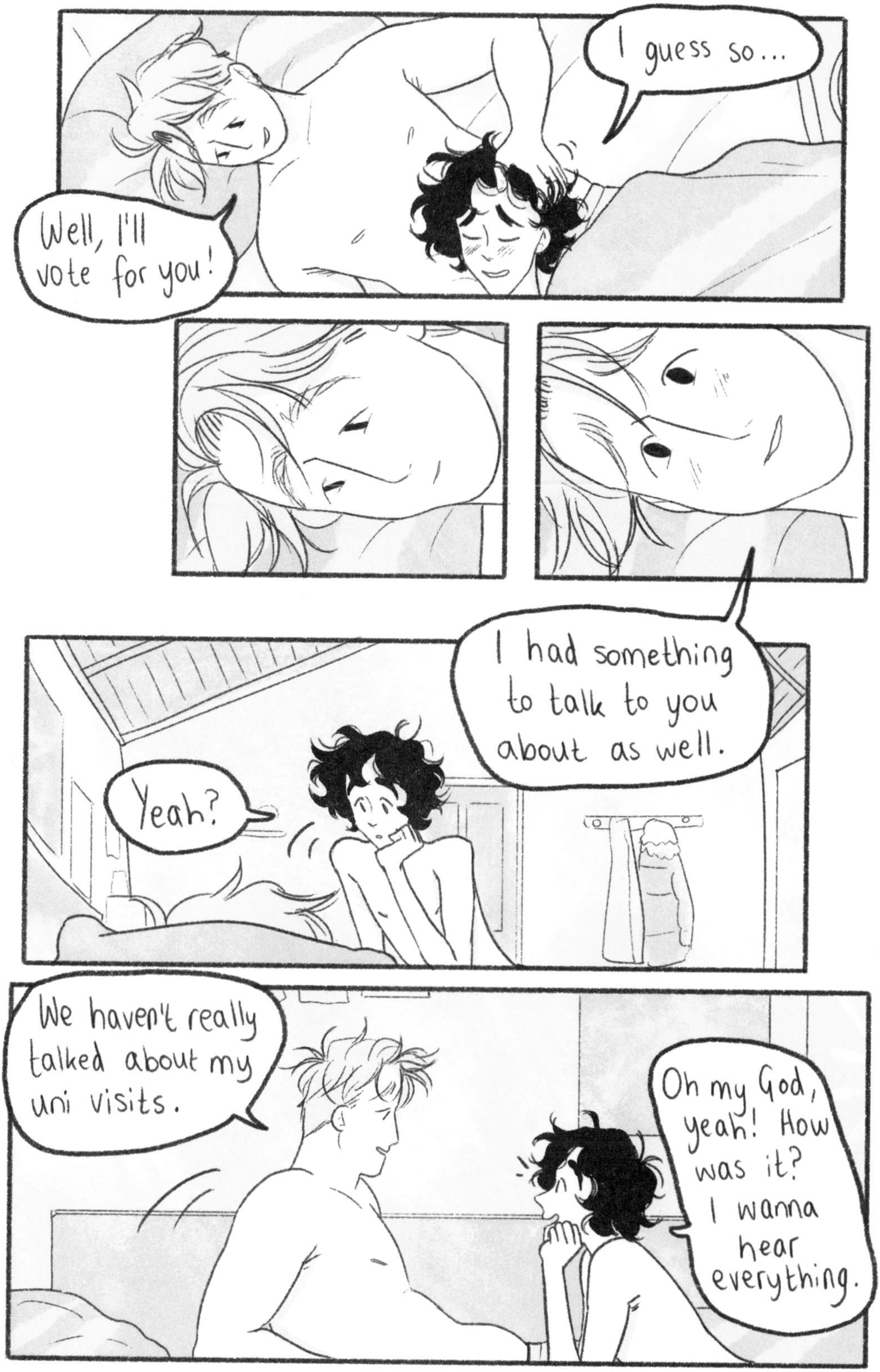
I guess so...
Well, I'll vote for you!
I had something to talk to you about as well.
Yeah?
We haven't really talked about my uni visits.
Oh my God, yeah! How was it? I wanna hear everything.

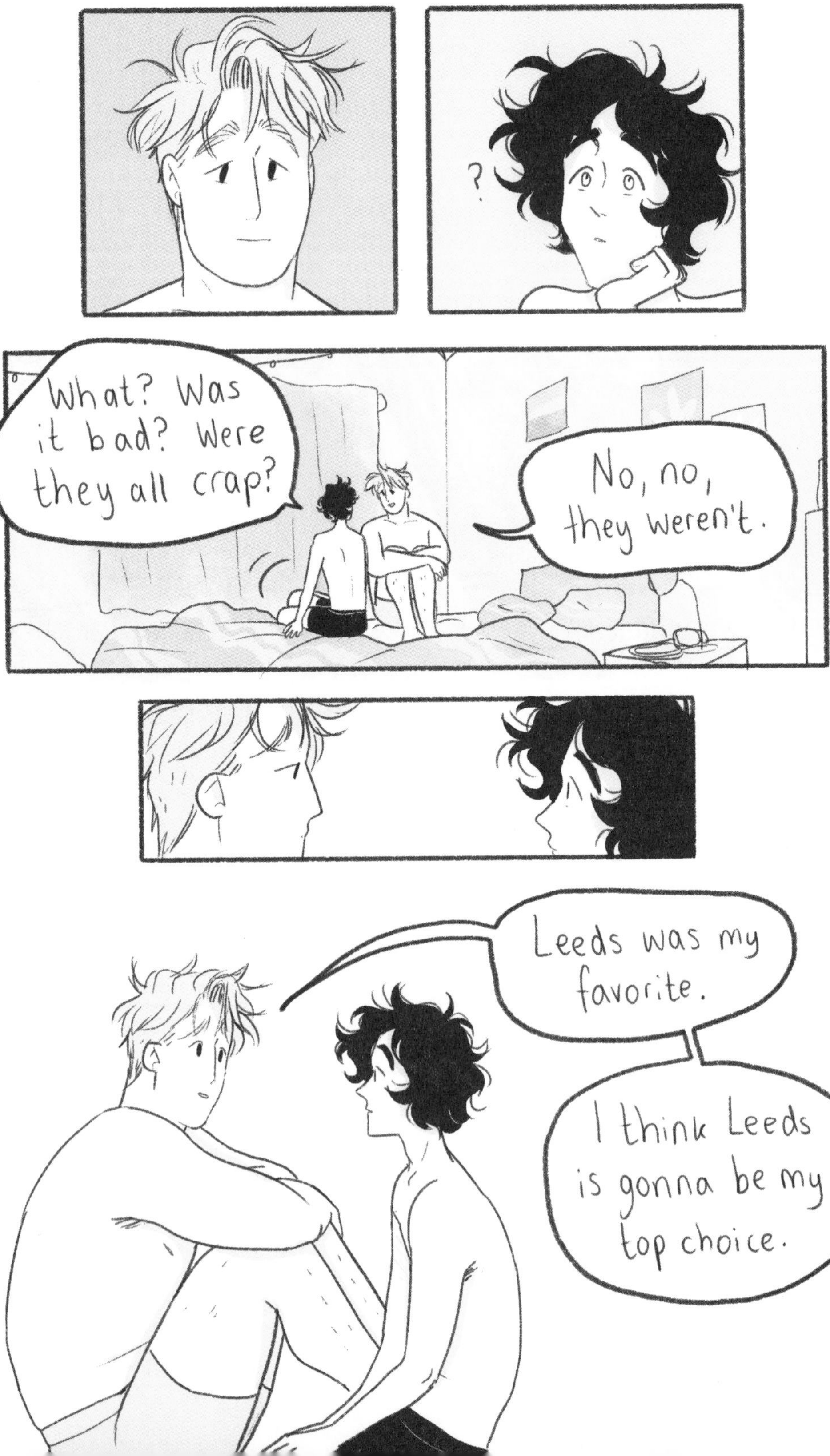
?
What? Was it bad? Were they all crap?
No, no, they weren't.
Leeds was my favorite.
I think Leeds is gonna be my top choice.

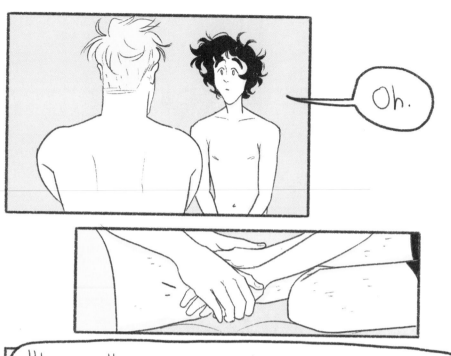

Oh.

It's a really cool campus, like, right in the city, and there's _so_ much to do there, and I got to see one of the rugby teams playing and they seem so cool, and everyone there seems really nice, and I think—

I dunno—

I think I'd really like it there.

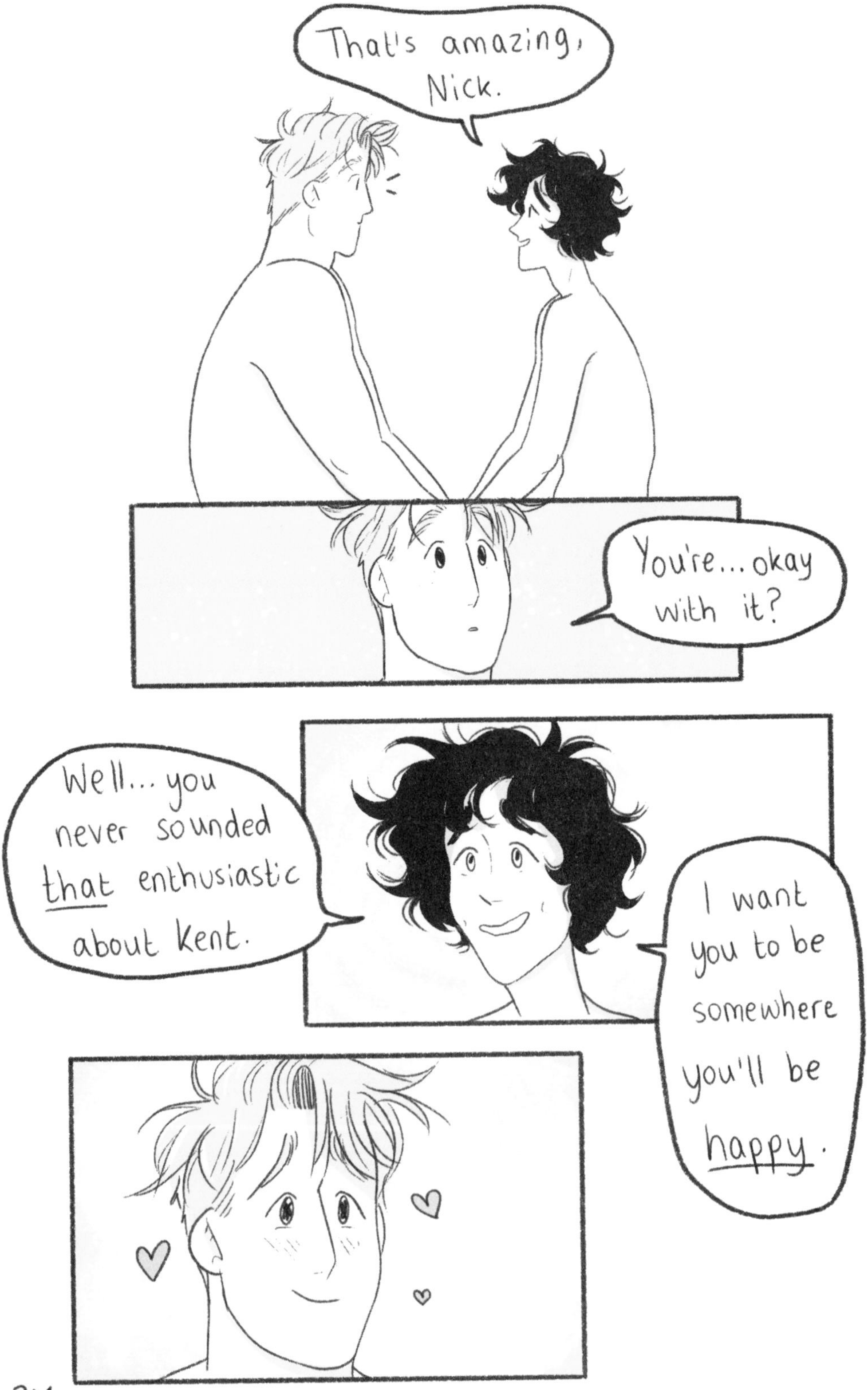

That's amazing, Nick.
You're... okay with it?
Well... you never sounded that enthusiastic about Kent.
I want you to be somewhere you'll be happy.

So, um...
How far away is Leeds?
TAP
TAP
TAP
to
Truham
4h 28
4h 10
3d
1d
Leeds
Manchester
Sheffield
4h 28 min
Tolls
Birmingham
Oh. Okay.

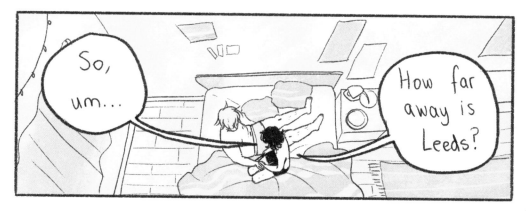

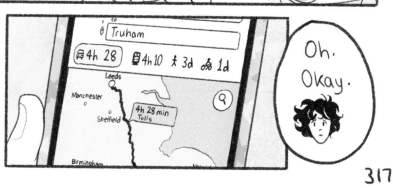

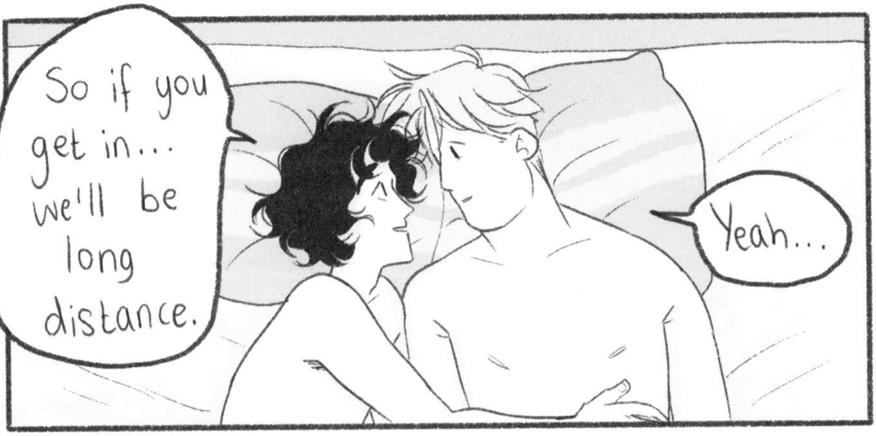
So if you get in... we'll be long distance.
Yeah...

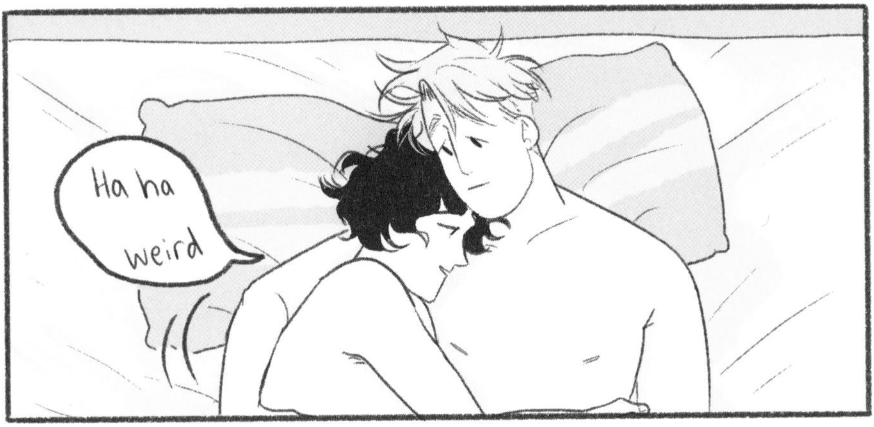
Ha ha weird

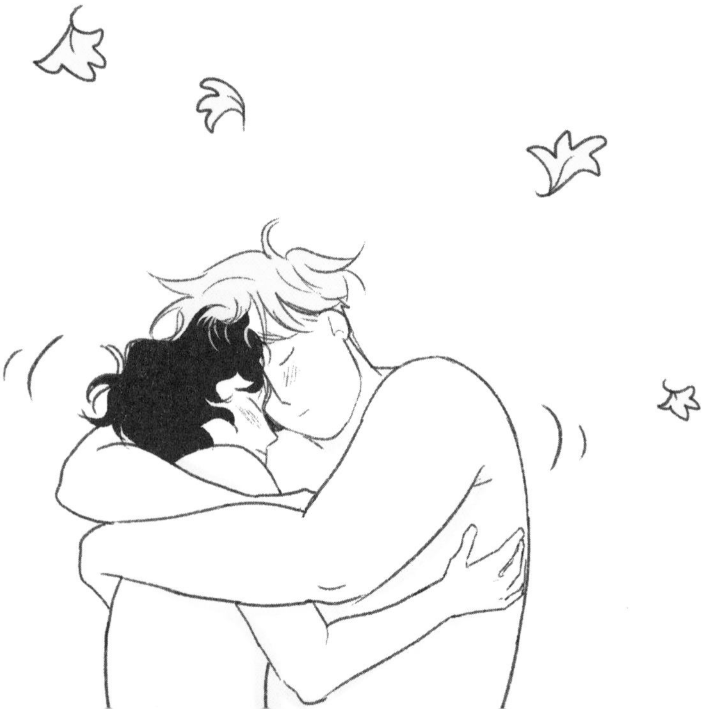

Heartstopper will conclude in
Volume 6!

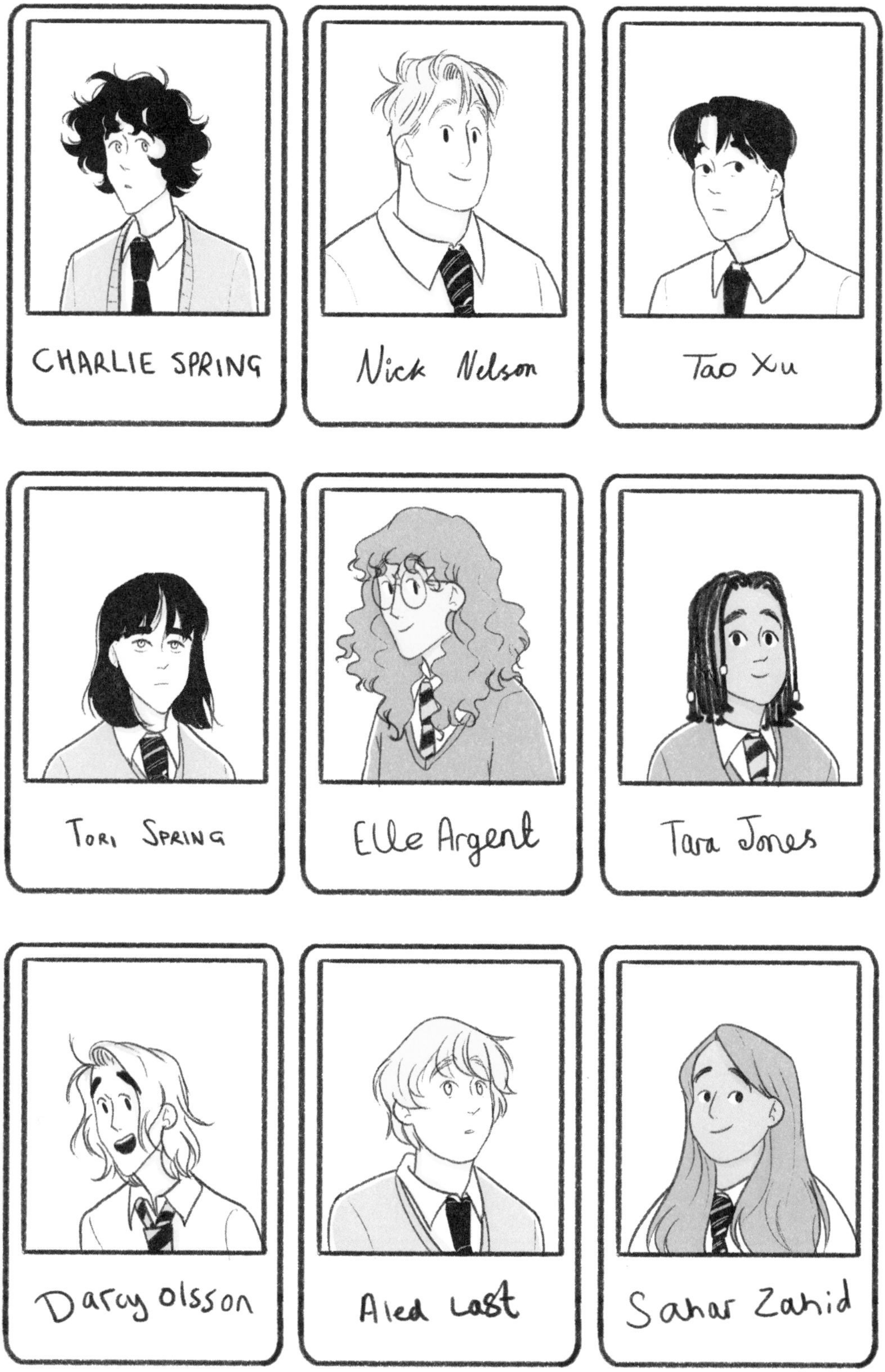
CHARLIE SPRING
Nick Nelson
Tao Xu
Tori Spring
Elle Argent
Tara Jones
Darcy Olsson
Aled Last
Sahar Zahid

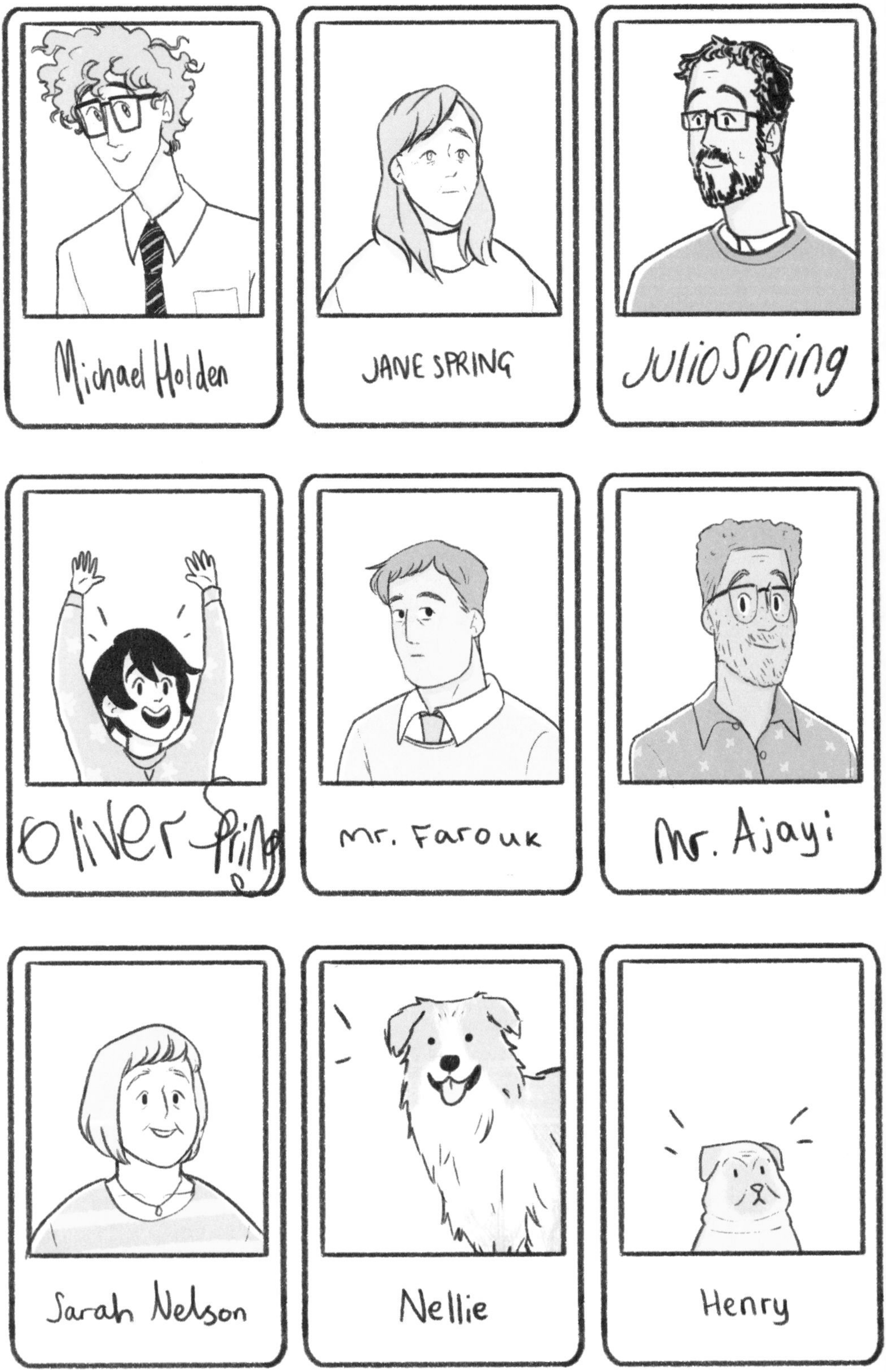
Michael Holden
JANE SPRING
Julio Spring
Oliver Spring
Mr. Farouk
Mr. Ajayi
Sarah Nelson
Nellie
Henry

Geoff

Sai Verma

Christian McBride

Otis Smith

COACH SINGH

MR. LANGE

Aleena

JAY

THE OSEMANVERSE

Year 1

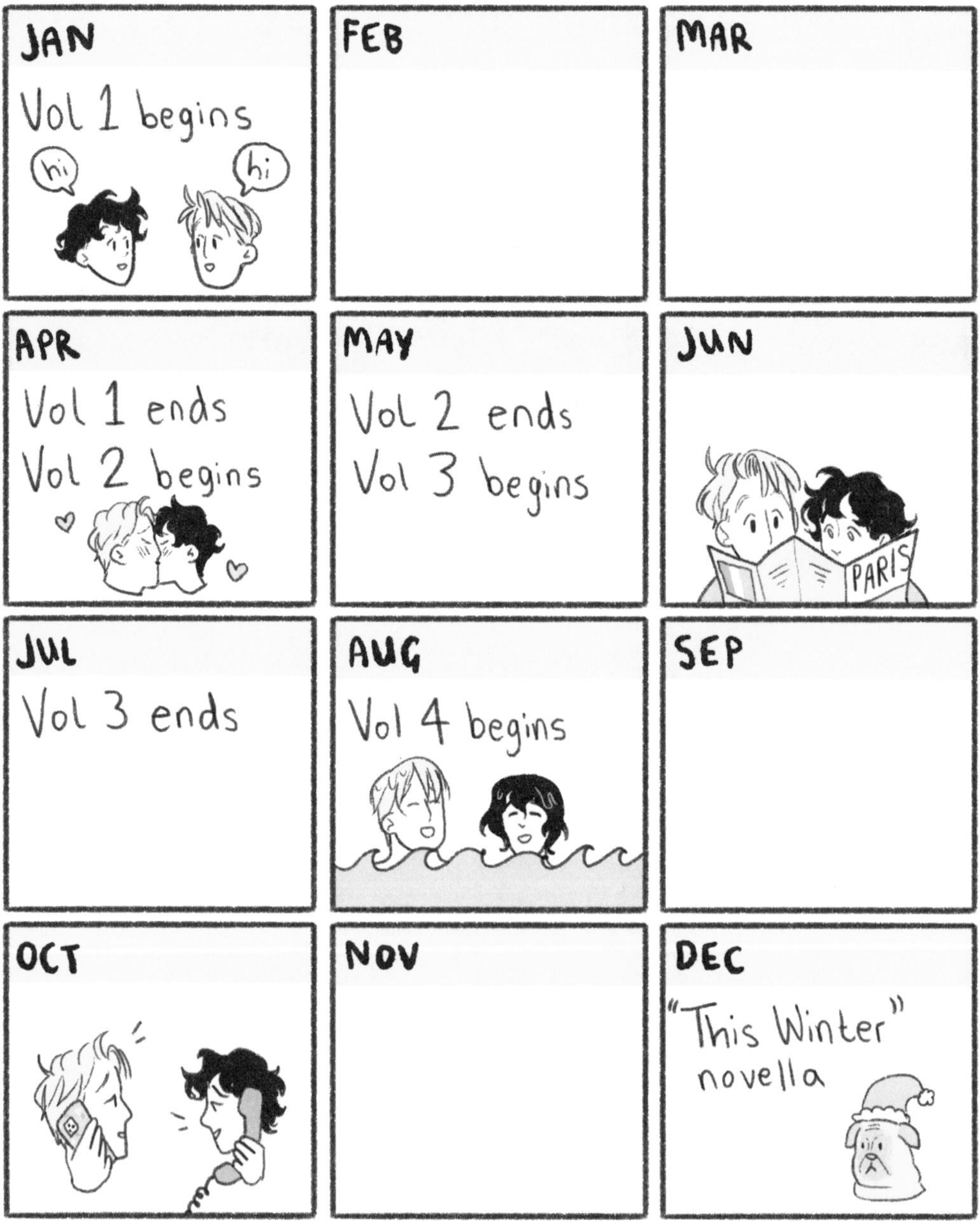

JAN
Vol 1 begins
hi
hi
FEB
MAR
APR
Vol 1 ends
Vol 2 begins
MAY
Vol 2 ends
Vol 3 begins
JUN
PARIS
JUL
Vol 3 ends
AUG
Vol 4 begins
SEP
OCT
NOV
DEC
"This Winter" novella

TIMELINE

Year 2

JAN ←—"Solitaire"—→ 	**FEB** → 	**MAR** Vol 4 ends 
APR Vol 5 begins 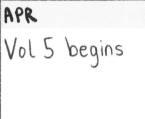	**MAY** 	**JUN** Vol 5 ends 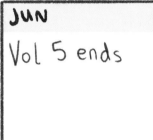

DID YOU KNOW?

Heartstopper doesn't take place in a specific real year

Vol 4 covers the most amount of time ...so far

The "Nick and Charlie" novella occurs in the summer of Year 3

Author's Note

Hello! It's been quite a while! I'm very excited to
finally be sharing volume 5 of Heartstopper with you.

Volume 5 took a long time to create because I've spent much of
the past few years working on the TV adaptation of
Heartstopper. It's been an incredible experience and I feel very
lucky to have an adaptation that I'm so proud of and happy
with. But without the comic there would be no show, so I
couldn't wait to get back to my desk and start drawing again.

We're careening towards the end of Heartstopper now. Last
volume, I thought this book would be the end, but it turns out
there needs to be one more to complete the story. I'm very sad
that the story is ending, but I can't wait to give Nick and Charlie
and the Paris Squad the most beautiful send-off in Volume 6.

My heartfelt thanks to my agent Claire Wilson, my editor
Rachel Wade, my publicist Emily Thomas, and everyone at
Hachette and Heartstopper's international publishers for all
your hard work and passion for the series.

Thank you everyone for your love and support for Heartstopper.
See you in the final volume.

Alice x

Mental Health Resources

For information, help, support, and guidance about mental health and mental illness, please check out the following resources:

National Eating Disorders Association
nationaleatingdisorders.org

Anxiety & Depression Association of America
adaa.org

Heard Alliance
heardalliance.org

The Trevor Project
thetrevorproject.org

Also by Alice Oseman

HEARTSTOPPER

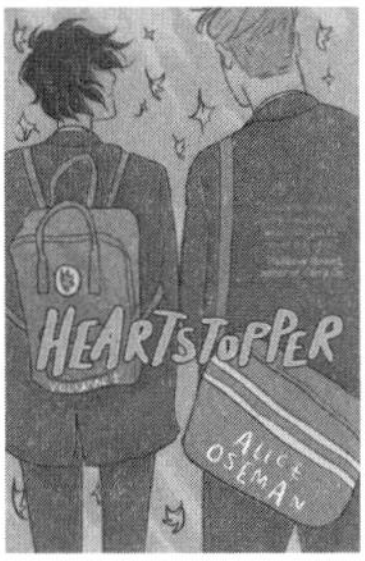
HEARTSTOPPER
ALICE
OSEMAN
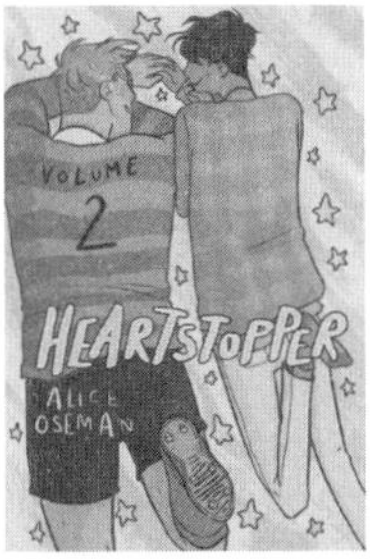
VOLUME
2
HEARTSTOPPER
ALICE
OSEMAN
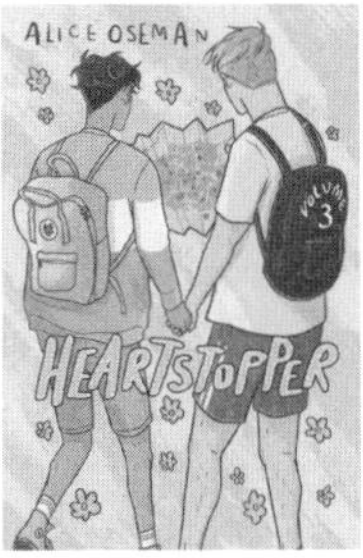
ALICE OSEMAN
HEARTSTOPPER
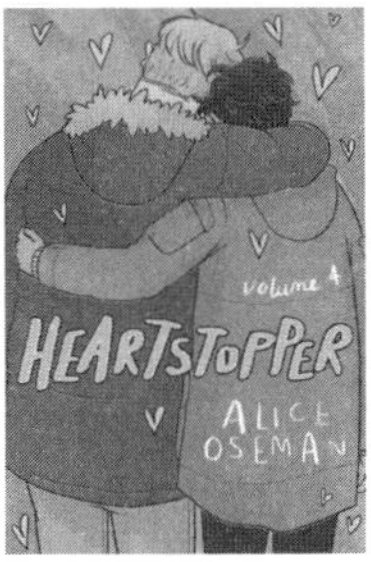
Volume 4
HEARTSTOPPER
ALICE
OSEMAN
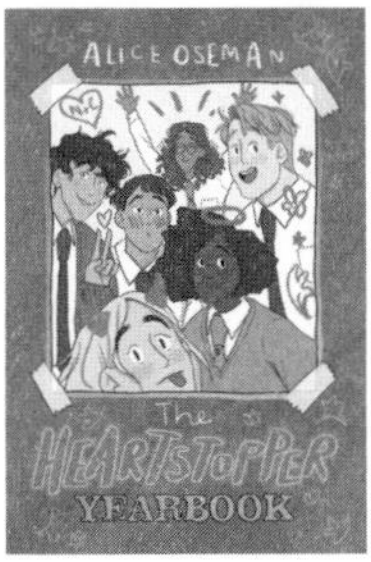
ALICE OSEMAN
The
HEARTSTOPPER
YEARBOOK
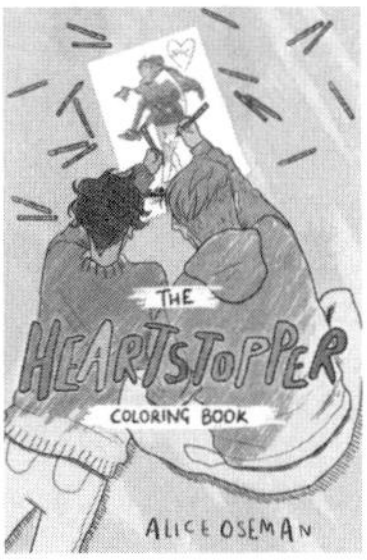
THE
HEARTSTOPPER
COLORING BOOK
ALICE OSEMAN

HEARTSTOPPER NOVELLAS

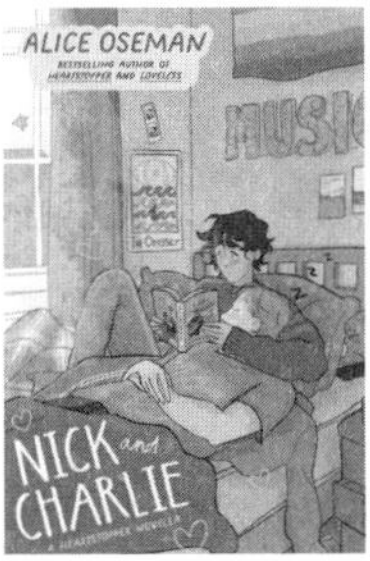
ALICE OSEMAN
NICK and CHARLIE
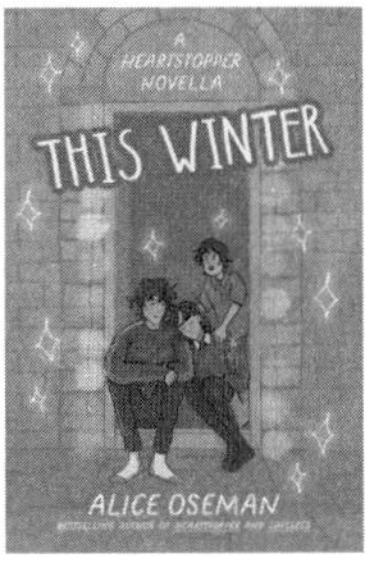
A HEARTSTOPPER NOVELLA
THIS WINTER
ALICE OSEMAN

NOVELS

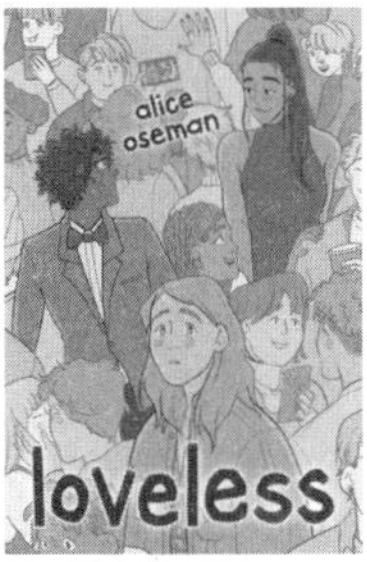
alice
oseman
loveless
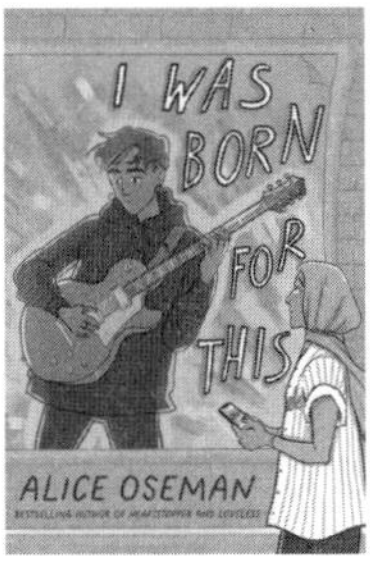
I WAS
BORN
FOR
THIS
ALICE OSEMAN
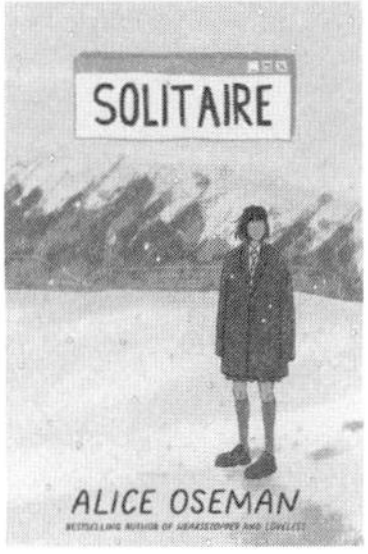
SOLITAIRE
ALICE OSEMAN

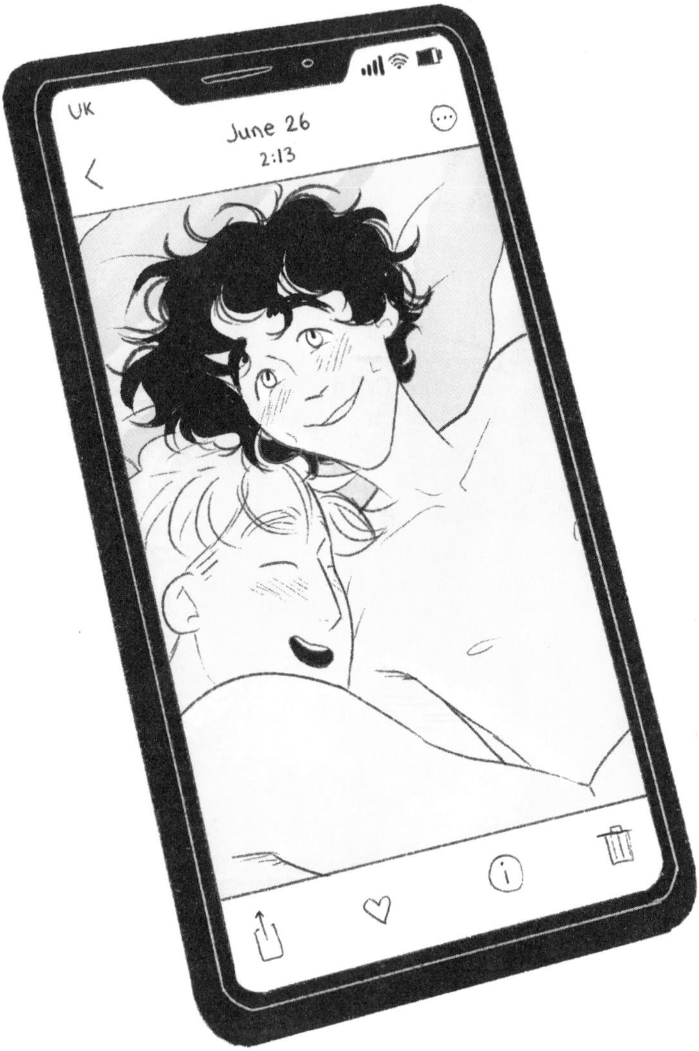

UK
June 26
2:13